MW00783887

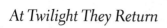

At Twilight They Return

At Twilight
They Return

A Novel in Ten Tales

ZYRANNA ZATELI

TRANSLATED FROM THE GREEK BY DAVID CONNOLLY

YALE UNIVERSITY PRESS ■ NEW HAVEN & LONDON

A MARGELLOS
WORLD REPUBLIC OF LETTERS BOOK

The Margellos World Republic of Letters is dedicated to making literary works from around the globe available in English through translation. It brings to the English-speaking world the work of leading poets, novelists, essayists, philosophers, and playwrights from Europe, Latin America, Africa, Asia, and the Middle East to stimulate international discourse and creative exchange.

Yale University Press books may be purchased in quantity for educational, business, or promotional use. For information, please e-mail sales.press@yale.edu (U.S. office) or sales@yaleup.co.uk (U.K. office).

Set in Electra and Nobel types by Tseng Information Systems, Inc.
Printed in the United States of America.

Library of Congress Control Number: 2016933041
ISBN 978-0-300-20071-3 (hardcover : alk. paper)

A catalogue record for this book is available from the British Library.

This paper meets the requirements of ANSI/NISO Z39.48–1992 (Permanence of Paper).

10 9 8 7 6 5 4 3 2 1

THE TEN TALES

At Twilight They Return

If you take ten dogs and let them loose in the wilds, in a wilderness through which no living soul passes, then in less than a few weeks these dogs will revert to being wolves.

So someone said one evening, and motivated by the emotion and the associations, complex in their immediacy, that his remark had on me, I started to recall some *old tales*.

This initial motivation was further strengthened—as a kind of reverse reflection—by the following lines from Paul Celan's "Todtnauberg":

Krudes, später, im Fahren,
Deutlich . . .

ZZ

First Tale

THE FIRST SLAUGHTERING

"Is there any place in the world more beautiful than this?" Thomas asked his twin sister, slowly turning his head toward her and not hastening to avert his gaze as usual.

"No," replied Safi-Lisafi, "there isn't."

She spoke without hesitation—why? because quite simply she hadn't seen any other place that she could have found better—but was also puzzled, catching her breath, since it wasn't often that she saw her brother's eyes, *looked into* his eyes, which she so wanted to do, but which he wouldn't allow (her or anyone else), yet now he was almost making her do so . . . Without doubt, there were no other eyes in the world like his: the one brown, a golden brown, and the other bright green like an emerald—who had ever heard of such a thing?

Then, as if satiated and a little dizzy from this unexpected good fortune, she turned to view the landscape he was pointing to, the place where they had been born and had grown up—far into the distance and down, down below—and where the others would be searching for them at that very moment. It was indeed beautiful, very beautiful. They nodded their heads pensively, their minds elsewhere; they saw things that they didn't see when they were down there, and they spoke, spoke under their breath, or recalled various things that brought them a sudden elation or a strange pang of anguish.

Now completely silent, the brother held out his hand to his sister, and like two shadows they slipped down into the nearest ravine. It would grow dark again and they were clueless.

We are somewhere in the north of the country, in a green and fertile stretch of land, once a renowned crossroads between provinces even more renowned, such as Bisaltia, Mygdonia, and Crestonia, where reliable sources inform us that during the 1868–69 academic year, there was a Boys' School with thirty pupils, a Girls' School with fifty-one pupils, and an inter-instructional school with eighty-nine children—and by the beginning of the century, these three institutions among them boasted five teachers.

In that time and place, then, when the boys reached the age of twelve, they weren't sent to war exactly—or to the temple to confront wise old men and ultimately the sins of mankind, not something in any case to be scorned. They were dressed in fine black-and-white garments, underwent a mock shaving—little bridegrooms, inexperienced and bewildered—and were led to the yard outside the house to slaughter their first beast, an act that symbolized any number of things, both obvious and inscrutable.

The ritual called out to all, as it will also call out to us, to watch it, as the knife gleams in the clumsy right hand, and gleams even more since the narrow place, before the boy arrives in the yard with his retinue, is quite dark and damp, covered with red earth, and extremely quiet, disturbingly quiet at that hour: day breaks . . . and gently it asserts itself and *prevails*.

The newborn beast about to be slaughtered—a lamb or kid being the most suitable for the occasion—waits sprawled out on the ground or on a bed of straw, its legs bound in pairs. Twisting its neck strangely, as if having discovered this ability only today after losing the use of its legs, it watches every so often the boy coming toward it, either by chance or with unexpected concern. And it opens its mouth to bleat, or changes its mind and closes it again in bewilderment (*really?*), intensifying in one way or another that sense of awe and menace that there is in the air and that grows ever more oppressive all around it . . . It jerks with little sting-like spasms, licks itself, feels ecstasy or inertia, or again gazes elsewhere, over its shoulder—various scenes play with its attention in these surroundings—and suddenly it again catches sight of the boy, who in turn twists his neck and shoulders and, disconcerted, watches the lamb, which presently he must slaughter, from an ever shorter distance . . .

There were boys who had no objection to this, who had no great objection, who took it quite lightly. Yet by the time they had focused their thoughts on what was about to happen, they found themselves with bloodied hands, knees, cheeks, and would never in their lives be able to say what actually *happened* then. Yet they would talk of nothing else, as the saying goes, until some other experience like the army or first love came to overshadow that of the first slaughtering . . . There were some twelve-year-olds who completely lost their senses that morning and some who never found them again. In other cases, boys wronged by nature, somewhat retarded in mind, with strange manners and gait, or excessively naive and moonstruck never looked back after this act, and no one dared make fun of them ever again. Of course, there were many who never made it to twelve, and others who did but whose fear lent wings to their feet and they escaped . . . Almost infinite cases, but whatever might be said, the custom lived on and prevailed and it would lose none of its power over time other than—even if it sounds paradoxical—to time itself.

In the house in which Thomas was born, almost every year there was some-one who became twelve years old, so that they said of their yard that it was *soaked in blood*. These children were offshoots of an indescribable tree, eddies in a merciless whirligig: a family so multifarious and with such flexibility in marriages and deaths, in successive marriages and deaths, official and unoffi-cial, producing so many children that to count them requires the fingers of both hands, and more than twice. When we think about it—and as this event had also triumphed in the previous generation and is being faithfully repeated in a third to date—it resembles the moves and unpredictability of an intricate game, of one of those *plans* whose conception, they say, belongs to the devil.

Of course, they say that at eighteen the devil, too, is handsome. No objec-tion whatsoever. But Hesychios,[1] father of Thomas and Safi-Lisafi and so many others, was more than handsome and from a much earlier age. Women fell into his arms in the same way that disasters fall upon others' heads. There were some who called him Fortunatos; others—with more or less the same idea—called him Misfortunatos. Anyway, it was his mother who, around his eighteenth birth-day, had christened him Hesychios (the name he had been given in church was Theagenis), precisely in order to exorcise, as the poor woman hoped, that interest shown by women. She pushed him half-naked into a stream one day as they were returning from the fields—she had made sure that there were others nearby, witnesses to see and hear—and chanting whatever came into her head, she sprinkled him in a few places and gave him the name Hesychios. He stood there without protesting, like the one in the Jordan—besides, what more bliss-ful than to be cooled down when it's a boiling-hot day—and after this event, she, at least, found peace and quiet: she died shortly afterwards, in a matter of a few weeks. And it was then that the girls, dazzled by his new name (which now inspired a certain trust and exercised even more charm—"*Hesychios*," they'd repeat to themselves in the darkness of night and wriggled with ecstasy, "*imag-ine Hesychios!*"), felt a real tempest raging in their souls, and peace and quiet was the last thing they would have from then on. And because not one of them wanted even so much as to imagine that such a thing could possibly happen to any other—not to fall in love with him, which was something even the soulless stones did, but to live just for one glance from him, one gesture—each of them

1. From the Greek word for "quiet." Cf. Hesychasm (from Greek *hesychia*, "still-ness, rest, quict, silence"): a mystical tradition of prayer in the Eastern Orthodox Church (translator's note).

shut her ears to the bragging and sighing of the others and saw him as her good fortune and only hers. Even though this too had an air of doom about it.

And indeed it did. It saddened many, but no one was surprised by the fact that both hearts and bodies bled at that time for the handsome Hesychios. Some died angelically gazing at the ceiling—to say died of pining would be too little; passion purified them absolutely before finishing them off. Others chose to die in a manner as if punishing their own fate, as if disemboweling it. One vanished. *Vanished.* That was all you could say about her. From one moment to the next, no one ever saw her again, neither alive nor dead; she simply *vanished.* But there were also several who suddenly and radically changed; their blood cooled and they entered into an alliance with the mothers of the dead girls, went from house to house, knocked on the doors and said, "Do you have any girls inside alive?" And if the answer was "We do," they gave them their counsel: "Guard them, bind them, tie them down, don't whatever you do let them see and fall in love with that Hesychios or you'll be weeping for them in their shrouds before long! Ahhh! THEAGENIS-HESYCHIOS," they foamed and jumped up and down as if they'd been bitten by a tarantula—"couldn't his mother and the priest have come up with some other name to give to that venomous cock!" Because apart from everything else, they had of course come to regard his sperm as poisonous (no need to explain that all this passion didn't exhaust itself in mere looks), for how else could such a pestilence, such an epidemic be explained? Quite simply, just as his good looks took people's breath away, so too his hidden member took lives away. "He has a blade between his legs," lamented those girls who had encountered it but had escaped at the last moment and were filled with anger, "the sweeter, the more poisonous."

Nevertheless, it was a blade that also granted lives; it didn't only take them. Six children had been born more or less together, naturally all his, who else's, and since none of their mothers had lived to see what was to be done with such an offspring, these too had been taken out on their strolls by their grandmothers (not one of them especially old, just the opposite, and all of them filled with fervor in their holy struggle to save those girls still left from certain death) and one fine morning had been left outside the front door of Hesychios's house. They got the slightly older ones to screech, shook the infants in their cradles to scare them so they would start bawling, and they themselves—with a whoosh like a swarm of jackdaws—ran all together and hid a little way off in some ruins and waited with bated breath.

Presently, they saw Hesychios coming down, somewhat stiff in his knees, in his movements, but not at all crabby in his expression or irritated, and stooping to pick up the infants, one by one, and hand them to his father behind him, to his sisters and brothers, who one by one had also arrived on the scene, all of them silent and ponderous. One of his sisters ventured to protest: "What are we going to do with so many children, Hesychios? Haven't we got enough?" but he quietened her very quickly and the girl lifted two of them up together in her arms, tossed her head back, and disappeared up the steps. It goes without saying that none of them were crying, shouting, or griping anymore. It was as though they were all at last where they wanted to be, or, at least, where they should be.

From the cover of the ruins, it was difficult for the old women to accept that the early-morning battle was over so simply and bloodlessly. Nevertheless, they continued to keep their eyes peeled, and one of the more suspicious and uncompromising of them muttered, "You think he's taken them in? Just the opposite! He'll get his sisters now to marry them off," and she made a gesture as if wringing clothes, but the others rapped her on the knuckles and shut her up. "We'll see," the oldest of them said quietly and with more than a little good sense.

And they saw Hesychios alone now, gazing all around at the sky, the trees, the clouds, the birds that passed and flew off, searching perhaps to find out for himself who or what had brought to his front door these infants, incarnations of his sins to put it another way, and eventually, fixing his — somewhat smiling — eyes on the ruins opposite, on the half-collapsed walls, focusing in particular on the gaps that the crumbling stones and timber left between them and through which fierce eyes were glaring.

The chorus of concealed women shook to the bone; they held their breath like never before, so that were any one of them to make even the slightest movement or let out so much as a sound, the others were quite prepared to make pulp of her; really make pulp of her. Hesychios lifted his chin even higher and shot a barely perceptible smile towards them, towards the gaps that is, before turning his back to go into the house, and this — his famous nod, the *sign* as they called it — brought with it an air of discord to the ruins . . . The dark silhouettes immediately stirred and stared, stared at one another, as if suddenly not recognizing the others. Not a bad thing either.

But the *best*, the most unexpected, was when one of them, in a cracked, confused, trembling voice, ventured to say, "He's good deep down, I didn't expect it."

Evidently she was not in her right mind, didn't know what she was saying.

"I didn't expect . . . didn't expect," she repeated with enthusiasm and complete abandon. "Even if he did for my daughter . . . He's good deep down."

They waited to see whether she would say it once again; she did: "He's good deep down." That *deep down* was beginning to get on their nerves . . .

It was Febronia who was speaking, her head lowered. She was one of the mothers of the girls who had died, leaving a foundling, and as she spoke, with her thumbnail she formed little shapes, half-moons that she immediately erased using the palm of her other hand. "Even if he brought my daughter to ruin," she said for the third or fourth time, as if it was precisely this that was the mark of his goodness. "He's good deep down."

There was a deathly silence.

Then, brutally like a stray bullet, one of the others shrieked, "Shame on you! Shame on you for giving in to his first look, as if you were in a world of your own. Those were the signs he gave your daughter once, or have you forgotten? And our daughters, too, and he was the ruination of all of them. That was the nod that the lecher gave us today. His *mothers-in-law*—shame on you for defending him, instead of cursing him and deriding him!"

She also said a lot more that made the others shrink back like tortoises before a hedgehog, but Febronia wouldn't hear any of it. She had already broken away from that chorus and taken her place in the other one, *of enchanted females*, and as she'd been a widow for eight years and was still not yet thirty-eight years old, that night she saw Hesychios—to her great delight and despair—nodding to her like a famished woodpecker, and she saw her reservations falling away like bits of rotten wood.

That same night, Christoforos, Hesychios's father, called all the family, ex-cept for those still not of age—who included not only his grandchildren but also some of his own children—to a family council that lasted almost till the morning. The parlor recalled a ship ready to put to sea, and as the captain it was he who came out with the first weighty pronouncement: "I count your mother lucky to be no longer alive—I count her lucky! Because I wouldn't know where to hide with all that's happened again," though he had to make it clear that he meant their last mother, Eftha, not the first one, who was no longer around to get caught in the flak.

The time has come for us to recall his own renowned background: around the middle of the century (for us the previous one, of course), the then young Christoforos married a certain Petroula, only daughter of a somewhat eccentric and highly strung local priest, who, believing that he was something of a new messiah, directly proceeding from the *lineage of God*, one day killed a shep-herd, no more no less, with a stone to the head because the shepherd didn't share his belief. Simmering below the surface, of course, were other differences, connected with land disputes, for five yards of earth, together with a few in-sinuations concerning conjugal fidelity . . . They caught the perpetrator, shaved off his beard, defrocked him, and shut him up in prison for life. After all this, his wife (and especially when she heard him shouting about how he'd covered his hands in blood because the shepherd had come out with some shameful insinuations that his upstanding wife had conceived their daughter with another man) preferred to find release by drinking from a pitcher of vitriol, and little Petroula—whose name was Parthena and whose mother had given birth to her at the age of forty—was left out on the street with everyone pointing a finger at her. With the passing of the years, the terrible scandal was forgotten, but because it shouldn't be forgotten completely, the name of the unfortunate daughter of the priest was changed from Parthena to Petra—wasn't it a stone[2] that had killed the shepherd?—and from Petra, because she was liked by all, being honest and hardworking and not at all arrogant like her father, it became the pet name, Petroula. And everyone wanted her, whether overladen or not, to work in their homes or their fields, but the house that Petroula liked most and where she decided to stay was the house of Lukas, a farmer-merchant with a large family, one of whose sons was called Christoforos. Christoforos fell in love with Petroula, set no store by her father's dark side and, from a servant girl, made her his wife, but forbidding anyone to call her by the name of Petroula. "Her name is Parthena," he said, "and you'll all call her Parthena from now on—enough of the stones she's had to bear." Nevertheless, it was difficult for him to get out of the habit of "Petroula," and even more difficult for him to oblige his tongue each time to say Parthena (it sounded strange to him, soulless), and so this wife of his ended the circle of her life as Petroula—till some grandchild of hers would be officially christened Petronia and one of her sons Petros.

Petroula and Christoforos had five children (more or less one every year), and just before the birth of the last one she received word that her father was gravely ill in prison and wanted to see her before he died. She dropped everything and went. During all those years, she hadn't visited him once—she wasn't even sure where his prison was, if he was alive or dead—and she appeared before him filled with remorse and pain that she, too, his only daughter, had abandoned him at his most difficult hour. Yes, he'd covered his hands in blood, hands that ministered to Christians, that baptized them, married them, buried them, yet this man was still her father . . . even if the air still echoed with the shepherd's claims to the contrary, claims that cost him his head.

"Forgive me," she said to him that day in the prison, not having the courage to look him in the eye, "forgive me for leaving you all alone then. I was only little, I didn't understand, forgive me."

In a wilting voice (which would often forget and become livelier) and with

2. *Petra* in Greek. See Matt. 16:18 (translator's note).

a welter of purposeless gestures, he told her that it was he who should ask for forgiveness from her and not she from him. "Damnation's fire awaits me," he said, "hell with its fire and its cauldrons. For all eternity I will be the shepherd's slayer. Who? Me! . . . No one will give my name to their children. No one, I'll say it again, no one will give my name to their children."

This matter seemed to concern him especially, and he repeated it, raising a fiery finger as though expressing his wrath rather than his grievance; even to Petroula it seemed at that moment pointless, inopportune—and what arrogance; people had been killed, lives lost because of him, and all he was worried about was his *name*—yet given up as she was to the darkest and most tyrannical emotion, she tried to mollify him, rubbing his chest, and said, "What makes you say that? Do you think I denied you even that? I've already given your name to one of my children . . . to the firstborn, in fact."

"Is it true?" he asked her, astonished, and you'd have wagered that he would live another thirty years after that.

"True! What, would I lie?" she said and her eyes filled with tears—besides what truth and what falsehood concerned itself with them?

And this haughty man, this wretched creature, mumbling something into the palms of his hands, gave up his soul.

Petroula returned to Christoforos and her children feeling ill, as if she had undergone all the hardships in the world during this short trip. And whereas for so many years she had said nothing about her childhood, from the time, that is, when she'd heard that her father had killed someone with a stone to the head to the next day when she'd seen some men carrying her mother half dead, with her clothes torn by her own nails, foaming at the mouth, jerking and howling in a way that rent the air, she only talked and murmured to herself about this after returning from her visit to the prison, all the images passed vividly again before her eyes, not allowing her to find things as she had left them. At times the images must have come so alive that they'd find her half unconscious here and there, with torn and wet handkerchiefs round her, bubbles of saliva on her chin, and imploring them (as she'd heard her mother do then) to leave her, to leave her alone . . . Once they found her with three teeth in her hands, without roots or blood, almost soft; they grabbed them from her to examine them more closely; they asked her about them, and she told them that they had fallen out themselves, that she had nudged them a little with her tongue and they had fallen out, but everyone knew that only vitriol seared and loosened teeth and anything else like that, and naturally they panicked and began hitting her to get the truth out of her, and she cried out in vain that she hadn't drunk any such thing, where would she get it, why were they hitting her, why wouldn't they leave her alone . . . Christoforos came and took her from their hands and held her in his own.

"Tell me," he implored her, "tell me if you drank any and I won't do anything to you, I won't let anyone harm you." But Petroula hadn't drunk any vitriol—she admitted that she'd wanted to, but she hadn't dared—and as for the teeth she couldn't remember anything, her hands were empty and she wasn't missing any teeth from her mouth. But nor would she open it so they could look, nor could they ever make her open it. Meanwhile—the climax of the mystery—the three teeth had disappeared; the person who had first taken them from her hand swore that he didn't know what had happened to them: he took them, saw them, felt them, but after that he knew nothing. And the same was true of the others.

Such were the sad and incredible things that happened; her mind had been affected, they said, by seeing again her deranged father—and how willingly she had gone to see him!—and before very long she departed on the longest journey.

In his chair, Christoforos wept for her and rebuked her. He felt terribly confused and helpless—as pitiable as she was herself—with her last wish, which was to give their last child, who was barely a month old, her father's name . . . "What's all this, dear?" he asked her, and he reminded her of how *that cloven-hoofed demon* had not only killed the shepherd but had killed her mother and had now killed her. "He's ruined me from one moment to the next and you want to give his name to our child? To your child and mine, who is without a mother now because of him? Well, no, we can do without that. And why didn't you remain with us to give him the name yourself? Do you think it's easy to leave it to others to do the work? How could you do it, you, a reasonable woman . . . But, of course, it's pointless asking you."

Yet since time moves all and conquers all, preserves all and softens all, eight years later, Christoforos gave the name of that accursed father-in-law to the first child that he had with his second wife, Eftha. He couldn't keep Petroula's last wish on hold any longer, he said, even though he totally disagreed with her then. As for Eftha, given that she had five children already from her own previous marriage—and since we're dealing with such stories and characters, we may as well regard second marriages as a prerequisite—and given that these children already had names ranging from the most unusual to the most common (there was a Cletia and an Eumolpos, but there was also a Marikoula, a Georgos, and a Giannis), it didn't bother her especially to christen her sixth child Theagenis, *of God's lineage.* In fact, she found it god-fearing—and God played more than a minor role in her life—though it was *this precisely* that caused Christoforos new worries. "Look," he proposed, "don't say that god-fearing name again, don't even think it again, because that's how the other one came to a bad end with that name, God's lineage and all that, and he reached the depths he reached. So enough, we don't want to be infected by the illness too—it's just a name and nothing more." Eftha reassured him that they would give something to charity and that would be that.

Theagenis then was the firstborn of Christoforos and Eftha or the sixth child of each of them separately, as well as being the eleventh in an already prolific family created in common by these two. Other children would follow, but Theagenis—first, sixth, or eleventh—was unique: he was the most attractive and loveliest boy to have been born in the past—what shall we say? hundred?—years. Even when he was still an infant, Eftha would dress him with his clothes inside-out, with the stitching and seams on the outside, so that people would find some blemish on him and not put the evil eye on him through their admiration or envy. When the child began to grow and, alas yes, to become shamelessly handsome, she would shear his hair like a goat, dirty his cheeks with charcoal, rub garlic oil on his neck, curse him and deride him, and generally do whatever passed through her hands in order to ward off the evil eye that she saw more or less honing in on him, and of course to temper his beauty, which was now tantamount to some kind of menace, something catastrophic. And when she saw that her hidden fears, alas, had started to take on flesh and blood and women gazed at him from their windows ready to die for him or, at least, to slip out of their house at his first sign, there was nothing left for her to do but take him to the stream and rechristen him Hesychios—a name, moreover, with which she shared a common feast day (Hesychios and Efthalia, martyrs, March 2), and this was how she came up with it. The goodly woman couldn't think of a better, more effective one, and with baited breath she waited for feelings to calm. But quite suddenly she died, bitten by a snake in the fields, and so she didn't see the most dramatic turn of events, the climax so to speak, of the feelings, which would result in that early-morning *harvesting* of children outside the front door . . . This is why Christoforos referred to her first of all at the evening council, counting her lucky that she was no longer alive—though he was sure that even her bones would be a little sad at that moment.

Then he turned to the cause: "Hesychios," he said, "you've brought us anything but peace and quiet, you and those useless looks of yours that grew where we had sown other seeds . . . I have called you all here tonight because it can't go on, something has to be done about you, you have to find a wife, I mean a mother for the six children you have already. Do something about it—."

"Ah, dear Lord, dear Lord, what a fool you are!" cried out one of Hesychios's older sisters, or rather half-sisters, a daughter of Eftha from her first marriage called Cletia. "Wasn't it enough that you had your way with the wretches, did you have to get them pregnant as well? Whose children should I clean first? I was born to clean children, but I've not had any joy of my own."

"Quiet," shouted Christoforos, "I'm speaking now! You can all speak when your turn comes!" And he continued to counsel and reproach Hesychios, to wave his finger at him and say, "Do something about it, you mindless wretch, I don't care how you do it, but find yourself a decent woman with a big heart who'll forgive you for all your past and help you raise those children so they don't grow up in shame—and if you want to have a couple more, then do it, but don't try our patience anymore, I'm telling you for your own good, we don't want any more of your shenanigans, enough. We've all loved and given fair due to women, you're not the only one. But remember: all in good measure, nothing in excess." He also reminded him that he could very well be much more severe with him and furious, that he could even throw him out of the house if he so wanted, disown him, but he would wait a little longer to see.

"All I have to do is make up my mind, father, and you'll see I will," was Hesychios's reply, which was provocatively prudent (but this was how he usually spoke), yet naturally the matter would not end there. All his brothers and sisters, half-brothers and half-sisters took the opportunity to give him a piece of their mind that evening; many of them had grown sick of his carryings-on—and Christoforos gave them all free rein, so long as they didn't all speak together.

"Whose children am I to clean first?" asked Cletia, impatiently starting up again and apparently particularly sick and tired. She showed Hesychios her hands, which had cracked from all the washing; the water had eaten away her nails, and only a few hangnails remained like scales. "Take hold of them and see for yourself . . . take them, what are you waiting for?" But as soon as Hesychios took hold of them—simply to do as she asked, not because he needed to see for himself—Cletia started to shake and stumbled. "I don't care," she said to him now, like a martyr who rejoices in his martyrdom and asks to give more; "all I want is for you to listen to my story, to afford me a little time . . . From the age of five, I've been cleaning babies and changing diapers. First my younger brothers and sisters from my other father, then the brothers and sisters I had from that father and the other mother, then all of you, with you first and foremost, and then the dozens of nephews and half-nephews. I gave up any opportunities I had, cleaning babies, lulling them to sleep, picking lice from them, dressing them, getting them out of bed, putting them to bed, carrying them, feeding them, making myself ill. My back has gone, I've no nails left on my fingers . . . And now these six have turned up, the fruit of your *peace and quiet*, each with a different mother . . . who can say? I've wasted away bending over water; I see the phantom of myself in it, but I don't care, I don't care about any of it. Just so long as you recognize it all."

Things very often took such turns—just so long as Hesychios *recognized it*, or touched it or even just caressed it with one of his nods. Very often and even in his own home, meaning among his own brothers and sisters, who, apart from anything else, had grown sick of it. They were at a loss; did he have all the luck in the world on his side? Or was the world a lucky place to have him living in it? Whatever the case, these latter, his brothers and sisters, had decided that evening to free themselves of the irresponsibility stemming from his charm, to be harsh, to rid themselves of that reverie in which his stunning presence, his usually few, simplistic words, enwrapped them. "Well, we do care and care plenty," said one of them ill-humoredly; "because we've been paying the piper for so many years, it's us that the old foxes stare at and smile to themselves."

And some of them began to touch more upon the ethical side of the matter—what would people say, how would those children be able to show their faces while they were growing up?—while the others touched on the purely practical and immediate side: how would they manage with six new mouths to feed in the already over-large family? "We'll have to take the food from our mouths," they said, "and cut it into six—is it right?"

It was simply a bit exaggerated. Because they had more than a little land, tobacco fields, wheat fields, vineyards, acres of citrus trees; they also had shops, a large inn, the largest, basically the only inn in the entire region, where, in parentheses, Saint Paul had stayed, *coming from Amphipolis and journeying to Thessaloníki.* From grandfather to grandfather, they told of Paul's passing through those parts and, yes, he had spent the night at that inn—which was different then, of course—and it was here he had met the fair Lydia, merchant in porphyry, a renowned idolater, who, nevertheless, tired of all the late nights and the marketplace, thirsted for something else, for something new to believe in, and so, after listening to Saint Paul, this, the first woman from among the Greeks and the Europeans, embraced Christianity, distributed her wealth, and followed him.

It was only natural, then, for an inn that still bore echoes of names such as "Paul" and "Lydia" to also attract many travelers or simply the curious to stay under its roof, and consequently many florins or banknotes to its erstwhile owners and their descendants. No, they had no complaints concerning the inn, nor from those years that were favorable to the crops, yet—one of the brothers again stressed to Hesychios—six wildling mouths in the house was by no means a negligible number.

The others had their say, too, and to which in any case he had no objection, while the night was now almost over and two of them had fallen asleep where they sat and couldn't be made to get up for anything. Only Julia, one of Hesychios's younger sisters, with red wavy hair and exceptionally soft skin, had not said anything all that time and could feel all the eyes—including his—weighing on her and waiting.

"Say something, don't sit there silent," they urged her, "it'll do him good, not bad."

"I know it'll do him good," whispered Julia, "but what can I say? . . . I can't think of anything."

"Tell me a proverb," Hesychios himself said to her, as if asking her for a favor; because Julia was fond of proverbs, as well as riddles, and following a grave illness she had undergone when small when she had had to be taken out of school, she had begun writing them in an exercise book; she would sit for hours beside the window and write or make up proverbs and suchlike; and if they didn't reproach her for wasting her time like that instead of getting on with her work, doing something more useful, it was at the orders of Christoforos, who had a particular fondness for her, the same fondness that he had for Hesychios—she was his *velvety*—just as she did for him.

"A proverb?" she repeated.

"There: tell him the one about *If you sleep with dogs, you'll wake up with fleas!*" said an elder sister, trying to help her.

"No, it's not appropriate," Julia retorted bashfully. "Dogs and fleas *for him?*"

"It's very appropriate, very appropriate," the other sister insisted. "He went too far with his flirtations and it's only right that he's now got lumbered with six sacks on his back—that's what the proverb means. But we've got lumbered too, and it doesn't say anything about that . . . So you find a better one then."

While the other sister was talking, Julia was looking out of the window at the early-morning moon, at the sky which had now begun to redden, to shine dimly . . . she also glimpsed a shadow flitting past, wondered whether it was real, whether she really had seen it, and what it could possibly want there at that hour . . . "Oh, so that's what you meant?" she murmured, surprised, without having heard it all. "Well then, this one might be more suitable: *Feed a wolf in winter and he'll eat you in the summer.*"

They all shouted, *Well done,* applauded her—*she took her time, but she came up with it!* But she wasn't pleased, she didn't want this kind of praise, and that's why she shot a quick look at Hesychios as if to say, *I take it back.* Then she moved away from the window and passing between them whispered in a deep, warm voice, one truly velvety and much more mature than to be expected for her age, "Everyone has had their say; time for you to get married, Hesychios."

The following afternoon, he went to think over what Julia had said to him. He went out of the lower door, saw the ruins opposite—as if he were seeing them for the first time—and headed off in that direction . . . Amidst the collapsed floors of a house of the kind that seems never to have been lived in, to have always been like that, amidst the crumbling walls, the gaping or not even gaping windows, and a pitiful jumble of bed frames, broken tables, chair legs, smashed kitchen utensils, sieves, vessels, tattered clothes (always we wonder what bodies these once warmed and what happened to those bodies, where did they go), and along with some stout mice that put the cats to flight, there, right there, in the heart of all this desolation, grew a renowned fig tree with spreading branches. Every year without fail these branches filled with figs. Countless small mauve figs that never ripened, never grew, never became edible. So no one touched them, neither the jackdaws nor the sparrows. Eventually they fell, rotted slowly on the earth, filled with worms and gladly dissolved, providing ever more fertile ground for their mother—the impenitent wild fig. Truly impenitent and un-relenting, yet providing enviable shade in the summer with all her foliage and enormous size . . . It was there that Hesychios went to reflect on his marriage.

He put a large stone beneath the tree—though there were many there al-ready that he ignored—searched for a kerchief to put over it, couldn't find one, blew the dust from it, and sat down. He considered it a tremendous undertaking to *see*, to imagine the face of the woman who was destined from that day to be-come his wife. He felt pressure, a weight in his temples, as though they were asking him to imagine the nose or the gait of God. And just how might God's nose be, if, that is, a God ever deigned to have a nose, or his gait, if he walked? And how—?

Yet sometimes such unprovoked thoughts merge with related events. So we might say, for at that very same moment a voice was heard behind him: "Don't be alarmed . . . it's me," and immediately, as if he had been softly struck with a whip, he recalled his mother, Eftha, who, when he was small and, of course, she was still alive, read passages from the Old Testament to him and his brothers and sisters. She would read them syllable by syllable, stressing every word, and then would explain it all to them in her own words, with vivid gestures and ex-pressions—she really lived it. Like when God catches Adam and Eve having eaten the forbidden fruit and his sandals are heard on the leaves and his thun-derous voice in heaven: "Adam and Eve, may fire rain down on you, what have you done? Come here!" But there was one time when he said it differently, more softly, strangely: "*Don't be alarmed . . . it's me.*" And naturally they were more than a little alarmed and with difficulty swallowed their tongues (Adam didn't even manage to swallow the apple—the bite stuck in his throat, and since then all men carry the painful memento at that point in their throat), just as Hesychios was now more than a little alarmed at that unexpected voice . . . He turned and saw a woman in black, nothing out of the ordinary at first sight, and yet he was transfixed. His hand, as he had turned to grip the stone, remained where it was.

"Did I scare you?" she asked him, terrified.

"No," he replied, uncertain, "why? . . . Who are you?"

She was wearing black clothes from head to toe, of the kind that were once other colors but had been dyed black out of necessity, so that the dye was dull in some places, in others bright and shiny and in others nearer to violet: as though she were wearing five shades of black. She had one sock rolled down to her ankle, so it looked like a thick bracelet—for a moment he thought it was a ruby bracelet! A shortish woman, neither plump nor lean, with her neck bent as though she had suffered something in her sleep, and with a noticeable lack of calm in her fingers.

"I know you, don't I know you?" he said, with that same lack of certainty in his voice.

"Mmm, where from?" she mumbled sorrowfully. And then, in a somewhat stronger voice: "I don't think you know me, I live far off," she said. She paused again and took a step closer and introduced herself, gazing at the fig leaves playing with their shadows on his cheeks, saying that she was Febronia, the wife of the cobbler Argyris F.

"Didn't he die years ago?" he asked, to show her that he remembered things—and immediately bit his lip: someone else's death, her youngest daughter's, two or three months before, would no doubt mean much more to her, this unexpected Febronia—and in recent years, in recent times, young girls didn't very often die in that place save only for his sake . . . He resolved not to ask anything more; let her ask the questions and he would answer as best he could.

"He died years ago, as you say," she said, "and my daughter . . . because you knew my daughter, seventy-eight days ago, I'm keeping count. And yesterday," she went on, "one of the children you found outside your door . . . the youngest, perhaps . . . was . . . hers, you know, my daughter's, the one with the beautiful eyes—I don't know, maybe they all had beautiful eyes! Pity . . . He's a boy, does he cry a lot? He has a mark the shape of a plum on his belly, he's probably the youngest of them all. If he cries a lot, I can take him."

"He doesn't cry a lot, none of them cry," he said, and he was unable to conceal how relieved he felt that she hadn't started throwing stones at his head or asking him extremely *difficult* questions. He stared at her almost with gratitude, and she responded with a gaze full of sorrow and worry, as though she were tormented by other things behind all that she had been saying, from which, however, there was no lack of grief or concern.

"Yesterday . . . ," she began again and moved suddenly, walking away, leaving the shade of the fig tree and going over to the ruined wall; she wanted to show him something and grabbed hold of a piece of timber as her feet slipped on the stones, but immediately, as if accustomed to it, she regained her balance. "There, yesterday, from here . . . here is where I was standing with the others and we all watched in secret as you took the infants . . . you and your folks . . . you took the little innocents in without any fuss. And I, when . . . when I saw you on your own—the infants were gone—I felt sad. I mean, I felt sad, *just that,* don't take it the wrong way. I thought you were . . . better not say . . . after all that happened . . . Ah!" she exclaimed, as if becoming angry. "Better not to pay any attention! I think one thing, say another, and mean to say something else!"

"Tell me what you think," he said to her calmly.

She looked at him as if not hearing what he'd said to her, but then her eyes filled with suspicion: "Tell you what I think? Don't go trying to get the better of me, though . . . I'm not my daughter!" she reminded him severely. Yet again the other feeling overcame her, the one that was wearing her out: "I felt sorry because . . . what does *good* mean, do you know?" she asked him, and without waiting for a reply: "Because you seemed good to me! . . . Deep down . . . The others were ready to kill me! But that's how it was, I wasn't expecting it, no, not expecting it, it was like a lightning flash, that's why I can't explain. As if I'm in a trance, as if I'm struggling with the air. Since yesterday! In spite of all that happened—as God is my witness! Since yesterday. I've been wearing her clothes, we had the same build, I dyed them black and I wear them so the evil that happened won't ever be forgotten. And yesterday you seemed good to me! Yesterday, since yesterday."

She said the last words quickly, raced through them almost without taking a breath, without any pause or hesitation, unlike with her first words, and yet she looked behind her filled with fear lest, just like yesterday, the other women would jump at her.

For yesterday, after the events at the ruins, in these very same ruins, she had hurriedly set off home with the other women following close behind her like Furies, in the same way that for a long time they had been following—she too— their rage for him. And when they were unable to enter her home—Febronia had quickly and forcefully slammed shut the lower door and bolted it so that the plaster had fallen from the side walls—they escorted her up all the stairs to her bed with demonic cries, a mixture of shrieking and wailing, that drove her crazy, made her whinny in reply. She shut the windows with a bang and stayed like that in the house for hours, like a winged horse that didn't know where to fly and where to stand. Her children returned, the two from the trade they were learning, the one from the fields, and finding doors and windows barred, they called to her, got no reply, and went to their uncle's, the miller. They came back again in the evening, when it had got dark, and Febronia had opened the doors and windows wide, but she wasn't inside. They imagined that she must have lost track of the time amidst the graves, that of Rodanthe, their sister—she went there every evening with the baby and wept—or that she must be still chatting with the other women, so they ate alone, filling the place with stones and crumbs . . . While waiting for her, they set to cleaning it all up so she wouldn't scold them when she arrived. Then they got tired and went to bed— she still hadn't shown up, where could she be? The eldest one—twelve years old—was more worried than the others and went out in the streets and to the houses round about, shouting her name, while the other two were asleep inside. They heard her in their sleep when she returned; heard her rasping breath and were relieved, turned over. She was struggling with herself, like a salamander dancing in the flames without getting burned, without falling lifeless, but without being able to escape, dancing as long as the flames dance and dying with them.

. . . She hadn't been to the graves or anywhere else, only to the ruins, to the gaps in destiny, and had been watching his house from there. What matter if no one forgave her! She felt her saliva thinning as with those on the brink of death, but what she longed for with all her soul was not to escape. She half-opened the window to let in a little air and fell asleep listening to her sharp wheezing breath . . . Then that dream came, a richly destructive dream, and however little importance you give to dreams, deep down you do give importance. And to such dreams as this, you more than give. You give in completely—*what defense is there against the body's sweet workings?*

She saw him with others, well-dressed, serious, hands behind his back, a little crumpled by age, in fact. He was chatting as though he had graduated from top schools, bowed his head to listen, hands perpetually behind him, raised his eyebrows, had the air of an experienced and highly interesting doctor. He was a doctor. And when he wasn't listening, he himself was talking and the others were listening. She was there too. It was his hands more than his words that drew her. The way he had them joined like that behind his back, in the queue, she held hers in the same way and started like sand to glide over toward him. She stood beside him while he was embroiled in the conversation, and while her fingers were perspiring and twisting, not knowing how to get closer to his, he had already grasped hers and was squeezing them. The unspeakable always happened behind their backs—no one else saw anything; she listened to him. She thought to herself with some bitterness, "*Experienced*—that's what it means, that's what he did with the other women. From in front a savior and doctor, from behind the serpent's naked." But these were powerless thoughts; in fact, she too had acquired thousands of years of experience, and they no longer knew, from one moment to the next, who gave the most pleasure to the other just by touching, nothing more for the time being, and with their fingers entwining like tentacles. The bowels of the earth rumbled in her ears, and it would become clear, the others would begin to get wind of it, their nostrils were quivering like those of swine, one even resembled her husband Argyris, he was standing right at the back at some distance and was looking at their hands as if hypnotized; it was impossible to say what he might do. Fortunately, Febronia recalled, he was dead. And someone dead couldn't become enraged at what he saw and beat her black and blue. Yet despite all this she wasn't sure, particularly about the former—the worry was already there and had added another feel to the happenings. And Argyris, who saw everything and was not at all pleased, dropped to the ground and wept like a little child. "A bullet got him in the belly!" a passerby told her, and Febronia went to lift him up, but instead she found an opportunity and sidled off, taking to her heels. "Wool over their eyes! I have to pull the wool over their eyes," she thought, and ran, ran, till she came to a sea, to the quayside in a large harbor, things she didn't know, that she'd never seen in her life—about the sea, the oceans, she knew a little. There was a mist and from out of the mist came an old man with white hair, white eyes, riding a beast. He cracked a whip, greeted her with an endless good da-a-a-ay, and vanished. Meanwhile, a blessed wind had got up, blew, blew, and dissolved the mist. But whether for good luck or bad, an old man, nimble and barefoot, appeared again, and quickly said to her: "Get up onto my shoulders, don't dawdle, he's waiting for you." She got onto his shoulders, hung her legs to right and left of his neck like braids, and he carried her like a bearer, but a bearer with devious skills, who lost no time in collecting his fee in advance: he did something with the collar on the back of his neck; the material grew hard, sprouted something like a nose, and this thing rubbed itself softly between her legs, on the underbelly, in harmony with his undulating step and the cunning movements of his shoulders, and thrilled her to the marrow, filled her with pleasure, overwhelmed her. She wondered whether she would tell *him* or keep it secret—now it was not only from her husband that she had to hide. "I have brought her to you, I surrender her to you, she remains untouched," the old man, with great solemnity, and of course with not a little sarcasm, said to *him*. And she once again found herself on her feet, without any beast of burden, and he took her, dismissed the old man, and laid her on her back. But the wind got up again, furious now, and lashed them, didn't allow them to come together, prevented them . . . "Leave it, leave it to me, it's from your girlfriend!" said Febronia—meaning her wretched daughter—and removing her socks and an earring, she gave them to the wind, otherwise it wouldn't have left them alone. Now being the sole master, he put her as he wanted her and with a simple touch, but which was like the first peck of a hungry bird in the wilds, he ripped off her clothes and began to inundate her from her feet up, ever up . . . Delight and despondence that are somewhere referred to were but drops in the ocean; given that their longing, which naturally (and fortunately so) can't be described, was endless and a thousand times more pleasurable than its very own consummation.

And at this point, Febronia's dream ended—or began.

If she had dreamt all this happening with a stranger, with someone who, how shall we say, didn't exist in this world (and sleep is teeming with such as these), perhaps she would have been content not to go looking for anything more than what the dream gave her—and that was far from little. Yet with the thought that this man was well known, that he existed and more than existed—at this point her daughter came back from the dead—that it was this same man who yesterday had picked the infants up from the ground, had handed them to his folks, and then had fixed his smiling eyes on the ruins; with the thought that he too was doing something in his own house at that same time, two score streets away from her own, or was dreaming of something himself, thinking of something as she was . . . with the temptation of such thoughts, anyway, Febronia forgot everything else—the mourning for her daughter, her oath to hate him as long as he lived (she didn't forget, it was what stoked the fire)—and, like a madwoman, she set out again for the ruins . . . Again, because it was already the second time. She had gone in the evening, as we know, as soon as it had got dark, long before she had had the dream, but then it had been different: she had gone completely blindly, feeling guilty and even unprepared, with disgust at that panting that came from her chest and *announced* her like the bells worn by lepers. At times, if nothing else, she felt so unbearably guilty, so full of miasmas and plagues, that she only just refrained on seeing a stone from taking hold of it and cracking open her head with it! But these were waves, large or small, that came and went to frighten her, to turn her back—woe betide if she expected from life (*from life*) to bring her into his arms without first making her go through hell, through whatever the waves had to throw at her, without all those trials and as many again, as had happened in the dream . . . where, here too, not everything had happened at the first attempt.

The first time she arrived, she found nothing. Just the stones, the timber, the wild grass, and, beyond, the fig with its leaves, the old clothes, and a few sounds here and there, creaking and suchlike, that may simply have been her imagination. Yet it was as if all this, even the clear darkness, had a second underlying element *that was looking at her* without her looking at it. She recalled that she had encountered someone on her way there, just before, who had walked past her, or, rather, whom she had walked past, lowering her head, without either of them exchanging a word. At the time, this was a relief for her, but now it began to torment her: perhaps the fact that he didn't talk to her, didn't ask her anything, didn't seem to recognize her, didn't even halt for a moment, meant exactly the opposite, that he had recognized her only too well and had suspected everything she was up to? Perhaps he had simply turned round and had followed her here? . . . Her blood ran cold: that was it: *someone was standing behind her.*

"My end," she thought, and motionless, like a pillar of salt, she kept her eyes fixed on Hesychios's house opposite, at the dull yellow light in one of the upper windows. "Now, it's too late, I can't even shift my gaze, and it's better that way," she thought. And she waited for the inevitable and redemptive punishment before even having partaken of the sin . . . But the time passed and nothing happened, except that the horrible feeling of that *presence* behind her grew and grew. "Dear Lord, why such anxiety?" she asked herself. "What have I done to him? What's he getting ready to do behind my back?" And as once again nothing happened despite the time she gave him, she realized that she had no more endurance for such unsettled business, that she had to put an end to this torment, and she suddenly turned round to face him: "What do you want here?" her shrill voice cried out.

There was something on the ground that at her frenzied turn moved off; everything went quiet, then, presently, it stirred again and reassumed its pose. Somewhere to her left, the woman saw two eyes gleaming uncannily, two golden-red phosphorescent jewels . . . The blood flowed again in her veins: she thought that she had fallen into the clutches of death, or even the arms of some fiend, the nails of her daughter — but they were the eyes of a cat! The kind of cat that the devil sends when he can't be bothered to go himself. "You scared me, you wretched cat, be off with you!" she said to it, waving her arm and taking care (only just remembering where she was) not to raise her voice too loudly. "Off with you!" she said more quietly, deeply, indignantly, and waved her arm again. "Are you deaf?" The animal condescended, unwillingly, to move again, to keep a respectable distance in fact, and when the woman persisted in driving it away, now stamping her feet and grabbing hold of a stone, it looked truly puzzled. Then, with those airy outstretched steps—without so much as a hint of a meow—it went elsewhere, away from her, leaving her alone. If that's what she wanted.

Such was the sad yet comical experience she had had on her first nocturnal visit to that place, with cats and ruins seemingly caring as little about her troubles as God did. Nevertheless, following this experience, everything seemed more natural to her, more balanced; her mind cleared a jot; she remembered her children, whom she hadn't seen all day, whom she'd left shut out of the house, left hungry; she remembered her little grandson, and who knew when and if she'd ever set eyes on him again, her daughter, whom she most definitely wouldn't ever set eyes on again (unless there is a life hereafter); she even remembered that the house of that ruinous and worthless man was exactly opposite her, still with that same light in that same window, and that she, innocent of innocents, was standing there without any particular precaution, not concealed behind the highest part of the crumbling wall as at least she had been that morning with the other women but exposed in a gap of sizable proportions—rather like a gateway—amidst stones that had once tumbled for good and had never moved again. If anyone were to pass along the street or open the door opposite, he would see her right in front of them—and if he didn't take her for a ghost, then he would certainly recognize her. "Am I out of my mind?" she mumbled to herself, "well and truly?" And she counseled herself, seeing that she was already mad even to be there, to conceal herself at least.

And so, with her body behind that piece that you could still call a wall, a remnant of a wall, she stuck out her head like a tortoise and looked at his house, enclosed as it was in the quietest darkness. If some noise, the distant barking of a dog or anything, made her think she was in danger, she retreated completely, shrank behind the wall, and then gradually, as soon as everything was quiet again, she got up courage and gazed out . . . either from the edge of the wall or through one of the large gaps that in any case were everywhere. She reflected that if any of those wretched gaps were made of quince or apple, she would eat it because she was hungry by now—she hadn't put anything into her mouth since the morning. And every so often she wondered what they could possibly want with that light up there, in a large window—had they forgotten it? Everything pointed to the fact that they were all asleep, in this as in all the other houses. And after who knows how long, Febronia saw at last a shadow coming up to the window. She immediately bent down, almost kissed her feet, as though the shadow would have been able from way up there to see her, she who had become one with the wall and the stones. Her heart was beating so fast that she was afraid she would die on the spot—her husband had died of his heart. And she allowed a few more moments to pass, to allow that mad fluttering in her chest to abate, before daring to straighten up again, to raise herself up, and to allow her eyes to search for a gap with the greed that a drinker searches for a glass . . . The shadow was still there, just as she was still here; it had its back turned, and from the slenderness of the angles of the back, from the thinness of the neck and all the hair that glinted as well, Febronia understood that it was a girl, one of his young sisters, and who knows what she was doing at that time of night . . . Yet what was she doing in her house, in her own house, even though she should be sleeping at that time instead of leaning with her back against the window? "Or perhaps I should be asking myself what I'm doing here, in this place, in the middle of the night," Febronia thought, "when even ghosts avoid it?"

But then again, she wouldn't have left, wouldn't have moved from that spot, if the girl (who didn't turn her back at all) hadn't suddenly made a movement with her arm over her head, waving it in the air or on the windowpane, as if she were wanting to say something with her hand . . . "Leave! Leave! Everyone's telling you to!" muttered Febronia, feeling hurt, as if talking to someone beside her who took no notice of words and gestures. And after crouching down again and climbing down as carefully as she could from the stone piles surrounding her and climbing up from some potholes a little way off (where she once again saw the cat's eyes gleaming), she took the path leading home, a prodigal and imprudent soul, as she saw herself. When she was outside the shock radius, when his house behind her had been hidden by others, she started running as if she were being chased by ten wild dogs. If anyone saw her and asked what she was doing out at that time, she would say that she had lost one of her animals and was looking for it.

She arrived and through the crack in the door heard her children's breathing; they stirred when they snorted, clicked their tongues, and went on sleeping. On tiptoe, she climbed the stairs—the wretched things creaked—and like a thief went into her own room. But there she had another fright: on her bed she found her twelve-year-old, Konstantakis, with a wooden swallow in his arms and a candle that was melting and dripping on his hand, and that, evidently, was his company.

"What are you doing in here?" she asked him under her breath.

"I was waiting for you," he said.

"I'm here, now go and sleep."

"I'll go—where were you?" he asked.

The child wasn't speaking bossily, he wasn't playing the role of the master, he was like her: hurt and at a loss.

"Where were you?" he asked again, lowering his head to his chest—if he had had longer hair, it would have been singed by the flame of the candle.

"You'll burn yourself! Go to sleep like your brothers and sisters," she told him.

"I'll go," Konstantakis said again, and sliding from the bed he got as far as the door with his candle and swallow.

"Aren't you going to tell me where you were?"

"An animal got loose and I was looking for it, searching all this time."

"Which one?" asked the boy in surprise.

He was irritating her—what did he care *which* animal?

"The black goat with the patch," she told him, and she knew that the boy would have seen the goat, that he would have fed it as he did every evening.

"I fed it . . . ," he said. "When we got back from the mill, I fed it—we went to the mill when we got home and didn't find you . . . the house was locked."

"You did right. Your uncle likes some company."

"And when we came back from the mill, you still weren't here. The house was unlocked, but empty . . . It was then that I fed it," Konstantakis explained.

"You fed it, I heard you. Then it got loose."

The boy didn't speak, it all seemed pointless; he puffed at the candle and it went out.

"That goat is cantankerous, it's broken loose twice before, don't you remember?" she said to him in the darkness. And it was a good thing that she remembered to say it—it may have puzzled him even more, but it may also have convinced him. "Do you hear what I say, Konstantakis? I can't see you."

Konstantakis pulled on a string and, tap-tap, the swallow flapped its wooden wings: he heard her . . . "And did you find it?" he asked then.

"Yes, I found it, did you think I wouldn't? It's downstairs. Now go and get to sleep, leave the candle here."

"No, I want to take it."

"All right then, take it."

The boy went out through the door, but before she had closed it behind him, he asked, "And the baby, where is it?"

"We gave away the baby," she told him. "This morning—yesterday, when was it . . . With a bit of a fuss, but now it's taken care of. We don't have nearly enough to bring up the baby as well."

"We do have enough," said the boy, "now that we don't have Rodanthe."

"*Now that we don't have Rodanthe!* . . . No we don't have enough . . . Don't fall on the stairs, Konstantakis, sleep well."

"*They gave it away,*" murmured the boy disappointedly, and walked towards the stairs; the boards didn't creak at all under his feet.

"Innocent little soul!" his mother whispered behind him. And then, with an almost childish malevolence, with a sense of satisfaction that stung and burned, she gleefully wrung her hands and chortled to herself: "We gave it, we gave it, and didn't try to save it!" The walls around her again began to dance, to spout flames . . . She gazed at herself in the mirror, where she knew there was a mirror, in which every day she saw her years pass; but without a candle she could see nothing. Stretching out her arm, she opened the window a little. It was a cool night in mid-June, but she was on fire, she needed a little air . . . Then came sleep, after the dream . . . And after the dream, there she was, setting out again for the ruins—a second time.

Day had just begun to break when she arrived—sometimes taking the same paths, sometimes others—and saw the same light in the window. "Are they having a family council?" she wondered, and looked for where she could best conceal herself, more safely and with more of a view. This time, she was helped by the first light of day, she didn't have to search blindly; and when at last she found the ideal position, the light in the window went out.

She felt abandoned; it was the coldest moment—another light had gone out like that before her eyes. She felt that she had been completely abandoned by her passion, her excitement, things which, after all, had come to her without her asking for them. What had brought her here for a second time? And since it had brought her, why had it left her now? She looked around her and saw everything as it was, and it was as she knew it to be. Even the cat had gone. She felt the dream going, with only the ground remaining beneath her feet—she had put herself through it all in vain.

She went back home, to her chores. The children were still sleeping—Konstantakis with one eyelid half open and trembling, one eye and his mouth; this scene made her tremble too, want to shout, to waken him, but she held herself back; the boy was breathing deeply, it was nothing. She left all three of them to sleep and went to milk her goats, the black one and the white one.

"You two are to blame for everything!" she said to both without differentiating between them. "Sluts! Hussies!" And when she took their milk . . . "There, there, there! And there!" She twice clouted each of the two oblong heads, the goats having no time to defend themselves, though they were in no way to blame, or at least were as much to blame as she was. Their eyes, a greeny white, like unripe grapes, remained impassive and reminded her of the eyes of the old man in the dream, of the mistman on his donkey who had said good da-a-a-ay to her, and this shook her right away (was she going to live with dreams?), but it also stunned her as though it were she who had had to endure the clouts, the *sour grapes* . . . "Don't take offense at me," she said repentantly to the two goats, "it all comes back to me."

She gave the milk to her children to drink when they woke up, and avoiding looking too much at Konstantakis (but there was something about his eye, still half open when awake; she wasn't to be fooled) she sent him back into the fields, sending the two younger ones to their trade, and towards midday she was back to herself and back on the path . . . For the third time. And in the light of the sun.

The early-morning frost, the coolness of the night had given way to a hot day that in a few hours would be a scorcher. It seemed strange to her that she had already got used to living and to walking without the baby—her three-month-old grandchild . . . She encountered four people on her way. No one spoke to her or asked her anything—we doubt that she was in any state for them to see her. If ghosts don't have shadows or reflections, as is said, Febronia at that moment wasn't even a ghost. She had gone out bodiless, in a world of her own—how else?—and as she was walking, voices were saying to her: "Where are you going? Such things are not for you, they're for others, for the mad, for saints, for the unborn—turn back, what are you after? Needles will pierce your eyes if you take a step farther, turn back!" She let them have their say. And not only that; sometimes she even answered: "And if they're not for me, then who are they for?"

Not that this *transformation* of hers went as far as blasphemy or conceit; quite simply she surpassed herself, ordinary things, at least in the way we're given to understand it. Or there were some moments, we don't know, when perhaps it did reach the limits of blasphemy—the unknown can't be defined with words, even less can it be divided with slide rules. The one thing certain is that the woman was herself afraid of this excess, this sublimity that she was experiencing willingly and not, and her existence—her flesh and what we call soul—was but a detail, an *occasion*.

It's pointless for us to go on; all this didn't happen, can't have happened as anyone else might have thought or described it—including herself—at that moment. "Perhaps I've died or I'm about to die?" she wondered. And continuing like this on a thread, between earth and heaven so it seems, she arrived at the ruins for the third and luckiest time.

She saw the back of his head beneath the fig tree, his back bent as if he were cutting his nails. He was wearing the same satin waistcoat, dark yellow like bronze, that he had been wearing the day before with the infants and it suited him like red suits poppies, but also in a way infinitely more compatible that she couldn't think of and it tormented her . . . When she got closer, right behind him now, only five feet separating them, she saw the shadows from the fig leaves that were playing on his back—not the slightest breeze stirred, but perhaps it was his back stirring, or her unhinged mind—and it was so lovely (that black fluttering on the golden back), so unsuspected, and so appropriate, that not even in her dream had she been graced with such a sight.

"Don't be alarmed . . . it's me," she said to him, amazed at the length of what was heard—inside her the same thing hadn't taken up any space. He turned to see her and remained speechless.

Yet what can we say about this woman who, on gazing at him for the first time from close up, felt what she hadn't felt either in dream or in waking: *awe*. His countenance, seen from this distance, was the most alluring abyss . . . and only now did she understand why her daughter had chosen the other abyss.

We already know something of what happened next in this unhoped-for and yet not unexpected encounter. They had already spoken quite a bit . . .

"And what brings you here today?" she then asked him, turning the conversation from her torment to his secret. "Do you come often to sit under this fig tree?"

"When I was younger, I used to come every day. But I still come even now, my house is only a couple of steps away," said Hesychios. "And what about you? What fine fortune was it that led you here?"

"What *fine* fortune? I lost my headscarf yesterday, when we brought the infants," she said, without the slightest remorse at such a gross lie, without even caring about any semblance of truth (by looking for it, by asking him if he'd seen it). "And what do you do when you come here? Think?"

"Yes, think," he admitted, "today in particular, I have a lot to think about. I didn't sleep all night."

"Ah! . . ." For Febronia, this was the equivalent of a dream—she didn't care why he hadn't slept, it was enough for her that he hadn't. Then she remembered the light in the window and very nearly asked him about it and so become trapped by her own words, though now that wouldn't be the worst . . . "But why? What were you thinking about that you couldn't sleep?"

His arms opened as though in admission, while hers fell as though out of weariness. "That I have children and I don't have a wife, that's what I was thinking. All night my folks had me with my back to the wall . . . but I admit it: I have to find a wife—one with a big heart, like my father says."

"How many children do you have?" she asked, as though she had no idea at all.

"Six," he said, "four girls and two boys."

"Hmm," said Febronia with sorrow in her voice. A sorrow that was next to nothing, next to everything—that simple. And she endured his gaze, just as he did hers, much longer than was required by a sound, unhurried weighing of the situation, by a secret agreement. And those voices in her head that previously had moved heaven and hell to dissuade her from going there now fell silent.

Six children belonging to Hesychios plus three of her own made nine. The fourth—the first of them, to be honest, her daughter Rodanthe, nineteen years old when she went—was gone in truth and, most likely, none of this would bother her.

Febronia was a full fourteen years older than Hesychios, something that, in addition to everything else, not only gave cause but also free rein to the people of that place and that year—by the following year it would have died down—for comments on their union of the kind usually reserved for the most heinous crime. They would speak, choked by holy indignation, even panic-stricken, about this unholy marriage, and feeling themselves personally threatened by such happenings—*signs of the times,* as they leniently put it—they began during those months to threaten one another without reason and to start terrible arguments among themselves at the slightest thing. And aside from this, if anyone seemed to them slightly suspicious or lax or had committed any small misdemeanor, they had the refrain ready: "Where else would it lead? There's no thunder without lightning—we're all going to sink in the same mire." This is what they said, not without some inspiration, for it seems that in truth the mire of lasciviousness dragged at least some down into its depths during that time; quite a few bonds between those unsuited (or blood relatives) were created, or perhaps came to the surface, so much so that the virtuous could have no complaints about business being slack. Yet of course the scepter of iniquity was held by Hesychios and Febronia—particularly by Febronia.

During one of those feverish days, Christoforos said to his newly wedded son: "I can say you've even surpassed me. When I married Petroula, my first wife, there were those who wanted to lynch me for taking the daughter of a murderous priest. Though there were others who saw it as a kind act—in what way was the girl to blame if the priest turned out to be a murderer—and it was they who in the end prevailed over the others. With your marriage, it seems, no one saw it with a calm mind, and so I advise you to guard yourself, don't let them see much of you till the fever has passed . . . As for Febronia, tell her to forget the things of this world for a year."

For the rest, he himself adopted a somewhat reserved attitude towards his daughter-in-law for some time, just as long as it took him to discern her traits but also her qualities and to value them accordingly. He saw that her soul was made of a sensitive fiber joined with bold sentiments that, inevitably, wounded her own self; however, in practical matters, he found her strong and capable (the age difference upset him a little, but it wasn't anything tragic), and so he gave them his blessing—six months after the wedding—together with a shop, numerous acres of land, and numerous rooms in the house for their own use, because of the particular profusion of children (already from the day after the wedding) in the more general profusion of the family traditions.

Before we cross this rich and thorny area in order to go elsewhere, we should mention, in parenthesis, the great alarm that the new daughter-in-law experienced on only her second day in the house on setting eyes on Hesychios's youngest brother, the eleven-year-old Minas, whom she hadn't seen before—how many could she get round in a day?—and who made her turn pale when she saw him, made her heart race. "Is Hesychios your father?" she asked him at a loss. "No, I'm his little brother," Minas said, "I lost my mother, Eftha, when I was only five."

If we imagine that—on seeing the striking resemblance between the boy and him—Febronia was afraid that she had got hitched to someone who had *more* than six children, from older adventures, much older, and we expect her to feel relief at learning that this boy was his brother and not his son, then our expectations will be in vain; her alarm was not lessened in the slightest. In any case, Hesychios couldn't have been fathering children from his own childhood—so it couldn't have been this that frightened Febronia even if she asked the question in such a way. Nor, most probably, could it have been the likeness itself, since Minas wasn't the only one of his brothers and sisters who resembled him: they all, some more, others less, resembled him in his features—or perhaps he resembled all the others—provided we remember that none of them reached his heights, none of them had the looks that he had.

So what was it, what sort of suspicion, that caused Febronia such alarm on that second day of her marriage and that—many years later—would also leave Hesychios speechless?

Meanwhile, over the next fourteen years, a new swarm of children came on the scene. Their first son was born—who was at the same time the tenth child in the new, unusual family—and they named him Christodoulos in order to distinguish him somewhat from the three or four Christoforoses who already existed in the family *court*, under the same vast roof. Christoforos, as we know, the father of Hesychios and of his many brothers and sisters, and all these, without being overly or unconditionally fond of his name, were nevertheless intent on giving it to their own children, evidently with an eye—though vainly—on the profit to be had from it: whenever he objected to some of their property or other proposals or when he had a completely different opinion, they reminded him of how much they respected and considered him: "We put your name above all else," they would say to him, "we never stop passing it down to your grandchildren—so do this favor for us now." Christoforos would raise his hand and cut them short: "You're wasting your time with all that children and children of my children business. My name, no name, means anything to me, find some other way if you want to get round me. Though you won't find it easy."

This Christodoulos had barely begun to walk when another boy was on his way to the *court of wonders*. They named this one Zafeiris, the name of one of Febronia's grandfathers, since her father's name had already been given to one of her sons from her first marriage. The following year, on the third anniversary of their marriage, the very day, the end of July, there came into the world a third boy, who was almost lost as soon as he had arrived, and for this reason they named him Sterios: to *strengthen* him! Both him and their marriage.[3] The following July—no fault of ours—a girl was at last born to them. We say at last because Febronia had begun to worry that, after Rodanthe and all the consequences, God wouldn't give her another daughter; there would be no second daughter as a kind of nepenthe . . . to relieve a little that unforgettable and unspeakable grief in her heart. But this second daughter came, and Febronia—just her and her alone—saw from the very first how much she resembled her first daughter, how it was as if she had simply given birth again to Rodanthe, and this filled her with a strange pleasure. And then it frightened her.

The fortunate thing was that, as often happens with newborns, after a few weeks, when her features began to *take shape*, the little girl presented a different face, and now everyone said, not neglecting of course to give praise to the Lord, how much she resembled her handsome father, the incomparable Hesychios. Perhaps what they meant was that the other little boys born at that same time by other women ought from then to guard themselves, along with those who had not yet been born? who were still on the way? In other words, Febronia once again had cause to be afraid—and if this was another kind of fear, if

3. In fact, this *strengthening* name came from something seemingly ungrounded, something suspended, from the name "A-sterios" or astral body; but they didn't have the time then for such connotative contradictions.

it wasn't related to her first daughter and her appearance, it nevertheless didn't help at all in forgetting her . . .

However, with the passing of time, Febronia's second daughter—whom she still left unchristened—adopted yet another face, a third *in likeness* so to speak, a third version, and this was it seems the golden mean between Rodanthe and Hesychios: more and more and even more astonishingly, her appearance now recalled that of one of her aunts, one of Hesychios's sisters: the docile and distant Julia. To the point that she even had the same red hair.

This red hair—since we have the opportunity now to mention it—was something only Julia had; no one else in the family had it, nor did they remember anyone else in the family having it. And this color would have remained a puzzle, the first puzzle concerning this girl, who would so love riddles when she grew up, if her mother, Eftha, hadn't remembered her mother saying occasionally that she had had a redheaded grandfather . . . Yes, this color went so far back, had bypassed so many generations before coming down to Julia—and sporadically bringing its faint hues into our own days . . .

After this and when, quite amazingly, she was already almost one year old, they were able to worry about what name they would give to this—almost protean—being. More than once, Febronia was niggled by the temptation to ask if they could call her Rodanthe. But she had no idea how this would sound to Hesychios's ears; she didn't dare ask him, not even in her sleep. Besides, she didn't really know herself how it would sound to her—at least she wasn't totally sure, totally ready, and so she left it to others to take care of the matter: whatever name they proposed, she would accept. Quite a few of the girls in the house already had the name of her grandmother, Efthalia, but it had also been given to one of Hesychios's other daughters, one of the *doorstep infants* that Febronia was now raising together with her own. Of course, there were many other names from long-departed grandmothers, great-grandmothers, and aunts who were just waiting to emerge again for a little from their oblivion—so many, in fact, that they couldn't decide on any. Until Hesychios asked his sister Julia, who wandered around the house always pensive and airy, to find him a name, just as he often found solutions to her puzzles.

"You're asking me?" she said to him. "Call her . . . what can you call her . . . Call her . . . call her Junia!"

"Junia?" he said in surprise. "Why Junia?"

"I don't know. Like I'm called Julia, you can call her Junia."

Hesychios stared at her thoughtfully.

"But if that's the case," chipped in Febronia, who had been listening to them without them seeing where she had come from, "if we're going to call her Junia, we may as well call her Julia straight out, like you! Aren't I right?" she asked her husband. "She was born in July, she'll be christened in July. Her aunt is called Julia . . . And she looks so like this Julia! Is it worth our while trying to come up with another name?"

"If that's the case," said Hesychios, "then why not have her aunt Julia baptize her?"

"I've no objection, but I don't know what the priest will have to say about it," she replied. "*Julia baptizing Julia in the name of the Father* . . . Hmm, I don't know. You'll have to ask him."

They asked him, and he didn't have any objection either—or rather there was nothing that surprised him with such a family. And so they christened their first daughter Julia, baptized by her aunt Julia, and they even managed to have the christening in the month of July . . . And this little red-haired girl, in so many ways a "Julia," would speak and walk exceptionally quickly, and become— literally speaking—the *shadow* of the elder Julia.

Around seven years later—it was August this time—when they were by now all convinced that they had had enough of these swarms of children, little Thomas arrived with his twin sister. For different reasons, we will spend a little more time on these two.

So the twins were born, a boy and a girl, and one of them, the boy, was born with . . . disparate eyes; in other words, each eye had a different color, something that before then no one had seen—and how many can say they have seen it even today? Very few we imagine, extremely few, and we're not talking about cats that, sometimes, do have different colored eyes. The colors themselves—brown and green, or, to be more exact, golden brown and bright green—in the eyes of little Thomas were not entirely *without justification*: Febronia's eyes were dark brown and Hesychios's were a brownish-green with yellow flecks. Of course, in his case, the brownish-greenish-yellowish that we're talking about was not so simple: according to the light or who knows what else, his eyes took on different hues, different glints or shades—Eftha once said that when she looked at him in the evening or in a dim light, she thought she was looking at a snake: his eyes would become olive-green, glazed and heavy, narrowed a little, frightening her. Then again, if they were in the light of the sun, they turned yellow, golden, shone in a different way—even red specks sparkled in that scintillating gaze. Then, at other times, it was green that clearly dominated, at others it was brown, a very strange brown. Yet all this—colors, hues, shades, and, of course, impressions—were wonderfully mixed and distributed equally in Hesychios's two eyes. But not in the eyes of his son Thomas. They were totally separate in his eyes: the brown went with all the deep, golden sweetness in one eye, and the green with all its dazzling brightness in the other. It wasn't even two different sides of the same coin—it was two different coins on the same side. And no one found it easy, not even his own mother, to stare at those eyes—so different from each other on a child's face—without getting a momentary dryness in his mouth. Apart from anything else, it wasn't very *pleasant*. Yet it was so astounding, so unprecedented, that no one could avert his gaze . . . And perhaps this was the reason, definitely this, that obliged Thomas from when he was very young, almost from when he was an infant, to keep closing them (almost every time he opened them), in order to avoid that magnetized, sick gaze of all the others. Or—as he grew older—to immediately turn his head the other way as soon as you went up to him or smiled at him or were about to say something to him. "I can't talk to your ears!" Febronia once said to him. "Turn around and look at me when I'm talking to you!" But as soon as Thomas did her bidding, she would lose her tongue—or cover her own eyes with her hand in order to talk to him . . . In time, of course, she got used to it, but it always made her start.

As for his brothers and sisters, consumed by curiosity, daring, and ignorance; they would plead with him every day "to let them look at his eyes for an hour" (though they were satisfied even with a few moments), just as the children of some future generation would plead with someone to let them into the cinema for free! And because Thomas refused good turns of this sort, the bartering and exchanging began: they would offer him delicacies, carved sticks, penknives, locusts or cicadas in tins (the first radios), colored stones, tufts of girls' hair, buttons, dead maybeetles, teeth, and whatever other small items of hidden or obvious worth they possessed. And in this way Thomas would sometimes succumb to the temptations and gave them what they wanted, and then the children would lose their previous vivacity, lose their great fervor—however much they tried to conceal it, something affected them, a kind of sunstroke . . . And yet the next day, they would start pleading with him again—their curiosity was unbridled, it was its own reward.

To the point that Thomas started to seclude himself, so that no one knew where he was, even though he was close by. In one period of his life, at around six, something else happened that among the members of the family would remain vivid for many years, and inexplicable at the same time: Thomas was terrified—and when we say terrified, we mean that he would jump out of his skin and a painful *eeiii!* would stick in his throat like a knife—at the sound of his own name. No one could call him anymore without wondering whether that *eeiii* would leave him dead on the spot. Ah, eventually this began to seriously concern them, to make their daily life extremely difficult. "If we can't call him by his name, then how should we call him?" they asked; *"Eeiii?"* And they set about trying to convince Thomas in whatever way and by whatever means they could to stop being terrified when they called him by his name, not to let it happen again—what was it all about? What connection was there? They called him to come to eat or in order to send him somewhere or to give him something; they weren't calling him in order to hang him or to tie him up—so why was he so terrified? "Put a stop to it, for your own good, or we'll all have to swallow our tongues in here," they said to him. And they began—in keeping with the hitherto unheard-of proverb *heal your stab wound by stabbing again*—to deliberately call out his name every so often, without any cause or pretext, at any time or moment, even when he was asleep in bed or going into the john, just like that, without rhyme or reason, simply so that he would eventually grow tired of being terrified, and they would grow tired of calling him. The place filled with *Thomas-Thoma-a-a-as* . . . And this rather harsh method had a completely unforeseen result: Thomas stopped jumping out of his skin, as before, whenever he heard his name, but before long he no longer even needed them to call his name: for example, Febronia would think of something to tell him, or call to him to come in from the yard or from the other room and Thomas— before any sound was heard or anything—would appear or, if he was already beside her, would turn his head and say, "What did you say?" or "What do you want?" Really. He would appear out of nowhere and ask her what she wanted, why she wanted him, at exactly the moment that she was getting ready to call him to tell him something or ask him to do something. And almost every time, she, because of her astonishment, would lie to him: "I don't want you for anything. What gave you that idea?" Or—if the boy was beside her and suddenly asked her "What did you say?" whereas she had said nothing, though she was thinking of saying something to him—she would answer drily: "What makes you think I said something?" Or, more gently, "I didn't say anything, Thomas, not a word." She would come out with lies like this every day and, not only that, she didn't get what she wanted either. Because Thomas was not one to persist: after waiting a little to see whether she changed her mind and actually wanted him, and since she persisted in pretending to ignore him, he would leave her and go away. "Oh, enough!" said Febronia one day: she had other things to do besides lying every so often to Thomas and to her own cost. So after that, she changed her tactics and as soon as the boy asked her what she'd said, she told him what—of course—she had been thinking of telling him. And sometimes, when he appeared in the doorway *without* her having called him, she would say to him: "Where were you? I've been calling you for ages!" always with a slight concern inside her as to his reaction, a curiosity concerning how he would re-spond to "I've been calling you for ages." Thomas, however, would simply say, "I didn't hear" (as if it were possible), and patiently wait for her to ask him to do what it was she wanted.

He was just as easily able to *hear* his father, his grandfather, and more or less all of them inside that big house and outside. "We told you not to be terrified when we call your name," Christoforos said to him tenderly one day, "but let us use it now and again."

The most difficult thing, though, from the time he was ten years old and afterward, was for him to let them look at his eyes. What we mean is look at them with that morbid submission that sickened him. His eyes would remain literally out of sight.

Even for his twin sister, Elisavet, with whom he had so many things in com-mon both inside and outside their mother's belly, his eyes were off-limits. Now this Elisavet (Safi-Lisafi, as it was decided to call her, since half her brothers and sisters called her Safi, and the other half Lisafi, and civil war almost broke out) loved him so much that she would even jump off a cliff with him. Never mind that he wouldn't let her see his eyes; she would prefer to have her hand cut off than for them not to let her hold his all day long, and she would prefer to be all alone with Thomas at the ends of the earth than to have them all with her or have everything but for Thomas to be missing. They said that she loved him even more than herself, and this was quite natural—though less than the truth, in the way that they said it—given that there was nothing for her without Thomas, given that their soul had entered two bodies. It was the same, we suppose, for Thomas, except that he didn't express so much this feeling of a *double existence*; he lived it more quietly, more like a boy.

The family had them sleep separately, but nothing could prevent them from having the same dreams every so often. Everyone tried through various ploys to keep them at a distance, to teach both of them to live their own lives, and would send Thomas somewhere on an errand and Safi-Lisafi alone with a present for her godmother or some sick relative; but if along the way Safi-Lisafi forgot about the present and burst out crying or started wailing, then even a stranger, some chance passerby, would feel in his own way that her twin brother was some-where in danger; and when some strange anxiety distorted Thomas's already strange and lonely face, they couldn't but suspect—but be anxious too—that something unpleasant had happened to Safi-Lisafi. And it was rare when the crying was meaningless, rare when the one face became distorted on account of the other without good reason.

Their best times were when the family would leave them alone together somewhere. Then Safi-Lisafi, so as not to put him in a difficult spot with regard to his eyes, so as not to do involuntarily what her other brothers and sisters did willfully, would arrange her tiny little body between his legs, rest her back on his chest, take hold of his hand usually and look in front, where most likely he was also looking. And she thought of his eyes, with a secret passion, she thought of his eyes: in other words, did Thomas see *what* she was seeing and in the same *way* that she was seeing it? Or perhaps those two eyes saw other things than what she saw—or the same, but in a different way? She was dying to ask him! . . . She was dying with the desire to see a few images with his eyes! To see, first of all, the eyes themselves—but to see them well, to gaze at them, to dive inside them, to have her fill of them . . . Besides, she thought that if she had *two eyes* like Thomas's, she wouldn't mind showing them to everyone! And even if she didn't show them to everyone, she would have shared them at least with her twin brother—she would have given them to him to see with whenever he wanted, they would go from one to the other like a pair of spectacles. But her eyes were like everyone else's, like most people's; no one had concerned himself with her eyes, just as no one concerned himself with the cat's whiskers or the cock's comb.

"Thomas . . . ," she whispered, feeling dizzy and half-turning her face toward his. But before he could even refuse her or grant her what she longed to ask him, she lowered her head again and fell silent.

Perhaps Thomas wanted to show his eyes *to her* . . . But there was that hesitance between them, a mutual hesitance.

And the surprises in store for Febronia never ceased: some two years after the twins, she gave birth to another child, another boy, as she was accustomed ("It was my fate to have *only* three daughters," she said, "*three only daughters*"), a son with green eyes, who, as was also the custom in the family, would take two names: Thanasakis and Barnabas (the wish of his godfather, who had lost both his son and his brother inside a year), but whom they called Benjamin until he came of age: it was the wish of all of them, including Febronia, that this child should indeed be the *Benjamin* of the family, the end of her fruition, the last child—she was weary now of birth giving and all that went with it, she was fifty-two years old, time for her to rest.

Let's not forget, moreover, that there weren't just these seven children that she had with Hesychios: there were also the other three from her first marriage (once four, let's not forget that too, as she always remembered it), and there were the six belonging to Hesychios from those six unfortunate creatures (and one of

these, the youngest, was also her grandchild, Argyris, the name of her first husband and his grandfather—and the naughtiest in the realm), in other words,
there were sixteen children hanging on to her apron strings and another thirty,
give or take, in the rest of the house. Enough.

As to their twelfth birthday, this was something that all the children awaited
eagerly, both the males and females, except that for the former it had an added
dimension: it had to be baptized in blood, the twelve-year-olds had to slaughter their first animal—even if it also proved to be the last—dressed, and made
ready as bridegrooms, without any bride waiting for them at night in bed. Only
the indelible marks and the deep thrill left from the morning's massacre.

For some boys, very few it has to be said, this ordeal had passed by without
their having to go through it . . . for reasons that had nothing to do, of course,
with their own reluctance or refusal, but because of some person who had recently died in the house: not more than three days previously. In this case, the
first slaughtering of the twelve-year-old "was excused," as they put it, and didn't
happen. This had been the case with Konstantakis, Febronia's eldest son, who,
on the day he was to do the slaughtering, was exempted—would that it were
not so—because of his sister Rodanthe, who had breathed her last, after drinking poison, two nights previously. But all it took was for some centenarian to go
from natural causes for one of his grandchildren or great-grandchildren to be
exempted. So we shouldn't be surprised by the fact that there were more than
a few twelve-year-olds at that time who, as their day got nearer, prayed ever
more intensely—secretly and racked by pangs of remorse—that someone in
their home would die, particularly if there was someone old or ill. But there
were few so lucky: life may have been jousting with death in some room, it may
have promised death to two souls the following month and three the following year, but—for that day and those days immediately preceding that day—it
kept all of them in its own bosom. So much so that it was said of the infatuated
Rodanthe that she did what she did more out of love for her brother Konstantakis—who was literally shaking at the thought of taking hold of a knife and
came down with a fever—rather than for the handsome Hesychios. Whatever
the case, we have to mention the fact that this slaughtering didn't take place at
just any time during the year in question, regardless of when the boy was born
exactly, the date of his birthday (which was not something that they attached
great importance to at the time, unlike today—unless, that is, it coincided with
something important or memorable), but took place only in spring, at the end
of March and right through April and May. Even if the boy had been born on

the last day of December 1868, for example, he would slaughter his first animal in spring 1880—or, better, would get a reprieve till the spring of '81. But spring, always spring. We suppose because it was then that the most newborn victims were available but also for its other associations, linked with age-old symbols, since spring was always *responsible for* and credited with a great deal.

The exact day of the slaughtering was fixed seven days before—"on the eighth," they used to say—and it couldn't be changed. If the boy and the animal got out of the specific day—due to some death—then they got out of all the others. (And the animal *too*, yes, that particular lamb or kid that had been chosen for the particular boy would also have the wonderful good fortune—rare for its breed—to be allowed to die of its own accord, to come to a natural end.)

Some would get their boys drunk beforehand, so they might accomplish the mission with as little fuss and upset as possible—though not infrequently, the drink took its revenge and the fuss and upset was doubled, the stumbling and excessive euphoria often ended more painfully and without mercy for both the boy and the animal. Christoforos, for example, just like his father, Lukas, and Lukas's father, Christoforos, didn't want even to hear of such things, and they guarded their twelve-year-olds like watchdogs, from the evening to the time of the slaughtering, lest someone secretly get them drunk with wine or something else. They had to have their heads clear, cool and clear like crystal, regardless of the excitement that shook these little spring suitors from head to toe, and to the depths of their souls. Afterwards, however, when the terrible act came to an end, then the drinking after the event, the boy's merry inebriation, was not only permitted but more or less expected: the older ones would pour the sweet wine from pitchers and give it to him to drink, sometimes even through the nostrils, and through the ears, and have him tell them what he did, how he did it, what he felt, what he thought, tell them everything and whatever else he wanted, what his soul had been dreaming of for twelve years and hadn't dared put into his mouth—the day was for heroic feats and fantasies, glory, boasting, gibberish, for anything and everything, even for vomiting, until the boy's eyelids shut and he fell onto a pillow, dead to the world.

Meanwhile, the women took him, undressed him, and threw his clothes into the waiting water. These clothes—worn for the first time, made especially for the occasion, or inherited from some older brother or cousin—had definitely to get bloodstained, otherwise it was almost meaningless. And if some boy— such things happened among so many other things—out of excessive concern or fear not to cut one of his own fingers together with the animal's throat, kept his distance, as though severing his arms from his body, with the result that his fine clothes did not turn sufficiently red, did not get as smeared as they should, then one of the older ones saw to it that these clothes, albeit after the slaughtering, got bloodstained; he would push the boy's trembling breast, his even more trembling knees, so that he came into contact with the slaughtered animal, so that what he was wearing would get splattered with blood, and like this he handed him to the women for the rest. If, of course, the blood dried, it couldn't be cleaned either with cold water or even less so with hot. Yet it wasn't this that upset them: on the contrary, it was one of their hopes that this clothing should retain its stains and mementos. Nevertheless, they had to be put into water to be washed, just as — punctiliousness on top of more punctiliousness — the water had to turn red, so that in three white cups three women could parade it around the neighborhood (exactly like some brides display the blood of their virginity on the bed sheets) and then throw it over three walls of the house for good luck. They used to say, sometimes with pride, sometimes as though washing their hands of it, that this was how they had found these customs, and this was how they would leave them.

If we forgot to mention that the twelve-year-old's shirt was black and his trousers, jacket, and waistcoat white, perhaps it's not too late to mention it now: he didn't have only similarities with a normal bridegroom but also some subtle differences.

It's also worth noting that on the evening before, some kind of instruction was given to the twelve-year-old: he was given some useful advice and guidance on how to use the knife, how to grasp the slender neck, and at what point exactly to strike (if there can be any *exactly* amid such frenzy), so that the animal's end and the boy's ordeal would not drag on. Very often they would drive the boy to extremes, saying to him, "Get yourself worked up, think to yourself, That lamb ate my mother and father, brought great harm to me and has to be punished, I'm raging and I'll slaughter it!" Then there were times when they advised him not to have this momentum only inside him, in his mind or heart, but to gather momentum with his feet too: to go back as far as he could and, when ready, to rush headlong . . . There were but a few boys who didn't accept such exhortations, or who at least made out that they didn't need them, that they knew, and who — even more rarely — proved it in practice. Most of them listened to the instructions with despair, learned them by heart but completely forgot them and became dizzy as soon as they were face to face with that *wild thing* that had no name.

Also worth mentioning is how most of the time, when boy and beast were side by side, the latter, though about to be slaughtered, appeared infinitely more fortunate, almost enviable, in comparison with the hell in which the boy found himself.

And, finally, if the need arose, if the sufferings on earth of these two strange adversaries were without end, the end was given by one of the adults present. In any case, the act, however far it went, belonged forever to the boy. And the sacrifice eternally to the other.

Hesychios too—still Theagenis—naturally had firsthand knowledge of this grimness, of this dark dizziness; he wouldn't be "excused" just because he happened to be a good-looking lad who often made Eftha feel sinful for his conception, a *pawn of demons* and suchlike. When, though, all these thoughts left her, she felt proud and chosen among women . . . only to don once again the yoke of sinfulness and so on, until she was racked by remorse once and for all and finally found peace and quiet. But we have plenty of time before then, another six years.

So in 1876, Theagenis was twelve years old, and had been born in April, an ideal coincidence. They fixed the date of the slaughtering by the date of his birth, it might be said. And precisely because he was a singular boy—what more modest way to characterize a beauty that was so out of the ordinary?—Christoforos wanted to mark the day especially. He ordered him the finest clothes, wonderful linen trousers and linen waistcoat, silk shirt (even beforehand the women felt uncomfortable about having to put such clothes into the water, didn't have the heart to do it), invited musicians so it would be a real celebration, and prepared his son in the way he thought best: "Bear in mind that it will be a very difficult moment for you," he told him, "very difficult. You'll be putting your hand into the fire. But bear in mind also that it's only one moment. When it's passed, everything will have passed, you'll feel as light as a feather, you'll remain with your mouth open . . . you won't be able to believe it. That's what you'll remember above all else: a feather."

But it wasn't destined to turn out like this exactly.

When the MOMENT came, Theagenis knelt down, clutched the animal's head to his chest, let the knife fall from his fingers—and from his eyes came a stream of tears. "He'll get over it," Christoforos said to the others, and they waited some time for him to get over it. But as Theagenis continued sobbing and did nothing else, Christoforos cleared his throat and went over to whisper something in his ear. The twelve-year-old let go of the lamb, got to his feet—let out a sob as though someone was whipping him—and after staying for a moment undecided, ran back (in the way that someone being whipped runs) to gather momentum and come back, in accordance with his father's advice. But he forgot to pick the knife up off the floor, and this—regardless of how he was going to use it even if he'd taken it—added something laughable to his abysmal wretchedness, something pathetically comical, that immediately became chortling and boisterousness on the part of his brothers, the ones from his parents' previous marriages, who naturally were among the first present at the festive ordeal. Derisive cries of *ouou-ouououou-ouou* raised the roof and it was too late for Christoforos to do anything about it . . .

The expensive garments, the dazzling looks, the instruction, the instruments, the choicest and sharpest knife, even spring itself, puzzled and unmoved at all these events, would, it seemed, go to waste right from the start, almost from the very first moment. With what delight those boys, the older brothers—just as in some biblical lessons or in folktales that arouse fear—welcomed the defeat of the special son, the crushing of all privileges.

And now it was they who sent him—who could control them?—to gather momentum . . . again . . . and again . . . "That's it, Theagenis, just once more, for me this time!" . . . "And for me next time!" . . . "Hey, that's not right, do it again!" . . . And the ridiculed creature obeyed, obeyed everything they said, went back again and again as many times as they wanted. Just so long as there wasn't just one time.

Concealed behind a wall, at the other side of the house, Eftha could hear all the hullabaloo. She didn't wish to be present at the event, she had never wanted to go, it wasn't just that day. Not even for the three sons she'd had with her first husband—and it was something of a relief to her that amidst all that barbarous *ouou* at least she couldn't recognize the voice of one of them, one of hers . . . "Such goings-on," she said, "first slaughtering and fiddle-faddle, it's not for me." And she was perhaps the only one of the well-known women who openly objected to the custom, disagreed, that is, with God himself—didn't everything come from him?—whom in everything else she loved and respected. No more days like this, no, she shook her head.

She heard the pandemonium and said to herself something that she often said: "I should. I should have been your real mother, not a stepmother, afraid of being called *stepmother*, and I would have sorted you all out. But if you come out with that *ou* sound again, you wretched creatures, I'll become your mother for real and much more beside!" She said it as if they had stopped with the *ououououou*, as if her threat fitted into some gap that they left now and then, before starting up again more forcefully. Or as if one of the voices wasn't that of her own Eumolpos, or of Georgos likewise, yet in her vexation she persisted in not recognizing them . . .

But already she was starting to wonder: was it only Petroula's boys who were shouting? Not that they weren't different from her own, made of different stuff they were from hers, then again at such times—her instinct about people was usually right—they all became the same, a rabble, a herd. "A little respect is what's needed . . . ," she muttered, and lifting her head looked at the clouds. Her moods changed like the weather. She no longer saw the respect that was needed so much in her own or the other mother's seventeen- and twenty-year-olds, who if need be could be excused some responsibility, as much farther, far beyond, in the Kingdom of Heaven, as she said, but she could hardly take on the Kingdom of Heaven. And perhaps this is why she was pious—at least, she believed in God, though she didn't go to church very often, not having the time, but she did read the Scriptures, the Old Testament, since she was fortunate in having a bit of learning, she fasted, took communion, knew some psalms and entire verses from the Bible by heart, talked to her children about God—but not to the point of being infatuated all the time with him, or of not investigating, in her own way, his unpleasant and dark aspects. And truly, strong-minded as she was, she found him overly severe at times, or unreasonable at others, and that tired her. And all that *ouou-ouou* infuriated her . . . And the more it infuriated her, the more unmoved it left her, leaving aside her total disappointment when, inevitably, she picked out the voices of her own boys among all that . . . "I can't understand," she said. "Truly, I can't understand. I thought there was a little respect."

Eftha's habit of speaking to herself was something she'd had from way back; it was her characteristic trait par excellence—her dowry, as Christoforos called it. She would talk, gibber to herself, even though awake, become impassioned, forget; her train of thought went in a thousand different directions, her mind was happy to stray from worldly anguish and go to find only heavenly indifference and from there continue to nowhere—and then suddenly to something current, next to her, that she had completely neglected and that, the very next moment, she would forget again. Yet she didn't feel at all unhappy at this quality or failing—of which, in any case, she was rarely aware. She rarely bathed in that chillness or perplexity when you catch your mouth waxing lyrical into the void . . . On the contrary, for her at least—being in no way a person happy in her own company—there must have been a large *audience* around her, an invisible and sensitive one, that listened without stopping her. Besides, if she got tired or remembered something, she stopped by herself.

Once, she said so much *to them*, to-ing and fro-ing in the room and telling them such a lot that she eventually felt exhausted and asked them to make some room for her to sit down(!), even adding: "And you should hear me when I'm talking to myself!" It was perhaps the only time then—at least, one of the very few times—that she became aware of what was happening, and she was completely taken aback, frightened by it. Just as on another day when, after she'd talked her head off, she turned and said in a conspiratorial tone: "So now you know *who* are the ones who talk to themselves, don't you?" And once again she realized what was happening, to *whom* she had said it, and she was left with a strong taste of the unpleasant *consensus* in his silence . . . "The realm is yours . . . ," she reflected . . . But the next day she had already forgotten, and the day after that she started again.

The others around her—not the invisible but the visible ones—naturally scolded her when they caught her talking, told her to stop, do something else; after all, who was listening to her for her to blabber on like that? But Eftha was in no way deterred by such things. On the contrary, she reminded them of what they wanted to forget or didn't want to attach due importance to: namely, that twins remain twins even when one of them dies! And she had had a twin sister who had died at the age of ten: they had been born together, had grown up together, had first walked together, had first talked together, had cried together, eaten together, thought together, though one had died without the other and the other had been obliged thenceforth to live without her. And this was difficult for both of them, it seemed, and again it was something they had to share . . . "Who told you I talk to myself?" Eftha said to them. "I talk to my sister, and I'll go on talking to her till I die! Because she wants me to, she needs it. And even if you don't see her, I do." They listened to her condescendingly; her twin grandchildren, Thomas and Safi-Lisafi, still hadn't been born, for them to listen to her with actual interest, with respect. And when they were born, she would no longer be living so as to enjoy it.

Besides, Eftha also talked to real people, to them, too—she may have not been totally immersed in reality, but neither was she totally cut off from it.

She had had sixteen children (some didn't survive), and she was a woman who was very close to the earth. No one would suddenly stoop while walking to take hold of a handful of soil as she would in order to say to it, "Well then? What do you think about us who tread on you every day?" And no one heard the rains or the showers as she heard them, believing as she did that when there was a shower, souls were speaking to us . . . but when it rained, they were angry and expressing their grievances to us. And if the others grew tired of her words and of the showers—particularly of those undying ones that lay heavy on their souls—Eftha reminded them of the droughts that brought catastrophe to them, and pointing to the earth and everything that they had sown in it and that most certainly needed moisture to sprout, said, "Don't say a word; those below are overjoyed!" She would say it with such conviction, such persuasiveness, that she made you think of thousands of infants under the soil happily suckling on the rain like milk—*overjoyed!*

And there is a lot more we could say about this woman, but because we have to limit ourselves to certain particular traits of the characters we chose—or who chose themselves—to give life to these tales, let us simply mention just one more thing: Eftha loved all animals, felt no disdain even for ants, and when she spoke to the domestic animals—particularly to a pig that no one saw as any more than ham for the winter—her gestures and expressions were in no way different from those that accompanied her most heartfelt conversation with a person or with her twin sister . . . But, it must be said, she had a particular *soft spot* for snakes. She knew so many stories about snakes and had such a knack for discovering them, so many ways to get close to their nests and eggs, such familiarity with their habits and their way of life, but also so much admiration for their appearance and flexibility, that eventually, inevitably we could say, this woman, herself charmed by her acquaintance with snakes, became a renowned snake killer. "Because every so often," she would say, "snakes have to be killed; otherwise they'll wrap themselves round our necks." And so in the summers, when the *slithering angels* were in abundance in the fields and didn't only eat the mice and the weeds but also sometimes bit people or set their eyes on babies suckling at the breast, if not on the mothers who were suckling them, Eftha became useful for many people and dangerous for the snakes. There was a day when she killed six of them! After this, she fasted for a whole month and on her knees begged forgiveness from the empty nests—feeling abhorrence for herself.

Her only tools were a sharp hoe and *the magic cane*. The latter was just a common cane, yet it had a very strange and mysterious effect on certain water-loving snakes: all it took was for someone skilled like Eftha to touch such a snake with the cane (along its spine) for it to become virtually enervated, for it to be caught unaware and disarmed—though not for ever: after a certain time, the effect wore off, but before then it was extremely easy to kill the snake without its understanding anything. If the need arose, Eftha also had her heel.

And her only rival in the extermination of snakes was a man from neighboring parts—who was often seen, however, in her parts, or she would reach as far as his—but who, it's said, was cruel and tortured the snakes before killing them, whereas Eftha had other methods, quicker if not gentler, to put them to death.

Yet with the last leaves of fall, this skill of hers would disappear—in any case, the snakes disappeared too—but generally throughout all the seasons of the year, people found some cause to talk about her, to extol her or to pity her a little, and Christoforos for his part used to say that *all his wives had something*: Petroula acquired it somewhat late, Eftha brought it with her along with her dowry. As for the third, he still didn't even know her name.

■

Returning now to the wall concealing her (without protecting her) from the events going on in the yard, we see her—since she saw no respect anywhere—ready to leave. Though previously she had uttered the threats of *a real mother*, now she preferred to leave, disdaining anything more, when—like a downpour that stops suddenly, all at once—the howling in the yard ceased. This made her suspicious because she knew that such pauses bode no good. But she didn't have time to think, didn't have time to understand: the air was rent by the anguished cry of the young animal, its violent and unbearable end. And then the clamor started up again, piecemeal and herdlike, the *ouou-ouou* again rose up, took on different tones, more panegyric, more devious, while Theagenis—who for the moment seemed not to have understood anything—broke out into more plaintive sobbing, a sobbing that made the stones beneath his feet scuttle away.

She lifted her dress right up above her knees—otherwise she would have torn it—and found herself in the yard, a veritable maenad. What came out of her mouth was an angry stream, a furious *wwwwwouou*, that culminated in an ironic crescendo: "Well done, all of you!" she said, "but it should be you—the Almighty got it wrong—you should be in its place. Or in his place!" She pointed to the slaughtered beast and, a little way off, to the humiliated boy, and only then did she allow herself to take a breath and let her dress fall. She also turned her angry gaze toward the older boys, especially her own, and blasted them too; the shouting and jubilation were extinguished like coals in water, their place taken by some expansive, perplexed gestures.

"Have you finished, you half-wits? Had your fill? Enjoyed yourselves enough for today?" Christoforos said to them, because, of course, it wasn't only Eftha who was so upset with them. He was even more so—after all, he'd seen more.

"You've no idea," he said to her in a strange, weary tone. "Don't say anything, take the boy and go upstairs; don't talk to him, don't ask him anything, close the door behind you. It's over, tell him, that was all." Then he turned to say something to his own brothers, while the musicians breathed deeply, without blowing or beating any of their instruments—the post-event festivities were put on hold.

Someone stooped beside Eftha (he seemed unfamiliar to her but it was one of her own brothers), knelt down on one leg, wiped the bloodied knife on the animal's own wool—three times on both sides of the blade and then kissed it—and lifted up the warm, lifeless carcass.

"Eftha, what do you expect?" he said to her in an apologetic tone; "some lambs have to be sacrificed too, not just snakes."

She didn't reply; she watched him walking into a circle that opened, then closed behind him of big, dark-clothed men, as if he were walking through a door. She lifted up Theagenis—if she had been carrying the slaughtered animal like her brother, it wouldn't have been any different—and entered the house, chasing away just with her gaze, words weren't necessary, a throng of smaller children who hadn't been allowed, or who themselves hadn't dared, to watch the slaughtering, and persons as unimportant as an ass's shadow in such circumstances, each of whom waited silently and anxiously in the house, and who, on seeing her entering with Theagenis in her arms, approached all together and surrounded her to find out . . . But on seeing her gaze, like a herd of young deer before murky water, they moved back, treading on one another, and slowly began to disperse (without actually going away), to sink into sadness and scratch their heads.

Second Tale

FROM THE YARD OF BLOOD TO THE
YARD OF THE WOMAN IN RED

The great ordeal in the yard had passed with not a little difficulty for Thea-genis; now another trial was awaiting him, this time deep inside the house. In the shape, first of all, of Cletia, who was in the customary room (which he him-self had heard about but never entered: a room with a skylight in the ceiling, painted in ochre, without windows), motionless between two tubs of soap and water, with her sleeves down, instead of rolled up to the elbows, and a very ten-der look for her brother after all she had seen from the window of another room.

"Off with you, I don't need you, I'll wash him," Eftha said to her.

As though not having heard, Cletia turned to the boy, who was still heaving from all the sobbing, even though the tears had begun to dry up, without, at least for the moment, new ones starting to run down his cheeks.

"Don't cry so much, you'll die," she told him; "those who cry too much die, didn't you know? Put it out of your mind, there are lots of other things, lots and lots, for you to cry about, oh yes!"

Then she altered the tone of her voice and, rubbing her back, said to Eftha: "As you don't need me, I'll go, my back is near to breaking . . ."

But she didn't go straightaway; she looked her in the eye mockingly and went on: "You didn't see anything even if you were the first to run to save him — you're shouting your head off without having even a clue. And don't expect the boy to tell you what happened."

No one, it seems, forgave her for her weakness in wanting to see with her own eyes the birthday *celebrations* of her twelve-year-old son, this same woman who charmed snakes out of their holes, wrapped them in her hands, and unwrapped them like lifeless rushes.

"Off with you, don't add to my grief," she said to her daughter.

"I'll go," Cletia repeated, "but mark what I say: don't put those clothes in the water, it's a pity . . . anyway, what's all the fuss about?" And she glanced at the tubs and all the other preparations as though regretting her efforts.

Another bout of wailing seized hold of the boy.

"There, there, enough, my dearest, enough, leave a few tears for us," she said, kneeling before him and kissing his hands one after the other and then his warm cheeks. "Oooo, I can't get my fill of those cheeks!" she said between all her kisses.

Eftha—who preferred to remain silent when someone else was speaking, this being another of her peculiarities—was obliged eventually to remind her that she was going beyond her duties.

"That's enough," she said, "those cheeks aren't meant to fill you, they're not grapes. And it's time for you to be going."

"Let him tell me himself when it's enough," Cletia replied, giving him another five kisses in quick succession.

Theagenis, ready to burst from so many kisses and tears, turned away and wiped his face with the back of his hand.

"He's told you himself," said Eftha, nudging her with her knee.

And Cletia at last obeyed, got to her feet, and went out. But as she closed the door, she said, in a grave and anxious tone: "I was thinking of bringing him some honey to lick . . . he's been through a lot."

She closed the door but stood there where she was, as though waiting for a reply; she even put her ear and then her eye to the keyhole.

"Your precious sister wants to bring you a little honey," Eftha said to the boy, "do you want some?"

He was still shaking so much from all the sobbing that one more nod of the head, a yes or no, was indistinguishable from the rest.

"You do want some . . . yes," the mother concluded, unsure actually, and Cletia got her answer and dashed down the stairs.

Presently she came back up more ceremoniously and quietly: she was barefoot and had covered her shoulders—more formal attire?—with a soft damson wrap with cinnamon-colored leaves, an old coverlet that still had a few silk tassels at the edges, and was holding close to her chest a copper plate with honey and lying horizontally across the plate a clean old ax with a short handle.

In case we're not familiar with this from other tales, in those times, when children were upset—and we're talking about the kind of fright that turns one's legs to water and renders the soul *a candle in the wind*, not just any old fright— they used to give them, and to adults too if in a similar state, honey to lick from an ax. The honey, with its well-known qualities, softened and sweetened the innards and the ax with its unusual contribution—and its generally avenging power—cut, so they believed, the panic and frenzy, subduing them. The sufferers licked the honey, not using their fingers but bending and sliding their tongues along the edge of the ax . . . Fingers were used only for what was left at the end by the women, the high priestesses of such an event, as was Cletia that day in Theagenis's case.

She entered and stared at him in astonishment, as if for the first time setting eyes upon such a handsome and wretched boy, while Eftha did her best to hold his hands.

"You'll lick this that I've brought you, my lovely boy, won't you?" she asked him, and swayed in front of him as she imagined the fairies did in fairy tales. "Otherwise, you'll go on weeping and wailing for five more nights. And what for? Downstairs, the others are celebrating."

"He'll lick it," Eftha replied on his behalf. "He'll tell us himself, you'll see."

He didn't speak, just stared at his sister's strange wrap, at the plate with the ax that she had brought him, and said neither yes nor no. He was afraid again, anxious: though twelve years old, he had never before had the need to lick an ax—he'd only ever heard them talk about it. We say "though," because other children were forced to do it at a much earlier age, when their tongues were softer than those of gazelles. Nevertheless—*though* it was his first time—he wouldn't make it hard for either his mother or his sister; it wouldn't be necessary for them to plead with him particularly, to coax him or to pamper him. Just wait a little.

And when he considered what he had gone through in the yard and what he still might have to go through, an ax dripping honey—because Cletia had by now dipped it in the plate of honey and was holding it up to him—didn't seem too frightful: he opened his mouth . . . But he opened it so much that for an instant she was taken aback, stopped short: whatever you give him now, even poison, she thought in alarm, he'll take. The image came into her mind of a boy she'd known who was ill, in torturous pain, to whom all you had to say was "This is medicine, to stop your pain," and he would open his mouth just like that, like a hungry little bird; and because there was no medicine for his pains, or there was no money for medicine, they would give him husked lentils or broad beans, and full of expectation, he kept opening his mouth . . . His folks didn't know what to despair of more: the pains that were gnawing at him, or the hope that wouldn't put an end to his pain. "But what's that poor wretch got to do with the boy," Cletia thought to herself, "or the lentils they gave him with the honey I'm giving to my brother?"

"Look . . . ," she said to him, nevertheless, "you shouldn't open your mouth so much, I'm not spoon-feeding you! Use your tongue to lick it. *Just the very tip, on this.*"

When Eftha was again alone with the twelve-year-old, she took him over to a chair—there was no bed in the room—sat him down, and looked at his clothes. "They wouldn't let me, those who saw it all, no, they wouldn't let me see you even today," she said to him, though she knew it wasn't the truth: it was she who had avoided being present even when they were dressing him up. So it was only now that she was actually looking at him in those clothes, now that she noticed them . . . As to how lovely and well-made they were and as to how much lovelier they looked on him, there was no call even for comment; but as to how clean they had remained despite all that had intervened—some dust and a few scratches on the black shoes, a few small stains on the sleeve—this seemed strange to her, if not a little suspicious. And the intimations of her husband and daughter—"You, you saw nothing, you don't know, keep quiet"—what did it mean?, she wondered. What had happened out of the usual with the boy, while she was lost in her thoughts behind the wall?

She left him for a moment and went over to the water, knelt down before the tub, put her hand inside, moved it back and forth . . .

"I don't know what to do," she mumbled. "I don't know what happened, and I'm not to speak, not to ask, not anything. And you, my fine water, you won't turn red today!"

She got up, ran her wet fingers through her hair, then pulled up a second chair and sat facing the boy, their knees touching.

"Why did you cry so much today?" she asked him. "Whoever cries a lot makes himself sick . . . And dies, just like Cletia said. So why did you cry so much? Won't you tell me so I might know?"

Theagenis took a deep breath that began, you'd think, from right down in his heels, and when it got as far as his chest, he again started sobbing uncontrollably and shaking, as if there were a mouth organ inside there that one mouth tried after the other, till his own voice faded . . . When it faded completely, Eftha caught his gaze and began again to ask him: "Was it your elder brothers that you were afraid of? Those smart alecks? Who when they were in your place squirmed like fish out of water and now like to have fun while sitting on the fence? Was it them? But that's what they all do, for heaven's sake, you shouldn't pay any attention, shouldn't take it to heart—the wretched are only happy when they see everyone else wretched too."

She was waiting for just one word from him, but in the drought she begged for even one drop . . .

"Ah," she groaned after a while, slapping her knees, "what was I thinking of? What eyes are those?"

The boy's eyes welled up, what rolled down his cheeks were not teardrops but huge beads and his sobbing, which just before had abated, now intensified again and multiplied as if wanting to finish him off. Because he was experiencing in his eyes everything that had gone before, which the ax with the honey might have softened somewhat, taken the sting out of, set apart but which still hung over him and frightened him, and this was reflected in his whole appearance.

"Ah," the woman groaned again, "what's this awful thing that I'm not considered worthy to learn?"

And she got up, grabbed hold of a towel from a stool, and came back; she wrapped the towel around his head and squeezed it gently, pressed it here and there, on all sides, even over his mouth and nose with him gasping for air.

"It's over, over, forget it, snap out of it," she kept saying to him, "don't let it get the better of you . . . they're all thoughtless, mindless! I wasn't in the yard, but I could hear them. Vultures lying in wait, who'd eat their own shadows if they could! *Lord, how have my oppressors multiplied so?*—wasn't that what your soul was asking? But look now . . . What was I saying? Shall we get these clothes off you? Throw them into the water? No—let me give you other things to put on, get out of those and put others on, never mind the water . . . Do you want to? Say something, you'll drive me crazy today. Look! Do you want a few of these raisins I've found here?"

She took a few raisins out of her pocket, pretended to count them out, put one in her mouth and stretched out her hand with the rest, offering them to him.

"You count them too," she said, and, after seeing his eyes move momentarily, without his counting them and without his showing the slightest interest in taking them, Eftha threw them in one of the tubs, then threw the towel onto the stool: "They told me not to ask you, not to talk to you, not to expect anything," she said, reaching the limit of her patience. "But I don't know: is it better I don't talk? That's all I want to know. Is it better?"

To no avail. The boy wouldn't speak.

"Am I pestering you?" she asked more openly, desperately, perhaps for the last time.

Again he didn't speak, but from the way a number of sobs stuck in his throat, it seemed to her that he had said no. And Eftha decided to sit there with him and wait as long as necessary till the storm passed, so she said.

Quite some time later, when all that remained of that inconsolable grief was a dim recollection, a trembling of the nostrils and, almost imperceptibly, of the shoulders, and when the boy himself began to yawn and look his mother in the eye more and more (though still not speaking, with his mouth still a tiny tomb filled with secrets), she said to him in a soft voice, as if forced to come out of a dream of her own: "You've made me sleepy, dear child, we're both as sleepy as cats. Cats, you know, don't talk, so they just look at each other and become sleepy." She got up with a new burst of activity and held out her hand to him:

"Let's go and get you to sleep in another room," she said, "I'm tired too with all your crying . . . There's not even a bed in here."

Theagenis slipped immediately from the chair, giving her his hand. His eyelids were heavy.

"Ah, you don't say no to sleep, you're more than ready," she said, somewhat annoyed; and she reminded him, shaking her finger, "But then you'll tell me what happened. I'm the only one who doesn't know."

Walking down the corridor, they saw Cletia through a half-open door and halted: she was from a distance devoutly staring at her image in a small round mirror she was holding in three of her fingers, as she might hold an apple or something more precious. She wasn't aware of them—the house was empty and she had her back turned to the door. But they were *seen* by her little mirror and this seemingly upset her; she put it down immediately (a spasmodic movement), and, as it was a mirror on both sides and half the room was bathed in the morning sunlight, a *ball* of light and infinite silence bounced off the ceiling to the floor and from there vanished in her breast . . . Other than this, she didn't even turn to look at them.

"Cletia is always looking at herself in the mirror and you don't talk at all," Eftha said to Theagenis, meaning that she didn't approve either of her or of him, and she led him into another room. Once they were inside and she had carefully shut the door, the boy stumbled towards the bed, but she dragged him with her over to the window.

"Let me first show you the poplars," she said.

Because she was still hoping to get a few words out of him.

But it had been a very confusing day for her. She thought that she had brought him to the room with the window that looked out onto the poplars, onto the meadow with poplars in the distance that in certain periods filled with water and that as a child she had gazed at from a window in her family home, and she couldn't wait, was immersed in a sense of nostalgia and trepidation, without knowing why. It was a sweet trepidation over something that had happened there when perhaps she had been much younger, or that would happen at any moment and was awaiting her, getting the poplars to call out to her, *Come, come* . . . An inexplicable sense, very intense, very elusive. When it was windy, when it rained, she would gaze out of the window at the poplars swaying: *Come, come* . . . And once, when she eventually was fortunate to find herself in that meadow with her second husband, at a short distance from the poplars that were neverending, that from a distance seemed to her to be close to one another but that she now saw were yards apart and the ground beneath was not flat but full of potholes with water and twigs, she asked him in order to discover *what trees* they were in fact that she had been gazing at from afar for so many years and had heard them calling her: "Those trees in the water, what water is that?" And he laughed so much that the trees and the water shook—he would relate it to others and again burst into laughter. "Poplars!" he replied joyfully. "Those trees in the water are not water but poplars!" That they were poplars, Eftha already knew. What she didn't know, what she *didn't* . . .not even he could tell her that.

Yet what a shame, she had brought her son to another room, with a bed in it yes, but whose only window looked out over the yard and not over the meadow with the poplars. "I got confused," she muttered; "today everything's going wrong, I can't do anything right—look where I've brought you . . ."; down in the yard, Christoforos (the very same who had once called in her ears "poplars"!) was filled with rage and waving his arms about, first at his brothers and brothers-in-law with a look as though he were countering accusations, and then at his elder sons and stepsons—would he still go on reproaching them? . . . But they didn't appear to have given up either: they were arguing with him, waving their arms about too, replying to everything he said (not much reached up there); perhaps they were reminding him of some past wrongs, various things, older events, who knows what—at any rate the atmosphere was tense, sparks were about to fly. And as if this weren't enough, all the children had come out into the yard, all those little *deer* that Eftha had chased away from under her feet previously, that everyone had chased away it seems, so that now they had found refuge under the feet of those who were arguing, to ask of them a little attention and tenderness, or at least to try to understand what was happening—and, naturally, they were wrong to do so: Christoforos turned around at some point and gave them a good scolding, told them to make themselves scarce, but given that they simply froze, he raised his hand and brought it down at random, his elder sons and stepsons started to do the same, and so did everyone in general who was anything over three feet tall . . .

"You see? The big hulks argue and it is the little frogs who pay," Eftha said sorrowfully. "That's how it always is."

And she pulled the twelve-year-old away from the window and into her arms, and like that they went over to the bed.

"I wanted to bring you here to see the poplars, not people, but I got confused," she said to him while sitting on the floor and untying his shoelaces, and while he took off the white jacket and waistcoat on his own and tried to undo the shiny buttons of the black shirt. "I still can't believe that you didn't open your mouth today to say something to me. What am I, your mother or some stranger? Seems you think of me as a stranger."

The boy raised his foot, tapping her lightly on the chest.

"Aren't I right in what I say?" she asked him. "Don't you have a tongue in your head to tell me? You prefer to use your foot? All right then. And now you're ready for bed, you're tired from all that's happened, and you want to sleep—the sun's shining outside . . . And me still not knowing . . . Seems I'm going to get angry with you, Theagenis! I'm tired! You won't open your mouth one way or the other, good or bad, right or wrong, who do you think you are? And what happened? Give me that jacket to take a look at . . . There, spotless, as if it's never been worn. What happened? Where's the precious blood? What happened with the slaughtering, with the water they'd prepared for you? Did they—don't be ashamed to tell me—did they make you slaughter it in some devious way? Did they take hold of your hand by force and . . . Give me your hand to look at."

He gave her his hand, which she examined like a palm reader, on both sides. But apart from the fact that it was so light, like a feather, and that it was still trembling, there was nothing else she could detect.

"Perhaps something else happened," she said, "and you're ashamed to confess it. But there's nothing to be ashamed about."

Her last words couldn't be heard, she pronounced them turning her head towards the door, a fraction of a second before it opened wide, and in charged two red-faced boys, not older boys or younger boys, but somewhere between, who most likely had taken up position in the yard from daybreak, though perhaps not in the front line. They caused as much commotion as an army in a peaceful lodging.

"We've found you!" they shouted triumphantly. "You left the room with the tubs, why did you? But we've found you!"

Behind them was a third, the seven-year-old Lukas, lame from birth because of a mistake by the midwife, but by no means any less boisterous than the others. Except that he wheezed more and had to stoop when he ran, take hold of his right knee in both hands and *pull* his whole leg upwards as if dragging it out of a shallow bog in order to free it; this is what he had to do every so often so as to, let's say, set it in motion again, that limp, trailing leg, provoking pity in everyone who saw him . . . But there was no pity to be spared for him that day: it was all for his brother, the most handsome and sound of limb of all.

"What are you doing here? Who said you could come in?" Eftha asked them and was about to throw Theagenis's shoes at them. But she didn't, not because she felt sorry for their heads but because she felt sorry for the shoes, and she ordered them outside immediately and told them to close the door behind them.

"Who's talking to you?" the oldest of them said to her, and for the umpteenth time she regretted not having been a sterner mother with her children, boys and girls, instead of letting them talk back to her like that. And of course, instead of going out, the older one bowed to Theagenis with a bow that was a caricature, and said to him, "What are you sniveling for, crybaby, seeing you didn't do anything? Seeing it was someone else who slaughtered the lamb?"

"He's not sniveling," Eftha cut in, with her mood again changing back and forth, "can you see him sniveling? . . And who slaughtered it, then?"

"Ask him to tell you who did it," the second boy said, pointing to his brother on the bed.

"He's told me everything!" she answered with what was left of her dignity, and turned to look at Theagenis. "Leave him alone," she said, turning back to the other three; "he needs some sleep . . . whoever slaughtered the lamb. I'm talking to you three—outside! . . . Haven't you gone yet?"

Not only hadn't they gone, but they were already getting ready for the torment of the reenactment with as much zeal and fuss as they could muster. A strange reenactment: "Isn't that what you did? Isn't that what you did?" the older one (though two years his junior) kept asking Theagenis, taking a run again and again from one end of the room to the other, where the little lamb supposedly was—and that now, alas, they were reenacting, forcing Theagenis to play the part . . . And all this was repeated by the other two boys, each one coloring it in his own way—especially the little lame wretch. For the knife, they brandished a carob. And it was an ordeal to match the real one, the one that had taken place in the yard that Eftha hadn't seen.

So that now she watched it feeling pity for her own eyes, nurturing hate for that leaden curiosity, sister to indifference we might say, that kept her fixed in the most protected corner of the room watching the constantly repeated *slaughtering* (till she realized what had happened), instead of rushing, till the end of her life if necessary, and snatching the twelve-year-old—slaughterer and slaughtered at the same time—from the clutches and ridicule of those outside; as in any case she had done that morning, as she had done on other occasions in the past for other children.

She mechanically turned her head to look through the window at other images—equally strange ones that would take her from a rock to a hard place: the reproaches and quarrelling had ceased; some were sipping at their drinks and shaking their shoulders as though coughing (most likely they were laughing), and they were all enwrapped in the calming vapors rising from the roasting lamb . . . Christoforos was chatting calmly with the musicians, rubbing his chest—perhaps he was giving them something, a token fee, even if they hadn't played . . . And even the younger children, who just previously had been on the receiving end, were now beginning to laugh and joke with their older brothers, to offer their cheeks for kisses and to take back harsh words, and it wouldn't have been at all surprising if they suddenly appeared there, laden with their own versions and their own carobs.

"*For innumerable evils have compassed me about . . . so that I am not able to look up . . . ,*" Eftha muttered, closing her eyes, far too exhausted to depart like that.

Theagenis wouldn't remember every day in the years that followed, when they all called him Hesychios and all the women would languish for him, the grim and miserable hours he had spent that day, first down in the yard and then—as though his endurance was inexhaustible—up in the room where his mother, Eftha, had brought him for refuge. He would neither cherish those days like relics nor would he shudder even sometimes at their grimness—memory, they say, has forgetting as its helper. But equally there were moments when these half-buried images once again crept into his head and tormented him as though he still owed something to life from that time.

When later he was married to Febronia and father to many children, he explained to a good friend he had acquired, an icon painter, what it was that had eventually delivered him from the hands of his raging younger brothers when they had kept asking him insistently, "Isn't that what you did? Isn't that what you did?" and fell upon him with their *knives*, without slaughtering him of course, though why not? He had reached the point where he wished they would slaughter him, the point of utter despair . . . Lying as he was on the floor, he turned to see where their mother was, why she didn't come to make them go away, to save him, but he couldn't see her, only her feet in one corner, but it wasn't the same, they weren't the feet of the woman he knew. And he remembered some tales that she herself had told them about motherly love but also about motherly heartlessness—some awe-inspiring tales. In one of them, the most widespread and well known, one son, in order to prove to a woman that he loves her more than any other in the world, even more than the woman who bore him, slaughters his mother and takes her heart; takes it as a present to his beloved, the shrew who was waiting; on the way, he stumbles and falls into a ditch, bloodies his face, and the heart of the mother whom he murdered stirs, alive again, and asks with all her eternal love and tenderness, "Have you hurt yourself, my child?" And in the other tale, the less-known one, the apocryphal one, the son is sick, on the verge of death, and his mother at his side implores Death night and day to let her take his place; but when Death comes with his scythe to take *her* in his place, life seems so sweet to her that she points to her son's bed and says, "There Death, there's the one who's sick."

And Theagenis imagined that this was what his own mother was doing that day—back then—and the darkest of thoughts flooded his mind. "It's the turn of heartlessness, it seems, better for me not to expect help from anyone," he said to himself. "It's my day and I'll either be saved by a miracle or my brothers will do for me." You see how they showed quite clearly, openly, that they wanted to tear him to shreds that day.

"... I was in despair," he said to his friend, the icon painter. "If they'd thrown me into a pit of snakes, the snakes would have treated me better; I think that I would have found a mother snake more compassionate . . . And suddenly it came to me: *the snakes!* I remembered the snakes that nobody likes, the tales they used to tell us—our own mother would tell us those too—about snakes . . . How snakes, when their head hurts, come out onto the roads so they can be killed, come out on purpose into the middle of the road and wait for you to pass by, to be frightened and kill them. *So that their head won't hurt anymore!* Of course, they told it like that in order to justify killing them, but what does it matter? And my own head not only hurt but I wanted . . . I wanted to die. Twelve years old, and I wanted to die, wished I'd never been born. And so this, *this* you're not going to believe . . ."

This, then, in total desperation, gave him the idea to shout: "SNAKE! A dead snake, there!" (even he believed it the way he shouted it), and he pointed under the bed, where only he could see, as they had him facedown on the floor. His three little brothers, in their excitement to do in one day what they didn't do in all the others, fell for it—almost before they heard it. They left him and dived under the bed—Theagenis had believed his own voice, but he didn't believe his own eyes . . . And as they fell upon each other, as Eftha, too, sprang out of some corner to see for herself, this woman who was renowned for her art in taking care of snakes, he found himself, unbelievably fortunate, the least concerned with the new battle, not needing even half a step to leap out of the room. And he leapt.

"Fibber, you fibber, where's the snake?" shouted one of them, running after him.

"In the same place that I am!" Theagenis replied mentally, and no one saw him again (which way did he go?) till late in the evening, when a forest warden found him in some far-off fields, close to the meadow with the poplars, up in a plum tree eating plums, still unripe, green and hard like their stones, but he was eating them and shuddering all over, with his teeth chattering. Without any jacket, without shoes, he was cold, anyway—April is not August.

"What are you doing up there? What are you, a thief?" asked the mustached forest warden.

They had called him a fibber, now he was being called a thief.

"I'm not a thief, I'm afraid to go home," answered the boy, and the forest warden proved to be an understanding fellow—besides, it was purely chance that had brought him there, nothing else—and he believed him without asking anything further, coaxed him into coming down, and took him by the hand and led him home without him having to be afraid of anything.

As they went, they became friends. And perhaps to vent his feelings about his mother's heartlessness, the boy told this stranger, who didn't ask too much, what he hadn't told her (and perhaps that was the reason for her heartlessness), who had so implored him to tell her . . . he told him of the lamb that had to be slaughtered that morning and how he couldn't do it, couldn't, and how in the end his father had done it—but which was just as terrible: to see it SLAUGH-TERED. It had happened behind his back, in the wink of an eye, when they had sent him to take another run at it, and coming back he had found the animal SLAUGHTERED.

He told him everything, everything except how he had escaped from his younger brothers—that he would tell only to the icon painter, many years later.

The forest warden listened, entranced almost. The beauty of this boy, more than his words, sent a most pleasant thrill through him, made him feel that he was accompanying a little angel who perhaps had never set foot on earth before, didn't know his way around, and that he had been called upon today to show him, and at the same time to learn better himself. He didn't dare open his mouth or look at the boy directly. He simply listened to his sufferings, and all he could do to show his empathy was squeeze his hand occasionally in his own. And to whisper now and again, "I understand . . . I understand . . ."

Yet he couldn't have understood everything, because for a third time Theagenis told him that his stomach was hurting from the unripe plums, and he didn't think of stopping and saying to him, Go behind a bush and you'll feel better.

"I ate a lot of honey . . . before the plums. And it's hurting."

"Honey?" the forest warden exclaimed in surprise. "And where did you get the honey from?"

"At home . . . they gave it to me."

"Who gave it you?"

"My sister."

"Just how many brothers and sisters do you have?"

"Lots!" Theagenis replied despairingly, and looked around him anxiously, so anxiously that he obliged the warden to look him in the eye.

"Oh . . . I see," he said spontaneously as though he had suddenly burned himself. "Now I understand—your tummy's hurting and you want to go behind a bush! Go on, I'll wait for you . . . take your time."

Like a tied-up animal suddenly set free, Theagenis bolted, disappeared behind a bush.

And unfortunately, twice more he had to let go of the warden's hand and run behind the bushes. "Take your time, I'll wait for you," he reassured him each time. At the third stop, the twelve-year-old felt the need to explain himself.

"While I was up the tree, I didn't feel anything. But now I've come down . . ."

"All that's come down too," the warden added jovially, with complete understanding, and happy that he could at last talk like a human being once more. Not that he'd swallowed his tongue all this time . . .

"That's the way of the world," he said to himself, "takes into account neither angels nor anything. If you eat unripe plums, you'll have a problem with your stomach—whether you're an angel or not! . . . And where did I get the bright idea that he's an angel and not just some poor little boy? When all's said and done, have I ever seen an angel? Maybe he is one."

Theagenis, meanwhile, disappearing for the third time behind the bushes, heard something of the mutterings of his older friend and protector and again remembered his mother, who also spoke to herself, who cut and sewed with her tongue like a dressmaker in a monastery . . . and who at the most difficult moment, however, had left him at the mercy of his brothers . . . of his brothers . . . yes . . . what were they all doing now . . . and Cletia, with the ax and the wrap . . . and his father, who had the knife, who went to wipe it afterwards on the grass . . . but they wouldn't let him wipe it on the grass . . . why, what was special about the grass? . . . and the inn . . . and the lamb, yes, ah . . . the lamb, why was he remembering it now? . . . and those fat folk musicians . . . how many were they, three? . . . and a fourth who arrived late . . . with protuberant ears . . . what was it he sang as soon as he arrived? . . . a slow song . . . *wretched bride, wretched groom* . . . for whom? for him . . . *wre-e-etched bri-i-ide, wre-e-etched gro-o-om!* . . . for him and . . . what was it that Cletia was wearing? . . . she got it from somewhere . . . it was like . . . and the honey . . . *Just the very tip, on this . . . Using your tongue . . . Don't cry so much, you'll die! . . . We'll be as sleepy as cats, Theagenis! . . . Take your time!* . . . There, now there was a spider in front of him, clinging to its web, should he destroy it? Take a jackknife and . . . no, why, what harm was it doing him? A spider couldn't harm him . . . it was quietly spinning its web . . . he got caught in its web and couldn't get free . . . Ah spider, little spider . . .

His vague thoughts spun their own web, a harmonious and irregular one, spun it, got caught and uncaught and followed his legs as these sought a more comfortable position, a little more room, each time he relieved himself, but he wanted more—he was suffering from diarrhea. It frightened him yet at the same time it pleased him: heaven help anyone who trod around there with their head in the clouds—they'd be cursing for a whole twelve months! . . . And he disappeared with trousers down and knees bent—and even worse, barefoot—farther and farther inside, as far as he could inside the bush he'd chosen, as though the bush were an abyss without beginning or end. But it eventually ended; he found before him only thick and thin tangled roots, or branches that looked like roots, twisted one round the other—and thorns! Loads of thorns, loads of twigs with thorns, so that, in trying to avoid the one, the poor boy stepped on another even worse! But he didn't make a sound, he endured it all, taking care only to finish in as short a time as possible—take your time!—so the warden wouldn't have to wait too long and start to wonder.

Each time that his little friend left him, the warden said whatever he had to say to himself and then walked away a reasonable distance; and from there he would cough to let him know that he wouldn't go any farther, wouldn't leave him, and he would begin whistling without any particular tune, but in an eloquent way: as though setting protective limits around the boy, warning anyone, even the lizards and tortoises, that they mustn't go near those bushes that he was guarding faithfully, albeit at a distance. And every so often he would put his hand to his mouth and call out again: "Take your time you, no one's coming . . ." *You!* He didn't know his name—each time he remembered to ask the boy what his name was, the boy wasn't with him; and when he returned, he forgot.

Yet no matter how confused, vacant, and fluid those moments were for both of them, we forgot to say that the second time they had to separate for a little, a small though fiery nettle behind the bushes stung the twelve-year-old on his buttocks, which made him, because he couldn't scratch it freely, even more late in coming out. He wanted to burst into tears again—the nettle's sting was worse, more real than the nettle itself! This had stayed where it was, small and untouched, as if nothing had happened, whereas he was carrying its sting like one carries one's sins. He felt like shouting and shout he did: "I've been stung! There's a nettle here!"

"Nettle? Leave it alone, it'll go away of its own accord, don't scratch it," the warden said, but the very next moment the young lad appeared before him with his skin inflamed . . . "It really stung you badly, eh?"

"It'll pass," the boy said stoically, comforting himself; "but it's burning."

And so the third and last time, he was especially careful, though in a hurry as always, not to get caught up in any nettles—the thorns were more than enough.

"See," the warden said, reminding him, "I didn't let even the birds come near you, but I can't prevent the nettles and thorns from growing where they want."

After that, Theagenis's belly found relief, and he found his friend at the other side of the path rolling a cigarette and still whistling. He said to him, "My father smokes too and my brothers . . . not all of them," and once again the warden was astonished.

"Just how many brothers and sisters have you got?"

"Ooo, lots," the boy said, yet again it didn't come easily to the warden — in fact he considered it improper — to inquire about his family or even to ask his first name. But he would ask him, they had time. That is, not too much time, because the path with its fine, sandlike soil that had brought them from afar, from the fields, was now different as it led them on: blacker, tighter, trodden, somewhat damp, with different turns — they were approaching the first houses.

"Which way is your house, where do you live?" the warden asked him.

Theagenis pointed at random: "That way . . . it's still far. I know the way by myself, but . . . No, I don't know . . . where's yours?"

"Mine? Close by, a little way up," said the warden. He halted for a moment, reflected, and went on: "Look, either we can go our separate ways here, a little way up, and you can go on alone without having to be afraid, or, if you want me to take you as far as your house, we'll have to pass by mine for a moment so I can tell my wife that I'm going to be a little late — she'll have been waiting for me for hours; I've been gone since the morning. And tomorrow I have one last shift."

Theagenis didn't care. In any case, since the morning, or was it afternoon, when he'd left his own house, he wasn't going to return before evening — and if the warden hadn't found him, perhaps he wouldn't even have returned in the evening . . . He shuddered at the thought of spending the entire night up in that plum tree, obliged to eat the rest of the plums!

"Let's go," he said willingly.

And so they passed by the warden's house, which was indeed close by, and his visit to which would constitute for Theagenis an event as equally important — for different reasons — as the drama that had befallen him that morning.

The man didn't call out to his wife but like a troubadour simply whistled a short melodic air, and she, after taking her time and so making him whistle again, came out, lowering her head in the small doorway that, like a cloth, quietly opened up in the lower part of the house, where they must have had the animals or a storeroom, and not from the top of the steps — wooden ones and dangerous without a rail — as he expected and so was gazing impatiently in that direction, nodding to his little friend, as if to say, *That's where my good lady will come from, from up there.* But she fooled them and emerged from elsewhere.

She was wearing a red, a striking red, pleated dress, with shiny rhomboid buttons in the same color, with unusual patterns and hems in various places, all very fancy (Theagenis had never seen any other woman in such a dress), and in her hands she was holding an enormous pair of black scissors. Over her shoulders she had a loose woolen cardigan, of another color, but it was as if this didn't exist: the red overshadowed it. And in any case, she soon rid herself of it, letting it fall to the ground.

"Are you down here?" asked the warden, puzzled. "What are you doing with the scissors?"

"I was looking for them to cut her nails," answered the woman.

She spoke to her husband and at the same time eyed the little unknown visitor. He was still gazing at her dress, nothing else: it was so red, Lordy, so insanely red! If he'd been looking at a red sea or a red river, it wouldn't have left him any less amazed! Even her breath, if he could have seen it, would have been red!

"What's wrong with her nails?" the man asked.

"They're long, like those of the dead," she answered; "the woman sent her away again. And she sent word that I should see to her, not let her go for her lesson again with nails like that. Just imagine! As though I'm the one who lets her, as though I were the one bringing her up! . . . And she won't sit still and let me cut them. I've been chasing her all afternoon; I go to get hold of her and she vanishes." She pointed with the scissors at the little door she had come out of. "Now she's hiding with the animals, between their legs; she's got them on her side, and they look at me with such eyes! . . . I'm afraid to go near"—she clutched at her belly with both hands—"I don't want to go and get kicked."

She was sick, her face full of blotches, marks, yellowing, and her belly was ready to burst like a bubble, large it was and pointed, so that it must have been far easier for her to bend backwards than lean forward. The twelve-year-old noticed it from the very first—you would have to be as blind as a bat not to have noticed—but, on the other hand, dazzled as he was by the red, he didn't have the time to think through what that bubble in front of her meant. He thought about it now: she would soon give birth . . . just imagine! He had seen his mother like that, and his aunts, and women from neighboring houses. They all carried their babies in there so they wouldn't get cold, the tiny babies, that's what they told them. And then they took them out, even if it was the heart of winter— now, they told them, they were too hot, they had to get out no matter what the cost. And the women themselves paid the cost with their cries and screams behind closed doors . . . While children like him were all locked together in a room in order to do penance and implore the good Lord in a loud voice to save their mother and their new little brother . . . It all happened with cries and tears.

The warden's wife appeared to be a little ashamed of clutching her body like that in front of an unknown boy—but how could she have hidden it? Only if she hadn't appeared at all.

"Anyhow," she mumbled, "she's a proper wildling, she makes me sweat blood with those nails of hers . . ." And with some irritation, she put the scissors under her arm and tried to button one of the three buttons below her waist that wouldn't fit into their buttonholes and that she left undone.

"Leave it, what are you doing?" her husband said to her, and she, as though not having any connection with either her buttons or her fingers, went on:

"I've been chasing after her all afternoon," she said, "all afternoon I've gone through the mill with her, what do you want me to do! Where are you? I've been waiting for you to give her a talking-to . . . *Who's that boy?*"

She asked the question half-closing her eyes, her hand on her brow, as though her head were suddenly hurting. The warden told her what he knew, or rather *how* he knew, because he hadn't heard very well a lot of what the boy had said when they first met, and he had got confused. But neither did the boy go to the trouble of correcting him or of confirming anything.

"Anyhow, I found him up a tree," he concluded (in the same way that he had begun, except for the *anyhow*). "He was stuffing himself with plums that won't be ripe yet for another three months! Afterward, until we arrived here, we were wandering around . . . bushes, nettles, bees—the day was full of incidents today, it wasn't at all boring like yesterday . . . Give him something to throw over his shoulders; he left his home just as you see him. He's not even wearing any shoes."

"Where am I to find shoes?" the woman said.

"All right then, give him something to put round him."

"You get the girl and I'll give him something to put round him," she said to him, and without waiting walked off hurriedly to the far end of the yard—they turned and stared at her: she resembled a red convoy being swept by the wind—went up to a small pile of wood, and pulled out a small garment that she brought back for the boy . . . "Put it on so you don't get cold," she told him.

Theagenis hesitated till he took hold of it in his hands, but then he put it on without any asking—"And remember to bring it back," he heard her say to her husband as he was pulling it over his head. It was a sleeveless knitted top, with a deep opening in front that fastened crosswise with elastic, and it had olive-green and yellow stripes. The elastic and the selvage around the shoulders was a dark green—one of those knitted tops worn equally by both boys and girls. It also had an embroidered letter on the left breast, so elaborate, with so many loops and tails—and upside-down as he was looking at it, out of the corner of his eye— that he couldn't work out whether it was a *B*, an *R*, or a *P*.

Then they left him in the middle of the yard to go and get their daughter. The man went to the left, to the side of the house, to a large door through which the animals went in and out, and the woman stood at the smaller, front door, to be ready in case the wildling tried to get away that way. Theagenis, being better acquainted with the man than with his wife, started to follow him.

"Psst, where'd you think you're going?" she whispered, stopping him. "Can't you hear what's going on? Do you want to get yourself kicked by the animals? Come over here."

He changed direction and went over to her. This woman could forget about him for entire moments, not pay any more attention to him than she would to her own house, which she saw every day, but when she did remember his existence, the surprise in her eyes was no less than in his own.

"I went through hell and high water," she started to tell him with a secretiveness that she hadn't had when she'd said it to her husband, "to get her to go to her craft learning this morning—I want her to become a seamstress—and they sent her away, sent her back to me. See to her, they told me. See to her? And who's going to see to me? Ha!" She opened her eyes wide: "She's a proper wildling, unruly!... And if you see her nails, so black and long... like garden hoes! What use are scissors with nails like that!... Come closer, don't be afraid—you slaughtered a great big lamb today!"

That's how she'd heard it from her husband, that's how she told it. And the boy did what he'd seen decent and modest folk do: he said nothing.

"But why don't you say anything?" she asked him. "Voices are to be heard. Or don't you have a voice?"

Behind the wall could be heard girlish shrieking and the shouts of the warden.

"They're quarreling . . . ," said Theagenis, finding no better way to prove to her that he did have a voice.

"Not quarreling, *playing*," she said, correcting him—or rather confiding this too to him—and staring at her scissors front and back. "I wish they were quarreling . . . I'm the only one who quarrels with her, but what's the use! The one's more afraid of the other." And saying this, she brandished the scissors and made two magnificent slashes in the air, one to the right and one to the left, as though forming a triangle without a base and at whose apex presumably were the heads of her and her daughter when they were quarreling . . . A strange woman; no one could have enacted those scissor slashes so well—she even laughed at what she had done, what had suddenly come to her to do, and naturally she didn't repeat it; she was smart, too.

On the contrary, she again became obsessed, periodically at least, with trying to fasten one of the three buttons that wouldn't button, while the boy, motionless beside her, with the voices on the other side of the wall sometimes getting nearer and sometimes moving away again, was imagining that she leaned towards him and whispered in his ear to put his hand on her dress . . . where exactly? *Here, here!* she showed him, holding his hand with her own on that warm throbbing sphere, and turning to look at the little door behind them: Nice, isn't it? — Oh, it didn't last very long, but it was bliss, a premature fervent passion in his mind's illicit depths that no one, absolutely no one, could even suspect or prevent.

"She's dangerous!" he heard her say as though she were counseling him to keep far away. "I realized it right from the start — she came out feet first, not head first, upside down . . . her hands crossed me, they opened like a cross . . . What I went through in bringing her into the world! And this here" — she looked at her breast, but meant something else — "she'll make me pay for it! . . . Ha, the little minxes today are ashamed if their mothers have a belly! . . . No, not ashamed, envious . . . Forgive me for being so open."

Theagenis forgave her, and mumbled something about his own little sisters, but the woman didn't hear; she was in a world of her own.

"You know those birds, those twenty-twoers?" she asked him, "that call out *coocoo-coo-coocooee?*"

"Yes, I do," he said, "we say that they're calling out twenty-two . . . twenty-two . . ."

"Now that's our language, and everybody can understand it, she said, "all that *coocoo-coo-coocooee* is another language, a foreign one, and it means *the little girl punished me! the little girl punished me!* That's what the poor birds are calling out, because when they went to drink from a spring, the little girl punished them. I know what I'm saying."

But Theagenis never managed to find out why she told him that story; the cries and chasing inside the stable suddenly reached the door (as if someone had fallen against it), and while the woman rushed to take up position beside it, holding the scissors like a trophy and unfastening a fourth button on her dress, he, stumbling — and with a vague sense of disappointment, as though she had once again forgotten him — moved two steps back. Now he would see her daughter, *the wildling.*

The little wooden door — which had no handle or bolt, just a hole for putting your finger through to pull the door open — opened again quietly, and Theagenis moved even farther back. From out of the dimness appeared the smiling and familiar face of the warden, holding by the scruff of her neck a vivacious little girl of about seven or eight years, hair disheveled, indomitable, with a trickle of green silk mucus running between her nostrils and her mouth, and two very bright eyes. Very bright.

"*Who's he?*" she asked as soon as she set eyes on Theagenis, making the stream disappear with her sleeve in the wink of an eye. Her appetite to learn could only be matched by the awe she felt.

"Never you mind!" came the answer from the woman in red.

"*Who's he?*" the little girl wanted to know, and her consuming interest in the unknown boy calmed her somewhat, so that she offered no resistance when the woman grabbed hold of her—just keeping her hands clenched and her head constantly turned towards him, no matter which way her body was pulled.

"Never you mind!" the woman said again tirelessly and took hold of both little hands together, putting the one wrist on top of the other as though she were piling stalks, and gripped them both in her fist, dragging her farther outside into the middle of the yard. "Sit down, and don't move, it'll soon be dark, and I can't cut your nails in the moonlight, have some pity," she said to her without coming up for breath.

The little girl didn't sit down, didn't hold out her nails.

"If you tell me who he is, I'll hold them out," she said, capitulating.

The woman, with a face as red as her dress, turned to look over her shoulder at Theagenis: "Tell us your name, dear child, for the sake of this unruly creature!" she implored him. "For her sake! . . ."

Theagenis advanced a little, but as soon as he opened his mouth and everyone was hanging on his words, the little girl wriggled free of her mother's hands. "Aaaa!" she screamed, and ran after her with such fury and agility, despite her weight, that Theagenis and the warden found themselves like innocents being swept away by the whirling red mass . . . She grabbed hold of the girl by her hair, next to the woodpile, and locked her superbly in her arms. The girl suddenly exuded all the weariness of the world and gave up.

"Don't try any more of your wiles," the pregnant woman warned her; "even if you fly up in the air like a bird, I'll catch you, do you hear? If you're a bird, then I'm a hawk."

The little girl shook her head as though she'd been encouraged to fly but didn't want to; she had grown tired of fighting over her nails, or some other miracle had happened and she was now being well-behaved, extremely well-behaved, even trying to hide behind the red dress or rubbing her forehead against the big, heaving belly.

"More of that and the baby will come out of my mouth; you'll be the death of me," said the woman, and the child, somewhat thoughtlessly, said, "Yes!"

That caused her blood to boil again.

"Yes, she says! I said that she'll be the death of me and she says yes! Whoever heard of a daughter coming out with things like that to her mother? Eh? Ah! . . . I won't just cut her nails, today I'll cut her hair off too, down to the roots!" And she dragged her with her in search of the scissors, which she had let drop somewhere when she was running to catch her.

She took them from the hands of Theagenis, who had picked them up and only managed to examine them a little, to see just how heavy and rusted they were. Taking them, the woman smiled at him faintly, almost vacantly; the little girl just stared at him: her eyes were both very dark and very bright, tiny flames in the black abyss.

Then mother and daughter sat facing each other on two smooth stones that served as stools in the yard.

"You two be on your way now, they'll be waiting for him," she said to her husband, pointing to the boy and arranging her belly and knees in such a way that the little girl could comfortably rest her hands there: "Hold them out," she said to her.

"Let them stay a bit longer!" the little girl asked imploringly, lowering her head, this wildling who had been tamed, who was now sitting like some quiet cats do when reflecting on their past as wild cats—at the same time stretching out her rosy hands with the big, dirty nails.

"And why should they stay?" asked the mother.

The little girl stared at her, with a somewhat impatient and gleeful look in her eyes, just as we look at someone who asks something . . . though he already knows the answer better than we do.

"Why should they stay?" asked her mother again, truly not seeming to suspect the motivation behind the request.

The little girl continued to stare at her with that fervent and wily look in her eyes, which both intrigued and irritated the mother.

"Speak," she shouted, "why should they stay?"

The girl lowered her head till she could lower it no more.

"To watch us," she said softly, her voice full of innuendo, coyness, and grievance all at the same time, an unbeatable mixture of shyness and sauciness that left the elder woman speechless.

Then she burst into bubbly chortling laughter, and her daughter started to laugh with her, as they looked into each other's eyes, rubbed their noses and laughed, made merry, split their sides . . .

"Did you hear what she said?" the woman asked, turning to the two men, but she saw only the boy before her and her laughter was cut short; with some delay the daughter's laughter was cut short too. "Where's my husband?" she asked Theagenis. Her husband had gone just previously to the front gate and was speaking to someone who had brought him something. The woman in red calmed down when she turned her head and saw him, as if it were possible for the earth to have opened up and swallowed him, leaving in his place that little unexpected visitor.

As for Theagenis, though he could have followed the warden without any-one preventing him this time, he preferred, on the contrary, to stay there, close to these two strange females, who seemed to pester each other and be at each other's throats all the time, though more because they were alike than because they were unalike . . . And, naturally, he had heard what the girl had said to her mother—she hadn't said it so softly that he wouldn't have heard it. So he stood there and stared at them, *he stayed there to look at them*, even if he hadn't dared to laugh too when they had laughed. Though he had chuckled to himself a couple of times: the first time, he didn't know why, the other time because he remembered his mother saying that *the other man's grass is always greener* . . . She used to say it when some child from another mother wouldn't want to leave their house—just like him in that house. Where . . . even the nails were greener.

There, now they were cutting the third one. And we ought to point out that these nails didn't get dirty easily just because they were long, but the little wild-ling grew them long precisely so that she could enjoy getting them dirty in any way possible. But now it was the older woman who was enjoying cutting them— no one would have imagined how gently and dexterously she cut them, and with such big and ungainly scissors, which were so old and cumbersome that if you tried to use them to cut a piece of cloth or even paper they just crumpled it, creased it, wore away at it, so that in the end, cursing, you preferred to tear it. Nevertheless, there were one or two points of just a few inches, imperceptible to the eye, that still cut fine, that had escaped the general lack of use and the thick coating of rust, and the woman in red—only she—knew where they were without having to look for them; and this is where she placed the nail in order to cut it perfectly from one edge to the other, almost without moving the tips of the scissors. They moved like the tip of her tongue hanging from her mouth, like painters when they perform their most delicate brushstrokes . . . the reddest tip.

When the first five nails had fallen into the lap of her dress—with the little girl gazing at them aggrieved, as if the moon had lost five of its phases, but also with aplomb because she knew that before too long her nails would be as be-fore—her husband came back over to them carrying a knapsack that appeared to be full of pointed stones, or at least pumice stones. He looked pleased; so did the woman as soon as she saw it.

"What have you got there?" asked his daughter, stretching out the hand that was still to be topped.

"Your dowry, and don't ask," answered her mother, and the girl didn't ask again; she wasn't particularly interested in what was in the knapsack; she could guess what it was, but she did want to look for the last time at her lovely and dirty nails. And show them to that nice, rather odd boy, whom her father, after putting the knapsack down at his wife's feet and remarking that the sun had almost set, took by the hand and set off with almost at a run.

"Who was it?" she asked her mother pensively.

"I don't know," she replied, "your father found him in a tree today, eating sour plums."

"Why?"

"Because something happened this morning at his house, some fuss or other, a celebration—hold your fingers straight! . . . *Seven!* Three more and I'm already tired, tired and hungry. I have to eat for two, you know."

"And why was he eating sour plums?"

"Because they're not ripe yet—do you know what I wouldn't give for a few plums? *Eight!* Even if they're sour."

"Will he come again?"

"How should I know . . . the door's open. Let him come if he wants . . . *Nine!*"

"A shoe!" the little girl exclaimed.

A shoe with its toe turned up like a tongue had slipped out of the packed knapsack; the woman stuffed it back inside and returned to the fingers.

"Why didn't we give it to the boy, he was barefoot?" the daughter asked.

"Because those shoes are big enough for another five feet like his . . . Besides, did he give you the impression of being poor?"

"So why did you give him my top if he wasn't poor?"

"Because he was cold. When the calves were keeping you warm with their breath, that poor little thing was cold . . . You won't lose your top, don't worry; your father will bring it back with him. Now, come on, give me the last one."

"Take it!"

The tenth nail fell into the red dress.

"And what are you going to do with them now?" she asked her, feeling almost fingerless without her long nails—but not for too long.

"I'm going to sow them over there in that corner, and wait for a hand to grow. It'll sprout flowers and branches—and the king's son will come! . . . He'll come again!"

The little girl was pleased; each time they finished with that tumultuous cutting of nails and she asked her mother "And what are you going to do with them now?" the mother would come out with some sort of story like that one. Then they would go and throw them in the fire and listen to them crackling like corn seeds.

We don't know over the following days how much these two, the woman in red and her daughter, wished to see the unknown visitor with the angelic face in their yard again. It was, however, something that he fervently sought in various ways. But it wasn't possible; he was unable to find their house again; he had completely lost his sense of direction. As though years had passed, as though it were a distant memory, a chimera that changed place every day. He tried going again to the plum tree in the hope that on his return he would be helped by recognizing some signs, some bushes, some white and then black dirt roads so that he might find that house again; but it didn't occur to him that one only arrives by chance at such plum trees. Besides, he didn't want to tell anyone or let anyone see that he was up to something. He simply wandered in unknown densely populated neighborhoods that reminded him of that one, in which you couldn't distinguish where one house ended and the next began, or which of the many front gates, yards, or staircases led to which house, and in which, of course, there was no woman—not even a sight of one—wearing a flame-red dress on a weekday or holding a pair of enormous black scissors. He was unable even to find the warden again, although he roamed about looking for him in distant fields—he even reached as far as the poplars, waited for him to emerge from somewhere and greet him, come over to him, but all he saw was a scrawny white horse with a bell round its neck looking for water between the rocks . . . It hadn't rained for some time, months; the place was bone dry. Like the horse, he too was looking . . . looking for what? There were moments when he thought that everything that had happened, from the plum tree and after, had been a dream, hadn't really happened. One day he asked his mother, while he had thread wrapped round his hands and she was winding it into tiny balls, when it is that women give birth! She looked at him, puzzled, stopped winding the thread and looked at him again. Then she picked up a new ball and began to wind it quickly. "When God says so," she replied, and like this, his last hope was gone—if, that is, his question involved any hope.

But one Sunday morning, two or three weeks later, he saw a crowd of children, of around his age and younger still, rushing out of church and racing madly to see who could outrun the other. And it immediately occurred to him that the warden's wife had given birth, that today was the day of the christening and that these children were running home to announce its name, to tell the parents and claim their reward . . . Because, at that time, the last to learn the name of the newly christened baby, officially at least, were its parents; the godfather and godmother were free to change their minds at the last moment, even violating some secret agreements, and give the child another name — with cases, of course, where such initiatives and surprises were not at all welcome to the parents and so ended in conflicts and strained relations that sometimes lasted years.

Indifferent to all this, Theagenis gathered momentum and ran behind the children who were running. He was sure that they would lead him to the warden's house, that even running now with his eyes closed, this is where he would arrive!

But, alas, his expectations proved wrong. The house into which the children entered like invaders was a different one, and the parents who were waiting impatiently to learn the name bore no resemblance to the warden and his wife — so little resemblance that Theagenis felt more sorry for them than for himself. Nevertheless, they seemed more than happy and scattered handfuls of coins over the heads of the children.

Two years later, summer it was, he saw something very strange happening in a desolate spot: two children, thin as reeds, a boy and a girl, were bending over a large, deep pit (a small chasm for them), trying desperately to pull something up, without success. It must have been something heavy and cumbersome, because a couple of times, in their struggle to pull it up, they were pulled down by it. Yet they persisted heroically, without speaking or complaining, and they were so engrossed in their labors that they didn't notice that there was someone behind them, Theagenis, watching them. He made several wagers with himself as to what it could be that they were pulling at with such zeal but that kept defeating them . . . And eventually, he made up his mind and went over to help them get it out.

"Don't! Get away, it's ours!" shouted the girl when he, still behind them, without them having seen him, simply asked them what it was they were pulling at.

"I don't want to take it from you," said the fourteen-year-old; "I came over to help."

The two children — obviously brother and sister, perhaps also twins — forgot what they were doing for a few moments in order to look at him: he was more than good-looking for those parts, polite and well-dressed . . . So they let him look into the pit. He leaned over and saw a cute little horse, very little, with shiny brown hair, seemingly as real as the three of them, sleeping peacefully, but sadly—so they informed him—it was dead: their mare had given birth to it that afternoon, but because it had been born dead, their father had taken the mare and thrown the foal into the pit. The children had been distraught and since then had been trying to pull it out . . .

"But why get it out?" Theagenis asked. "Since it's dead, isn't it better here? If you manage to get it out, what will you do with it?"

"We want to take it somewhere else," they said to him, "here, the crows will eat it."

They were right, but where else—unless they were to bury it like they do people—wouldn't the crows eat it?

"We want to take it somewhere else, it's ours," they repeated.

Theagenis offered to help them get it out, but on one condition: that they told him where they would take it afterward. They said to him: "Come with us and you'll see, we can't tell you now."

And he went down into the pit—it was quite deep and uneven—and there he lifted the small, though not lightweight, dead animal in his arms, until the two skinny children were able from up above to grip it tightly by its legs and finally pull it up onto the ground beside them. When he climbed back up to the surface, he saw them lying over the little horse, whimpering and caressing it as though it really were their brother . . . And then they got down to work: they tied its legs together in pairs with two ropes, tied the two ropes together with a third rope, and then began to pull it like two horses pulling a funeral carriage.

Clouds of dust rose up every so often, when the soil was plentiful and dry, and Theagenis followed behind in amazement—he was beset by the strange suspicion, or rather hope, that they would take it (in heaven's name why?) to the warden's house! . . . The two children and their precious cargo, without hurrying but without dawdling either, continued up hill and down dale, getting ever farther away from the desolate spot . . . And Theagenis—though constantly losing all hope that they would lead him to where he thought—followed them because he couldn't do otherwise . . . At some moment, he cast a glance behind him and saw nothing, hardly a tree even. "But where are we going?" he wondered. "To the ends of the earth?"

Nevertheless, from somewhere, no one could say from where, they were spotted by a restless soul, which, overcome by curiosity, very soon caught up with them from behind. The first to become aware of her was Theagenis, whose mouth turned dry when he turned and set eyes on the warden's daughter! What other girl was there with such a sparkling gaze and such a nimble body? And, of course, just as once she had given battle over her nails, so now too she would have done anything for a treasure being dragged along and exposed as was this dead horse. Her intentions were so obvious, and her designs on the poor animal so consuming, that she didn't pay particular attention to the thunderstruck Theagenis, or to the other two children, who gazed at her in fright, sensing what was about to happen . . .

For the time being, however, the newcomer—who couldn't have been more than about ten—kept on surprising them: just as they were afraid that she would grab the rope from out of their hands, she began to suck on her finger and entreat them, gazing at her feet, to let her drag the horse a bit, too; and just as they were about to oblige her, but only for a bit (and so as to avoid the worst), she grabbed the rope from their hands and vanished into smoke! If he'd had any doubts whatsoever concerning who she was—because he hadn't managed to get a good look at her, nor did he remember her all that well—Theagenis had no more after that spectacular escalation of her behavior.

The brother and sister, meanwhile, after being taken aback at first and left standing literally like reeds in the valley, chased after her and called her every name under the sun . . . But she too eventually got tired, or rather got punished: she was tugging at the lifeless animal with such haste and fervor that the rope round the hind legs came loose, and for her to go on dragging it from the one end only wasn't easy for her—apart from the fact that she was now on rugged terrain, full of stones, potholes, and thorns, whereas before the brother and sister hadn't made such a mistake. They would catch up with her, then, at any moment, and might very well tie her up now with the dead horse, so she, with things looking bad, abandoned her loot and took to her heels.

"Wasn't that the daughter of the warden?" Theagenis asked them, out of breath, when things had calmed down and she was nowhere to be seen.

"Daughter of the devil more like," they said, spitting to ward off any evil.

"Yeah . . . sure," Theagenis had to concede, "but isn't there a warden with a daughter like that?"

They told him without any ado that the warden they knew had no daughters, only sons.

"But there's another one that I know, who has a daughter like her," Theagenis persisted, desperate to get confirmation, but the two children had their own cares and were little concerned with his. They again bound their little horse with the ropes and pulled it out of the stones and thorns, patted and consoled it for the upset it had gone through at the hands of the intruder, and again began to drag it in the way that they knew, with Theagenis following behind.

And where was this mysterious trek going to end? At a chasm. Yes, at a real chasm—that's where they were taking it. In order to throw it into that deep and terrible chasm, they had taken it out of the pit that, of course, was far too small and shallow to play the role of a chasm — it would have been easy for the crows to see the dead animal and swoop to devour it, but also easy for people to jump down and take it! Regardless of whether crows smell their prey even without seeing it, or whether people usually are not so keen on stealing dead animals from pits. No, these were rational things, whereas the two children felt much more relieved, reassured, and safe by throwing their own dead horse into a deep, inaccessible ravine, and they looked at Theagenis — who naturally had followed them to the edge, to the point where the one mystery would be swallowed by another mystery — as if to say: Now you know.

In three or four years, Theagenis's adolescence would be over, concerning which, in any case, very little has come down to us, even more so given that his life from then on, enwrapped in the legend of his good looks and his fatal conquests under a new name, ironically innocuous, would take the lion's share in what would *remain* concerning him. Anyhow, making one last and brief return to the day that he became twelve years old, we see him going home alone late into the evening: the warden remembered something or thought up some pretext at one moment, and instead of taking him to his front door, left him before they even reached the ruins. And he also left him with the hope that he would pass by on one of the following days to see him, to find out what had happened.

He never passed by, however, not even to get his daughter's top, which, amid everything else that day, both of them completely forgot about. The only thing Theagenis managed to find out about was the red dress: he asked him where his wife had come across a dress like that, and he told him that it was from among the clothes *for the poor* that some people came and distributed now and again in the school or in church. "Last time, they brought such a lot of decent stuff," he said, "and she went and chose that red dress. At first when I saw it, I was alarmed, but . . . don't even think of telling her to take it off! She sleeps in it and wakes up in it, and if she didn't have her belly — she'll give birth soon — she would go swimming in it as well . . . But she'll go on wearing it afterwards too, says she'll take it in. What's to be said? She's even started believing that . . . it's her bridal dress that she dyed red. She's not without imagination. It's a good thing she doesn't go out very much — the dogs would run after her."

As for the twelve-year-old's family, they had been so worried by his disappearance, had searched for him so long in every possible place without finding him, that their minds turned to the worst (the previous fall a boy his age had hanged himself because his father had offended him with some harsh words), so that when they saw him returning like the prodigal son, they ran out to welcome him with open arms. The advice, the subsequent exhortations to him not to take to the roads at the first setback, and the questions as to where the heck he'd been hiding for so long, how he'd come by that strange top, how he'd managed not to be hungry or cold in his bare feet were all left for the next day.

And Theagenis talked about some of these things, but kept silent about others. He said a lot, for example, about the plum tree and the nettle that stung him, even talked about the kind warden who had got him down from the tree and had walked with him much of the way, had helped him find his way through those unknown places, but he said nothing about the woman and her daughter. He changed a lot as it came to him at that moment.

"When the warden brought me to the first houses and left me," he told them, "I went back into the fields . . . Not to the same ones, others, I don't know . . . I went one way then the other. But he found me again and brought me back. He left me next to the fig tree and waited to see whether I'd go back again. He watched me coming in and then left; he was in a hurry."

"He should have come in too, so we could've treated him to something," said Eftha.

"And who was this warden?" asked his father.

The boy described him as best he could (as he wanted), but neither Christoforos nor anyone else knew who he was—they thought they knew all the wardens—after all, it's not as if they were so numerous. He was also rash enough to tell them that they called him Giannis, which only confused them even more: there were many Giannises, but they didn't know any warden by that name.

"Anyhow, whoever he was, best of luck to him," said Eftha, and very quickly she and all the others in the house forgot about the warden.

But not Theagenis, who as the days passed began to bitterly regret not having described him correctly when he'd been asked, not having told them everything about the woman in the red dress and her daughter with her dirty nails. "Pity," he thought, "if I'd come out with everything then, they might have been able to tell me who he is and how I might find his house again." Whereas now he was searching blindly and was having no luck—and the time was passing; he would eventually forget them whether he wanted to or not, and that saddened him. He sat and reflected on what he knew about nails . . . He knew, so to speak, two women neighbors, Pulcheria and Daphne, elderly widows, who cut each other's nails, fingernails and toenails, because it suited them like that, it was a solution. He knew another woman too, a hunched-up and wrinkled old woman, Ol' Ma Maria, who occasionally came to their house—she was a neighbor, too—and asked the girls, his sisters and cousins, to thread a dozen or so needles—the poor thing could still darn, but she couldn't see well enough to thread the needles—and she lived in a house with only men; she didn't have even one daughter or granddaughter. So she would stock up for a dozen days or so. The same old woman would also come occasionally so that the girls could cut her nails, and she always had something in her pocket by way of payment: a roasted corncob, a few walnuts or chestnuts, an apple—and a pile of wishes with every nail that fell to the floor. She would even ask to see it, to feel it; she held it up to her eyes and would stare at it, and very often she would put this in her pocket too. Her bust, then, was full of needles like medals, and her old nails fell out of her pockets whenever she took something out . . . He also knew a story about one of his aunts, who in her youth, it's said, used to cut the nails of the elderly, and of the children, and her own, of course, and collect them in a bottle the size of a thimble. When the bottle was almost full and she was about forty, someone asked for her hand in marriage. But it didn't work out, and his aunt, out of grief and bitterness, threw them all on the fire and burned them in the same way that she might have burned her dowry. And she never married, but remained an old spinster, ever devoted to her brothers.

Yet all these stories and incidents to do with nails were of no help to him at all . . . On both occasions when his heart had fluttered because he thought that he had tracked down the warden and his family—first with the christening and then with the dead horse—it had fluttered to no avail: the first time he was proven wrong, and the second time not even that.

Third Tale

CUPID WITH HIS ARROWS

We are envious of a distant deity (perhaps Kali, perhaps some other), at least as we see her in one of her mythical depictions, in which sprouting out of each shoulder are fifteen arms, each one doing something different, and all of them converging. A privilege of this sort would help us, so we believe, to easily combine thirty stories (if not thirty, then even more) in one and would reduce the danger that often threatens us of getting lost in the labyrinthine paths of narration or of remaining with the thrill and incredible dismay of a beginning without an end—that is, of a consummate though ineffectual endeavor.

It is not only love and death or an environment with palimpsests of childhood fixation that has been drawing us for years now to explore and narrate it in detail; it is also something else, much more fleeting and individual, that calls us to this struggle with the ineffable, in which all the delights and enigmas of the written word have their origins.

We may even lose ourselves when writing, may not find again the way back to you—the sole pleasure that remains unpunished, it's said, is reading.

In front of the entrance to our inn, just before it was destroyed. Febronia, our fifteen children, and myself. The infant in her arms is Thomas "with the disparate eyes." The other infant is Elisavet. On the left is my brother Lukas with a horse. Memento, December 1899. Lest we forget.

This is what, in sloping but legible handwriting, Hesychios, formerly Theagenis, wrote on the back of a rectangular black-and-white photograph teeming with smiling and anxious faces, all intently turned towards the lens, so that if we were to imagine so many bodies aboard a boat, we would be right to imagine that the boat might very well have sunk. Having good handwriting, he wrote the same thing on the back of numerous other photographs, simply changing the names, showing his brothers and their families, all taken more or less on the same day, on the same spot, most of them now lost or hidden for another hundred years.

It was a *historic* event, however we look at it. Just as every six or twelve months he would bring a barber to the big house to cut their hair, all in turn, children and adults—because just imagine if all of them were to have to go separately for haircuts—and this meant that the lucky barber shut his shop that day and came with all his gear to the house, ate with them at lunchtime, and then continued work in the afternoon; or just as every now and again he would bring some other old craftsman or a little old woman, who would arrive with dark bottles underarm and leeches in the bottles so they could have a mass bloodletting in the house (those, that is, who needed it or those who wanted to prevent such a need), so also during the past ten or fifteen years, on the occasion of some exceptional anniversary or desire, he would bring a photographer with his canopies, backcloths, and plates to capture them, women and children all, for posterity. Photography was a big thing then, at the time of its beginnings; it was an *aberration* full of importance and grandiosity.

The idea for the particular instance in front of the inn came from one of those women who have still not made their appearance in our story; she had said to Christoforos on Christmas night: "This year will soon be at its end, and it's the end of the century. Why don't you get Alekos, the photographer, to come and photograph us all, so that people will be able to look at us when we're being eaten by worms?" Christoforos had to admit that sometimes women come up with good ideas, and so, early the next morning, he sent word to Alekos.

Alekos was a little fellow, a good two inches shorter than his tripod, but he would step up on a folding stool and so could grow as tall as he wanted. As a photographer, some considered him excellent, others, *in the country of the blind, the one-eyed man . . .* , and one woman once called him "an envious weasel" because she thought that in the photograph he'd taken of her she appeared "plump and cross." In any case, as soon as he heard that Christoforos wanted him to photograph his entire family with all its offspring, he rubbed his hands, drank something to give himself strength, and set off with jaunty, uncoordinated steps that made him look like a little woodland animal that had lost its way . . . Two apprentices carried his equipment, and as they always went with him they soon began, though without wanting to, to walk like him.

He started with the families one by one: first the eldest son with his wife and children, then the second, then the third—at the fourth, they had to stop because it was getting dark and because the camera broke, and they continued two days later, when the camera had been repaired. The remaining fathers with their children and wives began getting themselves ready and taking up position—always with the entrance to the renowned inn in the background—and Alekos was in his element: he counted and recounted how many steps in front, how many behind (all reckoned in keeping with his own dimensions), stuck his head in and out of the black cloth when he wasn't totally satisfied with something, ran back to his subjects, tapped or pinched a cheek or two to put some life back into it, turned their heads sideways or upwards towards the light, straightened the folds in the dresses so that they would all appear more natural, felt limbs, touched knees, pleaded with the little devils not to move for two minutes, occasionally drove away interlopers and those with no business there, and generally showed an intensity and an impatience as though it were the most crucial moment of his life. "The art, the art, the crucial click!" he would exclaim. "Ah, ah, ah," he would sigh then, "what I wouldn't give to be in your place: to sit like a pasha and have my photograph taken. But put yourselves in my position so you can see what art means! An art that, just think, immobilizes time, traps it like a mouse, not to be scoffed at." But such elation or bemoaning didn't stop those who were sitting like pashas and obeying him like dogs from also being overcome by fear, anxiety, and emotion.

Two of Christoforos's sons, Zacharias from his first marriage, a tailor by trade, and Lukas, from his second, a farrier, were both unmarried, "without wives, without woes," as with great delight they admitted (sometimes pitying their brothers with their large families, and no doubt seeing to it that some equilibrium was maintained), and on that day these two found themselves outside the hullaballoo of all the photography. However, they had cats and horses, respectively: from every shelf in Zacharias's shop and from every roll of material a cat would leap out of the blue . . . they all curled up, slept, and were content in there, and now and again, just for a bit of exercise, they would chase a mouse or two, and of course the Golden Horseshoe belonging to Lukas had more than its share of horses.

This is why Alekos had suggested to them from the beginning to bring their own dear ones with them and have a photograph taken as a memento.

Lukas liked the idea, but not exactly as the photographer had imagined it. He didn't go so far as to bring all the horses in his workshop waiting to be shoed and pose with them in front of that thirsty eye; he did something else: he went to each of his brother's families with one of his horses, a different one each time, and took up position to either the right or left of them. Alekos was overjoyed at the scenes, applauded, extolled his art, did somersaults in the snow, blew kisses in the air, and more than a few times had to crowd some of the children together till they were almost invisible in order to get the horse's tail in the photograph — which the men found highly entertaining, though some of the women wouldn't agree to sacrificing the children for the sake of a horse. But there was a solution for this, too: where there were too many children they were put on the horse —

much to their delight. In the end, the photographer asked Lukas to get up himself on one of the horses so that he could immortalize him like Alexander the Great on Bucephalus. Lukas, who, as we recall, had a limp, agreed to this, but unluckily for him the photographic plate was ruined, and so he never got to see himself sitting on a horse.

As for Zacharias, the tailor, not only did he not agree to come with his cats, he got annoyed when the photographer persisted and one of his sisters started begging him. He shut himself in his shop opposite the inn and zealously set to work with his needles and threads, while the cats purred, rubbing themselves against his legs with an excitement that they didn't have every day. "Quiet!" he scolded them. "Imagine wanting to be cherries on the cake just so that Alekos can indulge himself," and every so often he glanced out through the window because he wasn't totally indifferent to the whole affair.

Anyway, they got round him by sending two of his favorite nieces, so he came out to be photographed in the last and most wondrous shot: the one where it was mayhem trying to get everyone into the photograph, all the families of the house (they tried some amazing pyramids that began with the parents with their sons and daughters sitting on their knees and on their knees younger brothers and sisters, and on these even younger children, and finally on top of everyone the infants), and at the center of this congregation was Christoforos, the paterfamilias, with his unequaled pride imprinted enigmatically—almost stoically— on his face and, symbolically, with a rose in his hand.

Onlookers who gathered out of curiosity to watch this grand event in front of the inn, despite the cold and their winter chores, dispersed when Alekos signaled the end, folding and locking his tripod, and the snow began to fall as though it had been commissioned. All vanished inside their houses. The next day the snow stopped and unexpectedly the sun appeared with great promise, as well as a slight breeze that recalled spring—there was talk of some almond trees that had been fooled and blossomed from one day to the next. They celebrated New Year with sunshine. However, the snow returned and now the wind whistled, and on the fifth of January of the new century they all gathered again at the same place to watch—alas—one more historic though untold event: the flames of a relentless fire that licked on all sides and consumed the renowned inn . . .

The destruction was total; nothing was spared; and it all began with some barely perceptible tremors the previous evening. The tremors happened again—

longer this time and definitely perceptible—towards midnight . . . Everyone knew about earthquakes—"we were born with the earthquakes," they used to say, and many meant it literally, as it is well known that when the earth loses control a lot of waters break before their time—but the animals knew them even better. They could smell them coming long before the first tremors and revealed their anxiety to humans in various ways, but they didn't listen: the dogs barked all evening, the heifers lowed *without cause* and turned their huge eyes inward as though they were gazing at hell itself, the goats shook, and the swine grunted before invisible signs of danger; even Zacharias's cats chased one another or bit themselves, but the humans—as though they had all drunk of the distillation of some real plant called indifference—simply stared at them as a rational person might stare at someone acting out of the ordinary.

When the first tremors started, however, they too started to be alarmed, and when the second wave of tremors came, and the third and most frightening, they started to get ready for a major earthquake: most people left their homes, took with them whatever necessities they could, and went, in the darkness and in midwinter, to seek safety in the frozen and desolate fields. Their babies screamed, it's said, as though it were the night of the slaughter of the innocents. There was also a full moon and wolves could be heard in the mountains.

Christoforos's families were also up, of course, and on their feet—and what were they to save first, what were they to do to first save themselves; countless souls, abject fear in their hearts, anxiety verging on frenzy, panic and confusion. Febronia saw Cletia running like the wind and clutching something to her breast. "Never mind the mirrors," she shouted to her, "and take one of the children with you!" but Cletia was tired of the children. Calm, in the midst of everything that was happening, Christoforos rounded up all his sons who hadn't managed to dash off with their wives and went with them to the inn (packed as it was those days with hunters and livestock dealers) to evacuate everyone in it. The tremors were now competing in intensity with their movements—"If it goes on much longer, we'll get so used to it that we won't be able to live any other way," said someone, finding the strength to speak such words at such a time. They hastily got out of the inn all those who hadn't got out already (many were asleep and hadn't realized what was happening), followed by all the animals that were still tied up. There were children—some had lost their mothers, others were being looked for by their mothers. Christoforos and his sons ran in and out to see what else they could do; the women were shrieking, the men were shouting "Quiet so we can find out what's happening," and at the height of all this human confusion was heard the earth's unbearable roar, from its subterranean depths, which transfixed everyone and everything for a fraction of a second before convulsing them.

All the world a child's toy, a nightmare.

And then a relief verging on madness when, after preparing themselves more or less for the next world or similar, they saw that they were still alive, unhinged and unharmed, and saw that round about them the houses, walls, and belongings had all been shaken but were still in place. It seemed to them a lie, a terrible joke that they wouldn't forget for a very long time.

"It took us to the edge and brought us back," mumbled one ashen-faced man.

"That was it . . . *it's over*," said another, even more ashen-faced, hastening to reassure himself and the others. "Lady Earth couldn't get comfortable. She had worms in her ass, isn't that what we say? But now she's sitting again, she's got comfortable. With a bit of a fuss of course — but there it is, what can you do."

They all felt a new breath cooling their nostrils and new saliva moistening their mouths. But the earth was still not *sitting, still not comfortable*, had still not had the last word: two hours later, at around three in the morning, its hollow rumbling was heard once again — and this time many ceilings cracked, many walls crumbled, many houses collapsed, and many belongings were lost. But still it wasn't satisfied: Christoforos's inn caught fire.

Perhaps because of a lamp that had been left burning, though they thought that all of them had been extinguished, and had fallen, spilling its fuel — and anyway, what was to keep someone from having lit a tiny lamp after the (first) earthquake had passed? Perhaps because of the large fire that burned day and night during winter that, of course, they had extinguished, or thought they had. No one knew; the causes were as unknown as they were countless, infinite, given that the earthquake had played a role — and one spark in such circumstances is enough for the worst.

"While we were cleaning the stable, they stole the cow," was what people said in cases where, while recovering from one calamity, they were dealt the final blow. "While we were cleaning the stable, they burned the inn!" is what Christoforos's sons would say about that night — and no end of thoughts raced through their muddled minds: enemies, sworn enemies, bitter enemies, even bitter brothers . . . Ah, yes, this happened too; two of his sons from his first wife, Petroula, suspected, though without much to go on, two sons of his second wife, Eftha, whom she'd brought with her from her first marriage. "They," they said, "aren't even half-brothers of ours, they're nothing to us — why couldn't it have been them?"

And their suspicions caught fire too . . . Why couldn't it have been them? No doubt, being of another father, they wouldn't get much of a share of Christoforos's will; the substantial shares would go to them, his own sons, no doubt; to their way of thinking (given that Eftha had brought them there when they were small and they had worked in the home as much as all the others), they had been wronged—which, after all, they had said themselves on many occasions, had expressed openly. Why then shouldn't they want to take revenge before-hand for this injustice, for what to their way of thinking was an injustice? Why shouldn't one of them, like mice playing while the cat's away, taking advantage of all the confusion during the earthquake, have thrown a lighted torch through one of the windows and then run off? And in fact have been one of the first to come and shout *Fire, Fire*, one of the first to go and ring the bell? Why not? Who could have stopped them on their path of not-getting-anything-themselves-but-at-least-seeing-to-it-that-the-others-lost-their-smugness?

"Blood runs thicker than water, and water never becomes blood," they said to Christoforos. "They're not your sons or our brothers, not even from another mother, because we've brothers like that, too. They are nothing to you or to us; there are no blood ties at all—why couldn't it have been them?"

"Are you serious? Or have you gone completely mad to come here and tell me that?" asked Christoforos, upset with them, because nothing like that would ever have occurred to him.

They told him that they were deadly serious, and a fight began. The father drove them away, telling them that he didn't want to hear of such things, that even if a stranger were to come into his home, he would treat him as one of his own, and if a son from a hundred fathers bedded down at his hearth, he would treat him as one of his own sons: "So don't poison me with your suspicions, I've enough on my mind—off with you." He pushed them away with his hands, and they came back at him saying that sometimes he wasn't a *father* even to his own sons—how was it that now he didn't want to hear even one word about others' sons? Was it that they'd managed to get him on their side? Was it that they'd secretly come bearing gifts? "Or is it that your mind is only on marriages—despite your age—and on every Tom, Dick, and Harry that comes along with your wives?" Sick of hearing these things every time something went wrong in the household—even more so now that flames and sobbing were coming out of the inn—Christoforos showed the back of his hand to both of them.

The next morning they regretted what they had said, forgot the insult, and Christoforos too said he was sorry, and the brothers who had borne the brunt of the suspicions proved to be innocent, since at the time of the fire, both of them were in the fields with their families; yet it's true that all it took for this huge family, this endless family, was some kind of spark for discord to arise in its bosom, for its renowned equilibrium to be disturbed, and for the invisible cracks and blemishes to appear in its—otherwise well-knit and enduring—shell. And moreover they all had their own reasons for ruing the destruction of the inn. And for everything else that would be lost with it.

Smoke continued to rise from the ruins for a full three days, and people stared as though mesmerized.

"There it is . . . only yesterday, Uncle, we were all standing here and watching while you were having your photographs taken . . . How wonderful you all were! How wonderful it all was! And now . . . now this catastrophe—and what a catastrophe! To see the inn smoldering, turning to ashes, and we here unable to do anything about it. And your daughter as well . . . Oh, the pain of it!"

Silently and blankly, Christoforos gazed at the young woman with dull blue eyes who was saying all this—why say it? To console him?

She wanted to say more, out of sympathy of course, but his gaze discouraged her.

"Don't look at me like that!" she begged him, whereas he got the impression that not only was she gibbering away like a monkey, she was also talking to him in a foreign language: what he heard was an incomprehensible *don-tlookat-meli-kethat* . . . Then he understood.

"Uncle, don't look at me like that," she repeated, lowering her head, "it's as though, as though you were implying that I started the fire."

And she might have called him Uncle without being his niece, but she certainly wasn't unfriendly towards him (in actual fact, she *wasn't unfriendly* towards one of his sons—if he had been willing to open his eyes and see).

Christoforos turned to look at another woman next to her who still hadn't opened her mouth . . . Until she, too, could no longer endure his look and stepped back with head bowed, treading on numerous toes till she found another spot . . . Then he brought his eyes to bear on one of the men, then another, then all of them.

What had got into him? They were all looking at his inn as it slowly disappeared from the face of the earth, and he was looking at them who were in no way to blame and who had come to pay their condolences, to stand by him as best they could.

"Break it up," he said to them softly (he himself knew how *softly*—and those who heard him). "Don't you have cares of your own? Didn't the earthquake do any damage to your homes? Why is it my inn you're thinking about?"

Pain often renders you unjust, even ungrateful, they reflected. Why should it bother him if they put their own misfortune to one side and came to be with him and show sympathy for a catastrophe like the one he had suffered? Because, of course, it was one thing to have a crack in your ceiling and another to have an entire inn vanish—we don't mourn the roses when a whole forest is burning . . . Yet, Christoforos saw it differently; he didn't want their presence or their sympathy; he told them to break it up. And they, knowing that it was his despair speaking and not him, didn't reply, but simply obeyed, albeit half-heartedly, and moved off . . . They came back again as soon as he became absorbed again in the magnitude of the catastrophe and no longer cared who was and who wasn't there with him.

No doubt one part of his mind was working intensely despite the ostensible paralysis and incapacity. Having navigated numerous storms in his life, he wasn't going to let one more get him down, even if it was the bitterest. He would rebuild the inn, out of stubbornness if nothing else, or build something else in its place. What, however, he wouldn't find a cure, or even an explanation, for was the loss of Cletia in the fire. It was that, just as they were saying, "We can be thankful that no lives were lost at least," they suddenly found his poor stepdaughter crushed by fallen timbers and her body charred.

They couldn't believe it.

No one had missed her till that moment—for one person to be missing from a family like that, and at such a time, was a bit like a pin missing from a pin cushion: "Big deal," as she would have said herself; "Who knows?" But when they found her as they found her, they couldn't believe their eyes, couldn't believe in anything, not even in what they were saying. They swore that they'd seen her with them earlier, alarmed as they all were by the outbreak of the fire, running and waving her arms; how was it possible that now they had found her charred corpse?

Her brothers and sisters all shouted, "We saw her just before! Alive, alive and well . . . Before!" assuring each other of that *before* that was driving them crazy like a ghost seen by everyone but touched by no one.

And it was only gradually, after a little time had passed, that they began to realize that the *before* that they were all talking about referred quite simply to a very long before, to the past, an entire past when they had Cletia beside them, saw her every day, virtually ignored her—and she was now charred, unrecognizable, and indifferent beneath the ruins. The *before* was *now* with another face, but no mind is ready to grasp that without losing itself. And no word either.

Most likely it was Febronia who had seen her last, running around inside the house, then, when the tremors had started.

"I told her to take one of the children with her, running as she was like that, but she shook her arm at me as if to say, *I've had my fill of children!* She was clutching something to her breast—an icon, a mirror, what was it? She didn't seem all that well to me . . . But was I in any better shape? As though she had something on her mind, as though she were running not to get away from the earthquake, but to go somewhere, get there in time. I don't know, of course, maybe I'm just saying that now . . ." then, with a somewhat strange bitterness in her voice, she turned to her husband and said more quietly so that only he could hear, "of course, if *you* had asked her to take some of the children with her, she would have done it . . . She could never say no to you."

Hesychios's eyes darkened, blackened almost.

"If I had asked her to take some of the children with her," he said to her, "maybe the children would have burned with her."

She stared at him fearfully and put two trembling fingers to her lips; words are punished with words, but who could know what Cletia had hidden in her heart?

Eftha's first daughter from her first marriage, Cletia, as we mentioned, was the one who especially complained about having spent all her life cleaning other people's babies, about how all the washing had cracked her fingers, about having wasted herself over the water and so losing any chance for joy herself. She was the one who, when Hesychios, her brother from a different father, touched her truly worn hands and showed that he was in no doubt about her sacrifices in that house, softened immediately and succumbed again to her fate.

"Just so long as you appreciate it," she'd say to him.

Once, however, as a result of some chance event, Cletia's fate changed—at least her chores changed. It was again at such a time, a winter's night, several years earlier.

Christoforos, her stepfather—a longtime widower following the death of his wife Eftha—wanting to punish some of his younger sons for a mischief they had done that had greatly annoyed him, lined them up in front of him and told them to find the answers from memory to some arithmetical problems. This was a common punishment in the family, a tradition going down from father to son—for the girls there were other punishments. To be more precise, this punishment was applied during childhood, during which, if the offender didn't mend his ways, at least he exercised his mind. In fact, in time, it wasn't absolutely necessary for a boy to do something terrible in order for him to pass through the purgatory of multiplication tables—all it took was for the father

to want it, or remember it. Besides, again in time, it eventually became something of an *evening agreement*: almost every evening before dinner Christoforos
would line the boys up outside in the dark to tell him the multiplication tables.
Why outside in the dark no one knows—the explanation he himself gave was
so that they wouldn't be able to see any piece of paper they might have hidden.
Of course, even if he'd had them lined up before him in broad daylight, they
still wouldn't have been able to recite the tables from a piece of paper, but we
shouldn't forget that those were different times and people had their own ideas
and meticulous ways, and their own methods of applying them. So, then, outside in the dark and from inside he would begin:

"Two times two?"

"Fo-o-our," the boys would answer in unison.

"Two times three?"

"Si-i-ix."

"Two times four?"

"E-e-eight."

"Two times five?"

"Te-e-en."

Fine up to there and a little farther. But if he began asking them for more or
for more complicated multiplications—"five times five?" or "six times six?"—
the real darkness began for those sorry-looking souls of the darkness. "How are
you supposed to find how many are five times five!" each of them thought, with
awe looking at the boy beside him, who was thinking exactly the same . . . A
shambles, a dumb silence, incomprehensible things—and Christoforos from
inside asking continuously. They used their fingers to count on and got mixed
up halfway through, forgetting what they'd already worked out, with the numbers rolling around like marbles in their heads and them like little Sisyphuses
starting the uphill climb again from the beginning. And whoever, after a great
struggle or simply by chance, happened to find the answer, fine, got to sit at the
dinner table. But whoever didn't find the answer had to go even higher, to an
even darker room, in which the floor creaked, and perform twenty-five resounding acts of contrition or forty-two, shouting out the question and the answer
together, so that *five times five, twenty-five* and *six times seven, forty-two* would
be something that he would remember all his life. Or if he objected to so much
penance, he would go to bed hungry and dream of loaves of bread. In those
cases, Eftha did all she could to get something to the children being punished,
but often she was unable: Christoforos would keep her confined too, usually
between his legs, so that the children had to deal on their own with the hunger
that ravaged their innards. One solution was for them to struggle to sleep till

the morning, when the punishment would no longer hold. But there was also the sleepwalking solution, which, though in fact more dangerous, was also the more attractive: one of the boys would suddenly get up (they slept all together in one room—a hive that buzzed even in the stillest hours) and walk in circles with his arms outstretched in front of him and his eyes gazing into the void. If no one stopped him at this crucial stage, he would easily find the doors, walk down the stairs, which, if fortune were with him, wouldn't creak, open other doors, and fall like a feather upon a basket of bread or chance upon a cupboard with even choicer things. He would stand there. Find vindication there. And when the sleep-eating was over, he would return to his bed with the same vacant and docile look. It often happened that three or four boys would wander in the same way during the same night and in the morning the others would find empty cupboards and baskets with only crumbs in them. But it also often happened that Christoforos or one of the older brothers would be waiting for them at the end of their dreamy path or when they returned to their bed, and then it would all end very unpleasantly for these little sleepwalkers.

We may regard all these things as quaint and humorous, as old stories, but for the boys at that time the punishments were real. Fortunately, they eventually grew up, and the punishments—the same or analogous ones—would then fall upon their own children, who would also eventually grow up . . . "Too much freedom," Christoforos said, "is like a beautiful and unfaithful woman: first she makes a king of you and then a fool of you." And true to his principles, he never lost any opportunity to keep his children in check, even when they were coming of age, imposing on them, among other things, the familiar and traditional multiplication-tables punishment.

On that winter's night, then, two of his sons had again upset him. He told them to stand up and from memory do various multiplications and subtractions with double and triple figures, respectively. And though they were well practiced in such things, it wasn't always easy for them to achieve the required result at the first attempt . . . or the second. He, meanwhile, was in a hurry, because in reality he had a paper in front of him with bills from the inn and the other shops, with logistical problems that required a speedy solution, and so he had thought of combining *business and punishment*. Consequently, he was greatly irritated by the two boys' slowness and incorrect answers.

"There are three people here wasting their time," he said sharply. "I'm not getting my work done and you're not improving yourselves."

"And why don't you ask me?" Cletia suddenly asked him. She was sitting nearby, silent up till that moment and with her head lowered—she was roasting chestnuts in the fire and eating them herself.

Most probably she said it to break the monotony, but Christoforos didn't let it pass.

"Thirty-six times fourteen gives us what?" he asked her, turning his stool in her direction.

Cletia gazed at the hot roasted chestnut that she had in her hand waiting to be peeled; she brought it up closer to her eyes, moved it farther away, did this another couple of times, and said: "Five hundred four."

Was it simply a coincidence? Was it just an easy and manageable multiplication? Was it a magic chestnut that had inspired her in a magical way? Or did Cletia have hidden talents that no one suspected?

Christoforos gazed at her, scratching the back of his head.

"How did you find the answer?" he asked her.

"Using my brain," she replied.

"And where have you been hiding that brain all these years?" he asked again.

Cletia laughed as if making fun of her own laughter.

"How should I know where it was hiding? Under all the children I had to wash and clean," she said, showing her obsession with the same old topic.

"If you can give me one more answer like that," her father said, "I'll see to it that you won't have to wash or clean any more children."

"Ah, I see . . . now that they've grown up and they can do it for themselves," said Cletia, "and now that, for the time being at least, we're not expecting any more births . . ."

"Anyhow; tell me what eighty-seven times three comes to," he asked her this time, "and I give you my word on it."

Cletia took a chestnut from the fire, blew away the ash, rolled it in her hand a little till it had cooled, made the same movements with it in front of her eyes as before and gave him another three-figure number.

"Just a moment," muttered Christoforos and did the multiplication himself with pencil and paper. "Well, then," he said to his sons, "she's got the answer to that one too! And out of her head!" And he again gazed at her from head to toe. "We've underestimated you all these years, my child," he said to her with not a little emotion. "You're talented—you're just right for the inn."

And from then on, Cletia worked more in the inn than in the house. At first, she had the position of cashier, but as time passed, and she began to be careless with the bills (as though working with pencil and paper were at the expense of her innate talent to come up with the right numbers), her duties were restricted, or rather extended, to include the reception and care of the customers. She would see to their meals and the making of the beds, take care of the accommodation for their animals or children (because they would often bring their children with them), and, generally speaking, it was she whom Christoforos trusted more than his sons or grandsons who had been working for some time there, something which at first created a lot of dislike and disdainful looks. "It lends an air to the place—can't you see?—having a woman working in it," he said, trying to convince them. "And besides, your sister is not some flighty creature, nor some floozy."

That was true. Yet as time passed, Cletia felt an ever greater need—seeing how she had wasted her youth in the shadows, bent over cradles or tubs—not only to take care of the customers, but also of herself, of whatever graces remained to her. Of course, they had caught her long before, when she was still in the house, secretly admiring herself in the mirror and, even more often, wandering around with a little mirror in her pocket, and while she was lulling, swaddling, or cleaning one of the children, suddenly taking it out and looking at herself for a while in the way that a tippler takes his sharp, clandestine swigs. But as soon as anyone said anything to her, Cletia would laugh unconvincingly and reply, "To see my sorry state, dear! Even a crow looks at itself if the occasion arises, so what?" One day, Eftha advised her quite seriously not to look at herself so much because that satanic looking glass would keep her face for itself and she would remain *like that,* just a skull, but Cletia—again laughing half-heartedly and muttering, "What've I got that a mirror would be jealous of? What would that glass keep from me?'—feverishly took it out of her breast and looked at herself again . . . "And all of you who don't look at yourselves, tell me, will anything remain?" she remembered to say afterwards.

So there was a far from negligible underlying vanity that mocked itself if the need arose, and that now found the opportunity and the appropriate surroundings to come out more into the open, to express itself. Cletia *suddenly* started to take care of her appearance as never before; to be careful of her words, how she spoke to the customers, how she welcomed them, and how she saw them out. Above all, she began to show a special liking for the hunters, who filled the inn every fall and winter. Christoforos picked up on all this either with his ear or his eye and made a mental note of it, but as long as things moved within the bounds of what was permissible he said nothing; after all, it wouldn't be at all bad if a husband were to be found for Cletia, too.

However, there appeared on the scene a tall and strikingly handsome hunter (it was even said that he resembled Christoforos, rather like "a distant son"), with thick curly hair and a beard that were silvery in color, with boots that gleamed, with a waistcoat, scarf, and hat that were unusual, with carved bone pipes—

someone who had never passed through those parts before. Who would go out very early in the morning, earlier than anyone else, scowling and standoffish, and who would come back in the evening, less sullen but ever unapproachable. He always hunted alone, and anyone would have said that he thought of nothing else but hunting—anyone but the poor birds and animals, to be precise, that he *ought* to have targeted . . . His words were even less than measured—his bullets were unquestionably more.

This mysterious man, then, stayed for a few nights in the inn, paid, left, and returned within the week. And though he would think twice before saying even a good-morning to you, Cletia had it from his own mouth, so she said, that he had gone to be present at his father's last hour, that this wonderful old man hadn't been able to avoid his end, that he had accompanied him to his final resting place and had then returned to their hospitable inn and to the rich mountains in that area . . .

"And he said all this to you?" asked Christoforos and his sons in disbelief.

"And more besides," Cletia replied.

"Such as?"

"That I'm good at my job . . . that he's never encountered in any other inn where he's stayed such hospitality or such care."

"Perhaps he's in love with you too? Has he asked you to marry him?" Christoforos asked her sharply.

"It's my fault for even talking to you!" said Cletia angrily and turned her back on them.

The hunter left again the next day, and one week later returned again. He was called Marcos, the name suited him.

The following year, however, when this Marcos returned—decidedly more human and sociable—Christoforos began to be angry and knit his brow: one morning when he had returned especially early to the inn, when it was still dark (after Eftha had died, he would sleep at the inn, though now and again he also went to the house), he caught sight of Cletia cautiously coming out of the hunter's room . . . He followed her, walking on tiptoe, just like her, caught up with her, grabbed hold of her hair, and with his other hand immediately closed her mouth. "What's this man doing coming up behind me?" thought Cletia in terror, and the blood drained from her face—she thought she was about to be murdered, she felt his breath on her ear like a hot blade. And when she saw who it was, she showed herself to be even more terrified and confounded—she even smiled in bewilderment when he let go of her mouth.

"Who did you think it was grabbing you like that from behind?" he asked her under his breath; "that other man?"

"What other man? What are you talking about?" she replied, also under her breath.

"Where were you?" he asked her more clearly, dragging her aside.

"Where was I, where do you think I was?" replied Cletia in a fluster. "Here — didn't you tell me to sleep here because you would go to the house? Don't I sleep here at other times too?"

"I'm asking you about now!"

"Eh . . . I got up to see if everything is all right . . . I couldn't sleep, it's cold . . . I wasn't doing anything, what do you want?"

"I want you to tell me where you were, whose room you came out of just now, or you won't see the light of day, you'll be keeping company with your mother, I'll slaughter you like a she-goat, do you hear? Whose room did you come out of?"

Cletia waited until he let go of one of her arms so that she could point, in the dimness that was more oppressive than the light, to the door of the hunter's room.

"From there," she whispered.

"*From there!*" Christoforos was taken aback by her willingness or her audacity to admit everything straightaway. "From there you said?"

His stepdaughter nodded affirmatively.

"So from there! But of course! From the room of the hunter who came here to hunt . . . but hunting in the mountains is not enough for him, he's hunting in the inn too. You wretched girl! . . . What were you up to with him?"

"Nothing, there's no one in there," Cletia told him.

He raised his arm to hit her.

"There's no one," she repeated, avoiding his arm, "go and look for yourself."

He went towards the door of the hunter's room and she looked at him from behind as though feeling sorry for him. But before he entered, before he even went to open the door, he beckoned to her with his finger to go in with him. She went over and her expression changed — as though she was now sorry she had lost her sleep over all this.

"Open it just like you closed it before," he ordered her in a civil tone.

Cletia eased open the door with pointless caution.

"There," she said.

They found themselves in the hunter's tiny realm. The first light of day, dull and dim, was entering through a skylight, a few clothes and his belt were hanging over a chair; the tin bowl of water, the pitcher, and the towel were on another chair; and the bed was empty. Empty and made up.

"Where is he?" asked Christoforos, as if forgetting what had just taken place and what had brought him there.

And this manner allowed Cletia to reply calmly and with a sadness *within the bounds of the permissible:* "He's gone. He must have left early to go hunting . . . Or he may have simply left."

"And what about his clothes? Does he think we're so poor that we need his clothes? And how can he leave without paying?"

"He usually comes back," Cletia thought of saying.

Christoforos was fingering the pillow and bedcovers: they didn't seem that cold to him.

"That hunter doesn't like me," he said.

Her lips trembled as if to answer, *So what?*

"He's also got a red beard," Christoforos went on, walking to and fro in the tiny room. "Do you know what a hunter with a red beard means?"

"Where did you see a red beard?" she asked him. "It's gray."

"It's gray, yes, I know! Gray like this very hour, gray like a rat's back, it's even grayer than mine! But he reminds me of a hunter with a red beard, a rogue. Does it matter?"

He stopped pacing and looked at her as if waiting for some kind of reply . . . "What does he want me to say now?" thought Cletia, who really didn't know what someone was expecting when they ask such a question and look you in the eye like that . . .

"Why should it matter?" she mumbled.

"So, if he's not here, what were you doing in here?" he asked her, with a fresh glint in his eye.

She couldn't see any coherence in his questions, but at least she could answer this last one more specifically.

"Me? It's my job isn't it?" she said. "I got up to see whether anyone wanted another blanket, the cold's set in, haven't you noticed? I went to everybody, gave them all an extra blanket—next door is a family with two small children, they would have frozen . . . And I thought of bringing one for him, too . . . I saw what you saw—no one. So I just left it, there it is"—she pointed to a folded blanket behind the door, on top of a small chest—"and I came out."

"And if he'd been inside?"

"What do you mean?"

"What would you have done?"

"I'd still have left it, that's why I brought it."

"Would you have spoken to him?"

"If he'd woken up . . . I'm not a ghost."

"And why did you come out as if you'd been up to *something* in here?"

This time, Cletia took a little time to answer.

"Because . . . isn't that what anyone seeing me would have thought?" she said, looking blank, and reached out to put her hand on the chair with the clothes.

He grabbed hold of it by the wrist.

"I'm putting it out of the way," she said.

He allowed her to put the chair out of the way and to put the folded blanket on top of the bed.

"Are you expecting him to come back?" he asked her.

She pretended not to hear.

"Seems very strange to me," Christoforos admitted finally, "very strange."

"To me too," she said.

The hunter returned in the afternoon, much earlier than his usual time. He gave his horse to Lukas to be shoed and as he entered the inn—stooping as always as though afraid of knocking something over or of hitting himself—a cold blast of wind entered with him.

"That's a chill air you've brought in with you, sir," said Christoforos, who was at a loss with himself as to why he spoke to a hunter so formally! But given that he too spoke in the same way . . . "Did you catch much today?" he asked presently, pretending not to notice the empty pouch.

"Mmm, I didn't go hunting today," the hunter replied.

"Didn't go hunting? Pity. And you left this morning so early . . . We were puzzled. My daughter even came to bring you an extra blanket."

"Very thoughtful, your daughter."

Christoforos waited to hear more, he felt he had the right that particular day.

"To tell you the truth, I didn't return last night," said the hunter. "It wasn't my intention, of course."

"I don't imagine it was," said Christoforos somewhat playfully, casting a glance behind him in case Cletia suddenly appeared from somewhere. "And where did you sleep, if that's not being indiscreet?"

"I didn't sleep," replied the hunter, as though it were the most natural thing in the world. "And since I'm leaving tomorrow . . ."

"Leaving again?" asked one of Christoforos's grandsons. "And when are you coming back again?"

"Mmm, I'll be back, I'll come back again," replied the hunter, with the faint trace of a smile between his mustache and his beard, and then headed off to his room.

He left the next morning and *came back again* only in the following winter, which was—who would have thought it—the last winter for the inn and also for Cletia. Meanwhile, in spring, at the age of sixty-seven, Christoforos got married for the third time, and that summer Thomas and Safi-Lisafi were born.

Given the absence for so many months of Marcos, the hunter—though there was no lack of other hunters—Cletia began to lose her great interest in the inn and to miss the chores in the house, finding various pretexts—particularly after the birth of Thomas—to spend more time there.

"Don't you concern yourself with all that," Christoforos would say to her, now certain that some futile idyll had occurred between her and the mysterious Marcos and so, apart from his remarks, he had also decided to offer her some consolation. "Don't you concern yourself with all that, my dear, go on back to the inn just like before. After all, if he felt like you felt, he would have returned in so many months. And after all . . . if you were set on giving your heart to a man like that, wrongly, wrongly so, why didn't you tell me before I remarried? It's not like it would have been a sin—you're not my daughter and I'm not your father—and I think we would have made a good pair, the two of us. At least we'd have known each other's little quirks . . . I'm not talking nonsense, am I?"

"Lord above, Lord above, what are you saying?" said Cletia, almost choking, not knowing which way to look or who to address herself to. "You had so many children with my mother!"

"With your mother, not with you. Anyhow, it's in the past. We lost the chance. I simply thought of it and mentioned it—there's no need for everyone else to know. As for the other one, listen well: don't give him the bullets to kill you with, he has enough already."

"Who?"

"You know who. Him . . . And to tell the bitter truth, I didn't expect you, after avoiding all those *games* when you were young, to go and slip up now . . . Snap out of it, my dear, and find your peace of mind again. Love leaves scars; it's like an illness: even if you recover, it won't be like it was before you fell ill . . . But it's too late now for me to tell you all this—you're already ill . . . But forget him, nevertheless. As you can't do anything else, forget him. If I were in your place, that's what I'd do."

"Who are you talking about?" she asked again, despondently.

"About him, you know very well who I'm talking about," he said.

Cletia shrugged her shoulders as though none of this had anything to do with her. And she shut herself in one of those north-facing rooms upstairs that looked on to the mountains . . .

When she had first come to that house, at the age of eleven, she had been afraid of those bedrooms. They were dark and cold even in summer. They drove you away. And those unfamiliar *brothers and sisters* of the same age that she'd found there, fatherless children of Petroula (just as she had been fatherless herself), after glaring at her for some time or going away as soon as they saw her, cornered her one day and began telling her about the ghosts that roamed in their house, in those upstairs north-facing rooms, and in one of them in particular . . . She was scared. And whenever Eftha wanted her to do some chore up there, she wouldn't go—she preferred to be beaten rather than go up there. And when eventually Eftha discovered the reason, she took her by the hand and led her up to that very room, the northernmost and the gloomiest of them. "What ghosts are there in here?" she said to her. "This is a wonderful place! Look at how many things there are in here! Whoever manages to count all the things in here will get the hand of the king's daughter! . . . Or of his son, of course. And just look . . . just look what a view there is from the window, look at how beautiful the mountain is from here! Like a painting . . . They told you all that nonsense precisely so that you wouldn't come up here—so that only they would see the hunter who comes down once a year and chooses the most beautiful girl and takes her with him!"

Amazing—Eftha had talked to her of a hunter thirty-three years earlier! Of a hunter who comes down, she said, from that mountain slope once a year and chooses the most beautiful girl, the most worthy, and takes her with him! . . . Of course, she may have told her this to stop her being afraid of the ghosts, to stop her being afraid of going to that room—even to make her want to go. And from that time, Cletia did want to go—the odd thing is that from the very first the hunter prevailed over the impersonal ghosts—and from that time, Cletia wanted to be sent to that very room. And if she wasn't sent, she would go there on her own, and if sometimes she found the door locked, she would go crazy out of her desire to open it.

Until one night she was allowed as a special treat to sleep there (some treat, given that no one slept there: they used the room for storing and hanging whatever wouldn't fit in the other bedrooms or storerooms). Cletia must have been around fifteen, with two little humps on her chest, a soft matting of curly hair under her armpits, and scarlet blood every month . . . And what happened to her was something quite *amazing*. And because there is nothing quite like an amazing adolescent memory, let's try to bring it back to life.

Beneath the window there was an old bed with broken springs and a sunken mattress, stuffed with straw and whatever else you can imagine, that was covered in dust. It was summer, boiling hot, everyone was wilting under the heat . . . But not Cletia, who, on entering the room, found a coolness and dreamlike tranquility inside. How did she get the impression that everything was waiting just for her—her and the hunter.

"Ah, how wonderful—he might come!" she said to herself aloud, and got the bed ready, leaving the window wide open in front of her. "He might come tonight." Because in all the years she'd been waiting for him, she hadn't seen him even once . . . And her mother had married when she was sixteen—and most girls did the same. Why should she wait for the years to pass? If the hunter came that night . . . if he came . . . she may not have been the most beautiful, but she was certainly worthy . . . very worthy, and he would recognize her worth . . . Then again, if he came and took her with him, that alone would make her lovelier, no one would be able to believe their eyes at how much lovelier it would make her! . . .

And sunk in that old mattress, wrapped in a big sheet, surrendering to her unspeakable expectations, sleep came like another hunter and took hold of her.

It was all going nicely and well till the moment—just before daybreak—when everything changed: without her having woken exactly, and yet without her being really asleep, Cletia felt *someone* against her legs. And if it wasn't someone, it was *something*—even worse. With some delay, her mind went to the hunter. But, alas, that touch was so strange, it scared her so much, that Cletia would have preferred it if the hunter hadn't chosen her in that way, if she hadn't had him like that against her legs ever, never ever—there was no sensation more alarming, more unfamiliar, ominous, strangely warm, strangely cold, heavy, light, smooth like a playing card, soft like cotton wool . . . the poor thing lost her mind, what remained was an anxiety without before or after . . . And that *bogey* at her legs, doing whatever it wanted—what was wrong with it? Perhaps it had become entangled in the folds of the sheets, between her frozen legs, and was struggling to find the edge, an opening to get out; or, the most likely, unfortunately, it was trying to push its way further in—and in the end it wanted neither the one nor the other. And so, as soon as it began, it returned, without moving exactly, to its former position. It was a living trickle that expanded and contracted, a heart or a spleen that lived cut off from its body and was searching blindly to find a better home for itself. Cletia's legs weren't bad, but neither were they ideal, it seemed, for such demands . . . It most probably was bothered, too, by the heat—or better the coolness, because that place was so different, that bedroom, that bed, everything so different, that Cletia even thought she was feeling cold from the heat and was sweltering from that icy coldness, that the darkness around her was becoming light and the light darkness at the very same time.

To be completely honest, she didn't think anything herself—everything was provoked by *that*. And the worst of all is when an overwhelming mania caught hold of it and it started to judder between her legs! . . . *To judder*, how else might one describe it? It could have been a fan going back and forth at remarkable speed, a cat furiously scratching its ear, a hunter polishing his weapon . . . Whatever we might say, Cletia couldn't think of anything. And if occasionally this *polishing* stopped—it soon started again . . . And now there was nothing else: it stopped and started again, stopped and started again. Now if it weren't for those false pauses, even Cletia would have been able to reconcile herself to it, to get used to it, given that it had fallen to her. Yet, at fifteen years old, how could she reconcile herself with that dull and furious *krats-krats-krats-krats*, fine like cigarette paper . . . that, apart from anything else, reminded her of something, said something almost shameless to her, but was impossible, impossible for her to pinpoint?

She began calling on gods and demi-gods to save her, to awaken her—ah, certainly she was asleep for such things to be happening! *Won't I wake up?* her inner being cried out. *When will I wake up?* And yet she was awake and these things were happening, it was all happening. "And if I'm awake," she thought, "then there's hope . . ." Ah, she was *thinking*! That was a good sign. And she began quietly to make plans in her mind, to actually move one of her legs, very slowly, like the clock's hour hand moves . . . What a feeling of deliverance! Nothing followed her, the one leg was almost free, free of the nightmare, hers again.

And at the same time, what a fright! A large black bird squawked as it passed outside the window and that *squa-a-aw* robbed her of her wits. She leapt out of bed as though an arrow had pierced her eye—and like this it all came to an end, she was truly delivered: a cat jumped from the bed sheet to the other side—a cat! Cat. A cat had been on her legs all that time . . . She couldn't believe it, swallow it, forgive herself: a simple cat, a cat. Cat.

She stared at it. Everything was reciprocal, identical—Cletia stared at the cat and the cat stared at Cletia. The common fright that successively stupefied first the one then the other, the one as a result of the other, had completely equated them; they could have gone on staring at each other like that till the next morning, swapping faces with each other and still staring . . .

But their stillness, the silence, and the standoff was such that some paraphernalia hanging on the wall couldn't endure, it seems, for no one to note their own motionless existence for years on end and began—in God's truth, by themselves—to fall, to get excited and make a huge racket! A heavy tarpaulin jumped from its nail and fell on a sieve, the sieve onto a basket, which took with it another basket—this got caught up in a bunch of scythes and hooks and horseshoes, all this iron caught hold of a small spinning wheel, which collapsed together with the iron onto a cauldron containing glass, wire, flour, and a deer's antlers . . . This is the way that even inanimate objects sometimes go on a spree.

And while the cat again grew frightened and with each new bang and clatter jumped from one edge of the bed to the other edge, nothing could shake Cletia anymore. Nothing. She heard each thing fall and all the things together and didn't give a hoot—let the whole wall fall, big deal. The only thing that concerned her was the cat, the panic-stricken cat. And she followed it everywhere with her gaze and ferreted it out from wherever it ferreted.

"You, everywhere you, you and your accursed nine lives!" she cried in a hoarse and unfamiliar voice. For she had grown hoarse, had aged, had suffered more than a little anguish in bed on account of that cat.

That cat. Look at it . . . Now it had reached the door, the closed door, and was trying to get out, but how? It simply scratched at it with its nails for a while and stared at the ceiling, then the open window—look at her, at the sight of the window its back arched . . . But its young mistress climbed up on the bed, took two steps on her knees, and closed the window with great care—she could see the hunter another time.

"You, everywhere, you and your accursed nine lives!" she turned and said to it again in the same hoarse voice, though with somewhat less vehemence.

But the cat was sad. And when it realized that there was no way of escape anywhere, it surrendered completely to its torment—which also proved to be something of a torment for Cletia—and began, with whatever paws it had, to scratch its ear, its right ear: *krats-krats-krats* . . . *krats-krats-krats* . . . *krats-krats-krats* . . . stopped for a while, then started again . . . stopped and looked into Cletia's bust as though asking for a little understanding, a little mercy, and then started again . . .

"Got fleas in your ear, have you, you mangy creature?" asked Cletia, who all that time—since that blessed crow had flown past and had released her from her incredible nightmare—had thought of nothing else but *what punishment* would be the best for that cat. Should she bind its four legs together and tie it to the foot of the bed for ten days, leaving it hungry in that room? Or bind its four legs again but tie it to a string and whirl it round in the air till the cat sounded like a cicada? Or cut its whiskers with scissors, which for a cat is like cutting its feet off? Or should she perhaps—how far the thirst for vengeance goes—put it in a sack, as a certain Angeliki once did when she caught her cat eating the fish? Ah, just imagine that: to be so poor as to barely survive, to buy fish once every three months, to clean it, to fry it, and when you come with your children to eat it, to find the cat feeding out of the frying pan . . . This is what had happened to Angeliki, and when she saw what was happening, she became like one possessed. The cat, meanwhile, couldn't move from the weight of its stomach: it sat licking itself up to its eyes. Angeliki grabbed hold of it, made her children stand aside lest she grab hold of one of them, put the cat in a sack, tied it up, held it tight and began swinging it against one wall after the other . . . The cat never licked itself again. And Angeliki wept afterwards, for her fish, but more so for her cat. But to what end? The one had eaten and was dead, while she was alive and hungry—she didn't know which was worse.

"Hmm," said Cletia now to her own cat, "perhaps what you deserve is something like what happened to Angeliki's cat? At least it went with a full stomach—how do you want to go? With a flea in your ear? You mangy creature . . . What do you think of me stuffing you in a sack and going wallop-wallop in here? You'll lose whatever fur you've got, do you understand? You'll go with a big *me-o-o-ow* . . . And do you think I'll shed any tears over it? Eh? Like Angeliki? Like Menousis? Eh?"

Naturally, the cat didn't say anything—even if it had been able to, it was better that it didn't. It stood there pitiably and waited, every so often touching its infected ear with one of its feet, not daring to do anything more . . . and eventually, from thinking up one punishment after the other, Cletia grew tired, her anger subsided, and not only that, but—as often happens in such cases—she even started to feel sorry for it.

"You've got something wrong with your ear . . . what is it?" she asked. "Let me have a look."

The cat retreated—it couldn't be entirely sure of Cletia's new intentions. But it was already quite exhausted, and in some corner that it found to take refuge, supposedly so she wouldn't catch it, doing it in that hesitant ambiguous way that . . . made it easy for Cletia to reach out and take hold of it in her arms.

It was a lovely cat, also in its adolescence, with yellowy-gray eyes and orange and black spots, one of those that Mika-Mika had every so often with her sons, but inside its ear, deep inside, as far as the fifteen-year-old could see, she had got hold of something like honeycomb, a decaying blackish honeycomb that smelled strange. She took care of the cat for a few days, and it got better, the ear cleared up. Of course, it didn't try ever again to disturb Cletia in her sleep, but neither did Cletia ever sleep again (at least for many years) in that room.

However, she didn't miss the opportunity of assuring her mother and her brothers and sisters, half-brothers and half-sisters too, that there really were ghosts in that room—she at least had spent a night there with a ghost! She described it in all sincerity and without too much exaggeration: it came between her legs and did so-and-so—and naturally, since she had experienced it for herself, her account enjoyed the virtue of complete credibility. Except that she didn't relate the end—that is, she made up her own end: as soon as day broke, the ghost—which was perhaps a little child—left her legs and retreated to the wall opposite, where it became totally invisible and diabolical, and after throwing a pile of things to the floor and scattering them everywhere ("Go and see for yourselves"), it suddenly turned into a bird, a huge black bird, and flew through the open window with a *squa-a-aw* . . .

"I saw it all with my own eyes," she said, ending her tale, "and let the earth swallow me up if I'm lying to you!"

Her brothers and sisters, particularly the ones who had once talked to her of nonexistent ghosts purely to frighten her because she wasn't one of them, now gazed at her with open mouths and a little annoyed. And Cletia gazed at them with a little spark of vengeance in her eyes. And with concealed joy, from that time on, she heard them in the house talking of *Cletia's ghost* with the same awe and naturalness with which people then talked of a lot of things.

The following years were not especially *awe-inspiring* for her, though. Stooping like the branch of a willow over the babies of brothers and sisters and of halfbrothers and half-sisters (as she had been doing for quite some time), or at most looking at her sad, sardonic, and not unbearably beautiful face in small mirrors, she didn't go up much to that room unless it was absolutely necessary. No one had picked up the tarpaulin from the spot where it had fallen that morning (Cletia always had the impression that someone was sleeping underneath it), the bunch of scythes, hooks, and horseshoes had ensconced itself for good inside the old cauldron, the spinning wheel had become wedged inside the deer's antlers—it would have required something like what had happened that morning for all these things to come back to life again and change positions—and as for some nails on the wall that for some time remained bare and empty, they were very soon laden again with every ragtag and bobtail.

The bed was in its place, without sheets, and the window usually open in the summers and closed in the winters—now and again they would find birds' eggs, and a lot of cats went there to be healed (through fasting and abstinence) from their illnesses, some went to die, others to give birth or to eat the birds' eggs. Cletia would drive them all away at first and scold them, but then she left them in peace; she often felt the desire to look inside their ears, to examine them, and if any of them happened to scratch their ears in front of her, Cletia jumped with joy, her heart leapt. *Krats-krats-krats* . . . As for the hunter, she never thought of him again, she no longer believed in Eftha's fairy tales—until, that is, she was promoted to working in the inn, where she met the most real and most handsome hunter of her life.

■

So here she was once again in that north-facing room, believing once again in Eftha's words—at least recalling them, comparing myths with actual events—and waiting in case she saw *him* coming down from the mountain . . . For now there was a hunter, most certainly there was, but he was away most of the time. And that summer (her last) seemed endless to her; it seemed inhuman to her that there was no snow even from September, then September became October and October a heavy November, when so many hunters came again to their inn, but he—what was he waiting for? "Won't I wake up?" she said to herself with a weary sigh while standing in front of that mirror, with her hopes and the bad weather gnawing away at her. "Won't I wake up, to see that all this is an illusion, a chimera, and the hunter will never show up again?"

Nevertheless, one evening, in mid-December, one of her little nephews, one of those whom she'd done everything for barring breast-feeding, came to her flushed and out of breath—no doubt bringing news: his ears and eyes were crying out with it. Cletia felt on the verge of death, about to fall to pieces—she almost didn't want to hear.

"Aunt," the child said, panting, "what will you give me?"

That's how divulging some secret always started—secrets are too dear not to require something in return.

She was in one of the downstairs rooms, not even half an hour had passed since she had left the inn. And suddenly, as though the secret had already produced results, she felt annoyed that even the children could play around with her—whereas in fact only Christoforos and some of the hunters had suspected her suffering—and she looked at her young nephew with a great deal of reservation, not to say standoffishness.

"What will I give you—why?" she asked him.

"Because of what I have to tell you! . . . ," the child replied.

She put her hand into a deep dish and took out three raw chestnuts. She gave him three more . . . she gave him all of them, and the dish as well.

But children are relentless.

"Chestnut trees give chestnuts," he said.

"Well then, as I'm not a chestnut tree," she replied, "I'll give you this," and she handed him a red apple . . . small and slightly wizened.

Anyhow—the boy was in a hurry.

"Bend down," he said to her. She bent down so he could whisper in her ear. "There's someone dead in the inn! Grandfather is looking for you, he says for you to go! No one knows why he died!"

She broke her neck getting there, her mind buzzing like a swarm of bees: "If it's him, why is he dead? But if he is dead, what of it? No, don't say what of it, but what should I say? Better than never seeing him again! . . . Begone from me Satan, it's a sin, for heaven's sake, to put thoughts like that into my head! And yet to what purpose, what's the difference—as life hasn't united us, let death unite us, I'm only too happy to die, only too happy for anything, just let it be with him!"

Fifty yards before reaching the entrance, she halted and beat her breast, took some deep breaths so as not to appear too upset (though the place was empty), and continued at a normal—ever quicker—pace. She had forgotten even to throw something over her shoulders, it was freezing, sleet was falling, but she understood nothing of the freezing cold or the sleet.

Inside the inn, around the big fire, a number of the men in their alarm had formed a circle and were bending to see, the ones behind pushing those in front: "Move aside," they called, and those in front turned almost in anger and raised their arms in the air: "Wait! Wait!" they shouted. "Don't be like vultures, you'll get to see him!"

One of them saw Cletia entering—who at the last moment lost all her courage and couldn't go over, couldn't see him lying there like the game he used to bring back . . .

"Christoforos, your daughter's here," he said to Christoforos, who was somewhere in the middle of the circle.

Christoforos turned and with a quick movement of his hand motioned to her to go over.

"I can't!" Cletia screamed. Then she came round somewhat—she would betray herself, though nothing mattered anymore. "I can't," she said more calmly. "What can I possibly do? What do you want me for?"—and meanwhile she got closer . . . walking on a tightrope.

"To help us!" he said. "It's for times like this you need women, not just for ah-ah-ah! Who else can I call on? You work here! . . . Don't be scared!"

Cletia discerned something in that *don't be scared* that only she and he seemed to know: *What? that perhaps it wasn't the hunter? so who had she broken her neck for?* This is what scared her, perhaps, even more . . . She stood on tiptoe: *Who is it?* she asked him, using her hand. *Why did you call me here?*

But her stepfather couldn't answer—a thirty-five-year-old, well-built man with fair hair pushed through them all and emerged from the group in a bad condition; his eyes were red, he was waving his arms about and saying to someone else coming out behind him who looked like his brother:

"I'm amazed at how calm you all are! There was nothing wrong with the man, he was in good health—something harmed our father for him to end up like that, something killed him, we have to find out what did it!"

"Calm down, we'll find out," the other said; "he had a friend who was a doctor, though where are we to find him now . . . Calm down."

"I don't want to calm down!" the first one shouted.

Hapless he goes to drown himself, and the wells run dry, Cletia thought for her own part: *it's not the hunter, he hasn't turned up even dead . . .* And she felt her heart dry and empty, devoid of any feeling, either joy or pain.

She asked someone she knew, "What's happened now?" and before she'd finished asking, he pointed to the others and the others stood back so that she could see for herself: her eye caught sight of someone . . . But she circled round them and went to get a better look from the other side, thinking again of the hunter as she went . . . Perhaps, from then on, she wouldn't even be able to think of him.

One *like him* but not him, in a crimson-colored woolen shirt and everything else black, about the same age as Christoforos, a noble appearance, who was lying on the floor with eyes closed, half-open mouth and face turned slightly toward the fire—toward where Cletia had gone to get a look at him. He was pale, waxen, even though red reflections danced on his nose and cheeks. And with one of his fingers on his chest, slightly raised, bent like a hook, as though he had wanted to grasp something or get something out of there—or say something to someone. He never managed it. And though his eyes were tightly shut, his jaw like wood and his mouth a torn membrane, he appeared to be *waiting* for the woman who came and knelt down beside him.

He wasn't completely unknown to her: she had seen him the previous evening, when he had arrived at the inn full of vigor and in a good mood—later, as she learned from her father, his two sons had arrived. He was, as he told her, an old friend of his from the south and because he had once saved him from a disaster, every five or six years he would make a trip there, to his beloved Macedonia, to see him and, as a token of gratitude, to stay a few days at his inn, paying handsomely. This time, he had brought his sons with him. "A true gentleman," Christoforos said to her, "good family, good name—and a kind heart too. And a widower."

Cletia had only exchanged the usual polite words of welcome with him, and he had patted her on the shoulder and, laughing, had said to Christoforos: "This another of your daughters too, my old friend? How many daughters have you got exactly? Or is it perhaps your new wife?" And so she wouldn't think that he put her in the same age group as them, he hastened to explain: "I say that because I know how he likes to take young wives."

"Daughter of my second wife from her first husband," Christoforos replied. "But she's closer to me than even my own daughters. She's the one who runs the inn, not me . . . Her name's Cletia."

"*Cletia!*" exclaimed his friend. "Such a lovely name! . . . Who gave it to her?"

"A godmother with plenty of imagination. She has a brother called Eumolpos."

"Eumolpos!"

"Eumolpos, yes. As though we were in ancient Greece. I've a son too by the name of Achilles and another called Hesychios . . ."

Cletia left them alone to talk and went to prepare three beds, since she'd heard mention of two sons who had stopped somewhere and who would be along later. Then she went back home. The next morning she again saw the gentleman for a short time (but not his sons); she also saw him late in the afternoon sitting with Christoforos next to the fire, drinking tea and raki and talking incessantly. And she learned that the carriage that had brought them had been paid to go and come back in a week's time. So they were planning to stay there till then: his sons wanted to go up the mountain, *mountaineers.*

And now this same man was dead. Suddenly—not a quarter of an hour had passed. There where he had been drinking his tea next to the fire and talking with her stepfather, he had got to his feet, said that he felt something, something choking him, and the next moment, the cup had slipped from his hands and he collapsed to the floor—and stayed there.

His heart, that's what they all said—only a heart attack finishes a person off like that. Of course, his sons wanted a doctor to say that, but the man they sent to call the doctor still hadn't returned—most likely the doctor was away, just as many people were away, most of the locals in fact, because somewhere else, not too far, there was a big three-day livestock fair taking place, and everyone had gone there despite the bitter cold. In two to three weeks, with the new year and new century, that same livestock fair would take place here and then everyone and their animals would come here, but for the time being most people were away. Christoforos had thought of going himself, but his friend's arrival with his sons had forestalled him.

And now one of these sons not only wanted a doctor (who was also probably away) to come but had also got it into his head that something had *killed* his father, and he wanted to have him taken to the large coastal town—a night's journey by horse, in good weather—and to carry out, God forbid, a postmortem on him. He went on about it so much that he even convinced his younger brother, and now they both wanted it, as if there were any hope, with the postmortem, that their dead father would come back to life . . . Slightly uncomfortable, Cletia began arranging his clothes, rubbed his black shoes with her sleeve, not knowing what to do, how she might help, why they had called for her; she would have preferred to cry over other things (as well as for these), while those around her, particularly the fair-haired one, were calling out for horses and post-mortems.

"Now lads, don't get involved with postmortems," Christoforos said, trying to placate them. "I quite understand your pain, but don't get involved with things like that—it was your father's heart, take him home as is only proper. Or, if you prefer, we can bury him here. He's my friend, whatever I'd do for my own, I'll do for him—we've plenty of land even for the afterlife . . . enough for friends too. But what's all this about postmortems? Is this something you've dreamt up? Isn't your dead father enough? It's as if you suspect that I killed him, that someone here could have wanted to harm such a man—it saddens me that something of the sort even passed through your minds."

"Nothing like that passed through our minds," said the elder brother, the more fair-haired one, "but our father had no problems with his heart—how can he have died from his heart?"

Christoforos began to lose patience.

"But my wife too, this one's mother," he said pointing to Cletia, "didn't have any *problem* with snakes, but in the end she died from one! Others again expect to die from their heart and it's their liver that gets them. It's not as though the good Lord asks us, is it? Has he ever asked us? Or do you have to have a *problem* with something for him to take you? The same is true of your father. He *took* him. Before my very own eyes . . . The man opened his arms to fly and fell to the floor. Instead of flying, he fell. That's the way we are."

"Whatever way we are," the fair-haired one said again, "we have every right to learn what our father died of. And we can pay, for the doctors and the horses."

Christoforos took out his handkerchief and wiped his brow.

"Fine, then," he said. "As neither words nor postmortems are going to bring him back, have it your own way so at least you'll get rid of your suspicions. And I'll come with you—he may have been your father, but he was my friend. And tell me this: where do you think we're going to find four horses now with everybody away—and there's no question of a carriage, everyone's away." He turned to Cletia: "Cover him up with a sheet, with something," he told her, "and all those who have seen him can leave, can go outside . . . the stars will be out tonight."

She drove away the curious, sent them outside to look at the stars.

Outside, night had well and truly fallen and the sleet had stopped. Not a star anywhere. After much ado, they got hold of two horses from the houses round about (Lukas, of course, was also away; the Golden Horseshoe was closed), and others went to houses farther afield to find another two. "It's madness what we're doing," Christoforos kept muttering, "utter madness—we'll go and kill the poor man again taking him out on a night like this . . . But his sons want a post-mortem! As if it were as easy as pie."

Meanwhile, the one who had gone to get the doctor returned alone and told them that the doctor was away—he had been a long time because he had gone looking for a quack, but then he had thought that a quack wouldn't have been of any use. Four men picked up the lifeless body and carried it to the door. For a moment, his face was uncovered and it was as if he were saying to them sternly: *Who are you? Where are you taking me?* He was a strange fellow; even dead, his expression kept changing—with Cletia he was more pleasant. They covered him up again. They were helped by Zacharias, the tailor, who all that time had had no idea of what had happened in the inn—he worked, worked all night in his shop: he wasn't exactly overwhelmed by orders and clients, but he wanted to keep busy, keep his fingers active—it had become a habit, "that's the way my cloth was cut," he would say. Other people had come too, with women and children. Some of the children went up to the dead man's black shoes—no other part of him was visible—touched the soles, the toes, and then ran off to examine their fingers: "Mine have gone numb, they're going to get blisters," said one. "Mine aren't numb," said another; "I'm going back again." But Cletia stood in their way and wouldn't let any of them touch his shoes again. Then the other two horses arrived . . .

First, they loaded the man's body onto the best horse, tying him above and below and all round with rope so that he wouldn't slide off—and there was such a grim sadness, a chill three times like that of death, at seeing this rider, that some of the women wailed and began lamenting even though he was a complete stranger to them. Christoforos recalled an uncle of his and *his eyes misted*, but nonetheless he was obliged to take the lead in tying him to the horse. Then he and the dead man's two sons climbed onto their horses, all three of them wrapped up like Eskimos. Before they set off, he asked the two fair-haired lads—who couldn't conceal their tears or their awkwardness—whether perhaps they wanted to rethink the whole matter . . . But they said nothing, as if they wanted to let him have the last word, and he decided they should set off: for three living men and one dead man to get down again from their horses would have been more painful perhaps than getting on them. And then again, he thought, leaving postmortems and suchlike aside, the man had to be taken back home, and in the town they were going to it would be much easier to find a better and quicker means to take him.

"Let's go, and may this black night carry us there safely," he said, and set off first, opening a way through the women and children and turning to say to Cletia whatever he still had to say to her concerning the inn—she would take charge of it, since her brothers were all away, till he returned.

Standing beside her, when the last echo of the horses' hooves had faded, were three children, who were still trying to decide what their fingers *felt*, while Zacharias and a few men were still discussing the whole affair a little way off.

"What's a postmortem, Apostolos? Do they send the dead body somewhere?" someone asked a man called Apostolos.

"No, chum, what you're thinking of is something else. A postmortem is . . . when they open him up to see what he died of."

"How do they open him up exactly?"

"With a knife, I suppose! With their special knives."

"And it's allowed, is it?"

"Depends, how should I know!"

"What we've come to, damn it . . . First time I've ever heard of *postmortem!*"

"Have you ever heard of anyone else dying of postmortem?" asked another, who was among the last to arrive and was even more clueless.

"He didn't die *of postmortem,* chum—*they're going to give him* a post-mortem!" answered the one who'd never heard of it before and had heard of it that day for the first time.

"Phew! I'm tired of hearing all their voices and their prattle," Cletia said to Zacharias. "It was like the man had gone to sleep, and they're all standing over him arguing about why he'd gone to sleep! He's *gone to sleep,* what else is there to say? We'll all go to sleep. Even I go to bed . . . Ha, tonight there'll be me and myself in the inn! Do you want to come inside and I'll make you a nice cup of tea? No need to be afraid, not everyone who drinks my tea drops on the spot. Just to keep me company a bit."

But her brother—with whom she had neither mother nor father in common, but only their age, so Eftha had once had the idea to marry them, but they hadn't agreed to it—told her that he too had to get back to his shop, he had left a sleeve half done, but he would come the next morning to have a tea with her. And so they said good night to each other and went their own ways.

Cletia took good care to close the big double door, with all its metalwork on the inside, and after making some lime tea for herself and drinking it standing up in front of the fire, dunking three sesame cookies in it, she put a blanket down to sleep there in the same spot. "Not because a real gentleman chose this spot to die," she said to herself, "but better to spend the night being a bit afraid than being all alone."

Regardless of what it was that Cletia meant *exactly*, there really was no one else in the inn that night.

And because life is not as dull or as ungracious as we would believe, what followed that night might very well be a little tale of joy and mystery, with the title "Marcos and Cletia," that would overshadow for a while the renowned "Paul and Lydia," characterizing that inn from the depths of time.

Our heroine fell asleep and dreamt that outside in the street, in the coolness and tranquility of an uncommon hour, a silver lake spread out, and someone came in his boat, a face at once familiar and unfamiliar, a manly face, on whose account all the young boys and girls had come out of their houses and were starting up serenades and wedding rumbas, waving triangular kerchiefs before their eyes — hiding now one, now the other — and singing that well-known song "Up Lazarus and don't you sleep . . ." They were splashing a little in the water without being bothered, ever more closely encircling the boat with dances and movements that were constantly changing: sometimes their bodies bent and swayed like upright snakes, sometimes they lay on the water and sometimes they disappeared beneath it, sometimes they did something with their eyes so that only the frightening whites showed, and sometimes they danced the slowest dance, leaping deliriously, with their hands behind and their necks in front, emitting shrieks of *ay, ay, ay!* . . . The boatman could go neither backwards nor forwards — he had become trapped in those serenades, which were accompanied by no other instrument but their voices, their eyes, and their frolicking. He simply did a quick round on his boat and asked them what they wanted, why they were there. "Take out your pole so we can see it," they said to him. "That's who you are, isn't it?" (This was preceded by a name that sounded a little immodest, as one might answer back to Pluto — but jokingly and guilelessly.) "That's indeed who I am," he replied, taking his pole out of the water as though uprooting a tree . . . The rest happened as in an old Romanian legend that Eftha used to tell: the drops of water that sprayed all around flashed with the last rays of the sun like drops of molten gold . . . "Come," Cletia whispered, and turned pale. And a faint laughter, barely perceptible, echoed in her ears, and she felt a cool and shiny body wrapping itself round her neck and two yellow eyes gazing at her for a long time in the moonlight. "A thousand years," the eyes said, "a thousand years we've been waiting for you, you and only you!"

Cletia squirmed on her pillow, filled with fear, with untold terror, such as she had never known before, neither in sleep nor in waking. She opened her eyes and saw the fire, which was still smoldering — and she turned pale, and even paler: everywhere she saw those yellow, wily, and rather malicious little eyes looking at her and glowing like sparks. "Snake," she thought, "a snake sent by my mother to beguile me . . . And the boatman with his boat that carries you across to the other shore . . . Could the dream have been any clearer?"

She turned her head the other way and tried to forget it, to think of something else. But everything seemed in the present, everything had been infused by that dream, by the molten gold and that deep humidity that didn't end with it; and everywhere she saw dances, water, poles, whites of eyes, and shadows that alluded to a thousand and one things, *or one and only one*; from everywhere that weak, ominous laughter reached her ears.

And an old *chill* memory sprang up in her mind to ostensibly free her from the more recent one: when, when she was eight-and-a-half years old, Eftha had lifted her up by her arms and held her over her father's lifeless body so that she could kiss his forehead: that forehead was so fresh and smooth, so cold and white, that as soon as she touched it just for a moment a second skin stuck to her lips, an infinitely thin and transparent membrane, cold, faint, and odorless like hail, that wouldn't go, wouldn't come off till many days had passed. Many days! And she swore from thenceforth never again to kiss such a forehead, but oaths of that sort don't work, they don't allow you to keep them. And besides nothing, no *kiss* was ever like that first one when she was eight and a half. None. Apart from that dream: for whatever she did, however much she tried to think or believed that she was trying to think of other things, she was still swimming and trembling in it, still being beset by it. "Ah, everything's my mother's fault," she said, "all her fault . . ." She remembered her, that when a visitor came to the house she would bring him on a large dish all the *sweetmeats* together . . . "That's a tower," one visitor said to her, "not a dish for offering sweetmeats." "*They're all together so I don't have to keep coming and going*," she said to him — the same as she said to everyone — and after setting the dish down somewhere, she would begin the endless offering: she would give them the first sweet, talk, ask, listen, then the first glass of water, again talk, sit down, get up with some anxiety as though someone were calling her, then sit down, again turning her attention to the visitor (always unpredictable in her movements though never ungainly), move on to the second offering of sweets, then the third, the fourth . . . each in its turn, even though they were *all together* on the dish as though the end of the world were at hand.

"Yes, that's how she's doing it tonight," Cletia thought, reassuring herself. "She's brought me everything together, snakes, boatmen, songs to see how much I can bear. We had that man's death yesterday, not something to be ignored. But that doesn't mean for sure that my time has come! And, after all, I've been waiting *a thousand years* for a hunter, not a boatman . . ."

This last thought, about the hunter, came to her no doubt out of habit. She wondered whether, or better she hoped that, it was already daybreak so that she could get up—she didn't want to fall into that kind of sleep again. She looked at the time in the fire: the wood she had thrown on it before lying down hadn't burned up yet, so outside there would still be the blackness of the night, so—

What was that? Her ear again picked up an indistinct sound, fleeting, insignificant, nothing more than the noise a butterfly enclosed in a bottle might make. She thought that she had imagined it, that it was a vague recollection and nothing more, but then she heard it again—and she continued to hear it at infrequent and uneven intervals. It was something specific that was slowly approaching, like the steps of a tired horse on wet ground, or snow weighing for days on the trees and now falling, one clump from one branch, another clump from another—but fortunately, it bore no resemblance whatsoever to a boat gliding through the water or to that weak hapless laughter that had frozen her heart.

But when knocking was heard on the inn's wooden doors, really loud knocking, Cletia huddled up even more in her woolen blankets, afraid that the events of the dream were starting again . . . and without any pretext this time. The knocking had to be repeated several times (the pauses between were equally intense), a man's voice to be heard ("Open up! . . . Is no one inside?"), for her to be persuaded that she should do something other than huddle and shrink under the blankets. So she got up from her mattress.

"Who is it?" she asked, but in such a low voice that she couldn't even hear it herself.

She went over to the door with a feeling as though she were tripping over threads, over cobwebs, over her own hair, so fine and invisible were all the things obstructing her and at the same time pushing her to hurry, to run . . . *"I'm all alone!"* she remembered, with a clear head, but without daring to clear up what kind of panic it was that had gripped her—it might have been jubilation, it might be the hunter!

"Who is it?" she asked loudly and calmly when she got to the door, putting first her eye and then her mouth to the slit where the two large door panels met.

"It's Marcos," came the answer from outside.

She could feel his breath on her mouth—only a wooden door separated them. Naturally, it was impossible for her to speak, she needed A THOUSAND YEARS to take it in.

"Marcos . . . the hunter, don't you hear me? I'm sorry about the disturbance at this time of night."

What disturbance! She could very easily spend her whole life like that, with her hands stuck to the door's middle bolt and her breast fluttering like a bird caught in a net.

"Open up . . . What's going on?"

"There's no one here, they're all away," she said, without it being her doing the talking exactly; "someone died here in the inn yesterday—today—yesterday! . . . They've all gone. Back in the morning."

"It's another five hours till morning and I'm tired," said the hunter on the outside, "open up . . . what do you mean *there's no one here*? And you?"

"Me!" Cletia guffawed. "*You hunters* take a year to turn up! . . . Just a moment, the bolts are heavy."

And letting go of the bolts, she began searching madly (noiselessly) for something. First she searched in her clothes, surprisingly found nothing, then her fingers slipped beneath some salted food in the corner, where no one would suspect a little mirror might be hidden. She found it. She looked at herself anxiously in the dim light. She could see hardly anything—shadows and black undulations in the glass—but it was enough that she had looked at herself. Then, with amazingly reserved and dexterous movements, she released the three iron bolts one by one.

Christoforos returned in the afternoon of the day after the next day. He appeared exhausted, but on seeing the hunter before him and on learning when he had arrived, his eyes came to life and began looking round for Cletia. She appeared with a face like porcelain.

"What's going on here, Cletia?" he asked.

"I'm minding the inn, like you told me to," she replied. "The others came, too, today, Lukas, Achilles, Hesychios . . . What happened with your friend? Did they give him a postmortem?"

"What postmortem! Two different doctors saw him, said the same as I'd said from the very first and put him on a train home. What's been happening in the inn while I was away?"

"What do you think? The usual . . . An old customer turned up," said Cletia, and her eyes—only her eyes—turned in the direction of the hunter.

"So I see," was all Christoforos said, though clearly with his mind full of thoughts.

That same evening, he said to the hunter as though wanting to scare him: "That friend I was telling you about, whose life I once saved, and who died the other day in my inn while we were talking, just like we are now, was a bit like you . . . understand what I mean? When we expected him, he didn't come—he always came when we weren't expecting him. A bit mysterious. Splendid fellow but a bit mysterious. But the most mysterious thing of all is this: just a few days ago, he left his home, all his things, all his comforts, his obligations, and came here to die! He journeyed for three full days in the snow, to come here and die in my inn! . . . Don't you find it strange?"

"Mmm, strange indeed," the hunter admitted.

"Not only strange—it's uncanny, beyond all ken," said Christoforos.

"Mmm . . ."

"I don't want to alarm you, my dear hunter friend, but how can I put it; since all this happened in my inn, I've started to be afraid when anyone comes here after a long time," Christoforos said, stroking his beard.

"You mean you're afraid in case he's coming here to die?" asked the hunter.

"Mmm, exactly . . . I can't get the fear out of my mind."

The hunter stroked his beard, too.

"No need to have any fear of that with me," he said; "I've no intention of dying while I'm here."

"Perish the thought," said Christoforos, feigning surprise. "I was just saying . . . Sitting round the fire in winter, everybody has something to say. Somebody says one thing, somebody else another . . ." And discreetly scrutinizing the hunter's face, he tried to imagine what might be going on in Cletia's heart at that moment . . . "Are you married?" he asked him softly and straight out, without standing on ceremony.

"Me? No," replied the hunter.

"Engaged? Courting perhaps?"

"No."

Christoforos slapped his knee and stood up, not knowing what else to say . . . Then he thought of something and sat down again.

"I got married three times, for my sins," he confessed. "The last time was just a few months ago."

"Mmm, yes, I know, your daughter told me," he replied.

"Have you been talking with my daughter, then?"

"Yes . . . a little."

"Which one? I've got hundreds."

"Cletia. I don't know the others—didn't you yourself just say that in winter people talk round the fire?"

"I did indeed, as God's my witness, that's what I said," answered Christoforos. "And what else?"

"What else?"

"What else did you talk about?"

"Oh, various things . . . The place here has made me . . . mmm, more talkative. Normally, I'm not someone who likes to talk very much."

"The place or Cletia?" Christoforos asked with due accord, as though dangling two dewdrops from his fingertip and asking the hunter to choose.

He chose both: he said that Cletia was a very gentle soul and had a name that he never believed he would hear in those times, and that the place itself was a little wild, uncompromising in many ways, and that the two together left him far from indifferent.

Christoforos adopted an expression as if hearing secrets that he shouldn't have heard, and yet they weren't sufficient for him to reach any conclusion.

"Mmm . . . you've got me saying that *mmm* now! . . . *The more I proceed, the more the road lengthens*," he said ponderously, and also a little fearful of such uncomfortable situations; and he got up again. "That's what my first wife used to say when what she meant was *I'm not getting anywhere!* Or perhaps it was my second wife, I can't be sure."

And he left the hunter poking the burning logs in the fireplace with a long iron poker. The glowing red embers crackled and the sparks shot up to the ceiling. It passed through Christoforos's mind at that moment that perhaps his inn would catch fire like that one day . . . But like so many things that pass through the mind, though some of them — in retrospect — prove to be *premonitions*.

Meanwhile, for Cletia the days went by full of enthusiasm and feeling — she hadn't known a happier period in her life, though no one knew exactly what had happened or what would or wouldn't happen between her and the hunter. In the house — though it was less than three hundred yards from the inn — no one really paid any attention to those two. They had other things to see to: first of all, there was Christoforos's third and inimitable wife, by the name of Persa, who had also been married twice before (a kind of symmetry that you don't even find in embroidery patterns), and then there was the latest child of Hesychios and Febronia — another inimitable couple — one of the twins, the boy, who had been born with disparate eyes, each a different color, completely different, and everyone in that place, even the teachers at school and the loafers in the cafeneion, were talking about it. If they had seen an eagle with two heads, it would have made less of an impression on them. He had been called "Thomas Two-Eyes," not because everyone else only had one, but that's more or less how they felt after seeing this unheard-of *dichromatism* in the eyes of an infant. And what's more, not the infant of just *any* parents . . . The fact was as rare and inexplicable as something which had happened thirteen years earlier: twelve people had gone to unearth an old woman, to dig up her bones, that is, and put them into a little chest, and instead of bones or anything similar — a not fully decomposed corpse for example — they found an enormous black spider in the rotten and empty coffin, a spider that was motionless and still like a dark jewel, but as soon as they blinked at the sight, the spider vanished in a flash! At any rate, they all saw it, all managed to see it, it even ran through their legs — unless it was a case of mass hallucination. And at any rate they didn't see, didn't notice, didn't find anything else in the opened grave, however much they searched with their eyes, with their hands, with sticks and poles, to find even one little bone belonging to the dead woman . . . So how were they to come up with a solution? They all turned to the priest who had officiated at that unspeakable disinterment: "What do you think, Father? We're all looking to you," they told him. And though as troubled as they were and after asking them for a little time to think about it with God's help, he said the following: "What we witnessed could mean one of two things: that the woman buried here three years ago was a paragon of good-ness and purity, an unsung saint, or that a more sinful woman has not been seen throughout the centuries!" But, of course, who could possibly feel satisfied or even relieved with an answer like that—not even the priest himself—yet, on the other hand, what else could they all say, what other explanation could they give of their own? And so they accepted this solution, which was a new enigma, a new riddle.

When Thomas was born, then, even though his stunningly disparate eyes had nothing in common with the black spider found instead of the old woman's bones, they all said that for him to have one eye brown and the other eye green means one of two things: either God had forgiven the union of his parents (for how could anyone forget a union in which the woman married the lover—and cause of death—of her daughter) or the marriage would remain forever unpar-doned. They didn't want to give a third *explanation*—which might be seen as the tacit acceptance of the inexplicable. They also said about the child itself that either he would live for a hundred years or the thread of his life would be cut before he reached twenty.

And the time passed with one thing and another: with Thomas's eyes and with "a Persa was all we needed, and now we've got her," so that Cletia could live the first and last love of her life untroubled—unsung, we might say. Deep down, she expected, without admitting it, that all hell would break loose concerning her idyll, but there wasn't so much as a flutter: some people heard something, got wind of something, but didn't attach any further importance to it. There were times when she was gripped by anger, the outburst of someone without any tomorrow, and wanted to take hold of them one by one, at home, on the streets, and say to them: "Haven't you got eyes to see with? Why are you look-ing elsewhere and not at me, this love-smitten woman before you?!" But even if she had done it, even if she had proclaimed it left and right, they might very well have taken her like that kindly, guileless man by the name of Dounis, who said to anyone he encountered: "I'm pitiful, pitiful; you have a pitiful soul be-fore you, pitiful, pitiful!"

Her stepfather at any rate was not one of those who *didn't look*. On a num-

ber of occasions he tried to squeeze out of her what was going on exactly between her and the hunter, why her face had been as pallid as the moon and she
had shrunk to half her size until those innocent words the two of them had exchanged in the inn together with those strange looks he was sure he noticed.
Cletia simply sighed and turned away, keeping silent. Now that someone was
asking her, that there was no need for her to shout it out on her own, now it
was that she kept silent. And if Christoforos persisted and became angry at her
silence, she would get angry too and say to him in a stifled voice: "I'm tired,
leave me alone. Leave me alone. I'll only end up telling you untruths." "Fine,
then tell me some untruths!" Christoforos said to her one day. "In any case, what
have we understood of the truth?" and Cletia decided to rise to the challenge:
"The hunter and I love each other!" she said, and watched her head trembling
in his eyes like a pinhead. "Perhaps we'll never get married, but we love each
other, he's my betrothed, so now you all know!"

"So, you've exchanged engagement rings, have you? Have you pledged yourselves to each other?" Christoforos asked in amazement.

"We've not exchanged anything, that's what people do who are afraid,"
Cletia replied.

And before he had time to ask anything else, a customer called to him, and
she hurriedly headed toward the house.

"God didn't see fit to give me daughters or stepdaughters," Christoforos kept
thinking to himself during all that time; "he gave me enigmas."

And for his part, Marcos, the hunter, stayed from mid-December, when he
had arrived, till the New Year—during the last days, he went out neither hunting in the mountains nor even for a walk. He had definitely become more ame-
nable and cordial with other people. In the evenings he would sit around the
fire with the other hunters, playing drafts with them; they all heard his laughter
and saw his white teeth, which they hadn't seen before then. It was he who filled
the wine cups, it was he who tended to the fire morning, noon, and night and,
in general, he was a different man altogether. One day when Christoforos asked
one of his sons to help him with some difficult chore and the son told him that
he didn't have the time, the hunter offered to help. And the following day, of his
own accord he asked Christoforos whether he had need of any help.

"I've any number of needs," Christoforos told him, scratching the hair on the
back of his neck, "but first I want you to help me with a question I have."

"Out with it, then, what kind of question?" the hunter asked (there were no
longer any formalities between them).

"Look here. You're a hunter and you know about animals, whereas I'm an
innkeeper and I don't know much, not about my customers, not even about my

own children! Perhaps you know then . . . This is the question: If someone says to you, 'I'll only end up telling you untruths,' and when they do open their mouth, and come out with something from the very depths of their heart, should we take it as true or untrue?"

"Mmm, that's a difficult one," said the hunter. "Anyway . . . mmm, it all depends. It depends . . . If they say it from the very depths of their heart like you say, then probably it's true."

"It's true? Let's leave aside the probably," Christoforos said impatiently.

The hunter threw his arms up in the air; and like a mirror the door opened at that very same moment and in walked Cletia, an innocent accomplice to her fate. They were unable to go on with their conversation nor did they ever have the opportunity to go back to it.

On New Year's Eve, after the episode with the famous photographs, which Marcos had watched with great interest—without it being totally ruled out that he, too, had been captured in the background of one or more of these—something happened that would be long remembered by those who saw it.

There had always been mice in the rooftops and the basements, especially in those houses with a double ceiling (the two-story houses all had double ceilings—like saying that the ceilings too had a floor and ceiling), but during those days the mice had grown particularly bold in the inn: it seems their holes weren't big enough for them and they came out for a stroll or chased each other on the broad wooden rafters above the people's heads; they had literally turned into house pets and the traps with cheese that Christoforos had set in order to teach them a lesson simply ended up as games for them. But even when some got caught in them and were unable to run again, there were so many more behind them that it was enough to drive anyone to the edge of despair on hearing the wild patter of feet and that slight *tak-tak* that came from their plump little bodies. Christoforos regretted time and again that he hadn't heeded the advice of his late-departed Eftha when she had told him to put a snake in the inn (she would find it for him, a baby one, just out of its egg), and she would raise it on milk and with care so that the snake would grow accustomed to him and work for him and his inn, exterminating the mice. But he wouldn't listen to her, he didn't want a snake in his inn—"I'll lose my customers," he said to her. And now he was in danger of losing them because of the mice . . . And where was he to find a snake now when he wanted one, at that time of year, and without Eftha's help! Even cats didn't like such big—and so many—mice. They had already tried shoving some cats into that large double ceiling, shoving them into that darkness by opening some holes for this purpose and closing them up behind them, but the cats wouldn't take even a step farther inside. They grew wild in surroundings like those, stood there with their fur bristling and simply wailed (which, of course, had some effect, but only a transitory one), and when they unblocked the holes and let them out, they looked as though they were emerging from a madhouse.

So Christoforos had the idea, as a last resort, to ask the hunter's help.

"Can you find me a weasel?" he asked him one evening, on the eve of New Year's Eve.

"A weasel?" the hunter exclaimed in astonishment.

"A weasel, yes. But a live one, very much alive. Only a weasel can save us from this plague of mice," he said, pointing to the ceiling.

The hunter admitted that what he was asking wasn't easy, but he promised to do what he could to find him a weasel. And he left that night—they were all so concerned about the mice that no one was afraid, not even Cletia, that he might not come back.

He didn't head for the mountain, nor for some distant wooded region—he knew that weasels didn't live far from human habitation. He might even find one in a stable or in an odd pile of wood and stones, in which they liked to make their soft nests, give birth to their babies, and spend their days unnoticed, before going out at nightfall in search of food—again unnoticed. So it would be fairly easy to locate one, though not so easy to catch it alive.

But neither was it impossible for him: at daybreak he returned to the inn with a cute, bushy, and terrified weasel in his arms . . . Its fear and distrust gradually began to recede, and it got on quite well with its hunter (it greedily crunched on whatever he gave it on the way, as well as on his nails and his buttons), yet it grew terrified once more when he brought it in front of so many people, and it began biting his fingers with those fine, pointed teeth—and, very nearly, for a moment, got away from him and escaped all of them.

Then the weasel—before the hunter even tried to regain its trust with a few nuts, and of course before it was necessary for him to show it the way to the double ceiling—flew like an arrow out of his arms and onto the floor, stood there a while on its two hind legs turning its sharp-witted little head in every direction with its nostrils quivering insatiably (living up to its name), and with a leap, quicker than the hunter's eye, found itself on a thick rafter, and from there leapt onto another one, nimble and predatory as it was, and completely in its *element* . . . The mice, no matter how quick they were to try to disappear and stop their noise, sensed the end of their reign.

The hunter, too, was quick to get out of the inn, along with the others.

When they went back inside some time later, they stood with open mouths and crossed themselves profusely: the floor was littered with shriveled, lifeless mice, the rafters were empty, silent and uninhabited. Presently, they saw the weasel coming out from somewhere, from nooks and crannies in the ceiling that not even Christoforos knew of, and holding between its teeth two more half-suffocated victims that were struggling feebly and vainly to escape . . . It stopped in the middle of the rafter—as though for everyone to see it—laid its victims before it, and, after sucking them dry, threw them down with the rest.

"So, the weasel doesn't eat the flesh then?" asked someone, when they all started to recover their speech.

Some of the others looked at him without venturing to answer—as if they should know that weasels like blood so much that they turn their noses up at the rest?

Marcos clapped his hands triumphantly to awaken them from their stupefied state and decided to take hold again of the little heroine, which, now satiated, was more relaxed, put up little resistance. At the same time, Cletia, her stepfather, and two of her brothers came with some long-handled wooden brooms and made a pile of the scattered pathetic little bodies. It really was like a pile of empty corn leaves: such was the power that this cute little weasel had in its pointed teeth.

"My, my, there are more of them dead than there were alive!" said Christoforos, who was almost starting to feel sorry for them. "I mean it: now that I see them like that, I feel a bit sad," he admitted.

Nonetheless, they shoveled them into a sack and took them behind the inn, where they lit a big fire. They all gathered around it and tossed them onto the fire like dice.

All of them. Marcos remained alone inside and made his way to his room to sleep a little, taking with him the weasel, which now seemed completely at ease with him, but also a little ill, hurting—was it about to vomit? And Cletia too, standing still at one end of the corridor (in the same place where her stepfather had grabbed hold of her by the hair one morning), was waiting for them.

He halted before her; and from the way that he looked at her feet, at the point where her dress ended, perhaps wanting to tell her something but deciding not to, Cletia immediately understood, sensed, that he was getting ready to go away again, to leave her. She sank into a sea of blackness—no joy was worth such pain. The celebration for the extermination of the mice seemed ludicrous to her. And yet she invoked it.

"Are you going?" she asked him, also avoiding looking him in the eye; looking from the weasel's hanging tail to the quiet ceiling up above, but more than this she looked at his feet, just as he was at hers: as though there were little mirrors on their shoes and through these they could see each other still—eye to eye—and communicate. "Are you going again? Now that we've gotten rid of the mice! . . . And tomorrow's New Year . . . The people in these parts celebrate . . . Why don't you stay and see for yourself? You'll like it."

"Unfortunately, I've promised some of my relatives to go and see them for New Year—mmm, exactly . . . it's tomorrow. They're old and on their own."

"Is he telling me the truth? Is it a lie?" Cletia wondered. "At any rate, he said *unfortunately!*" She was overcome by a longing not to let him leave the inn again, to cast a spell over him if at all possible, or to vanish with him, to leave and never be seen again. Oh, better a thousand times that she should vanish too than that it be only him, with her waiting again another year—no, she didn't want even one more *day* to dawn without him.

"Our inn," she whispered, "you said that you'd never come across any other inn like ours!"

"And it's true," Marcos said.

"So, then?"

"But I'm not going to any other inn, I'm going to visit two aging relatives of mine who are on their own."

"If there are two of them, they're not on their own," said Cletia, swallowing most of what she really wanted to say.

"They don't have any children, they don't have anyone at this time of the year," he said.

"And are you coming back? And when? Next winter?" she asked him in quick succession, believing that outside she could already hear the dead mice laughing at the way she was trying to hide her feelings and her anxiety, though in fact baring them.

"No," replied the hunter, "I'll be back in a few days . . . mmm, I don't aim to be gone long."

Aim! Why not *promise* instead of *aim*? He aimed with his rifle at the birds and animals . . .

"Will you take the weasel with you?" she asked him.

The hunter smiled; opened the legs of the weasel that was curled up on his chest and began stroking it on its satiated belly with his five fingers—his hand was larger than its entire body.

"Mmm," he murmured, "if this is what kind Cletia wants, I'll leave it here—after all, I brought it for the inn, didn't I?"

"Take it," she said as if presenting him with it, "take it, because otherwise . . . I'm no *kind Cletia!*"

He stared at her as though he had been saddened by what she said. And Cletia regretted it at the same moment. Besides, give a dog a bad name and hang him; and faced with the void that was opening like a chasm before her, she too—both good and bad sides—reached out her hand and stroked the weasel's belly. How contented it must have felt! . . .

"It likes being caressed," the hunter remarked.

Cletia didn't need to say "Everybody likes it, so do you and so do I." She didn't need to say it because from then on (for some time), everything was ambiguous: they said it and intimated it at any and every chance, to hear it and understand it themselves.

"It likes it," she agreed, "it's pampering itself . . . it's sick, it wants to bring up what it drank."

"Cletia! . . ."

"What it drank . . . It'll bring it up, you'll see."

"Oh Cletia . . . why do you say that?"

"If it wasn't for our inn, would you come back?"

"Yes . . . Where are the others?"

"Outside, no one's here, don't worry."

"Don't *you* worry, let's go farther inside."

"This way . . . ," she told him.

"Can anyone see us?"

"Shh . . . don't be afraid."

They went down stairs, and more stairs, no one saw them, everyone was outside, because of the mice and the fine weather. Even the weasel left them and, in a daze, jumped to the floor, went into a corner, and slowly began to vomit, doubling up and then undoubling its whole body . . . Every now and again, it would turn and look at their feet for a little, very little, while waiting for the next wave that would double it up again over its own vomit, which had become a pool . . .

"I'll clean it up, don't worry," whispered Cletia, with the hunter's white teeth so close to her tongue that nothing, not even death itself, could have been very far away.

It might have been him who said *don't worry*.

The next day, New Year's Day—with a sun that glistened on the dirty snow and slush—some fifty or so men went out into the streets with a stout white bullock on which they had set up (they were holding it so it wouldn't fall) a painted wooden boat. Hanging and swaying on its rudimentary masts—tied with colored strands—were wooden horns, mandarins, pieces of salted meats, small apples and sweets, while passing from hand to hand was a long pole that ended in a strange *icon:* a series of small silverfish held together with wire formed something that, with a little imagination, might be read as TWENIETH CENTURY. They had forgotten the T, or, rather, it didn't fit—one of the letters had to be sacrificed.

The celebration that day surpassed all previous ones—they were afraid that some of them would drop dead on the spot through so much revelry and drinking. Only Christoforos had woken up in bad spirits, and when they passed by his inn to usher in the New Year and entered prancing and wiggling their shoulders and hips like oriental belly-dancers, he behaved to them as he would have behaved to a herd of madmen and fools—up until the previous day he had had the gray rabble, now he had this motley lot. "Good-for-nothings, haven't you got work to do . . . if the fate of this century depends on you lot, we're done for!" And of course, he didn't exempt those of his sons who were trailing along in the hubbub, and while the wife of one of them was in the house burning up with fever. "Good-for-nothings . . . bah! . . . dolts, all of you," he muttered, huffing and puffing. And he didn't turn to take even a sip from their bottles they held under his chin as they pushed and shoved one another to be the first to wet his mouth, the first to dull his own wits. "Bah! You and your bottles . . . Good-for-nothings . . . I want none of your wine!"

"It's a grave sin you're committing, Christoforos, not to drink with us on such a day," one of them said.

"I like grave sins," he replied ill-humoredly. "I like celebrating on my own."

Cletia, however, standing beside him, watched this intrusion into the inn with bright eyes and a shining face. She felt happy at the thought of the hunter, of the exquisite moments they had spent together, and now his absence made them all the more exquisite. She was impassioned by his absence that day, the thought of how he would view all this *if he were there*, of how he would smile with surprise, with astonishment, with sympathy . . . So she watched everything through his eyes—with the same longing and generosity with which the pregnant women of her times would eat *for two!* Or, at other times, in her mind she described it all to him (in anticipation of his return), and all this imbued her with an almost otherworldly appearance, such that, had she and her stepfather at that moment been a couple, they might well have been called *the Scowler and the Starry-eyed.*

"Cletia, my fairest—and do you like *suffering* on your own too?" someone asked her, deliberately altering Christoforos's words.

It was Haris, a jolly fellow who, given the festive day, was even jollier, her second or third cousin, an aspiring hunter himself (for the time being a worker in the tobacco store), and very unlucky with women—only his mother loved him. He wouldn't have said no to trying his luck with Cletia, though she preferred to try hers with someone else, something which he had become aware of (the tobacco store was behind the inn), and this gave a melancholic dimension to all his jolliness, an air of vulnerability.

"And rejoicing with others," Cletia answered without much hesitation and without refusing the wine that he offered her.

Haris, however, had his own appraisal:

"Drink to forget your woes," he said to her conspiratorially, "and don't come out with lies to me—lies have no legs to stand on, they're blown over by the breeze!" And as he said this, he knelt down before her, at her feet, and from down there, whispered to her: "The hunter's gone again, hasn't he? I saw him leaving early this morning like a vampire—is that why you're *rejoicing?*"

"He'll be back," said Cletia, stooping to reassure him. "And why do you call him a vampire?"

"Because he's sucked you dry, and you run after him like a lamb running after a wolf!"

"Shh!" she said (Christoforos kept glancing at them, his eyes filled with pity, which was at least better than anger), not knowing how to get him away from her legs or whether she too should become angry with such *jokes* or begin for real to rejoice that, if nothing else, the fact that someone else was talking to her so openly about the hunter was like a validation of that inner sorrow, a further level of significance.

For the time being, she found Haris's words pleasing to her, the good and the bad that he'd said, but if the hunter were to delay, if, God forbid, he were not to return, then even a hair on her shoulder would be unbearable for her.

"And if that cur doesn't come back, I want you to know that I'm here!" Haris went on undeterred, and slumped on the floor like a cripple, wrapped himself around her legs, wanting to kiss them, wanting at all costs to kiss them, and when the others came between them and pulled him away, he wanted to kill them all. "Get your hands off me, damn the lot of you!" he began screaming. "I love her! I know how to love women like that—you and all your kind!—who are in love with someone else!"

And just how all his merriment and good spirits turned into weeping and wailing only the double-edged wine can say. And the human heart, of course, so inflammable and defenseless.

"Get him out of here," said Christoforos.

"Love has no legs to stand on, it's eaten by the crows," sang Haris, tottering and weeping between Cletia's knees and at the hands of his friends, who were struggling to pull him away while he kept finding variations for his own words and their allusions.

Was all this his, improvised or designed; no one else said such things, and it was this exactly that most worried Christoforos because they reminded him of another *jolly* fellow, who also *played* with his songs and with a load of allegories — it wasn't so long ago — and who, in the end, had life play badly with him.

"Take him out of here, enough," he said again to Haris's friends. "Take him to his mother, she knows what to do to calm him down."

Without more ado, they got him to his feet, and like the guilty he didn't know where to hide his face or the tears furrowing his cheeks.

"Not to my mother," he said, "she's lost two like me, let her die like a human being, let me kiss Cletia's legs, kiss them, oh oh oh . . ." — he collapsed again — "the hunter with his shot, any bird he pierces . . . with his arrows . . . oh oh oh the de-e-e-er . . ."

"Pick him up, get him out of here," Christoforos said for the last time, throwing his arms up in the air. "Off with you all, enough! Go and take your New Year to someone else's door!"

One by one or in little clusters, they all went out of the inn, casting glances of disapproval and fear not so much at the one who was driving them away as at his daughter by another father.

"The day has made a femme fatale out of you, my dear," he said with pronounced irony when they were once again alone in the inn; "your luck's in, how else can I put it? It seems that when you fell in love with the hunter, everyone else fell in love with you. Pity you didn't know it before, you'd have been married by now. With someone else, of course."

In the bad mood he was in, his tongue turned her into a wreck, ruined the festive day. But as long as the hunter remained in her heart — and it was impossible for him to escape from there — nothing frightened her of all the rest.

Night fell, and the area with its mountains round about was still humming with the festivities and the singing that left openings for confused sentiments and vague premonitions.

The following day and the day after that had their own joys, though slightly more subdued. The sun continued to play hide-and-seek with the wind and the clouds, and to shine for a few hours and be hot as though spring had already arrived — everything seemed full of promise, everywhere a sense that something was about to happen, even in the peaceful slumbering of little children.

Cletia had turned her attention once again to the children, to all her nephews and nieces, half-nephews and half-nieces. She was happy to return to her old habits now that she no longer had need of them *in order to live*, now that she had another reason to live. The new year, even the new century, might have found her alone as always, but the thought of the hunter, and the thought of him alone, heartened her in her solitariness. And this was the only new thing for her, truly special, since, as for the rest, the new century in her life meant absolutely nothing to her, she saw no fish flying in the air or crows turning white. But the hunter, he transformed everything. Even when he didn't return, so to speak . . . but no, just thinking of that caused her so much pain that the pain itself prevented her from dwelling on it anymore, just as someone close to us who's just died prevents us from thinking of him, of *how he's spending* his first nights in the ground.

On the evening of that third day, Thomas, then five months old, suddenly got an unending bout of hiccups, and Febronia was in another part of the house with her sick sister-in-law; so he and his sister Safi-Lisafi were being looked after by Aunt Cletia. She stared at the twins and wondered that one was convulsed with hiccups while the other slept beside him completely unperturbed. Something which wouldn't have surprised her had it been any other two children, but which placed her in a grave dilemma with these two: What should she do? What was easier? Stop Thomas's hiccups or wake up Safi-Lisafi? Something told her that if she were to wake up Safi-Lisafi, the little boy's torment would cease . . . However, something made her try the more difficult way. And so she left Safi-Lisafi alone sleeping and with the ardor afforded her not only by her long experience with babies but also, and above all, by her late-flowering love, which would lead her she didn't know or care where, she grabbed hold of the boy, wrapped him in three sheets, and went out with him into the winter sun before it set and they lost it. She sat down on one of the steps and sat the baby on her knee, face to face with her.

"Little rainbow-eyes," she said to him teasingly, "look into my poor eyes and those mad hiccups will stop!"

And she began, with his every spasm, to give him a little slap on the cheek: "hic" went his throat—"thwack," she replied, imitating more or less the sound of her hand, "hic"—"thwack!" "hic"—"thwack!" . . . The baby stoically accepted these slaps, but neither of them saw any improvement in the hiccups. And gradually a crowd of children gathered around them, Thomas's brothers and sisters and cousins and other children from the neighborhood, and asked Cletia why she was hitting the baby.

"To stop the hiccups," she told them.

"But they're not stopping."

"They'll stop, it's up to him."

But it wasn't up to her.

"Shall I show you how to stop them?" asked one little girl with a blue hood and beautiful—though slightly squinting—eyes.

Cletia let her show her—love makes you humble, patient, indifferent, concordant with children, with everything, and with nothing. Then the little girl, whose name was Calliope and was known to everyone as Lope, removed her hood and revealed a torrent of wavy jet-black hair; she ran her fingers through it and tossed it this way and that to make it even bushier, and when that shiny undulating mass had become the center of attention, she leaned over so that her head was between Cletia's breast and the baby. She waited for a few moments completely still and then stirred again . . .

"What's he doing?" Cletia asked.

"He's looking at it," she replied.

"What else?"

"Nothing."

Thomas was indeed staring at the wondrous sight with unblinking eyes—and what eyes!—nevertheless, he showed no intention either of touching that marvelous hair or of freeing himself from the hiccups that had been troubling him for so long.

"Get him to touch it, get him to touch it!" Lope said impatiently.

"He can't, he's all wrapped up."

"Get him to touch it, I'm telling you! With his mouth! Kiss it! . . . And the hiccups will stop."

Cletia did what she was told: she pushed the baby's face into Lope's rich black hair . . . Undeniably, he shuddered all over, like a young boy who touches and smells a woman for the first time, but the hiccups—after a few moments of great anticipation—returned.

"Ooo!" said little Julia, Thomas's sister. "Enough, move away—my hair will make it stop."

And taking off her own green hat, she revealed an auburn torrent, full of swirls. She did the same—tossed her hair, ran her fingers through it, made it bushy—and offered it to her brother, asking him to kiss it so that the hiccups would stop. And the requisite kiss was given, and given again, but the hiccups wouldn't give up.

Lope, meanwhile, who wasn't too pleased about being excluded from the *effects* of the hair, again came between Cletia, Julia, and the baby, and now set to subduing the hiccups with arduous gobbledygook: "Eren-teren, seren-tereren, I'll turn you into an owl so the hics will fly away! Eren-peren . . ."

"Eren-teren, seren-tereren, i'll turn you into an owl so the

HICS WILL FLY AWAY!" sang out all the other children, joining in with her and rhythmically swaying arms and legs and heads: "EREN-TEREN, SEREN-TEREREN, I'LL TURN YOU INTO AN OWL SO THE HICS WILL FLY AWAY! EREN-TEREN, SEREN-TEREREN . . ."

And, of course, amidst so many voices, so many hiccups jostling in the front line of battle, it was impossible for Cletia—the only one watching silently—to see whether the baby's devilish hiccups had indeed been vanquished . . . It was only when the voices quietened and faded one by one and they were all waiting with the greatest anticipation that—God forbid!—the incorruptible, unsubdued "hic" was heard again.

And Cletia burst out laughing and began to kiss Thomas, kiss him on the cheeks, on the eyes, on his swaddling clothes, even on the mouth of his hiccups—kiss him everywhere, as she had once kissed her brother and his father.

This was the episode the children would remember above all of Cletia, as that day was her penultimate day.

But it was also the episode that Cletia would remember of the children, as that night she was woken by a knocking on her door (she was now sleeping in the house), and when she went to open it, she saw her brother Hesychios's wife, Febronia, clutching in her arms Thomas's *other half*, little Safi-Lisafi, who was writhing from all the spasms . . .

"What a bout of hiccups, Lord! She won't let me get any sleep," Febronia said to her.

"And what about the other one?" Cletia asked her, hoping she wouldn't think she was asking about Hesychios.

"The other one's sleeping blissfully," said Febronia. And she expressed her puzzlement: "Those twins will drive me crazy. Usually the one is hurting and the other cries, or you feed the one and the other feels full . . . But this evening it was just the opposite: she's choking from hiccups and the other one is sound asleep, dreaming."

"Wake him up," said Cletia bluntly.

"Wake him up? Why? He's sleeping so peacefully . . . It's this one I don't know what to do with—can you tell me?"

"If Thomas doesn't wake up, Safi won't stop," said Cletia, revealing her secret.

And this is what happened; she went with her to the cot where Thomas was sleeping and woke him up, taking him into her arms as though stealing his sleep from him. Safi-Lisafi's hiccups stopped immediately, and Cletia said good night to Febronia, who was left speechless.

■

The next morning saw the start of the big cattle market that would bring hordes of people and livestock to their area, and—with the oncoming of night— something more: a major earthquake. The biggest and most terrifying earth- quake. And the fire.

However, we still have a little room for noting that, during all this time since the hunter's departure, a short time and yet long, Cletia had not only the chil- dren in the house, her chores in the inn, her thoughts and hopes: she also had the weasel. The hunter had left it in the same way he might leave her his ring or something similar, and Cletia fed it and took care of it as she'd never taken care of anything in her life *except him.* She literally treated it like a princess, as the embodiment of his promise that he would come back.

But all this care and love suffocated the weasel, made it feel captive, and it did nothing to conceal its longing to get away . . . For her part, Cletia, not want- ing to lose it—at least not till the hunter returned—actually did keep it captive, shutting it in the north-facing room (and tying its leg to the bed). Locking the door, she even took the key with her . . . It was a large key that looked like a pair of scissors; she hung it from her belt over her left hip, and whatever she did in those next days, wherever she was, wherever she slept, her hand would go down every so often and feel her hip in order to make sure that the key was still there. The key never left her. Besides, for most of the time (especially at night), she locked herself up in the north room with the weasel, and we can only imagine what caresses that unsuspecting animal got and how many confessions it heard that were intended for another . . .

And besides, Cletia never stopped dreaming—in the short time that she slept—that the years had passed and the hunter never returned . . . She would wake up hurt, as if she had been beaten in her sleep, and she didn't know what was more preferable: to sleep and have such dreams or to wake up and not see him. It was the latter that seemed to her more hurtful—she had no latitude for dreaming . . .

It was from that room, then, that she rushed in terror when the first men- acing tremors began on that fourth night in January, and what she was clutching to her breast when Febronia saw her was perhaps the hunter's weasel and not a little mirror. Perhaps it was both.

How and why she ended up in the inn when—with the second quake at dawn on the fifth day—the fire started, and how the flames trapped her and pre- vented her from coming out again, or how, perhaps, it was she who didn't want to come out, these are questions that found no answers at the time, nor is there much hope that they will find answers now.

Most people didn't even know of her love for the hunter, so as to attribute some blame for her death to him. They wept for her as a virgin and unfortunate who at least deserved a somewhat gentler, tender end.

Virtually all alone, her stepfather strove to link vague movements and images from the previous days with what had transpired afterwards, to discern some *forewarning* in some of her last unsuspecting words, wanting—amidst all his sorrow at the disaster—to find an explanation, some rudimentary explanation for the loss of Cletia, who, *if nothing else*, was the dearest of his stepchildren.

But there was nothing to help him—all they found in her hands was the backbone of a small animal (a cat, they would have supposed, had it not been for the odd case of the weasel), and in the ashes of her dress a broken, charred mirror.

And the hunter did return, but only the day after, like a phantom on his horse, at the hour of her funeral. It was, they say, the most evocative, the most anxious moment: as soon as they saw him coming down the path in the cemetery they all stepped aside to allow him to stand in front of the still open grave, even those who didn't know who he was or who were frightened by his presence—his face was darker and more unexpressive than ever, he had eyes for no one, only for that hole in the earth.

He let his horse—that is, he didn't let it, he spurred it—go right up to the edge . . . and it was only at the last moment that he restrained it and stopped it from actually going inside! But he began making circles around the grave, stamping on the grassed-over graves on either side, bringing new turmoil to the living, and terrifying out of their minds the two old gravediggers, who had only just let go of the ropes and taken hold of the spades; they thought he was bearing down on them, that his horse's hooves were going after them, and in order to avoid the danger they held the spades like shields in front of their chests or over their heads and slipped into the pit, not knowing how much deeper in they could go without getting Cletia out . . . It was pitiful, and the hunter didn't bother to say, "Don't be afraid" . . .

Eventually, he again halted at the spot where he had halted the first time and asked them to open the coffin lid.

Everyone froze. The gravediggers looked at him as if they hadn't heard properly, the priest—nervously shaking his stole and taking wheezing breaths—told him that her soul wouldn't want that as it was now seeking peace.

"Yes, it would," was the hunter's emphatic reply, and, to confirm it, he looked Christoforos in the eye—the only one whom he deigned to look at.

Christoforos, however, seemed to agree with the priest.

"Why do something like that? It's pointless," he said to the hunter.

But he waited, holding the horse's reins in a way that spoke volumes . . . Christoforos felt the same fear that the gravediggers had felt and went up to him, told him again in a low voice that it was pointless, why do something like that? It was not something that had ever happened before.

"I didn't ask whether it had happened before—I want to see her," replied the hunter.

"You're talking like someone pigheaded," Christoforos said to him. "What do you think you'll see? Charred remains, not her."

"I WANT TO SEE HER!" the hunter's voice drowned out his words, while the horse—which he was at once restraining and also spurring—almost lost control of itself and reared up on its hind legs, letting out a whinny like a flame from its mouth.

"All right, all right," Christoforos said, giving in, "just a moment while I explain to everyone." And he turned to the crowd: "It's her betrothed," he said loudly, struggling between fortitude and futility. "Yes, Cletia's . . . Let him have his wish . . . We kept the engagement secret—sadly the fire, the end, came first."

His sons and daughters and daughters-in-law and his third wife were more surprised at what he said than any of the others there.

"Eh, yes, secret from you too," Christoforos said sadly, "secret from everyone—the two of them decided it themselves . . . and confided in me alone . . ."

He stared at the coffin: if the dead are affected by our actions, he could be sure that Cletia was happy to hear his words. Then he stared at the hunter: there was nothing in his mien to contradict what he'd said, though he didn't appear to be really listening.

And so that strange and rather macabre wish was granted, and the lid was opened by the two old men with the spades; the shroud was removed from her face—only for most of the people to recoil or turn their eyes away. Only Marcos stood there motionless, rooted to the spot, and gazed at her from up above . . . He could recognize nothing other than her mouth, perhaps, which had remained wide open, a chasm, stuffed with cotton wool. Cletia—

He put his hand into his pocket, his breast pocket, and everyone thought he would pull it out, holding something to throw into the grave. But he remained like that, a one-armed man. Then, with a nod, he motioned to them to cover her up again.

No one failed to see that reddish sheen in his gray eyes or the way he restrained his throat *with a bridle almost* like the horse's, and the whispering that arose from the mouths of the one and the other covered, together with the moist earth and the last hymns, whatever was still left to cover.

Over the next days, no one spoke so much about the fire or the earthquake as about the hunter, that secret suitor who appeared, albeit at the last moment—and whatever glory Cletia had failed to experience while she lived and lived her love, she experienced after she had burned.

Christoforos, meanwhile, following the funeral, opened his house to him, let him cross that threshold too. There was no longer any inn. But even if there were, the dinner of thick beans, the sweet wine, and that sugared pilaf at the end (which some quite bluntly called "that bedamned pilaf") could only be offered at the house, in the big parlor that was heated by three braziers. A lot of people, invited and uninvited, turned up: for Cletia, for the inn, to observe the custom, to fill a few hungry stomachs, but also to get a look at the hunter.

The family, the close relatives, looked at him with some reserve, even servitude in part, but also with a certain hostility in their faces, with bitterness; but the most difficult of all for them was to understand what had happened, what had been going on so long behind their backs so that, just like a cuckold, they'd been the last to find out about it. Above all, Hesychios, perhaps being accustomed to the privilege of having so many women die on his account, didn't appear to easily digest the fact that his very own sister had died on account of a stranger—but he may simply have been too sad and dejected at her death. At any rate, during those hours, he said nothing, would listen to no one, and withdrew early from the parlor.

His father, on the contrary, went on talking to the hunter till after midnight. He described to him how his recent great ills had started, *with the earth's stumbling,* and how he was trying—hoping, more like—to discover from him how Cletia had been lost together with the inn.

But if he knew nothing, the hunter appeared to know even less.

"Why didn't you come earlier?" he asked him. "If you'd been here, we wouldn't be grieving over so many *things.* If you'd only come a day earlier! . . ."

"The snow prevented me," said the hunter, whose demeanor recalled the unsociable and solitary hunter of the past, the very same that Cletia had fallen in love with, starting what was to be a slow and magical transformation that there was no longer any point in continuing. While Christoforos was talking to him, he kept looking straight in front of him, just as in the cemetery, and only on one or two occasions did his gaze light up somewhat at the appearance of the red-haired Julia, the younger sister of the deceased, following her movements for a while as—shaking from head to toe—she refilled a cup or plate and then went away again.

Christoforos wasn't happy about this, and he told Julia to go to bed, there were other women to take care of the parlor. She obeyed and didn't come back.

"Perhaps we're seeking an explanation that's closer to us than we think?" he subsequently asked the hunter in a different tone of voice.

He knitted his brows—what did he mean by that?

"Perhaps you've been making eyes at another woman lately and Cletia understood?" the host said outright.

"No," replied the hunter calmly.

"I have many daughters," Christoforos continued, "more than the plagues of the Pharaoh—perhaps you had your eye on one of them and Cletia was only a front for you?"

If the moment and his character had permitted him, the hunter would have laughed.

"If you mean the girl with the red hair," he said to Christoforos, "I was look-ing at her . . . mmm, because she reminds me a bit of Cletia."

"Cletia? Where on earth? They may have had the same mother, but they didn't have so much as a hair in common," Christoforos told him.

"I'm not saying they look alike," said Marcos; "it's just that there's something . . . about the cheeks, I don't know, that paleness . . . and about their movements . . . She reminded me of Cletia . . . Mmm, but don't worry, Cletia is the only reason I'm here."

Christoforos got up and walked over to the window; he opened it, as though consulting the darkness, the chill air, shut it, and returned to his seat. He filled their glasses with wine, pouring a few drops into the tray of sand with the extin-guished candles and said:

"All of us here tonight—even you!—with her gone . . . With the inn gone . . . I can't believe it, hunter. When I think about it, I don't want to live. As though everything's gone up in flames."

Some relatives of Eftha's first husband had come for the funeral, two sisters and three nephews of Cletia's real father, all from another place, and the two women were complaining in a roundabout way to two of Christoforos's sisters that they hadn't been informed sooner, when their niece took ill . . . Didn't they want to accept that Cletia hadn't been ill, but had burned like a torch from one moment to the next? Or did they put it that way, implying that the poor girl hadn't found happiness in the house of her stepfather? That evening was full of such unpleasant insinuations.

At the other end of the parlor, Christoforos pretended not to hear, but he had his ears pricked to everything that was being said. Eventually, he could no longer contain himself—one of the women was saying, feigning quietness so as not to be heard by those around: "If her father, our brother, had been alive, he would have had our Cletia married these past twenty-five years, she would have had ten children of her own by now and no reason to be looking after others' kids or to be running and getting burned alive for an inn or whatever!"

He was unable to put up with such insinuations and leaving the hunter alone went over to the garrulous mourner from the other family.

"If you've come here to talk like that," he said to her, "and not to grieve for your niece, you can get up and leave. Cletia fared no better or worse in this house than your children in your houses. Or are you the kind of parents who only bathe their children in happiness from morning to night? Try asking them . . . Or perhaps," he went on, "you're those lucky parents who never had to bury one of their children—because I've buried four of mine, Cletia is the fifth—and perhaps that's why you're shooting your mouth off so easily today."

The woman was dumbstruck, shrank in her seat, and her sister (who had been just as outspoken) wagged her finger at her as if to say, *That's enough, he's right.* And so the risk that the grief of that evening might dissolve into bitterness and re-crimination was avoided. The woman found her voice again and said to him that though she hadn't fully understood what he had said, she hadn't meant anything of the sort; all she wanted to say was that Cletia had met with such a death . . .

Christoforos declined to waste any more time on her, and with some bitterness he remembered his role and said to everyone: "Eat, drink to Cletia's soul, weep, laugh if you wish, but don't speak badly of me. For whatever wrongs or ills I've done in my life, I've paid in full and more."

And he went back to the hunter.

"If women had *only* tongues," he said to him, "I'd prefer to have cut mine out rather than marry three times."

The evening progressed. And it's true that more than a few, even among the close relatives, the immediate family, ate and drank as though they had for-gotten what had happened—the living sorrow became a vague mourning and almost whet the appetite; the funeral, the fire, the earthquake had exhausted them, and at the same time it was as though a long time had passed since then . . . Moreover, there was no shortage of laughter, and roaring laughter at that, when someone recalled two women years before, cousins or just friends it wasn't certain, neither of them in the prime of her youth, who, whenever and wherever a fire broke out would put on their best clothes and *go to see!* They would go to the fire as if they were going as guests at a wedding. So much so that when people saw them dressed up and made up and there was no fire, they fully expected one to happen—they were seen as harbingers. There was one time when instead of throwing his bucket of water on the fire a man threw it over them and drenched them from head to toe! They swore at him accordingly, but didn't stop their practice. And they would also get dressed up to go to any public dispute ... Eventually, of course, they died.

Someone else recalled that a few years earlier, when a country chapel on the foothills of the mountain had caught fire and they all ran to put it out, they had chanced upon an illicit couple: a married man with his brother's wife! They had been ready for anything, but not that. Things took their lawful course: the woman's deceived husband killed the couple and attempted to commit suicide. But the bullet went into his eye and he was *just* blinded and went to prison. The only person to be saved was the wife of the other man, the one who'd been killed, and she couldn't decide whether she should weep or rejoice that she'd been saved from any more adultery. Eventually she found consolation with another of her husband's brothers, a widower himself, because it seems it's not easy to break such *bonds.*

They also told other stories with fires and monasteries, while Haris—who naturally wouldn't have been absent from Cletia's wake—sat subdued and solitary in a corner and hummed the same song to himself: "Whatever heart Cupid pierces with his arrows ... whatever heart is pierced ... with his arrows ...," and hitting his feet with a cane, as if he were being urged to continue, he graciously added: "The rest we let go, the rest we don't say!" Occasionally, instead of gazing at his feet, he cast a few deep glances at the hunter, gently waving the cane in the air ... At one stage, he went into a room and asked the women for a glass of water. But before they could bring him one, he leapt out of the window and dragged himself like a cripple to the graveyard's closed gate. We never found out what he did there, where daybreak found him, or what happened to Haris in his life. At any rate, he provided the title for this tale.

As to the hunter, one of Christoforos's elder sisters, in Cletia's absence, made up a bed for him in one of the rooms and silently led him to the door. "See you in the morning," she said, and left him, while he was just about to say or ask her something, perhaps. But he didn't persist, nor did she alter her proud—in actual fact ambivalent—stance.

And the sun rose the next morning, was well and truly risen, but the hunter didn't come out; downstairs his tea was getting cold; they warmed it up, and it got cold again. Some of the women had work to do in that room and began to be annoyed at his aristocratic desire to sleep until midday—this had on other occasions given a bed to other people in that house, but no one had forgotten to wake up. So they got their kids to make a noise outside on the stairs, and they pretended to scold them for bothering their aunt's betrothed . . . But nothing; the door didn't open. And moreover (they put their ears to the door), nothing could be heard from inside; the strange suitor showed no signs of life or of awakening . . . From their impatience to hear something, they undoubtedly did keep hearing some noises: sometimes one of the floorboards creaking slightly (but they were unfortunately obliged to admit that it was one of the floorboards *outside* the room that was creaking under their own weight), sometimes, though, they felt sure that the window inside was being opened slowly or that he was clearing his throat while polishing his boots! . . .

Nevertheless, daring to call out to him by his first name, they received no reply. Until the sister who had brought him to that room decided to open the door—after knocking on it more than a few times—and see what was going on. And she found no one inside. The bed was more or less unused, the sheets were cold.

It wasn't enough that he was strange; now he had become unsettling. Who was this man who came and went like the wind? Just a hunter for the mountains? For partridges and wild boar? Or perhaps something else? His behavior had something uncontrollable about it, methodical and uncontrollable—they didn't like to say it, to let their imaginations run wild, but if they had to liken him to something, they couldn't help but recall that *Death* too (in no way impersonal for them or without attributes) had always borne many names: hunter, charmer, horseman, exterminator. Even suitor—there; and this one here was all of those.

They went downstairs, each one more agitated than the other, and told their husbands.

"The hunter's gone again!" (They were all now aware of his previous similar disappearances.)

"He'll have gone over to the inn," they said.

"What inn? Is there an inn anymore?"

And, in fact, a good deal of time would have to pass before they got used to the idea that there was no longer an inn. As for the man in question, though they didn't go to the extremes of their highly imaginative wives—to identify him, that is, with all sorts of crazy things—the husbands nevertheless couldn't deny that his behavior in general confused them too.

They went outside into the marketplace, to where their building had once stood and where now the wretched cinders were still smoking, and there someone told them — he'd already said it to others too — that he had seen the hunter very early at daybreak, when everyone else was sleeping. He had seen him wandering around these ruins, and it had made an impression on him — at first he had thought that it must be Christoforos, inconsolable as he was. He himself had been returning from the house of a sick friend and was walking quickly home when, suddenly, that tall and slender dark shadow that was wandering around as though looking for something had made him stop. He saw the horse a little way off and recognized the hunter . . . Whom, it should be noted, he had seen no more than twice — once the previous day at the graveside and once a couple of years before at the inn — but he could have picked him out of a thousand. "Hey! . . . Hey! . . . ," he called out to him, waving his arm again and again, and he was kind enough to wave his arm back once. "Are you looking for something?" he asked, jumping over some obstacles and going up to him with the aim of asking him more questions, to ask what he was doing there at that time — hadn't Christoforos anywhere in his house to put him up for the night? But the hunter, without exactly turning his back on him, moved farther away. It was very dark, more like nightfall than daybreak. He understood that the hunter was in no mood for conversation and so he left him, again jumping over the obstacles and finding himself back on the road. But he couldn't find peace without hearing the hunter's voice at all: "Hey! . . . ," he called out again from there. "That was the inn belonging to Cletia, to Christoforos . . . Do you want me to tell him anything?" The hunter, as if expecting some such offer, said to him in a clear voice, "Yes. Tell him that I bid him farewell, that I had to leave." "Anything else?" "Nothing."

"I told your father a good few times," he said now to Cletia's brothers, "but he listens to me as though I were making it up! He doesn't believe me. And yet I saw the hunter with my own eyes, even if it was still dark. I heard him — he said what I told you, not much but exactly that. Now I hear that he left your house like a ghost. I don't know what to say . . . there's nothing I can do about that."

It wasn't that Christoforos didn't believe that he had seen the hunter; it was that he was upset by the way that the hunter had left. He had put up with all his eccentricities till now with good humor (some had made him angry but he had gotten over it), but this last act of his — to leave while they were still sleeping — annoyed him particularly, especially after all that had happened and changed. It stayed gnawing at him.

But he didn't want to show it too much — at the supper table, with all the adult and younger members of his family — and he said: "The hunter had a job to do, very early, and he had to leave—he told me last night but I forgot. I forgot . . . But he'll return. Like he told me, he'll return."

"Bite your tongue, you old fool!" one of his sisters said—the one who had prepared the bed for the hunter. "What else is there for him to burn?"

And as for Cletia, among all that everyone said or thought concerning her death, the one thing that was the most important and the most likely totally escaped them. What, that is, Death himself had said to her as he wrapped her in his suffocating embrace: *Let me be the one to take you now, and let others search for the reason later. O Cletia! . . .*

Fourth Tale

LIVELY SOULS AND *SIANKES*, THEIR SHADOWS

Some referred to that big quake as the big *shake-up*. It wasn't just the fire it caused in the inn, destroying it beyond all repair; it was also that the quake brought about considerable damage to most of the houses. Some people thought that all they had to do was simply bolster their cracked or half-crumbled walls, but as soon as they attempted to do so, the walls—like the proverb that says *I wanted to fall so it's good that you pushed me*—collapsed completely, almost crushing them. And this didn't happen only to one or two but to many. And some of these people, who, it was generally agreed, were poverty-stricken and could not find the means to rebuild their houses, were aided, it's said, by some notable gentry from the nearby big town, perhaps from all over the country, at any rate by some benefactors or state officials. So what were for that time large sums of money were given, sometimes in the form of a loan, sometimes in exchange for a little plaque on which would be forever engraved "So-and-so, benefactor," and that spring the place was literally in a state of rebirth and reorganization.

And those who until then had never known a sunny day and suddenly found themselves with a new house which recalled nothing of their old dilapidated abode were the ones who referred to the quake as a *shake-up*, since thanks to this, albeit in an unorthodox way, fortune had shone on them.

Of course, the place perhaps lost something of its old *color* (though there was as yet plenty), but this was a complaint that would be voiced by the more sensitive of those who were still children, when they were grown up and recalled their past in houses that were more complex and expressive, and in smaller rooms . . . For the time being, for the adults of the time, and especially for some of the older and more hapless ones whose lifelong dream had been to build a new house even if it killed them, the house was built, the dream was pieced together, and—in more than a few cases—their wish came true down to the last word: they died without being able to enjoy it for very long. Others enjoyed it, however.

Whatever the case, Christoforos's home, that *complex* of houses joined together all around, suffered next to nothing. Just some minor damage, a few cracks here and there as though roots had sprung from the walls, which were quickly covered over, patched up, or which stayed like that indefinitely. But his inn suffered so much, such was the destruction, that no one was envious of the proverbial endurance of his house.

The winter passed, and while it was still fresh the wound hurt and howled, but it would hurt more—or at least differently—when it began to fester. Spring, in any case, found Christoforos with more wrinkles and a more melancholy look, but also with the heroic decision to rebuild his inn on top of the ashes.

So the required craftsmen and master craftsmen came, the ground was dug up deep and wide, three cocks were sacrificed because one wasn't sufficient, the new foundations were laid, and it was about at this point that Christoforos changed his plans and decided to build a sesame-oil mill. The reason for this was his restless nature—he wanted, he said, to try his luck with sesame, let Cletia take the inn with her—but also without doubt the fact that some people (two smart brothers, his distant nephews) had taken advantage of the destruction of his inn and had hastened—behind his back and while he still wasn't taking it seriously—to build another inn on their own account. "How could we ever imagine," they said by way of an excuse, "that you'd find the courage to build a new inn!"

Such things had also happened in the past. Being a pioneer in many things, Christoforos aroused not only admiration but also enmity among his fellow villagers, with the result that many were simply waiting for an opportunity, and when he suffered something or when things didn't go quite right for him, they themselves reaped the benefit of his ideas. Of course, he had inherited the inn from his father just as his father had from his and so on; but the way he managed it, particularly during the last years, the conditions that prevailed there, as also the three shops surrounding it (aside from the smithy and the tailor's) with merchandise both common and rare, difficult to find even in the neighboring town, all this was new for the times, novel, and ideas out of Christoforos's head, but something which could be exploited by his successors—or stolen by others. Even his many marriages had found imitators, especially in his own family: one of his daughters remarried *without a second thought* when she was widowed, and two of his sons, when they became widowers, kept buzzing around him like flies and were forever mincing their words: "You know, father, it's not easy to raise so many children on their own . . . No matter how well we take care of them, there's nothing like a mother . . . Not that we're particularly keen, but there you are! . . . There are women just waiting, who want nothing more than to bring up motherless children."

"Never mind the excuses and all that motherless children nonsense," Christoforos said to them, "you've found something to grab at and that's the truth of it."

Anyway—as for the sesame-oil mill—he was certain that no one would dare copy him before a good number of years had passed since he was one of the last (of the few) in that area and beyond who knew the secret of *crushing the sesame*.

Building it took four years and a few months. It would have been finished much earlier, but the weather conditions hadn't helped at all. After the earthquake and the fire, none of the other natural elements wanted to remain uninvolved: raging months passed with so many gales and so much snow, but mainly with so much rain, so much flooding, that all the water made the stones soft, and some strangers who had been trapped there for days waiting for the rain to abate a little asked—thirteen years later, when, in another place, they met some younger men and learned that they were grandchildren of Christoforos— whether it was *still* raining in their region! Even then! . . . That's how difficult it was for them to forget those days.

So after this had happened, after they'd also been hit by a hailstorm of the kind that comes once in three generations, everything took a turn for the good and the place rediscovered its normality. Lush vegetation sprang up where not even weeds had grown previously, the crops—which had been absent for two years—now came twice as rich, and Christoforos's sesame-oil mill was finished and was soon in operation, providing work for more and more hands. For they didn't just get oil from the sesame (which was then a basic necessity, olive oil was still unknown in those parts, and was brought in later by the refugees from Asia Minor); they also made tahini from the sesame seeds and halva from the tahini. People had their bellies filled.

It was then, too, that they finished the houses, the new ones from the *shake-up*, that had remained half-built, so that whatever cataclysms they hadn't already been subjected to could pass over them.

At that time, Hesychios was forty years old, fine and handsome as ever, *like an angel with wings (but also cloven hooves,* thought Febronia, who was tormented at times by incredible suspicion and envy, the kind that poisons the body, but doesn't destroy it), and she herself was fifty-four, just two years previously having brought into the world her last son, Sakis or Benjamin. Thomas-two-eyes and Safi-Lisafi were already five, and all the other brothers and sisters followed, or rather preceded, with their own ages that were not very different the one from the other. There was also Konstantakis from Febronia's first marriage, who was already a grown twenty-eight-year-old man, married with two children and a third on the way, just like his two younger brothers. There was no Rodanthe. But there was also the fruit of her onetime love for Hesychios, the most difficult and unruly of all of them: Argyris—and let's not forget his various other five brothers and sisters, the ones from the other poor wretches like Rodanthe, all children between about sixteen and eighteen, whom we can't mention one by one: it's inevitable, given that we chose such a labyrinth instead of an easier path, that some characters will remain in the shadows and in silence so that light might be shed on others, or so that these too might appear eventually and speak elsewhere.

On the other hand, in the same sprawling house there were also Hesychios's seven brothers and sisters, without including all those who departed when still small, forgotten by time, and also without our ignoring the five elder children from Christoforos's first marriage with Petroula, as well as the other five from Eftha's first marriage. These ten were now middle-aged, with their own children and grandchildren—and, to be truthful, half of them were already dead, the most recent being Cletia.

With Persa, his third wife, Christoforos had no children, and so many bets were lost. Anyhow, she had seven from two previous marriages (a blessing, they said; it could have been fourteen), two of whom, men the same age as Hesychios, visited her from time to time, while one of her daughters lived there, but no one had ever seen the other four, who were scattered in distant parts.

It should be of no surprise to us that Christoforos himself had many brothers and sisters, though his parents, Lukas and Georgiana, limited themselves to one marriage; and besides both of them died quite young, one after the other. All of them with their families lived, if not in the same house, then in adjacent or neighboring houses: they were separated only by a common wall, between the yards, the parlors, or the backyards, and they were united by regular bickering caused by these party walls; all this kept them in contact and alert, given that grumbling is sometimes also communication. When the sisters got married, they naturally went to the homes of their husbands, to the common walls and rows there. But there were two sisters still unmarried, one older and one younger than Christoforos, and these remained and died in the family house.

The latter, the younger one, was not exactly their sister; Lukas had adopted her when, while still only small, she was left orphaned by her parents, who worked on his holdings. They had met a tragic death; they had run beneath a tree to shelter from a sudden summer downpour and were struck by lightning. In front of them, almost untouched, was the half a watermelon they had been eating, the forks still plunged into its heart . . . Their little daughter had the lovely name of Violetta, and they called her Letta for short, then later it became Lily to make it easier: "Here lili, switi gimmi," all the other kids would say to poke fun at her, meaning, "There's money, give me a sweet," but, unfortunately, instead of money, they would pinch and punch her plump and tender flesh. But the biggest misfortune—after the lightning bolt and also before it—for the Lily in question was not her nickname with its consequences. After all, it was a rare thing for someone not to have a nickname at that time—there was one man who till a ripe old age was called Chooey by everyone, because, when still only small, he had slipped down one day in the snow letting out a loud *aaachoo* (sneeze); if you asked for him by his actual name, no one knew who you meant . . . No, the biggest misfortune for the Lily in question was that she had been born deaf and dumb, both she and her brother, who was a little older than her and who had been taken and raised by others.

In time, of course, she turned into a sharp-witted, auburn-haired girl, with eyes the color of almonds and a particularly well-defined mouth, and no one suspected at first sight that this pretty and lively girl could neither speak nor hear. Besides, she understood everything, had fashioned her own language, rich in gestures, facial expressions, and inarticulate sounds, and it was up to the others, those who could speak, to make sure that they understood her.

Meanwhile, Petroula, hounded by another kind of misfortune, had come to Lukas's house (not as a foster-daughter but simply as a housemaid), and Lily suffered greatly when before anyone else she got wind of the fact that Christoforos—who till then had made eyes at her even though she was dumb, even though she was his adopted sister—had now turned his attention to the new orphan girl in the family. Yes, she suffered greatly.

Indeed, when she saw that marriage arrangements were being made . . . and sensing that she would be unable to change anything, she left them all and went to her real brother. She found him beside a few sheep and as many dogs passionately playing a flute. She waited patiently, but given that she couldn't hear the sound of his flute, though neither could he hear—in any way—the twigs that snapped behind him, under her feet, or in her hands, Lily began to grow impatient, to flare up . . . She fell to the ground sobbing, surrendering herself to the most unrestrained and frenzied crying and bringing the twigs down on her own head—her hair filled with thorns, her mouth with earth, her lips were split open. And for her to be writhing like that behind her brother's back and for him to go on playing without a care in the world was for her UNBEARABLE,

something that pushed her mute suffering to the limits, turning it into rage . . .
Even his dogs, which at other times would bark or run as soon as they heard
or smelled the slightest thing, were gazing now towards her with their heads
slightly raised and their eyes expressionless, as if they saw nothing, as if, when
beside the deaf and dumb, the animals too lost their senses.

It doesn't take much for a person to lose it or to surpass his misery by experiencing it to the full. A hair's breadth is all that separates us from everything, and
Lily covered the distance, picking up a rock . . . The dogs appeared to wake up,
and her brother stopped playing, and was about to get up, but it was too late:
the rock came down on his head. How, when did it happen? She felt so helpless—certainly she didn't want to do it, it wasn't at all her intention to kill her
brother. Her brother! . . . She wondered what was left to her from then on, what
else could life offer her . . . What else other than abhorrence and the ultimate
bravery of returning to a house where they had adopted and betrayed her, with
a rock in her hand, without saying or concealing anything.

As soon as she stepped into the yard, the thought came to her: *Now I'm
not only more beautiful than that bashful Petroula, who they preferred for their
brother's wife, but I'm also worse than she is: I killed my brother the shepherd—
I didn't wait for someone else to do it, I didn't wait for some unknown shepherd!*

"What's that, Lily?" Georgiana asked her, sitting behind some railings and
darning socks.

*My-brother-sent-it-for-the-wedding-of-your-son-with-the-daughter-of-the-
priest-who-killed-the-shepherd!* said Lily, with her fingers opening and closing
like a pair of crazed scissors in front of her mouth.

"And why are your eyes red, what are you crying for?" Georgiana asked her.

For nothing, she said.

"You should be happy that my son is going to marry Petroula," the woman
remarked, bending over her darning again.

Why should I be happy, nobody's happy, said the dumb girl. And at that point
she awoke . . . it was all a dream.

A dream that she had gone to find her brother in the hills, the flute and twigs,
too, were a dream, the sleepy dogs, her desperation that had led her to fill her
mouth with earth and take hold of the rock . . . Only the joy of Christoforos and
Petroula—the most unbearable thing of all for her in that present period—was
not a dream, only that. And their joy had been consummated the previous day.

And when she went out into the yard and saw the new bride doing chores
and walking strangely, with her legs somewhat apart, weak-willed, with circles
around her tired eyes, Lily—who in spite of her dumbness was foul-mouthed—
went up to her and said: *So did you get your fill of his poleax last night, eh, Miss*

Prissy Priest's Daughter? Come up to here, did it? (And she drew a line with her hand from the lowest to the highest part of her belly.) *Went in a candle and came out a wick, did it, eh? Ha ha. Pretending to be coy and not to understand. Who do you think you're fooling?*

But Petroula really didn't understand Lily's expressive and merciless tongue—and she took to her heels.

These two together, living in the same house and eating at the same table, sister-in-law and daughter-in-law to all intents and purposes, never got on well despite their various efforts—valiant yet half-hearted—to get on better and try to understand each other. *We've nothing in common, we never did,* Lily said to everyone; *when my belly is rumbling from hunger, she asks where's the bird that's warbling—the only bird is in her brain!* And for her part, Petroula would grumble: "I don't know what I've done for her to dislike me so much. If I say white, she says black, and if I start to say black so as not to provoke her, she says white—there's no getting to the bottom of it." Anyhow, Christoforos, half-jokingly, often counseled her to guard herself against the beardless and the lame, against the hot southwesterly and the locusts—and last of all against the spite of that deaf-mute, Lily. He never thought of counseling her to guard herself against her father the priest, who, beardless, was rotting in prison and no longer appeared to be a danger.

Nevertheless, at Petroula's untimely death, Lily cried more than anyone would have expected, even though they all knew how sensitive she was to various events and how, while shouting and raging at someone, she could, the very next moment, smother him in hugs and kisses, or feel smothered herself by her pangs of remorse for upsetting him . . . Whatever the case, Christoforos had a hard time tearing her away from Petroula's coffin (and there wasn't an ounce of pretense in her grief), so much so that he began to suspect—but without saying anything to anyone—that perhaps Lily had had a *hand* in Petroula's death (she was capable of anything), and it wasn't because she had returned pallid and upset from her trip to the prison. And anyway who would have returned fresh and contented? But then again who would have died in such a short time like that, senselessly, if other causes, perhaps more difficult to be named, hadn't intervened?

Yet when you don't have evidence, suspicions alone are pointless and are soon forgotten.

With Eftha, his second wife, Lily got on like a house on fire—*on fire* with all that this might possibly entail—during all the years that they lived together under the same roof. Of course, they argued and were cold to each other for short periods, but without little things like this it would have been like a river-bank without any greenery . . . And with Eftha's children too, both those she brought with her and those she acquired in that house, Lily was kind. She was useful when they got sick or when they fought over who was going to eat the best cherries and who would be left with the stalks. Besides, their aunt Lily—as we're talking about cherries—had the fewest (or the most eccentric) demands, and her delight was to eat the wormy and rotten cherries that the others threw away. She said she found them sweeter and riper. So when—at some crucial stage of their growth—the cherries were subjected to heavy rain and filled with worms, with the result that they all opened them up before eating them or, if they saw *something* inside, threw them away, Lily found ready and abundant food. On the contrary, in better years with very few worms, it was now Lily who had to open up the cherries and look inside . . . and if she found no worm inside, she would leave them for the others: such was the extent of her eccentricity. She even persuaded some of her nephews and nieces to do the same, so that the *best* cherry in those old and unsung days, the cherry of discord as we might say, might not always have been the one that a proper and less adventurous cherry eater of today might imagine.

But Eftha had also caught her doing *unprincipled things* to the kids, par-ticularly to the unsuspecting infants. As, for example, secretly squeezing and pinching them, causing a great deal of heartrending crying, while she turned her face toward them with the most angelic expression, with the greatest loving care, puzzlement, and concern over their crying . . . Then the young and later adolescent Cletia would go—or was sent by Eftha—and take the infant from Lily's arms, as decorously and discreetly as she could. The crying stopped after a while, if not immediately, and Lily would smile somewhat condescendingly at this *common situation,* or purse her lips and leave.

At other times, Eftha had caught her eating the food (creams with starch, with crushed fruit) that was intended for one of the babies. Lily would offer to feed it, but in actual fact she would torment it: as soon as it opened its drooling mouth, she would quickly put the spoon into her own and then dip it again in the bowl—out of ten spoonfuls, it was questionable whether three went into the baby's mouth. And so it remained with its mouth drooling, amazed in front of the bowl that emptied without it filling its stomach, and often it didn't wait for the pinches from its lovely and speechless nanny as dessert to burst into tears . . . Eftha also caught her doing something far worse without any compunction: when the food was somewhat more solid and it was only natural that someone would first chew it and then give it to the baby, the still toothless infant, Lily, after having chewed the food and put it into the little mouth (which was waiting eagerly), would often take it back—with fingers like soft and flexible hooks— and put it back into her own mouth, for good this time.

These babies had their fair share of crying at her hands. And *gaping mouths*.

With the older ones, those aged from around five to ten, Lily did other things. Such as pretending—whenever it was her turn to go upstairs to get the beds ready—that she was afraid of the dark, afraid in case her lamp went out, and she wanted one of the kids to keep her company; she explained by gestures and a mass of facial contortions that when she was small some adult would always take her for company as soon as it grew dark (it appears that at that time the children maintained a good relationship with the dark, whereas the adults had lost theirs). So she would choose one and go upstairs with him or her—in fact, she would follow the child up the stairs, sometimes tickling it under the arms or pinching it to make it run, to make it hurry. Upstairs, she would begin to make the beds, going to and fro without paying much attention to the child's presence and, at some moment, when she was shaking one of the sheets to open it, the lamp, puff, would go out! Lily would jump with a shriek that reached up to the ceiling, panic would take hold of her, the panic would get to her heart, and then, half-swooning, she would ask the child, boy or girl, to rub her a little *here*, on her breast. At first on top of her clothing, while she herself sat on the edge of the bed or of a chair, and then under her clothing and lying down now—even on the floor—with sleepy eyes. Later still, she would ask two or three of the children to go upstairs with her for various jobs, even if it was midday, and it was rare for her not to have some problem with her heart while up there . . . And so a multitude of little fingers would dutifully massage her from her neck to her belly, and when Lily *woke up*, she had nothing wrong with her. She would appear not to remember anything, while they were out of breath and trembling.

Silently and ponderously, Eftha observed all this through holes or cracks that the need opened up for her. More than a few times she lost her time, left her work unfinished to go see what Lily was up to with the children and be astounded, annoyed. She said nothing to Christoforos because she didn't want any fuss and because, in general, she was of the opinion that we shouldn't confess every sin to the priest. However, she would speak now and again to the children themselves and urge them to be obedient to their dumb aunt, not to defy her, because they would give her cause to be angry and everything would turn bad—but, she went on, they were not to do everything she asked them to do, because then no one could say how far things would go.

For her part, Lily evidently discerned this *leniency* in Eftha's behavior, and for this reason her feelings for her were often expressed so profusely and loudly (inarticulate cries one after the other like those of a happy monkey came straight out of her throat), that they literally terrified the others, completely pushing them aside. She gave Eftha to understand that if she had that kind of *contact* with the children and if sometimes she *took them* with her, it was not for what the clever busybodies thought but because God had deprived her of *that*, her speech.

Eftha believed her; she couldn't do otherwise. "I know that you're not a bad person," she said (gesticulating the way the other did), "you're just dumb and that's enough." What she meant exactly even she didn't know, but that's what she felt and that's what she said.

Nevertheless, once she saw something that really got her back up, that was beyond all leniency. From an internal window that went up and down like a guillotine, covered with clothes on hangers, with a sheet over the clothes so they wouldn't get dusty (there were many such windows in the house, in the walls between the parlor and the other rooms), she saw Lily lying down in a strange position, supporting herself slantwise on one elbow, with her belly resting half on the bed and one shoulder turned back, but, heaven forbid, with her skirts rolled up to her pelvis . . . with her mouth open, trembling: four children were around her, sitting at her knees like the newly converted, drawing with their fingers the sign of the cross on her lily-white legs and then stooping and kissing the cross! . . . With her finger, Lily showed them where else to do it . . . and where else . . . till her longings brought the crosses and the kisses up to her left buttock.

"O, this is going too far!" said Eftha, and unable to control herself, she brought her hand down on the window—it didn't smash, but the entire wall shook.

Inside, Lily, sensing rather than hearing the noise, quickly covered up her legs and the four little boys found themselves huddled up, their hearts in their mouths, under the bed.

Eftha—and it was a miracle that she didn't fall down the stairs—ran to the inn and confessed a few things to her husband concerning his dumb sister and what kind of things this precious woman was teaching the kids. She was really upset and expected all hell to break loose in the family.

"We'll all be consumed in the fires of hell after what my eyes saw today," she told him, shaking and spluttering.

But instead of what she had imagined all the time that she had said nothing, Christoforos didn't appear to be unduly angry, or even to be all that surprised.

"Calm yourself, woman, don't work yourself up," he said to her, "she does all that unthinkingly, she doesn't understand, she doesn't have any conscience."

"And you think it's all right, do you, when people don't have any conscience?" asked Eftha, whose mind, of course, went to someone *unscrupulous*.

But all Christoforos meant was simply someone *unaccountable*.

"She doesn't have any, there's nothing we can do about it," he said, "she's innocent."

"Innocent!" exclaimed Eftha. "How can you even use the word? Not even God is innocent in such cases."

"Even so, we still arrive at the same conclusion," retorted Christoforos.

"Listen here, I don't know what you have to say—you seem to me to be a bit lacking in *compunction*, yourself—but all this business with Lily has to stop," said Eftha. "I turned a blind eye all this time and said nothing out of fear that you'd be harsh with her, but today I opened my eyes and I wish I hadn't. Once again I'm the one who comes out the loser . . . I don't understand it. You'll end up by telling me that I shouldn't have said anything to you—perhaps I should go and kiss her backside too?"

"If you'd told me about it earlier, we might have been able to put a stop to her," said Christoforos, "it wouldn't have got as far as her backside."

"There, it's all my fault again," concluded Eftha, who, whenever she felt herself being stabbed by others, continued the business on her own, plunging the knife even deeper.

"All right, don't carry on like that, I'll talk to her," Christoforos promised, "I'll put her in her place."

And sure enough, before long, they sent Lily elsewhere on the pretext of caring for an elderly couple, childless but not penniless, in the nearby town.

But after two months, like cats that never lose their sense of direction, wherever you bundle them off to, Lily returned to them. With her hair styled a different way, with something different in general both in her appearance and her dress, slightly more plump and smelling of lavender and rosewater—perhaps to remind them that she was called Violetta. She told them that the two old folk had accused her of stealing from them and thrown her out, or rather that she had preferred herself not to put up with such slander, and she humbly asked them whether she might still consider as her home, her refuge, the big old house of dear departed Lukas, her father to all intents and purposes.

"Even if we send her away again, she'll come back," Christoforos said to Eftha, who viewed Lily's return somewhat cautiously, but not—paradoxically perhaps—with hostility.

"What do you say?"

"I say that God finds a nest for the cross-eyed bird," Eftha replied, and in this way she let all of them understand that she considered it all water under the bridge and welcomed back the prodigal daughter as an integral part of the family.

Lily stooped and kissed her two hands.

"But promise me," said Eftha (who decided to take the opportunity to adopt a more severe attitude towards her, to assert herself and not turn a blind eye in future), "promise me that you won't get up to such things again with the children, otherwise there'll be trouble."

I promise you! said Lily and, crossing her two forefingers and making a cross of sorts, she gave it a smacking kiss as a sign of her promise.

Eftha's eyebrows rose and fell.

Shortly afterwards, they learned that the couple in the town with the snow-white hair and the silver grips on their walking sticks had died—first the woman in her sleep, then the man while he was eating his breakfast in the kitchen.

"It was you who finished them off and we've only heard about it now," Eftha said to Lily without believing it completely.

Me? I never did any such thing! Lily retorted, feeling offended, but meanwhile Eftha hardly had time to take out of her case a whole selection of unknown dainty objects: a little bronze statue, a long woman's hat pin, a tiny bone dog, an empty powder case, a neck scarf, a handful of beads from a necklace . . .

"Where did you get all these things, Lily?" she asked her.

They gave them to me, they gave them to me . . . they were throwing them away, they didn't want them anymore, she said.

Eftha kept on pulling things out, and in one corner she found something round and shiny, flat, and when she pressed it at one point, it opened up and became a little double mirror: the one side showed everything magnified, unnatural, the other showed everything normal. But this soon vanished; other hands took it.

As for the rest of the things, given that she couldn't return them to their rightful owners, Eftha put them here and there around the house, using them as decorations so they wouldn't be wasted. Among them was a lovely bottle containing a blue-and-yellow butterfly that was still alive, half-alive (how strange; how did it get in or how did they get it into the bottle?), which a few days later— maybe because of the change of environment, maybe because it had completed the cycle of its strange life—ceased to make even the slightest, the faintest movement.

After that, Lily behaved herself. The children passed by her, passed by again, waited for her to call them, to make suggestive faces at them, sometimes they even provoked her with the old "here lili, switi gimmi," but Lily would just chase them away, she even threw stones at them sometimes, and when they went away and they came back to look at her, they would see her standing for hours in the same spot, totally still, indecisive, as though not knowing what it was she wanted.

"Everybody grows up eventually, even Lily," remarked Christoforos, thinking that it wouldn't be at all a bad idea to look for a suitable man to marry her. But at that time, it was easier for a camel to pass through the eye of a needle, as Eftha said to him, than to marry a woman who had turned thirty, and a deaf-mute as well, like his adopted sister, even if she had her own charms.

Besides, Lily herself, when she found out what Christoforos was up to, was furious, felt offended, glared at him, and said something to him that she wouldn't have said even if she'd been able to use her tongue: *Don't even think about it,* she told him, *you stay faithful to Eftha and I stay faithful to you! Or do you think that I've forgotten?* (She depicted faith by joining two fingers from each hand in circles and linking the circles together; in just the same way that wedding wreaths symbolize the newlywed couple as being of one flesh and one body.)

At the same time, however, it's easier to lose your soul than your habit. And the following spring they caught Lily in one of the fields, beneath a pear tree, reveling with a little Turkish boy.

This boy, or rather his parents and two elder brothers, had once been in Lukas's employment, but afterwards this foreign family was split up and each of them found work with one of his sons. They were so-called bondsmen, which sounds strange when one considers that the Turks then (and for three centuries previously) were occupying the country . . . Nevertheless, situations and needs arose, and some of the Turkish occupiers (the hounded, families that were destitute or decimated) left their own parts and came there to earn their living, working in the houses or the pastures of those under occupation, and even calling them *effendi*. This young boy, then, Orhan was his name, and his mother worked for Christoforos. They lived in one of the lower rooms at the back, with their own customs and their own prayers, and every Sunday they would meet with the father and the other two brothers and eat all together. They even observed Ramadan.

The woman in her yashmak (who, it should be noted, secretly believed in the Virgin Mother of the Christians, but only in the Virgin Mother) worked in the house in winter and outside in the fields in summer, while young Orhan went wherever he was told and wherever they sent him. So Lily must have told him to go with her one day and, naturally, he went . . .

It was Eftha who saw them, yes, Eftha again—it was her fate to see such things. And here's what she saw this time: Lily lying on the ground, rollicking with laughter (and her laughter was no different from that of any woman) and jerking her legs up and down, with Orhan, sometimes sitting beside her and sometimes going around her, tickling her under her arms, on her neck, under her feet, sometimes with his fingers and sometimes with a long feather. Lily's pleasure must have been so great that her tongue was hanging out of her mouth and her eyes were glistening and brimming with tears of mirth.

Behind the bushes, Eftha crossed herself and withdrew. *After all*, she thought, *for a little Turkish boy to be tickling a dumb woman isn't exactly improper—it could have been worse.* So she went off, but before going far, she changed her mind and went back: "I've started to turn a blind eye again," she said out loud to herself; "not improper for a young boy to be tickling a grown woman? Of course it is! There are those *who whet their tongue like a sword!* . . . Phew, it's a bit strong to talk like that about a dumb sister-in-law, but it suits her to a T the way she had her tongue hanging out like that! . . ."

But she found no one when she arrived back at the pear tree. Unless she had taken the wrong path and this was a different tree. Or unless Lily and Orhan had gone somewhere else in the meantime.

Very soon, someone else saw Lily eating from a plate of beans with Orhan. There was nothing reprehensible about the scene, except that from then on, every so often, others would see them eating beans or broad beans or chickpeas from the same plate, but not with two spoons and not entirely fairly: Lily was the only one with a spoon in her hand, and though she would only put one bean or chickpea in Orhan's mouth, she would put two in her own. With infinite care, she would pick them up each time on the tip of her spoon and say to the boy in some hoarse, slurring yet encouraging vowel sounds: *eee . . . aa . . . eee . . . ii . . . iii . . . oo . . . eee . . . ooo . . . aa . . . eee . . . ii . . . iii . . . oo . . . eee . . . oo . . .* In her language: one for you, two for me, one for you, two for me.

"Why do you give only one to him and two to yourself?" someone asked her. *Because I'm a grown-up*, replied Lily.

"And you, why do you let her only give you one? Are you stupid?" the same person said to Orhan.

The boy raised one of his shoulders, slowly rubbing his chin on it and gazing at Lily with dark, mysterious eyes.

But one day things changed. Now it was Orhan who held the spoon and in a thick yet comic idiom—because he too had been late as a child in learning to talk and had a speech impediment so his Greek was *orhanic*—he would say to Lily: "Hawon fer'ye, edu f'miii," and acted accordingly, giving one to her and two to himself, one to her and two to himself . . . Lily not only didn't complain about this inequality but actually took pride in him . . . "How come? What happened?" Eftha asked, and she replied: *Why not? Now Orhan has grown up!*

She explained this with significance, with a gleeful look in her eyes, a look even more mischievous than usual, so much so that Eftha felt a cold shiver running down her spine, and pushing Orhan and his spoon aside, she asked Lily just what she meant, what she meant exactly by that *has grown up.* But Lily, after opening her mouth and virtually slamming it shut, began with two fingers to pretend that she was sewing it with needle and thread—in other words, that no one would ever get a word out of her not even in the ages to come!

And one evening, everyone was alarmed by the sound of cries like laments mixed with cussing and swearing, by banging and thudding at the back of the house. Orhan's mother was in a rage . . . She had caught him arm in arm with Lily in her own bedroom! She had popped out to go to the house next door to see one of her other sons who had been sick for days, intending to spend the night there and return home the next morning: she had done this twice already. She had left Orhan on his own. But she came back a little after midnight, probably to get something and then leave again, and she was taken aback by what she found there: she saw the dumb woman and the boy in her bed clinging to each other like blind puppies. And she went crazy. She cursed the day and the hour that she was born, and her mother for giving birth to her, that she had found herself in that place and that house serving those heathens and having her children abused by deaf-mutes and a thousand and one other things. At the same time she wrecked her own home, throwing her mattress and covers out the window, together with spices hanging on the walls, strings of garlic, stools, cushions, a sack of walnuts, even her own slippers, even her yashmak . . . without finding peace. And, of course, renouncing their Virgin Mother for good.

Orhan was whimpering as he dragged himself from corner to corner. She had beat him black and blue with a leather belt belonging to his father—it was a wonder that she didn't hang him by his toenails.

Lily had managed to rush outside, to find her own folks, who didn't know what to do with her . . . One of Lukas's sons spat on his hands and began to beat her.

Her eyes blackened and with pains in her kidneys, Eftha—she had tried to stop her brother-in-law and had herself felt the weight of his hands—reflected that Sodom and Gomorrah didn't exist only in the Scriptures but also between Lily's legs, and she was afraid that she herself would turn into a pillar of salt at any moment. Nevertheless, the time was rapidly approaching when she would give birth to another child, prematurely, paying in this way for this latest rumpus in the household.

In the same period, two of her daughters (one from each of her marriages) and one of her sisters-in-law were also expecting, if not for the first time. Such a thing—mother and daughter being pregnant at the same time—was not something rare then or reprehensible: aunts and uncles, nieces and nephews grew up together and being of the same age were more like cousins, something that—though common—also caused a bit of a headache: how could you accept as your uncle or aunt, when you were five or even twenty-five, a boy or a girl you went to school with, played with, or with whom you stuck out your tongue at the grown-ups or at each other? Not to mention that there were some nephews and nieces quite brazenly older than their aunts and uncles! Personally, we can recall—as children of one of the last children of this chain—that we called one of our father's sisters, in other words our aunt, *Grandma* until the day she died, and this didn't seem in the slightest bit strange to us. On the contrary, it was difficult for us to accept that such a woman was *only* our aunt, given that she reached an almost mythic age and had so many children, grandchildren, and great-grandchildren (perhaps even great-great-grandchildren) that even a ship's crew would be envious of their number. By the same reasoning, we called all her children—who were, of course, our first cousins—aunts and uncles, and we thought of their children as our cousins, though we were their aunts and uncles . . . Real hodge-podge!

But let's turn back again, to a hundred years earlier.

It was summer, and Lily was under close supervision—she complained that they didn't even let her fart on her own. On the other hand, in the back wing of the house, underage marriages had taken place: after the episode with Lily, Orhan's mother had hastened to get him married to a girl of their own ethnicity, from a family like theirs living in a nearby house. There weren't so many such families in that place, but at least there were some—and it goes without saying that these families were closely knit.

The bride was only twelve years old and Orhan—who looked ten—was fourteen. They still smelled of milk and chased black beetles, but Orhan's mother insisted, having thrown a fit, and so the two children found themselves married. To smooth over all that had happened with Lily, Christoforos generously endowed the newlyweds, giving them a separate room—but not in his house: he arranged with one of his brothers for them to go to his house and, naturally, to work for him. The two kids still couldn't understand what had happened to them, what had changed in their routine; the girl was still playing with rag dolls and Orhan brought her walnuts that he'd cracked with a pestle, putting the pieces into her mouth one by one and sometimes leaving his finger inside to be licked by her tongue . . . Isn't this how it all begins?

And once, following her eyes that suddenly became fixed elsewhere, somewhere over his shoulder, he turned round and saw Lily's face behind the window, with her hands curved round her cheeks and brow, gazing at them as she might gaze at a distant, unforgettable *nightmare*. Just this, then she rushed away. It was a very long time before they saw her again; she left them alone.

Eftha was still two and a half months away from giving birth. But what with the beating and everything else, when still in her seventh month, while exerting herself to finish a job in the fields with Lily—so that they wouldn't have to come again the next day—she clearly felt the premature signs. Panicking, she sent her dumb sister-in-law to quickly fetch a woman from one of the other fields.

Lily ran to the top of a low rise and saw only empty expanses all around her, golden-red and drowsy in the setting sun. To call for help in the hope that someone in the distance might hear her was not possible . . . so she waved her kerchief in vain and went back to Eftha—who was already in labor.

Don't carry on like that, don't be afraid! she said to her using her hands; *I'll help you! I don't know what to do but I'll learn, you can show me!*

Eftha was heaving as though she had an entire mountain inside her body that was pushing to get out. This didn't frighten her overly much; she had been through it many times and knew that eventually it would be over and that all that remains of the *mountain* is a *mouse*—but she was afraid of the consequences that the slightest wrong or sudden movement by an inexperienced midwife might have, even more so given that it was from such a case that one of her children, Lukas, had been born a cripple; she didn't want a repetition of this for anything in the world, and she said to Lily outright, almost insultingly, to stand aside, get out of the way, and not interfere—she would give birth on her own, without any help, whatever happened.

Lily, crawling virtually on all fours, went and hid behind the trunk of a walnut tree and presently she started to cry and nervously clutch at her clothes as she secretly watched Eftha's torment on the ground and saw other things as well that she had no idea a woman could do . . . *Even if I'd had a tongue, I'd have lost it now,* she thought to herself.

And so, before losing what she didn't have, before going crazy and finding herself up the tree and leaping from there (because that's what she thought of doing), she raced like the wind back to Eftha and, though completely inexperienced, knowing just how little confidence she inspired and feeling scared and nauseated at the sight, she undertook to deliver the baby.

In her dizziness and exhausting efforts, Eftha was still gesticulating *no* with one hand and shaking her head as if wanting to chase her away again, but Lily simply ignored her and, guided purely by instinct, exhausted herself by her own courage, by the most agonizing and voiceless emotion, she managed so well in the end that now it was Eftha who was crying and thanking her. "Maybe your destiny is to deliver babies just as it's mine to give birth to them?" she asked her. But Lily had done and seen so much that day that she had no mind left for any answer.

And in this way, Minas, albeit two months prematurely, joined the family maze, while just a few days previously, in one of the house's high-ceilinged bedrooms, the wife of one of his older brothers gave birth to her third daughter in a row (each time they set their store out for a boy and each time they found themselves with a girl), and in the following month two of his sisters gave birth to two more girls—all nieces of the still minuscule Minas.

As for Lily, she had found her path, they said, after listening to Eftha's counsel and training for nine months with the oldest and most skilled midwife in the area. After four months, she allowed them to cauterize and remove two of the nails on her right hand (this was a sacrifice imposed by the profession, the art of delivering without causing any wounds or infections in the innermost parts), and from the ninth month on she did everything and her teacher simply supervised, intervening only if there was some special need. So that eventually (who would have believed it) she herself, an ignorant deaf-mute, became the most skilled midwife of her times. And if at first the parturient women hesitated to summon her, taking into account what they had heard about her and the children she gathered around her—all this was set aside: no one had fingers like hers when it came to delivering.

Five years after Minas's birth, in that very same field, Eftha was once again writhing on the ground, but this time for another reason, a much more serious one: this woman, who had killed snake after snake in her lifetime, and sometimes hung them on the fence for passersby to see (and for some of them to take and claim as their own handiwork), who required no more than a barely perceptible ripple on the ground or in the air, a sss less audible than that of a passing fly to recognize in what direction she had to go and where she should wait till the unsuspecting reptile emerged for her to pin down, was now journeying herself, in terrible pain, to the other world, having been bitten on the leg by a little poisonous viper.

On the other hand, they said that on that day Eftha was out looking for death; that if the viper hadn't appeared, Eftha would have forced it out of its hole without any ado; that, in a manner of speaking, it was time for her to make her peace with the snakes.

"She had woken up different that morning—like every other day, but different," said Christoforos, "and as we were on our way to the field, she must have asked me at least five times what day it was. 'Who are you expecting, woman?' I asked her. 'No one,' she said, 'just asking.' 'But you've asked so many times.' 'Yes?,' she said. 'I don't recall.' And her eyes were strained and wandering, her mouth a mere stripe."

When they arrived, everyone set to work apart from her. She kept going over to two of her little grandchildren, who were tied by rope to a tree so that they wouldn't wander off, and asking them, "What is it that's making you so restless today? Do you want water? Be good and Grandma will go and bring you some water . . . Which direction do you want her to go? This way? That way?"

They nodded, pointing in the direction they wanted her to go (and sometimes each pointed a different way), and Eftha would go off every so often for water . . . they would lose sight of her . . . then see her again coming and going over to the children . . .

The same thing was done systematically by one of their lazy neighbors—a next-door neighbor and a next-field neighbor. He so disliked working in summer, the digging, the gathering, the reaping or harvesting, that his delight was to take his wife or one of his younger children with him—the stork visited them very often too—in order to have an excuse every so often; and at the child's slightest murmur he would put down his spade and rush over to ask it, "What is it then? Why is my good little boy crying? Is he thirsty? Does he want some water? Ah, Daddy's going to go now and bring some, he'll go and bring some water straightaway!" And he would set off with a jug in his hands, full-grown man that he was, to go to some tap at the back of beyond—ignoring others that were much closer—to bring water to his child and escape the work . . . When he returned—and always something would happen to delay him even more— "My, my," he'd say to those who were bent over working and saw the sun between their legs, "you must have thought I'd forgotten you, that I don't want to do my share," and he'd take up his spade again for a while. They hardly had time to see him digging before he was back again, beside the child, asking if he wanted water . . .

Eftha did the same that day. Except that she didn't go off with a jug in her hands, but with her spade under her arm—and the others saw her from afar, somewhere different each time, searching or *spying* the ground like a diviner.

"Where on earth do you keep disappearing to?" Christoforos asked her during one of her brief returns. "And what's all this business with the water and the kids all the time? Has that dad of theirs, the water-bearer, died and you've taken over his job?"

"Don't joke about it, Christoforos," she said to him, "there's a treacherous snake circling around us today, but I can't catch it, it makes no sound. That's why I keep asking the children. It's not only Jesus who loves children, the Serpent loves them too—they might be able to show me where it's hiding . . . Little hands pointing at random, they're the ones to trust!"

In a world of her own, he thought to himself, and he told her to leave it for another time and help them a little, because the work was going slowly and he had to get back to the inn early that evening.

"You're right," she said. But before long they were looking for her again.

In the afternoon, Cletia came with little Minas. She brought them cold pumpkin pie with diluted sour yogurt to refresh them, along with her broken back as she put it. And she also had unpleasant news about Theagenis, recently rechristened Hesychios, grievances, objections, and suchlike, but she couldn't see his *godmother*—as she had christened Eftha—to tell her and get it off her chest. When she learned that Eftha had been chasing a snake all morning, she was puzzled: she had never wasted so much time, she said, on an oversized worm.

At that very same time, when the sun was scorching hot, Eftha—on another of her inexplicably persistent searches, soaked to the skin with sweat and a good few fields away from her family, on another patch of land that also belonged to them—passed like a shadow beside the lazy neighbor . . . lying on his back, far from the shade of any tree, naked from the waist up and with his trousers down to his groin and saying, his eyes closed, in a slow and expressive voice: "Cast down your rays, O sun, and burn us, wretches that we are! . . . Cast down your rays, I said! . . . Wretches that we are! . . ." At the same time, he tipped the flask of water he had on his chest, and as it dripped he cooled himself somewhat. When he got fed up with this, he emptied the rest in one gulp into his mouth, without opening his eyes, without sitting up—so that he choked, began to cough, to fling his hair back and curse the damned water . . . before seeing, as he was getting ready to lie back down again, a woman like Eftha just a few yards in front of him, who at that moment was turning her eyes away from him to continue, stooping, on her way.

The swift and almost frightened turn of her head made him feel uncomfortable, and he pulled his trousers up to his waist and searched for his shirt. "She'll tell my wife," he thought, "but it's not as though she saw me doing anything, is it? I was sunning myself . . . And anyway, where's she going to in such a hurry? Maybe she's afraid lest I tell her husband? Just look at her . . . As if she were walking on air."

He watched her getting farther away, not quite in a rush but with a certain ease of movement; a sharp and slightly irregular movement, that sometimes seemed to bring her back, sometimes to carry her forward, and all this without the slightest noise and while around her feet, and everywhere, the hot air rising from the scorching earth rippled and steamed visibly like a veil covering her . . .

Unable to shout, he picked up the empty flask and threw it after her—he didn't hit her, not even on the hem of her dress, but the thud made her halt. She turned toward him after thinking about it for a moment and, putting a finger to her lips, asked him to be quiet.

"Is it a snake you're after?" (whereas when you asked him to talk, it was too much of an effort for him). "I saw one."

"Where?" said Eftha, immediately showing concern, though in a weak voice.

"Yesterday, if I remember rightly . . . A big one . . . Over there somewhere," and he pointed behind him, to the east. At the same time, he got to his feet and sluggishly walked over to her, or perhaps to move the flask out of the way.

"That one . . . a big one, you say, greenish . . . *quick* like you. That one can't find a place to die, it won't harm anyone—that's not the one I'm after," said Eftha.

"Ah, so you're looking for the one that can't find a place to bite."

" . . . "

"Well go and look for it elsewhere, Ma-Eftha, not here, I didn't come here to be distur—"

"Shh!" she cut him short.

Was it she or the deep commotion? A deep commotion . . . Her face shone transparent in the sun—for everything there's a last time.

According to what the neighbor said, the *commotion* came suddenly from behind a clump of withered and pitiful briars, not at all far from the spot where Eftha was standing. She didn't move at once. And yet he didn't see how and when she moved away from him and got there. Not moving from the spot, afraid as he was of snakes, like most people (as for what he'd told her about the snake he'd seen yesterday . . . someone else had seen it and told him), he very soon heard MERCY, MERCY from a voice the sound of which made him shudder from head to toe. And then a NOW . . . NOW — MERCY again. That voice didn't remind him of anything, it didn't sound like Eftha's, and yet her hoe was going up and down like a whip and he stared at her through the bare branches—until her frenzy brought these down too, most of them, and she began trampling on them as if she were up against a whole tangle of newborn snakes.

"Come and look," she called to him. "I didn't spare it! . . . Come on, don't be afraid, I've killed it! I've killed this one. The varmint!"

Crazy words, yet he got up courage—seeing her taking a rest, arching her whole back and resting her brow on the shaft—and he went over.

"Look at it! It's eaten a whole bird . . . that's what it was struggling with," she said, "I wasn't in time."

A brightly patterned snake was in four pieces. In the last piece, a suggestion of life was still squirming, in the first—just below the head—there was a relatively large bulge, in which there was also perhaps something still squirming . . . Eftha had seen off the snake and the snake had seen off the bird. And everywhere there was that quiet and that sense of *done*, something that flounders between relief and retraction.

The neighbor was shaking like a sinner on Judgment Day.

"You've killed it, let's be off," he said, "I can't stand to see all that, I don't have the stomach for it . . . I'm cold."

"Get back to your work," she said, "I'm going to stay a while."

"What? In case another comes along?" he asked, horrified. "Haven't you had enough with one?"

Eftha made a movement that made her look forty years younger. And throwing aside several twigs, she knelt, and with her two fingers stroked the battered head of the snake.

"*Be merciful unto me, O God: for man would swallow me up; he fighting daily oppresseth me. Mine enemies would daily swallow me up . . . O thou most high, be merciful unto me.*"

She was weeping.

He was trembling as if afflicted by every fever imaginable, he couldn't believe it and gazed around him as if looking for help.

"*For many are those who oppress me, for my soul trusteth in Thee . . . in the shadow of Thy wings . . . until these calamities be overpast. Put Thou my tears . . . they have prepared a net for my steps; my soul is bowed down, be merciful unto me.*"

He simply could not believe it: she was grieving for the snake that she'd killed with her own hands, she was stroking it. And something else, she was speaking in its stead! From what little he understood of her words, she was speaking in its stead!

"Are you crazy, have you lost your mind, let's go," he said again, frightened out of his wits. "You . . . was it you who was shouting that *Mercy-Mercy* before? Was it your voice? It fair shook me . . . who else, now I see. You kill the snakes and shout *Mercy!* If anyone had told me, I wouldn't have believed it—let's go. I can't wait here anymore, let's go . . . I'll count to three . . . to thirty, and I'll call you. Otherwise, I'm leaving on my own . . . Damn it, I wanted to sun myself a bit today!"

"Take your child some water," she told him.

He went on entreating her, but from farther off, throwing two small stones into his water flask and shaking it like a bell, but she wouldn't come (she was even undoing the straps of her apron and searching in her pockets) and he left alone. Undecided and not in the least bit at ease—other demons assailed him and told him to go back and take her with him, by force, it was his duty, but he was already running, and all he did was to turn around and look back at her every so often from a distance . . . even when he was so far away that he could no longer see her.

Well, he said to himself, *well!* . . . and forgot what he wanted to say—well . . . ah, yes! He'd soon reach Christoforos and he'd tell him to go back for her, after all, she was his wife. He'd also tell him—he couldn't not say it—"For years, I'd heard that your wife kills snakes, but I'd never seen *how* she kills them. And what she does afterwards!"

Nevertheless, he came back himself, out of a curiosity that wouldn't stop gnawing at him, accompanied by Cletia and Christoforos. They heard groaning and scraping on the ground before they even saw her . . . And they found her a little way off from the disturbed briars and those four pieces, with a greenish-bronze color that distorted all her features and in spasms and shaking all over, her teeth chattering like castanets and covered in the coldest of sweats. This is what they saw and heard—the expressions of a pain that made all others seem like caresses.

They gathered round her, in vain asking her how it had happened, what had happened. "But you'd killed the snake, how could it bite you?" Cletia implored her to tell them. But she was incapable of uttering a word and struggled with her finger, like Lily, to show them something . . . that obviously meant snake, but what else? Was there another snake? Not the one that she'd killed? She said yes and again lost her strength, only groans and froth coming out of her mouth.

It was difficult for them to even guess what had preceded, what had intervened—the neighbor's descriptions were not sufficient to explain such a dramatic end to all that had taken place previously before his eyes. Not, unfortunately, a little while previously, because they hadn't set out straightaway to find her: they thought that once Eftha had taken care of the snake, she would come back on her own. But she didn't come back and they started to worry—the three of them arrived in haste, but not in time.

The neighbor felt the burden of responsibility, more so even than the responsibilities already burdening him: it wasn't only that he had left her and run away, but now to find her in the throes of death? For the other two to be looking at him as if to say, "This is not what you told us, nothing like." And yet what else could he have told them? Could he have even imagined, poor man that he was, that something else, other than what he saw, could possibly happen? Was what he'd seen insignificant? Not at all insignificant, but then again not like what they were seeing now . . .

"I swear on my mother's bones, on the bones of my brother who died only a year ago," he said, "I left Eftha caressing the snake there, that one there, in pieces, that she'd killed . . . chanting psalms to it. Sorry, I don't mean that she was crazy, but that she was in the best of health. The . . . best . . . of . . . health. The same Eftha we've known for so many years, that's how I left her. My mistake, of course, for leaving her, but what I'm looking at now . . . this, no, she wasn't in this awful state when I left her . . . how could I ever have imagined, when I brought you here, that this is how I'd find her! . . . Eftha, say something! Tell them that what I said is the truth, that I left you in the best of health . . . say something, call for mercy, why don't you? Who else will?"

He began to cry; he was the first to cry for her before she was even dead. And it was the first time he'd ever found himself in such a difficult, such an unenviable position.

Yet if he had been a little less upset, he would have seen that Christoforos and Cletia were gazing at everything—including him—with anguish and despair, but not mistrust, not with the mistrust of someone unsuspecting or unprepared for the worst . . .

"You go looking for trouble, dear woman," Christoforos said to her, stroking her cold forehead. "But you'll get well, it'll pass," he said, without believing it himself, of course, without hoping for a miracle.

Meanwhile, they were searching for something to cut open her leg, the spot that was bluer and more swollen than the rest, where she had suffered the venomous bite, in the hope that *maybe*, maybe something could be done, maybe they could stop the poison before it spread everywhere. But they couldn't find anything. What irony. Eftha always carried a small knife with a blade that folded into its wooden handle; she said that she wanted it to peel apples, but actually she saved more people from snake bites with that knife than she peeled apples for herself. And now they couldn't find the knife in her pockets. The sharpest thing around was her spade, or at best Cletia's little mirror. But who would dare to cut her open with those?

They lifted her up and carried her to another spot, with a little greenery and shadier. To their misfortune, there wasn't anyone nearby with a horse to get her back to the house, but not even the swiftest horse could outrun the *galloping* from the other side . . .

"I'll leave this field unsown, unsown, for a full ten years, forever," said Christoforos, gazing at it from one end to the other, as if this afforded him or would afford him the slightest consolation. "Unsown, unsown, not even grass for grazing!" And though he was holding Eftha's head in his hands, with her groaning and trembling breaking his heart, he saw her like a vision approaching from opposite with her spade, with her wide dress lifted from its hem and tied behind her back to allow her legs to breathe—then she was gone again.

"Unsown . . . Mmm, then all the snakes will make their nests there," said the neighbor.

"Let them—there are no more snakes," said Christoforos.

"That's one reason. And those almond and walnut trees, what will happen to them?" the other asked.

Eftha's husband shut his mouth; the suffering hold their tongue, those sympathizing use it. Eftha could do neither with hers.

Meanwhile, Cletia had gone to the other field to tell the others. How was she to hide it, for the time being, from the five-year-old Minas? This concerned her, too, amidst everything else. On the other hand, she regretted having left her mother in such a state in order to go tell the others. It was something the neighbor could have done, so why her?—what thoughtlessness! *And what if I never see her alive again?* she reflected. *If I'm not in time to tell her I'm sorry for arguing with her yesterday. For sometimes talking sharply to her, for snapping at her? When other things were to blame, I always took it out on her—how will I be able to live with that? Dear Lord, let her still be alive—she always believed in you . . .*

Halfway there, she ran into some of the others, told them the bad news, and sent one of them to the other field. In this way, she was able to get back to Eftha while she was still alive.

During this time, others had come too—bad news travels quickly—some came with potions, antidotes, sharp blades, but could do nothing. All that happened was that Eftha regained her senses for a short while (but not without hallucinating), and her voice (unrecognizable: as if it were coming out shrouded in a pile of kerchiefs, like a cuckoo's), and so they were able to find out from her own mouth just what had happened: she had made up her mind to leave that place and was searching for her little knife to open up the snake and take the bird out of its throat, perhaps she would be in time, but she couldn't find the knife, she'd dropped it, couldn't find it; so she decided to go; but at that very moment a viper came, a small gray viper, she hadn't heard it, she didn't even really see it—the smallest and quickest viper, a sudden and devious flash in the earth. That was it.

Then she started raving. No one could make any sense of what she was saying, apart from the odd moment or two.

"How many years has my husband still got? Twenty? Divide them up and give me ten. Ten? Give me five of them, three . . . I'm not ready to die yet, I've small children, a sick daughter. Even if I'm only a shadow of myself, let me live. Do you hear? Three, two . . ."

She was *bargaining*. It's one of the last stages before final acceptance. She stopped as if listening herself to what she was saying.

"Forgive me, Lord, for interfering in your work!" she said afterwards, and her words once again dissolved into those changeable and vague *assumptions*, beyond all ken.

Strangely enough she had no more pain or even many spasms. However, she did have one last lucid moment. When she opened her eyes and saw so many people around her, she asked for tea with lemon. There was no tea to be had in such a place, so someone brought her water. Instead of taking the water, Eftha took hold of the cane, a long thin cane, that the man was holding in his other hand, and using this began to point at them one by one (they had sat her up in the meantime) and to say their names: you're he, you're the other. All of them, even the strangers, she took them to be her sons, daughters, or ancestors. She asked that the others come too, saying the names of people who had been long dead, and more too. She stopped a little longer at some of them, to make a comment, ask an unexpected question or—this too—to make a joke. She knew which of the women would remain unmarried and was concerned about them: she said to Christoforos that if he intended to get married again, he should take Violetta, who had been waiting for him for so many years and who wasn't his real sister; she asked Cletia what she was waiting for and why she didn't marry Zacharias given that he wasn't her brother (and though neither Zacharias nor Violetta was there, she pointed to them with her cane in the persons of others). Laconically and incomprehensibly, she reminded Theagenis (who was also not there) that he had a *hollow tooth*—but she also mentioned Hesychios as though he were someone different. At one moment, she turned her head and told some-one, whom no one saw, to come and stand before her too. She asked one of her daughters-in-law what the blood was that she had on her hands, just under her sleeve . . . And when they brought the five-year-old Minas before her—whom they had been keeping away from her, but whom she kept asking for—she tried to smile at him, to be playful with him, but her expression changed and she asked them to cover her.

Three hours more or less after the bite, she expired—it would have made little difference if they had managed to get her back home. Till then, till the final moment almost—and while she had fallen into a coma and her eyes never opened again—she had waved her right hand in the air every so often, as though giving a handshake. Such a thing was familiar to them, unfortunately, and decisive: they knew it meant that she was starting to meet up *with the others*, that they were welcoming her.

It takes nine months, they say, to escape from the spell of the dead. To be able to remember the dead and refer to them in conversation without expecting them and without feeling hurt as in the first weeks. Not that before these nine months have passed, the process of letting go or, better, of conciliation hasn't already begun . . . Nor, of course, that after these nine months have passed, everything is suddenly healed and the definitive absence of the dead doesn't surprise us or hurt us. But there you are, at around nine months something happens—a kind of *welding*, perhaps, without any sparks—and everything goes back to normal, whether we want it or not. So they say.

When they brought Eftha back, followed by a crowd of people, some of whom had heard the news earlier and got ready, whereas others only heard then and came out of their houses to join the disorderly and noisy procession going to hers; four little girls—six, five, and four years old, grandchildren of hers—had put down a red kilim in one of the upstairs rooms and were dancing, tightly clutching each other round the waist, cheek to cheek: the six-year-old with the five-year-old and the two four-year-olds together. For them, the death of their grandma Eftha meant above all a *funeral*, and a funeral meant a *festivity*: so many people would come to the house that they would come out in spots; they would collect pennies, kisses steeped in tears, and there'd also be plenty of pastries for them to eat, because at such times people don't have their minds on closed cupboard doors; on the contrary, they open them and share out what's inside *for the good of the departed souls* . . . the bells would toll mournfully, the words would become laments, the house would take on a deep glow from the smoke and incense . . .

Only the six-year-old, glancing for a moment out of the window at all the people entering the yard like a dark cloud, became aware of something more than what they were looking forward to and, not knowing how to express it so that the others would understand, turned and slapped her five-year-old cousin with whom she was dancing. Dumbfounded, she returned the slap—only to receive a second and a third, in quick succession. No one expected their dance to take such a turn. The other couple beside them, the four-year-olds, supposing that they too might get their share, slipped to one side arm in arm, away from the red kilim (from what had been agreed, that is), held on to each other even more tightly, and began to whimper.

"But it was you, you were the one who told us to dance because she'd died! . . . ," they said to the elder girl.

"I was the one who told you? There! . . . Little scaredy cats!" leaving the five-year-old and struggling to separate them and drag them back onto the kilim, even if she didn't care at all about the dance anymore. "Well, now I'm telling you that they're *bringing her, carrying her,* and you don't understand . . . There! And there, so you'll understand!"

And she slapped freely to left and right, even if her slaps didn't always find the target, not that she knew herself what the target was.

The five-year-old joined in the fray, the first to have been the recipient, and though anyone would have expected her to take the side of the younger girls, exactly the opposite happened: she too began slapping away to left and right, till the younger girls began to get infuriated too, *awoke,* and there was no longer any hand that wasn't slapping some cheek . . . So that in the end they all became a single weeping mass on the red kilim.

This is how they were found by the mother of one of them, one of Eftha's daughters, who, unable to imagine what had gone before but adjudging that such a situation was completely normal—for four disheveled little girls to be crying for their grandma—opened the door even more and showed them to some others who had come up the stairs with her, before they brought up the dead woman.

"See how even they are crying, even though they don't understand anything!" she said. "How everyone and everything is crying today for Eftha—a dear, unforgettable mother, who wouldn't hurt anyone. She wouldn't hurt anyone and they've taken her from us!"

And so it was with those little laments that the great lamentation began in the house, that heartrending dirge "Everyone is here but there's one soul absent" that makes one shrink, unable or afraid to set it down with all his being on paper . . . And Eftha, whose children, all of them, her own and the others, called her—lovingly or angrily—"Mother," henceforth became, completely spontaneously, "Mama Eftha," just as Christoforos's previous wife had long before become "Mama Petroula"—even for Eftha. The two together gave a singularity to each of them: as if they were two queens who had gone into the past, and of equal status, albeit with a different name, a different character, and at the same time as if the ground was being prepared, still vaguely so, for a third queen.

Minas, the youngest of the children to be left without a mother, was the only one never to share with his brothers and sisters the common name of "Mama

Eftha." For him, she was always "Mother," his mother, even though when he got older he couldn't recall what she looked like or the sound of her voice or anything else about her. Except for the day when, with a load of syrups and fairy tales, some women in the house had done their best to keep him away from her, so he wouldn't see her. But when they lifted her to take her elsewhere and new cries and laments followed in her wake, he had managed to escape from the protective hands. He surged like a boat without a rudder into the street and wriggled his way between the legs of first one and then the other, of people he knew and didn't know, grabbing hold of clothes, hands, and hair, and asked insistently:

"Where are you taking our mother? Where are you taking our mother?"

And no one was able to tell him, no one.

Fifth Tale

THE BLACK SHOES, DEKATESSARA . . .

What's more, an illness of the intestines by the name of *sisaibeoma* was afflicting a number of children at that time. Among them was the eleven-year-old Julia: in the space of a few weeks she turned as yellow as a sovereign and her red hair fell out in tufts. This happened the previous February, six months before Eftha had taken her leave of them, and at the time when the whole place was being rocked by the stories about her eighteen-year-old brother, Theagenis-Hesychios.

They took her out of school without any ado—something that saddened both her and her teacher, because she had an aptitude for learning and the most sensitive *ear* in the class—and they had her in the house following a course of therapy with herbal medicines and lotions. But her skin just kept becoming yellower and yellower, and her hair didn't stop falling out (every morning her pillow was covered with it), while she was so weak that you could have blown her over. They decided to take her to be examined by doctors in the large seaside town before the situation got any worse. It was around Eastertime, and for those in that place it was a time for dark dealings between twelve-year-old boys and newborn lambs, and it was better for Julia that she got away from it.

Eftha dressed her in her best clothes, wrapped her head in a coral-colored cotton kerchief, hung a wooden charm on string around her waist, underneath her clothes of course, and handed her over to Christoforos, who was waiting in a freshly painted carriage drawn by two horses and driven by a coachman. As Julia passed by it, one of the horses snorted—and the girl almost collapsed. If it had been just because she was startled and not because of her illness, her terrible weakness, everyone would have laughed; but now they simply pretended that they hadn't noticed anything. Eftha would go only if it proved necessary for her daughter to stay for some time in the hospital, something that they all hoped would not be necessary.

So it was because of the sisaibeoma, which showed no mercy to the children, that the eleven-year-old set out on a trip she would remember like a dream, full of vague allure and anxiety, of the kind that you don't know whether you want it to end or to go on. Hers ended in six or seven days, but its haze would surround her for many years more.

Once the coachman had been paid and left them, they initially found themselves in a place where there was a well surrounded by acacias, and a little farther, beyond the acacias, were some whitish grimy walls without windows. Julia gently let go of Christoforos's hand, daring to take some steps on her own towards the well, while behind her he cleared his throat and spat.

"If that's not a prison, it must be a hospital," she heard him say, "but where's the door to get in? I can't see any door . . . That opening there, do you think it's a door? It's you I'm talking to."

She turned to tell him that she didn't know, all she was looking at was the well, but her father was speaking to someone else. He had stopped a stranger, a nightmarishly bony man with a long shiny nose, long fingers, long crowlike hair that was also shiny, and one eye that was dull and motionless and stared at you like a viper. Where his other eye should have been there was a round hole with some hairs round it and inside something milky and completely vacant. He was neither young nor even middle-aged.

"The door is on the other side, ye'll have to go round—who brought ye round s'eere?" he asked. "S'eere, through that opening as ye put it, only caskets come out . . . if I'm making myself clear! Ye've come to the backyard of hell and I'm the warden—what d'ye want s'eere?" he asked again, changing his tone from one of irony to a more official one.

Julia wasn't surprised so much by that *backyard of hell* as by that *s'eere* that he kept on saying: did it mean "this here"? "in this place"? And if so, why didn't he say it, instead of using that *s'eere?* As if he were rasping.

"My daughter here is feeling a bit weak . . . it'll pass—she's lost her appetite and her hair has thinned out a bit . . . Am I talking to a doctor?" said Christoforos, who, while beckoning her to come over to him, suddenly went himself over to her and whispered to her not to be afraid.

"Seems more than a bit weak to me, what's wrong with her? And yellow—have ye been feeding her on cockroaches?" the stranger asked, with the curiosity of a studious type.

"She's just a bit weak, my dear man! Just a bit weak," Christoforos repeated, obviously annoyed, as he gazed with half-closed eyes at the man's own miserable condition: a bag of skin and bones like this talking about the weakness of others! A scrawny, jaundiced, one-eyed old man wondering at why his daughter's cheeks weren't glowing red . . . He was amazed at such audacity.

"Come on," he said to her, "let's go round to the other door, here there are too many people trying to be smart—great minds think alike. Or is it fools?"

"S'eere I'm the boss!" he repeated, pointing with two wide-open fingers to the grassy paved yard.

"S'eere you may be," Christoforos said to him, making the same gesture, as though finally communicating with him.

They found themselves in the street. Not knowing exactly in which direction to go (what with all the rest, they hadn't had time to ask the *warden*), they walked at random . . . though not exactly at random, as the hospital was beside them; they saw its roofs, but they had to find where the main door was, and not end up again in some backyard . . . On top of a low wall that obviously surrounded the entire complex, separating it from everything else, were black iron railings, and sticking out between these were long green branches with bright yellow flowers—it smelled of spring. Christoforos halted for a moment and stared at Julia: all that was left of her were her eyes, big, stark, dark green, and a half-open linenlike mouth. And two red hairs that stuck out from beneath her kerchief and cast their shadows, two faint lines, over her anemic face. He reflected that even a hair has its shadow.

"Can you walk?" he asked her, trying not to offend her.

Laced with invigorating oils from the previous day but also because of the excitement of the trip, she told him that she could; and to prove it, she again let go of his hand and took several steps on her own . . . She looked like a fairy who had had too much to drink—anyway, she was walking more or less normally; she couldn't be expected to dance as well. With two of his steps, he caught up with her, took hold of her hand again, and they leaned for a few moments against the low wall; he talked to her about all they could see around them, strange houses, strange streets; he pointed in the direction of the sea (he wasn't so sure himself, it wasn't as though he saw it every day), promised that he would take her there as soon as they were done with the doctors, and then they continued to walk.

"Why did that man with the black hair keep saying *s'eere, s'eere*?" she asked him.

"Because he's obviously from down south, didn't you realize?" he said to her. "Down in southern Greece and the Peloponnese, that's how they talk, all *s'eere* and *th'eere*, or is it *th'are*, I might be getting confused. And they use that *s'eere* all the time . . . Yes, I've some friends from there. They come here on business and they think we're simpletons because we're not wily like them. Once, one of them, from the Peloponnese I recall, Morea as they call it, was arguing with me and called me a Bulgarian. Can you imagine! . . . He turned round and called me a Bulgarian, a Serbian, and whatever else you might think of. It suits them to think of us northerners like that, because there are Slavophones in these parts. And why wouldn't there be, I ask you? All these Balkan areas are one big melting pot . . . But I told him that his mug reminded me of Omer Brioni[1] and so I got my own back. What clowns we all are."

"*And with one eye,*" said the girl timidly.

"What, are you talking about the warden of hell? That's nothing. There are others who don't have any," replied her father. "Aren't you tired from being on your feet for so long?"

"No, I'm happy that we're talking."

There was one good thing about that illness: because of it, she could ask her father questions and be sure that he would go to the trouble of giving her an answer—this was not usually the case unless you were ill. Also because of the illness, her father would leave his inn every so often to come home and see how she was, to bring her spleens (even though they ended up being eaten by others), to feel her forehead, to himself put a compress of vinegar on it and to give her a kiss on the cheek before leaving, or simply, and even better, to rub his own cheek—which wasn't exactly a cheek, but rather an *arena* of small, soft prickles—against hers. Oh, those *little prickles!* . . . What she loved most about her father—who still didn't have a beard—was those little prickles, his unshaven face when he pressed it against her own hot and feverish cheek. And the more the fever rose, the more the prickles pricked deeper, whereas the more the fever . . . *unfortunately* dropped, and did so steadily (as had happened at other times in the past when she had fallen ill for a short time), the more the prickles withdrew and she sought them, even at the cost of a new bout of fever . . . You see, in a house where almost every year a new little brother or sister arrived on the scene taking pride of place over all the others, neither the mother nor the father had any time to spare to show a little tenderness to the older ones—in fact, the father didn't really show very much tenderness even to the younger ones. So for the older ones, at least for the more sensitive ones, for them to come down with an illness now and again or some sudden nocturnal fever that lasted a few days was something of a privilege: it obliged the parents to remember them, to give them a little attention.

Of course, Julia's fever lasted months: it rose and fell of its own accord, and this wasn't very pleasant for anyone. And perhaps we should take the opportunity to point out that it wasn't only the fever that afflicted her or her hair that came out in tufts when you touched it; there were also the shadows that passed

---

1. An Albanian by birth, he was a leading figure in the Ottomans' attempt to suppress the Greek Revolution (translator's note).

over her at night . . . the shadows, the notorious *siankes*. No one could say exactly what these siankes were—particularly given that they themselves were unable to approach their own existence . . . Perhaps they were restless dreams in suitable bodies, unique impressions that gave substance to nothing, giving shape to the air and making phantoms of it. Perhaps they were just normal dreams that ended as nightmares, in a black ethereal cloud, a whirling *wisp* of darkness that, as it got closer to the sleeping or half-sleeping body, choked and became mortally fraught, offering explanations that surpassed all logic and frontiers.

Anyhow, whatever they were, whatever they weren't, some of the girls in that large family, and in others too, would talk now and then of the sianke that passed over them *again* the previous night, of how it had terrified and tormented them, and above all they would show (as evidence) the black marks on their bodies, *fingermarks*, mainly on their bellies and chests, that they hadn't had before and that no common ailment could have caused. So it was, in keeping with their fixed ideas, from the sianke's passing, from its unbearable grip, its embrace, till they awoke and were saved and could return to their right senses.

And in time, with repetition and unintentional suggestion, the sianke for each one of these young and impressionable girls became in a manner of speaking *her* sianke, a kind of desperate guardian angel that threatened her, needed her, and used her (not always roughly) till she had grown up—and somewhere there, it abandoned her. Somewhere there, each girl lost it, together with her innocence.

It would most likely be some time before Julia lost hers, however, what with the fever and all its consequences and her own disposition. And some years later, she wished she could have described it, at least as best she could, had been able to *sketch* it, given that this shadow had touched and left its mark on a sizable expanse of her nocturnal otherworld, between her pre-adolescence and the end of her youth, yet on the other hand we know only too well that these are experiences so variable, so incommunicable, so dim and secret that they risk being dissolved when we try to grasp them. Or of swallowing us up if we get too close . . .

That day, before she entered the hospital, before the entrance had been found, she would lose her father. It happened in the simplest and most unexpected way: he had her sit on the wall with the railings, between the branches, and wait for him: he rushed over to the other side of the street to look at something that interested him in an arcade with hanging merchandise, and after examining it and feeling it with his fingers while she watched him from the distance, he continued carefree into the arcade and—she lost sight of him.

It seemed to her that he was a long time in coming back, and she began to worry, to imagine all sorts of things, but she didn't think to get down from the wall (it was high for her, she would have had to jump), afraid lest the slightest change or movement in such a strange and important town might result in her father not finding her. She was already afraid that he was wandering in alleyways, in other arcades, had come out elsewhere, was searching elsewhere for her . . . she grew frightened: perhaps it was really she who was lost and not him?

The moments disappeared, taking on the dimensions of hours, and two men whom she saw in the distance both seemed to her to resemble her father—except that neither of them looked towards her, no matter how much she strained her neck . . . A third man did look, but he certainly wasn't her father: he passed by her walking slowly, admiring the polished tips of her shoes, and without wanting to she stretched out her leg slightly and touched his sleeve: he raised his eyes and, startled, looked at hers, then at her coral-colored head, and then continued walking. She was alarmed at the thought that perhaps her kerchief had slipped down and that everyone could see she had no hair. Or perhaps, without anything having slipped, everyone had understood what she was suffering from and why she was sitting on that wall. She saw a fourth man in the distance . . . She felt like calling to him, jumping down and running and throwing herself around him, but, in the end, using both hands, she simply moved her body a little farther to the right . . . and the branches around her swayed as though they had been shaken by someone behind her. Thinking that she was to blame, that she had caught them accidentally, she stayed where she was, as though being punished, completely still, but the branches moved again, more wildly and impatiently, and she turned her head to see.

"What's your dad thinking of, leaving one like ye all alone?" said a voice familiar to her. "Aren't ye scared?"

It was that S'eere again, what a fright! . . . *S'eere himself and none other.*

"Ha, ha," he said, carefully pulling aside some of the lower branches that were in his way, "S'eere I'm the boss, like we said. Look! . . . Hey, ye . . . s'eere, psst! . . . Yellow face, hey, death face, s'eere! . . . S'eere, I'm telling ye . . . look!"

Out of instinct, she was ashamed to look and turned her eyes away, blinking like someone blind who is told to wake up . . . yet she couldn't help but see a small silver disk that shone between his long dark fingers, a brand-new coin that he was playing with like a mirror in the sun to dazzle her, while with his other hand, with the entire palm of his hand, he made big slow circles over the hollow of his belly, circles that got continually smaller, smaller and lower, till suddenly—how did it happen?—from out of his palm appeared something blue and brown like a hanged man's tongue, like the impudent head of a tortoise, like the wailing of an alley cat.

Her surprise slowly yet completely inundated her, as when you throw a little red paint into a pot of hot water . . . it ate away at her. This, coupled with her in-expressible fear and the unusual composure it required for her to understand and link those two gestures through the branches, the enticing coin and the other (even if there was no hope whatsoever on the horizon), caused her cheeks to turn red, deep red, and they were never red, not even before she fell ill. And she felt that the hair was starting to grow again on her head, but hard hair, prick-ing her like needles.

She suddenly turned round to the front and jumped down from the wall without taking anything into account. It was as though she had suddenly been cast out of the clouds . . . The branches shook again furiously, madly, as though this man behind them wanted to make arms of them in order to catch her.

"My daddy's coming!" she shrieked in a panic — perhaps she wanted even to protect him?

Her answer was a grouchy "Hey, hey . . . we were having a good time, weren't we?" with one last shake of the branches, which now returned to their natural slant and balance after a passing disturbance. She heard his steps getting farther away — a sudden crucial blow *and fleeting* like in guerrilla warfare — and his voice laced with irony: "Her daddy's coming . . . yea!"

Exactly on cue, her father appeared at the other side of the street, having emerged from the arcade — she'd forgotten that she had lost him and thought it insignificant now — and he was talking with someone, holding a big box close to his chest, and with his hand he gestured to her happily that he was coming.

This then. And afterwards in the hospital — after a long process, papers and more papers that even if you were well were enough to make you ill — they were left to wait in a sitting room. On the wall were pictures of human intestines and limbs — as well as others of tranquil landscapes and snowcapped mountains. Christoforos cast sideways glances . . . He tried to concern himself more with what he had bought wholesale in the arcade — various tools for builders and farm-ing gear that were intended for his own shops. He showed them to Julia and every so often would get up to stretch his legs — smoking wasn't allowed, and he felt as though he were being deprived of oxygen. The waiting was becoming long.

"Have an apple, aren't you hungry?" he asked her.

No, that was the problem, she hadn't been hungry at all during the previous months. Nevertheless, she took out one of the apples that Eftha had given them, blew on it, rubbed it on her cardigan — and that was it: she had no appetite for biting into it . . . Or, timidly and inquiringly, she would look him in the eyes be-fore putting it back in case he wanted it.

"No, no, I don't want an apple right now," he said to her. "Listen, my dear girl, to what I'm about to tell you." And he gave her some fatherly advice: when they came to take her, if, that is, they ever came to take her, she shouldn't be afraid; she should tell them how she felt, what was wrong with her, what she had been going through since February; she should show them her head and not be ashamed, they were doctors, not prospective bridegrooms, and if they didn't see her they wouldn't be able to tell what the problem was . . . "And if you allow me to come inside too, I will, otherwise I'll wait outside . . . Above all, don't be afraid, life's long."

This was something he would always say, especially when life was getting him down and there was nothing more to be said.

They both fell silent till, quite unexpectedly, Julia asked the question: "You mean . . . I won't die?" and he laughed, reproached her, told her that he hadn't brought her *s'eere* (spreading two of his fingers) for her to die, but because the doctors had to live!

At that moment, two tall, stout nurses appeared and took Julia with them, almost swallowed her up like waves.

"Those carthorses . . . ," he muttered to himself when he was alone. "Where are those carthorses taking her?"

And he followed them at a distance — to see through which door they would go — and somewhat unsteady on his feet, as if he hadn't moved his legs for a long time. Deep down he was worried, gnawed by the same thought: he knew how easy it was to have children, but also how easy it was to lose them. And if he was going to lose them, then why have them? And . . . where had she suddenly got the idea from, an eleven-year-old girl, to ask about dying? And without any hesitation, she, who was usually so hesitant? Not that children didn't die at eleven or even earlier, at eight, at five, but at least they didn't know what was happening — they were *children*.

The two nurses weren't in the slightest bit concerned about whether he was following them or what thoughts were going through his mind. And after fingering their patient left and right and telling her that she was all skin and bone and that she would die if she didn't eat, they opened a door and handed her over to two doctors. The door closed behind her.

One of the two doctors looked like an owl that rejoices at the light of day — he was all smiles, coquettish, made faces, shook his legs as though he were hanging from the branch of a tree, kept tossing his head back, and had hair that rippled and glinted. The other was wearing black-rimmed glasses and green trousers beneath a white coat, and he seemed very serious, almost angry. They took her with all the care due to someone of her age and with the ailment she was suffering from and had her sit on a high leather couch. There may have been no green branches or railings, but there were other things in there.

She would not remember much from the scenes that followed in that room. Only that every so often she would hear her father outside coughing loudly and spitting into his handkerchief, and the two doctors both looking towards the door each time as though someone were coming in without knocking . . . Then they would bend over her again as if there had been no interruption. The hardest moment was when, after a good many questions and a lot of going back and forth to drawers and cupboards, one of them, the serious one with the glasses, slowly undid the scarf around her head; and though she was expecting it and had prepared herself, she hid her face in her palms and cringed as if they had stripped her naked. Besides, she felt cold without the scarf, she had become accustomed to it . . . Absentmindedly, the doctor put it down somewhere, while with his fingers he gently pressed her head with the little hair she had left—mainly around her forehead and on her neck—but keeping his thoughts to himself. He exchanged glances, however, with the other one . . . And presently both of them were examining her head as if it were a tiny globe of the world.

Eventually, they said to her: "We heard from someone that you had very beautiful hair before you fell ill. And red hair—is it true?"

She didn't know how to answer; *yes* would mean she was boasting, *no* would mean she was telling lies.

"Who told you?" she asked.

"A little bird!" said the one who looked like an owl.

"A little bird outside the window . . . just before the nurses brought you here." And he made a charming little hop with his whole body, just as birds do when they are tired of singing in one direction and make a half turn on their branch. "So, then, Julia," he continued, caressing his tiny chin, "if you show patience—because the illness has progressed somewhat, we'll have to fight it—and you are a good girl and take the medicine that we give you, you'll grow new hair, even more beautiful. But you'll have to have patience, it will take months. And the medicine won't be pleasant . . . but you have to take it."

"I'll take it," she promised them, greatly relieved that they gave her back her scarf.

These, however, were only preliminary tests, they weren't over. She would have to stay at least four days in the hospital so they could give her more tests, blood, urine and others. They would have to talk to her father in private. To begin the injections that same evening—preferring not to hide from her the fact that they would hurt a little, not so much the actual needle as afterwards. Injections in the abdomen and in the stomach.

She was patient, which was a surprise to them. They usually had to hold or even bind other children to stop the needle flying into their own eyes . . . Whereas she looked at the needle while the nurse's fingers prepared it and then closed her eyes and took the deep breath that they told her to. As soon as she let the breath out, the pain began—a pain that felt as if she were being burned alive.

They gave her ten such injections inside five days, bombarded her with more words (that's how it had to be, they said), hoping that they wouldn't have to subject her to another ten the following month. Meanwhile, Christoforos had found a way to inform Eftha that everything was going as well as it could and that they would soon return . . . He spent his evenings at an inn called the Lovely Nights and, in truth, he felt strange, he couldn't accept that he, an innkeeper from his cradle, had to wait for them to show him where he would sleep and tell him what the cost of a night's bed and board was. Of course, it wasn't the first time that he had slept in someone else's inn (and especially in this one, given that he often came to the town to buy things), but he had never spent more than a couple of nights, whereas now it was already six. He spent a good few hours of the day at the hospital with his daughter, keeping her company, and only moved away from her bedside when it was time for the injection, then approached again when the syringe was empty, and inside he whimpered like a little dog hit by a bullet . . . he caressed her, touched her with his beard, held her up to his shoulder so she could cry more easily, told her stories about the future . . . and when her pain eased a little and he suddenly felt drowsy, he would lie back and sleep in a chair beside her bed ("Wake me up if you hear the carthorses," he'd say to her), as if he weren't getting enough sleep at night. But he justified himself by saying that it made him drowsy to watch the other two girls in the room, with unknown ailments, who were always sleeping: a deep and inauspicious sleep that was not interrupted by either visits or any other happenings.

Nevertheless, he also went out into the town, as it was an opportunity for him to do the rest of his buying, to see the sea a little, the streets, the women (who here were not all in long black dresses at forty, as in his parts, but wore European clothes and hats), perhaps even to bump into a friend by chance, to walk, to savor the different air, and, of course, to make sure not to forget the hospital entrance . . .

Coming to her one day, he told her that he had encountered that skeleton, that S'eere, straddling the railings like a wild goat, and that he had asked him how his daughter was (he concealed from her his actual question: "Is that little corpse you brought here the other day still alive?"); and that he had later learned, from one of the nurses, that he had been a renowned doctor, the Napoleon of medicine, but he had lost his wits, and now they couldn't get him out from under their feet—he wanted, come what may, to perform the duties of a warden and frighten people. He didn't look it, but he was over seventy, perhaps already touching eighty, and he had lost his eye as a result of one of his own acts of madness, one of his experiments carried out on himself, and this had affected his entire nervous system.

Julia listened in silence to the news. She catalogued it with her own from that very same morning and wondered how much longer she could keep it secret from her father: very early in the morning, before the nurses came with their thermometers, she had woken up abruptly as if someone had nudged her, as if someone had breathed on her . . . On opening her eyes and for quite a few moments more, she hadn't understood where she was or recognized anything around her—it seemed to her that a window was hanging from the ceiling, that a head was sinking there where she thought her feet were . . . everything upside down, unfamiliar, and with her much closer to the edge of the world than to herself. Yet there was someone standing in the background, and this obliged her, somewhat forcibly, to reconnect with the environment: it was S'eere. He had slipped quietly through the half-open door and was again rubbing his belly and whispering that "psst . . . hey . . . ye . . . s'eere," just as before behind the low wall with railings and branches . . . She didn't have the slightest idea how she might be able to drive him away, how to defend herself—it was in a similarly sneaky way that the siankes would appear, but they didn't do anything and not even one of them had dared visit her in the hospital . . . The old man moved away from the half-open door—unfortunately to come farther in—and in her fright she leapt out of bed and stood there.

Strangely so, did this make her invisible? Did it remove her from some magnetic belt? Because he, responding to her dumb panic with a disdainful "all right then," appeared to hesitate somewhat between the other two girls, who were fast asleep, whose beds were closer to the door—in other words, closer to him—and whose faces were shining palely in the dim light, devoid of all expression or expectation, and turned—both of them—towards her: the eleven-year-old had spent hours and hours gazing at them . . .

"Don't disturb them!" she told him (not even she understood where she had found that voice, that courage). "They're sleeping."

"Sleeping more than is good for them," he said mockingly. "They'll have to wake up sometime or we'll be mourning them—call that life? More like misery." And he nudged the one closest to him: "Hey, wake up," he said to her, "haven't ye slept enough?"

Not even her breathing changed, but Julia was alarmed, stifling what would have been a very long shriek. And not having any way of stopping him from doing something similar again, she picked up one of her shoes from the floor and hurled it in the direction of the door.

His one eye revealed surprise that turned to anger. He stared first at the shoe and then at her. "S'eere—," he started to say, but then had another idea: he picked up her shoe, examined it on both sides, and then put it in his pocket like a stolen egg and went.

Julia was left with one shoe. A few moments passed, and the loss of the other one surprised her rather than upset her (deep down she believed that he would bring it back: what could an old man do with a girl's shoe?), but for good measure she took the remaining one and hid it with her clothes in the tiny cupboard. The next day, she would leave the hospital and that town. Yet how could she leave? With only one shoe? And what would she tell her father about the other one? That it had disappeared . . . what else? That, perhaps, someone had stolen it—though . . . who would steal one shoe and leave the other? Unless he were one-legged . . . or one-eyed! Her head was swimming. She began to look around her, to search . . . Perhaps it had only *seemed* to her that he had put it in his pocket? Perhaps he had simply dropped it or craftily tossed it into a corner?

The door suddenly opened while she was on her knees searching between the other two beds—and certain that it was him, that he had brought her shoe back, but it was someone else's voice she heard.

"Is no one here?"

She got to her feet.

It was a patient in a long nightdress, she had seen him before, wandering sleepless through the corridors all night.

"That old crock!" he said. "He scared you, right? I saw him coming out . . . Did he *touch* you?"

"No," she said hesitantly, "me . . . no."

"What . . . them? Was he envious of their peaceful slumber?" he wondered, gazing at the two sleeping girls. "He's done it before, no need to be scared, no one pays any attention to him," he said to her and left, carefully closing the door behind him.

She had no time to share her concern about her shoe with him, to ask his help, but . . . even if he had had more time for her or had asked her more questions, she still doubted whether she would have found the courage to ask that kind of help from a stranger. She began searching for it again . . . With as much hope of finding it as the two girls beside her had of waking up with the light of day.

In the end, she decided to *lose* the other one too. Everything is for the best, she told herself after her father had left that evening without learning any-thing—neither he nor anyone else. That night, they would give her the final injection, and the following morning they could leave, go home . . . Everything is for the best, she told herself again; for some time now, for the past two years at least, she hadn't liked those shoes: they weren't hers, for as long as she could remember she had never had her *own* shoes, but had always worn the shoes that her elder sisters no longer wore, that no longer fitted them, and so were handed down to the younger sisters—and these here were not even pretty or appealing: they were rough-cut (or, from another point of view, strong, made to last years), with soles that never showed any signs of wear and tear, and the design of the shoes . . . did they have any design? Nothing, just a black color that became blacker every time they polished them, two rounded tips, two thick soles, with a wide lace to tie them. She didn't like them. But her father wouldn't get her any others so long as these were still sturdy. And when they no longer fit her, the *new* ones they would give her would again have been worn by her sisters, again they would be like these here, but a bigger size. Unless . . . unless she lost them: in a strange place where she wouldn't be able to find them again, in a hospital like this one, and had nothing to return home in . . . Then her father would be obliged to buy new ones for her, to go to the expense on her account . . . Her timid heart with all its secret desires felt sorrow at all this, but given that she couldn't do anything else . . .

And so, after waiting for the last night to pass—with one last *hope* for her lost shoe, which, of course, simply smiled at her a few times in the darkness— the following morning, just before the nurse came with the thermometer, Julia hurled the other black shoe out of the window.

Her father kicked up a fuss when he came to take her and learned that her shoes had disappeared—he had practically the whole hospital buzzing with his shouting and protesting, and, of course, held the nurses and the cleaners re-sponsible. They knew nothing, swore that they had seen his daughter's black shoes under the bed every day—if they had suddenly disappeared, what could they possibly know about it?

Julia felt like jumping from the window herself rather than have things go as far as they had. Besides, she should have known that her father wouldn't allow such an odd happening to go by just like that.

"It's not about the shoes," he said to the other patients who had gathered around to find out what was happening, "if I want, I can buy her five pairs of shoes! But it's *why* and *how* a little girl's shoes can simply vanish in a hospital and *no one knows anything!* They've robbed us already with the cost of all the medicines and injections—they don't have to steal our shoes as well!"

If the patient in the long nightdress, the one who was awake all night wandering the corridors, had been there, he might have been able to shed some light on the matter (or embroil her even more) by coming out with a few of the things that Julia had kept quiet about. But he would collapse exhausted onto his bed when all the others were waking up and so he wasn't there, and naturally no one thought to wake him. Just as no one suspected the nutcase in the backyard: all of them knew more or less about his senile carryings-on, but up to then at least no one had heard anything about his stealing shoes. At any rate, they didn't even give him a thought, he skipped their minds completely.

After he'd calmed down somewhat following his outburst, Christoforos took Julia by the hand and they stood together in front of the two beds with the two girls sunk in their hapless sleep, who hadn't woken up when they'd arrived and who wouldn't wake up now that they were leaving . . .

"Good night," he said to them, bowing his head.

It sounded a little strange at a time when the sun was streaming in through the windows . . . He wanted to say something else too, but he simply said it to his daughter once they were outside the door: "They certainly didn't steal them."

So without shoes, walking in her lovely silk socks, Julia went down with her father to the room where the two doctors had seen them. There was only one of them there, the one who looked like an owl.

"My daughter has lost her shoes," Christoforos said to him on entering, without even so much as a "good morning."

"I heard. But she's won my heart!" said the doctor, with a little glowing smile.

They stared at him in surprise, but the doctor continued in all boldness: "Didn't your daughter tell you that I'm in love with her?"

"What! . . . ," Christoforos exclaimed.

"But of course. There's no what about it. I'm in love with her, I've fallen in love with her," the doctor went on, "and if I hadn't been in a hurry to get married ten years ago, I'd have waited another ten years till she'd grown up!"

"If you like, I have other daughters too," Christoforos said, somehow finding the courage, evidently meaning that he wouldn't have to wait ten years for them. "But if you say you *were in a hurry . . .*"

"In a hurry, in a hurry," the doctor repeated, opening Julia's mouth to examine her tongue. Then he moved to the whites of her eyes and said, "Perhaps *I* stole her shoes to stop her from leaving!"

Julia's eyelids almost beat against him as he was holding them open, and they fluttered in fear.

"Ha, ha," he laughed, full of high spirits, "I'm saying all this so she'll remember me . . . because I've taken a liking to her. It's the first time I've taken such a liking to a little patient—what is it about her? Did you keep her in honey when she was born?"

Such words, of course, did not require any response; he left them alone for a while, explaining that he would soon come back with his colleague for the last few things.

"Just fancy . . . He likes to be playful even if he doesn't show it—he has the look of a gloomy owl," Christoforos said to his daughter once they were alone.

"He's happy, full of jokes," she said. "it's the other one who's sad . . . with the glasses and the green trousers."

"Ah, yes, there's that other one," Christoforos conceded. "But I get them confused, which one is happy, which one sad . . . It's not that I've had any dealings with them before now. And . . . hm, what happened to your shoes? Who'll answer that for me?"

Julia lowered her head and kept it lowered.

When she raised it—someone outside knocked on the door and her father shouted "Come in"—she saw an ugly nurse walking in and holding in two fingers one of her shoes!

"The little girl's shoe . . . ," she said calmly, though with a good deal of spite, while looking at Christoforos. "They found it in the garden, under her window—just the one. As for the other one, no matter how much we searched . . ."

So Julia found herself once again with one shoe, how wretched! She felt like crying, beating her breast, grabbing it and hurling it once again through the window—in front of everyone now—so it might find its black and shabby partner.

But unfortunately or perhaps fortunately, she didn't have time to do any of this. She couldn't nor did she need to do it. The two doctors walked in. The serious one was more serious than ever (even his trousers today were dark gray; he had changed that rare green pair) and, laconic as always, he simply said to her father: "We only just managed to save the girl. But she will have to go on taking the medicine for some time."

He took off his spectacles (his eyes looked unhealthy without his spectacles), breathed on them, cleaned them with a soft cloth, put them back on, and gave her a parting pat on the cheek.

The other one was as always more generous: he closed her hands in his, gazed at her tenderly, comically, sadly, grimaced, as though crying or reminding her of their secret agreements, and in the end he said to her—also speaking on behalf of his colleague—that they would love to see her again, though it would be better for her to get well and never have need of them again.

Wrapping the scarf round her head, with her eyes fixed on the other doctor's gray trousers, she had the pleasure of hearing his voice again one last time: "If in the next twenty to thirty days she doesn't start to gain weight or grow new hair, you'll have to bring her back."

And as she left the hospital, walking beside her father with one shoe (the other foot was wrapped in gauze with a *sole*—the obnoxious nurse had taken care of that), she also had the painful experience of again seeing for one last time the branches behind the low wall moving wildly, as if dogs and cats were going at it behind them . . .

"Ha, ha, and just where are ye taking your precious with one shoe," the voice of the old goat was heard to say, "to find a groom?"

And without them actually seeing him, the other shoe fell from the branches.

In order to find a carriage to leave, they had to go to an eating place that acted as a kind of agency; in other words, it was frequented by cart drivers with their beasts. When they arrived, it was virtually empty, but it soon filled up.

It smelled of barrel wine even from outside. On their entering, there were other smells too mingling with the main one, like that of the beans stewing on braziers at the back, of freshly cut onions, or of the dampness coming up from the dirt floor—not an unpleasant smell when it wasn't wintertime.

Incredible objects decorated the walls—among them a dead eagle on a board, the head of a wild boar on another, and lower down in one corner, among sprigs and dried flowers, an entire fox with glazed blue eyes ready to spring!—and instead of normal tables with chairs there were just wooden couches, long wooden couches with particularly high backs. When two or three or four people were sitting on the couches, these backs were released by some bolts at the left and right and unfolded—passing over the heads of those seated—to become long, narrow tables in front of them, quite stable, and without leaving their backs without any rest: there were other, permanent backrests behind them, even higher than the others, the movable ones. Naturally, such couches-girds held the diners captive and if it happened that a person wanted to get up before the end of the meal, he couldn't—unless he jumped over the side or the back.

All this seemed exceedingly strange to Julia, though not to her father. First, he had been on other occasions to this eating place, he was known there, and second, when he was a boy, as he told her, he recalled his parents and grandparents eating on two such "couches that became tables," while for the little children there were low round tables (which still existed in the homes), together with the high tables that had been made meanwhile.

He told her to choose the one where she wanted to sit, and with a grand gesture he passed the couch's *two-sided* backrest over their heads: Julia watched, turning her neck as though a giant wooden bird was passing over them.

"Now we're locked in, and we have to eat," he said, leaning over to her.

The girl, of course, wasn't hungry; it was still too soon for her to be hungry again after what they had given her for breakfast in the hospital, but Christoforos asked the cook's son to squeeze *seven lemons with three spoonfuls of sugar* for her, to bring a jug of wine for him and something for them to nibble. Others had already started coming and going in the place and stared at them as if they had never seen a father and daughter before.

"Don't pay any attention to them," he said, leaning over to her every so often (which only made them stare more), "it's the time when they don't know what they want—they're hungry, but they can't decide what they want to eat. A coachman will be along soon, and we'll be on our way . . . Look there at how many lemons that boy is carrying! You'd think I'd asked him for a whole grove!"

The cook's son, a teenager covered in spots, with catlike eyes and a mouth that constantly trembled without uttering a word, three or four years older than Julia, came over to them with his apron full of lemons. His legs were long and thin and seemed odd and excessive given that the cuffs on his trousers only reached down to an inch or so above his ankles—and with the lemons, he brought whatever else they had asked for (the wine, a plate of meat and potatoes, the bread, and forks), but also whatever he needed himself to cut and squeeze the lemons *in front of* them.

"Steady, Son! . . . I didn't tell you to do yourself an injury," Christoforos said to him. "Not even Santa Claus comes loaded down like that."

As though not hearing, the boy put everything down on the table, cut a lemon in two and asked him somewhat curtly: "Didn't you tell me to squeeze fourteen like that?"

"Bravo," said Christoforos, pleased, "you're good at arithmetic—fourteen halves make seven whole ones. But squeeze them with all your might, don't hold back."

"Do you see me holding back?" he said, cutting the other six lemons in half and squeezing them with all his might into a glass.

Then he added three spoonfuls of sugar, shook the mixture a little, and then proceeded to empty the juice from the first glass into a second and from the second back into the first in order to dissolve the sugar. He did this many times, with the distance between his hands and the glasses getting ever bigger, and with a speed that revealed experience—even climbing onto a stool so that they could see him better . . . When he had almost sent his little customer into a daze—she stared at him with a smile that came and went and revealed her anxiety lest he spill any of the juice—he leapt like an acrobat from the stool (emptying for one last time the one glass into the other), and he handed it to her with the greatest respect.

She took a sip and winced—it was still very bitter, the lemons were especially keen.

He took it back from her, threw in another spoonful of sugar, and began the process again . . . But this time it was her father who became dazed by it all.

"Enough!" he said, "we asked for juice, not froth"; and taking the brimming glass from him, he handed it to his daughter: "Don't ask for any more sugar," he told her, "because it will be like treacle."

She was almost frightened at seeing his brow darken as though there were many things suddenly weighing on him. They had both been so well together during the previous few days, despite the illness, the medicines, and the black shoes, that she didn't want to spoil everything through some mistake, perhaps, on her part; so she took the glass, took two sips, saying that it was fine now, and hoping that the cook's son would take the rest of the lemons and go away from their table. But to her great surprise, the boy began cutting up the rest . . . She didn't know where to look, which way to turn her head.

"Hey, what are you doing? Who are those for?" asked her father, sharing her concern and aware that it would be an ordeal for her to have to drink another seven lemons.

"She might want some more," said the boy, unperturbed. "Besides, it won't get wasted: I'll give it to my sister."

"You have a sister?"

"Why shouldn't I?"

"Because as many times as I've been in this place, I've only ever seen you—so where is this sister of yours?" asked Christoforos.

"She doesn't come out, she's ill," said the boy, and Julia stirred in her seat as if they were talking about her.

"Ill?" the father asked again.

"Yes, though even before she fell ill, she didn't come out . . . why should she? Now she's ill as well . . . We took her out of the hospital the day before yesterday."

"What's wrong with her?" he inquired, again showing concern (his daughter wouldn't have dared).

"What's wrong is what's wrong . . . ," said the boy, casting an anxious glance in Julia's direction. "We only just managed to save her, so the doctors told us. My father said it's nonsense, that it's what they always say so we'll feel indebted to them! But the poor girl was on the verge of death . . . Now we're counting the days and waiting for her to grow her hair again, she lost it all . . . I squeeze a mountain of lemons for her every day so she'll get her strength back—all you have to do is blow and she falls down. She's inside. We have the eating place here in front and the house is behind—we don't have a mother. That's where she is, there . . . She's waiting for her medicine."

He spoke and flicked the lock of hair hanging over his forehead, while his hands worked with unflagging energy, either cutting more lemons or emptying their juice from one glass into the other—into a third one, that is, which he had brought in the pocket of his apron and taken out at the last moment.

Julia stopped looking and listening; she had turned her head to face the wall with the head of the wild boar, because it was now her turn to become gloomy, to be overcome by a rather unpleasant and unwelcome feeling: as if they had taken her glass away to give it to another girl . . . And if it was only the glass, she wouldn't have cared—she was only drinking out of a sense of obligation—but it was something else too, something more vague, that reflected strangely on two small glass surfaces with a black frame all around, and this feeling upset her, disappointed her, turned green into gray . . . "*We only just managed to save the girl!*" So they said it about all the girls, without exception. Hmm . . . it was also her father who had come out with: "You see? You're not the only one," certain that he was comforting her like this.

And on the other hand, as if he too were playing with words, he left her alone . . . Because he saw an old acquaintance of his coming into the place and called to him to come over and sit at their table, but his friend didn't have time; he told him that he had brought his wife's little sister to see the doctors, and they would keep her some days in the hospital till she got better (he didn't have to mention the illness, they all knew), and he was now looking for a cheap inn where he could stay at night.

"Let me show you where I was staying," said her father immediately, "it's neither expensive nor very far. Besides, I have to go back there to pick up the things I bought." And lifting first one leg then the other, he jumped over the side of the couch that was keeping him fenced in. She got up with him, but he made her sit down again.

"What are you doing? There's no need for you to tire yourself too," he said. "I won't be long."

She looked him in the eyes, ready to cry.

"I won't be long," he promised, "this time I won't be long, I won't stop to talk

. . . we have to be going. As soon as I'm back, we'll be going. Wait for me here like a good girl."

She felt as though she had become a speck on the edge of the couch, all alone, no longer having anything truly pleasant to remember from the hospital . . . other than those grimaces of the funny and tender doctor, but these too were quickly losing their appeal.

Her father halted in the doorway of the eating place, tall, very tall, slender and dark against all the bright light coming in from outside; he halted as though remembering something or wrestling with some dilemma . . . and she sat up. But in the end, turning half round, he motioned to her to sit back down in her place and repeated the same thing—that he wouldn't be long and she should wait for him, not go anywhere.

Not go anywhere!

While she was waiting for him, perhaps because it provoked some sympathy seeing her head poking out of that corner of the table as though she were without a neck and body, the cook left the money he was counting in the drawer and dragging his two swollen legs came over to her and lifted up the couch's wooden rest, which no longer had any reason to be serving as a table. He fixed it again to the back of the couch so that it became an enormous backrest, but at least he had freed her from that obstacle in front of her that had been hiding, not to say suffocating, her all that time. From her hands he took the glass that had only a drop of lemon juice still in it—thick like soup from the pulp and all the pips that she held back with her tongue . . .

"The blockhead," he muttered, "I keep telling him to use a strainer, but he just does as he likes . . . Was it good the one time? Did it give you strength?" he asked her, raising the opaque glass.

No one in her place would say no, unless they were in a mood for pointless chitchat.

Tired, the cook sat at the other end of the couch and sighed deeply, tossing his head back and fanning the tip of his chin with the edge of the large red towel he had flung over his shoulder. Sounds like gargling were coming from his chest, as though he had chestnuts roasting inside him . . . For a few moments it seemed as if the two of them had pricked up their ears and were listening . . .

"A-s-th-m-a!," he said to her at last, conspiratorially. "The doctors call it a-s-th-m-a! The wretched fat doesn't help . . . Imagine a-s-th-m-a! By the time I'd learned to say it, it had got worse . . . If you had it, could you say it?" he asked her.

She shook her head uncertainly: it really did need a little effort to be able to pronounce this abstruse word the first time. And in his effort to pronounce it correctly and letter by letter, the poor cook sounded as if he were saying *as-*

them-eh! . . . Besides, until a few years previously, Julia had had to make a great effort to pronounce *skull* "skull" and *school* "school" so that those around her wouldn't laugh, but who, of course, because they wanted to laugh, had her say the words over and over again . . .

"No," she said to him shyly, "I . . . I don't have that."

"God forbid that you ever should!" the cook retorted. "There's nothing worse!"

She could have said the same about her own *asthma* . . .

At that moment there came a familiar sound of dry reeds clashing together (familiar from the time she had sat down on that couch), and the cook's son came out of a narrow opening at the back, next to the braziers, which, instead of a door or even a curtain, had hanging reeds; reeds, that is, cut into thin strips and attached by string from top to bottom so that if anyone passed through them, it was as though a crowd of gypsies with tambourines was passing by. Among the reeds were also some large blue beads, to ward off the *evil eye*, like the eyes of the fox, and some tiny animal bones—no doubt from those left on the plates—tied with thread as a kind of afterthought.

The teenager (whose legs recalled somewhat the hanging reeds), not seeing his father in his usual place—and without it passing through his mind that perhaps his father could see him from some other place—did something unseemly that made you wonder why he hadn't at least done it earlier, before the clashing of the reeds: he leaned over and very quickly rubbed his hair with one hand over the dish he was carrying, scattering dandruff all over it like salt and pepper, perhaps with a hair or two as well . . . Then he immediately set the dish down in the place he was supposed to—and at the very same moment, a towel came down on his head!

The reeds clattered more loudly than ever before—then again, even more wildly, as the terrified son was followed by the furious, asthmatic father, pouring out a shower of abuse . . .

Julia reflected that she couldn't go on sitting on the couch waiting for her father—particularly because in his haste the poor cook had lost one of his shoes and she considered it her duty to pick it up. As for the men who were gathered outside the place in the sunshine, they had, it seems, heard the reeds clatter in that way many times before, and so they didn't budge from their seats; a few of them simply turned their heads laughing . . . Julia was expecting them to ask her what was going on (and what would she tell them?), but it was questionable whether they even saw her, given how dark it was inside and with their eyes accustomed to the strong sunlight outside. Nevertheless, the smell from the braised meat on the dish reached their nostrils and she heard one of them say: "There's a smell of incense in the air, pal! What time is it?"

Holding the cook's large shoe with its worn heel, she went over to the reed-covered doorway . . . She gently pushed aside the reeds and saw a yard.

She stepped back and closed her eyes because the first thing she saw in that yard was three slaughtered hens. She would always leave the house whenever her mother was going to slaughter a hen; she would go to one of her compassionate aunts who lived nearby, an extremely compassionate, tender, and suffering aunt, and there, hidden in her aunt's skirts or in the cellar, she would stop up her ears until evening so as not to hear, as she believed, the hen's throes . . . She would return at night—if they hadn't been looking for her in the meantime—and again she would wonder how she would manage, what she would face, while the others inside were licking the last little bones and calling to her through the railings: "Come on in Julia, don't be afraid. The hen's not in pain anymore, now it's laying its eggs elsewhere." In the way they said it to her, they made her hate them, not want ever to go near them, yet on the other hand she saw quite clearly that the hen—that particular hen, at least—was truly no longer in any pain, was no longer screeching, was no longer alive.

And so now, too, she reflected that these three hens were no longer in pain, they couldn't have suffered anymore after having been butchered; so . . . she *could* see, and, moreover, she *wanted* to see other things too (which her eye had only just managed to catch sight of) in that strange yard—and so she once again pushed aside the reeds.

And she saw a girl, thin as a rake, like her, perhaps slightly older than her, who was furiously plucking the hens . . . She was sitting on a low wide stool, and despite her awful chore she was without doubt the cook's daughter who was sick with sisaibeoma: round her head in plain sight was a similar scarf, in another color of course, duller, more befitting the illness (only someone like Eftha would wrap a hairless girl's head in a coral-colored scarf), and her cheeks displayed the same sad paleness; she had the same weak legs, the same bony fingers and all the rest and all the rest: the afflicted recognized each other even if their *suffering* was not immediately obvious, even more so when it was . . . And they had no particular liking for each other, as others said or as they let others think. Nor does one of them even accept that they are like the others . . . the others are always in a worse condition (without knowing it and simply deluding themselves), the others are always more pitiable and miserable . . .

O at that moment, Julia's heart became a tangle of emotions impossible to unravel on seeing her likeness, who, like someone blind or half-blind, had her nose almost touching the feathers her fingers were tugging at with short, sharp movements—sometimes they didn't tug at anything—while every so often she would turn her head to the left, to the far end of the large yard full of stones and puddles, to where her father was beating her brother next to a brick oven. And now and again, she would even go to the trouble of calling out, "Don't, you're ill, he won't do it again . . . Don't hit him anymore, your asthma will start up again." But she said it without much expression in her voice, without spirit (and she pronounced *asthma* "asma"), as though she really wasn't concerned about either her father or her brother. And she didn't even notice Julia, though she glanced once or twice in the direction of the reeds. On the contrary, whenever she remembered it, she leaned down and picked up her glass from the ground and drank from it greedily, or rather she drank nothing, having already drained it, and simply sucked the air out of the empty glass, then put it down again before getting back to the feathers with even greater intensity. Two of the hens were in her lap, the third on the stool beside her. Her fingers were red from the slit throats and her clothes stained.

Exhausted, as though someone had placed her in front of the most heartless and dispiriting mirror, Julia moved her eyes away from the scene . . . then brought them back. And she kept moving them away and bringing them back and this went on and on.

"Stop it, I'm tired of you," shouted the girl in a still expressionless voice to her father and brother—but it was as though she were saying it to Julia.

"And I'm tired of you, too, off with you!" shouted the cook from behind, letting go of his son, and then wringing his sock from his shoeless foot after stepping in one of the puddles. "You good-for-nothing. Off with you and find my shoe," he said to him, "or there's more where that came from! And find my towel too—you lazy ne'er-do-good! Mangy numbskull! I'll have you lick your heels! And mine too, off with you!"

Dizzy from all the cuffs and the *promises*, the boy didn't see Julia in the doorway holding the shoe and stumbled over to his sister.

"Have you got his shoe?" he asked her, gripping her bony arm.

"I haven't got anything, and take your dirty hands off me," she said.

"I . . . I've got it!" shouted Julia, making use of the reeds around her and their *cric-crac* to announce her hitherto unseen presence.

The boy's sister cast a questioning glance in her direction, in fact over her head, as though she saw Julia's voice in flight . . .

"Who was it that spoke?" she asked her brother.

"You called my hands dirty, I'm not telling you!" he replied.

"I call them dirty every day," she retorted. "And who might you be?" she said in a louder and expressionless voice, asking the unknown girl directly and gazing up even higher than before—truly . . . as though Julia were a head higher than she actually was!

"What should I say?" she wondered. "Can't she see?" And timidly, she descended the two steps after the reeds which led into the yard with its puddles.

"Who are you? What are you doing here?" asked the girl again, fixing her tiny deep-set eyes on Julia's feet now, on her black shoes.

"Nothing . . . I'm bringing the shoe," she answered.

"What shoe? What's she talking about?" asked the other girl, turning to her brother, but since her brother was no longer in the place she thought, she stretched out her arm and waved it cautiously in front and around her: "Where are you? . . . Stavros? . . . ," she called out.

Blind. She was . . . blind!

Julia got a fright, a terrible fright. Not because she had chanced upon a blind girl, but that for so long—*as if blind herself!*—she hadn't realized . . . And apart from this, she panicked at the idea that this girl might have been blinded as a result of the sisaibeoma. Up until now, everyone knew that the worst thing that this illness could cause was to leave you without hair and without appetite for anything—no one had talked of blindness. But perhaps this happened too as the final blow? Besides, she thought, the two can't be unrelated: there was no way this girl could have sisaibeoma *and* just happen to be blind—for two such misfortunes to befall the same person was simply too much. Or perhaps the yards were to blame, those backyards that hide so many things?

Trembling, she handed the shoe to the cook, and he took it laughing, coughing, and waving his hands like someone who has learned many lessons in life and is now teaching them to others.

"Is it my daughter Marietta you're looking at?" he asked her, slipping from one puddle to the next while putting his shoe on. "Poor thing can't see, but look at her handiwork, look at the work she does—for three! She's the one who killed the birds, she's the one who cleans them, and she's the one who'll put them in the pot. She does it all."

Julia shuddered to her bones: she imagined the birds and the twelve-year-old girl searching for their necks! . . .

"And look," the cook went on, slightly lifting the scarf from his daughter's forehead and telling her to sit quietly, "look . . . my darling girl is growing new hair. Just like you, no? You two have not only grown new teeth, you'll grow new hair too—I should be so lucky . . . May the good Lord forgive me for talking like that." A seething sound was heard from his chest, a cat's purring.

"Who are you talking to?" his daughter asked, pulling the scarf down to the eyebrows.

"To a girl just such as you," he said, winking at Julia.

She didn't like that—it was too true not to hurt.

"Bring her closer," the cook's daughter said, emptying her lap—she put the two hens down on the stool together with the third and shook the feathers off her—as if she were *preparing* the whole area for Julia. "Tell her to come here," she said again.

"Come over here," the cook urged her, "come on, don't be scared. She doesn't pluck people, she just wants to see you—she sees with her hands."

Julia said the shortest prayer that she could remember from her mother ("... Lord, have mercy!" ... and at the same moment the reeds clattered again), and she went up to the girl as she would to the edge of a precipice.

The girl reached out her hand, searching for Julia's.

Julia helped her to find it, to take hold of it . . .

All she wanted was to hold it, to feel it . . . She left her a *rose* of red fingerprints, held it a little longer, and then, without saying anything, let go of it and again took hold of one of the hens, placing it in her lap. And through her teeth, she asked for another glass of lemon. And for something to eat, she was hungry.

"You're hungry?" said her father, surprised, and stared at Julia: "Did I hear right? Did she say *I'm hungry?* She's not been hungry for months!"

Julia was unable to hold herself back:

"Did she go blind from the sisaibeoma?" she asked him.

He stared at her in amazement.

"No," replied the girl with that same flat and guileless voice that the sightless usually have.

"From the sisaibeoma? Whatever made you think that?" asked the cook. "My Marietta was born like that . . . she touches blood but can't see it; everything for her is black and blacker." He tapped her gently on the back to accompany him back into the dining room and whispered in her ear: "And don't think that she's unhappy about it . . . She doesn't know that life for us has other colors—how would she know, the poor girl?"

"I know," came the harsh sound of her voice from behind them. "Stavros told me so I'd be jealous, told me everything. But I'm not jealous—I hope you enjoy your *colors.*"

She said it as she might say *collars*, starch, stuff and nonsense.

The cook sighed sorrowfully: he had forgotten that Marietta might not have been able to see, but she could *hear* and sometimes even the thoughts of others. He sighed again.

"Right then . . . let's go," he said to Julia. And he added somewhat vaguely: "I didn't mean to . . ."

Strangely enough, she didn't want to leave anymore. But she followed him, leaving Marietta alone. She *gazed* at their feet with a sad, slightly spiteful expression, and hearing the reeds closing behind them leaned over and said something to the hens.

On seeing her come through that reed-covered doorway, Christoforos waved to her. He was back from his business, and if he didn't seem too worried at not finding her on the couch, it was because the cook's son had told him where she was. So he was standing and waiting for her while conversing with another three men, who were waiting to eat, and holding a new cypress-green hat.

Perhaps because she felt calmer now that he had returned, perhaps also to punish him for having taken so long, though he had promised not to, Julia returned his wave very fleetingly and stayed close to the cook, almost brushing up against him.

"Aren't you going to go over to your father?" he asked, puzzled.

"I'll go," she said; "aren't you going to take some food to Marietta?"

The cook remembered and jumped to it—he went over to the steaming pans of food.

"*Food for Marietta!*" he said. "Do you know how long it's been since Marietta asked me for food? Mo-o-o-onths, I can't remember how many! But months. How did her appetite suddenly come back to her? Was it because she saw you? Up until yesterday, I had to beg her to eat . . . Hey, you!" he shouted to his son.

The boy was standing beside him in front of the pans, filling plates for the impatient customers who were sitting at the tables, with his eyes fluttering at his father's every movement, his spots shining stars in the steam, and his mouth constantly moving as though in mental prayer . . . Hearing the angry voice, he stopped dead with the ladle in the air and sucked in his lips.

His father took the red towel he had previously brought down on his head (now it was hanging from a hook), shook it like a duster, and hit him with it again on the back of his neck: "Did you blow your nose into it for seasoning?" he asked him, taking care that the others sitting at the tables didn't hear him.

The boy just cowered and shook his head. He seemed particularly upset.

"Uncivil are we? Don't like being talked to like that in front of a girl, is that it? And who told you to shake your hair into the plates, eh?"

"I didn't shake it into the plates," said his son, in a tight corner. "But that man who asked for the roast meat . . . he kept making fun of me."

"Why was he making fun of you?"

"He called me spotty-face . . . and spike-haired . . . and a load of other things."

"Make fun of him back, call him spotty-face," said the cook.

"And that my lips are like two maggots . . ."

"Tell him that his eyebrows are like maggots! Whoever heard of such things!" He turned to Julia, who had her head lowered: "A child learns its manners from its mother," he said to her, as if wanting in some way to justify his son's not always blameless behavior and perhaps also his own. "Do you have a mother?"

"I do," she replied, as though feeling slightly guilty about it.

"Take good care of her," he counseled her, "a mother's worth more than ten sacks of gold. I didn't know my mother, I lost her when I was young. And the same with my children, runs in the family. If I'm not mistaken, neither my father nor my father's father knew his mother—like I said, *runs in the family* . . . Three and four generations without a mother, how can we be expected to get on?"

"And why didn't the fathers get married again?" Julia ventured to ask. "When his first children lost their mother, my father got married again."

"Ah, you see, we never thought of doing that," said the cook, "once bitten . . . how does it go . . . twice shy. A wise counsel. Though wisdom too is something you get from your mother." He turned again to his son: "Leave that to me," he told him, "I'll be the one to feed the hungry maggots—you take a plate of food to your sister. She's *hungry*. Our Marietta's hungry again, she's regaining her strength."

That's what the doctors had said to her father too. "When she gets hungry, when she asks for something to eat, it means that she's regaining her strength." She herself still hadn't asked. If they gave her something to eat, she would per-haps eat, but she still hadn't *asked herself*—Marietta was fortunate.

The boy passed through the reeds again with a steaming dish, a large piece of bread, and a spoon.

When he came back (not straightaway, as his sister had grabbed the dish from him and asked him to put the hens into boiling water), he said to his father: "You should see how she's eating! . . . She's eating and her tears are falling into the plate! . . . From joy, I don't know from what else. Where's the other girl to hear it?"

The fat cook hit him again with the towel.

"Which other girl? Isn't one enough for you?" And he added in a dramatic tone: "The other one's leaving."

"Leaving?" The teenager ran to the big front door. "Are you both leaving?" he asked Julia's father.

"We didn't come to stay," he replied, and gave him to understand that it wouldn't be a bad idea if he lent a hand to help load the boxes and cases onto the carriage that was waiting.

The boy helped—he could have lifted mountains . . . his eyes searched for Julia.

She was inside the dark carriage, between two unknown women who were impatient in their black attire and who evidently would be traveling with her and her father. It resembled a kidnapping.

It really did resemble a kidnapping. And before the coachman sat in front and took hold of the reins, and before Christoforos jumped into the carriage, the cook's son started acting crazy, as though something had stung him.

"From my sister! . . . This is from my sister!" he said to Julia, searching desperately in his pockets. "From my sister—don't go, she told me to give it to you . . . where did I put it?"

"Never mind, you can give it to her another time," Christoforos said to him, and nudged the coachman to get going.

"No, *now!*" the boy shouted.

And he stood in front of the horses opening his arms and legs—then he lowered his arms to search once again in his pockets.

"Get out of the way, you spotty squirt, we're in a hurry," the coachman said to him in a puzzled tone.

"Now . . . now . . . I'm getting out of the way . . . why such haste? Let me find it . . . where is it? . . . from my sister . . . where did I put it? She said I had to give it to her . . ."

He stood there muttering to himself, searching for a feather, a large feather that, instead of being blown away by the breeze—because the breeze might have taken it, no one else would have been quick enough—ended up being stuffed into his pockets.

And neither he nor Julia would understand why such haste for the horses to gallop off leaving behind them an enormous cloud of dust, which would cover everything for a few moments and plunge everything into a silence like that of the grave.

He went back into the eating house and slowly passed by the couches-tables; he really did appear to be sad, to have had his wings cut.

"Hey . . . Have your ships been scuttled?" his father asked him. "Did that little sick girl make your heart throb? Don't be despondent, we have our Marietta."

The boy reflected that they had indeed been left with their blind Marietta again and with the familiar daily customers, the familiar daily events.

"Or perhaps she didn't make it throb?" his father asked again, fastidiously.

"Marietta liked her," the boy said to him after a brief hesitation; "she wanted me to give her . . . because she was ill too . . . a whole hen."

The cook was taken aback:

"A whole hen! What got into your sister? Has she found her appetite and lost her marbles? And what would the customers eat?"

"It was me who put the three of them in to boil," said the boy sulkily.

"I should think you did—otherwise I'd have put you in to boil instead," said the cook.

"She gave me a beautiful feather to give her . . . But I lost it, where could it be? And why did they leave so quickly? Has war broken out?" he asked, pointing towards the door, where the cloud of dust still hadn't settled.

"Think I know why?" said his father. "Women . . . They're like whirlwinds, we hardly get a good look at them."

Julia was already too far away to be able to hear what the two of them were saying. But she herself felt suspicious of the two women who were sitting next to her, at the right and left of her, looking as if they weren't at all disturbing her—and what's more, as if they were actually doing her a favor by taking her with them on that breathless return.

They had arrived at the eating house so unexpectedly . . . Suddenly, everyone stopped eating and talking and turned to look at the women . . . They certainly weren't black shadows, they were real women . . . Out of breath, they went up to the first coachman, paid him whatever he asked, and told him that by five o'clock that afternoon, they had to be at Dekatessara, a well-known crossroads at the time, where one of their kin would be waiting for them with his horses to take them to another place (on an urgent matter, they said, that couldn't be postponed) by roads so rough and impassable that iron wheels couldn't possibly pass over them, only trained horses.

"And why didn't you come earlier? Did you only decide now?" asked the coachman. "How are we going to get to Dekatessara by five?"

They told him that they had had things to do earlier—and gave him a bit more.

With so much money gleaming in the palm of his hand, the coachman agreed to run the legs off his horses and melt the wheels on his carriage so as to arrive at Dekatessara by five.

But why Christoforos had been in such a hurry to leave with them when he could have taken another carriage, just for himself and his daughter, was still unclear. He told his daughter: because they had come to town with the same coachman, and because if he were to delay any longer with his friends, who were everywhere, and all the conversations he kept striking up, night would fall and they still wouldn't have set off—and Eftha, the inn, the house, the shops, and the fields were waiting for them . . . They had been gone six days, and he didn't want to be gone even one hour more—that's what Julia thought. But he went on: "A happy coincidence, a happy coincidence," he kept saying reassuringly, squeezing her knee, which was shaking (as was the entire carriage), since the two horses, spurred on by the whip, were galloping wildly.

And it was only the beginning. When they left the town behind and took some devilish little roads, shortcuts, supposedly to arrive more quickly at Deka-tessara, Julia wished she had never arrived at that town rather than for the journey to end like this. Her own father, too, was making her upset, amidst all that turmoil and hardship, by finding the courage—oblivious to everything around him—to exchange smiles with the two unknown women in black and to make eyes at them from under his heavy eyebrows, eyes about which her mother had said to her in moments of despondency or perhaps resignation: "It was those eyes of his that made me fall for him. One day, they'll make me fall into my grave." Julia thought it amazing that she would recall those words while her father's eyes were bearing down on *other* women, on two unknown women—this had never happened before, at least not in front of her.

But the most incredible and outrageous thing was not those smiles—which had already elicited a response—or even those eyes. It was that the two women sitting on either side of her kept *changing*. They changed like silkworms, how might she better put it? While their heads were rocking back and forth from the shaking of the carriage and the jolting up and down, they kept pulling rib-bons and fabrics out of little blue cases under their feet and changed . . . putting on other clothes, so that from being dressed in black, they became saucy little things, without stripping completely, and without it being possible to under-stand what was going on with them. And they tittered and shrieked as they helped each other to button up the new clothes and fix their hair, up till then tied up and hidden beneath large black scarves. They used Julia as a kind of *bridge*, given that the workings of fate had arranged it so that she was sitting be-tween them . . . And under her nose she saw their hands, no longer concealed by inelegant sleeves but ringed with fancy bracelets, crossing. They glanced a couple of times with deep surprise at the coral-colored fabric wrapped around the head of this terribly pale little girl—but went on with what they were doing . . . If Julia could have got up and walked away or simply shown indifference, she would have taken a road directly ahead of her and vanished like a spirit, even if it had meant her father losing her too; but how was she to escape from that wretched *ark* that was heaving over the stones? Nevertheless, she did what she could: she got up, using her hands as legs and attempting to meet her father's eyes (without actually succeeding), and went to sit in another corner, not particularly close to him, but far enough away from them. They just laughed or something of the sort; anyway they weren't upset, didn't clothe themselves in black again.

And what of him? Quite simply, he had forgotten her. That is, he was pretending to have remembered his purchases in their boxes, was supposedly sorting through them or examining them again to assess them more soberly, but his eyes struggled in vain to free themselves from the legs and the frills of the two women . . . Though often, just as at the beginning, he would stretch out his hand and squeeze his daughter's knee: "Happy coincidence," he said again; "don't be scared because the horses are racing."

When still in the doorway of the eating house, Julia had overheard the coachman whispering to him: "They'll be in such a hurry over some will or other, some father or uncle of theirs must have kicked the bucket and they're rushing to make sure they get their share" — and her father whispering back and nudging him: "What will, are you blind? Black on the outside, fire on the inside — they're rushing to be in time for the cavalry, haven't you heard?"

What will, what cavalry, what fire? Julia looked from under her eyelids at the two changed women (they had even put on shoes with bows now and were digging out lace fans), without being able to make sense of it. And then one of them — what was she thinking of! — pulled out a little red velvet purse and handed it to her.

"Take it," she told her.

Julia looked at her father.

"Eh, take it if she's giving it to you," he said.

And she took it, reached out her hand and touched it, looked at it, looked at her, looked at it again, didn't know what to do with it . . .

"Take it, it's *for you*, she's kind and she's giving it to you," the other woman hastened to add.

Imagine being eleven years old, suffering from sisaibeoma, beset by siankes, a bit starry-eyed, and chancing upon two female harpies who suddenly give you a velvet purse!

"Take it, what are you afraid of?" they both said again in one voice.

She was mistrustful, hesitant . . . She wanted it, of course, it was a very beautiful purse, she held it in one hand, but . . .

The first woman, the same who had given it to her, took it back, held it in front of her almond-shaped eyes, up to her nose, inhaled rapturously as though she were in the vale of roses and gave it back to her saying: "It smells gorgeous! Do the same — so you don't get dizzy with the galloping of the horses."

Julia held it in front of her own eyes, not far from her nose (it smelled like liquid cinnamon or pine oil dipped in . . . in what else?), breathed in a little deeper to smell it better and held it there: it wasn't pleasant so much as over-powering . . . it held her fast in a sweet fear . . . and she heard their double and triple breaths as they waited for her to say something, heard the horses racing like the wind, the whip cracking, the wheels creaking.

"Are you dizzy now?" they asked her in the sweetest of voices.

She didn't condescend to answer—from the sides and from underneath she could still see everything . . . She accepted, however, the humiliation of staying like that with the purse in front of her eyes and the bitter self-deception that now she was no longer dizzy, no longer saw, no longer wanted to see. But they told her to smell the velvet purse some more, to smell it *deeply*, very deeply, and to count up to ten! She counted up to ten as fast as she could and at that point her strength deserted her, everything went black—at that point the evil spirits, as Eftha would say, won: she saw her friend Marietta running with open arms and cute bandy legs, like babies have when they first start walking, and falling upon her like a feather, she felt velvety female hands laying her down on a straw mat-tress and heard her father from above, from far away, coughing and talking con-stantly, talking incessantly, as when fir trees rustle and like a flash a story came into her mind about someone who didn't eat anything, who fasted all the time (and yet whose existence depended on this), and who, when the others weren't watching—when they were sleeping like her or were far away from him—*sang*, wore himself out singing, lest the others thought, given that they couldn't see him, that he was eating in secret!

Julia smiled—what a confusing story with fasting and rustling . . .

She awoke at Dekatessara; it was her father who woke her up. The horses were no longer galloping, they had been unharnessed and the carriage was lean-ing with its front part resting on the ground—so she awoke with her head point-ing down and a little heavy, fuzzy, as if she were being pulled from the depths of a lake. He shook the straw from her elbows, her dress, and her cheeks, and helped her to slowly climb down with him and emerge from the halted covered carriage. Without saying anything, Julia went back on all fours and in a panic: the kerchief had fallen from her head, and it was only when she got outside into the cool air that she realized—the thought that they had seen her with her head bare made her want to die! She found her kerchief, put it on, and sat down again on the straw . . .

Her father reached out his long arm and tugged at her feet. "No one saw you," he said.

"They saw me," she said, hiding her face in her hands.

"Who? I want to—"

"God, He did!"

"No one saw you," he said again, "do you think God has got nothing better to do? And anyway, it's not bad to let the air get to your head now and again, the doctors said so: you should take it off when you're asleep . . . You slept like a little lamb, do you know? I called to you, but you didn't hear—we got here a good half hour ago."

He was speaking like the other one who fasted, who sang, that is, while she kept touching her right cheek: she felt that it was swollen, as if there were something wrong with it, something stuck there that wouldn't come off.

"It's from the straw," he said, "you slept with your cheek on the straw and it's left a mark . . . your hair's getting thicker, did you know? Your mother will be pleased"—and with the back of his hand he stroked her cheeks . . . "*You're to say to your mother, if she asks you, that we left the hospital in the afternoon and passed by Dekatessara for a while to see the horses*"—he said this to her almost as an order, and in a particular way: making clear to her something that she must not forget, or say in any other way, or even ask why—neither now nor later. "Come and see," he said, pulling her over to the place where the coachman's two horses were grazing and pointing to the coachman, who was sitting on the grass. "Look, he's got the food out to eat . . . They have lovely spring tomatoes here, we have salted sardines, and cheese, aren't you hungry? . . . But why am I asking? Of course, you're hungry."

He gave her half of one of those large bright red tomatoes, fleshy, sweet, and soft, that people called apple-tomatoes because they ate them like apples.

She held it in her hand and remembered the purse . . . She knew, even if she never opened her mouth, that *a-a-a-all* that her father had told her was nothing compared to *a-a-a-all* that he wanted to hide from her.

"Or is it an apple-apple that you want and not a tomato?" he asked her again.

"Apples? Did someone ask for apples?" asked a short and swarthy fellow behind another coach. "If it's apples you want!" And nimble as he was, he poked around in a barrel and jumped down with an armful of apples: "There! If it's apples you want! Let everyone have apples—let the rich eat and the poor have their fill!"

"Give us a few to try," Christoforos said to him, "we're from a line of apple eaters."

The man emptied the armful of apples into a basket, filling it with as many more.

"A good few pounds there, and the basket too," he said, wiping his mouth (he had four fingers), "here, we give them away, we don't sell them—do you see around you? It's festival time in Dekatessara! We're not selling them, I said, today we're giving them away!"

Christoforos took out a few coins and handed them to him because, a merchant himself, he didn't believe in gifts. The man counted them in a jiffy, threw them into a pouch, took hold of two or three apples (from their basket), and raced off after three bent old women.

"Apples?" he shouted to them too. "Did you three pretty things ask for apples?"

"And where will we find the teeth for apples?" they asked complainingly, "have you got any figs for us?"

"Figs in August, together with the snakes," he retorted.

Coming from the other direction was another man, barefoot and wearing a robe, with his finger raised. And if you had patience and were in a good mood, you would hear words such as these:

". . . Your light should shine before people for them to see your good works and glorify your heavenly father. And whoever wants to live without sorrow should carefully seal his lips and not speak rashly. And prudence not anger should govern man's actions. For which is the wildest of all animals? Man when he is angry! And who is the companion who doesn't forsake us at the hour of our death, as do worldly goods and family and friends, but who accompanies us to the courtroom of God? It is our good deeds that accompany us and plead for our deliverance! . . . O Holy One, haven of all who beseech you, hear the prayers of your unworthy suppliants! . . ."

Dekatessara had been a well-known crossroads since olden times. But once every year, it became literally steeped in glory: on the occasion of an anniversary celebrated faithfully by the inhabitants of the surrounding villages—the pastures of which nourished exceptional livestock and in particular a renowned breed of horses—Dekatessara was transformed into the Promised Land, and for three days and nights it became a land of milk and honey for traders. The road, or rather that *star* from which a host of roads, paths, and bridges radiated out, was blocked during those days by the goods that piled up, by the animals carrying the people to see them and buy them, and also by the animals that many people brought to sell.

Nevertheless, the most characteristic thing about Dekatessara wasn't the fair or cattle market of the kind held in many other parts and at many times of the year. It was the *horse mating* that took place there every spring and lasted three days: the best or more common horses from throughout the land, and also from throughout the Balkans, were brought there to mate with other horses of similar breed or, at any rate, of similar strength. Naturally, they were accompanied by their owners and usually by all the members of the family—and during these days, Dekatessara was teeming with people, voices, yelling, cheering, neighing, goods for all purses and tastes, with children and old people, men and women, and whatever anyone could possibly imagine. Which is why, if you were in a hurry to get to the next province, you avoided Dekatessara on those days, even if it was on your route. Just as others did their level best not to avoid the temptation of passing by there, even if it was out of their way.

The Church, moreover, resented it if this horse festival—they called it horse *idolatry*—coincided with Easter (as was the case that year: it had begun on Holy Thursday) and saw it as an aberration on the part of any Christian who ignored the Church's ban and went to this place of shame instead of going to the service—and from this point of view, there were exceptionally few Christians who were not guilty of this aberration during the days of this *double* Easter. And the Church had made efforts to persuade the inhabitants of this area that was so renowned for its horses to at least change the date of their festival if this fell at the same time as Easter, to move it to a date before or after. But the inhabitants replied that their festival was not a movable one, that it always began on April 23, so—they said—it was a good thing that the Church had not made Easter an immovable feast. They couldn't come up with a solution.

For some, however, it was one drop too many, and they also brought their dogs and donkeys and sheep and goats to mate at Dekatessara, which did not give rise to a wave of protest: everything seemed natural and permissible, and the people too—for three days each year—were innocent and guileless like their animals.

Anyway, this particular year, when Julia and her father were to pass by Dekatessara, coincided with something else: an important Carpathian prince would be there, they said, with all his horses and cavalry so as, with his presence, to honor the festival, the one and only such festival so it seemed, but also to stop at the places around Dekatessara, wild and idyllic places, for a short time. And this, whatever anyone might say, lent a special *flavor* to what was in any case a special festival.

That's why we could say that those women perhaps acted with excessive naïveté or caution (unless this excited them) in dressing modestly and coming out with the story to the coachman about someone waiting for them with his horses at Dekatessara—and all the rest about the urgent matter that couldn't be postponed—when during those days, Dekatessara was far from being simply a crossroads, nor was it possible for an experienced coachman not to know what went on there . . . Yet even if the coachman happened to have forgotten the festival and to have been uninformed about the additional *Carpathian visit* (as proved to be the case), the same wasn't true of Christoforos, who, of course, immediately twigged the real reason that these women were going to Dekatessara . . . and the fire that was smoldering beneath their black exterior.

As for the rest, whatever this was, only his daughter could tell us. But they put her to sleep . . . This at least became known to us as a nebulous end to that journey which would enwrap her in an equally nebulous way, forever: shadowy and blurred scenes — and how was this very different from a blurred memory? — given that, months and even years later, she would remember the scenes and it would seem to her that they had never happened, that she always remembered them . . . Yet that's our lifeblood and our riches, because events end constantly in order to become memories, and memories slowly dissolve. But not their *effects*.

The person who wouldn't keep his mouth closed about what he went through was the coachman, who, after having quelled his hunger with a small mountain of salted sardines and sweet tomatoes, entrusted his carriage and horses to a professional guard and set off with Christoforos and his daughter to make a closer tour of the place of the festival. It was then that he discovered that only one of the four coins given to him by the women was in fact genuine — the one of smallest value that they had given him at the end, supposedly as a tip. The other three, for which he had risked life and limb and almost crippled his horses, were counterfeit.

His legs collapsed under him. And the women had vanished. He was angry at Christoforos, too, not because he laughed, but because he said so lightly: "Did you have your eyes shut or something? Didn't you see what stuff those two beauties were made of? I got wind of it from the very first, before I'd even seen them! And anyway" (he said this now), "I knew them, I'd seen them before outside the Lovely Nights . . . Women don't hang about outside inns at night without reason! Unless they're . . . butterflies of the night."

"And why didn't you tell me?" asked the coachman lamentably, "why did you let them rob me?"

"What was I to say . . . I wasn't certain that it was them," said Christoforos, looking now for excuses, evidently regretting having said more than he should — for apart from the coachman, his daughter was listening too.

The deceived coachman walked back and forth like a caged animal. He couldn't stomach the fact that he'd had the tables turned on him.

"Where are they? If I get my hands on them!" he growled. "Just show me where they are—you're the one who gets wind of such women before you even see them! Which way did your butterflies go? That way? . . . This way? . . . Just show me and I'll fix them! That way?"

Clearly regretful now, Christoforos tried to calm him, getting hold of his hands.

"Calm down, my dear chap, don't go on like that—what does *this way* or *that way* mean here? Can't you see what's going on all around? Calm yourself. They'll think we're mad, getting worked up about a couple of miserable coins."

"It was three! And those with money talk like that, not friends," the coachman retorted. "Let me find them, I'll hang your two butterflies by their hair!"

A crowd gathered around them—one of them was talking about butterflies with hair!

Julia began to find it enjoyable (the kind of enjoyment that stings), whereas her father began not to find it at all enjoyable; he stepped away from the coachman and pushed the onlookers away, telling them to mind their own business, to get back to the festivities: "This is the sticks, the wedding's over there!" he told them, and he pointed to an open space a little way off, lower down, where at that moment a white horse was rearing up on its two hind legs in excitement so as to be able to fall like a whinnying avalanche of snow upon the other one waiting . . . The air filled with applause and cheering—"Run and watch!" he said, pushing them again, and they forgot about the butterflies and ran back to the horses.

But the coachman had remained where he was and was still demanding *explanations* from Christoforos, narrowing his gaze at him more and more, as old needlewomen do when they are trying to find the eye of their needle . . .

As we'd say today, Christoforos was in a fix.

"What are you looking at me like that for, my good man," he said to him; "what did I do? Was it me who gave you the counterfeit coins?"

"*Was it you . . . was it you . . . ,*" screeched the coachman, not being able to find the words to express what he had finally begun to get wind of himself. "*Was it you . . .* Was that why YOU came up behind me like a hobgoblin while I was whipping the horses and told me that the ladies inside couldn't stand the sight of the whip, were getting dizzy, and wanted you to draw the curtain behind my back? Mmm? *Was it you?* WHEREAS I only draw that curtain when I'm carrying a corpse or a woman in labor, and ONLY THEN, not when I'm carrying a normal fare! And I took all of you today as a simple fare—you and your butterflies!"

In vain, Christoforos tried to shut him up, and in vain Julia struggled to feel sorrier for the coachman than for her father: the enjoyment that had stung her just previously was now taking on a greater dimension and a most unexpected turn.

"Anyway, anyway," said Christoforos, "let's not allow all this silly business to get out of hand—I'll give you cost of the fare! And for the two women, too, I'll pay everything, in double and triple—but let's forget it."

Yet, alas, as he went to take his wallet (to pay the coachman on the spot) from his inside pocket, where he always put it, he saw that the wallet had vanished. For a moment, his mind stopped working. "Keep calm," he told himself, "your mind's muddled, my man, keep calm." But no matter how much he searched, whether calmly or desperately, whether in this or in all his other pockets and side pockets, his wallet was nowhere to be found! And if he managed to contain his anger for all that had already been more or less revealed, his sadness and disappointment were depicted on his face and in those gray-green eyes with their thick, curling lashes . . .

"What have you got to complain about?" he said to the coachman, "I'm the one they robbed, you got taken in, that's all. Those harlots . . . So much the worse . . . Damn and blast! . . . But let's go and take a look in case I dropped it in the carriage and I'm getting worked up for nothing."

On finding a fellow sufferer, the coachman started to calm down.

"Let's go and take a look," he said. "But if it's not in the carriage, what you said still holds, Christoforos: you'll pay me the whole fare, and for the women too. All of it. There's no charity where my coach is concerned—I earn my living from it, just as you do with your inn."

And so they went back to the carriage to look, but, of course, all they found was straw and the boxes of things.

"Why on earth didn't they take those with them?" Christoforos said, puzzled and bitter.

"Be thankful they didn't take your daughter too to sell her at the market!" said the coachman. And he continued in the most genial and relentless tone: "But you've broken my heart, Christoforos, I've lost every idea . . . You who caught on to them right from the start, even before you saw them, and on whose account you came and closed the curtain behind my back—something no one has dared to do before now—for you to have been taken in like me! What am I saying, *like me?* Twice as bad . . . What will you tell your wife?"

"Leave my wife out of it," said Christoforos, his eyes glazing over.

He looked at Julia; her eyes had glazed over too . . . The young girl was weaving her fingers in front of her belly and stretching her chest back—it was a characteristic gesture of Eftha's (passed on to all her daughters and granddaughters) when she wanted to show discretion, or solidarity at least, complicity, stoicism

. . . Those women had brought shame on him, all women—the ones he'd married and the ones he couldn't marry because they were his daughters or sisters.

He picked two big fluffy leaves from some tall wild plants that the coach's wheels had half crushed and blew his nose on them (alarming the horses). It was his own characteristic gesture—on leaves, on handkerchiefs, on whatever he found—when he wanted to clear his head . . . And he usually said: "God, too, when he's tired, blows on everything and finds rest." He omitted to do so this time.

"Damn and blast!" he exclaimed again. "To hell with it all! Those two were *gutterflies*, not butterflies. From the gutter . . . Rodents—are we going to concern ourselves with them? They're partying at this very moment with the prince's cavalry—so what? Tomorrow the cavalrymen will be wailing, the day after the two women themselves—the rope and the rod have got two ends . . . I'll give you double the fare, do you hear?" he promised the coachman in a tone that brooked no objection. "And you . . . you," he said, turning with emotion to his daughter, "such beautiful red hair will grow again on that poor little head of yours that the prospective grooms will be like flies around you asking for your hand, but I won't let anyone have you! I'll tell them: First find another girl with hair like hers and then come and ask for Julia, that's what I'll tell them. And they'll run off to find another with such hair so as to win you! That's what will happen . . ."

He had been gripped by *what* remains, together with gentleness, when all else is lost.

Of course, all that had been lost now was a little money—not something to be ignored or disregarded—but more than this, his so-called honor had been lost, his good reputation, and this—no matter what anyone may say—stung, hurt him . . . But he wasn't going to let it get the better of him: after all, only one thing, as he said, is inescapable.

It was sufficient that Eftha didn't find out about any of this. Not that she would have killed him with her hoe or given him a mouthful of abuse, but she was more than capable of behaving towards him with subtle disdain for a couple of months, which would have brought him to his wits' end, so that he might have ended up by killing her (she had already got away with it by the skin of her teeth more than once). In any case, he preferred to let it pass, no matter how much it stung, and to draw strength from all this unpleasantness.

He left Julia with the coachman and went off to look for a friend or someone from his village to lend him some money till the following morning, when he would be back in his inn. He would pay the coachman there, but he wanted this money now for Julia: he had seen her (when the three of them were nonchalantly strolling around the fair) looking at some shoes, gluing her eyes on them—but without, naturally, saying anything to him. Just as when she was smaller she had glued her elbows on a crate of grapes or peaches outside their shop, again without saying anything, and this meant that she wanted a little bunch of grapes or a peach. All the other children simply took what they wanted without wasting much time, whereas she—if you didn't give it to her—was quite capable of drooling over it with her elbow on the crate till nightfall! So he wanted to get her those shoes (and without saying anything to her), to make a present of them to her after a journey like that . . . the guilt he felt might not have been so tragic as to demand punishment, but nevertheless it demanded some kind of atonement.

The few coins he had left in his pocket were not enough for such shoes, and so he was trying to borrow some money.

He ran into two of his older sons from his first marriage, who had come to Dekatessara with friends. They asked him what he was doing there, where Julia was, how he was, and all the rest, and, though having decided against asking to borrow something from them, Christoforos eventually did so, for time was passing. They found it strange: their father asking them to lend him money? They knew that he always went into town with enough money for his purchases and never returned with empty pockets.

"What happened? Did someone rob you?" they asked.

"Rob me, are you serious?" he said. "It's simply that with the doctors and all the medicine, I've nothing left."

The sons, however, only had the bare minimum with them for their trip to Dekatessara—he wouldn't hear of depriving them of it, and in any case it probably wouldn't have been enough for the shoes. He asked them simply if they wanted to leave with him in a while, in the same carriage, but they had only arrived that afternoon and were counting on staying till the day after next, when the festival ended.

"And where will you sleep?" he asked them.

"On the grass," they replied. "In the fields. Where everyone sleeps."

He didn't persist in trying to persuade them to go with him—the two hip-swaying phantoms that would accompany him along with Julia's third eye were more than enough for him.

"Be careful," was all he said to them, "there are some very fragrant roses around here but with big thorns."

A little farther on, he saw another of his sons, Lukas who had the limp, with one of his uncles, a brother of Eftha. When he was fourteen, Lukas had been apprenticed to this uncle to become a blacksmith, and as he showed great skill at it, Christoforos thought of handing over part of the inn to him after a few years, as well as a few more square feet of empty space, so that he could set up a smithy there for himself and for any of his sons or nephews who might want to work with him. He himself had had a liking for blacksmith work from the time he was small, but then it passed, and he devoted himself to his inn.

"What brought you two here?" he asked them (a somewhat superfluous question for two men who shoed horses from morning to night, even if they didn't ride them).

"We're here to look at the horses," they told him.

Then they too asked him about Julia and where he had left her, and he showed concern to find out what had been happening back home while he had been away. But to ask for a loan from one of his wife's brothers, that . . . Well, he would have to have had far less of a guilty conscience to do that. He was scared in case the brother asked him for money—he was already looking at him strangely—to buy a horse.

"What's the matter?" he asked him.

"Eh, nothing," replied the brother-in-law, "it's just that . . . I'm looking to borrow a bit of money, have you got any with you? I saw a horse, fine frame, one year old, and going for a bargain—you see, I didn't come prepared to buy horses, just to look at them."

"Afraid not," replied Christoforos sadly. "I'll empty my pockets out if you want, but I don't have anything. The doctors and the medicine for your niece cleaned me out—daylight robbery!"

There, *he had said it* and felt relieved, as though a weight had been lifted from him. He left them to manage on their own and went on searching himself for the wherewithal to buy Julia's shoes.

Crowds of people were coming and going all around him—he hoped he wouldn't suddenly come face to face with the two butterflies! . . . And he was sorry for hoping he wouldn't come face to face with them, because—if it weren't for his sons and wife's brothers being at the fair—he would *very much* like to come face to face with them, *very much*, he wouldn't have left a stone unturned in order to find them again and show them another side of his character, not only the one that they imagined, and . . .

"What a to-do, what a to-do!" he kept muttering, giving vent to his anger and trying to forget with everything that was happening around him: most of the horses were now being rested and generously fed so as to be at their best the next day . . . The other animals, which had been brought there simply to be sold, were chewing melancholically on their usual fodder as they awaited their new masters. But there were others, too, asses and mules, that were running to and fro or prancing around and coming out with cries of overexcitement—unhappy deep down: they'd had their rumps rubbed with turpentine to make them appear more lively and virile in order to increase their market price . . . Elsewhere, half-naked men were wrestling with each other for fun—those contests that start out as a game, with bravado and banter, and often end up as mortal combat. In other places, they were drinking, dancing, and kissing, offering their bottles to anyone passing who wanted to sink into that happy trance that sometimes turns into a bad dream. Gypsies had come too with their dancing bears, and Gypsy women who were selling green sieves and reading people's fortunes in their palms. Nor was there an absence of the blind, the dumb, and the paralyzed with their paillasses. Some people were talking of a certain Antonio Rades, from Portugal, who ate live lizards! The renowned *Goliath* was also there and was bending iron bars and sticking knives into his belly, and *Nero*, too, who breathed fire from his mouth and shouted "Rome! . . . Rome! . . ."

At one end of a bridge—under which there was no longer a river; it had been smothered by bushes and rocks—the man with the robe and the raised finger was saying to one or two listening to him that if they ever found themselves among people with one eye, they, too, should shut an eye and that if they had the faith of a mustard seed, they could say to this mountain, *Move from here,* and it would move! . . . They stared at the mountain, with the setting sun bathing its peaks in red, shut one of their eyes as though they were themselves one-eyed, but seemed to feel pity or simply be too bored to tell the mountain to change its position . . .

"Next year, I'll have to bring Eftha here," Christoforos thought. "She could wrap a couple of snakes round her neck, hitch up her skirt to the knee, and we could come to Dekatessara—she would make a name for herself, win renown, and we certainly need it . . ." Squinting, he looked around for the foreign prince, the blueblood from Carpathia with his cavalrymen, who instead of tassels on their hats had, they said, foxes' brushes—like the Carnival dancers in his own parts . . . Hmm, so it was so they could giggle in those brushes that those two *gutterflies* were in such a hurry, though they had had time to fleece him and make him look a fool . . . (Enough! Whatever he did, he couldn't get them out of his mind!) But their beaux, the ones with the brushes and the braid, either hadn't arrived yet or, more likely, had arrived and were resting (for the evening, when the festivities would start up again with the outdoor feasting) behind the gray, rocky heights of Dekatessara, where, quite unexpectedly, sloping expanses overflowing with trees, birds, and streams opened out. There were even some small waterfalls that gushed behind those rocks, and it's said, no less, that still to be seen roaming in those parts was *the woman of old Europe with her fawn*. Did they mean Genovefa? Or perhaps our own Artemis?

Christoforos heard and saw many things, then went back to Julia and the coachman to tell them it was time to leave because he had grown tired, had started to long for his inn and his peace and quiet. And he hadn't been able to borrow any money—he would buy her shoes another time, make sure he wouldn't forget.

But on getting back, he found his wife's brother and Lukas there, with some others, and a horse as fine as spring water.

"Where did you disappear to?" asked his brother-in-law. "I got the horse, here it is! I was looking for you to tell you and bumped into Julia, who was also looking for you."

Julia was sitting on the grass, all alone, and was plucking it, seemingly bored.

"Why were you looking for me?" he asked her; "didn't I leave you with the coachman for company?"

The girl raised her hand and pointed to the carriage and the two horses that were still grazing.

"He left, too, right after you," she told him, "then the guard had to go somewhere else, and they left me to watch over everything . . . I got tired."

"We'll be on our way," he said to her, "before nightfall, we'll be on our way." He turned to his brother-in-law: "And you, how did you pay for the horse?" he asked him, "with what money?"

"Ah, but I came up with some," he said, "if your luck's in! . . . I ran into an old acquaintance who owed me even I don't know how much or from when— the shirt on his back. And he was always moaning, I haven't got it, I can't, I'm broke, wait and wait some more. And I came upon him today, of all things, just as he was about to buy a pair of horses. Not just one, but *two!* The same one who didn't have enough to pay me for the horseshoes and the ropes was actually buying *two* horses! And without too much bargaining, acting like the lord of the manor! I stood behind him playing possum. And as soon as he pulled out his wad of money—more like a sackful than a wad—to pay, I went up to him and gently took his hand. Do you remember me? I asked him. Of course I remember you, he said. Do you remember what you owe me? I said. Eh, well, what . . . he protested. What and what a lot more! I told him; either you give it to me today, right this moment, and in front of all these people so I can buy a horse, or I'll drag you into court with a dozen witnesses! You should have seen him . . . Whether he wanted to or not, you see, he took out the money and gave it to me. He pretended to have to give back one of his own that he'd just bought, supposedly because he didn't have the money for *three* horses, but that wasn't of the slightest concern to me. I got back my dough, got my horse, and had some left to spare. If you want, I can lend you some."

Favored by the new circumstances, Christoforos didn't have the time to be difficult: whether from his wife's brother or from an enemy, he had to accept that money and get the present for Julia before his pangs of remorse abated and he forgot about it.

"All right," he said, "I wouldn't have asked you, but since you have it, lend me a bit till tomorrow. I want to get some shoes for Julia that I know she'll like" — he didn't even have time to hide it from her anymore, to let it be a surprise as he'd planned.

She was over the moon, got up from the grass with a changed expression: without losing her old, unenviable shoes, without her asking him for anything, he would buy new ones for her! . . . He held out his hand to her and she gave him hers, letting the others wait while they went to find the Jew who was selling them.

The Jew didn't waste any time either. We don't mean that he had already managed to sell the shoes to someone other than Julia but simply that he had used all his craft and his acumen and for those three days had constructed an entire temple of trade in those dry meadows of Dekatessara (the grassy ones were at the other side, behind the rocks), even expanding his business up on the rocks . . . but also *down* below the rocks, in some niches rather like caves formed by their enormous and intersecting outcrops. It was in here that a part of his goods was being safeguarded by a woman (evidently his wife, though she resembled him so much that she could have been his sister), and these goods were silk threads, wonderful embroidery, rare fabrics, and expensive jewelry—only rich young ladies went anywhere near there (and it's worth noting that there were such ladies who came to the fair at Dekatessara; it wasn't only for simple folk or for princes). However, strewn over the rocks and a little farther, on the dry grass, were threads and fabrics of the brightest or dullest colors that the poorer women could buy for a little money or exchange for poultry so that these hungry women could also have something to wear. And naturally, next to these was a pile of fancy jewelry to suit every purse. And, in addition, shoes—many, very many shoes, for all ages, in all styles, and all types: leather ones, woven ones, cloth ones, elastic and rubber ones, even wooden clogs. An entire army of shoes just waiting for feet to come and put them on.

And out of this entire army, the two that caught Julia's eye were a pair of blue suede sandals, not shoes, as her father had thought. Yes, *blue*, the only blue ones among so many others, and yes, *suede*: without doubt no other girl at that time had ever worn blue suede sandals.

Except that they were a bit big on her, very big unfortunately, and of course there were no smaller sizes (or larger, for that matter) in the same color and design—they were unique from every point of view. And Julia wouldn't look at any others, better none at all than others.

"But how are you going to wear them? They'll come off," Christoforos said. "Are you going to walk barefoot and carry them in your hand? And what's more, I brought you here to buy shoes—I thought you wanted some real shoes, not *sandals*. Sandals, eh, they're just sham, all holes and straps . . . they let the rain in and the toes out."

"I'll walk barefoot then, they're the ones I want," Julia said, replying to his first comment only.

"But, my dear girl, why walk barefoot?" the Jew's wife said to her in the voice of a hoarse goldfinch and through thin dark-red lips, suddenly coming over to the shoes and cheap fabrics and leaving her expensive caves; her skin was lily-white, smooth, and plump despite her indeterminable age, her eyes were dark blue, beady, and deep-set (full of sweetness, yet cunning too), her wavy brown hair was gleaming beneath a violet gossamer net, and her body, not at all scrawny or weathered, was wrapped in silk: naturally everyone looked at her first and then at what she was selling.

"Why barefoot?" she again asked Julia, touching her with the softest fingers in the world. "You'll grow eventually, won't you? So your daddy will get them for you now, and you'll wear them when you've grown. The years pass like birds overhead."

"You're right," said Christoforos, "but till then, till . . . the birds have passed, what is she going to wear?"

"O . . . till then! . . . There are lots of shoes . . . ," she said, with a weary smile and pointing randomly at the multitude of other shoes.

"That's what I've been telling her too—lots of other shoes!" said Christoforos. "But she has her heart set on these blue ones with all the holes."

"But, naturally," the woman agreed in her warbling voice, "I'd be the same if I were in her place—they're the ones that stand out. And if they're a little big for her . . . eh, her feet will grow before too long. What would happen if they were too small for her? There'd be no hope then."

She wrapped you in her words, it was her job after all, but the one thing you couldn't escape was her smile: a smile as though she were mortally tired of life and of people and, at the same time, a disarming smile, irresistible, full of seduction and endless allusions, sober, intoxicating, able to trap even the wiliest of foxes.

Julia's father looked toward the mountains: *If you have the faith of a mustard seed . . .* He glanced behind him: there were others standing there, some lean-looking men with four or five pairs of rubber shoes in their hands, with even more children around them and with wives indifferent to their cares or ready to fall apart, who were waiting for them to finish their bargaining so that they could begin theirs. Some had really beautiful eyes, but the way they were looking at the attractive saleswoman, you'd have thought that they were ready to sacrifice even these, to exchange them (together with the eggs in the wire baskets and the live hens they were holding) in order to get hold of two yards of fabric and a bauble or two for their necks. He felt sorry for them and decided to finish with it so that they could have their turn.

"And how much are those blue sandals?" he asked the saleswoman.

She told him a price that seemed to him not unreasonable (though everything that came out of her mouth was not unreasonable), and she pointed with her jeweled hand to a tent in front of the rocks, quite a way off, in the entrance to which was sitting the fat and red-faced Jew with his black attire, his glasses, and his black beard, ready to take the money.

"Tut, tut, tut! . . . Jews, everywhere Jews!" he murmured as he went over there. "Whatever stone you turn up, there's a Jew underneath! And with all his Jewish kids . . . Look how many he's got! More than I have . . . I don't know if they're all his sons, but it's an entire tribe."

Holding on to his arm with one hand (and on to the sandals with the other), Julia walked with head bowed, skipping steps and missing breaths, as though following the rhythm of a joyous song inside her. "That," her father reflected, "is something we haven't seen for a long time . . ." And he tried—though not too much and not too persuasively—to bring her back to reality, by showing her, among the fabrics and voile strewn over the grass (which they took care not to walk on by jumping over them or stepping to one side) the many young boys of her age and slightly older, all clad in black, who were hawking, in still unbroken high-pitched voices, the abundant wares of their father or at least of their employer.

"All the same tribe!" he repeated, circumspectly, as if it would be any less strange if each of them had belonged to a different tribe.

But Julia had other things on her mind, which eventually became too much for her, it seems.

"She was nice, that woman, wasn't she?" she said to him.

"Ni-i-i-ice," he replied with some reservation, wondering what in fact she meant: after her experience with the other two, the ones who had knocked her out in order to fleece him, he wasn't expecting her to talk like that about a third woman . . .

But Julia had taken a liking to this woman in the same way that we often take a liking to something from the first moment, whether or not there's any reason for it, or in the way we dislike something without bothering to search for the reason why.

"She was nice," she repeated to herself, and they weren't just words to her.

And so they found themselves before the Jew, who was waiting for them with much the same smile, he, too, *in full regalia*, but, being a man, his expression and his whole demeanor carried more weight.

"You look very much like your wife, did you know?" Christoforos said to him, aware that it was a good ploy to make a compliment—he hoped the other would take it as a compliment—if you're planning to ask a favor, and the favor he wanted to ask for was to let him have those sandals at a better price as it would take another ten years before his daughter would be able to wear them. "Of course, she's a woman, different again, but there's certainly a . . . *resemblance*," Christoforos said, clarifying himself.

"Most definitely, most definitely," the man in the black attire conceded, "don't you know that all couples resemble each other? Eh, yes," he answered his own question, "living together over so many years, the same years, with the little habits of the one that get on the nerves of the other, but that the other eventually comes to acquire too; all these things, my dear fellow, do their work without anyone being aware of it. And *solid work* . . . If someone were to see you with your wife, he'd think that you looked alike, perhaps take you for brother and sister or first cousins. Isn't that why we talk about being *joined together in marriage?* But," he said—as though it suddenly occurred to him—"where have you seen my wife?"

"Where have I seen her!" replied Christoforos. "Wasn't it her who charmed my daughter into wanting these sandals?"

"My wife's inside with the silks," said the Jew calmly, pointing with his thumb behind the rocks. "The other one with the shoes is her sister . . . Eh, yes, exactly, I live with two women. Ruth! . . . *Ru-u-u-uth!*" he called out in a singing voice. "Come out here for a moment."

Ruth! It was the first time that Julia had ever heard that name; back home there were a lot of unusual names (Eftha, Cletia, Eumolpos, Mama Petroula who was no longer alive, an uncle by the name of Epainetos, another one of Eftha's brothers, his wife Epesteme, and Theagenis who would later become Hesychios), but no Ruth, they didn't have a Ruth. And what could her sister's name be? Would she find out or would she have to guess? *Thur* perhaps? Who could say?

Ruth stuck her head out, followed by her rounded shoulders—her fingers gripped the rocks, but they were too white and plump to recall an eagle's claws—and she asked her husband what it was he wanted.

"They want to see you," he told her.

"To see me?" she said, surprised. "Let whoever wants to see me come inside and see my silks and my threads . . ."

It was clear that she really was the other woman's sister, though with slightly more striking characteristics and at least five years older; but the same voice, the same mischievous eyes, the same fine and desirable skin, the same shining hair in a hairnet, that same dangerous playfulness on the fine, ruby-red lips.

Julia thought that without any doubt the handsomest man she had ever seen was her brother Theagenis and the most beautiful women these two sisters—especially the one with the shoes—even if they weren't *exactly* beautiful . . .

"So much the better," said Christoforos to the Jew when she went back inside like a caterpillar into its cocoon. "You look like your wife and like her sister. If, and let's hope not, you lose the one, you'll still have the other . . . But really, didn't the other one ever get married?"

"She got married and got divorced," the Jew informed him. "And you know why? Just a moment . . . Because he forbade her to smile! . . . Of course, yes, that's how much . . . No, no, they'll have to go elsewhere for medicinal herbs, this is an emporium . . ." (He was replying at the same time to two black-clad boys who had come to ask him something.) Yes—what was I saying? Ah, yes, so the Smile came to live with us—in our language we call it Lehkhahyekh—and the worst thing is that she smiles at me too! You see, I'm not her husband to forbid her! But the strangest thing of all is that her sister, my wife that is, smiles at both of us!" A ringing bout of laughter gladdened his entire body and caused some passersby to stop or come closer: "So I can only smile too, and whatever happens, happens. You'll ask me why I'm telling you all this! Because you asked me, of course . . . We're living in harmony for the time being, wherever church bells and festive tambourines call us, and we have four children. Ruth gave birth to all of them . . . But your daughter, why is she so pale? Eh, my child?" he asked, turning towards her, his glasses reflecting the light, "your mother feed you on ants, does she? O, I know, it's that difficult age . . . If Ruth were your mother, she'd feed you on silks. And the other one on smiles . . . Well then, what's to be done, will you take those sandals, or shall I let some other girl have them?"

After all that he'd told them or allowed them to guess about his personal life, he showed that he hadn't forgotten about the sandals.

"So, can you give us a better price?" Christoforos asked him. "We want them even though she's not going to wear them, but just because she likes them. Pity to throw money away like that."

"There's no way it'll be thrown away," said the red-faced merchant.

Christoforos had no doubts about that, nevertheless he persisted in bargaining over the price, pointing out how small his daughter's feet still were and how big the sandals were, while the merchant simply kept saying "yes, yes," but without reducing the price.

Christoforos made one last endeavor, leaning over to Julia: "Haven't you considered," he said to her, "that by the time you've grown enough to wear these sandals, some better ones might have come out?"

"I don't want any better ones, I want these," she said.

"They're the ones she wants—why do you go on tormenting her?" said a stranger waiting in line behind them.

So he got them for her. He gave his last penny almost, hoping he would lose his last pang of remorse with it and his last recollection of what, for both of them, had been an unfortunate experience.

The sun was going down as they left the crossroads with the meadows, the bridges, and the rocky hills and set off home, traveling all through the night.

"*Today, hanging on a wooden cross,*" the coachman reminded them acrimoniously, as he made fast a couple of poles on the side of his carriage, those with the curved ends that, joined with the other planks and the canvas, form the *dome* overhead; then he cracked his whip a couple of times in the air (not bringing it down on his horses, they had been whipped enough), and they set off again. He had hooked up the part of the canvas behind his back, the curtain, let's say, with a wire so that no one, other than him, could lower it—and he asked Christoforos if it was all right by him . . .

"And if my daughter is cold during the night because of the chill?" Christoforos asked.

"If your daughter's cold, let her tell me so *herself* and I'll lower it," said the coachman.

Lukas had come with them—the uncle and the older brothers had stayed behind.

Just before Dekatessara vanished from sight, Julia drew back the little canvas curtain at the back of the coach and looked out . . . Between those tall and irregular rocks, tongues of fire could be seen and every so often, as if being deliberately thrown into the air, black calpacs with golden plumes, horses' manes, swords, cries, and laughter.

"Is that the cavalry?" she asked her father, but he had already curled up on the straw mattress, with his two hands under the side of his face, and had closed his eyes.

"Yes," he answered (when she no longer expected a reply), in a tone of voice that reminded her of the eyeless Marietta.

Then he opened one eye and, seeing that she was holding the sandals in her arms as if taking them as a gift to one of her elder sisters, closed it again, saying to her: "And now see to it that you get better and grow up quickly, or the other girls will have them from you."

She spent part of the night conversing in a low voice with her brother Lukas about how things had transpired at the hospital, what they had brought her to eat, whether the injections they had given her were painful, *where* they had given her the injections, and so on and so forth, and when he too fell asleep (and when the coachman no longer kept looking behind to see or, if he looked, saw nothing but darkness, which became even thicker when he lowered the canvas), she unwound the kerchief round her tender fluffy head, put the blue suede sandals on her feet, and all alone, racing without even moving, she continued that unforgettable journey.

Sixth Tale

RAPINAS NOCTURNAS (*IT WASN'T A WINTER'S TALE*)

Life is a bridge, said life itself, revealing its secret to someone; pass over it but don't build your house there.

Thus Julia also passed over a bridge—which may not have been a whole life but just a few days in her life—without having the time to build or even think of building a house there, but nevertheless bringing back with her from that journey, which was rich in strange and extraordinary events, all her future, we might say, and engraving her own enigmatic character on it.

The years that followed seemed to be a *simple* extension of this journey.

Eftha had risen from the night and very early at daybreak on Good Friday. When she heard the horses entering the yard below, she hurriedly pushed the basket with the red-dyed eggs beneath one of the beds in the old bedroom— just managing to cover it with an old sheet, to remove from it two dead hedgehogs, so that the little ones wouldn't find them and polish off all the eggs before Easter—and eagerly descended the stairs, catching and knocking over an old scythe with the hem of her dress.

They were already being welcomed by the dogs from all the neighboring houses, their own first and foremost, which Christoforos was shooing away from under his feet and patting any which way, at the same time examining the front of his house to see if there was any change after so many days—even if only a few—that he had been away. Always people believe that the world must have changed in their absence, though they invariably find it just as they left it.

Eftha saw Julia getting out of the carriage with her head still wrapped up, whereas she had dared to hope that a miracle might have taken place in the six days and that she would see her with her hair again . . . Yet never mind; simply seeing her again was enough. And as for the miracles, she thought to herself, if they don't happen in six days, they may happen in six months. And from that moment on she would be counting the months, without knowing that her own months were numbered.

Easter Sunday and all the following week passed with numerous house calls and get-togethers. A whole host of relatives and neighbors came to see Julia on her return from the hospital (in the meantime they had had the funerals of two children whose parents hadn't been able to save them), bringing her pies, preserves, and sweetmeats to humor the already retreating illness and help with her recovery, and sometimes also showing an insatiable curiosity to learn everything and in every detail: what happened, how it happened, what the doctors said, what they didn't say, whether there were other girls like her in there, how many and what their names were, whether her hair was already starting to grow back and what color it was now, as though there were as many colors of hair as there were of flowers.

Julia had grown tired of their questions, and above all she didn't want—nor was she *obliged*—to tell them everything.

At any rate, Eftha had persuaded her not to be afraid anymore of removing the kerchief from her head, since it was a fact that something had again begun to appear up there: faint and soft down, nothing more for the time being than the first plumage on fledgling birds, nevertheless it was something, a new start, a blossoming, that you could neither ignore nor put too much hope in. She even encouraged the visitors to touch her daughter's head and waited with childlike anticipation to hear their impressions . . . Not even as many siankes had ever passed over Julia as the fingers of the men and women who touched her during those days.

For a while, things resumed their normal rhythm. The stories of her brother Theagenis with the women-who-wanted-him-and-whom-he-never-refused didn't make for peace in the house, but that summer Eftha shoved him into the waters of a river, a stream anyway, and baptized him "Hesychios." As a name, this soon caught on, but as a *characterization*, alas, it brought anything but the peace and quiet they longed for, and the handsome Theagenis was simply transformed into the fateful Hesychios . . .

Christoforos, meanwhile, worrying for quite some time about Julia, afraid, that is, lest she divulge his little *irregularity* on their return trip to Dekatessara to someone, and seeing that Julia hadn't done so but had kept it all to herself, came to appreciate her—over and above the special affection he had for her—so much that he was as concerned about her recovery as he had been when the illness was at its height, and he had allowed her a *golden corner*, as her brothers and sisters called it complainingly, where the girl was able to do something that no one had ever thought—nor had the time—to do then: *to write!* What? *Sagas . . . incomprehensible things*, as the others said, whenever they occasionally stole a look.

And in the afternoons or the evenings, Christoforos would talk to her, when he came from the inn to eat before going back; he would talk to her in a kind of code, which the others heard and felt themselves to be superfluous: "Julia," he would say to her, changing his tone of voice, "he himself and none other!" and burst into laughter pointing with two open fingers first to the floor and then to the ceiling. Or he would come out with some improvised songs, look-ing her in the eye, warmly and foxily: "'The sad owl gave / medicines bitter to taste / and the other one turned green . . . ,' no, 'and the goldfinch became hoarse . . . ,' no, not that either, 'and the goldfinch grew jealous . . .' I've muddled it up—and *what?* what did *it* give?" he would ask Julia, waiting for her to find a word that would rhyme with *taste,* because at such times people have a hanker-ing for lines of verse. Julia didn't disappoint him usually, and never said no to such games, as long as the moment was right ("and the goldfinch gave sandals that wouldn't go to waste," she said to him), while the others listened as though it were gobbledygook, as though they were undeserving of such entertainment.

Until the poem got onto the subject of a Jew, and no matter how condescend-ingly they listened to it at the beginning, as though to the ranting of some idiot, eventually they showed genuine interest in finding out about the Jew in ques-tion, whether he was a real person and where they had seen him, and eventu-ally they all learned it by heart and recited it at the first chance, so that it passed into the traditions of that *community,* if and given that we can't really call it a family. It went: "True, how true, said the Jew, / and sighed anew, / and from joy untold, / when we gave him our gold, / in his breeches he did a miracle of old."

Such verses were often heard coming from Christoforos's mouth and no one knew: were they his? from out of his head, made up on the spot, or were they of old, once often heard and now half-forgotten, that he, when the situation called for it, some unexpected event, came out with and presented as some-thing new? Then again, he would make them think that he was hard of hearing, that he had some problem with his hearing, and could make neither rhyme nor reason of what people said. Or simply *pretended* to have a problem so that he could come out with his own stuff. Once—and this is one of the least unusual things that we're able to recall at this moment—rushing into the house with a thousand things on his mind and asking the children playing in the yard where their mother was . . . he shouted out in amazement, "ANGRY 'N CROSS? Why is she angry 'n cross? Angry because I'm asking for her?" And this was because, when he asked them, they had replied, "hanging the clothes." Meanwhile, he had become angry himself, but evidently because of everything he had on his mind and not because of Eftha, who was hanging out their clothes to dry . . . Just as on another occasion, he answered someone bidding him good morning by nodding his head and saying, "Marmalade, marmalade!" Taken aback, the other asked what he meant. "If you say to me *honey* this morning, why wouldn't I reply with marmalade?" Christoforos retorted. Had he heard *honey* not *sunny*? Had he really heard that? The two sounds aren't so close . . . Though not, it seems, so different.

However, more serious distortions than these had occurred, and some of them took on huge proportions. Others became legendary. Like the one with the town crier.

Every Saturday afternoon a town crier would come to the marketplace and shout "Gentleme-e-e-en-gentleme-e-e-en!" numerous times, alternating between sharp and deep tones, until all the men were gathered around him. Then, from his waistcoat, he would take a piece of paper, sometimes rolled up and sometimes folded into four, and he would read them the news. News mainly concerning their village and their district (that the tobacco merchants would be arriving in a few days so they should get their tobacco ready, that there would be a collection for the construction of a country church so they shouldn't all leave their houses, that a storm was expected or wolves were roaming in the hills so they should take precautions, that a field was for sale in such-and-such an area or at such-and-such a price, that a mule with one ear had been lost on such-and-such a day and in such-and-such a place and that there was a reward for anyone finding it and handing it in, and similar things of a rural nature), but also news from the entire region, of a more political and social nature, since newspapers at that time were so rare; as rare as those Saturday town criers are today. Once, then, the town crier grandiloquently read out a proclamation or some such thing by King So-and-So the First, and in a formal language that was hardly familiar or *recognizable.* When he finished, he carefully folded the paper, put it back in his waistcoat, took out a handkerchief, wiped his mouth and his brow, and said as a finale to the silent crowd: "So the king has said!"

Among those at the front of the crowd, very close to the town crier, was Christoforos, who jumped up, shouting "What? The king has fled. Why has he fled? Has someone stolen his kingdom from him?"

At first, of course, they all took it to be one of his jokes, the kind he fabricated himself, and they all laughed . . . though the people at the back heard what Christoforos had said better than they had the town crier and a wave of intense curiosity arose to find out what exactly had happened with the king, what the ones in front were saying, and when they found out, they too laughed at Christoforos's pranks and gradually the Saturday assembly dispersed.

The next day, however, and the day after that, the wave arose again because a certain someone went and said with the utmost secrecy and all due caution to certain others who had been absent from the Saturday assembly that a suspicious rumor was circulating that the king down in the capital had fled his throne, but, for reasons of security, it hadn't been announced to the people, and perhaps it wouldn't be announced even in a month's time, and, who knows, perhaps they would go on being governed like that in the name of His Majesty! . . . Anyhow, this certain someone counseled those certain others to keep their mouths closed too, not to tell anyone, because you don't risk your head by revealing the secrets of the palace. This, then, is what he had to say to them, and they agreed completely, no question, except that indiscretion is not one of the rarest human characteristics: so they too couldn't refrain from telling at least one person . . . who told another . . . who in his turn told another, till hour by hour the rumor grew—they may have denied it, but it continued to grow, just as a fire grows with the wind against it—and some of the more hot-blooded ones, unable to bear this secrecy and uncertainty, after being patient for a few days more, went the following Saturday and came up behind the town crier as soon as he opened his mouth for the customary "Gentleme-e-e-en-gentleme-e-e-en": "Enough of the Gentleme-e-e-en-gentleme-e-e-en," they told him, "tell us the truth about the king: has he fled or not?"

The poor man was not only lost for words, he lost blood as well, for in the wink of an eye they had him sprawled on his back, holding his arms and legs tight and threatening him with a large pear that they'd stuff it in his mouth if he didn't tell them the truth about the king. Or did he prefer that one—and they showed him an even larger pear.

Fortunately, Christoforos came between them and the town crier was saved: "The king," he told them, "has NOT fled, why would he be so stupid? It was a piece of false news designed to spread confusion, but the town crier had no responsibility for that, let him go, he's only doing his job—that's the news he was given, that's the news he transmitted, how is he to blame?"

And that's how it was: you didn't know to what degree Christoforos was playing and to what degree he was being serious, to what degree he really was hard of hearing and to what degree he preferred not to hear well. In any case, as he approached old age (and this is when the episode with the town crier happened), he began to go deaf in both ears, and communication with other people was, on his part, unending versification, indefatigable and incomprehensible inspiration . . . And towards his end, blissfully submerged in other levels of life, he spoke only with signs, with infinite gestures, that recalled—in softer tones—those of the first woman he had loved, his adopted sister Lily, Letta or Violetta, for many years now at rest.

We might mention in parentheses that less than two weeks after the episode with the king who *so said* or *fled*, the king was bitten by a monkey—which he kept as a pet—on the royal estate at Tatoi. The wound festered, gangrene set in, and within thirty days the just twenty-seven-year-old monarch surrendered both his crown and his soul. There was uproar throughout the land, a scandal: for a full-blown king to die from a monkey bite! It sounded more like a joke than a tragedy. And yet it was tragic, rather like the viper that sent the uncrowned Eftha to her grave.

As for the royalist supporters in Christoforos's village, they stared at him with a suspicious and icy look for a long time, and though they didn't go so far as to attribute the existence of the satanic monkey on the royal estate to some devious plan of his, they nevertheless accused him of speaking ill of and so putting a jinx on His Royal Majesty.

The king, meanwhile, was buried with due ceremony in the royal cemetery and quickly succeeded by a new one.

So let us return to that summer when they were all still alive (so to speak) and Julia's hair had begun to grow again. This didn't mean, of course, that the sisaibeoma had entirely left her from one day to the next—on the contrary: the recovery took time, and always with the risk of a relapse. This is why they didn't allow the girl outside too much (not that she wanted to go outside very much), they didn't take her with them to help in the fields, and they did not let her take care of the younger ones in the house for fear that she might infect them: even though the illness wasn't considered contagious, they preferred to be cautious.

So the eleven-year-old girl was still extremely pale and weak, and her new hair (redder than ever and curly like rings) could only just be wrapped round the fingers when Eftha died leaving her motherless . . . Her absence was immeasurable, inconceivable, more *alive* even than she was when living . . . Like shadows stumbling in the darkness—all of them, even the children that weren't hers but whom she had brought up—they felt incapable of finding a space in their minds able to contain the sudden news, able to accept it. Whether their mother or not, mother or stepmother, she had certainly been the most important presence in that house for the previous nineteen years. And death, even though a part of life, is always a *blow* unlike any other. Just the evening before, she had made them two large pumpkin pies with sugar, a surprise for the end of the meal, and while the pies were hot, she served them, one or two helpings to each—and to Julia, who always ate only a little, she gave three helpings. She herself, from what they struggled to remember afterwards, didn't have any . . . perhaps only tasting a bit from one corner. And she put the few pieces that were left over in a shrine, saying that they were for those who *didn't put their hope in wrongdoing and had no wish for quarrels.* She would often come out with such things, to which no one attached any importance, though someone once asked her, to tease her: "You only care about the dead, you put everything away for them," and she replied: "We call them dead, but they're happy, they've no need of food and they don't cast any shadow." *They don't cast any shadow!* . . . They found it so meaningful and original (she had never said it before, it was new for her too) that they forgot to ask her why, then, she was leaving pumpkin pie for them if they had no need of food . . . Better look for a needle in a haystack. The next day, her daughter Cletia opened the shrine, took the pieces of pie, and carried them to the fields to be eaten by those who work under the sun and cast shadows as long as cypress trees. And there would have been nothing at all special or unusual in all these actions if, just a few hours later, they hadn't had to carry Eftha, dead, back to the house.

A widower for a second time, as though an unruly child were playing with the lives of his wives, Christoforos, in his new despair, compared the two deaths and concluded that the first, that of Petroula, was more fortunate—if you can describe it like that. And he asked the invisible God, the ever merciful, why he couldn't have given to Eftha—always faithful to him—a little time, as he had with Petroula; a little time to prepare herself, for those around her to prepare themselves; why hadn't he given her a grave illness at least, so that they might get used to the idea that they were going to lose her, just to the idea, never mind all the rest; why did he have to take her like that, from one moment to the next, using a snake as his intermediary—what of all the other ways? So many gentler and humbler ways? Was it necessary to use a snake?

And if until then, he had shown himself to be the calmer—with Eftha still alive in his arms, albeit already condemned—now that he saw her dead, *dead*, it was another thing, as different as day is to night. And he went up and down the stairs as though drunk, or paced to and fro in the parlor, outside the *best room* they had, banging his head sometimes against the walls and sometimes against his hands—and kept on asking the same thing, getting angry at the same thing: What in heaven's name, is there no justice in the world? no order? no coherence?

Yet equally he accepted in the depths of his heart what, among so many other things, Eftha used to say until only yesterday—that thing about *everyone dying as they lived*—which was apt in her case, and in a way that was capable of overshadowing his grief . . . of making him shudder. He was unable to ponder these thoughts, they slipped like water through his fingers, at any rate, it wasn't only, let's say, the more obvious things that deprived him of his wife: in life she killed snakes and it was a snake that led to her death . . . But it was also something else, something much more intangible and powerful than mere recompense and that, with its final *exaltation*, intimated at all that had gone before.

Very early the following morning (Eftha would still be washing herself or rubbing her eyes: how could she suddenly dismiss habits of fifty years?), an unknown woman came to his house and formally asked to see him. She was quite pitiable, with sparse hair like Julia's when she was at the first and second stage of her illness (you could see her scalp between the hairs, grayish-yellow it was and it sent a shiver up your spine . . . but she certainly didn't have sisaibeoma, which only attacked children and adolescents), a torn dress whose fibers had not decayed yet but still held together, with a bodice in equally bad condition, through which you could easily discern two scrawny, sagging, wizened breasts, like tobacco pouches, scraggy and gawky, like the scarecrows they made and set up in the fields to frighten away the birds, and two or three children around her feet, who had nothing to envy of this woman who had brought them into the world.

As soon as Christoforos went outside and saw her, he forgot Eftha, his grief almost disappearing: so strikingly wretched was this hapless woman. Meanwhile, from the windows and various railings, other faces popped out, with eyes red from weeping and lack of sleep, to see this terrifying visitor . . .

"You asked for me? What is it you want?" Christoforos asked her, trying to ignore as best he could her appearance.

"I live near the mountain," she told him, "in a wattle hut, and your wife sent me to tell you —"

"From where did my wife send you," he said, cutting her short with a shudder, "from the wattle hut?"

"No, from the dream I had last night, through God's good grace, and she told me . . . I saw us washing together in a river, and as she was beating the clothes with a stick, she turned and said to me, through God's good grace, that, look, I'm dead and I've left my husband a widower with motherless children, she said, and as your husband has left you, too, go and tell mine, given that you have children too, without a father, go and tell mine to take you in, tell him not to see you as poor and wretched, but to take pity on you, and you'll become for him good and worthy like I was, she told me . . . through God's good grace!"

She finished, crossed herself, and bent her knees. The three little creatures round her legs took their fingers from out of their mouths and did the same.

Christoforos gazed at her as if he had been hypnotized by her; and if he hadn't been drowning in such despondency, perhaps he might even have been amused by that simplicity of hers, a simplicity so absolute and disarming that you didn't find it even in children, perhaps only in the mad. Even that singular ugliness of hers, her teeth that hung like wet ash from her gums, and you expected, when next she opened her mouth, not to see them again, for her to have eaten them — perhaps teeth can't be eaten, but ash can — yet even these paled beside the simplicity and immediacy of her soul or who knows what need that had brought her so early in the morning to his door.

"And what do you want from me?" he asked her. "For me to listen to your dream and marry you?"

"Yes," she said (she wasn't going suddenly to spoil her image).

Nothing's sacred, thought Christoforos, seeing in this *image* — in this measureless simplicity — hubris too . . . together with a fair deal of indifference to his grief.

"What's your name?" he asked her.

"Moira," was what he heard her say.

"Moira . . . like fate?"

"No, Myra, from Myrofora, the bearer of myrrh," she explained to him.

"So . . . Myra from Myrofora . . . Does such a name exist?" he asked her.

"Of course, it exists. My godmother's daughter, through God's good grace, was also called Myrofora — I was given her name because she died very young, in the bloom of her youth. But I wasn't so lucky."

"And so . . . ," Christoforos broke in.

"But I'm also like fate," she just managed to say, "I can sense a lot of things, I know when there's going to be an earthquake and I can save people if I want — the one last year, that big one, I sensed it before it happened, but I didn't tell anyone, they all deserved what they got."

"So, it's like that, is it," said Christoforos, shaking his head, "it's a good thing we don't have big earthquakes every year; you'd sense them and wouldn't say anything to us."

"I'd tell you," she said, looking him in the eyes.

Unconsciously, he stretched out his arm and waved his fingers, as if not wanting — for heaven's sake no — to lose whatever distance there was between them, while she, this simple and horrifying Myra, seemed intent on narrowing it.

"Look here . . . I lost my wife yesterday, and I can't think straight," he said to her, "for your own good, if you have needs, if you're hungry, I mean, I can give you something, I can help you without your owing me anything, and then you can be on your way — on your way, understand? I don't want you round here anymore."

And he turned to leave, to go back into the house and send one of his daughters to give the woman a crust of bread and a few coins, but she shouted to him: "Wait!"

"What do you want?"

"And the dream?" she asked him, as though, with his movement, he had turned his back on the most important thing. "I really did see your wife and she told me—"

"I heard what she told you! She told you nothing! My wife didn't come to me in my dreams, yet you're telling me she managed to come to you?" shouted Christoforos, starting to lose his temper, and he pointed to the gate behind her: "On your way! Enough, go back to where you came from. There . . . take that with you so I don't have your curses on my head," and he reached into his pocket and took out a few coins, which her children rushed to grab from him and then waited for more. He took out a few more—their mother looked at his hands just as a coachman had once looked him in the eyes . . . That look, which normally would have angered him, on the contrary appeased him, or rather it put him in an even more difficult position. He sighed and asked her who her husband was, who had left her a widow.

"No one," she told him, "he abandoned me and went off with another worse than me."

"And who was it? What was his name?" Christoforos asked again.

"Even if I were to tell you, you don't know him, you don't know us," she said, "I came to these parts on my own three years ago, when he left me, and I live with these torments (she pointed to her children) close to the mountain, in that hollow, Marazi as you locals call it, only fit for lepers. Yesterday, I caught this one (she pointed to the middle one) with wood in his mouth, it's God's truth, he was trying to chew it . . . We've nothing to eat, we go to sleep hungry, that's how it is. You don't know us, but we know you, I knew your wife too, she'd come every so often and show me a little charity, she had a soul, may she rest in peace, and myrrh in her bones."

She stopped to get her breath, licked her lips, and asked him what was going to happen.

"Nothing's going to happen—I can't marry you, if you want me to talk straight, too," Christoforos said to her.

"Why, because I'm poor and ugly? That's why I came . . . But you don't know my heart . . . So take me as your servant, me and these here."

"I've no need of servants, I've lots of children, from two wives, I have all the helping hands I need, I don't need any more," Christoforos told her.

"So give me one of your sons if you have so many children, give me to one of your sons," she said to him.

She was like one of those mosquitoes that don't leave you alone no matter how many times they bite you.

"In the name of God!" Christoforos shouted. "We've just had a funeral in this house, can't you understand? If you're so keen on getting married, find a husband on your own, the place is seething with men. But leave me in peace."

"There's no man for me," she said, "and I'm not keen on getting married, I'm in need, things have come to a head, that's why I've come to you. I'll die with these three if you don't do something, and you'll have to live with it. I wanted to come the day before yesterday, to plead with your wife, but I wasn't in time, I heard that she'd died in the fields. I waited for you to bury her and came. When a person's suffering, it's then that he helps; when he's happy, he forgets everything."

Perhaps Myra sprouted there where she hadn't been sown, but she also knew how to get a foothold there where you didn't expect—on some sensitive spot.

"And the dream?" Christoforos asked her now, strangely afraid—how ironic—that the dream—if not everything—was a lie, a cheap pretext.

"The dream is true, but through God's good grace I had it six months ago," Myra said to him, "when your wife was still alive and came and showed me charity. I even told her about it, I'm not one to hide things. And she said to me: Look, for you to have a dream like that, who knows, maybe I'm going to die soon, and my husband will become a widower and you'll marry him."

"And so? Did she tell you to come the very next day after her funeral and ask me to marry you? Did Eftha, my wife, say such a thing?" asked Christoforos, not at all expecting to hear such things.

"No, she told me that in the dream, you're getting confused, in the dream— through God's good grace—she turned and said to me, while we were both washing the clothes in the river, Look, I'm dead, she said, I'm no longer alive at this moment that I'm talking to you, I'm dead, and I've left my husband a widower and my children motherless, and because you're in no better state, she said to me, go and tell my husband to marry you, not to see you as poor and ugly, but to take pity on you! That's what she told me in the dream, as true as I'm standing here. But she was still alive then, it was only in my dream that she was dead, she was still alive, so I couldn't very well come here and ask such a thing of you, I'm not one to come between man and wife," said Myra, and without giving him the time to sort out for himself what of all she'd said was a dream and what not, she went on: "And when I recounted it to her, she turned and said to me, Look, perhaps I'll die for real, and things will turn out in that way and you'll marry my husband—only mountains don't come together, she said to me. But she was alive and well in her health . . . In fact, another time that she came to see

me, a couple of months later, as she was stooping to enter the hut, I said to her,
Well then, my dear woman, when are you going to die so I can marry your husband? I could have choked on my words! . . . But I said it jokingly, not to make it
happen! But it did happen, she did die, the dream was prophetic. And I came."

"And why then did you tell me that you saw her *last night?*" asked Christoforos.

"All that about last night was a lie, the only lie," she admitted, without feeling
any discomfort or saying she was sorry.

During all this time they had been talking in the doorway to the house, he
in mourning and in a daze, she in her poverty, which equipped her with such
immediacy and a rare kind of clarity, others had come out too and were listening to all this questioning and answering and were trying to understand what
was going on, what that woman was doing there, and why she was talking about
Eftha as though she were her sister . . . It didn't take them long to understand,
and they began to get worried: Christoforos's older children looked at him perplexedly, while the younger ones looked grim and also frightened: they could
easily see their father going and getting married again and *to her!* They would
sling stones at his wedding! They would sling their hooks, leave home to show
him they were opposed to it, they would deride him to the four ends of the
earth, even go so far as to put their necks in nooses and hang themselves from
the trees so he'd be racked all his life by remorse! . . . Such were the tales they
were making up in their minds, such family dramas, and they were looking at
him as they were looking. Grim and frightened.

Lily too came out from inside, pale and beautiful from all the weeping and
sighing, in a wide jet-black dress, and she gazed at Myra like an eagle smelling
possible prey. But Myra just stood there apathetically, waiting for her host's next
words, for what he would say next. Lily went up to her little children, examined
them, touching their clothes, smelling—and pulling a sour face—those filthy
necks, thin like twigs, their ears . . . (*Where there's muck, there's stench*, she allowed herself the thought). They stood there letting her smell them, letting her
see the grime they had accumulated from filthiness and their grim wretchedness . . . She went up to Myra too, and drawing back like a curtain the rags covering her bust, she cast a more than fleeting glance at her breasts, which provoked
only pity and were anything but sweet-smelling. Myra allowed her to look, she
had no wealth to hide. As for the others, they were far too stunned by the whole
affair and the indescribable presence of this strange woman to prevent their own
Lily from doing such things.

Ugh! grunted Lily, full of disgust, as anyone who had a tongue and could
speak might have done. She let the gray rags fall back over the woman's breast,

went into the house for a moment, and came back out with a belt round her dress, and a staff and a half-open leather knapsack filled with cloths and instruments—she had to go to two women about to give birth.

Before they lost her for hours, perhaps even for days, she said something to Christoforos about Eftha (*Eftha* in Lily's language was a coil in the air, like the symbol of Hippocrates), as though apologizing to him because his beloved wife had died and she had to rush off and be midwife to others, but duty is duty she told him. Furthermore, she advised him to be careful of this strange woman, this brash and intrusive woman . . . and discerning a look of surprise on the woman's face—perhaps she had only just realized that she was dumb—she again went up to her and opened her mouth wide like a hatch, coming out with a hoarse and horrible *Aagh!* To frighten and discourage her.

But scarecrows, as everybody knows, can't be frightened, no matter what.

With a big heart rare in our times—perhaps rare in theirs too—Christoforos took Myra and her three children into his home . . . despite the wailing, the threats, and the cries of protest of his own family, both the older and the younger ones. Not in order to marry her, ah, no, there wasn't the slightest possibility of that—even though Eftha (another big heart) had, herself, in a manner of speaking given her permission or at least hadn't excluded the possibility . . . But in order to see for the time being what he might do for this hapless woman who had sought refuge at his feet. And first of all, he made sure she had something to eat, and her children, too, who were starving, were nothing but skin and bone. But to eat with measure, not allowing them any more (he likened each additional spoonful to a knife wound), though they appeared capable, mother and children, of eating for three days nonstop after so much deprivation and hunger . . . "You'll die if you suddenly overfill your stomachs, can't you understand? Don't you know what happened to the hungry goat when it ate more than its fill of barley?" he said, when they were begging him to give them a little more *to fill their bellies.* But he was implacable.

On the contrary, they washed and cleaned Myra for three whole days to get rid of the filth that had penetrated deep into her pores like dry rot in wood, and for three months they took care of her generally to make her into a human being again, make her presentable.

"What will people say about us, WHAT WILL THEY SAY?" shouted some of Christoforos's older daughters, who had undertaken—had been obliged to undertake—this rather unpleasant task (and while they were still in mourning).

"I don't know what people will say, mama Eftha anyway would say that you were doing a great act of charity," he replied patiently.

"Acts of charity like that we can well do without!" retorted some of the bolder ones.

Yet the work was carried out, and Myra changed day by day.

When the three months had passed, even her very own children could hardly recognize her. Myra had completely changed appearance, and we can confirm that she wasn't so ugly anymore. She was quite attractively plain, with something indefinable about her characteristics (which remained sinister nevertheless, like those of a bird of prey), perhaps something in her smile (which you rarely saw anyway), that recalled Eftha's face and smile . . . And this *resemblance* was ever more notable the more indefinite and uncertain it became. There were moments, that is, when this wild bat, this female vulture, anything but *resembled* their own dear Eftha—and they were puzzled as to how they could even think it, how on earth! Yet there were also moments when a certain *something* passed quickly and splendidly through that hawkish gaze, that face with the high cheekbones, that so tormentingly reminded them of the other woman . . . only to vanish again, only for the impression to dissolve, as in some random people on the street, or in portraits of strangers, where at one moment you see the underlying expression of someone dear to you and at the next moment you lose it, it escapes you as though you'd never seen it, and you desperately try to grasp it again.

And then Christoforos decided—as he had always liked to find brides and grooms for *difficult* people and make a match for them—that the time was right to find a husband for Myra. He began with those he knew best and, what's more, with his own sons: Eumolpos, Eftha's son from her first marriage, had prematurely become a widower and was the right age for Myra, and Petros, his last son with Petroula, was still unmarried . . . But they thought he was out of his mind: however much Myra had changed her skin, she still remained for them the horrible and hapless figure they had first set eyes on in their yard on the day after the funeral. Petros, in particular, who was quite a bit younger than she, regarded the very suggestion as an insult. Eumolpos as mockery. "We don't mind you wanting to be charitable, Father," they said to him, "but not to the point of marrying your sons off to a scarecrow!" Whichever way they saw her, she was still a *scarecrow* to them, at best a *hawk*—they would never see her as a fellow human. As for the little ones, her own children, when they wanted to refer to Myra, and even in front of her, they would call her Teyim: "Teyim has teeth like pearls . . . Teyim will eat you alive . . . Teyim has eaten and belched . . . Be good or I'll hand you over to Teyim," and suchlike, as the poor creature not only said "tey 'im" instead of "tell him" (or "tey 'er," "tey me"), but when she started with that *tey* in her conversation, she couldn't stop, she kept coming out with it over and over again. Because—given the opportunity—despite the fact that almost everyone

in the house with the exception of Christoforos treated her with disdain and re-
vulsion, Myra, either because of her proverbial apathy or to show her gratitude
to the man who helped her, never stopped speaking to them in the way that she
always spoke or seeking to associate with them, even with the younger ones, who
looked at her as if they were looking at a blockhead who wanted nothing but to
eat all the time and made fun of her or openly avoided her. And in this way she
gradually managed, on her own, to get them to start to tolerate her, and later, to
actually like her and accept her. At any rate, she became stuck with the name
Teyim: only occasionally in her presence did they call her Myra—but whenever
they spoke about her among themselves, they always referred to her as Teyim.

As for the mute in the house, in her language, Myra was expressed as a nod
toward the breast accompanied by the sound "paah," a euphemism in a manner
of speaking for that "aagh" she had come out with the first time.

Meanwhile, the time passed as always, and between the memorial services
for Eftha, Christoforos did all he could to find a companion for Myra—now
from among his nephews or his cousins, from among both relatives and non-
relatives. But no one wanted her. Though she no longer had anything repulsive
about her or anything to cause pity or displeasure, her first image was ingrained
in all of them, that first sacrilegious arrival of hers at Christoforos's door on the
morning after his wife's funeral, and no one wanted to bear the burden of such
a woman . . . though there were more than a few who wanted to sleep with her
secretly and illicitly, since her "crooked wooden body," as they called it, and her
expression, voracious like a nocturnal carnivore, had something extremely enticing and primitive about it.

Till someone was found who showed interest, by the name of Apostolos, a
saddle maker by profession, an only son and without parents for three decades
and more, in whose arms not even a cat would settle—so radiant was this hapless man to look at, so little *human* or, rather, so *divine*. He made his saddles in
a large and dark workshop—more like a cave, it was—not far from Christoforos's
house that he had inherited from a childless uncle of his, so that Christoforos
was at a loss as to why he hadn't thought of him before as the prime candidate
instead of pleading with all those other stuck-ups. Yet Apostolos had already
heard talk of a *Moira*, without having seen her, who was looking for a husband,
and he sent an aged friend (he didn't have any young ones) to tell Christoforos
that his neighbor the saddle maker was interested . . . so now the question was
whether Myra would want him!

But this was something said jokingly by others, those who live on the stories
of others and stick their noses in everywhere, though it was no lie that this
Apostolos—Apostolakos, as he was known—was so unfortunate when it came

to looks and finesse that he rarely emerged from his cave, to keep people from seeing him and crossing the street to avoid him. Moreover, so it was said, this is why he had made his workshop so dark (the place had already caught fire twice, and he had done nothing to remove the black soot from the walls), so that those who went in wouldn't easily be able to distinguish him. All his tools were black too, like the clothes he wore, black also the leather and straw he used, black too the thick cloths like sailcloth that hung for no particular reason from the ceiling or covered things that by chance happened not to be black. He had become one with the darkness of his workplace, and the only white inside there was the white of his big, lethargic, and slightly puffed eyes with their glistening, deep black eyeballs. Once, it's said, when they brought him a white mare to be measured for a saddle, Apostolos had to close his eyes, he couldn't stand so much light, such brightness; he measured it as though blind, using his instinct and his touch. The mare, it seems, was so angry with him, or became so haughty at those strange conditions, that it kicked him again and again in the belly and on the legs, leaving him crippled.

But the most characteristic thing about him, the most terrifying, was the hair on his body. He had hair everywhere—black, impudent, sleek hair all over, all over his face more or less, right down to his fingernails, up to his eyes, his neck was covered in hair, his ears covered in hair, his chest like a forest, even his back was black and soft from all the hair. Only his heels and the lines in his palms were free of hair. It's said that he had tried various means to rid himself of the relentless growth of hair—he had gone to doctors, to quacks, to old wives who had fleeced him—but with no result, the black undergrowth was everywhere. In fact, some medicines had exactly the opposite effect. And so, finally, he accepted his fate, he had no other choice, and devoted himself to his work and shut himself up in darkness. For him to find a wife, a companion in there, even one with drawbacks, was beyond all his dreams. For friends he had some old men whom no one wanted, or who had no one, dry leaves in the wind who found shelter in his workshop and in his solitude. Mothers threatened their children that they would give them to Apostolakos to put under his hair or sew into his saddles if they didn't behave . . . He had become the bogeyman, whatever was most abhorrent, though he wouldn't have harmed a fly. Even when he was once bold enough to go to church, to take communion at an evening service, the priest scowled at him, not because he wasn't a member of the Orthodox faith but rather as if he wasn't a member of the human race, as if a black sheep had walked into the church. And the saddest thing of all, in fact, was not the priest's reproachful look but the behavior of the rest of the congregation: for after the priest had begrudgingly put the spoon with the bread and wine into

Apostolos's mouth, the others—those waiting in line behind him—declined to take communion after him, but scattered like innocent doves and gave each other bygones for their sins.

Of course, not everyone always behaved like that to him—we've mentioned only the bad. The farmers needed him as much as they needed their animals and came and went to his workshop without fear, or if they happened to be passing outside they would shout good morning to him. And women from the surrounding houses would also go in often to ask him for favors that weren't really his work but that his kind and empty heart was always ready to undertake, and there were not a few fights between couples where the woman would say to the man: "I wouldn't mind your having Apostolakos's bad looks if you had an ounce of his heart and pride!" Moreover, his closed and solitary life, those black sailcloths hanging from the ceiling, the charred walls that were worse even than those in coal yards, his bitter sunless eyes and the way he turned them to the vaulted door whenever he heard footsteps outside or sensed that someone was looking at him from there while he was bent over working, provoked people, especially the children. And very often Apostolos had a tingling feeling in his backbone that, though he was working all alone in his shop, a thousand eyes were *secretly* watching him . . . And then, sometimes, he would suddenly leap up and clap his hands as though chasing birds away, or would threateningly raise a piece of wood or iron—and in truth a swarm of urchins would fly in alarm from the roof and the walls outside, from slits and cracks through which they had been watching him . . . though they weren't really frightened, but chuckled and made faces at him, pulled their tongues out or winked at him, as if to promise that they would be back for more of the same. But he didn't know when. And sometimes he would leap up suddenly from his sewing and clap his hands or grab hold of a stick . . . and no one was there, anywhere: and the black walls around him would laugh.

This, then, was his life, until the day he heard of a certain *Moira*. And he thought, For a woman to have a name that meant fate and not to find a man to marry her, who knows, perhaps she'll accept me?

Anyway, he waited some time in case someone else turned up . . . And when no one did, he sent his proposal to Christoforos, and Christoforos passed it on to his house guest. She said yes straightaway, but he, knowing better than to count his chickens, said to her, "Wait till you've seen him first."

And wasting no time—so that he could see her too—he rounded up the women of the house and begged them not to object to what they were going to hear from his mouth. They had their suspicions, but didn't know exactly what it was about. "Go on, we're listening," they told him, and he said: "Get hold of

Myra and I don't care how you do it, go over her from head to toe and make her beautiful for the evening after tomorrow. But with moderation, not too beautiful, we're not for suchlike—Apostolakos is coming to ask for her hand."

The women softened at the sound of that name. Naturally, their minds immediately went to their neighbor the saddle maker, but because the name that was very common in their region from olden times was Apostolos (as we said: the Apostle Paul had once passed through those parts and had stayed at their inn; so in his honor, the local inhabitants gave the name Apostolos to their children—or, at any rate, *this name too,* in other words the abundance of the name, was invoked as an argument by the researchers of today in order to prove that the Apostle Paul actually did honor their land with his presence and a few sermons, that it wasn't just a groundless legend. Of course, there are the doubters who ask themselves, And why then isn't the name in abundance Paul, this particular Paul, and not Apostolos, when there were many Apostles and not only Paul? Perhaps the whole troupe of Apostles had passed through our parts, they say, ironically, while we believe that it was only Paul? But we're not the ones to solve such puzzles), we'll simply say again that, because the place had no shortage of Apostoloses, the women thought that perhaps Christoforos meant another one, though plain Apostolakos, without any surname or other qualification, could mean only the saddle maker.

And it was, indeed, him, as Christoforos assured them. And they were totally at a loss.

"Fine, we'll do what we can to make Myra beautiful, but . . . *who,* pray, can do anything with that poor wretch?"

"God will take care of him too," said Christoforos; "you take care of Myra, and let God take care of him."

And the women took care of Myra.

"Up to now, we've managed to make a human being out of you," they said to her; "now we've got orders to make you into something at least a *little* beautiful: the day after tomorrow, Apostolakos is coming to ask for your hand! . . . Do you know Apostolakos?"

"No," said Myra, "I don't know anyone here, apart from all of you and apart from your mother who'd come and show me charity. Is he young, through God's good grace, is that why you call him Apostolakos and not Apostolos?"

"No, he's not young, he's your age," they told her—surprised that this was the *only* thing she had to ask about Apostolakos.

But Myra really was content with little, in her own way of course, and she was only interested in the bare essentials. She had an irresistible appetite for food— could eat the tablecloth and not put on an ounce. And since, besides this, she had now been blessed with having a man ask for her in marriage, Myra, for the moment, could ask for nothing more; she wasn't interested in details. (It should be noted that the father of her children had left her unmarried for nine years though she called him *her husband*, like you might say, for example, "my snake in the grass." So there was no risk of her being accused of bigamy.)

Furthermore, let's not forget that during all these months—roughly seven—since Eftha had died, Myra had not been sitting with folded arms waiting for her daily bread. She earned it in Christoforos's house by doing whatever chores they gave her to do, and she proved very able and quick at packing the tobacco leaves, even though she claimed they didn't have tobacco in the parts she hailed from. But no one was exactly sure from where she hailed exactly. Even the three years she had lived at Marazi were a mystery to most—only Eftha, according to what she herself said, used to go and show her a little charity now and again, but now Eftha wasn't there for them to ask.

Christoforos wondered just how much more Eftha had concealed from him concerning her doings . . . just how much would he uncover in time concerning her secret—though not necessarily reprehensible—deeds.

Just one day before the likely engagement, when they decided to clean the house—and before beginning Myra's *beautification*—they would discover still more about her . . . It was when she was mopping the big staircase leading to the large parlor—and we say "big" because there were many other smaller staircases in that indescribable house, in different directions from one another, on the same or different levels, just as there were also smaller parlors, or rooms resembling parlors. She had begun mopping from the lower stairs and working up (in general, she had *contrary habits*), and when she was nearly done, only four or five stairs remaining, she stopped, froze to be exact, and grabbed hold of the rail on her right, desperately contorting her mouth. She would stop, of course, at every three stairs or so, to breathe on her calloused hands and mumble something—but this was different: she stood frozen, in fright.

"What's wrong?" asked Georgiana, Petroula's eldest daughter, who at that moment was treading the verandah with a red-mud paste and couldn't move till it had dried.

"What's the matter?" asked Cletia too, who was sitting on the smaller and lower staircase opposite and feeding two babies.

But Myra just gazed at them, her eyes wide open and glazed, without uttering a sound: something terrible was going to happen.

"Huh!" exclaimed the one with the red-mud paste. "Is it an earthquake you can sense? What kind of eyes are those?"

"Not an earthquake," whispered Myra, "but . . ." And as she said "but," she opened her legs slightly and raised her dress in panic, as Eftha used to do when she smelled a snake in the bushes . . . Two children, meanwhile, had come up behind Cletia, and a man had appeared from somewhere, and all of them, their eyes raised, were looking at Myra up there on the staircase and Myra was looking at them down below, or rather at herself: without doubt something terrible was happening to her, something that no one had seen before, not she herself: quickly like an arrow that nothing can stop, a long white snake, thin like a cord, slipped from between her legs and fell with a small unpleasant thud, lifeless, wet . . .

The children beside Cletia screamed, Georgiana stepped on the red paste on the verandah to see better and very nearly slipped and fell, which would have been more than a little serious for her.

"*What is it?*" screamed Myra with a tragic expression. "Did it fall from me?"

Alarmed, Cletia had jumped to her feet, holding the two babies, who, though hàving seen nothing, began whining, while the two older children cowered, their legs shaking. A little way off, at the foot of the big staircase, the man, the husband of one of the other sisters, perhaps out of alarm and ignorance, perhaps out of disgust, squeezed, *scrits-scrats*, a bunch of keys he was holding in his hand. And from the large parlor, higher up than Myra, appeared Lily, who obviously had no idea . . .

Yet when she saw Myra standing in front of her, livid; when out of instinct, her eyes went straight to her feet, to that formless and slimy mass, like a cast-off cuttlefish or an umbilical cord without the child—that was steaming in the cold atmosphere—she, too, dumb though she was, let out a shriek.

"What is it?" Myra screamed again, this time with an even more tragic expression and stepping down one of the stairs to get a better look. "A worm?"

Not exactly, but she wasn't far off: it was a tapeworm, that worm in the intestine that had been feeding off her, even though she had gone hungry for so many years . . . She had escaped, that is, from her most treacherous and inconspicuous enemy—or competitor during the last few months that her stomach had not been underfed.

The puzzle was solved by Christoforos's elder sister, the old spinster Polyxeni, who lived in the same house and knew, as a consequence of her age and virginity, about many such things (they often called her "Polymathi"). "Be happy and don't stand there like a plank of wood," she said to Myra. "In two days, you've found a husband and rid yourself of that worm—you spewed it out from below, you crafty madam, for it to fall out so easily you must have been bare underneath. You'll see that before long your body will get its shape back, you'll look like a woman—instead of a scarecrow."

And, through God's good grace, the next night, the last day of February, with snow and bitter cold, the unprecedented meeting would take place.

Those enterprising women had succeeded in making the *scarecrow* unrecognizable, in literally making her up. They did it out of curiosity: to see what they were capable of or she was capable of; but they also did it to be rid of her, to send her off to another house. So they dressed her in some sweet folksy clothes in brown, mauve, and dark yellow, all cast-offs, which they altered exactly to fit her body, because even though none of the women in their family was plump or stout, neither was any of them so thin that you couldn't distinguish their necks from their shoulders, as they said, chattering away like real seamstresses.

After trying this nostalgic dress over and over again, and before putting it on her for the last time, they held it up for a while: "Let me see it! Let me gaze at it a little longer!" they said to each other, pushing one another aside, like mothers taking their leave of their child for the last time. And at the same time, they felt merry, were bursting with laughter—but without knowing why. Perhaps the garment would be just right for a little girl, for their emaciated Julia, let's say, except that the hem would fall half an inch or so too long—and with what was left from the width, they would be able to make a second dress almost, but for whom? For Teyim again? "One's enough for you," they told her. The same with the tight-waisted jacket that they had had to take in a good deal more for her: they held this up too, repeated the same things, laughed again, sighed.

However, on Myra, these clothes stood out like pearls on the neck of a poorly dressed woman.

As for her teeth, though, there was little they could do; in fact, they could do nothing, they remained gray and hollow like splinters of petrified ash. They all thought it a miracle how she ate with those teeth without chewing them up too! . . . "There's nothing we can do, not even *through God's good grace*," the women told her, "we're sorry. But here's a piece of advice: even if Apostolakos says yes, don't smile at him: he'll take it back."

To get her own back a little, Myra smiled at them . . . (Some years later, she would get new teeth, false ones, after all of hers had fallen out. But her gums, meanwhile, had become so set and hardened that whenever she wanted to eat, she would take out those *bones* as she called them and would put them back in when she was digesting, when she was returning again to this world. And what irony: in the lower part of her mouth, one of her own teeth, just one, had remained untouched by her sufferings and wretched life of so many years, completely untouched; and it was visible, it was right at the front, just left of center:

healthy, slightly pointed, large—especially so, as all the others were decayed or missing—not at all rotten or gray, a strange remnant we could say of a race that had vanished . . . So the false set of dentures they had given her was missing a tooth. And they said that, in reality, Myra always ate with one tooth—this one.)

When it came to her hair, though, miracles took place: some of the twelve-year-old Julia's medicines, some of those distasteful bitter pills and syrups that—in small doses—she was still taking for her hair, so that the new growth of hair wouldn't stop (if Apostolakos had heard of this . . .), benefited Myra enormously: within two months after winning her way into that house, and with that scanty hair on her head, and after they had had her take some of the medicine in question (either she'll lose the little hair she has, they thought, or she'll grow a few new hairs), her head literally sprouted. Julia secretly looked at her quite shocked; the others gasped in amazement. And on the day that Apostolakos would come to ask for her hand, Cletia, in a moment of magnanimity, with a pain in her heart (she was over thirty and, though a beauty next to Myra, no one had come to ask for her hand), decided to present her with a wedding gift, anyhow one of those good deeds that you don't let your left hand know that you're doing: to curl her hair! Because Myra's head may have sprouted a crop of hair, but it was so straight and inelegant that if anyone other than Apostolakos had seen her, he would have thought, What are those brush spikes on her head? Doesn't she have any hair? Of course, there were kerchiefs for women which could easily conceal even a bald head or any other imperfection up there, but not for women whom the prospective groom was about to see for the first time, not, that is, for the prospective bride: both had to appear with head bared, since the hair counted as a positive or negative attribute when it came to match-making. And if this particular Apostolos didn't have any right whatsoever to complain about the hair of whatever Myra, they had, nevertheless, to take care of this detail too, given that the whole business was taking place in the house of Christoforos. And everything would have been easier if that hopeless hair were longer, so that they could braid it and tie it up behind her head . . . But Myra herself had taken some scissors and cut it just a few days before because, she said, it was a nuisance, it got in her eyes. So hair ends were sticking out everywhere, and this, according to the host of the event, was not seemly.

So Cletia had her sit next to a fire and took a long thin iron tong and revealed to her one of the beauty secrets of the time: she curled her hair, which was as straight as a leek, heating the tong every so often in the fire and wrapping the unruly tufts around it one by one. The task took a long time, and it was well that Cletia had thought to start the whole process quite early while the other women were still poring over the mauve dress with the yellow pheasants on the breast. Myra was scared that she would burn her hair with that tool, but when she saw the first results in the mirror, she sat obediently, surrendering herself into Cletia's hands, and said no more. Besides, Cletia knew to what point she should leave the tong to heat so as to curl the hair without singeing it—for years she had been curling her own hair, at least in front, in this way, as neither had she been fortunate enough to be born with curly tresses. Naturally, some hair didn't escape getting singed and the room smelled of burning, but what were a few beside all the rest?

Apostolos, on the other hand, during that time, had no one to take care of him. But there were some who claimed they had seen him heating water in a huge cauldron, behind his workshop, and getting into it wearing only his birthday suit. The chilly weather pierced right to the bones, but he set to soaping his neck and arms with a bar of green soap that kept slipping from his hands into the water, and he would keep plunging deep inside to find it again. But you should have seen his fright, they said, when he began to suspect that there were those who were secretly watching him, though he had gone to amazing lengths to avoid anything of the sort . . . They thought they would never see his head coming out of the water again, thought they had lost him—he was so ashamed or scared or hurt. And the hairs on his back, they said, swayed on the surface like black grass . . . They felt sorry for him (what got into them?) and called to him: "Apostolakos, we're going, spruce yourself up in your own good time!" And so that he would believe them, they leapt up and left making a loud din and shouting, albeit they had come noiselessly . . . They heard a *splish-sploosh* behind them and they weren't sure: had he taken heart and lifted his head out of the water? Or had he sunk to the bottom? One of them turned round to look. "Let's be on our way," he said to the other one, "he's lifted his head out . . . he wants to get engaged, not to drown."

Two grown-up men were relating all this in the marketplace (taking pride in it perhaps?), and not two young children—the children showed more respect for him on that day.

Everything was ready in the large high-ceilinged room, *heavy* from the rosy warmth and impatience—the fire was blazing, the walls around had been covered with red kilims to keep the heat inside—and any moment footsteps would be heard in the yard, if the wind allowed them to be, that is. Christoforos didn't neglect to send two of his relatives to bring Apostolos, given that he had neither relatives himself nor friends, aside from those old men, and given that it was part of the formalities to be accompanied by two witnesses. It was also decided that Myra's children should be present at the gathering, though under normal circumstances the children were absent from such events—they brought bad luck, it was said, *bother*. But Myra was unaware of such superstitions, and the host wanted them too. "They'll spoil the affair," his sister Polyxeni told him, faithful to the customs. "There's no way that children can spoil it," he replied, trusting his own feelings. Besides, it wasn't every evening that engagements took place between such *creatures*, for success or failure to be decided by such details.

As for the dark despair surrounding Apostolos, his hair that is, no one had thought to prepare Myra (nor had she thought to ask anything more about his person), so this too remained for Christoforos to do. He went up to her, at the last minute, and quietly asked her if the women had said anything to her about Apostolos.

"Said what to me?" asked Myra.

"If they have told you!" he said again impatiently, but without being specific.

"They told me, through God's good grace, that he's a good man and needs a woman in his life," said Myra, making it up out of her head, as they hadn't told her even that much.

"And nothing else?" he asked.

"I don't recall . . . what else?" said Myra. "Does he have children too? That—"

"No, no, children wouldn't be any problem," he said, interrupting her.

"Then what?" she asked him, "does he only have one eye or one leg? Tell me, I don't care. The way you're talking to me now with the fire reflected in your face, it's as if you only had one eye . . . the shadow is covering half your mouth. Tell me what you want, I don't care, even if he's as ugly as sin, just so long as he has a good heart."

"He has a good heart and more—no one has a heart like his. But he has hair too," he told her, "lots of hair . . . a *forest!* Do you understand what I'm telling you?"

"So what?" said Myra, hearing this; she let a few moments go by for it to sink in. "So what if he has a lot of hair? I wouldn't take somebody with no hair . . . And my previous man, curse him, had a lot of hair. Yes, I wouldn't say a forest, but he wasn't without his share of hair."

"This one is a *forest*," Christoforos stressed once more.

"A forest then . . . I'll be a *spring* in the forest," she said, finding inspiration.

"Well, let's let divine providence take care of it from now on, I can do no more," Christoforos muttered to himself. And he cast a glance at the others: there were two daughters and a son and daughter-in-law, Myra's three children, who, well-dressed and groomed, were eating carobs next to the fire, Polyxeni, of course, who now replaced Eftha in many things (though not to the point of sleeping in the same bedroom with her widower brother), Lily, who kept coming in and out, unsure of what attitude to adopt, and a couple more relatives. Twelve people in total, including himself, and the three who were on their way, fifteen: a goodly few; usually there were no more than between seven and nine in such cases, but again it was his own idea for so many to be there, to warm the atmosphere a little, to have a mixture of voices and faces, so that the two of them wouldn't feel so *alone* or *different*, obliged to stare at each other from beginning to end.

And when Apostolos came in, stooping slightly and in clean and black clothes, clasping his hands as though crumpling paper or as though getting on with his work in his workshop, accompanied by the other two, who, unconsciously, to lend support, were also stooping; when he halted for a moment, at a loss and not knowing whom and what to look at first in there . . . and when his eyes finally came to rest on *her* (all the others were familiar to him, only she was unknown to him . . . unknown and strange like her name), and when at last neither he nor she gave the others the slightest indication of whether it was the first excitement at seeing each other that had rooted them to the spot like that or perhaps the first reciprocal disappointment—it was then that the host, tireless, upright, and *beguiling*, got up from his chair and went over to the guest in order to salvage the proceedings or to facilitate a better outcome.

"Well, my friend," he said to him, opening his arms and wanting to add a note of cheer to whatever was going to happen. "Didn't anyone ever tell you not to choose fabrics and wives at nighttime?"

"Well yes . . . they did," Apostolos replied timidly, "but . . . such things . . . aren't they better done at nighttime?"

This pleased the host no end.

"Nighttime, yes, nighttime!" he agreed, emphasizing it. "A proper baptism . . . for all! Eh? What do you have to say, Myrofora?"

She put her hand over the pheasants and gave a reply like an oracle: "Me the nighttime," she said.

And everything turned out well. The night proved favorable, the flickering of the flames in the fire enflamed them all in a way that was detracting and mysterious, the wind howled like a hyena outside the windows, Myra's three children slept sweetly, and Polyxeni brought stewed quinces with melted brown sugar.

With the coming of summer, Christoforos also got Eumolpos married, for a second time, to a woman who had also been widowed while still young, and—

three years later—with some reservations at first, he also got Hesychios married to the widow of a cobbler. The place found peace for some time from all the stories about him, and the descendants in the big house multiplied and multiplied. So much so that some childless and distressed women came around from other neighborhoods and from other parts to ask Christoforos *how* it was that in his house children were born one after the other: his wives, his daughters, his daughters-in-law, all bred like rabbits—what was it, was it something in the water? And where was that water so that they too could go and sip from it? Didn't the good Lord have eyes, that to some women he gave in abundance and to them nothing?

They asked and actually expected to learn some secret, some *method* unbeknown to them, and Christoforos's mind gathered steam, unwillingly, when he heard all those stories about something in the water . . . "Go home, maybe you're not the ones with the problem, it could be your husbands," he said, trying to console them, "send them to see a doctor, it might be their fault."

Yet who could ever possibly believe at that time that it was the man and not the woman who was to blame for being childless? "Ah, you know and you're not telling us—seems that your secret is costly and we're only poor," they would say to him complainingly—so that his mind swirled from all the love and tenderness for these underprivileged women, who were so desperate for a child . . . And with him a widower, too.

But the fecund water also brought fresh sorrows to the family. First of all, he lost Marigo, one of his sisters, a particularly unfortunate and tormented woman, who couldn't have been more than thirty-five at the time but who looked forty-five. She had turned the world upside down to get married to someone her parents didn't want—he was too much of a troublemaker and a drunk—and once he'd married her, that was the end. People said he was the death of her, and they meant it. And at the very end—after this torment had gone on for ten years and a baby boy had been born after nine of those years—he kept her locked up in an attic, ill and half-crazy, and lived with his mother. None of her own folks could see Marigo, the mother and son downstairs chased them all away; they had a dog, and when anyone went near, all three of them would start barking. In addition, they accused the sweetie Marigo, saying that she had got what she deserved because of this, because of that . . . but who paid any attention to them? They brazenly spoke ill of her, but not even the children believed what they said.

Christoforos had made efforts to get round her husband, used kid gloves on him. He would go now and again and remind him of the *good old nights* (which only the devil would consider good) when, still betrothed to his sister, he would come to their home, with his friends, to see her . . . But his father-in-law, Lukas, would drive him away because he was blind drunk, both he and his entourage, and as they passed by they would leave nothing standing. But he, of course, would insist on coming inside to see his betrothed, would shout with all the air in his lungs that he had the right—in fact he shouted a lot of things whether or not they had to do with his betrothed. And terrified upstairs, Marigo, so as not to hear all this (and because he, in his raving, was quite capable of flaring up), would go and wake her brother Christoforos, being the eldest and most easy-going, and beg him to go down and sort things out . . . For his sister's sake, he would go—followed by his children or his younger brothers to watch. And all this would take place in the middle of the night, when people wanted to get a little rest. And as soon as the drunk saw Christoforos, he would forget about Marigo and his father-in-law and begin a different kind of merrymaking: "It's you I want," he would shout to his brother-in-law, "it's you we came here for, come on, hop-hop. . . . Another round, that's it, for a bit of a dance, that's what we came for, not to kill you in your sleep!" And whether Christoforos was in the mood or not, he would begin dancing with him and his cronies, would do whatever they wanted: hands high? high; even higher? even higher; one more round? one more round; a song from him too? a song. His younger brothers joined in the dance too, and his sons, that is, the dance went one way and their feet another, the song went one way and their voices another, no one knew what they were supposed to be doing, where they were stepping, yet supposedly it was all for one and one for all, and they were on the brink of true togetherness. And that was it; then they would be on their way and leave them in peace and in a daze. And then a couple of nights later, the same would happen again, again they would have a longing to come and see Marigo . . .

This irksome betrothal lasted a full five years (Lukas passed away in the meantime). Plus the ten years of marriage that followed.

So Christoforos went and reminded him of all this, though he took no plea-sure in remembering it: "I was never against you," he told him, "perhaps my father might not have been all that keen on you, but I never said no to you, I always went along with you." And of course, he said all this to him in the hope that he would let him see his sick sister, or if necessary—though this would be more than could be wished—let him take her back to her family home, to take her out of his hands. "And once she's well again, she can return to you, yours again, I'll bring her back myself good as new to this house," he said to him, going so far as to make himself seem ridiculous with such promises just to soften him a little, because this man was the most obstinate and pigheaded critter, "next to whom our husbands"—as some women with cantankerous husbands (though not to that degree) admitted—"are angels with wings."

And truly not to that degree. And it is not our intention to eradicate from the face of the earth this cross-grained and surly man or to classify all men in this category; it's not unlikely that women worse than him may make their appearance on the planet or that there may be others beside whom he pales. Anyhow, he was what he was: one of that caste of miserable wretches who, even if a rose were to grow by mistake in their hearts, would eat the thorns in order to nibble on the roses . . . And if, when he was still young, he would waver between his drunken bouts and somewhat moderate his miserableness, with the passing of the years, everything became ten times worse, and not even his mother—with whom he had much in common—could ask him for a favor.

And only Marigo's groans and coughing emerged from high up behind that window with the iron bars and, occasionally, her hands. Months had passed, and not one of her own folk had seen her. And as for her little son, had anyone seen or heard him? Christoforos was infuriated when he realized that he didn't have to deal simply with a stubborn and pigheaded man, even with a spiteful and malicious one, but rather with someone cruel who was torturing a woman not because he loved her or hated her but because he was incapable of anything else. And he felt himself even more hard-pressed when someone came and told him that he had heard Marigo calling from the window, "Tell Christoforos to come—what's he waiting for? For me to die?" Even if this someone had said it as a busybody, simply to open up wounds or light the fuse, Christoforos realized that the limits of patience and tolerance had been reached, that Marigo was calling to him from her hell, and that either he had to kill his brother-in-law or find some other way to go to his sister. At the risk of proceeding with the first (and extreme) solution, the weather helped him to decide upon the second—it was winter again.

Winter, and the other man hardly went out, his mother—so it appeared—was confined to bed, and the wolfhound that they had to guard the house was found one morning frozen solid in the snow. He cursed it, spat on it, kicked it in case it came round, but didn't seem to show much sorrow. Nor did Christoforos.

The next night, he brought a tall wooden ladder and climbed up to Marigo's window. The vertical iron bars were rusty, and with a little effort he bent the middle ones, but he couldn't get through, the opening wasn't big enough (nor would it have been even if he had bent all of them), while from inside she stared at him terrified and cowering in a corner. *She* was a phantom of his sister, not his sister—only a shadow had remained that kept coughing up blood into a handkerchief. He called her over to him, clasped her two hands and said, "I've come, don't be afraid," though he felt overcome with shame for not having come sooner . . . But there was no time for more, they would say what they had to say back home and in comfort, now they had to hurry. "The child first," said Marigo; and she handed him the little boy (who would have passed through an even narrower opening), and he promised her that he would quickly return with one of his other brothers to take her too, they would bring a rope with them to lower her down—but what was he saying in his turmoil? If Marigo could get through that window and climb down the wall with a rope, then she could also climb down using the ladder—the problem was the window. Only if they were able to take those darned bars out . . . "No, they won't come out," she told him, "but there's another door to the house, a back door . . . I don't recall . . . only through that . . . if I can find it." He told her to try to find it, to get out through there, to wait for him below, and wrap up warmly—he told her where exactly. "I'm not sure, I'm not sure . . . I don't recall," Marigo groaned, filled with fear and doubt, while he had already started climbing down the ladder with the child in his arms. "Try to recall, we've no time to lose," he told her, "try, don't be afraid, I'll be back, I'll be back for sure." "When?" "Tonight . . . in a while."

But when he did come back—with another of his brothers and more equipment—the weather was against him. The snow was falling much thicker now and swirling, blinding them, forcing them back or stopping them from making any headway, and it was only the thought that Marigo was waiting for him and worrying—this alone—that kept him going on his course. And he eventually arrived there again, but it was as if days had passed: the snow that had fallen during the time he had gone and come back didn't allow him to recognize much, virtually nothing, and the wooden ladder—which he had left on the ground behind the house—was nowhere to be seen, covered over by the snow. While searching for the ladder, he also looked for Marigo—perhaps she had climbed down, perhaps she had come out from the other door—calling out in a muffled voice, "Marigo . . . Marigo . . . can you hear me?" Not even his brother could hear him, and he was following behind him, searching too. Eventually they found the ladder, shook the snow from it, and leaned it up against the window, of which only a small black hole was visible. He started to climb up again, with the danger of the ladder sliding—of course his brother was holding it below, but who was holding him? The swirling snow made them dizzy, threatening both of them, as well as their ladder—and halfway up, he heard the sound of her coughing from inside . . . as though she were making herself cough differently, as though wanting to tell him, "Don't climb up any farther." He understood, but he couldn't go back; her husband was with her in the room, waiting for him behind the bent bars.

"I've come for her," Christoforos said to him. "You'll either give her to me peacefully—"

"She's in a bad way, that's why I have her in here," he replied, "can't you see?

If I let her come downstairs, she'd infect us all, my mother's already caught it—what do you want? Do you want us all to get it? She's coughing up blood from morning till night, that's all she does . . . Fine women you have in your house, real pearls, each and every one! . . . And this one takes the prize."

"You'll have time to say all that tomorrow, now give me my sister," Christoforos told him; "in our house, we're not afraid of illnesses."

"Why would you be?" the other retorted ironically. "Is leprosy afraid of lepers? Ha! . . . I caught her looking for the door. *What door? The other one.* What other one, there's only one door to my house, I don't need another one. Imagine, looking for the *other* door! . . . She's not right in her head anymore . . . Take her!"

And he gave her to him. After all those years, all those months, that he had been draining the life from her drop by drop and wouldn't let anyone near her, suddenly—no one can see into another's soul—he gave her back to her own folk as easily as he would unburden himself of a small sack on his back.

It was a bolt out of the blue for Marigo too, not only for Christoforos.

He went back down the ladder floundering in the white blizzard and rushed into the house through the normal door and ran up to the attic. He was worried lest some other surprise be waiting for him there—but he found her alone, doubled up and huddling against the wall. "Get up, sister, let's get away from here," he said to her, "let's go home," but she was scared and told him it was a lie, all a lie . . .

While he helped her down the wretched staircase step by step, while he took her through that old door and lifted her up—after wrapping her in the blankets that his brother gave him—to take her back home, Marigo never stopped whispering in panic that it was a lie, all a lie, or asking where her son was, or where her comb was so she could comb her hair a little . . . she didn't want her father seeing her in such a mess.

"Our father's dead, Marigo, these past twelve years, what on earth made you say such a thing?" her brothers asked her. And halfway along the way, they heard her softly crying for their father who had died and asking forgiveness for *being so heavy*, as she passed from the arms of one brother to the other, from one embrace to the other . . . and meanwhile day was breaking because it was a particularly difficult return, slow, endless, the snow was up to their knees, to their thighs, no matter how they struggled the one to clear the path for the other, they were eventually forced to halt and wait in the hope that someone else might appear and help them, still having as far again to go; so that Marigo would not be cold, they both took off their thick overcoats and covered her on top of the two blankets already wrapped round her.

But Marigo was unfortunate right to the end. They brought her back to the family home without being aware that they were carrying a dead body; they thought she was tired and had fallen asleep, that she was so heavy in their arms because of the many covers, because of the cold that weighed on their own limbs. And if her body became more and more of a *dead weight*, more and more stiff, they no longer had the fingers—they were numb—to open the covers to see . . . This was done once and for all by the others who were waiting on the doorstep.

And they fell upon her sobbing. Some years before, in similar fashion, with one or two slight differences in the details (just enough to emphasize what was in common), they had carried Eftha from the fields . . . incomprehensible women in that house, *each and every one*—as though there weren't any beds for them, no easier ways for them to depart.

Stupefied, Christoforos couldn't but recall the words of that blackguard who had given him his sister back when she had only had a few hours still to live, those words about real pearls . . . "And this one takes the prize," he had said to him. And it was true (though not in the sense that he meant it) that Marigo had surpassed even Eftha—and Petroula—by a long chalk. And other older women . . . At least they . . . At least? What point was there in recalling everything again from the beginning, in comparing the incomparable? "Everyone has their cross, but in some crosses the nails are especially sharp"—so Polyxeni had said, and that was sufficient. And each new death simply stole a little of the *gleam* of the previous one. Just as Polyxeni *stole* his thoughts from him: when she turned her head, completely crushed, and asked him choking with tears, "And now, who's going to surpass our Marigo? Who, my dear brother? What more does the good Lord have in store for you?"—it was exactly what he was thinking, but he hadn't dared to come out with it as she had. "Shh, don't speak like that," he scolded her. "That *our* was her undoing. We all waited for everything to get out of hand before we remembered her. *Our* Marigo." "That's how it was going to end," said Polyxeni. "I'm not trying to take away any responsibility, but that's how it was always going to end. Right from the start, the sharpest nails are destined for those who are special. And Marigo was special."

Marigo, Marigo . . . They hadn't set eyes on her for months, the speed of her consumption left them speechless, she hadn't visited her family home for months, they didn't know whether her son had been baptized—when, how had she given birth? Who had been beside her to help her? Everything behind a window, through which not even the sun sent its rays. All alone in a hellhole, when in paradise no one is alone. Marigo . . . If someone died in his prime, when everything was going well and his mature years and sweet old age were awaiting him, they wept and wept at this misfortune, for the things he hadn't managed to enjoy from the fruits of his labor, to see, to learn. But when someone goes as Marigo did, in the snow, even in the arms of two of her brothers, what should they weep for first, what should they lament most? For the years she hadn't managed to live? Or for the ones she had lived?

And the weather wouldn't allow them to bury her, *not even that*—it was an unprecedented winter, no one recalled such snow. There were plenty of arms willing to carry her, but where were they to put their feet to take her to her final resting place? Before the following morning, the snow was higher than the height of a man, the downstairs windows of the houses didn't look onto snow-covered roads or snow-covered yards but were covered themselves by snow, the gates and front doors wouldn't open, and those that had remained open were blocked by the snow—they were unable to go out even for their physical needs. Where were they going to find a carpenter for the casket? Where would they find a priest for the rites or relatives to send her on her way? Who was going to clear a path so that even a small procession might pass? "Winter, winter . . . harsh, rough, and irresolute," Christoforos would say every winter, rubbing his hands next to the fire. What could he say this year, when it was harsher and rougher than any other year, and not at all *irresolute*? Three days had passed since they had brought her back to her family home and they still had her there. Laid out in an empty room, wrapped in the blankets that had frozen solid along with her. Every so often someone would go upstairs to see her, stay a couple of moments with her and leave—not even a white wolf could stay longer up there. And Marigo endured all this, she neither spoke nor complained—*she slew them*. Better for another two to have died than her, and like that.

On the fourth day the snow stopped, a frost set in, and on the sixth day they decided to bury her. Without any rites, without even a coffin, and just her close kin—and of these, only as many as had the guts to undertake a procession over the ice, as far as the foothills of the mountain where the cemetery was. A veritable Via Dolorosa. They didn't wear any shoes—if you did wear shoes those days and went outside in them, you couldn't get them off again. And then there was the other thing: that even those soles with thick treads slipped on those glassy paths and made you fall—even more so when you were carrying a corpse on your shoulders. So they cut up covers and other woolen blankets, wrapped their feet in these (putting dry grass inside, and ash), bound them with thick strands and set off. Three of her brothers and as many cousins. Seven counting her. They took with them three large spades and as many pickaxes. Polyxeni had got ready too, but after thirty paces she went back: would it make any difference anyway if she had set her mind to going too? Marigo had gone without demands and grumbling. Night had fallen by the time they were through, nor was there any moon to look down on them. They lowered her in just as she was, wrapped in covers . . . One night more on this earth, one night less . . . Incomparable Marigo.

Usually after a death—then, at least, and even earlier, in those parts—they would empty the large earthenware jar of water they kept in the house. They did so. Because it was in there, they said, that Charon dived and cleaned his sword after severing the soul. So they too washed the wide-lipped earthenware vessel to get rid of the blood and filled it again with clean fresh water. Those who didn't have earthenware jars did the same with their pitchers, which were also big enough for a sword, as was a jug if necessary. Charon may not have done any favors for these people, but he always found clean water to wash himself after the act. And in addition, even the room where the conquest—*the last slaughtering*—had taken place was always whitewashed, because—according to what they believed—the blood splashed as far as the walls and even splattered the ceiling. Even if they couldn't see it with their eyes—in any case could they see Charon? The one moment that they would see him would be his moment and not theirs. They did the things they knew—we shouldn't think them simplistic or insignificant.

So Polyxeni, too, had wanted to empty their earthenware pot and to whitewash a wall or two, at random and symbolically, for Marigo, in the belief or under the delusion that, as they hadn't done anything for her before, they should do something for her now at least: a kind of atonement for the house. Besides, there were others too who died like dogs, others who didn't simply expire in their beds, who were brought home *ready* and unrecognizable, from who knows what sudden and violent, slow or quick encounter with the inconceivable; nevertheless the jars were always emptied in their wake and at least one wall in the house received a new coat of white. (They thus satisfied their *imagination*, because most probably they—or others before them—had seen some *images* that haven't come down to us.)

But how was Polyxeni to move the earthenware jar? The water had become ice—even a sword would have had difficulty in piercing it. So she took a hammer and began, *crak-crak-crak*, to chip away at the frozen surface . . . and she cracked it in a couple of places, and a kind of network was formed under which there was some sign of life . . . She grabbed hold of a few ice crystals and a few drops of water and tossed them around her—she could do nothing else. And which wall was she to whiten, given that the whitewash was as hard as rock and the walls like glass? She left everything for the spring. Or at least for the first day that the weather would have improved a little.

But before this happened, other things happened. Twelve days after Marigo, one of her uncles, Elias, a brother of their father, Lukas, also fell victim to the snow. He lived next door, the houses were side by side. His two sons didn't dare go to the mountain for wood, and so he went himself; one evening they missed him, both him and his horse from the stable. They went out looking here and there, but thick snowflakes again began to slowly fall, the ground again began to rise, and the area again to whirl, and so they returned home empty-handed. For three whole days they waited for him: the snow stopped and began again, they set out and returned home again, not a sound came from their mouths. On the fourth day, their father appeared on his horse with two armfuls of wood on either side. The horse was walking very slowly and before it was even through the gate (and before they could run outside), it collapsed. With his back erect and threatening, their father . . . fell *slowly* to one side, heavily, unbending, the way a column would fall. Tiny icicles were hanging from the rim of his hat, two streams of ice ran from his nose to his lips. His eyes were half-open, motionless—beads of crystal shone in his eyebrows. "He's playing a hard game," his sons thought, hoping that only his body had frozen and that it would unfreeze, that it wasn't the end, that they could save him, that there was still time to take him to task.

He didn't speak to them no matter how much they asked him, how much they touched him, how much they breathed into his mouth or slapped his cheeks. One of his nephews, a brother of Christoforos, cupping his mouth with his hands, put it to his frozen ear and shouted loudly: "Uncle! . . ." And even louder: "UNCLE! . . ." Enough to wake the gods on Olympus . . . but he didn't wake up. "He's gone," he mumbled to himself, "what am I shouting for?"

Four of them brought him into the house, close to the fire, seated on their hands as on the back of the horse. They had never seen from close-up what someone's perfect *statue* is like in full attire and in one of his favorite positions—and they saw it then, carried it like workmen: the folds of his black overcoat, the sleeves on the inside, the rigid trousers, the laces, the bridle, and his clenched fingers, his face with its wrinkles and the sullen expression, his legs, neck, trunk, all a statue—just like a statue. Except that their statue was not a thing of beauty or something to delight in . . .

And gradually, in front of the fire, whatever there was on him that could thaw—of his expression and his clothing—did thaw: the frozen snow melted, dripped and dried. But he himself didn't thaw out. His back didn't bend, not even his neck.

They kept him in the house for two days, not like Marigo in an empty room, but downstairs in the warmth, among them, propped up on stools and cushions, surrounded by their silent presence, because till the very last moment they kept their hopes up. Till the very last moment, it seemed to them that their father was *playing* with them, that he wanted to play the hard snowman, as long as their nerves would endure—and his too: his expression, his posture, though characterized by the most incredible rigidity, retained something of the living—and the bitter—expression and posture of this man when, up to not very long before, he would sit in front of the same fire, silently gazing at its flames . . .

Up to not long before, however, but not anymore. The mirror they kept putting again and again to his mouth didn't mist over, however much they wanted it to, however much they prayed for it to . . . He had died days before on his horse, bringing the wood that he had managed to gather.

There were more people who went to his funeral; the roads were now passable, yet no coffin could be found for him either, though the carpenters had returned to their workshops; but his knees wouldn't bend at all, his body *never left the saddle.*

They put him in a deep grave, more or less sitting up, next to his equally unfortunate niece. "Now you can chatter away together to your hearts' content—without in any way being envious of us here!" was Polyxeni's heartfelt wish for them.

In another place, they had also buried the horse, which had arrived home alive, bringing them their loved one, and then had expired.

And that winter wouldn't have gone had it not taken with it the *last one,* someone whom everyone believed that God had forgotten about: the father of this same Elias and of Lukas, Christoforos's grandfather, also called Christoforos. He was the oldest man in the area, the remotest past that still stirred beside them, and had lived those past twenty years in one of the rooms that belonged to his grandson with the same name, though he had many other grandsons, with and without the same name: all middle-aged or older, and granddaughters too, who felt like children beside him, born only *yesterday.* He had no sons left (with the exception of Elias)—none of them had survived. Nor daughters. Only grandchildren and great-grandchildren.

So this Ol' Christoforos—and to call him a centenarian would be doing him an injustice—was like the trees: without asking why, without the others around him asking why. No one was in a position to say for sure if he could still see well or not, if he could hear anything or not, if he was ready to die now or live as long again; in his face you could see the emotions that had furrowed it and the memories that prevailed in him, as you would see them in the face of a Sphinx. He didn't speak, didn't answer you—though sometimes he did, completely unexpectedly—nor, of course, did he laugh or cry, he was not astonished in the slightest by the things that astonished others, he didn't even sleep at night: each evening someone would put him to bed, tuck him in, and as soon as he went the old man would get up; he would sit on a stool or in a chair, with his stick between his knees and his gaze directed upwards like the blind Tiresias, until someone again came in to tell him that it was daybreak. Often they weren't sure if he really was alive, if he was breathing—he seemed as if carved in stone. If you gave him something to eat, you saw his plate hardly touched, if you gave him some water, he would drink just a few drops; if you didn't give him anything, he wouldn't ask—they had forgotten when the last time was that he had asked for anything.

And his sole pastime—if we can call it that, if we may be permitted by an interminable existence—was to hold his hands out now and again and gaze at them, on one side and the other, to gaze at them intently, as a mineralogist might do with two of his favorite stones, which no longer hold any secrets for him. Or perhaps they did. Sometimes, one of those around him said how much he would give to know what the old man was thinking of in these moments, just *how* he passed his inconceivable time, so much time . . . One day, Christoforos heard him counting his fingers in a low, hoarse voice . . . When he reached ten, the tenth one, he stopped, and his grandson wondered whether he would go on to eleven or back to one . . . But the old man didn't go on. And not to miss the opportunity, the grandson went up to him, leaned close to his face and said to him loudly and clearly:

"I see you can still count, you're counting your fingers . . .why?"

He looked at him surprised, not surprised, probably recognized him, but said nothing in reply.

Nothing at that moment, because the same evening, when Christoforos was accompanying him to his bed, he quite unexpectedly said to him in an elevated voice: "Carried amazing things that morning!"

"Who?" asked Christoforos.

"These," said the old man, showing his hands with their outstretched fingers.

"Your hands? . . . What amazing things did they carry? . . . What morning?" asked Christoforos . . . as though suddenly *a vein of gold* was opening up before him.

"I count them. To see if I remember," the old man told him.

"If you remember how to count?" he asked.

The old man said nothing.

"And do you remember?" he asked him again.

He nodded again and again—yes? no? who knew?

Christoforos didn't know: should he stay? go? ask more? — then the old man spoke again: "She scolded me when I got back because I was late, she and her mother were scared that I'd got lost because I went to get a hat. What are you scolding me for, I said to her. Life is full of adventures."

The grandson felt a slight numbness: what story was this?

"Who scolded you?" he asked the old man.

"My daughter."

All this reminded Christoforos of something, like something he'd heard; some strange tale — coincidences? He having once been late . . . A new cypress-green hat . . . his daughter Julia . . .

"Which daughter?" he asked his grandfather.

"That one," said the old man.

"Which one? Don't you remember? Which one of all of them? What was her name?"

"No, I don't remember," he told him.

Christoforos waited a little while longer; the old man looked at his hands again.

"Shall I stay?" he asked him.

"Go, go," said the old man, tired, and he turned toward the wall, closing his eyes.

Christoforos knew that as soon as he was outside the door, the old man would get up again. He went out. He reflected on the old man's words while he made his way to his own bed, while he fell asleep: all that about the daughter scolding him, about being late in returning because he'd gone to get a hat and she scolded him . . . Damn it if it wasn't a lot like something else, something concerning *him*, that time with Julia, after the doctors and before Dekatessara, something the old man couldn't possibly have known about! . . . Could Julia perhaps . . . had she spoken of it? No, it was out of the question, years had gone by since then . . .

He fell asleep without having understood. He dreamt of his grandfather strutting about in the world at large with a new hat . . .

And the next day, leaving his own story aside, he said to his other brothers: "Our centenarian is still alive and can feel. Can feel and remember! I asked him something yesterday and he answered me! . . . All right, I asked him in the afternoon and he answered me at night, but at least for once he answered."

"What did you ask him?" the others wanted to know.

"Something," said Christoforos.

Concerning whether he could *feel*, they shouldn't have had much doubt; it had often happened during all those years — and we're talking about since his old age had gone beyond the limits of wonder and had become something else, perhaps the beginning of another life, another concept—that they had discerned traces and remnants in him proving that he wasn't so unfeeling as they thought, he wasn't the sacred crock who had forgotten to die. They had seen this whenever someone died in the house, grandchild, great-grandchild or whoever. Then, like smoke from a dormant volcano, something seemed to rise from those depths . . . And he would astound them by his appearance in the dead person's room—usually unaccompanied—and by the way he greeted and left everyone speechless: he would take off whatever he was wearing on his head, throw his stick on the floor, and thrice prostrate himself before the deceased in the coffin, a sign of utmost reverence and humility, and also a plea for forgiveness, which usually is made only by the younger ones to the older, not to say that many considered it unnecessary, or considered it outmoded, and simply kissed the dead person on his hands and forehead, crossing themselves of course. But this decrepit old man was intent on bidding farewell to those dead and much younger than he ("or on welcoming them to the other world," as some in the crowd said with black humor) with those prostrations of the body to the ground, which in no way signified any servility, no lowly or shallow emotion. By the third prostration, his knees and jaw were trembling . . . He didn't kiss them (or very rarely), nor did he sit with the others chitchatting around the coffin; with his fingers he asked the others to hand him his stick from the floor—it was too difficult for him to bend down again—and put his hat back on his head, and then asked someone to take him out . . . He would walk off slowly, dragging his feet, and those taking him out said that they could also sometimes see tears in his eyes, those tears that well up in the eyes without actually falling, or that he would sometimes come out with a strange "Ah," an "Ah" as if he were clearly pronouncing someone's name, a specific and important name, completely different from all the others: "Ah."

And if a few passing illnesses had visited him in his old age and afflicted him for a month or two, now none ever came near him and no one could imagine—when it came to himself of course, but especially when it came to this old man—when and how and from what he would die. And if.

Concerning his granddaughter Marigo, they didn't tell him anything; he might not have even remembered her (that's what they said; he, however, appeared to remember everything); they concealed her death from him, particularly the details. When all was said and done, had there been any real funeral in the house at which everyone had been present? Had anyone come from another house to pay his or her respects—had anyone else even learned about it? No one—everyone would learn about it after the snow had gone, with the coming of spring. And could this decrepit old man have gone to the room where they'd had her laid out for five days and prostrated himself before her too? Let it pass, they thought, on top of everything else—better that he shouldn't know.

But he surprised them again, leaving them speechless. When the six of them had set out to bury her and Polyxeni, the seventh, had come back because the snow was far too deep and slippery for her, she thought of going to the grandfather's room to see if the fire was still burning. Because he was quite capable of staying without a fire in such weather and of not protesting and because, when they brought him down to the large sitting room where they all gathered in the winter so as not to have many different fires and burn up all the wood, he would get up unconcerned and return to his own room . . . So she thought she would go to see what their living ghost was up to and whether he needed anything that he hadn't asked for. And she found him sitting before the fire, moving the coals back and forth with the poker and talking to himself. She carefully closed the door behind her—he seemed not to have noticed that anyone had come in— and pricked up her ears to hear what he was saying:

". . . sesame three kegs. In the first one the sieving, in the second, the brine, the third with water. Afterwards in the oven and then the millstone. Dolts, don't you understand anything! he shouted at us. First in the oven and then the millstone! And put blinkers on the horse when it goes round so it doesn't get dizzy . . . It's not as if we knew. We were just kids, we didn't know how to do work like that, our father sent us there because he'd fallen ill, pneumonia, we worked there for two winters and then he took us back home. But the other one had us at his beck and call and scolded us. What—"

"Grandfather, who are you talking to?" asked Polyxeni, stopping him. "When we ask you to say something, you don't open your mouth, and when you're alone, you wag your tongue . . . What's all that about kegs and sesame? Who were you talking to?"

The old man didn't speak; he stopped raking the coals with the poker and raised his right hand to the level of his brow as if he were looking at his visitor from inside there. She stepped from the doorway and went up to him.

"Who are you talking to?" she asked again, nudging him gently in his side with her knee.

"When I was small, I worked in the sesame mill," he told her.

"That's something I never knew," said his granddaughter. "And where was that sesame mill?"

"A long way away. We didn't know and he scolded us. But afterwards, our father got well and he brought us back home. Sesame, three kegs! he would tell us each morning. We'd forget and put out four. What's that for? he'd ask us and then and there he would push our heads inside, with the brine on top, so we'd learn our lesson. But one day he had the legs pulled from under him: his little daughter fell from the trapdoor, fell into the sesame, into the mill as it was grinding . . . his darling girl, his only child. Ooooh. His world came to an end. She was called Marigo, he wanted to hang himself from the highest tree, leap into hell's fire. There was nothing left of the girl, little she was, like us, even littler, a girl to bring joy to your eyes. There was nothing left of her; dead as a doornail. From then on, her father never scolded us again, was like a lamb. Then our father came and took us back home, he got well, we left the other man. We owed him, and because our father fell ill and didn't have the means to pay him, he sent us to work for him for two years."

"What was his daughter's name?" asked Polyxeni, who, yes, had clearly heard him say "Marigo," but during those days, all she heard was "Marigo," it was what was gnawing at her.

"Marigo. Like ours whose husband used to beat her," said the old man.

"Do you remember Marigo?" Polyxeni asked him with a feeling of faintness in her breast. "Our Marigo?"

The old man nodded several times (they had him down as a dodderer).

"Do you think I wouldn't remember Marigo?" he said to her.

"And how do you know that her husband used to beat her?" she asked him. "Did she tell you so herself?"

She received no answer.

"He *used* to beat her? Doesn't he beat her anymore?" she asked him again *craftily*.

"No, he doesn't beat her anymore, where would he find her?" said the old man.

Polyxeni was reluctant to question him further — anyway, the old man only answered when he wanted to. And anyway, she felt a sense of shame or irony because they thought that they were hiding things from him, when, in fact, he was way *ahead* of them. She cast a few more pieces of wood on the fire, rubbed her hands over his clothes to see if he was warmly dressed, told him that she would come back with some warm soup for him, and left him. As she was shutting the door behind her, the old man spoke again.

"Marigo's found peace, don't feel sorry for her. Wherever he hit you, the bones went farther in, sank inside, his hand was a heavy one. A shameless one. Whoever felt it can tell you . . . She found her peace years ago, eight to be exact! And I was eight then too."

"Perhaps he's talking about the other Marigo," thought Polyxeni, "perhaps about ours—there was nothing left of either of them." Aaah! She wanted to cry out but restrained herself and went some way off so the old man wouldn't hear her. Then she did let out a cry: "Aaah!" and began cursing between her teeth: "May he hang from the highest tree! May what he did to her all those years become needles to pierce his eyes! May dogs eat his remains! May he have his head crushed in a millwheel!"

And so she cursed her sister's husband (she didn't have a husband of her own) and dissolved into tears, wiping her eyes and choking, while stumbling along with her feet wrapped in rope and pieces of blankets . . . If anyone had seen her in that state and, nevertheless, been obliged to tell her that in a few days her uncle would also come home dead, we can't say what might have happened: the most probable thing is that she would, with a little fear and reservation, have let such a person go by . . . but she might also have chased after him or showered him with curses.

And so this happened too; her uncle arrived home just as her sister had. And this time it was the old man's son, his last remaining son, not one of his countless grandchildren—this was not something they could hide from him, their consciences wouldn't allow them. It was Christoforos who went to tell him.

"Elias from next door," he said, coughing, "Uncle Elias . . . ," and the burden wouldn't let him continue, let him come out with the *word*.

But the old man was very talkative during those days and we might say fully conversant with his surroundings.

"What?" he exclaimed, "has he gone too?"

"We don't know . . . probably. He returned from the mountain frozen stiff."

The old man slipped into an eon of silence. Then he got to his feet, took his stick, his hat, and was getting ready to go—Christoforos restrained him.

"Where do you think you're going? Do you know what the snow is like outside? Do you think you've ever seen snow like that in all the years you've lived?"

"I want to see it now," he said.

"I'll take you myself," said Christoforos, lifting him up in his arms and carrying him, the old man a mere snippet, skin and bone.

He left him in front of the three steps leading up to the door—he wanted to climb them himself—and simply watched him . . .

"Why did you bring him? Why did you bring him?" asked two women, sticking their heads out of the door.

"He wanted to come," said Christoforos, "we can't *celebrate* everything in secret."

"And what's there for him to see? What?" they muttered, despondently.

"To see Elias, that's what," said the old man *proudly*.

And it seems that what he saw that day was something he had never seen before throughout his long and varied life. And the third prostration that he insisted on doing before this strangest and saddest of his sons was his undoing, leaving him in a heap.

They carried him back to his room with his mouth open, as if through paralysis, and his eyes dull, very dull. That night he didn't get up from his bed; they found him just as they had left him . . . yet still breathing, as they discovered by putting a mirror in front of his mouth. Anyway, they hadn't left him alone in the room, there was someone with him all night . . .

And every so often over the next few days, his last (though once again they wouldn't believe that *for him* these could be his last—"he'll see this through too," they said), this grand old man would raise his exquisite hands, clasp them together, unclasp them—his fingers had become unimaginably longer and finer—would tap on the wall beside him as a butterfly might tap it with its wings, or would rub his eyebrow (his mouth had closed), the underside of his eye, his nose . . . persistently, more expressively than anything, than anyone . . . he reminded them of cats when they were *preening* themselves, and they would bring some visitor to the house. Each day like this, every so often, without his uttering a word, without his casting even a glance at those around him who were looking at him. Later, when the first of these last days had passed, he again raised his hand . . . but he could no longer bring it up to his eyebrow, nor could he even bring it back to its original position, and someone had to help him do both. They couldn't believe it: was he taking his leave of them? They had become as used to him all those years as they had to their own hides, to the air they breathed. They didn't even remember him ever as being someone who was *getting old* and would inevitably depart. All of them from their childhood—and they were all now approaching old age too—remembered him like that, carved in time. He didn't speak to them (as he hadn't spoken to them then), but then at least he would get up at night or occasionally say something, just to surprise them. Now his lack of movement made them numb; whether nightfall or daybreak, his silence had no end. Except for one night, when Polyxeni suddenly opened her eyes (she had moved into his room to sleep on a mattress across from him, with a lamp that burned dimly till morning) and saw him sitting up in bed trying to *put on* what he was already wearing. She rushed and got hold of him by the shoulders.

"What are you doing? Where do you want to go?"

She knelt before him and continued to ask him, to shake him till he looked her in the face.

"Why are you talking?" he said to her. "Do you think I know where I want to go? I'm not myself."

And he willingly let her put him to bed again and tuck him in.

The woman tried not to go to sleep again; she called one of the other women, and they sat opposite in two chairs with their legs stretched out on a stool in the middle, and as the lamp just barely lit their faces, they looked like the queens in a pack of cards. They chatted and ate raisins so as not to feel sleepy . . . And suddenly one of them, Polyxeni again, opened her eyes, and the breath went out of her: the old man had his head on the floor and his hand, with its five fingers stretched out like hooves, was trying to *stand* somewhere. She went over to him again, waking the other woman up, and then they saw a stranger: his face had become wild, had turned blue and hard like a fist—it wasn't him.

"What do you want?" she asked him, scared.

"To leave!" he told her, full of anxiety, like someone who is tired of hiding.

And the very next moment—not like *a passing storm*, but something much quicker, something that you don't believe happened even though you saw it— his face softened again, mellowed, and his head turned, weary and light, on his pillow.

And at daybreak—what persistence—she found him again sitting up in bed, bent over, searching on the floor with his fingers, close to his feet or as far as he could reach, in the same way that she would poke around to find a pin on her couch.

"What's going on?" she asked him; "can't I get a few minutes' sleep? Do I have to have my mind on you all the time?"

"Go to sleep, what's stopping you?" he said. "I'm looking for my shoes."

"What do you want your shoes for? Where do you think you're going? Up until yesterday, you couldn't even rub your own eyebrows, and now you're looking for your shoes?"

"Yes, it's my shoes I'm looking for," he said quite lucidly.

"Lord above!" exclaimed Polyxeni, crossing herself profusely. "What do you want your shoes for? Where is it you keep wanting to go *all this time?*"

He stopped, silent, at a loss, raising his body up a little and looking all around him . . .

"Don't know, where do I want to go?" he muttered, and an unvoiced ignorance (or awareness) rekindled and at the same time crushed his expression.

His granddaughter felt sorry for him—only a human being can feel sorry for another human being in that way when life is ending but not the clinging to life . . .

"Tell me where it is you want to go, and I'll take you, I'll help you," she said, falling in front of him, holding him by the knees, ready to give him whatever else he wanted. "There are your shoes, waiting for you."

He nodded his head, looking now at the shoes, now at the door, now at his pillow; he appeared to prefer the pillow. She helped him lie down again.

And he didn't try to get up again. He had his eyes closed, and everyone thought that he was sleeping, resting, but unexpectedly he opened them again and looked at them: however old someone may be, when the person looks at you like that, you feel ridiculous and useless because you're still on your feet and you can't become one with his most silent thought . . . They saw that the strong tree doesn't fall at the first or the third blow of the ax, but only after the umpteenth blow.

"Is it going to take you five years again to tell us another story?" Polyxeni asked him one evening.

He turned his face to the wall, tapped it noiselessly (in any case his hand had been raised and resting on it for hours), and only at daybreak did she hear him say: "I've reached a ripe age . . . *a ripe age.*"

"Eh . . . we've reached a ripe age too," she said. "You know that I'm your granddaughter, not your daughter, don't you? And do you know how old I am?"

"You don't understand me," he replied. He was talking, no doubt, about his *own* ripe age—and toward the middle of the day he took his leave of them.

The next afternoon, they set out on their familiar course through the snow, without reindeer to pull the *sleigh*, only themselves. In one of its interim blizzards, the winter—when the trees were slowly falling (we didn't have time to recount it)—also took Marigo's little boy, a mere gulp for the winter. The following month, it took Christoforos's eight-year-old grandson—and before long his daughter-in-law, the child's mother. *That's how people went then* (just like today) . . . An unusual dirge was heard as the company beneath the snow grew bigger: "The wolf a hundred years old, and the wolf cubs a hundred and ten, oh-oh-oh, and the wolf cubs a hundred and ten . . ." It was *red water* that flowed from the earthenware jar in the house when they emptied it in the spring . . . It was no winter's tale, no it wasn't, no: out of desperate (though pointless) remorse for her act, the mother of the eight-year-old had plunged her slashed wrists into it.

Seventh Tale

THE BELL-WEARERS; *VELVETY* AND THE *WEREWOLF*

"We're nothing. We're left all alone, and in the end nothing," said Christoforos to his close kin that spring, counting the names of young and old who had departed in the blizzards. "That wingèd trickster"—and he wasn't referring to some bird like the cuckoo that leaves its eggs in other birds' nests—"is forever emptying our homes . . . Wherever he finds us, he falls upon us and brings our ruin."

No one disagreed, but as long as they were living, those who *were* still living, it was that *nothing* that kept them going. Besides, in a house like that one, it would take the end of the world to empty it truly, to bring it to ruin.

And once again the years passed as only they know how to pass. One more of his widower sons (the one who had lost his child and his wife in the space of twenty days) got married again to a timid little girl whom he told each evening—when she was reluctant to give herself to him, to take the place of his previous wife in bed—that, with respect to the other woman, it wasn't just the death of her poor child or any curse on *this* house. "Her own blood was to blame," he explained, "the blood she brought from her own house, from a *hemophiliac* ancestor of hers, as both her father's brother and her grandfather before had done the same."

"You mean?" asked the frightened young bride.

"That they too were hemophiliacs . . . how else can I put it?" he said.

"So you mean?" she asked again, frightened.

"I mean that they couldn't bear to live with the fear of even a pin . . . *now lie down!*" he begged her.

She lay down on the very edge of the bed, as though she were lying on thorns, wrapped the sheet tightly around her, and tucked it under her chin.

"With the fear of even a pin . . . ," she murmured, looking up at the ceiling, "you mean?"

"I mean that when a person is born a hemophiliac, better for him not to be born," he said to her once again, "better for him not to be born, because if he suffers so much as a prick from a thorn, he may very well die! Or from a needle prick—from nothing at all! I mean that his life is a nightmare!"

"A nightmare . . . And that's passed down into your children?" she asked him.

"No, only into one of our children, only the firstborn inherited it . . . and he went before his time. But it doesn't pass into all, it passes into some and not into others, its ways are a mystery. And it's far less likely to pass into women than into men."

"You mean?" she asked with half a breath.

"I mean you'll be the death of me! I've told you a hundred times, but you don't listen, you'll drive me mad with all that *you mean—you mean!* . . . I'm telling you, and don't ask me again: my previous wife was a hemophiliac, I found out after we were married—perhaps she, too, didn't know or was hiding it from me, I don't know. At any rate, her grandfather and her uncle were out-and-out hemophiliacs—you weren't born then, you didn't know them, they both committed suicide . . . And we thought that it didn't pass down into women, that they simply transmit it, but it passes into them too. Rarely, but it does. And my wife was one of the rare cases . . . And unfortunately, our child, our first boy, inherited it too. Unfortunately. But all that's in the past now, now you're my wife—come close to me. Don't be afraid anymore, and don't ask questions, don't keep tormenting me."

But she—who had agreed to marry him because she was from a very poor family, while he was from one of the most well-off and prosperous—was still tormented herself.

"So you mean your wife . . . not me, her . . . committed suicide because she was . . . how did you call it?—or was it because she lost her child?"

"For both reasons, the poor thing. Because she blamed herself for our child being born with the illness—and he died because of it. So when we lost the child, she no longer wanted to live. And she slashed her wrists. And as the blood in hemophiliacs gushes like a spring . . ."

"You mean?"

". . . we couldn't save her. Just like we couldn't save the child—a stone no bigger than your thumbnail hit him on the forehead, no bigger than your thumbnail."

"So he didn't commit suicide then?"

"Of course not! An eight-year-old doesn't commit suicide just because he happens to be hemophiliac! . . . He got hit accidentally. The poor lad always took care from the time he was small; his mother was always warning him, Be careful, be careful, don't play with the other boys, you're not like them, you have to be careful . . . And the poor lad did take care; all the other boys played, squabbled, fought, laughed, and he would watch them from a safe distance and be envious of them, he was afraid to join them. But one day a stone hit him on the head, just here, above the eyebrow . . . No bigger than your thumbnail—any other boy wouldn't have paid any attention to it. But for him it was all it took: in twenty-four hours we'd lost him. From a hemorrhage."

"You mean? . . ."

The girl wasn't stupid, she was just scared—*afraid* . . . Which is why, if anyone happened to pass outside the marital chamber on those evenings, instead of hearing the bed creaking or stifled groaning, they heard that frightened "you mean, you mean?" coming from her mouth and wondered what was happening. But eventually, the creaking and groaning were heard too. Eventually, the new daughter-in-law lost her fear and within a few months began to mature and to bear children in her turn, also taking care of—together with her own children—the other two boys who in her frenzied passion the other woman had left motherless.

No one remains behind. Nine years had passed since then, since that ruthless winter, and no one would leave *his field unsown* for such a long time—for whatever reason. A decade was coming to an end, but also an entire century. No, Christoforos hadn't remarried, even though a respectable period of time had elapsed following the death of his second wife, and even though there was no lack of proposals or hints at such a thing during this period. But he held out. He was, after all, sixty-seven years old.

During that last Carnival season—they called it the last because the century was coming to an end, not the Carnival—the *sardanapalla* took place once again in their village. They might not have known where such a word came from, but they knew only too well what luxury, what carefreeness and letting go came with those two days of the year, the Carnival days (especially *that* year), which began two weeks before and ended as all the big festivals end.

Perhaps we should, before anything else, explain that the Carnival that took place in these parts was not something that happened just anywhere. Others too may have worn fancy costumes on occasion and danced and jigged for a few hours, but nowhere else from what we know—in our times, at least, and in theirs then—did people transform themselves with such pious devoutness and such craft into *bell-wearing goats*. Perhaps someone might not have room in his home for his children or for stretching out his legs, but the full-length black *goatskin* that he would don once a year always occupied a prominent place.

They had sewn many similar pieces—many goats, that is, had been sacrificed—in order to make this garment that covered all the upper part of the body and went down over both legs like trousers. They had corresponding sandals for their feet, as well as the gold-trimmed and exceptionally fanciful mask, which didn't hide only the face but covered the whole head—together with its incomparable top piece: the tall calpac, colorful and ornate too, from which hung the tails of whatever wild and semi-wild animals each one had, with pride of place given to the most bushy and beautiful: the golden-red brush of the fox.

And, of course, there were the bells, the five enormous bells that were tied—with ropes passed over the shoulders—around the waist. Four of these were roughly conical, iron, shiny, extremely heavy (actually small bells with smaller ones inside and even smaller ones inside these), with sounds worthy of their size, two being in front of the thighs and the other two on the sides of the buttocks. The fifth differed: this was bronze, bigger but lighter, roughly round in shape with a small aperture, with what might be thought an inferior though sharper sound—the necessary discordant note in the quartet of heavy tones—and this hung at the back from the tail, clumsy but not hard to move, and known as the *batali.*

If not all then almost all the men—but also some women who had the heart for it and, of course, the necessary body—donned the goatskins and girded themselves with those ringing iron bells every February or the beginning of March, depending on when the anniversary fell, threshing the air and the ground as they passed with their springing dances and those songs—born of deep sorrows—that tried to compete with the wild and deafening bells:

"Four oranges, my dear / two rotten all through / four fine young lads, you shrew / lost because of you" . . . "I wanted to come at night / but got caught in the rain / you should have come you liar / even if soaked to the skin" . . . Or the other one: "I've never killed a man / I've never kissed a woman fair / but they've given me a bad name / thief, liar, and murderer" . . . Songs of grief and disdain, usually slow, that five or six would sing arm in arm and with heads lowered (struggling to make their calpacs fit into that huddle), and with every pause, with every new verse, they would open up like a lotus flower and dart this way and that, shaking ecstatically or jerking their bell-laden bodies . . . before joining again and continuing their slow, plaintive song, often bent down to the ground, kneeling like beggars with enchanting voices, while at the same time the other group some way off would be opening up and dancing, and farther off another would be closing and singing a dirge . . .

Others, especially the tall ones, would appear colossal with those ungainly and pointed calpacs on their heads, these too from animal hides, with their tails and their colored ribbons flapping from the top, with their long mustaches (also from black or white horsetails), with their wooden swords, and of course with those impressive and *inexpressible* bells that framed not only their bodies but, we might say, their very existence.

As for the mask that covered the face, this had to be seen to be believed or at least to get an idea. Its special name was "the unchristened," in other words, the indescribable. It was literally terrifying to look at and captured the gaze; children were subject to attacks of panic—a fair amount of time had to pass before they got used to it and didn't scream at the sight of it . . . Yet they couldn't do any differently, they had to get used to it, and from very early on, given that the event wasn't something random or unexpected but just the opposite: it was the event most awaited at the end of each winter, on the verge of spring.

But for the others too, the women and younger members of the family who were obliged to help in the preparation of a *Goat*, it wasn't easy: suddenly their loved one, known to them, ordinary, common—so to speak—ceased to be a person or, at least, someone familiar: he became a Goat—yet even as a Goat he was different. And if behind the two slits, beneath the plumed brow, two gleaming eyes, familiar until a few days previously, blinked slowly or fluttered excitedly; or if behind an elaborate membrane in the center of the face, two wet nostrils heaved, and below this, protruding through another hole were two red lips, swollen from the excitement—these half-hidden (and distorted) human characteristics in no way lessened the pagan character of this beastly yet night-marishly beautiful mask.

These Goats hailed from older times, much older than they themselves knew or even imagined. Later, the custom became shrouded in other myths in order to be acceptable to another state of events, and so they said that it was Saint Theodore, a general or some such thing, who was once obliged to dress himself and his soldiers as goats in order to trick some renowned enemy. Or that it was Saint Paul who did this with a group of the faithful for similar reasons. The Church, anyhow, though doing all it could to propagate the new myths, would always have its reservations and objections to the way these people insisted on becoming wild and excited as Goats during the Carnival, instead of dutifully playing the faithful flock persecuted by other religions—without bells, of course, or masks or calpacs—on the feast day of Saint Theodore, just for a few hours . . . Though there were more than a few who had no compunction about getting dressed up on the feast day of Saint Theodore too, in the way that they knew, not as the Church would have wanted it—and the result for the Church was doubly unpleasant.

In the end, it closed both its doors and its ears on those days, with the idolatrous remnants raging outside.

■

In any case, the Carnival brought with it the day of *forgiveness*, the purification of souls. Starting out on his noisy wanderings through the streets and lanes, laden with all his accoutrements and paraphernalia, each Carnival dancer made sure he was also carrying a large white handkerchief, tied at its four corners and preferably passed over the arm not carrying the sword. This handkerchief was filled with oranges (*oranges!*) intended for the older relatives and friends: the Carnival dancer barged festively into the houses—your heart stopped on hearing the bells *rattling* the steps and bearing down on you—and arriving at the corner where the oldest and therefore most revered person in the family was sitting, he would kiss his hand in deference and give him one of the oranges, asking for all transgressions to be forgiven; or using the more general and one-word expression "bygones." Then, in his joy, you'd think, at what he asked for and received, but also at what he offered, he would do the most festive of jigs in the room, moving his body back and forth, successively, with great strength, so that the batali lived its most glorious moments, reaching high up the back, falling down low again, and then again reaching up high . . . And we shouldn't forget, of course, that all this functioned as a pretext, a noble pretext, for the people to then eat an orange! . . . It was such a scarce thing—this precious fruit—then, in their days and in their parts, that it was well worth the trouble (so they said) to grow old simply to be able to eat an orange!

And truly, there was no greater honor for an old man or woman than to be offered an orange. Uncomplainingly, then, they went without it for three hundred sixty days of the year for no other reason than to have the rare satisfaction of savoring it at Carnival time, when—on the eve of the Carnival—whole caravans arrived in the marketplace laden with oranges, and they spared no amount of money in order to acquire them. And so these fruits, so desirable because of the long period of deprivation, were in abundance during those days, just those days, and their formal offering to the old folk by the Carnival dancers—apart from any symbolic significance—also had a practical aspect.

Besides, in later years, the venerable old man would give an orange *too*, would also kiss the hand of the masked dancer and ask to be forgiven for his own transgressions.

So the oranges were endless, the kerchiefs became lighter and heavier again in the very same moment, and dancing and yelling the bell-wearers would even go so far as to where, now silent, their dead relatives and friends were, distributing them even there with the give-and-take of forgiveness, so that the poor could go the next day and eat them—so that the poor too could eat oranges!—since, however we look at it, *those casting no shadow* have no need of nourishment. Not even of this choicest of fruits.

Even with the silencing of the last bell, of the final echo, the air went on for days pulsating and humming in people's ears: the festivity ended but not its aftermath . . . And just as others are accustomed to the plashing of the sea or to the restless rustling of a birch wood and go on hearing the plashing and the rustling even if—for some reason—the waves cease to break or the birches cease to sway, so they too went on for days afterwards—with a somewhat melancholic disposition—hearing the bells of their Goats in the breeze and finding it strange that the Goats themselves were nowhere to be seen . . . Or just as when it rains incessantly for days—and then suddenly stops: isn't it then that we *actually do hear* the rain? The sound of which we had grown accustomed to so that it no longer made any impression on us, and which we only really perceived when it stopped? Doesn't it happen that when everything is quiet outside, we think *It was raining*, whereas while it is raining, both the event and its sound escape us?

So they, too, would hear the splendid pandemonium when everything had ceased and routine days would follow those special ones.

It was early on the eve of Clean Monday, the first day of Lent for all Orthodox Christians; the great festivity would end in a few hours for this year too, the last year of the century, perhaps would end only in the morning, for the breeze to continue it on its own . . . A Carnival dancer, sweating in the frost of that Monday (which coincided with the second day of March, a bitter March to be precise), passed before Christoforos's house for the umpteenth time, gravely and hastily, panting like a hunted bear, casting strange intense glances at the facade and the windows, as if seeing new things now that he had removed his mask with its calpac—after wearing it constantly for three days and nights (and after two years of carnivorous love that had just about devoured him).

He felt as though headless without the calpac—a kind of cold emptiness from the neck up—nevertheless streams and beads of sweat glistened everywhere on his face and were dripping from both his chin and his nose. At such a time, when the dull aftermath was starting, many bell-wearers removed their calpacs (because they were heavy, they weren't made of paper) and carried them sideways in their arms and it was a sad sight—even more frightening—to see a Goat with a tired *human* face, lined with all the excitement that had exhausted him . . . Others lay down or sat resting against a wall or in the middle of the street, slightly uncomfortable with their bells, but completely incapable of anything else, and waited for someone to gather them up and take them home—it goes without saying that the raki flowed in abundance, it was one of the basic accessories.

This one was around forty, with blue eyes, a ruddy face, strongly built, and with his sword in two pieces that were struggling under his arm to keep from falling, while the ferocious calpac in his arms was in no danger whatsoever of falling: it maintained the privileges of a newborn or rather of an indestructible prince. He slowed his step and held his breath when, in one of the windows, he *at last* saw her . . . She (and it was of course the once eleven-year-old Julia, the redhead with the ivory face) disappeared as soon as he raised his hand in greeting and . . . he dropped the sword from under his arm—two misfortunes: she had disappeared and he had appeared ridiculous. He took a deep breath and then blew the air out from his lungs, but instead of stooping to pick up his sword, he kicked it in the direction of her house's big wooden gate. It was broken in any case.

Christoforos was cutting wood in the yard, with his back to the street, and he turned to see who had struck his gate like that.

"Bygones, Christoforos!" the Carnival dancer shouted (during those few days, that's how they all greeted each other, there was no "good morning" or "good night").

"Bygones, bygones," he replied, somewhat dejectedly, bending again over his work. "Same old stuff!" he said to himself with a little more zeal as the pieces of wood he was cutting shot this way and that like sparks. "Bygones today, same old stuff tomorrow," he said, continuing his monologue.

Then he wedged his ax in the large base—from a tree trunk—on which he was chopping the wood and sat down carefully beside the ax, taking from his pocket his tobacco pouch and cigarette paper. Cletia was in the inn, and he had come to chop wood because his sons and sons-in-law, with the exception of Zacharias, had disappeared from the house those past days—such was their obsession, their craving to be Goats with bells.

The Carnival dancer, who might very well have been one of them, came through the gate (after having picked up his sword) and entered the yard.

"I don't have any more oranges—*a-a-a-all gone ro-o-o-otten*," he said to Christoforos (the last part he chanted in a voice full of heartache and innuendo), "but here you are! . . . chop up these pieces too" (he gave him the remnants of his sword), "and throw them on your fire so your daughter won't get cold!"

"I've five hundred of them—which one is to get warm first? . . . ," said Christoforos, who liked to brag about his six or seven daughters and all the stepdaughters he had.

"I'm not talking about the five hundred, I'm talking about the *one*," said the Carnival dancer, "the one with the red hair and the white velvety neck—I'm talking about the lily that ends as a poppy!"

"You're looking to build your nest up high and it might easily topple," said Christoforos, somewhat teasingly and still despondently.

"That's a song I don't know, though I know a good few . . . *What's it supposed to mean?*" asked the other, equally *teasingly* but not *despondently.*

"It means you've set your sights high," Christoforos said to him, slowly licking his rolled cigarette as though trying out a mouth organ. He knew that, for a couple of years now, this bareheaded Goat had been after Julia and had been hanging around her like a wolf around a lamb; and probably he was content not to be able to catch her.

"She's the one who's set her sights high," retorted the Carnival dancer with the same sobriety, and put his calpac down on the woodpile as he might put a baby into its cot. "What does she think, tell her . . . the time flies, the day will pass before she knows it and it'll be too late."

"We've begun talking in allegories, but I don't see her coming round," said Christoforos.

"Better that way," said the Carnival dancer, looking for somewhere to sit down and passing his hands under the bells.

"You're like those women who lift up their frills so they don't get muddied," commented Christoforos.

"You like your irony," said the other. "I'm like a lamb being led to slaughter."

"And who told you to get dressed up as a *Goat* on top of everything else? Wasn't one bell enough for you?" Christoforos continued, with the same irony.

The other one wasn't obliged to give an answer to everything.

They both fell silent for a time and stared at each other: he too was a widower—he had lost his wife at about roughly the same time that Christoforos had lost Eftha. Neither of them had remarried since then, but now the one had taken a fancy to the other's daughter, and a strong fancy at that.

"I've seen you for months, I don't recall how many, going up and down this street like you were under a spell, like you were looking for something," said Christoforos, when he decided to open his mouth again. And after a significant pause he added, "What is it that you want"

"Just one thing," said the Carnival dancer, "make me your son-in-law, give me Julia."

Christoforos puffed at his cigarette and blew out the smoke, looking only at this. After a good bit of time, he turned his gaze back to the other man.

"Julia?" he asked.

"Yes, Julia. If my wife were alive, I wouldn't be asking for anything . . . But . . . widowers, widows have a habit of entering your home—why shouldn't I? At least let her leave yours and come to mine . . . what's wrong with me?"

"There's nothing wrong with you. But you're a little old at forty-five."

"You're overdoing it," said the Carnival dancer, "first I'm only forty, not forty-five, and what's more, if you were to get married again, you'd be . . . sixty-five, wouldn't you?"

"Leave me out of it. First, I've no intention of getting married again . . ."

"And what's more," said the other man, remembering something, "it's not as if Julia is just out of the cradle, is it? She has a few years on her too."

"No, she's not just out of the cradle, but there are those who've been even longer out of the cradle," said Christoforos. "Why don't you ask me for Cletia, she's more suited to you. In everything . . . age, character . . ."

"Because it's Julia that my heart is set on," the other said plainly, "and anyway Cletia has the hunter."

"Cletia has the hunter as much as you have Julia," muttered Christoforos.

"Why are you set on dampening my heart on a day like today?" the other man asked him. "If you want an apple, would you settle for a pear? Or if you wanted a pear, would you be happy with an apple? No, you'd take what it was you wanted. And what I want is Julia. Cletia may be good too, but I want Julia. After all . . . it's me alone she'll be marrying, I have no children, nothing. She'll come into my house, and she'll be the lady and mistress, everything is waiting for her. *Everything!* . . . I mean, she won't have any children round her feet from the very first day, or in-laws always counting her faults or anything. I'm alone like a lone dog and it's her I'm waiting for."

"Tell her," said Christoforos over his shoulder, having got to his feet to chop more wood before nightfall. "Why do you tell me and not tell her all that?"

"She won't stay and let me tell her; as soon as she sees me she disappears."

"Find a way to make her stay . . . be tough with her and tell her," he repeated, but in the way that we all say things we don't believe, but say them anyway to get a *grip* on the other.

"*Be tough!* . . . ," exclaimed the Carnival dancer. "I look tough with all these bells, with this calpac . . . but deep down, eh? I'm begging at this moment like a poor beggar."

"That's what you're doing, yes! . . . ," Christoforos agreed. "Instead of taking what's given to you! . . . Cletia! . . . Even if she is a bit older than you! . . . Even if she loves the hunter! . . ." (with each phrase, he chopped another piece of wood). "Take what you're given . . . because if you wait to be given what you want . . . the day will pass, like you say . . . and it'll be too late!"

"Aagh, here we go again," said the Carnival dancer, getting up.

"Look . . . I've not let you into my yard so we can quarrel . . . though you let yourself in, if truth be told . . . but if she doesn't want you . . . what can I do about it?" said Christoforos, putting down his ax again in order to light another cigarette. "I'm not one of those fathers who always have their eye on their daughters and then marry them off."

"I'm not asking you to do that, but . . . as her father, you could talk to her, tell her—"

Christoforos raised his hand and stopped him, forcing him too to turn his head to see: coming out through the front door was Julia herself, who stared at them in a dumb panic as though having heard everything—there were times when it seemed that she was the mute in the house and not her aunt Lily. At the very same moment, a loud increase in the noise of the bells (which hadn't stopped ringing) from the top end of the street, in the marketplace, close to their inn, increased the panic in her gaze and also caused the two men to wonder.

She ignored them and ran to the gate, grabbed hold of the closed half of the gate with her right hand, and leaned outside to see: four Carnival dancers were hanging onto each other like beasts standing on their hind legs; you couldn't tell whether they were embracing one another in order to sing or whether two of them were fighting and the other two had stepped in to separate them—most likely the latter, given that two tails were already missing from the calpacs, as in other cases it would have been hair or hairpins that were missing. There was a huge fuss; it was as though their bells were fighting rather than they, while all this time, the other Carnival dancer behind her never stopped looking at her: how she moved and twisted her body . . . that body was all he longed for.

Julia saw her sister Cletia coming from the inn, but instead of looking at the Carnival dancers who were fighting in front of her eyes, Cletia was looking toward the house . . . unsure as to whether she should continue or to return to the inn—she saw Julia and motioned to her with her hand, as though asking something.

Julia didn't manage to answer: running up from the bottom end of the street were another two Carnival dancers, whose bells were making even more noise than the galloping of ten horses; they were not wearing calpacs (or carrying them underarm), and on seeing her they began crying out and beating their breasts. The girl stopped leaning outside the gate, stood upright, hid behind the door, and raised her gaze upward, as when one is expecting an inevitable downpour . . . She also put her hands behind her back.

Christoforos pulled the ax out of the wood, throwing down his cigarette and stubbing it out with his foot, and went over to her.

"What's going on here?" he asked her. "Is there a fire somewhere, and we can't hear the bells ringing?"

"Those who are coming will tell you," she said in a stifled voice, her eyes blinking with fear, perhaps fortuitously, at the other one still standing next to the wood and still staring at her as though there were nothing else and nothing happening around her. He eventually decided to move, but only to touch his calpac lying on the wood—without taking it—and look at it again . . . She knew those eyes, blue, motionless, servile, which found her in places where she could never have imagined—the most amazing place was one evening the previous summer at the threshing floors: she too had gone to help, the only woman among her brothers, and when they had sent her to bring something from behind a stack of bundles, Julia went and saw before her those eyes twinkling like blue fireflies—lurking and lying in wait for her. She stifled the cry in her throat and ran back to her brothers to tell them that she hadn't found anything . . . And when one of them was about to go himself, she stopped him: "I'll go back and look more carefully," she told him, "you get on with your work." And she went back. And the eyes were waiting for her again, but now she was prepared: "Get away from here," she said with her heart in her mouth, "because my brothers will see you and they'll kill you—off with you!" "Better that you kill me with your own hands, not your brothers," he told her. Well enough: she got what they had told her to get and went back to them. She never dared go back to the threshing floors any other night, but those eyes were everywhere, always before her. Now they had even come into the yard of her home, were glued to her like a fly to honey. He was favored by the circumstances of the moment . . .

The two Carnival dancers arrived at the gate out of breath and embraced Christoforos, shouting "Uncle! Uncle!" Both were much shorter than he was without their calpacs (though even if they had been wearing them), just striplings, and they struggled to bring his head down to their level to tell him something confidentially, as if it would remain confidential for much longer: "Covered in blood, in blood . . . unrecognizable . . . covered in blood, Uncle!" This is what reached Julia's ears again and again, but she already knew it, fond as she was of standing at the window, particularly the back windows of the house . . . and it was to one of these that not long before someone had come and said to her, "Where's your father? Your aunt, the mute one, the one your family adopted . . . someone has hit her, maybe two or three of them, I don't know! . . . They've left her covered in blood, close to the school . . . No one dares touch her, it's a shame . . . a woman without a voice!"

Now it was her father's turn to be stunned by the news.

"Who? Why?" he asked the two young bell-wearers who had told him.

"We don't know, Uncle, close to the school . . . by a stream, a place where people don't go . . . in a ditch. Covered in blood . . . we saw her with our own eyes, Uncle, you wouldn't recognize her. We were going to bring her, but no one wants to touch her, there are others there, they're afraid to lift her up . . . Run, no one knows, Uncle! . . ." They almost swallowed their tongues, the sweat running down their faces.

"Enough, I don't want to hear any more," said Christoforos; "just show me where exactly, come with me — I can't make head or tail of what you've told me."

And he went with them, still holding the ax, which he had put down and picked up again three times — finally leaving it: he threw it down while running and shouted to Julia to take it. Meanwhile, others had heard the news, the street slowly filled with the curious and with bell-wearers, most of whom were without calpacs, and only those four who were fighting beside the inn didn't hear anything apart from the sound of their bells . . .

Julia rushed and took the ax from the ground, from the middle of the street where her father had dropped it, and returning — to avoid the people and their questions (naturally they would go to the inn and question Cletia) — she shut the large front gate with the iron bar. Let her father come back . . . her aunt Lily, or anyone else from the family, and she'd open it again.

But the other one was waiting for her in the yard, and the house was empty; they were all out except for two children, ill with mumps, whose mothers had dosed them with Sleepies, a concoction of poppies that induced a deep and peaceful sleep in children, so that they could both go out too on such a day — and they still hadn't come back; it was almost nighttime and still neither of them; they must have gone to call on their folks or old friends.

Angry at all this and upset, Julia made out that she didn't see the blue-eyed man next to the wood and proceeded to go into the house.

He took two steps forward — his bells frightened her — and without even bothering to ask her about her mute aunt, he said to her in a grave and clear voice: "What you haven't let me tell you for the past two years, I'm going to say to you now. And if it's not to your liking, cut me in two with the ax you're carrying, but don't let me go on living without your love."

Her eyes misted over.

"No . . . be off with you, go . . . what do you want . . . I don't . . . ," she stuttered.

He took hold of both her hands, while she was still holding the ax, and pulled her to him — his mouth smelled of sulfur, his bells were as hot as coals. The ax wedged itself between his legs, she tried to pull it away, but he held it there, gripping it with as much strength as she was gripping its handle.

"But let me go . . . be off with you, what do you want from me . . . I'll scream

. . . I don't . . . let me go . . . let me go," she told him in a low voice, the way you would talk with someone mouth to mouth, and only the *gos* could be heard, because she would have liked to have shouted, to have pierced his ears, but she didn't want the others to hear her. "Let me go . . . they'll kill you, one of my brothers will come . . . They can get in through a closed door . . . they know how, let me go."

He didn't let her go, but clutched her even more tightly.

"I'll kill myself, I'll do it myself if you don't want me," he told her with far less panic than hers, "today, tomorrow, what's it matter — I've . . . I've . . . ," he didn't know how to say it to her without it seeming negligible or ridiculous, without his seeming pitiful or risible, *"I've fallen in love with you,* does that mean anything to you? I'm sick with love for you, gravely sick — no sickness is like this one! If you love me too, even a little, just a little, I'll let you go, we'll tell your father together as soon as he gets back, I've already spoken to him, got him ready . . . I'm not the person you're afraid of, I won't harm you, I won't — you just have to love me too . . . *learn to love me* if you don't love me!"

"No!" she told him; she didn't know why she said that *no* with such force, she felt her head rolling beneath black hides, beneath goats that themselves didn't know which way to go and were trampling on her, tormenting her in her impasse . . . She was no longer saying no, she had closed her mouth and was imagining the worst: who was to say how much more torment and trampling underfoot till *she loved him too!*

And he suddenly let go of her. Someone outside was banging on the door.

"Julia, open up!" — the voice was familiar, the demand reasonable, someone who lived there.

"I'll come back again at the same time tomorrow, I'll ask you again in front of your father," he said to her hastily, wet with sweat; "now go and open up for your brothers — wait!"

He pulled her back to him and was about to stroke her tangled hair, but he didn't dare, and simply blew on her forehead . . . And as soon as he let her go, he again pulled her to him and kissed her hand, deeply on her palm. As though he were kissing her on her navel, as though he were touching her with hot irons — in her other hand she was still holding the ax.

"Same time tomorrow," he reminded her.

"Hide yourself!" she advised him, throwing down the ax.

"No," he said, picking up his calpac, "I haven't killed anyone, why should I hide?" And he let out an undulating yell: ". . . *I've ne-e-ever kissed a wo-o-oman fair / bu-u-ut they've gi-i-iven me-e-e a ba-a-ad name / thi-i-ief, li-i-iar and . . ."* He had become a Carnival dancer again, the Carnival festivities were ending, and stumbling among the wood and searching for the *recollection* of his sword, he was singing old and well-known songs that didn't revoke anything.

Julia went to open the gate, giving—she hoped—the impression that she had run out of the house, from deep inside the house. Outside the gate Hesychios was waiting with some of Febronia's sons, and behind them were a few others with no connection. He too was without his calpac (Febronia, pregnant again, was holding it in her arms), and he too was sweating and hot, he too smelled of goat hide, except that he was . . . more handsome even than when he wore normal clothes—that handsomeness that brings languor, weakness, Febronia knew this better than anyone and examined, searched the face of anyone looking at him, even those of his sisters . . .

"Why did you lock it? Did they bring her back?" he asked his sister.

"No . . . not yet," she replied.

"So why did you lock it?"

"So people wouldn't come in . . . What about you, didn't you go to see?" she asked him.

"I'll go. But first I want to get these off," said Hesychios, and he took his calpac from Febronia to go inside and change.

It was then that he bumped into the other one, who was on his way out.

"Hello . . . Hesychios, bygones," he said to him, and repeated it to the others, gently swaying his own calpac.

"Bygones," Hesychios replied, somewhat surprised. "Did you hear what they did to our mute aunt today?"

"Yes, I heard . . . I'm sorry. I hope it's nothing serious," he said.

"*Covered in blood*—isn't that serious enough?" asked Hesychios, glancing at the others who were listening.

"*Blood* . . . ," he said. "Sometimes it's better for the blood to flow rather than remain inside and clot."

"Why do you say that?" asked Hesychios. "Was it you who hit her?" (He didn't mean it, of course, but . . . who knows?)

"Me? Good Lord, no . . . I had no reason, and why would I have done it? I don't have children."

They didn't take note of this then, but later it would be used—or rather it wouldn't be used for anything.

"And what are you doing here at this time?" asked Hesychios.

"Oh nothing, I was having a chat with your father just before," he said, and he headed off up the street.

Hesychios raised his eyebrows. And leaving aside the event with their mute aunt and before going inside to change, he introduced Julia to one of his friends, Kimon the icon painter, who had arrived that day to see their Carnival—who had been twice before, but Julia hadn't happened to meet him. She lowered her head and smiled, but she had other things on her mind.

And as he was going up the street, the other one stopped for a moment and gazed at them—heard the name: by a devilish coincidence, he too was called Kimon. There wasn't any other Kimon in the whole village and now suddenly there were two for Julia.

Before long, and before Hesychios had managed to go, they brought Lily back, covered in blood. And it was Christoforos again who was carrying her— "How many more of your women folk will you have to carry?" some of the women asked him, ready to begin the dirges. She had been beaten badly on her head, her face, and her back, hands, and chest. Her clothes were in a bad state, her legs were covered in scratches and mud, and she was unconscious.

Who or how many had done this—and why? What had a speechless woman done for them to beat her so badly? The questions came thick and fast and required answers, explanations, but first and foremost the woman needed to be taken care of. They had to wash her, clean her, bring her round. But she had blood running continually from her nose, and that worried them. And she wasn't speaking—she couldn't speak in any case, ever, but she did nothing to make them understand, she didn't seem to understand anything herself.

Three days had already passed, the wind whistled and kept whistling beyond the last echoes of the bells . . . eventually it stopped.

Julia also had another worry . . . On the day following that not very *clean* Monday, she decided to go herself in broad daylight to the house of that man who was in love with her and tell him—or rather write it on a piece of paper— not to come that evening to their house, she implored him, because they were all deeply distressed about their aunt . . . Fortunately, it was awful weather, and people stayed indoors, and she managed to reach his house without, let's hope, anyone seeing her. Of course, he saw her from his window and came outside, opened the door for her, elated . . . As if well and truly trapped, Julia looked at him, and her eyes filled.

"Don't be afraid," he said to her, "come in . . ."

"No!" she said, as though waking up, and throwing the piece of paper into the air, she took to her heels.

On the way, she was afraid lest the wind had taken it, given the way it was blowing . . . lest he come that evening, impetuous, and ask her in front of her father—she was afraid until evening when an unknown boy came to their house, shivering and trying to find a thousand and one excuses for coming (he was wearing a knitted bonnet that covered everything but his eyes), until Julia understood, and giving him a crust of bread and a few olives led him to the front gate. There, the unknown boy took from out of his bonnet a crumpled-up piece of paper, let it fall in front of her, and ran off. She picked it up, shoved it into her stocking, and ran up to one of the upstairs rooms. She locked herself in and unfolded it, shaking from head to toe. Written in large letters, in black pencil, in some places thick and in others less so, it said:

I UNDASTA-ND
I WILL CUM IN ONE WEAK NEXT TUWSDAY
I LUVE YOU ALL-WAYS. KIMON
KIM/WHO LUVES YOU

I'm not going to get rid of him easily, thought Julia. And on the morning of the following Tuesday, she again put pen to paper.

Meanwhile, her deaf-and-dumb aunt was in danger of losing all her blood from that unstoppable nosebleed, despite the March chill and despite all they did to stop it. The blood was streaming from one of her nostrils as if from an open tap—they recalled their hemophiliac daughter-in-law who had slashed her wrists . . . but from what they knew, Lily wasn't a hemophiliac—that's all they needed, for *her* to be one too, and to have waited so long to show it! . . . But no, they had seen her bleed before, it wasn't the same: those passing cases of bleeding had no connection with the present instance, which was so very worrying, that—apart from anything else—it didn't allow Christoforos to devote himself to finding out what had happened, finding the one or ones who had done this to her. And those of his sons who did try found nothing, no one. And it's better when these things don't drag on, because when they do, they get forgotten. Or things come to light later when other matters are under investigation.

On the fifth day, Saturday, Myra came to their house; yes, Myra, whom we may have forgotten, but she had never forgotten the good that Christoforos had done for her by taking her into his home and marrying her to Apostolos, and she always endeavored, in every way, to repay him. So when she heard about Lily, the moment she heard, even though Lily had once more or less shown utter contempt for her and in general was fairly scornful towards her, she did everything she could—for the sake of Christoforos, not of Lily—to find a way to save her. So she sent Apostolos to go and fetch her mother (whom she hadn't seen for more years than she could remember, though she knew roughly where she was living), because she was the only one who knew how to heal such things. Apostolos had to go by train to find his mother-in-law—and the trains at that time corresponded, especially for a humble and unsophisticated saddle maker, to something like today's spaceships.

And there they were then, Myra and her mother, at Christoforos's house. He himself was away at that moment, but this didn't stop the mother from immediately going over to his adopted sister, who was unconscious and virtually not breathing from exhaustion. Without wasting time, while the others stared at her dumbfounded, as they had once done at her daughter (though not with exactly the same feelings as then), this tall unknown woman asked for an egg, broke it, emptied the yoke and white onto a plate and threw the shell onto the fire. She waited for it to toast and turn brown, taking some bracelets from her arm, with quick, austere movements that nevertheless did not conceal from anyone her amber-colored nails . . . Though her eyes too were a color not very different . . . When the shell had blackened completely—had burned without being burnt—she took it from the fire, rubbed it in her fingers the way you might rub dried oregano, and when it was a fine black powder in the palm of her hand, she took a pinch of it and put it into Lily's nostril. At first, the first few times, the blood streaming from her nose simply swept it away, but the tall woman neither appeared worried nor gave up: she kept putting a little of that black powder into the open nostril every so often . . . until the blood began to lessen significantly. She kept on applying it—put the last grains there—until the flow of blood stopped completely.

Meanwhile, Christoforos had come back and was standing behind the door and staring, more dumbfounded than anyone.

When all this was over, and Lily began to open and close her eyes and move her mouth, to look at them and seem as though she was vaguely starting to recognize them again, Myra introduced her mother to the master of the house.

"Uncle," she said (she too now called him "Uncle"), "this woman here, by God's good grace, is the woman who bore me, Persa . . . a *witch* of renown—not an evil one, but how good exactly I don't know. I knew that she was the only one who could find a way to save your sister."

"I don't know how to thank you enough . . . both you and her," said Christoforos, at a loss.

"I'm the one who should still be thanking you," said Myra.

"And why is she called Persa?" asked a long-legged lad, one of Christoforos's grandsons. "Is she from Persia?"

"It comes from Persephone."

They made both of them stay to eat with them that evening. In fact, Persa could stay at the inn for a few nights if Myra didn't have room at her house now that the number of her children had doubled, could sleep there without paying, of course, or—if she didn't mind—in their own home.

And Persa did stay a few nights in the inn and then stayed in the house too.

The days—the hours—were getting closer for Julia to *next Tuesday.*

On Monday evening, she confessed her secret and her concern to Febronia, with whom she was more at ease than with her sisters, and the best that Febronia could say to her by way of advice was to marry him, to accept him, and in time love would come.

"Love isn't always something that comes at first sight, it can come *slowly,*" she told her.

But Julia shook her head insistently.

"You're twenty-eight years old, what are you waiting for? A prince to come?" Febronia asked her.

"You were thirty-eight when you married my brother," Julia said gently, without spite, "but you got the one you wanted."

"Ah, yes . . . ," replied Febronia in much the same tone, "but I was only sixteen when I married my first husband. And I hardly knew him, hardly knew whether I wanted him or how much he wanted me—it was our parents who got us married. And Eftha too, from what I know, your mother and my mother-in-law—who I didn't meet though I've heard so much about her—was only sixteen when she first got married. And there are so many others like me and Eftha . . . but you, who didn't rush to get married before your time like we did, now's the right time for you to get married, if you want my view. And as this Kimon seems to want you so much . . ."

"I don't love him . . . how can I get married to him?" said the redhead gloomily.

"Love's not everything," said Febronia gloomily.

"Of course it is," the other disagreed.

"Love . . . comes, I mean, it happens gradually," said Febronia, absentmindedly—since the subject came up—stroking her belly. "And besides, too much love can be dangerous, don't you know that?"

" . . ."

"Anyhow. What do you want from me? How can I help you?"

"How can I stop him from coming tomorrow . . . or the following Tuesday, or ever? How can I make him understand, accept it?"

"Ah, you *not only* don't love him, you're *also* asking a lot of him," said Febronia. "Look, if he loves you, he won't accept it easily."

"I'll write him a note again telling him not to come."

"He'll only write back that he'll come after five days; letters will only make it worse."

"No! This will be the last one—I'll write to him that he mustn't come again, that . . . I . . . I don't . . . that . . . *I love somebody else!* What do you think?"

"Do you love somebody else?" Febronia asked.

"No, but I have to say it, otherwise he won't take no for an answer."

"Do you really love somebody else?" Febronia repeated.

"No, I told you. That is . . . Perhaps, I don't know . . . but *he doesn't know that*—no, *he doesn't know that*," said Julia, surprised herself at what she was saying, but evidently she was *preparing* herself for the letter—don't they say, Believe what you say if you want others to believe you?

"My husband has some very strange sisters, I've come into a very strange family," said Febronia suddenly and without the serene and melancholic tone that she had had until now. "Cletia is in love with a hunter we never see, you love somebody who doesn't know it . . . And all the other sisters loved *something* before they got married or love *something* and don't get married . . . Perhaps it's Hesychios you all love?" she suddenly spurted. "Perhaps you've all forgotten that he's your brother?"

"What are you saying again, what are you saying?" asked Julia fearfully, and her green eyes became like broken green glass.

"What you heard! Perhaps you love your brother, your handsome brother? Perhaps that's why he calls you *velvety?*—You're his *velvety* aren't you?"

"He says that . . . about my skin, not about me," said Julia.

"I once had skin like that too," said Febronia, "but not one of my brothers, in fact I only had one, ever called me *velvety!*"

"How can you possibly say things like that?" asked Julia, completely taken aback. "How can you possibly even think such a thing?"

"It's not difficult," replied Febronia provocatively, "given that you can all think such things . . . and given that I, his wife, your sister-in-law, can light the way for you all! I deserve it . . . deserve what I get!"

When the curse of jealousy blinded her or injected her with its venom (and this happened often), Febronia didn't know what she was saying or how far she might go—it wasn't only her tongue. Often from the depths of her being, full of shame and despair, she wanted her husband to die and let her die herself the very same day (she had no doubts about that), rather than seeing him year by year become more good-looking and younger, as if he had made a pact with the devil, instead of getting older and losing his good looks like everyone else; and rather than seeing women still looking at him as they did in the past, and seeing him look at them—only for him to come to bed afterwards and tell her that the more he looked at other women, the more he appreciated her! She didn't want such appreciation! He was the only one she loved, and it didn't matter if she didn't wildly appreciate him, and she wanted him to love only her, look only at her, and never mind if he didn't appreciate her so much. And even if she didn't have his good fortune not to age with the years, not to lose her looks, not to grow decrepit, not to, not to, not, not to . . .

Ah, jealousy was a hell on earth. She didn't know whether there was a heaven or hell in the next life, but Febronia knew only too well the hell here on earth; she lived in it every day, boiled in its cauldrons. Only for a short time, every now and again, did it leave her alone, for a very short time, just enough for it to flare up again even more fiercely. And she would hear the women saying to each other in secret, "Make a cuckold of your man and no need to bewitch him," and she couldn't understand what they meant, how these two things were connected . . . When she finally did understand, she felt like letting out a scream, like getting a stick and beating herself to death with it for not having thought of doing the same, of making a cuckold of him a few times and of watching his legs give way beneath him, just as hers had given way at his carryings-on. Because for him the saying changed, becoming "Make a cuckold of your wise wife and no need to bewitch her, it's unnecessary." But it was too late. Febronia was almost fifty, though she was still bearing children, and he was only thirty-five—another reversed and inexpressible situation that now, with the passing of the years, appeared even stranger and the difference greater: she looked like his mother and he like a young stripling, as when she had seen him from behind the ruins—perish the thought . . . And then again, these things have both a *wooden stool* and a *throne*. Fortunate is the one who manages to sit on the throne. And woe betide the one who is left with the wooden stool: even if he sometimes goes towards the throne, from sudden good luck or pure desire or revenge, the throne will seem uncomfortable, the other one won't believe him, won't take him seriously—he has become *habituated*, you see, with the wooden stool. Just as Febronia had become habituated with it over so many years—wretched and unenviable *habit*.

And, moreover, why should she take a stick and beat herself to death, since till her death she would always have that jealousy flailing in her breast?

That's why she told Julia with so much bitterness that love isn't everything—because *that* love was everything, black love that was not begotten in the light and offers you nothing to drink but your own blood. And if they hadn't seen her being bashful about her late pregnancies, when others at her age were dancing their grandchildren on their lap, it wasn't only because it was God who sent these children, but also because Febronia herself, fertile as ever, sought them in her mind's conflagration so that the others would see at least that it was only with her that Hesychios had so many children, that he was no longer sowing his seed in other fields.

And if at this point we should say that the present indiscretions of Hesychios bore no comparison to the dramas and storms of the past and that it was Febronia's ailing heart that made mountains out of molehills, we should also say that on a long road even hay is heavy. And it was a long road for Febronia, very long: to take as her husband the father of her grandchild, the lover of her dead daughter.

Eventually, of course, weariness, that beneficent indifference, would get the better of her; she would see how useless it was to suffer from matters so major and how even more pointless it was from what was small and insignificant. But till then . . .

Julia had shrunk into a corner and was afraid to look at her. Her eyes kept filling with tears, as happened every time people put her in a difficult position (this weakness was something she had acquired relatively recently).

"If I'd known that you thought such a thing about me," she told her, "I would never have spoken to you about the man. I asked you for your advice and you . . ."

Yet Febronia wasn't always this woman poisoned by her suffering and her suspicions. There were times when she foamed and became a wreck, and times when it was a joy to listen to her—in this she resembled her mother-in-law, Eftha, and it was a real shame that these two had never met. And as suffering begets knowledge, not just ruin, she always had wise things to say, and there were many who asked her advice, including her father-in-law. Besides, not to go on too much, no one suffered more than she did herself when she lost her self-control: "You know," she said to her husband, "even the craziest person, when he loses his head, suffers by doing so, he doesn't do it either for a good reason or because he likes it." And she would say this when she herself had lost her head— and also when she had calmed down, when she brought it to mind . . .

"Don't pay any attention to me, you have to understand my position," she said to Julia, and pointed to her belly, because the rest, what went much deeper, wasn't something she could show so easily with her hand.

"I do understand. That's why I always take your side—don't you always tell me everything? And don't I always show understanding?" asked her sister-in-law.

Febronia would have had to have been very mean to deny it or not to recognize it: this sensitive girl with red hair and frightened eyes was her best sister-in-law, the only one never to have held her marriage to their brother against her, the only one—though little then, motherless and ill—who accepted her with kindness from the first day that she came into that house (and who, moreover, had been the first to see her from a window that daybreak when the family was still in counsel, roaming around in the ruins . . .). All the others, either more or less, had made life difficult for her in the beginning, and were the opportunity given to them again, they would no doubt take it.

"I can't forget what you did for me, or rather what you didn't do," she told her. "And I want to help you . . . about that Kimon, then. Well, I have a feeling that you won't regret it if you say yes to him. That's why I'd advise you to give it a little more thought."

"No!" said Julia once more.

"She says no and goes to pieces," Febronia thought to herself, "why so?" And she looked her in the eye for a few moments . . .

"All right, let's go inside now," she proposed; "it's going to rain."

Julia followed her.

To talk about their secrets, they had withdrawn into the backyard, into a sort of shed which was missing the bigger section of its upper part and so was in effect roofless, and the weather was looking like rain: by the time they had reached the house, the first big spots had already started to fall and the black clouds flashed extensively . . . and thundered. Febronia stood and watched them, putting her hands on her hips: and this movement also very much recalled Eftha when, unexpectedly, she would leave her worldly chores and gaze at the *celestial kingdom* . . . What's more, if Hesychios often called his wife Febra, it was for that reason: *Febra, Eftha*, even their names matched as peculiar sounds, and that confusion between the presence of the one woman and the memory of the other was not unpleasant. She was also called Febra by whoever else in the house wanted to—just as she had once been called Febra by Argyris, her first husband. And the month of February was her godfather, or at least the reason why they gave her that name: she happened to have been born in one of those years when February had twenty-nine days, on the twenty-ninth day in fact, and so her parents had thought it prudent to christen her Febronia: an uncommon name—to ward off the bad luck of the leap year.

"Did your mother tell you when you were little not to look at the lightning because needles would go into your eyes?" she asked Julia.

"Yes, she used to say that," Julia replied.

"Needles did go into my eyes from a lightning flash: when I saw your brother . . . ," said Febronia earnestly. "And since then, I can look at other flashes without fear . . . O Lord above," she groaned, "when poison doesn't work on you straightaway . . . better that it does work on you straightaway! Otherwise, afterwards that is, you take it and ask for more . . . It gives you strength."

"I'll write to him on a nice piece of paper that he's not to come again because . . . and don't take it wrongly again—because . . . *I love someone else*," said Julia, going back to her own subject with that pensive and distant expression that characterized her whenever she took hold of a pencil and started to write—no one knew what, no one had ever read her notebooks. Only sometimes something may have caught their eye and it was only to Febronia that she had said that—aside from proverbs and *chronologies*—she also wrote other things. "What?" she had asked her. "The things that happen, the things we feel," said Julia, and taking a notebook out from under her mattress, she put Febronia in a difficult position: "I don't know how to read," she said, "I only went to school for two years . . . and what little I learned, I've forgotten." "I'm not giving it to you to read," said Julia, "just for you to see." And she had quickly skimmed through a notebook, holding it upside down, a useless precaution given that Febronia couldn't read (and even if she could, she wouldn't have had time), and then she held it upright, so that Febronia could see the image on the cover: it showed the crucifixion of Christ, but it was a crucifixion like no other she had ever seen. It wasn't only an image of Christ on the cross, there was a cock to the left on a low wall from which ash, tridents, and lighted torches were coming—and it was crowing to the Lord. On the floor was a lantern and beside it a long green snake coming from the lantern and sticking out its red tongue toward a fallen pomegranate or apple. A little above the apple were three dice, above the dice a skull, beside the skull a purse from which florins were pouring, and beside this a rope, beside which—and to the right of the cross now—was a ladder hanging in the air. In the air: only the bottom of it was touching the ground, the upper part *nowhere*. Nevertheless, resting on this were a sword and a lance that had on its tip a sponge with vinegar. Beside this was a silver bowl and jug, and behind red flames in the fields. And up above the sky a greenish-blue and black, and on the left—over the cock's head, like a halo—a red sun or moon. And a few birds in the background, on bare yellow boughs coming out of the clouds which were probably lightning flashes . . . "Seems we can see everything but the crucifixion," Febronia said at first glance. "I've written a story about the picture," Julia confided in her. "Really? Read it to me." "No, I don't read them to anyone." Febronia looked at her slightly reprovingly, then looked again at the *crucifixion* . . . "Never mind," she said, "it makes me shudder just to look at it—just imagining hearing a story about it!"

"And what paper will you use to write to him?" she asked her, as they both went under the roofed verandah with the rain now beating down on the stones and tiles. "Will you tear a leaf out of that notebook of yours with the cruci-fixion?" (Though months had passed since she had seen it, nevertheless she re-membered it.)

"That one's full, I've another one now," said Julia.

"With the crucifixion again?"

"No, with something else . . . I'll write to him exactly what I told you: It's pointless for you to come round again for no reason, I love someone else. Julia."

Febronia shrugged; she found it a bit sharp and abrupt, not in keeping with Julia's usual manner, but if this was what she had decided in her stubbornness . . .

"Should I tell him that I'm sorry?" she said as a second thought. "Or wish him . . . *good luck?*"

"Ah, no, that would be too much," Febronia immediately retorted, almost becoming angry again. "If I were in his position and on top of everything else they wished me good luck . . . No, forget the bit about good luck—you can't cut somebody's hopes like you were cutting his throat and then tell him good luck! No, that's too much, it's not right."

"You're right," Julia admitted, "I won't tell him good luck."

"But you have to tell him *who* it is you love," Febronia reminded her, "be-cause he'll ask you."

"How?"

"By letter, how else? He knows how to write too . . . Or he'll make it his busi-ness to find out from others. Then what will you do?"

"Who should I tell him that I love?" Julia asked her.

"I don't know, you know. You're green-eyed and red-haired—there must be someone you could love, someone who could love you . . . Say that it's that other Kimon, I don't know, your brother's friend. He doesn't know him, he's not from round here, he's already gone . . . I think he's the *best person.* Because whoever else you say, from round here, he'll be able to go and ask him if he wants."

"Yes, but what if things get complicated because they're both called Kimon?" Julia wondered. But since Febronia said nothing, she made her decision: "I'll say it's him. He saw us together outside the gate . . . He'll believe it."

"Tell him and . . . see if he believes it," said Febronia, again shrugging, and they parted, each of them going to her room and to her own concerns. Outside the rain was coming down in sheets.

The next morning it was still raining. Julia crept into a storeroom, got hold of a large canvas sack, stuck one of its corners into the other, making a cone of it, put the cone over her head—the rest covered all her body right down to her knees—and set off again on the rather long way to the neighborhood where Kimon lived. Such a long way, in fact, that . . . it wasn't raining there. Or at least, it had stopped by the time she got there—at any rate, the ground seemed dry: as if not a drop had fallen there for hours.

It surprised her that people were looking at her from their windows not as a stranger or as someone suspicious, trying to guess who she might be, but rather as a person who didn't know what was happening, given that she was wearing that strange covering even though it wasn't raining. Gradually, of course, they would begin to be suspicious, but Julia—feeling uncomfortable in any case— didn't take it off. So she passed between their houses and traversed numerous narrow lanes, clumsily covered by that sack, and provocatively too, like some virtuous ladies of older times who went out at night for debauchery wearing beggars' clothes—this, we suppose, is rather how she saw herself, and she was out of breath by the time she reached his home . . . This time she avoided the main entrance, she hugged the low stone wall that enclosed a small garden with some fruit trees he had in front of his house, and from there she saw him scattering corn to a few hens and a cock—his broad back was all she saw, his body from behind. It seemed to her that he was barefoot. And ready as she was, having wrapped the paper round a stone, she threw it in the direction he was throwing the corn and ran off down a back lane, hiding her face in the canvas cover, almost without seeing where she was putting her feet.

That evening, he didn't show up. Nor did the boy with the bonnet. Nor the next evening. She imagined that he must have found her letter, respected her wishes, and so hadn't come. Yet she was a little puzzled that he hadn't written to her that he would come again in a few days . . . Of course, she had told him— asked him—never to come again because *she loved someone else!* . . . But nonetheless, was it so easy for him to decide not to come? Strange. She waited the third evening, and the fourth. And again no one showed up. And this girl with the red hair, who thought that she would be pleased at this, would be relieved, was neither pleased nor relieved. She went to find Febronia and confided in her: "If he sends me another letter, I'll say that . . . that I've thought again about the *someone else*, that . . . perhaps, if he has patience, my feelings might change."

Febronia saw that they would change. So she advised her to write to him straightaway, without waiting for his letter.

"And I'll take the letter myself," she said, "I don't care if anyone sees me."

But no, Julia didn't want to right away, she was scared, didn't have the courage.

She again shut herself up in a room and reread in secret—secret from whom? Did the walls have eyes?—his first and only letter . . . She looked at her hand, at the *burn* from his kiss . . . She wanted to see him again.

It was during the days that Lily had started moving around again, eating, vaguely communicating with those around her—though, regarding what had happened to her on Clean Monday, she didn't seem to remember very much. But her eyes had acquired a somber look of fear, of distrust, even of madness, and she stared at everyone, aside, perhaps, from Christoforos and Persa, as the poor wretch might have looked at whoever raised a stick or a stone against her . . . It was impossible for them to learn even the slightest thing from her mouth; they would have to begin their investigations again in the dark; it was difficult in any case, but it was made even more unpleasant by the fact that they had to go to other people's homes at random and ask the householders whether any of them had hit their mute sister or aunt on the first day of Lent, or whether they themselves suspected anyone or had any idea that might help them, that might lead somewhere . . . Naturally, no one had hit her and no one had any idea. They thought it an insult that the family could even suspect them—and, of course, most of them were right: one or two or three at most had hit her, not all of them. Yet how was the family to find that one or those two or three? All of them, even the ones who had a somewhat shady past because of some act of theirs, appeared to have their hands clean or an airtight alibi. Besides, she might have been hit by someone from another place: there were many strangers there at Carnival time—and trying to find the person afterwards would be nigh to impossible.

One day, Hesychios remembered something and said to his father: "That Kimon . . . not my friend the icon painter, the *other one*, with the blue eyes, the widower . . . who happened to be in our yard one afternoon when I came home—he said he'd been talking with you—do you know what he said to me? *And why would I have done it? I don't have children.*"

"What did he mean exactly by saying he didn't have children?" asked Christoforos, whose mind was burdened those days, filled with many and various concerns, and he was unable to grasp *nuances*.

"What indeed! I'm equally puzzled," Hesychios said, "and that's why I didn't attach any importance to it. But today, I thought about it again . . . And he may be right in what he said. Lily might have been up to her *old tricks* with some little child . . . and been caught by the father, and—anyhow."

"And how did Kimon, who doesn't have children, know that our Lily would sometimes get up to tricks with children?" asked Christoforos. "*Used* to get up to tricks, because she doesn't anymore."

"Not anymore, but when she did," Hesychios reminded him, "everyone heard about it, things like that become public knowledge—why shouldn't Kimon have heard about it too? When it rains, it doesn't only rain on a few."

"That's something," said Christoforos, reminding him in his turn, "that I said when your stories were raining on everybody and you wondered why every bitch in heat was after you. You can't teach me anything. And yet . . . you might have something; that Kimon might be right. Our Lily might have been up to her old tricks again with some child."

And with this new lead, as we might call it, in their hands, they began their investigations again. Now they didn't go round asking the adults so much as children, young and old, and did all they could to find out from their own lips whether anything strange had recently happened to them in connection with their mute sister . . . The children would do all they could to remember, but in the end could remember nothing. They asked Lily herself—asked her straight out without beating around the bush: "Tell us whether you've been interfering with some little child so we can find out who hit you," they said to her. But she shook her head, just like the children.

Meanwhile, there had been other cases—one before the Carnival period and two immediately after—concerning a gang of rustlers. This dangerous gang not only stole animals, preferably horses, but also beat their owners if they happened to try to resist. They had long rifles, and used these to hit with—fortunately, with-out having fired a shot yet. So this gang of thieves also passed through Christo-foros's mind. Though again, the thought ran through his mind, why would they hit Lily? Had they seen Lily on a horse and she had refused to give it to them? And Lily often did find herself astride a horse, astride various horses—when she went someplace to deliver a child—but she was always accompanied by the hus-band, father, or brother of the woman, at any rate by whoever came by horse to get her and bring her back. Or perhaps these rustlers saw Lily on her own, a mute woman and not at all uncomely for her age, in a remote spot, and had their mind on other things, and when Lily refused them they hit her? Or was it impossible that both things had happened—that they had their way with her and hit her to boot? Things like that didn't happen every day, but occasionally they did. And far worse things. So Christoforos began to incline towards this ex-planation, and suspect the unknown bravos, and naturally it rankled him that he couldn't find them and have it out with them. But he confronted Lily again and began asking her once again, not about little children this time but about men who stole horses and abused women—that's how he said it, straight out, to try to draw her into admitting it. But Lily, after learning to shake her head from side to side, kept on shaking it in the same way.

Things, then, had reached an impasse when at a remote farm something even more tragic happened: the rustlers shot and killed an old man and his wife for the sake of two horses. The horses belonged to their sons, but they weren't at home—one was playing cards in the cafeneion and the other had gone to town, both unmarried, both with some years on their backs. Their father was in the stable feeding the animals when the thieves came in. The man raised his hands and begged them to leave him one of the horses at least. When they took the second one too, the old man in his despair grabbed hold of the horse's rump and wouldn't let go—still begging and crying—no matter how much they tried to push him back with their rifles . . . One of these went off and the bullet hit him in the shoulder. And amid the confusion, another one finished him off. Worried, his wife came out of the house holding a lantern to see what was happening, but before she had time to realize what was happening, they killed her too.

This double crime, so outrageous and heinous, made even the stones shudder, filling people's souls with panic and anger. Nevertheless, the place started to calm down again: ten days had passed without the rustlers having shown any signs of life, so everyone thought that was it, they'd had their fill, they wouldn't show themselves again. But they, stealing two more horses, left them two more dead bodies.

Benumbed, as was the very air, by the event, Christoforos couldn't—didn't have the heart—to go on looking for those who had hit Lily. And since at least her nose had stopped bleeding—thanks to Persa—he decided to forget about it, to let it rest.

Julia, too, decided to forget about her concerns with Kimon, to let it rest, though for her it was a little more difficult. She had feelings of guilt: everyone was sad about the two old folks, everyone hoped the killers would be found and hanged, and she was hoping that she would again see this man who loved her so much and whom she had chased away. Because he still hadn't shown up. This man, whom she used to see everywhere except in her sleep, had—since she had thrown him that letter with the little stone, that rash letter—now disappeared. And his silence ate away at her, filled her with sorrow, worry. She began to see him in her sleep too . . . To read and reread that laconic, badly written, misspelled, yet so very serious letter of his, as if behind every word there was a well that she was unable to fathom, whose depth and importance she was unable to see at the first couple of glances only—as if she had to lean right over till she too disappeared into that cold darkness that painfully echoed his inexplicable silence . . .

In order to forget, she wrote in her notebook about the murder at the farm: what she heard from others and what she made up, with grief more than verve, using her own imagination. She also wrote about the funeral and the two coffins that passed outside their house and she saw from her window: she went from one window to the other (many windows, not to forget), and from each she saw a different scene, a different aspect of the same scene: of that black, grief-stricken procession . . . till it disappeared from view or till the many windows ran out, though she continued to run in circles in the house. She wrote about the tears that welled up in her, as if her own parents, both together, were traveling in two similar coffins, or even, even . . . *she and him . . . She and him . . .* "*Me and you.*"

And naturally, she also wrote about Persa, who now slept in their house, and how her father showed great respect towards her—but also the same familiarity that he once showed to Eftha, her mother: perhaps . . . (who knows what the moment holds in store) he intended to make her his third wife? Perhaps the children from his second marriage, like her, would also have the good fortune to live with a stepmother, as the children from his first marriage had?

To put it bluntly: her father had come straight out with it, telling her brothers and sisters: "I'm thinking of marrying this Persa in my old age . . . Old age, whatever anyone says, is not pleasant for anyone. And the recluse who goes off into the wilderness goes to the *wilderness,* marries the *wilderness* . . . He doesn't live alone, I mean."

"If you do that, father, I'll lose every idea that I had about you," said one of his sons. "And forget the parables about the wilderness . . . *I'll lose every idea!*"

"And you'll be right to do so," he replied.

And perhaps he didn't say it indifferently or cynically, he may perhaps have *meant* it, have been answering himself, a reproach, a kind of self-irony. Nevertheless, he was still sitting on a low wall when he said it, with his one leg bent and the other hanging and swinging in the air—and his sons who saw him couldn't help but wonder, *What old age?* He looked younger than the young lads, all he needed was a sling in his hands, and he was announcing his third marriage as if he were telling them a fairy tale about someone who got married three times and something that till now no one had questioned or frowned upon, since—as in a fairy tale—other rules applied, other standards.

Julia wrote or thought about all this, but every so often she would close her notebook, hide it in the most unprecedented and incredible places, and rush to find the expectant Febronia to talk to her about Kimon—about the one care that she had inside her . . .

"Why don't you go and give him another letter?" she said to her; "I told you from the beginning—what are you waiting for?"

Julia wanted it more than anything now: a letter telling him to forget the two previous ones and to come and ask for her—to ask for her hand, to make her his wife, *she wanted him . . . more than anything else!*

Yet she still couldn't find the courage, she was still scared . . . or still hoped.

And she immersed herself in a recent past, which she hadn't appreciated and given attention to as much as she should have, and which now was punishing her, taking on an inconceivable gravity.

This is what had happened just three years earlier.

A law had been passed opening evening schools for those, both men and women, who hadn't been able to learn to read and write when they were young—for those, of course, who *wanted to*, though in the end it became compulsory, given that most *didn't want to*, either too ashamed or too bored to go at their age to recite the alphabet and learn to write on white paper or black slates. "Leave us alone to plow our fields, to dig better, and wipe the sweat from our brows," said some, for whom, after all, plowing and digging was something they had learned from an early age and without having been taught in some special school. "What are we to do with reading and writing? Can you teach an old dog new tricks?"

But they too were compelled to go. And this *schooling* would last nine months, this was the minimum length of time, while for those who wanted to continue—they heard this and rollicked with laughter—there were an additional nine months. For those with numerous obligations or numerous children, both men and women, the law was more flexible.

For Julia it wasn't difficult, or unpleasant in itself, to recall the day when she learned—not without a little fear—that she could continue her schooling from where, fourteen years earlier, she had been obliged to end it because of her illness. She was once again in one of the upstairs rooms, at one of the windows, and she was brushing the hair of the younger Julia, her niece and godchild (four years old then, talkative, and an attentive listener), and telling her stories . . . when she heard a loud voice from down below: "Is there a Julia who lives here?"

The voice sounded slightly mocking, since the person asking seemed to be sure that he hadn't come to the wrong house.

"There are two Julias living here," they heard Febronia say to him, "which one do you want?"

"The elder one," he said.

"They're asking for me," she said to the younger one. "Wait here for me, I'll be back."

"And they're asking for me too," said the younger one. "Aren't I Julia too?"

She took hold of her by the arm, and they went down together. Waiting in the yard was a local constable, a friend of her father it seemed, who in recent years acted as a constable and wore high boots and a gray uniform with lots of pockets; he was standing holding a paper, and on seeing her he pulled a pencil from the top pocket of his jacket and said to her, "Julia, my dear girl, come and put your signature here so that you can go to school!"

The younger Julia was, of course, still not of school age—but even less was the elder Julia, who at that time was almost twenty-five years old.

"There must be some mistake," she said timidly, *"I'm the elder Julia."*

"Yes, you, it's you I came for," the constable said; "your father lost no time and enrolled you among the first in that new school, since you were bright as a child."

"What school?" she asked, because word still hadn't gotten around—her father may have been among the first to hear about it, but not her, not most people, at least not most women, who didn't rush to hear the town crier every Saturday.

He explained to her. And she, after remaining for a few moments hesitant and undecided—because he told her as well that it wasn't compulsory (it would become compulsory later when nine out of ten had refused)—let go of the younger Julia's hand, took the pencil and paper from him, went aside, and put her signature.

"If you can't," he said to her, "put a cross, most people will have to put a cross, what else?"

But Julia wasn't so illiterate, she wasn't at all illiterate to be exact (for the times), given that she had managed to learn quite a lot by the time she was eleven, and since then she hadn't ceased to scribble whatever learning she had in secret notebooks.

So when she gave the paper back to him and he saw how nicely she had written her name and surname, he was astonished.

"What's this? You're more cut out for a teacher than a pupil," he said. "I can't understand why your father wants so much to send you to that evening school . . . and why you want to go."

"I know how to read and write a little," she told him, "but . . . there's much more that I don't know."

"Very well," he said, and took his leave, making his way to the next house.

Then the other Julia, the younger one, sat squarely on her lap and from there looked at her like a dolphin that raises its head out of the water and shows its friendly and playful teeth: "You're going to school! . . . ," she said. "Will you take me with you?"

"Yes, I'll take you," answered the elder one.

"Only in the evenings?"

"Yes, the evenings."

"And what will we do during the day?"

"We'll talk . . . I'll brush your hair . . ."

"And in the evenings, we'll go to school! . . ."

"Yes."

"And the school . . . where is it?"

"There where the other one is."

"Where's the other one?"

"There . . . don't ask so much."

"Why?"

"Quiet now, let me think."

"I want to think too."

"Think without talking."

(When both Julias were talking, the birds would stop their twittering.)

"And what will I think about without talking?"

"Ohhh, Julia, quiet—I'll smack you!"

"Ohhh-Julia-quiet-I'll-smack-you."

"Oh don't start saying everything I say again!"

"Oh-don't-start-saying-everything-I-say-again."

"Fine . . . talk on your own, I'm going."

"Fine-talk-on-your-own-I'm-going."

"And don't follow me!"

"And-don't-follow-me."

And, naturally, the younger one followed the elder one everywhere she went, everywhere, she followed like a faithful shadow with red hair, but not always. Especially to the evening school, when before long it opened, she went only two or three times. Then she found it boring and didn't go again. The elder one continued, however—and would spend eighteen months there.

She sat at the same desk with two twin sisters: Olga—who had a long, heavy tress that she hung in front of her, reaching down below her large breast—and Eugenia, who separated her hair into two smaller tresses, which also reached down to her breast, which was also smaller than that of Olga. They were known as "the twins with the three tresses," the daughters of the butcher. They were known for other reasons too. For example, for the fact that though twins they didn't resemble each other in the slightest, even though they had been born with only half an hour's difference. But mainly for the work they did: they slaughtered the animals bought by their father! . . . And to put it more *soberly*, from the time that they had lost their mother when still only small, they had learned, instead of sewing and embroidery, to mix with the animals that were brought to the back of their house, where, in a few days or a few hours, their

father, the father of these two girls, would slit their throats and skin them before
their eyes. We can't say whether he obliged them to be present at this ancient
ritual, nor can we say whether their panic at first, the horror that gripped them
making them clutch hold of each other, became, day by day, *acceptance* and
routine, so that it eventually became their own work, their own expertise, so now
it was their father who watched—and sometimes not even: they slaughtered
the animals at home while he waited for them in the shop and talked with his
friends—only when they were large animals did he stay to help himself.

He had no sons, perhaps we should say this, which at that time was a great
disadvantage for a father. Nor any other daughters. And that house that very few
people ever went near—save only those who brought the animals—was a long
way from the shop that people saw every day and where most went to exchange
their mite for a piece of meat. So when Olga and Eugenia finished their work at
the house, they had to load the meat onto a wooden cart and bring it to the shop
to be sold, traveling up and down a host of streets to get there.

Literally up and down: that bloody cart went nowhere without stirring up a
frenzy of cries, clapping and jeering . . . The clatter of its wheels on the cobbled
streets was perhaps no different from that of other carts, perhaps even its load
wasn't so unusual; but the two *Amazons* on top, the twins with the three tresses,
these two who did the talking and took care of everything with a knife—ah,
people's curiosity about these twins never abated, and everyone would rush to
see them whenever they passed by. In any case, there weren't many other opportunities to see them: the two girls didn't go out of the house except for this unpleasant and difficult trip . . . Many children would hang from the sides of the
wooden cart or manage to climb up and stick their legs between the iron spokes
of the wheels, either to make themselves fall or to halt the smooth—if we can
call it that—running and force the twins to get down and chase them away—
and enable themselves to see them from close up, to touch their leather clothes
or, in the best of cases, to tug their tresses a little: O the little rascals went wild
for such things . . .

They both wore trousers, when for women this was not exactly *forbidden*, but
rather unheard-of, unthinkable. Eugenia also wore skirts, but the way she always
covered them with long dark-blue aprons, worn over the neck and tied in three
places (around the breast, the waist and lower down), not even her own dress
recalled that of a woman. In general, Eugenia differed: she was thinner, more
ungainly, more timid, something of an expression of her own genteel name, we
could say, or a kind of unconscious identifying with it—as well as the *surplus*
of the overbearing and imperious Olga. Olga was the first to roll up her sleeves,
it was Olga who decided on the order of the animals, then it was Olga who got

into the cart first and took hold of the reins, again it was Olga who got down
first and started to unload, holding her tress in her mouth. Often, beside her,
Eugenia seemed unnecessary, to have nothing to do in particular, something
she showed through little indecisive and completely imitative movements: Olga
would take up the whip and she unconsciously raised her arm too; or Olga
would suddenly turn her head to say something to her father and she suddenly
turned hers too, without having anything to say. Some believed that it was only
Olga who brought down the knife and that Eugenia did what a mirror does, but
it's not certain. And from the fact alone that the younger sister showed such
devotion and awe towards the elder one (because, whatever anyone says, there
was in their case this difference), we can surmise that she also showed great obe-
dience to her. And Olga was blessed with playing the *leading role*, but not with
being able to do everything on her own.

Julia once recalled how, four or five years previously, during the days leading up to Easter, when the cart with the twin sisters had passed once again
along their street laden with newborn lambs, piled one on top of the other—not
slaughtered yet: this time, one of the very few, the sisters were making the opposite journey—from the shop to their house—with the cart not empty as usual,
but crammed with these little living animals that were bleating weakly though
incessantly, and no doubt were going never to return again. They knew it in
their hearts . . . And through the slits between the wooden planks of the cart,
yellowish liquid was dripping and wetting the street . . . At other times, almost
all, drops of blood would fall from there making Julia's eyes fill with tears; but
now, from her surprise, from this unfamiliar emotion, or rather suspicion, that
gripped her, she was unable to resort to tears, to let out her feelings—she had
her eyes clearly open, wide open, and fixed there: on the iron wheels that were
bumping with a dangerous instability over the cobbles (but which nevertheless
jumped over every obstacle) and on that yellow liquid that was dripping and
spraying the cobbles . . . And because of the different way the others that day
were looking, without yelling, without commenting, all of them with their eyes
fixed *underneath* the cart, the twins also bent their heads to see. And the elder
one was heard to say, "What are we to do! They had a mother too." "They . . .
mother too . . . ," her sister was vaguely heard to say, *the echo.* "They know where
we're taking them!" shouted Olga again, waving her whip in the air and bringing
it down on the horses' rumps to make them go faster.

And then Eugenia got up without anyone asking her to, took hold of the
wooden pole beside her and, leaning halfway out of the cart as it careered down
the sloping street, she shouted with incredible strength, in the name of no one
but herself: "THEY KNO-O-OW! . . . And out of fear . . . OUT OF FEAR THEY'RE

WE-E-ETTING THEMSELVES!" It was as though she were asking for help. Everyone who watched the scene was dumbstruck—this time there was no clapping or yelling. The rebellious twin hid herself again, and the cart vanished round a corner. And Julia couldn't remain standing in the doorway any longer—she rushed into the house and collapsed onto a bed, weeping.

The following year, or maybe the year after that, by coincidence and by virtue of that unusual law concerning evening school, she found herself sitting at the same desk with the two twin sisters . . . They smelled of blood, of actual blood. Their clothes, their hair, their skin. Just like women suckling infants or working in the tobacco store smelled of milk or tobacco, so these two smelled of the blood of the animals that struggled in their hands and lost. At first, Julia felt great displeasure, wanted to be moved to another desk. But there weren't many desks, they all had to accommodate themselves at the few there were and in the same place the teacher put them on the first evening. On the contrary— and a surprise for him—the adult women who wanted or were obliged to learn like little girls were quite numerous, surpassing his every expectation. And Julia didn't know whether the sisters sitting beside her had themselves wished to learn to read and write at the tender age of thirty or whether the law had made them, given that they had neither children nor other serious obligations (other than their rather peculiar occupation, that is) . . . She would find out on the second evening, when the gray-haired and mellifluous teacher, instead of a lesson, asked the women one by one, "And you, my dear girl, what made you come here?" Or on an even more personal note, as he leaned over and looked them in the eyes, "Tell me, my dear girl, what is it that brought you here to me?" And in the beginning, most of them replied, "The law . . ." Or "Because I couldn't when I was little . . . because I couldn't learn then." But as he asked them, ever more sweetly, ever more gently (though compellingly), all the others began to say to him: "Because I wanted to . . ." and all the first ones to correct themselves: "Also because I wanted to . . . not just because of the law."

And if they hadn't wanted to right up to the previous day, they all wanted to from that moment . . .

Julia said the same, almost weeping in her anxiety until her turn came, without adding, though, that she already knew quite a bit, she wasn't entirely a beginner. The teacher looked her in the eye a little longer than the others, smiled, but not in a way to worry her. And when he asked the same question to the girl beside her, one of the twins, she didn't know what to say and looked at her twin sister, like a drowning man searching for something to hold on to . . .

"Are you sisters?" he asked, more out of intuition than because he was prompted by some obvious likeness.

"Yes," said the stouter one.

"And what brought you to me, and both together, my dears?" he said again, asking his constant question, which none of them found tiring.

Eugenia waited in vain, she looked at Olga and waited for her to say something again: but she had lowered her head and kept her lips sealed.

"Shall I say?" she asked her.

The lowered head moved slightly.

And with a great deal of faltering, she started to say something about a constable who had come to their house and told them that learning was good for people . . . and because they hadn't been able when they were little . . . and because learning is good for people . . .

"Isn't that what he said?" she asked, looking to Olga for support.

She raised her head for a moment and fluttered her eyes.

"And did you come because he told you it was compulsory? Or because you wanted to, my dears?" the teacher asked more plainly.

"A bit of both," said Olga, opening her mouth.

"*Yes, that was it!*" spluttered Eugenia, with a feeling of deliverance.

They always came to the lessons in women's clothes, both of them, with their tresses combed, still wet, and it was clear that they didn't have the courage to speak to the other women. Nor were the others in a hurry to encourage them — something, however, that Julia did from the second week: she turned to them one evening, while they were waiting for the teacher to walk down the corridor, and asked them whether they lived very far . . .

"Yes . . . very far, didn't you know?" Olga asked her at one end.

"How should she know?" asked the other, in the middle, looking at her sister. "They all know!" she said.

"Because? . . . All? . . . ," said Eugenia in surprise, taking hold and playing with the end of one of her tresses.

"I . . . I don't know your house, I've never seen it," said Julia (she was afraid in case her question, which she came out with at random, just to make conversation, caused some friction between the twins), "but I do know that it's a bit far . . . Aren't you afraid, when it's dark, to go home alone?"

"We're not alone, we're together," said Olga.

"Together . . . alone? . . . ," the other whispered or half asked.

The way that she was always in the habit of parroting the last words of her elder sister, even if she varied them a little, reminded Julia of her own game of *I'll-say-what-you-say* with the younger Julia . . .

Nevertheless, as the weeks passed, it was the younger of the twins who started to show some initiative, still imperceptible and questionable, that the elder sister either missed or *conceded*, given that she was the first to slide her bulky body into the desk, then curled up in the corner and . . . warmed the cold wall or supported it so it wouldn't fall, as the teacher would say about those mature pupils who liked to glue themselves to the wall and hide, instead of sitting upright and looking straight ahead at him and at the blackboard! But Olga didn't appear to be wise to the fact that he was *also* saying this about her, perhaps more about her even than the others; she didn't even raise her head when he said it again and again, smiling with unrestrained hope in the direction of her distant and still corner . . . Just the opposite; if it had been possible to open a big hole in the wall and crawl into it, she would have done so with pleasure.

"You don't pay attention to anything—we've not come here for that," Eugenia said to her one evening, almost scolding her.

"Eh . . . so!" said Olga.

"Eh . . . so? Do I say eh . . . so? . . . You won't learn anything if you don't look at the board! The teacher is talking to you too!"

"Eh . . . so!" Olga repeated. "You can learn."

And only once (when Eugenia, fed up with her, said to her, "You're like a dumb animal!") did she come out of her blissful state, appearing to be a little surprised, and—gazing at her sister somewhat severely, somewhat . . . as if she had overstepped the mark—asked her, "And you, what do you think you are?"

In general, however, she didn't appear to be sad or troubled by the fact that, in class at least, she seemed to lose some of her elder-sister privileges—which she most likely ceded to her sister—just as her sister didn't appear worried or to be in any hurry to acquire them . . . Perhaps in the unspeakable work they did at home, it was Olga who always had the upper hand, but in learning—in that late literacy that both of them were going there to acquire for the first time—it was Eugenia who stood out through her unassuming interest.

Julia grew more fond of them with each day that passed, grew accustomed to their *odd* smell (which became even more odd and *somber* when they tried to drown it under various fragrances), and when school was over the three of them would often go off together and walk quietly in the twilight till their paths parted.

"They're nice what you're wearing . . . and *blue!*" the younger twin said with admiration to Julia one evening in the fall. "Don't your feet get cold?"

"No . . . I've got used to them," said Julia, who from the age of eighteen or twenty had been able at last to wear her blue suede sandals: not only was able, but never took them off save only to go to bed or in the depths of winter. Otherwise, as long as the weather permitted, until the heavy rains and snows came—and ignoring the frosts and chills of fall—Julia would wear her sandals and only these. And because the cold in that mountainous region was no joke (even in October), she would wear them with socks, often woolen ones (they were big enough), otherwise—whatever might be said—she would have been cold. Of course, she took care of them, took great care of them, and willingly took them off and held them in her hands if there was a sudden rainstorm or if, by mistake, she found herself on a stony dirt road. Yet they proved to be exceptionally sturdy, indestructible, got old without looking old, without really becoming worn: that woman seller with the unforgettable smile on her thin red lips had been right to insist so much that her father buy them . . . The sister of Ruth! Lehkhahyekh . . .

When, that year, winter came, and it fell dark early, the twins started coming to school with their *buggy*, in other words, their cart, covered now with canvas and skins, and with the boards inside covered with warm fleeces. Afraid lest they ask her to get into it with them sometime (because her torment was that she never forgot anything—and in the case in question, it wasn't so much those two she-devils who had once tricked her father and put her to sleep *in a carriage like that*, as the slaughtered animals and, above all, those little lambs that were still alive and that could sense their end . . .), and in order to avoid any such proposal on the part of Olga and Eugenia, she found a way for the first few days to leave with the other women. In fact, some of these women, some third or even fifth cousins, had actually seemed annoyed by her *friendship* with the butcher's daughters and once or twice had rushed to take hold of her arm as they left the classroom with an air of concern and a display as if they were laying claim to her: "Ugh! What are you doing hanging around with those two? Is it that you want them to take you home with them?" they had asked her, almost taking her home with them instead—clutching hold of her almost the whole way. Julia was scared: the twins at least had never taken hold of her like that! . . . Of course, she was afraid whenever she saw them in their buggy (that's what they always called it: buggy) because other things were stirred in her memory that she didn't want to remember . . . but not to go out of the frying pan, as we say, and into the fire.

Nevertheless, one evening it was so cold that only she, the twins, and another three women turned up for the lesson—a total of six, that is, out of the twenty-nine in the class. And when the lesson was over, earlier than usual, the twins suggested that the other four get up on the buggy and let them take them home . . . The cold was so diabolical that not one of them declined their offer, not even the one who lived quite close by: so all four climbed up. "Ah, it's so warm in here!" said one of them, and the other three agreed. "Like a crib! Only baby Jesus and the little lambs are missing," she said, not missing the opportunity to have a dig.

Dig or no dig, that little episode broke the ice, removed certain reservations, and from then on—whenever it was bitterly cold—other women, too, asked the twins if they would take them in their buggy and drop them off near their homes, and they, of course, never said no to anyone. Yet they couldn't conceal their satisfaction, their joy, we could say, when it was only Julia who got into the buggy with them, and the three of them went together as far as the point where their ways parted, so that she could arrive home quickly on foot, while they still had a long way to go to arrive at their home. "Good night . . . Till tomorrow," they said, and perhaps one of them would correct the other: "The day after tomorrow," but usually they left it like that.

The lessons were three times each week, every other day, and they had literally begun with their ABCs. Christoforos's daughter was the youngest in the class (most of them were over thirty or even approaching forty) and the only one who wasn't completely *unlettered*. All the others, more or less, were learning for the first time that there was something called an alphabet and that it had twenty-four letters, just like the day with its twenty-four hours, and that whatever we say or think can also be written down.

Each of them learned first of all to write her own name and some showed as much surprise as a native presented with a mirror.

"*That's* . . . that's me?" one of them asked in astonishment when the teacher wrote her name in calligraphic letters, accents, breathings, and all, on the blackboard—and a name that was truly unusual at that: "Heliostalacti Tundras."

"You're that and a good bit more, my dear, that's only your name," he said to her, being scrupulously fair.

All of them, for the first weeks and—why not?—up to the end, would delight in this Heliostalacti. First of all, she was sixty and not forty, but full of verve and vigor, as if the sun were dripping on her from morn to night just as her name suggested . . . In the evenings, she would be transformed into a backward, inexperienced pupil and always came late to class with a frightened and worried look as if she were entering some cheap dive. Or like an engaging rodent that has found itself by mistake in a ballroom and everyone turns to look at it . . . She didn't know even the letter o. When the others had learned how to differentiate omicron from its brother omega, she was still wondering what in heaven's name that round empty egg might be that the teacher kept writing on the board and asking her to tell him what it was . . . "I'm waiting, my dear Heliostalacti," he would say to her, "what's that?" "Just a moment," she would reply, "just a moment, please . . ." "What is it, my dear?" he would ask again presently, resting the tip of his cane in the circle. "Just a moment to think . . . Putting your cane like that helps me," she would say to him; "it's . . . it's like a ring from a goat that fell." "What fell, my dear? The goat?" he asked her calmly, despite the raucous laughter shaking the desks in front of him. "No, the ring," she said, "it fell, and you're trying to lift it with the cane . . ." "What you say is good," he said to her, "but I want you to tell me what letter I'm pointing to with the cane!" "I told you," said Heliostalacti, "ring . . . Link! . . . no?" "No! Do I have to get angry for you to wake up? It's the letter OMICRON!" "Ah, yes, omicron. I knew that's what it was," she explained to him, "but I couldn't remember what it's called."

Nevertheless, despite the chortles that were provoked by her simplicity, she herself, of her own free will, came "to listen to some learning" at that age, given that she had no children or grandchildren; in fact she had no one apart from a few animals and the only person to have once been a companion to her, Ol' Tundras with his nice stories who always greeted others like an eagle with wings outstretched wherever he passed by, had died the previous year, suddenly, and if his presence was missed by many, it was missed by her a thousand times more. That's why she would go there in the evenings.

Anyhow, after some time, she too had learned the omicron and the omega, and also learned quite a bit more that would help her, as she said, to read the inscription at the gates of hell and try to find some better place—but always she had the fixation, as well as the knack, of likening almost all the letters to *things* that her hands knew well. The teacher might have had a sister five years older than she who spoke of pianos and fine sentiments (he had brought her twice in the spring to see and talk with his pupils), but Heliostalacti—just like Olga, in fact—knew far more about metal links and meat hooks and talked more about these. Olga didn't talk even about these.

When the women finished their lesson, the men with surly faces would come into the same classroom and find the desks warm. For them, the time of the evening lessons was even later, and while they were looking at the letters on the blackboard, they could also see the moon through the windows nodding at them strangely, deceptively . . . There were clearly fewer of them than the women—there were more than enough desks for them: how had so many managed to get away with it?

Even Christoforos came for three evenings, out of curiosity: he had heard his daughter singing the praises of the teacher (both the women and the men had the same one), telling him how many wonderful things she learned from him and how he spoke to each one of them as though she were his own daughter, and he came to meet him in person. And meet him he did; in fact he made him into a customer at the inn. But what he was teaching the others, the *ignoramuses* let's call them, Christoforos already knew, and so he didn't go a fourth time. Even that "my dear" that the teacher said in such a sweet way to his women was something that Christoforos also said to his—he even made them his *precious* whenever he wanted to mock them a little.

On the contrary, Julia wasn't at all bothered at hearing some things she already knew. There was always something new to be learned among the old—and besides, there were other things that she heard about for the first time and that fascinated her.

And there in the doorway, going out one evening, she saw Kimon for the first time. She didn't know him. She didn't know his name, who he was, that he even existed . . . nothing. And if his eyes hadn't been so blue so as to stand out *of necessity* from all the other eyes and things, she wouldn't have remembered that . . . she had seen him *somewhere* before . . . yes, there was no mistake, she had seen those eyes before when he was much younger and she only small (where and when exactly was something she couldn't recall, nor did it concern her overly). She simply *recognized* him, then, without knowing him: significance often lies in the unsuspected.

Besides, she would be obliged from then on to see him often, given that he too came to the evening classes with those few men who succeeded the women at the desks. But obliged also because of future events (not all had taken place yet) to *see him again* by recalling him in her memory: recalling with painful pleasure those momentary and chance encounters of theirs when the sun was setting or had well and truly set . . . At first, they did happen by chance, even on his part.

As on one evening when she dropped her pencil case as she was going out . . . there, in the doorway again. And though she immediately stooped to pick it up—and other women with her—the pencil case rolled as far as the feet of someone who was standing to one side, almost hidden by the open door. A woman handed it back to her, she barely managed to get a good look at the man, but—she recognized him now even better—it was him, the one with the blue eyes.

As on another evening when she was walking down the stone steps outside with the other women, and there was an icy, fine hail coming down, and it was windy . . . A little way off, in the schoolyard (a yard that was more like a trodden field), he was there again, standing with his collar turned up, blowing on his hands to keep them warm—this time next to a wooden *platform* on four legs with casters, next to a moving stall, that is, on which were lined up *birds!* . . . What an impression it made on her—birds on a table! . . . It didn't take long, however, to see that they were stuffed: hooks and wires were securing their feet to thick blocks or rectangular wooden bases, and that stance, full of intensity and anticipation, had something so final about it, so futile, that she felt a pang in her heart as she gazed at it. She felt a pang and remembered . . . a fox like that, and an eagle, and a boar's head . . . and she distanced herself a little as the other women went up to the table with those birds and began to touch their beaks, their wings, while she watched them from a little way off, afraid to go near. One or two fell over like wooden soldiers from the women's touching, but also from the wind blowing . . . And he, the blue-eyed man, picked them up, taking hold of them as though they were pricking his fingers . . . "What are you doing here on a day like today? Selling birds in this cold weather?" one of the women asked him. "They're not mine," he said. "Whose are they?" "Someone's . . ." "So what are you doing?" "I'm watching over them," he said, "he went to talk with the teacher . . . He asked me to watch over them." He kept blowing on his hands and rubbing them together; he was cold and like a little school-boy who had exchanged his lesson to do a chore . . . The birds were cold too: the plumage on their breasts (and on their backs, but more so on their breasts) was slightly quivering, and tongues of it rippled with the blowing of the wind, just as with live birds when they nestle in winter on the wood and the fences — they were cold even though dead.

The women were cold too, and left.

On the way, Heliostalacti, tiny and garbed in sheepskins and rags like an Indian squaw, said, "In winter, those with blue eyes feel the cold more than others." "Why?" they asked her. "Eh, why! . . . Have you ever seen the sky staying blue in winter?" That was something they had never heard before. "So then we shouldn't call you Heliostalacti anymore till the sun comes out again in the spring," one of the women said to her, "we should call you . . ." "Call me *Snowstalacti*," she herself proposed. They all laughed, and that warmed them a little.

And the next day, or the day after, they saw in the classroom, on a shelf on the wall, three of those birds: "These *taxiderms* — please make a note of any words you don't understand — victims of man's arrogance and greed, once soared in the heavens . . . ," the teacher started to say in his calm, emphatic voice.

One evening at dusk, at an hour that teeters — as the French say — *entre chien et loup* . . . , at such an hour, then, a few days later, they again encountered the blue-eyed man on the street, at quite some way from the school this time: they had finished the lesson and, hungry, were hurrying home, whereas he still hadn't gone — they saw him just as he was taking his leave of a group of men and waving to them, as when you don't have time for anything more . . . "News at ten!" turning his head to them and smiling, as in a moment or two he would cross paths with the group of women. He passed them by as if they were reeds . . . "What . . . what was it he said?" one of them asked, slightly peeved at his indifference, half covering her mouth with the palm of her hand. One said,

"I didn't hear," another said she had, "Nine out of ten," none of them understood anything. A little farther on the other men were waiting . . . and when the women had passed by them, unspeaking, indomitable, serious, beauties of the twilight, each of the men came out with some complimentary remark for each one of the women . . .

But what had he said? How Julia now, only now unfortunately, would have wished to have given all her attention *then* to his words, to his movements, to anything of his—or even of his friends, those who knew him, who were close to him, loyal to him for years or only passing acquaintances, it didn't matter.

But she had remained as far away as she could: the most cautious, the most emotional of all of them, the most amiable, but also the most distant, the most *embalmed* for anyone who spent his time looking at her. Besides, Kimon was almost the only one who still didn't look at her—quite some time would pass, that first *year of evenings* (and for many the last) would almost be over, before for the first time his gaze would fix itself on her. And it would remain there forever.

The snows melted and spring slowly made its presence felt. One evening, while the women were still having their lesson, the breeze brought to their ears the sound of bells . . . At first distant and indistinct, as though a herd were scattering on a hillside somewhere, but the next moment it was as if three sets of bells were ringing right beside them. The teacher stopped the lesson and went over to the window to see, the women understood and took a few clandestine breaths—a shiver ran through them: the lesson was good, but to hear the bells was even better!

The bell-wearers arrived at the schoolyard, scraped past the walls, climbed the steps, came into the corridors, and were soon standing outside the door. It wasn't yet Carnival time, just the last few days before, but they had already got dressed up and come like that to the school . . . Being new to the place, the teacher wasn't aware of the customs, only knew of them by hearsay—now he could *hear* them for real.

"Can we come in? Or will you turn us away?" asked one of those outside.

He took out the watch and chain from his pocket: the time—and especially the expectation in the eyes of his dear women—convinced him to open the door. So he went over with great dignity to open it.

Yet it was with far less dignity that he moved back when they rushed into the classroom wildly and yelling, shaking their calpacs and brandishing their swords, so that the women dissolved into laughter that brought tears to their eyes . . . And in order to contribute to the pandemonium, not to be left out, they started to climb up onto their desks like yearling goats or to dive beneath them, shouting, coming out with whatever sounds the teacher still hadn't managed to

teach them—while the men chased them, lunging with their wooden swords
and thrusting with their calpacs like goats do with their horns . . .

Real pandemonium, and it was in vain that the unsuspecting teacher tried
to raise and impose his voice: "It's a special day—A SPECIAL DAY, I see that! . . .
But calm down, ladies and gentlemen, so I might understand what's going on!
. . . Besides, you're deafening me—calm down! . . . Control yourselves! . . . I'm
talking to you! . . . Cease! . . . I'll take out the whistle made from human bone!"

At that point, they all fell silent. The women got down from the desks, arranged themselves, shook themselves, brushed back the hair that had got caught
in their eyes and noses like gossamer thread, while the others, the four bell-
wearers, came over docilely and awkwardly . . . reminding him of peacocks that
fold up their magnificent wings to peck at a crumb or two.

There had been other times, more than once, when he had threatened—
more like promised—to show them that *whistle made from human bone*, but he
always said afterwards that he had forgotten to bring it with him. It had become
a rare thing to see—perhaps even for him too—and what if he had forgotten it
this time too, what if he was telling them the same thing again! . . .

Fortunately not. The teacher said: "Here it is!" and he took from his pocket
a green leather case, and from the case a smooth white bone with several holes
in it: he stroked it with reverence and blew into the holes to awaken them—
then he put it to his mouth and the bone whistled deafeningly! . . . He gave it to
them to feel, to try. It was a well-wrought whistle—if not entirely natural and un-
worked—with a strange shape and a sound that was truly enviable . . . "But," said
the bell-wearers, "how do we know that it's made from human bone; it might
just be ivory!" He assured them that it was made from human bone, it had been
given to him by one of his relatives who was a sailor, a seafarer, from Africa—and
there, he said, nothing goes to waste.

And so, with this agreement, they got to see a bone whistle, and he was able
to examine close-up their incredible attire of black goatskin, the bells, the hanging tails, the colorful tiny disks of shiny metal that decorated their masks and
their cheeks and glittered in the dim light of the classroom like slivers of gold . . .

Yet before this, while the three bell-wearers were chasing the women on the
desks and playing with them as-though-time-had-been-wound-back, far back,
to their childhood relationships, the fourth had stood in front of Julia *and was
seeing her for the first time*: he was leaning over her with all the fullness of his
calpac—she was the only one, together with the twins sitting beside her, who
hadn't been carried away by the other women in their mad dance—and closing
her in with his hefty arms at right and left, imprisoning her in that position, he
searched her eyes . . . At first, it seemed as if he simply wanted to frighten her

or amuse her, but if you were to remove that indescribable mask from his face, what he really wanted was something else. And his eyes, however distorted and wild they appeared through the two slits, were so blue, so *thirsty*—

Fortunately, the others pulled him away and he left her. But her eyes had time to mist over from a feeling of danger; and she gripped the notebooks in front of her as she would have gripped her chest had she been alone: her heart was pounding like his bells.

"*Him*," she heard Eugenia beside her say. "You should have heard him cry when his wife died!"

"Why . . . how did he cry?" she asked in fear (not knowing that he had a wife who had died).

"He *wept*," Eugenia said categorically. "There's no *how*. And now look at him . . . *Flirting!*"

"Were you at the funeral so you can be sure he wept?" Olga asked her from the other side, unable to hear well—perhaps not at all—that *last word* her twin sister had voiced so meaningfully and so quietly.

"No, I wasn't at the funeral; some of our father's friends in the shop were talking about it and I overheard. It was years ago," said Eugenia.

And it was then—*at that very moment*—that Julia remembered where she had first seen him: in the graveyard! When she was eleven or twelve years old (and how old was he?) and her elder sisters would take her to say prayers at the grave of Eftha, their mother. It was there that she had first seen him, when he would come and stand at one of the graves and wipe his eyes every so often, his shoulders shaking . . . It was there that she had seen those blue eyes, which then, from so much crying, were blue-red. And because the graves of her mother and his wife were close together (she didn't know then that it was his wife's or whose it was), she would stand a little way off, between, and stare at him with sympathy for his grief . . . From behind, from the side, not directly facing him. She was unable to see his face: he had his head lowered, and naturally she would never have dared to go up to a man who was crying . . . And if he chanced, sometimes, to turn in her direction, she immediately lowered her own head or turned her gaze and pretended to be looking for something in the distance. Nevertheless, once or twice, their eyes had met. Fortuitously, inevitably. He in his grief and she in hers; a grown man, she still a child. And she remembered those eyes— no matter that they had long gone out of her mind . . . She remembered them.

Except that, if Eugenia hadn't helped her (albeit unknowingly) that day, perhaps she would never have remembered where and when she had seen them for the first time. Perhaps, for many years more (like Heliostalacti with the omicron), she would have known that it was *him*, without knowing who *he* was.

"Good Lord!" she thought to herself, almost aloud, as her heart was still pounding from what had just passed and from those things so long ago; while he and the other three were trying the bone whistle, and if she picked him out from the others it was because his mask was looking toward her and because he put the whistle to his mouth as though it were an angel's trumpet. "How many twists and turns time brings! Where am I?" . . . And spontaneously she turned and asked Eugenia: "What's his name?" "Who?" she said. "Him with the bells . . . who you said wept then." "Ah, he has a name like cumin . . . Kimon, Kimon, that's his name," she told her.

That same night—and we shouldn't forget that all this happened three years earlier and Julia was remembering, just as then she had remembered things that had happened thirteen years before that—so then, that same night, when she returned home and went out again to take some clean sheets to the inn, she saw someone with bells leaning against a wall: he was doing something with his head hidden behind his right arm and holding his calpac under his other arm. She suspected that it was him—it seemed to her from the way he moved his shoulders every so often that he was crying—but she couldn't be sure about anything. When she passed behind him (with the lightest of footsteps) and found herself on the other side of him, closer to the inn, she hesitated, hesitated greatly, but in the end turned her head: it was him . . . She took a step forward, then turned back, because once again she wasn't sure: it was him—how could she have any doubts? The man at the graveyard, the man at the school. Him. And he was vomiting against the wall, or rather he had just finished vomiting and was waiting with a strange, slightly forced, smile that was not directed at anyone, perhaps he hadn't finished, perhaps there was a little more to come . . . Every now and then, from slight movements or spasms, a bell would ring softly, something which worried no one but her—he himself was totally absorbed in his upset stomach.

She reached the inn, keeping her gaze to the ground, as though there was a possibility that she would see the same man there too in the same position, and she only returned home much later, with her father, when darkness had begun to fall. She again made out the figure with the bells, this time close to their door . . . He was looking toward her as though he didn't believe it was her (he didn't expect to see her out on the street at such an hour, he hadn't seen her on her way to the inn . . .), and as soon as he realized, as soon as he was certain—also because of the presence of her father—he picked up his calpac, which he had put down upright on the ground, turned his back, and began to walk away down the street: his bells echoed loudly and somewhat pointlessly, out of place at that

quiet hour. "Who's that over there?" asked her father, without being all that concerned as to his identity. "Dressed up from now? Not to miss out? . . . Lost soul."

From then on, their encounters wouldn't happen so much by chance, at least
not on his part. She saw him everywhere; it was unusual for a few days to go by
without her seeing him somewhere, not only at the school (besides, it closed
for the summer) but anywhere at all. He would look at her—repeatedly from
some distance: quick, clear looks, *justifiable*, or sometimes risky, exceptionally
piercing, yet always as though not wanting anything more from her than that
she should know that he was looking at her, that his life had no other purpose
and hers no other alternative.

She felt as if blowing over her were a warm, eerie breeze, in gusts, even sen-
sual or, just the opposite, dark, as if it were being sent by his dead wife . . . and
she was scared to go out of the house. And yet, after she had not been out for
days and she knew that he was looking for her up and down, she was worried, literally suffered at the thought of his worry . . . and went out again. Or she would
open one of the windows and stick her head out. On such occasions, it was rare
not to see him passing by on the street . . . Or if she had gone down onto the
street, it was rare for her not to encounter him face to face . . . And the *hide and
seek* began again . . . Where would it end?

When the evening school opened again, she asked her father: "Do you want
me to go this year, too?" "Why are you asking me?" he said to her. "If you've a
heart for it, for learning, then go this year, too. You're a grown woman now." And
so she went—following the innermost and implicit call of her heart, which perhaps wasn't only for the learning.

That year, only fourteen of the women returned, and only three of the men.
Just as we heard it: only three. Nevertheless, the gray-haired teacher didn't appear to take this abstention personally: he knew very well how many agricul-
tural concerns the people there had, so that they were satisfied at having done
their mature school duty for a full nine months. So he did his own thing with
those who had the time and heart for another nine. Heliostalacti, for example,
was once again present (justifying herself on the grounds that she had *acquired
the habit*—as though it were some forbidden addiction), whereas the twins were
absent: only Eugenia came now and again, exceptionally, just to see Julia, who
now shared her desk with someone else. And there were another dozen or so
women, who were absent occasionally, or more often.

As for the three men, the teacher didn't think it worth the trouble to have
a separate lesson: he put them in with the women, making it a mixed class,
though he had the men sit at the back with two rows of empty desks between
them and the women.

One of the three was, of course, the widower with the blue eyes, and we should not be in any doubt that he went there again simply on account of Julia: he could gaze at her neck, her shoulders, her red hair, her spine, gaze at them all he wanted, without her being able to escape him. And she, with her eyes and half her attention directed to the front, knew what was happening behind her and silently, fatalistically even, allowed it to happen. In general, though, she avoided him or, better, half-avoided him, and always shuddered whenever she saw him before her.

And so the time came round again for the next Carnival, and the one after that. This one would bring him very close to her, so close that her face would burn from his breath . . . and her hand from his kiss, the first one without doubt, even though her heart still strongly resisted out of fear.

And yet when the burning flame reached that far, he would disappear.

Twenty days had already passed since that rainy (though dry elsewhere) morning when she had gone as far as the wall of his house and had thrown her second letter, without any reply—neither good nor bad, neither warm nor cold—from him, when, before, not a day or second day would pass without her seeing him standing slap bang in front of her. If this wasn't a mystery, what was?

Febronia kept on urging her to go and give him a third letter—which, in any case, she had already written and which was what was needed: she told him that she wanted to see him again, that she had thought it over and had had a change of heart—and because she was scared (ah, she was still scared) to tell him outright that she loved him, she wrote it in the most secret and ingenious way: she put a second sheet of tracing paper over the first, the letter, and wrote on the second, down at the bottom: *I love you.* She pressed hard with her pencil on the eight characters, on these priceless and precious words, so that they also *came out* on the letter paper: a white presentation on the white surface, manifest and yet invisible, unexpected and yet undeniable, depending on the powers of observation of the recipient . . . Yet given that she was still undecided about going to give it to him, all this seemed pointless. "No, I can't . . . I can't find the courage," she said again and again to her sister-in-law. "If it were gold, you'd find it," she replied, but only once.

Nevertheless, she did find the necessary composure to go one day to the graveyard. Yes, there. And how this came to her, how and why, remains unknown. We don't suppose she had any *hopes* that he, after so many years (and after his love for her: a love so evident, though so secret), would be standing over the grave of his former wife and weeping . . . so that she might see him again. Nor do we suppose that just by going again to find his wife's grave this would help in some way.

And yet she roamed around *like a criminal* in the area where she remembered her mother, Eftha, was buried and read the names on the wooden crosses, trying to find *her*—she would recognize *her*, so she thought, from something she would recognize it. And afterwards? . . . There was no afterwards, and that's what she expected: the older dead gave way to the newly dead, and Kimon's wife—just as her own mother—for years had been living in some small chests, brown in color, deep brown, that were piled one on top of the other in that little building that was called an ossuary. She went toward it . . . And a woman (who looked unfamiliar, but who was known to her after all) waved her hand to her from a nearby grave and asked her with great secretiveness, "Who are you looking for?"

It was a sixty-five-year-old woman in black, chubby, round-faced, by the name of Alexandra, who had lost three brothers in recent years and, as she herself said, "My path now is this one," meaning the path to the cemetery, where she would go every so often to light the lamps and lay a few flowers. And in general, *her path* . . .

"Who first?" sighed Julia. "We've got so many here too . . ."

"So you've come to spend a bit of time with them!," she said, as if congratulating her.

"Yes . . ."

"You're Christoforos's daughter aren't you?"

"Yes . . ."

"Mm! You know, there were once feelings between your father and me!" Alexandra said, leaving the graveside and coming closer to the path down which Julia was walking. "In our eyes, of course—we had nothing more than our eyes then. But in the end, he married someone else—and that was that. And I married someone else. If you tell him: *I saw Alexandra today,* he'll know which Alexandra! But all that, my dear, is in the past . . . Now my path is this one . . . I lost all my brothers inside two years, lost my husband four years ago. I come every Saturday and once in midweek to tell them the news . . . and I ask them for theirs. But they don't hear me! They don't tell me anything. But I come here—*faithfully!*"

Julia didn't know what to say to her. The other woman helped her: "Don't go looking for your mother here, she's in that little building. She *grew old* and they've changed her place. My husband is there too . . . Their bones that is."

"When . . . *do they change their places?*" asked Julia.

"Now that's a fine question!" replied Alexandra. "Where on earth are you from to ask such a thing? After three years, they move them! Don't you remember when they dug up your mother? The others, so many from your family? . . . Unless they're still *in one piece,* if they don't want to decompose in three years.

Then they leave them for another two. Then, straight to the little building! And when the building's full, they cast them over there! Where we'll all end up!" She pointed to some fences. "But I'm off now," she said to her, "because I've jobs to do in the other house. My regards to your father! From Alexandra, tell him, he'll know who." She waved her hand in the direction of her brothers' graves and took the path home.

Alone again, Julia went down towards the *little building,* as the other woman had called it, the *little house* according to others, the *nesting place*—and various other pet names for a building so desolate and companionless as the ossuary. Its tiny door was closed with a rope on the outside that was hooked onto a large nail in the wall and unhooked easily for whoever wanted to enter. She unhooked it . . . She entered, took a few steps and halted. She couldn't go any farther: what cold, silent, and close adyta these were! Who was she looking for? "Welcome!" they seemed to say to her for a moment. Like voices in a dream? Like the waves that the darkness sometimes whips up in our thoughts? No, not this either— TOTAL SILENCE welcomed her. Silence and a multitude of tiny chests reaching up to the ceiling and jostling below on the floor next to her sandals. Entire walls of chests; in rows, one after the other. If you didn't know what they were, you'd have thought that you were in a storeroom with crates, in a pirates' lair. They also had *faces;* on which yellow or white scribble jostled in two or three lines to say a name, an age, a final line of verse . . . On some, there were also painted flowers or crosses with dots all around. Like a parody, a voice came to her ears: *"Apples? Did they ask for apples?"* — *"Where are we going to find the teeth?"* . . . She had once heard about a flood, before she was born, that had swept the chests away, and the bones had poured out "in sackfuls." And another time when they had fallen over and become mixed up because, so they said, of a rat! . . . And yet these were all people. Entire generations.

She found and rewound the rope around the large nail—they were neither keeping her nor chasing her away, alone she had come there. She turned her head in the direction that Alexandra had pointed to previously: there was the deep ravine into which they cast the bones in heaps when there was no longer room for new ones in the little building. The leaning, wind-beaten fences wouldn't allow any more. It was the bed of all those who were absent.

She took the path back home and made an effort to recall or to understand what had brought her there and whether it was *now* or many many years ago . . . Then she remembered Kimon.

And following this experience, every so often she mentally decided to go and find him at his home, and if he came out and said to her, just as the first time: "Come inside . . . don't be afraid," she would go inside even if she was still afraid.

And perhaps—by the time she got inside—she would no longer be afraid . . .
Mental decisions, or rather gut decisions, because of the anxiety gnawing away
at her. And she was always in two minds: *to go or not go.*

And one day, she went a step farther and went to her brother the tailor, to his
shop, because she had seen Kimon going in there on several occasions in the
past months—before he disappeared, of course. She herself was not in the habit
of going to Zacharias, with whom she shared a common father and an equally
obvious solitariness, but she would see his shop, and him behind the window,
when she was on her way to the inn—and they sent her often to the inn, from
the time she was little: to take clean sheets, to collect the dirty ones, to bring her
father a little warm pie, to give something to Cletia . . .

Now raising his eyes and seeing Julia hesitantly opening his door, he, Zacharias, got up from his seat not knowing what to do, how to welcome her. He left
the article of clothing he was sewing on the seat, pulled the needle from the
thread to put it between his teeth, and waving his hand pointed to where she
might sit, anywhere she wanted, all the shop was at her disposal. In his flurry
to appear worthy of the honor she was doing him, he moved aside two piles of
material from one of the shelves, pushed them farther to the right, then to the
left, then took them and moved them somewhere else . . . and his cats purred
lazily and stretched out their tails. Their backs became like arcs of the rainbow:
some outlining the shape upwards and others downwards—genuine felines that
occasionally awoke.

"Ah, you have so many cats!" Julia exclaimed, at that moment forgetting
everything else.

"Hmm, just so," he said. "You know what our father says? *Whoever doesn't
have customers has cats.* It's me he says it about."

"But you have customers too . . . no?" his sister asked, amazed that she had
been given the opportunity to allude to *him* . . .

"Of course, of course, I have a few customers—those who come and want
me to alter their wedding clothes, the ones I made for them twenty years ago!"
said Zacharias, again threading his needle, while Julia had rested her elbow
somewhere, and one of the cats was sniffing her and pawing her shoulder.

That "twenty years ago" that her brother had said rang in her ears so strangely,
so *specifically*: it made her think—for the first time so vividly, almost with a pang
of jealousy—of Kimon's *wedding* to the other woman, a woman by the name
of Chrysanthe: for him to have lost this Chrysanthe so soon, fifteen or sixteen
years earlier (something she had learned from Febronia), it was not unlikely that
they had got married twenty years ago exactly, it wasn't unlikely that her brother
was speaking literally, was actually referring to *him*.

"And is it only those who were grooms twenty years ago who are your customers?" she asked him.

"Eh, more or less," he replied. "And even they sometimes disappear."

"Disappear?"

"Eh . . . how shall I say, disappear, hide, who knows what they're up to."

Julia couldn't go on asking—the more her imagination raced, the more her tongue stuck in her throat, when she ought to have spoken up about some things. She pretended to remember the cats: she stroked—as many as allowed her—their long curled tails, their soft heads, their magnificent backs, picked up more than a few silk hairs on her fingers . . . then said to her brother:

"So . . . I'll be going now, I just stopped by."

"Stop by whenever you want," he told her.

"Has no one else come by today?" she asked, daring one more question.

He stared at her a little astonished.

"I mean . . . a customer," said Julia.

"Ah . . . only two all morning," he told her.

Anyone by the name of Kimon?—oh! why didn't she have the courage, as Febronia would, or Cletia and perhaps numerous other sisters, to ask this too?

She left like the inexperienced fisherman who got his feet wet but caught nothing.

She wanted to go the next day too, and she got him a couple of pieces of a cake she had baked in the house. Zacharias only came in the evenings and ate with them; at lunchtime one of his other sisters, not a half-sister, one of Petroula's daughters, would take him food to his shop, and Julia waited for her to leave, for him to eat, before setting off with her cake: she knew that the other sister hadn't put any in his lunchbox. As she got closer, she saw a crowd of people outside the inn, and also farther away, around the spot where the four bell-wearers had been fighting. She also saw the wall where *he* had once been vomiting . . . and an idea came into her head. She decided to walk around the crowd of people, who in any case weren't blocking her way as she was going to the tailor's and not to the inn, and it wasn't the first time that people had gathered around there: it was the center, the heart of the marketplace, at least of one of the two marketplaces—the other one was close to the church. But she saw her father in front of the inn, with some other men around him, sitting on a stone with his head in his hands, shaking it from side to side: he couldn't believe—though it was as clear as day—what the others were telling him again and again . . . She stared at him through their legs that, every so often, changed position as though they were playing *hopscotch*. And Cletia behind them, her arms crossed over her breast and her hands under her armpits, was also listening. "Come on, let's go, so you can see with your own eyes! . . . What are you shaking your head for?"—so one of them seemed to be saying to him; before he too tossed his head back and spat forcefully and with anger into the air.

At the same moment, seeing her, a boy broke away from the other group that was closer to her. She didn't know him, and his sudden and sideways movement frightened her somewhat, making her halt, while he came towards her hurriedly, yet dragging his legs to the side, as though he was unable to run in any other way. *What a strange boy!* she thought; and when he came up to her, he became truly strange: he completely turned his back on her and, with the same hurried, sideways steps, did a turn—that is, he did a half-circle before her, like a sickle cutting in reverse—and then immediately left her and ran back to the older men. From there, he turned his head, fixed his eyes on her, and then immediately turned away again. *What a strange boy!* Julia thought again. *Why did he do that circle?*

And it was only then that she recognized him: it was the boy with the bonnet (who wasn't wearing it that day), the boy who had brought her the letter! . . . Though motionless, she was panting, her heartbeat trebled—there was no doubt that it was him! She was now more unsure of whether she was Julia than whether he was that boy! And what did he want to say to her now, almost a month after the letter, with that reverse dance that he had done under her nose, with that turning of his back and those sideways and peculiar steps that no doubt concealed some *message*, something very important maybe—and yet something of a reproach, something of a dismissal that perhaps she deserved? And why hadn't he found another way, as then at her house, to draw her to him so that he could tell her what he had to say to her or give her a letter? Because without her realizing it, she was once again following on his heels and had almost reached the large group of men . . . and she was ready to give him whatever she was carrying in her hands, whatever else he had a whim for, so long as he told her something plain and not in riddles or with sideways dances, so long as she could prize from his lips or from his hands what she had been waiting for all those days.

But the boy, truly strange, had disappeared among the older men—*he had nothing more to tell her.* This pierced her like a knife, her pain turned into hatred for him, her breast heaved, she was shattered. And she abruptly turned her back on him too and rushed off in the direction of her brother's shop.

Inside the shop, she encountered two other men, and she couldn't have imagined that they too would cause her just as much grief.

"I've brought you something, some cake," she said to Zacharias, panting, nervously unwrapping it as though she wanted to loosen her tongue at the same time. What she had lacked in courage the day before was now made up for by that heated state, by the shakiness and quavering of her mind, which wouldn't allow her to think normally, just as in a shattered mirror you can't see even a single finger entire.

"What's happening in the marketplace today?" she asked him, "why all that *fuss*? . . . Aren't you alone?"

"Alone?" replied Zacharias. "Does all this unpleasantness leave us alone?"

"What's happened?" she asked.

Her brother was holding the needle without any thread, a large needle, and it was with this that he motioned to the others to speak.

"What's happened *again*, you should ask," one of them said to her.

"What's happened again?" she acquiesced automatically, on the verge of exhaustion.

"Hmm!" he exclaimed.

The girl was almost dropping to the floor.

"What's happened again?" she asked the other man.

"Eh . . . don't dwell on it. People like you, like us, have no connection with things like that, better to stay well away," he said to her, as his mother had probably taught him to say in similar circumstances.

"What does that mean?" asked Julia. "*People like me, like you . . .*"

"Eh . . . didn't you hear from your father?" he asked her.

"From my father? I haven't seen him since yesterday."

"He's already gone," her brother added, pointing to the inn. "He must have gone to the walnut tree."

She too looked out of the window; there was now no one outside the inn, nor even from the other group—Cletia was on her own sweeping the entrance.

"They've all gone to the walnut tree," Zacharias said again slowly. "To chew on the *good* walnuts; the *good* walnuts."

"What walnuts? Why don't you tell me?" she asked all three of them.

Her brother took hold of her by the arm: "My dearest sister, go home and don't ask," he counseled her. "None of us are to blame for what happened, beyond the fact that it happened on one of our walnut trees."

"On one of our walnut trees? What? . . ."

"Somebody hanged himself."

"Who? Why?"

"Why I've no idea. As to who . . . ," Zacharias waved his hand; it was difficult for him to say, his head was swimming.

"Who?" she asked him again, pleading.

"*Him!*" he replied, confusedly and pointing to an olive-green jacket with black stripes that was on a hanger, right at the front and at a distance from the other garments, which were also arranged on hangers, and hanging from a steel rail high up. "He brought it to me two or three weeks ago to be widened because he'd broadened around the shoulders he said—*the good life,* he said . . . perhaps with a dose of irony. At any rate, he was in a hurry: *fix it quick, I'll be back in two days to collect it.*"

"And he didn't come back," said one of the others bitterly—more like a question.

"No, he didn't come back. Not in two days nor in twelve," said the tailor. "And I left everything else to fix his jacket . . . And it required work, it wasn't easy: unstitch the shoulders, unstitch the sides, the seam at the back . . . it was his wedding suit. I was the one who made it for him twenty years ago! And now he wanted it widened, was in a hurry . . . *In two days!* I did my best, and waited for him."

"And didn't you suspect anything when he didn't come?" one of them asked him.

"What should I suspect?" said the tailor, "it's not as if he was the first! Another one left me two pairs of trousers before Christmas and he still hasn't come to collect them, and he was in a hurry too! . . . I don't understand: is he going around in his underpants? Or does he have so many pairs of trousers? Ah, I should start selling all the things they leave me for alteration, or I'm not going to manage. Sell it all! Or make them pay me up front—in the hand, slap down! . . . Then you'd see how quickly they'd remember to come and get their things."

He looked at his sister: he was the one talking, he'd got carried away and was talking about the difficulties of his work, and she was still waiting with clouded and cracked eyes for him to tell her *who* had hanged himself, *who* owned that olive-green jacket, shiny like a fish's back from so much ironing, that wedding jacket . . .

"You go home," he told her again softly, opening the door for her. "You don't know him . . . Someone by the name of Kimon."

And so end some hapless loves or so begin others even more hapless. Most likely, Zacharias had no idea about the relationship between his red-headed sister and this desperate man by the name of Kimon; most likely his concern that she should leave his shop and go home was not motivated by any particular worry or suspicion, nothing more than a brotherly wish to keep her as far away as possible from such things, and more generally away from men, just as he kept himself away from women . . .

Yet at that very same time—if we have to leave Julia in her despondency—Christoforos was going through some of the strangest feelings of anxiety in his life: if this crazy lad had done what he had on account of his daughter (*if!* Because he may have had other reasons . . . though, by choosing one of his walnut trees, it made it seem less than fortuitous), then it was likely that he had left a note explaining the reason, accusing her, and then Christoforos's family would really get itself a bad name; it would be the last straw for his already much troubled and, in part, curse-ridden family; then the stone throwing would begin, as Eftha had feared even in the past, before all these worse things had happened. And the others had listened to her and simply laughed. But they might not have been laughing if she were alive to say it today . . . They might not laugh anymore—if this lad in the tree had left a note . . .

He called him *lad* because he still couldn't believe this business with the tree . . . and if his worry about the accursed note didn't allow him to feel sadness or abhorrence at the event itself, feel sad for the man who had gone in this way and so forget his own concerns, it was because he still couldn't really believe it, get his mind round it, accept it.

And yet everything around him, with the breeze as the main instigator, seemed to be calling out: *Kimon hanged himself, Kimon hanged himself.*

"Alive, my lad," he said to him mentally, "alive, I'd have put up with any amount of trouble! Any amount of times you could have come into my yard and asked me for my daughter . . . I'd have given her to you! Eventually, I'd have given her to you! But this one thing now, why have you done this one thing to me now when you're dead? Why go and hang yourself on my walnut tree, instead of coming to hang yourself around me, around my daughter, become a nightmare for her, a nightmare and a pest, until she accepted you—eventually she would have accepted you! All women say no in the beginning, but in the end she would have said yes. Why didn't you persist, you silly lad, why did you have to resort to the walnut tree? I'd like to know what happened, what else happened . . . What do you have hidden in your pockets!"

He kept shaking his head and all those round about him thought it was because he still couldn't believe what had happened, whereas he had already come to believe it, but he was still shaking his head because he was saying to the lad things that he didn't want the others to hear. And he went with them to Megali Morphina, one of his farthest fields, which Kimon had chosen as his ideal spot . . . There was also Mikri Morphina, much closer, but there were no walnut trees there.

They weren't even a third of the way there when others caught up with them and told them that some of Kimon's relatives had gone, accompanied by two constables, and had cut him down and taken him home.

They turned back and took another path home . . . They passed by the place where his sister Marigo had once lived—if you could call it life and not misery. He felt a sudden pang in his heart when he saw the window with the bent bars, with no more than half a shutter flapping in the wind, with the jackdaws now living there, and perhaps the occasional owl at night. He halted and crossed himself: "One of my sisters lived here once," he murmured. The house was in ruins everywhere, after her, all of them had died: her mother-in-law first, then her husband . . . and her child, of course, very soon after her—Marigo had left no accounts to settle.

But one of the others took hold of his arm and pulled him away—that day they were going elsewhere, they didn't have time for his sister.

"And he chose, my friend, one of *your* walnut trees, one of *your* trees!" someone said to him again (it was a forest warden, one of those who had found Kimon while they were searching for the others, the ones who had killed the old couple). "The whole area full of trees and whatever, but he chose that place! He went and made a noose for himself on one of *your* trees! Seems he saw everything, examined it all, weighed things up, weighed himself—including the bells!—and decided that yours was the strongest, the best bet. And he hanged himself *on that!* . . . Just imagine! Where did he find the guts? How he took care of that noose as though he were taking care of his share? What can you say about him!"

Such events stemming from extreme despair or enormous composure arouse you in a strange way, make you search with tooth and nail, or with words, not the cause—who can ever discover that?—but that which *embellishes* even the most obscure cause, that which attracts the others, the talkative and the dumbstruck, to congregate round such a body.

"My name's Vassilis," said another one, blue-eyed like Kimon and with curly hair—fair hair, in fact, that here and there had started to turn gray, like Kimon's. "I'm a simple builder—I can't read or write and I never went to learn. But from the moment I guessed what the whole business was about, I mean, all's well and good, but we're all here to die, there's ONE THING I want, for someone just once to come back from the other world and say to me: *Vassilis*, to whisper in my ear, *death is a narrow passage, a hole, a turn* . . . But for him to tell me something I can understand: WHAT DO WE SEE when our time comes?"

"Is that what you're bothered about most or that you'll die?" another asked him.

"That's what I'm bothered about most, in God's truth, THAT's what bothers me most!" said Vassilis with passion, flinging his hands in front of him just as when he flung the trowel with the mortar on the walls. "After all, I know that I'm going to die, what the hell . . . But *what do we see at that moment? What's* there at the *moment* that we pop our clogs? What opens? What closes? A door? A garden like the Gospels say? Does some narrow passage suck us in like a whirl-pool? A precipice? A hole? An abyss? What? Does a fox run five paces in front and there everything vanishes? A wolf? A dolphin? A shark? What? That's what I'd like just one person to tell me one time! Not why we die or what happens afterwards. WHAT WE SEE AT THAT MOMENT! What's the last image! . . ."

"Ask Kimon today," someone else told him. "He was a builder like you, and he's a recent case . . . Perhaps he'll tell you."

"I will, I'll ask him! There's not been a single dead person I haven't asked!" said Vassilis, inflamed by the paroxysm of this matter, his ignorance of which so tormented him . . . "But again he won't tell me! No one has told me . . . I'll die with that disappointment . . . What do our eyes see at the very last moment! What's there? A hole? A narrow passage that turns? A gate? A stairway?"

"Why do you keep on about holes and narrow passages and you don't say anything about some beautiful woman who takes you in her arms," one of them asked him, "or about a fine white horse that you climb up onto and go-o-o-o?"

"That too . . . it's not out of the question," said Vassilis, but without assimilat-ing it as quickly, without being able to include this new imposing *scene* in with the others, the humble and restless scenes that suddenly came into his mind or encircled him like autonomous parts of some dream he had forgotten, some significant dream.

"And what might God be?" another one in the big group on its way to Ki-mon's house found the opportunity to ask.

The question fell into a black void. The only thing that someone found to say—with a mouth that seemed rather to gawp than to articulate any words— was: "He's probably asking the same thing about us at this very moment: *And just who are those human beings, then, and where are they going?*"

"I know one thing: today we're here and tomorrow we're not. That's what I know and I've no wish to learn anything else," said another.

"Don't say anything, you, you're content with little," yet another one said to him, "you're not like Vassilis here . . ."

"But I'm happy with little too!" he started up again. "What am I asking for? For God to make me immortal? No. Just to let me know *what it is we see at that moment!* Just that! *What we see, how it appears to us . . .* Just that!"

"All right, we've understood that. But what we've not understood is what you mean by that moment . . . where do you put it exactly: while you're still alive? Or after you've popped your clogs?" one of them asked him.

"How should I know! That's exactly what I'm asking! That's what I'm ask-ing!" retorted Vassilis almost resentfully. "That *in-between*, that *life-in-death* . . ."

"That's something not even Socrates found," said the man beside him. "Do you know who Socrates was?"

"I've heard of him," Vassilis mumbled, still engaged in his own questions.

"Well—I'm telling you: it's something not even he found. And he died *intentionally* to find it. Not us! . . ."

"What are you poking around at? Death is death. If it were something else, they'd give it another name," said one of those who had just been listening up till then.

"Christoforos is the only one who hasn't said anything," someone remarked. "We've done all the talking, and he's not uttered a word."

"Christoforos is thinking about his walnut tree," said the forest warden.

They all turned and gazed at him without stopping walking. He gazed at them too.

"I'm thinking about Kimon," he said to them—and they all waited for him to continue, to say something else.

"And what do you suppose we're thinking about?" sighed Vassilis, given that he didn't continue. "Kimon and . . . *what he saw*."

"*What did he see?* I have to admit that I'd like to know too," thought Christoforos. "Anyway, none of you have had anything to say yet about my daughter! . . . Either you don't know anything or you're keeping it for me till the end."

He hoped they didn't know anything.

And so they reached Kimon's house. From inside came the sound of voices lamenting—aunts or cousins of his, as he had neither wife, nor sister, nor mother—and outside in the yard were two apple trees, two apricot trees, and a pear tree that would no longer be tended to by his hands.

"Look, trees here too! . . . There were trees here if he'd wanted," said the forest warden, as though someone had paid him to say it. "But not for him—he preferred your walnut tree! At the back of beyond, but where *your* walnut tree was!"

"Stop going on all the time about my walnut tree," Christoforos said to him, still with some composure, before he lost it and got angry.

"I'm not saying anything, I'm not accusing you!" said the forest warden, defending himself from a wrongful reproach. "But as he chose your walnut tree and not anyone else's, what else am I supposed to say?"

"Stop going on about it. There are other things we have to think about," Christoforos said to him.

And he went first through the half-open door, against which, so that it wouldn't close—because the door of a house with someone dead inside mustn't be shut—they had put a metal cat. Christoforos bent down and picked it up (by its front legs, just as he might pick up a living, wiry cat) and held it a few moments before his eyes. Who knows why he did that . . . Perhaps he asked it something about its master that only it, being lifeless and omnipresent, could know, perhaps for a moment he longed for its lifeless and guileless presence.

It was one of those black metal cats with triangular legs, with a straight, elongated, flat body, raised high neck and equally raised tail that, in pairs, adorned every fireplace in winter (one at each side), and at the same time held the wood and logs so they wouldn't fall or, if you were to put them together, performed the duty of an eight-legged trivet. They used to tell children that they were once real cats, but because they never moved away from the fire, God turned them into metal to protect them.

Christoforos put it back down again, in the particular place and for the particular purpose that they were using it that day, and all he did was to gently push it back with his foot to open the door wider and let a little light into the dark hallway . . . He failed to hear a voice from inside speaking to him, and one of those behind him nudged him: "They're talking to you," he told him.

He turned his head.

"Who are you? . . . Are you one of his friends? . . . ," the voice from inside asked again. A girl, thin-boned like Julia, had emerged from one of the interior doors on the right, had put her arm high on the doorjamb, and on this was resting her face; a face completely exhausted, cracked and shapeless from all the crying.

He hesitated slightly before answering her.

"Y-y-yes . . . a friend of his"—he didn't know who this girl was or *why* she was asking him.

She leaned even more on her arm, almost dragging her chin over it, gazed at the others who had started to enter, taking off their hats or brushing down their clothes, even though there was no mud or snow outside, and gradually, constantly rubbing her face on her sleeve and starting to cry again, she turned it towards the inner part of the room, unable to let go of the door or even bring her arm down—and she let out a cry between her sobs: "Your friends are here, my dear brother! . . . Your friends, my dearest! . . . Open your eyes to see them, those lovely blue eyes! . . ."

"Who is she? Did the poor lad have a sister?" asked Christoforos quietly, turning back towards the others.

"It's his wife's sister," someone replied equally quietly, implying that *something was going on* . . .

"Yes, yes," one of the others confirmed, "after he'd lost his wife, of course . . ."

"What?" he asked, astounded. "Kimon and her loved each other?"

"Something like that, perhaps not exactly . . . One of those things up in the air . . . She wanted him, waited, whereas he didn't want to do that to Chrysanthe, share the same bed with her sister . . . don't you remember which song it was he sang most?"

"No, I didn't know him all that well—which?" asked Christoforos.

"The one that goes *No more, no more . . . I've had enough of the woman next door . . .* He meant with his sister-in-law, his wife's sister."[1]

"With her?"

"Eh, who else? He didn't have any other sister-in-law."

"Don't talk like that, she'll hear you!" Vassilis said to them angrily, though equally softly.

"Even if you beat drums today, no one's going to hear you!" she said from the doorway with passion in her voice.

They froze. Had she heard what they'd said and wanted to put them to shame? Put them in their place? Or had she heard . . . *he'll hear you* and was talking about her dead brother-in-law, who, no doubt about it, couldn't hear even drums anymore. But she might have been talking to the other women inside, perhaps they had said or done something to provoke her caustic outburst . . . Whatever the case, she left them speechless, made them forget what they were talking about. Christoforos stepped aside, let the others go first towards the room, and then followed behind—O how well he knew that passing into such rooms, how it resembled a hiatus or a slip, and yet how it prepared them, all of them without exception, for the other *passing,* their own, from here to there . . .

When he got to the doorway where she was still standing, he halted and bowed his head to her silently. From the grief that tingled and burned in her eyes, he understood that she wasn't only crying for her sister's husband . . .

He went towards the dead body, up to the bed where they had laid him, now knowing a few more things about him and his personal life, but which wouldn't help him to unravel anything before its time.

Never, before that day, had Christoforos happened to go to Kimon for something. Nor he to Christoforos, for that matter, save, of course, for an exchange

1. The rest of the song: ". . . each morning she stands at her door and asks: *Where were you last night, my bonny lad? The night before last where were you? Yesterday I was at my mother's, the night before at my sister's, but tonight, my black-eyed beauty, we'll sleep side by side.*" The last line, from what we can gather, was not sung by Kimon.

of greetings and small talk on the street if they happened to meet (they weren't enemies), and apart from that evening on Clean Monday, a month before, when Kimon had gone to him with bells and songs and had revealed his love for the red-haired Julia. He recalled how they had begun that conversation in a roundabout way, like Carnival banter, and how it had gradually narrowed down and become serious on Kimon's part . . . Then all the rest had come, with Lily in the ditch, and Christoforos hadn't given any further thought to Kimon, hadn't had the time. And then the others had come and told him that they'd found Kimon hanged on one of his walnut trees in Morphina! . . . "If life isn't crazy, then it drives its children crazy — it made you crazy and it's slowly turning me crazy," he said to him, bending to touch those cold and crossed hands with his lips, without being heard, of course, by anyone, but also without managing to touch him since he was still gripped by the fear that as soon as his relatives saw him and recognized him, they would show him the door, throw him out, for having dared to come and pay his respects . . . But nothing of the sort happened (the people saw him, those who knew him well spoke to him, even expressed their regrets concerning the business with the walnut tree . . .), nor did he feel himself threatened by anything in the atmosphere, other than perhaps by the face of the dead man, which they had covered with a white cloth down to the shoulders.

He looked around to sit on a chair and tried to picture the man's face under the cloth . . . He might not have had eyes for anyone, or anger or pity, but it was better that he saw him covered. On his forehead, on top of the cloth, they had placed a weight, a round flattened iron weight, attached by strong thread in four places, as though from a gust of wind or a touch the cloth might fall off and reveal the ineffable. Similarly, they had tied his wrists with red cord . . . And bent over his bare, blue-black and very swollen feet were two women, who were struggling to put them into clean, unworn socks — the last difficult job (given that they had proved capable of dressing the rest of the body), the last and most difficult as the time passed: the socks were very narrow for such feet, even though they had chosen the biggest, but it was mainly *those* feet, which submitted to their efforts about as much as two hewn rocks . . . One of the women was weeping so much that instead of taking hold of the feet she groped and grabbed hold of the other woman's hands. And the other one became cross and said: "Where are you looking? You're going to do me an injury!" But above all, the feet themselves seemed to be asking both women: *Why are you struggling in vain?*

Until a third woman came with a big pair of scissors in her hand: "Cut the sides," she said crying, almost angry for not being sorry about this — "otherwise, let's leave him like that, barefoot, no one's going to take it amiss." And using the scissors they cut the socks, opening them up at the sides, so that they would at least cover his soles, just enough so that the dark blue color wouldn't appear. They didn't even try to put on his best shoes, they left them beside him.

All those who had come with Christoforos paid their respects one by one, as did all the others who kept coming, and before long the man with the coffin arrived. He told them that the church wouldn't agree to give him a funeral service, not even to toll the bells, but someone would come to the house to chant the customary prayers. It was the last thing they cared about, aside from one of the suicide's uncles, who was deeply religious and who said, sorrowfully, that if the church were to do that, it would be like handing a noose to a strangled man.

Vassilis stood longer than all of them over the covered face with the weight on the forehead. He stood silent and motionless—both of them builders for so many years, together they had worked with the mortar and the spirit level—and eventually he sat on a chair that someone put behind him and began talking to the dead man.

"Old friend," he said, "do you remember last fall when we were finishing that crazy house for the signore,[2] we were putting the last tiles on the roof, and you had a headache . . . a real headache, so that you dropped whatever you tried to pick up? Do you remember what you said to me? *When I have a head like this, I feel like making a noose and hanging myself!* . . . Did you have that head again, Kimon, and you did it? Eh? Tell me. It's your friend Vassilis, your workmate, and I'm asking you. Was it your head?"

There was a long pause, made to seem eternal by the sobbing of the women all around.

"And what did you see—I can't not ask you that, too, today—what did you see when everything faded? A ladder? An open roof waiting for you to construct it? What did you see? Tell me . . . A narrow passage? A bend that swallowed you up? . . . Tell me this!"

And others, too, would talk about Kimon's headaches—we mean that his closest kin and friends knew about it, because there were others, like Christoforos, who had no idea, but found out about it then thanks to Vassilis, who spoke about it openly, and to some others who confirmed it and, though mincing their

2. He was talking about an aged Italian aristocrat, Signor Boroni of Florence, who had built a beautiful though eccentric house in their parts because he liked the climate and their luscious green hills. He would live there for the next ten years, would die there, and would ask to be buried there.

words, let it be understood that it was no common headache, but *the wolf.*[3] And that whenever he suffered an attack by the wolf, there were no more songs for Kimon, or painkillers.

"*A horseshoe, Anna. It's a metal horseshoe that grips me from here to here. And it tightens round me, tightens, drives me mad . . .* That's how he described it to me a few months ago. I didn't know, it was the first I'd heard about it. I asked my mother, and she said yes, his head's been hurting him for some time—she knew about it. But not me, it was only then that he told me . . . when I happened to find him in pain. *From here to here. A horseshoe, Anna. It's driving me mad.*"

That's what Anna, a forty-year-old cousin of his, said, pointing with her two hands—as he would have pointed for her—to the whole of one side of her head (an arc stretching from her right ear to her left temple), and tightening it as a large horseshoe would tighten it, a pair of pliers, while her mother beside her, his mother's sister, sorrowfully nodded her own head and waited for her daughter to finish so that she could say what she had to say: "When he came at Carnival time to kiss our hands, to bring us the oranges as he did every year, I asked him, I see you've got dressed up again this year, son, doesn't your head hurt? *Of course it hurts,* he said, *now it's found me, it won't go away, it goes from bad to worse.* So why are you wearing that calpac, I said to him, to aggravate things even more? He didn't answer, just did a whirl in the room . . . his bells echoed . . . *dang-dong, dang-dong* . . . Perhaps he thought that the calpac and the bells would scare it away. But it wasn't a dog to be scared, it was—what it was in the rocks and mountains! It was that wolf that finished him! . . . And with me, too, whenever he talked about it, he called it that *horseshoe*—accursed horseshoe! *It's tightening round me, tightening, Aunt, how much more is it going to tighten?* That was it, it tightened round him once and for all, and he at last found rest."

"With me he called it a *crown*. It had become a crown that was constantly getting tighter round his head," said one elderly man, also an uncle. "He told me about a week ago. Of course, I've known about his headaches for months now, but I didn't know that they were continuing, getting worse . . . I came by a few days ago to see him and I found him going through his own Holy Calvary . . . or unholy one, more like. *A crown,* he said—*not of thorns, but of nails! When they put it on me, even my eyelids hurt, the hairs on my head, each and every one!* . . . I said to him, Why don't you go and have a doctor look at you, what kind of state is that to be in? *What doctor,* he said to me, *there was only one doctor for*

---

3. *Wolf* referred at the time to an illness for which they had as yet found no more appropriate name. Some had the wolf in their bellies, others in their stomachs, others in their heads, others in their chests . . . Later, it was given the name *cancer*.

me and that doctor's gone. Of course, he meant . . . who else but her? What else could that crown have been? . . . Though he didn't want to say it, to call it by its name. He thought that he'd exorcize it by not saying it. But even unnamed, it just got worse and went on . . . And wearing that calpac the last time didn't help, it seems. It was the last straw, as they say."

"And when did all this start?" asked someone who had known nothing about it till just now.

Someone said a year ago, perhaps more. Another insisted that it wasn't as long as a year. Someone else said just a few months. But they all agreed—all those who had known about it—that the pains had increased during the last few weeks, even the last few days. In fact, his neighbors, without having seen much of him during those last days, had seen the worst.

"The other day, it was in the evening, I saw him coming out into the yard with his head wrapped up as if he were a maharajah," one of them said. "Some maharajah . . . He was dragging himself from wall to wall like a casualty, he was stumbling, falling . . . he'd shrunk to half his normal size in the space of only a few days, he was unrecognizable. Hey, Kimon, I shouted to him, do you want anything? He didn't even hear me, he just went back inside . . . He wasn't at all well . . . Seemed shriveled up."

"His face had become unrecognizable," added a woman, in confirmation, "like when you see a stranger, one . . . that's scary. His body had wasted away, his clothes were hanging on him—where was that man we all knew? That fine young man . . . He'd wasted away, only his eyes were still plainly his. But what can you do with just eyes? Three days later when I next saw him, he didn't have even his eyes left to show."

"No need to look far!" said one of the others who had taken him down from the tree. "Hadn't he hung bells from his belt? Hadn't he filled his pockets with stones and metal to add weight to him so the noose would do its *work*, not leave him *dancing?*"

Those who were listening shuddered—those who already knew and those who were hearing it for the first time.

"Did he gird on his bells?" mumbled Christoforos, wiping his dry lips with his tongue, with his Adam's apple bobbing in his throat.

"Eh, see what he did—didn't I tell you?" said the forest warden, jumping in. "But you went into a world of your own at one stage, you didn't hear anything."

"You were talking to me about the walnut tree . . . you didn't say anything about the bells," he mumbled again.

"I told you about the walnut tree and about the bells," said the forest warden. "You heard the one thing and missed the other, it's not my fault."

"Kimon was no longer a man, he was a *wolf man*, a *werewolf*—in the other sense of course," said a friend of his, the last person to have seen him alive. "But he didn't want me to fetch a doctor, didn't want one . . . He said the same thing to me: *there was only one doctor for me and that doctor's gone, doesn't exist.* It's time that you forgot her, I told him the other day, to come round, remarry, take care of yourself. *All right, all right, I'll forget her,* he said to me, *I'll come round, go now.*"

"It was a mistake, a big mistake on our part that we didn't take him more seriously, that we didn't concern ourselves, didn't do something," said his relatives, "we left him on his own with the wolf . . . And then it was he said, If it's going to finish me, I'll put an end to it. And he put an end to everything with the noose."

They had all stopped mincing their words: they all inclined to the belief that it was *the wolf* that had led him to this final act of despair.

Then there was Chrysanthe, his wife. When they stopped talking about the horseshoe and the crown and the wolf, they would all start talking about her. They had lost her sixteen years earlier, and at around the same time, *midway* between winter and spring—on a day with a clear sky and a sun that burned, like that day. She had died of eclampsia during the birth of their first child: another riddle this eclampsia, this *light burst*, an illness with such a name (recalling anything but an illness) that afflicts only pregnant women—perhaps not anymore, but at that time it was common . . . We imagine it as some kind of *exceptional* flash that hurled the women up high, made stars of them—them and their infants (some of which, nevertheless, sometimes survived). And so it took Kimon's wife, who was only twenty-two years old—age meant nothing to it—and him twenty-four. A marriage that was the result of a great love: he had run away with her. For three years they hadn't been able to have children, and in the fourth year she died together with the child. And from then on, so they said, however much Kimon seemed in good spirits those last years, however high he leapt at the Carnival and sang his heart out, there was a worm inside him—till it became a wolf—eating away at him without Chrysanthe.

It was a different worm that ate away at Chrysanthe's sister concerning him . . . *About this* no one would speak plainly—either plainly or even mincing words. Besides, there were those among the relatives (and they had all known for years) who didn't find it at all reprehensible and told him there was no reason why he shouldn't marry her, though others again didn't agree at all: of course they wanted him to remarry, since he had been widowed so young, but to another woman, not his sister-in-law.

Yet his sister-in-law's eyes revealed much that day—*revealed* or *concealed*, we don't know how to put it exactly—so that neither encouragement nor reproach was needed to change her heart in the slightest (perhaps that "Even if you beat drums today, no one's going to hear you!" might have been referring to her own heart).

Yet she too was obliged to talk about Chrysanthe and not about herself, given that—the most painful thing in this love—he didn't want her nor had he ever given her any hope . . . And she, who was loved by others who sought her, refused them all, turned them away, waiting for something to change in Kimon's heart, for something to happen that would bring him close to her . . .

Unfulfilled, one-sided loves like these were never absent from the time the world's clock was first wound up. But perhaps in those times, they had an absoluteness, a hermetic aspect, that has been blunted and lessened in later and modern times.

Christoforos still couldn't believe that his sullen, vulnerable, and suspicious presence added nothing to this already burdened house . . . Or if it did add something—of which he himself was more and more certain—the others couldn't see it, didn't know it: none of them, absolutely no one among the relatives and friends, could boast that they knew all Kimon's secrets, just as he, Julia's father, until the previous day that is, was also ignorant of most things, of everything, and the only thing that made him remember *something* was the fact that to accomplish his task Kimon had chosen a walnut tree belonging to his own ancestral holdings . . .

Besides, they would eventually get round to discussing the walnut tree, its time would come too—they say that what you don't talk about while you're alive, you hear about when you're dead. So Kimon would hear them too—and in the case in question also Christoforos—expressing their puzzlement as to why he should choose that tree, so far away! . . . Yet just as they would if he had chosen some other tree, one in his own yard. From the moment that he had decided upon the noose and tied it—as one person said—he would have found a tree even in the desert! Even more so given that Morphina, their own *desert,* was strewn with walnut trees, chestnut trees, and many other trees . . . the majority of which, after all, belonged to Christoforos and to his children and not to the exiles of Galilee. Even that forest warden, the only one who seemed to want to insist on this detail, on this particular choice of tree, even he in the end was either persuaded or simply gave up: it was chance, blind chance and an inauspicious hour, that had led Kimon to that walnut tree.

But Christoforos knew, could feel deep inside him that no, it wasn't just the invisible and malicious workings of chance, it was also Julia's refusal—so it was *also* Julia and *his* Julia: the final roll of the dice perhaps in that game that was secretly being played for such a long time under that very roof, with the only player a man, even if with a wolf for a partner—the final roll, then, but not the least important. Or simply as important as every *occasion* that ends up being fatal.

And so he, who happened not to know what all the others knew about Kimon, found himself in the end knowing what all the others didn't know: that *the only doctor* that there was for him (*and this one too no longer existed*) was not his wife, Chrysanthe, dead for so many years, as all of them thought, but his own daughter, the ethereal and hesitant Julia.

And he, he again, who at first, during those first few moments he had entered that house, felt like when-you-are-preparing-to-go-down-one-more-step-in-the-dark-but-there-is-no-other-step-and-your-foot-lands-clumsily, now, exactly, now that there was no outcry, no reproach, no curse, found other steps for himself, and other threads that led him farther down, brought him closer to the edge of the secret—which in this case, however, was a *wall*.

And so, though more and more certain that something had happened recently between Kimon and his daughter, he didn't know what; doubting less and less about something that the others didn't even suspect, and yet tormented more because he knew but without really *knowing*.

Naturally he would go home and ask Julia herself, press her till she did talk, hang her by her fingernails as they say, but something told him that he wouldn't get much out of Julia's mouth, not much more than from Kimon's mouth . . . He would, of course, find her notebooks, wouldn't stop at either her first or at her last refusal. Her notebooks, which he had given her the permission to keep when his other daughters didn't have time even for scratching their nose, while she was concerned about where to put a period—he would find them, and they would tell him something . . . Provided that she hadn't burned these too in her desire for secretiveness.

He was sitting among Kimon's elderly relatives, opposite the forest warden, Vassilis, and the others, and he was the only one who said almost nothing. It was as though his interest had faded from the moment that he discovered that Kimon hadn't left a note, no note had been found in his pockets, filled as they were with stones and weights, or on his pillow—whereas, on the contrary, Christo-foros's interest had been rekindled, and whatever had put his mind at rest for a while previously now pestered him even more. At any rate, he said virtually nothing, simply letting the others speak, and he just listened or gazed occasion-ally at Kimon, who was now at their feet and not on the bed: they had placed him, picking him up together with the bed sheet, in the casket, and they pre-ferred to leave this on the floor, whereas they remade the bed and pushed it back against the wall, as it had been until the previous day, so that more people could fit in the room.

He gazed at the line of his nose which was clearly outlined beneath the white cloth, with something of the hollow cheeks, of his eye sockets, even of the un-certain curve of his mouth since the cloth—a thin, cotton cloth—was soften-ing, almost wet now from the fresh flowers they kept piling around him, and it was gradually becoming like a thin mask, like a membrane that, even though remaining opaque, covers and sticks to the features, highlighting them in a strange way: making them more hollow or swollen, more disturbing, and above all *motionless* . . . There, close to his eyes, those once blue eyes, two stains like bruises could be discerned, these too motionless, perpetually still, or—if more appropriate—*concentrated.*

The thought crept up on him like a snake: Did Kimon have his eyes open underneath; had they remained open? Is that why they had covered him? mainly because of that? It was on account of this, then, that a shudder suddenly passed through him, a horrible suspicion, swift as an arrow, cold and rapid like the passing of a reptile over his exhausted breast.

He took a very deep breath, filled his lungs, and expelled the air through his nostrils shakily and slightly whistling: from looking so much, from looking so intensely for some moments, not only did he suspect that Kimon's concealed eyes were open, icy, but that the cloth over them was moving, that the face underneath was trying—at certain moments—to uncover itself . . . They heard him suddenly coughing, clearing his throat as though he had swallowed some threads or thorns, and one woman stared at him questioningly: "A little water?" she said to him quietly, but he shook his head and tried to concentrate, to drive out those crazy thoughts by moving his gaze away from there. "I won't look at him again," he promised himself, even though he'd never been afraid till now to look at a dead body, that is, he had never avoided standing over or across from a face like that or observing one . . . observing it despite his need to forget it, to not see it . . . But all this today with Kimon was—how might he put it—something more than just a *dead body*: it almost surpassed in terms of chillness and mad-ness even his uncle Elias, who, seated in a chair, with eyes half-open and fists as if they were cracking walnuts, received the last farewells and the terrified gazes of his relatives.

"How much more," he reflected, "are we going to have to witness . . ."

And he noticed for a third or fourth time that from the upright of the door and from other spots, the sister-in-law, Chrysanthe's younger sister, who would now be a little older than Julia, was looking at him — much the same way as he was looking at Kimon. Her eyes half-closed and narrowed, as she raised her head a little, and stared at him with some bitterness, an inexpressible resignation.

"Is she staring at me or am I imagining it?" Julia's father wondered. "It's as though she knows something . . . or thinks that I know something."

But every time that he caught that gaze of hers, she immediately turned it in the direction of the corpse, and her face became clouded again by that familiar — perpetual we could say — despair and devotion. And every time she rushed up to him, if she wasn't there already, knelt beside him (letting her dress be stepped on by all the others), and was the only one who dared, now that there was nothing stopping her, to caress him over the cloth, to draw her fingers over his nose, cheeks, eyes, up and down between his brow and his chin, and to come out with the tenderest of words from her mouth — constantly mentioning, of course, her sister's name: "Chrysanthe, Chrysanthe, Chrysanthe — don't be afraid," she said to him, "It's her hand that's waiting for you . . . waiting for so many years to caress you . . . her hand — no one else's, don't be afraid! . . ."

"She'll go mad if she keeps harping on like that today, her wits will soar into the sky like a sparrow," said one of Kimon's aunts, said it, that is, in the ear of one of her friends, but she was very close to Kimon and the other men and they overheard. In any case, they all felt a kind of insecurity about this woman: a passion that she had nurtured by herself, for some eight years, was emerging from its hiding place at last and encircling the dead man, using as a bridge (still) the name of her sister, of his wife.

Till, eventually, she put her hand among the flowers at the right of his head and they saw her withdrawing it, moving at the same time an edge of the cloth that was covering him.

"Eh, no!" cried one of his aunts. "Not that too today. Stop!"

And she went over, took hold of her hand and hit it.

With the "eh, no!" she had already let the cloth fall back in its place and waited for the aunt, simply pulling the upper part of her body back, like a little girl who has been up to mischief and stands waiting for the customary punishment.

When the aunt hit her on the hand, she put it back on top of the cloth.

"Chrysanthe, Chrysanthe," she started up again, "no one can see that it's only Chrysanthe today, my dearest brother . . . my dear . . . that you don't want to see anything else today, that you don't have any song to sing to us . . . Only Chrysanthe, don't be afraid."

They all felt uncomfortable at her persistence, dizzy, even annoyance, or stifled a chortle—some of the men went out into the hallway to get away from it, some women too to get a breath of air—but in the end they all felt pity for her, reproached her but felt sympathy, just as sometimes you chastise a naughty child so he'll cry more . . . and so you'll feel sorrier for him, love him more.

It was a pity that Kimon hadn't given her any love even of that kind, if only out of pity for such patience and devotion—a pity since even he, there where he had given his own love for the previous two years, had had it returned to him, had had it rejected.

Better, then, Chrysanthe—ambiguously as her sister said it: *only Chrysanthe.*

Eighth Tale

"AN EVIL ANGEL PASSED BY AND THOUGHT IT GOOD TO TOUCH ME"

Julia was hounded by shadows. Even after the news had widely spread concerning the *wolf* in Kimon's head that had made him do away with his own life, not much changed inside her—at most, the shadows that hounded her perhaps slowly acquired the shape of wolves.

She shut herself in a room (at first keeping close watch on the stairs, lest anyone come up and catch her, but then forgetting) and took out from the hem of her dress, from her brassiere or underwear, or from some hidden inside pocket, his letter, that precious piece of paper with its dark words—words that had invisibly cracked open, had expanded and become blurred because of their now permanent contact with something more or less moist, organic. She fondled it, breathed it, rubbed it on her breast devotedly and completely absorbed, turned it to the other side, the side without any writing (which allowed her to read it that way too), and in her hands this inanimate thing acquired a significance, an entity, that no animate thing had—not even he himself when he wrote it to her, as in no way could she imagine him dead—not even his form as a living being, either whole or in part, would consent to stand for a moment before her when, afraid, she sought this . . . All she had, then, to preserve this love and her regrets was this piece of paper—and the deep wells between the lines that had now become a thousand times deeper.

Persa, on the other hand, was the most impressive woman that any of them had set eyes on during those past years, and perhaps during all the previous ones. Tall, regal almost, on the brink of her third youth, with narrow red-brown eyes, strongly outlined cheekbones, and a somewhat hooked nose. There was nothing particularly endearing about her characteristics, in any case, particularly given that she was in the habit of *wearing colors* (colors that matched her eyes, but excessively so: gold and purple), of putting round her neck a triple string of deep-blue pearls, of fixing her bun on the left side of her head and not in the center (and adorning it with a red semi-circular comb), and of hanging from her ears two shiny green earrings in the shape of lightning flashes: two slanting Zs. No other woman of her age—and widowed twice at that—would ever decide to do something like that, but this was Persa, and not only did they have to put up with her, but they also secretly admired her. She was, in other words, just as her daughter Myra had presented her: a *witch*—not a wicked one, but how good no one knew.

What's more, she liked tobacco; whenever she remembered, she would put her hand into a deep pocket and pull out a metal box with worn edges and take from it a tight round cigarette that she had rolled and prepared herself. Usually she would light it with coal from the fire, and it was a whole ritual until she managed to get hold of a piece of coal with the tongs—get hold of it properly—and bring it up to her mouth . . . As she exhaled the first cloud of smoke, everyone else stood back and sighed. And when, occasionally, she was so absorbed that she forgot to flick the ash, one of the little kids would go up to her and nudge her gently, with his eyes fixed on the ash waiting to fall. Persa would smile and flick the ash with the finger of one hand, pushing the child away with her other hand. Sometimes, it was Christoforos himself who went up to her with a brush and pan. "Woman . . . ," he would say, leaning over her: and with the brush he would flick the ash into the pan and then *empty* it in the fire with all the other ash. Of course, there was a note of surprise about his excessive, servile, and stoic concern for her ash . . . But Persa would smile at all this with lips sealed, probably looking to discern something of the things to come in that light eddy of smoke that engulfed them all. None of them had ever seen another woman smoking, but even today when we can see many, not one of them, we believe, surrenders to the fumes as she did: if she weren't called Persa, perhaps we should have to call her Pythia.

Her nails were yellow, deep yellow rather like her eyes, amber—all ten of them: those that the nicotine didn't color, she colored herself with *kna*[1] or plunged into the hot juice from walnut shells. One of her grandfathers was from Circassia, and had come by boat from the Black Sea to the Aegean, but the boat had sailed back without him. So this wanderer—then still young—found dry land on a large island, married one of the local women, and over the years became a wealthy raisin merchant—and cardplayer second to none: he would lose, they say, simply so as not to get bored by the others' losing, and would pile all the winnings—inevitably—next to him. Later, his children would arrive at the Peloponnese while his grandchildren scattered wider afield and also took

1. A kind of yellowish dye from plants.

to the sea. Persephone was his only granddaughter, the daughter of his only daughter, and he always talked to her in the other language, his mother tongue, because he didn't want this to be forgotten. The little girl learned quite a few words, as many, at least, as were necessary so that they didn't have to resort to Greek (she was fourteen when he died), and so many that she still remembered most of them in her own old age and still used them whenever she wanted to say something *strong* without others understanding her.

And apart from the bracelets on her wrists, she also had two round her ankle—perhaps, they said with some acerbity, she had a Gypsy or an Egyptian grandmother, nothing could be ruled out. But apart from anything else, the fact that she was Circassian was enough, both to kindle their imaginations and to justify most of the rest.

This woman with the foreign face and the little yellow nails had married twice. Her first husband had been lost in a storm, and in the hope that he would one day return alive she had lived for another five years with her father-in-law and all his relatives, who didn't like her especially. But neither did she like them—it was a reciprocal tolerance that sustained them, rather like fellow passengers in a crowded carriage. The old man was a *born tyrant*, as Persa always said. When he sat down at the table, no one dared to pick up a fork before he picked up his, and as soon as he put his down, they all had to put their forks down, whether they had filled themselves or not. Persa had often remained with an empty stomach as she couldn't always manage to sit down before the others had finished, since she had three small children who never left her in peace, being little tyrants themselves. Her bones were sticking out from lack of food and that living widowhood, and she was obliged to get up in the night and secretly eat apples, a mere pittance, and whatever else she could find in baskets and on shelves. One night, her father-in-law caught her and almost twisted her arm off. She got away from him, but the next day he got hold of her again—while she was eating black sunflower seeds in the laundry room and looking at the steam from the boiling pot—he held her elbows behind her back and led her to a door with two holes like the huge eyes of an owl that Persa had never seen before. To a family torture chamber, as she would soon realize. There, helped by two of his sons, who liked her about as much as she did them, he untied her long, wavy hair, divided it into two strands, and passed one *strand* through each hole. Then he went behind her, from where you would look at that wretched door, took the two strands and joined them together again in one long, neat braid—a braid down to the very roots of her neck, where her hair grew less and less, where she had no more than two hairs to join with two more. And he left her like that, trapped by her hair, till the next morning.

And that evening, her children came to see her—to see her braid, that is, hanging from the closed door—and primed by the old man asked her, "Will you do it again or won't you?" They went on like parrots, again and again: "Will you do it again or won't you?" "What exactly?" she said, becoming furious, and asked them, "What exactly, you devil's spawn, just like him! Mockingbirds, monkeys!" But they couldn't tell her; they had no idea what their mother's sin was, and they just kept asking her, "Will you do it again or won't you? Will you do it again . . . ?"

Nevertheless, urged on by another voice inside them, they were able, secretly and quickly, to stroke her hanging hair, to tug it in another sense (before the old man came to get them and shut them in another room), and from the other side of the door she could feel that fleeting caress and find a bit of consolation, take courage and continue to move the weight of her body—like lead from so much standing—from one leg to the other, until it grew dark and she became sleepy. But every time she let herself slide and started to nod, the roots of her hair sent pricks of pain through her and forced her to hold her head up again. Those holes were exactly at her height—had they measured her and made them? She could hear the unmoving blood in her legs humming, whistling almost, and wondered just how far this punishment for a mere morsel of food would go. And whenever she moved a little on the spot, thousands of pins and needles racked her body . . . Exhausted, she began to cry out: "Is there no human being in this house? Christian, Muslim, atheist . . . a human being to untie me . . . to cut my hair with scissors—I'll make a gift of it, let him cut it and take it! . . . Is there no human being in this damnable house? A rat to gnaw it and release me . . ."

She had no need to worry—the next morning, her father-in-law came and cut it with a saw! . . . "Eh, yes," was how Persa swore wearily all her life: when day finally broke, when a little daylight finally entered that dungeon, someone came behind the door, and she heard a saw going back and forth against the thick wooden panel, almost against her back. She didn't understand at first—she, who had felt that forbidden and fleeting caress from her children on the hair, was now asking herself what he was doing with an entire saw behind her back . . . When she began to realize that the saw was going back and forth on her braid, close to the two holes, two fingers' breadth away from her neck, she almost fainted and was about to fall. But from behind he pulled her back—he wasn't done yet. When he was done, Persa collapsed to the floor without any hair. Then the door opened and she saw the old man in the full light of day throwing the braid into the air and kicking it towards her: a lifeless fragrant *kitten* fell onto her face and she remembered no more.

After this, she would have to keep her patience for a few more days: the following week, an unknown rider brought them a letter with the news that her husband was long dead, and that same night Persa took all she had, her children too, and left. Having learned, meanwhile, that all the other women in the house (the tyrant's wife, his daughters, his daughters-in-law) had at some time passed through that ordeal with the door and its two holes . . . For the shorter women, there was a stool—there were no taller ones. And instead of abandoning him and leaving one by one, they stayed with him and partook of the bread of misfortune. She didn't envy them: let them envy her.

Her second husband was several years older than she, but he, too, had a father. Fortunately, however, while the other one had been an *old vulture*, this one was just *old:* a meek and lovable man, quieter even than his own shadow, forbearing, quiet-spoken . . . who had a chronic problem with his hands—total ankylosis—which prevented him from opening his fingers: he kept them always tightly closed with his thumb inside, and naturally, being in essence without fingers, only with great difficulty could he grip his fork or spoon: someone had to feed him. Persa confirmed once again that life was strange and unpredictable: it had had one man saw her hair off because without his permission she had eaten a wizened apple, a pittance, and it had put another man without fingers in front of her who waited to eat a bite of food from her hand! Life is certainly strange, and it was only through its unpredictable *appetites* that it brought some balance and respite . . . So she generously undertook to feed her second father-in-law (in exchange for a wealth of blessings each time), since her two sisters-in-law, the wives of the old man's younger sons, said that they had grown tired of feeding and taking care of a *child* like that. They said it with not a little grievance as they hadn't acquired children of their own, neither the one nor the other, and most probably—they intimated—it was not their fault. But the old man, too, felt aggrieved that he had lived for so many years without being blessed with a grandchild. "Just one," he found the courage to say to his new daughter-in-law one day; "let me see just one grandchild, and I'll die in peace. Let me see him come to me . . . eh! and rest his little face here!" and he showed his stiffened thumbs or leaned forward and rested his own face there, to show her how much he wanted it—how much he wanted it, without it having happened.

To console him a little, Persa reminded him that she had brought three children to his house—albeit from another family: "They may not be actual grandchildren of yours," she told him, "but if you want a grandchild so much, think of these as your grandchildren." "That's how I think of them," he said to her, "but, eh, I'd still like another, one with my own blood, one . . . eh! who would come and rest his face *here!* . . . Let me just see that before I close my eyes." "You'll see it," Persa reassured him, "why do you think I came here? Why do you think I married your son?" "Ahh," exclaimed the old man, without much hope, "when my two younger sons haven't given me grandchildren, and the son you married . . . who's well on in years now . . . I don't think so, no I don't think so." "If we put a wager on it, you'll lose," Persa said to him, taking care, however, not to shake his hand on it.

And in fact, before she too was well on in years, she provided that sweet old man with not just one but four grandchildren. One of these was Myra. And Persa taught them when they were still small to go and rest their cheeks on their old granddad's stiffened fingers and thereby give him the greatest of happiness . . . They would kneel down in front of him as if adopting a pose in front of a mirror or as if resting their little necks on an altar so that someone might paint them—what we mean is that their action wasn't always spontaneous. But the old man, half-blind on top of everything else, didn't notice this; his joy was immeasurable. And this joy, rather than closing his eyes, enabled him to go on living a good few years more. So many that Persa's life with him—as with her first father-in-law—proved to be longer than with her second husband: he died in his bed a few months before the fourth child was born.

Persa left this house too when the old man died. And when her own children grew up and went their own ways, she went to live with one of her brothers.

After all this, for her to have a third husband without a father seemed almost unthinkable. "What can we do," Christoforos said to her; "you came after I'd lost my father . . . If we'd met ten years earlier, I'd have been able to introduce you to my father's father as well!"

Even so; Persa found so much more in that household that the *lack* of a father-in-law was soon put behind her.

Their wedding took place in one of the rooms in the big house, quietly and without fuss, without guests and merriment, even without all his children being present. Christoforos had asked a young priest to come, without telling him exactly who was getting married. When he arrived with his official vestments (besides, most weddings at that time took place at home), the host welcomed him, took him up the main staircase, pushed him into the room, pointed to Persa, his sister Polyxeni, his adopted sister Lily, his soon-to-be-granddaughter Myra, a cousin of his called Aspasia, and two of his daughters-in-law ("The seven fates who are waiting," he said to him), and—for some time—things remained like that . . . up in the air: with the two men talking about all things under the sun, and the seven fates waiting in silence.

"Well then," said the priest at last, clearing his throat, "so . . . where's the bride-and groom-to-be?"

"The bride and groom, father, are me and her," Christoforos said to him, pointing to Persa, blooming in her everyday clothes and *in fine fettle*, it has to be said, for all her years.

The young cleric was dumbstruck and stared at her hanging green earrings as he might the horns of a forest demon.

"Of course . . . forgive me . . . I hadn't understood," he mumbled, and started to prepare whatever was necessary for the wedding ceremony.

Meanwhile, the door behind them opened and two or three scowling men came in, each ostentatiously carrying an infant in his arms: they were the groom's sons with some of his most recent grandchildren.

So this was the woman who was going to succeed Eftha, who herself had succeeded Petroula, in that indescribable house. There were times when even Christoforos himself thought it incredible, as though it were happening in a dream-that-was-weakly-trying-to-make-him-accept-that-it-wasn't-a-dream . . . During the ceremony, he recalled some prophetic words spoken *then* by Kimon: "If you were to get married again," he had said, "you'd be . . . sixty-five, wouldn't you?" Words that he had uttered like that, without much thought—a cursory reply to something that Christoforos had said to him . . . When had that happened? That *he* had said *then* as though it were something in the distant past, long gone, whereas he only then realized how recent it had all been (not even two months back), and he felt like flapping his tongue like an oar, or leaping like a frog here and there: in that short period of time, Kimon had hanged himself and he had remarried! . . . No one ever went short of the unexpected.

It goes without saying that at first almost all his children more than once pulled a face at that marriage, showing that they didn't consider it necessary. Some of his sons swore never to speak to him again just as before, never to waste a smile on him or his new wife. "Nothing is as it was anymore," one of them said, scowling (and melodramatically), in the same way that he might have been stressing the difference between heaven and hell, and one of his daughters from his first marriage, Georgiana, added: "I feel like crying, but I can't, the tears won't come. I forgave you for the second marriage, but not for the third . . . I swear it: not the third!" At thirteen years old, she had seen another woman take the place of her mother in that house, and this was something she couldn't forget—whatever had happened since, it was something she couldn't forget. She had simply got used to it in time, she had *accepted* it at any rate—taking into account her other brothers and sisters, who, motherless from such an early age, were in need of motherly or at least stepmotherly care. But now, at forty-five, for her to see a third woman take her mother's place, this really was too much and entrenched her in the bitterest intolerance . . . "I'll never forgive you for this!" she said to him brusquely whenever she saw him without Persa, and when she did see him with her, she raised her hand—without any peace offering in it—and walked past them.

Except that she hadn't reckoned on the fact that time was at work always and concerning all. And that such intransigent attitudes—particularly when there is no deeper motive, actual hatred or spite—fade without as much as asking us . . . Besides, Persa, clever rather than particularly good-natured, knew how to take the side of the *wronged* children whenever they disagreed or quarreled with their father, something which mollified them, duly relieved them—without really upsetting her husband or making an adversary of him. Because being a mother is a natural state: a bit like the birds that sing in the trees. But being a step-mother—and especially during those difficult years—required craft and versa-tility, and this is something that Persa seemed to know very well. Better, it has to be said, than Eftha, who was always well-intentioned, but always more sus-ceptible to *discrimination*.

And we should also remember that Persa hadn't brought her own children from previous marriages into this household (apart from Myra, who was already there but living in another house), and this undoubtedly eased the situation right from the beginning, or at least didn't make it any worse.

In the same summer, a little before that unexpected though otherwise in-evitable wedding, Febronia gave birth to Thomas, the child with the disparate eyes, and to his twin sister, Safi-Lisafi. Now the household as well as the wider circle had a new *event* with which to concern themselves—something which, moreover, brought to the fore an older event: namely, who had beaten Lily on the second day of the Carnival? She had been beaten by another mute—her very own brother.

A mute story this with mute developments that was very difficult for anyone else to follow . . .

Her brother, a little older than Lily, was called Gabe (Gabriel), and he had been taken in by another family after being orphaned—he worked as a shep-herd. But the most *difficult* thing about Gabe—both for himself and for us—was that he had been born with deep wrinkles on his face, wrinkles that didn't fade with the passing of the years, while, in addition to this, his body didn't age, didn't keep up with the passing of the years . . . He wasn't a dwarf: you can't call a child with normal dimensions a dwarf, but when these dimensions remain unchanged for whole decades, then, alas, you're dealing with a rather sad freak of nature.

This, then, was Gabe: a deaf-mute with the face of an old man and the body of a child, and, what's more, with the muscular strength of a giant—which he normally didn't need to use: all he had to do was to open his mouth to put even wolves to flight . . . That *ououou* of Gabe, they said, that *ououou*, was enough to make even the moon shudder.

(We can't say whether those times *favored* such people—not that there are not such people today, but we don't see them, or hear them, because they are shut away in asylums, herded behind walls—or whether it's some tormenting need of ours that draws us every so often to times, tales, and people who open their mouths and, *without fail*, invoke the abyss . . . May we be forgiven. And let it be an occasion for asking ourselves if, in fact, the act of writing, manifold in its voices and ways, is not perhaps a tacit *plea* in the course of time.)

Gabe—since the time has come to talk about him—didn't come down often into the company of people: from a young age (if, that is, his age had such stages), he had become used to living in the hills, in the clear air, together with a fair number of sheep that followed him, or that he followed, and three dogs that surrounded him, their tongues hanging from their mouths and faithful unto death. His boss had given him a flute and told him to do whatever he saw the other shepherds doing with their flutes. So Gabe would take it out of his knapsack and put it to his mouth with a tragicomic passion, after stopping every so often to gaze at it with tremendous interest . . . But from then on, it ceased to concern him: unable to hear what his lips and fingers were doing—anything at all. Whenever Lily happened to see him playing the flute (given that she, too, could hear nothing), she burst into laughter and ran, and he would chase after her, yelling and pelting her with stones, or would send his dogs to bring her back . . . This is how they would express their love and solidarity as brother and sister.

In winter, he would come down for a while, but also sporadically throughout the year they would see him now and again among them. His master's old mother would take care of him; she was sorry for him but also afraid of him, and in her house he had his own bed, underneath which was a pile of old children's clothes (his permanent clothes), with darned socks and woolen caps. Nevertheless, Christoforos—since Gabe's parents had once worked on his family estate—one day asked Zacharias to make a regular suit for the mute: for him to wear whenever he came down from the hills.

That was it. From that day, he came down much more often, went to his bed, changed his clothes and headed for the marketplace. Nothing either in his build or his gait recalled a human being, a child, or an old man—nothing. And what we referred to as *the face of an old man* and *the body of a child* is but a manner of speaking—we had to describe him in some way. Besides, his face was truly wrinkled and his body small, *stunted*; but Gabe was also much more that no description can do justice to.

And so, puffing and wheezing, he would head for the marketplace, waving his arms as though he had no joints in them and dragging his legs like dogs do when their ribs have been broken, and with an amazingly changeable range of grimaces from his narrow forehead to his lean chin, grimaces that had the fluidity of sand when tunneled underneath by some reptile or when swept by the wind, and no one knew where they were directed or what caused them. And suddenly the surprise: he was able, instead of going through a gate, to take a run and leap over it, passing like an arc to the other side, or, if you were especially friendly towards him (usually out of fear), he was able, taking hold of your hand, to do half a dozen somersaults in the air. And besides, his usual handshake, whenever he wanted to honor someone with this, always ended in a jumble of somersaults, shrieking, and other such joys and scares.

If he were to see a familiar house, or someone who seemed familiar to him, it was rare for him to walk on by: he would go inside with remarkable ease, and if he found women knitting socks, he would push in among their needles, pull them one by one from the knitting, throw them aside and begin to wildly unravel (he had a mania for socks) till he himself was all wrapped up in a mesh of threads—and then began the devastation and the real highhandedness that terrified the women . . . And if they didn't dare resist him or take hold of him, as you might think, and throw him like a cat down the steps, it was because none of them knew *how* Gabe saw things: a YES or NO on their part might move him, break his heart, and leave him in a heap of tears at their feet, or it might also provoke far worse.

All this, we should recall, had started to happen regularly and even more regularly from the time he had had the suit tailored for him—previously Gabe would come down from the hills much less frequently, and when he did he preferred to stay home, do odd jobs, and sit quietly somewhere and (with that surge of odd grimaces and spasms on his scrawny face) watch the children playing a little way off or simply the passing of a cow. Or he might give his entire attention to a procession of ants: in truth, this might keep him busy for hours, all hell might break loose around him, but he would continue, as if hypnotized, to watch that black undulating *line* on the ground . . . Of course he would go farther afield, as far even as the marketplace, but not for very long, just long enough for people to remember him in order to forget him again.

But from the time that he had had that garment tailored for his body, Gabe began to feel, it seems, somewhat on a par with everyone else and to seek relations that till then had not interested him. And so every now and again he would leave his sheep to his dogs and to another adopted boy and come to see them and be seen by them . . . At the same time, he started to reveal his own hidden talents, such as those incredible somersaults, his *arcs* over gates and dividing walls, his crazy grunting, and even more that bloodcurdling *ououou!* . . . And at first they all seemed to be getting on well with him, to be in need of such a presence, and particularly—it goes without saying—of its comic side. So they would call him into the cafeneion and treat him to thick, sweet coffee, Turkish delight, and heady *tintoura*[2] only to see him down everything in the wink of an eye, grimacing uncontrollably and gesticulating, and then doing whatever they asked of him, whatever provoked the loudest and most heartrending laughter.

There was no one to match him when it came to how tortoises chase each other in the mating season—in this even the tortoises themselves would stop to watch him: he would put his sack over his head and crawl on all fours under the tables, getting between the legs of the customers and the chair legs, or he would even go outside the cafeneion, tumble down the few steps and come back, and all this with the speed of a lizard, or, at least, a lizard with a shell on its back, and coming out with those high, piercing shrieks that the male tortoises make when they are chasing the difficult females among the bushes or on bumpy hill-sides (he would chase whatever they threw on the floor—and whenever he got close to it, they would kick it farther away), shrieks that very much recalled the cries of a newborn baby when it's in pain or hungry, while the breathless racing, the clashing of shells, and the way they ignore obstacles and dangers in order to reach their goal do not very much recall what we know of the slow and cautious tortoises . . .

"What's happening, for heaven's sake!" some people would ask, not of course about the tortoises, but about the deaf-mute impersonating them: "He can't hear anything, so how does he know what sound they make when they're *crawl-ing*—or make *that* particular sound? He could come out with . . . I don't know, *aaa-ououou*, whatever he feels like, something completely unconnected . . ."

2. A kind of liqueur, fortified and slightly *colored*.

But he came out with those particular wails, shrieks that were fine like hair and loud like *crescendos*, which only the tortoises let out in spring when they fight to the death for the perpetuation of their species.

"Nature has many secrets," others would reply, unable to say anything more. And they would stare at Gabe with a note of fear as he crawled as if cut in two by the legs of one and the knees of another and waited for the second round of treats in order to do even more tricks for them.

In the end, these pitiful spectacles with the deaf-mute crawling around the cafeneion came to recall strange rites, *chthonic* ones, more or less.

A little later, however, came the first improprieties: one day he got hold of and beat a little girl before a hundred people. Just when no one was expecting it. Here is what happened: There was a wedding in one of the houses, in the foothills of the mountain, and they had put tables outside for the feast. A little girl, six or seven years old, perhaps slightly older, kept going up to her parents, grabbing a piece of meat from their plates, and running off with an arrogant expression, supposedly to eat it on her own. Of course, she wasn't really hungry after so many morsels that she had already downed, but she did it *anyway*, and with that expression, till someone would have enough of her and put her in her place, or rather till the other kids, the shyer ones farther away who had surrounded her and were watching her mouth, would grow jealous of her. One of these was Gabe . . . The little girl returned his longing and languorous looks with a good deal of spite, trying also to imitate (though extremely clumsily and humiliatingly) his endless grimaces, while other children of her age wouldn't think of looking at them. And after she had extended her tongue and licked the meat all over—focusing her eyes on the tip of her nose so she could watch herself—she then threw it down, trod on it, spat on it, said "boo!" to him like a bogeyman, and went, ever more haughty, arrogant, imprudent, and inelegant, to snatch another morsel from her parents' plate . . . In short, she was becoming unbearable for all the other children, even for some of the adults, who were watching her from the other tables or from the fences a little way off, but she was the groom's only niece and the next day would be a bridesmaid and so was not lacking in boldness.

But when she returned once too often to the place where the deaf-mute and the other kids were, carrying this time a whole rabbit's head in her fingers, Gabe grabbed hold of her, put her between his legs and in the space of a few seconds—before the others realized what was happening and the music stopped—he had beat her black and blue and left her to them.

Explaining himself that same evening at Christoforos's house (where he had taken refuge and Lily was questioning him in a cellar), he said that he couldn't stomach the little girl, that she was loathsome and greedy, a real little turd, and that's why he'd hit her—whatever they couldn't understand directly from his mouth, Lily, his sister, would translate for them. Naturally, Christoforos gave him a dressing-down, told him that this wasn't acceptable behavior, heaven help us if we beat everyone we couldn't stomach black and blue, that if he handed him over to her parents, they would have him thrown into a cell full of rats; and after he had put the fear of God into him as best as he could and saw him wiping his eyes on his sister's apron, he helped him get away back into the hills, asked his master to keep a more watchful eye on him from then on, and not allow him to come down, and then he went to sort things out with the parents of the little girl, since a certain amount of the responsibility for what had happened (because of the suit he had had made for him) rested with him.

Shortly afterwards, his partial ward was accused of having beat another little girl. And this was because, he said, he had seen her pulling out one of her teeth after loosening it with her tongue, then wrapping it in a piece of bread, and throwing it on the roof tiles! . . . He found it outrageous. He had gone up to her and asked her, grimacing profusely, whether, perhaps, she wanted him to climb up and bring her tooth back, but she—on seeing him in front of her—began screaming and calling for help. And this had made him see red.

And shortly after this, he had stolen an old woman's savings, throwing the gold sovereigns into a trough (at least they recovered them) while he made boats of the paper money and sailed them on the surface of the water simply to pass the time—and when he had got bored, he had jumped up onto the lip and started to urinate on them to sink them . . . That's when they caught him.

One day Christoforos was obliged, secretly in the inn, to strip him of his clothes—he cringed at the sight of that stumpy, disfigured body—taking back his new clothes (which, of course, had become soiled and blackened long ago, yet still remained his *other* clothes, his *best* ones) and clothe him again in the old ones, those rags he wore in the mountains, in the hope that this would dampen his appetite for coming down so often.

But Gabe had now learned the path and kept coming (more often at night now) and complained to his sister Lily that that devil, her false brother, had stolen back the clothes that he had given him! But he would get his revenge.

The following New Year, the deaf-mute went out to sing the traditional carols. He did it every year, it wasn't anything new. He went on his own to as many houses as he could, coming out with his inarticulate and indescribable cries and banging on the closed gates with hands and feet. And if someone inside didn't open to give him a few dried figs or damsons, a breadroll or a carob, Gabe would thump on the doors till the hinges creaked and bent. There were no carols more nightmarish than his—or more destructive. Once he took a door panel away with him, lifting it from its hinges and putting it on his back; he paraded it through the streets till daylight, and whoever saw him wondered who was being buried at that time of day: they took it for a coffin lid . . . Which is why most people now waited for him behind the gate and when they heard him leave the neighbor's and come in the direction of their house would open the gate before he raised his foot and give him what they had to give him—so that he began going round with a cart because he was unable to carry so many treats in his hands. And when the other children woke up and went round to sing the carols, he had already finished and was on his way back to the hills.

But that particular New Year, full of spite at having been deprived of his best clothes, he went out with a hatchet for company—in the blackest hour of night, much earlier than he normally had in previous years. And he passed in front of a host of front gates without even turning to look at them, without anyone getting wind of him, before stopping in front of Christoforos's gate and starting to try out his sharp hatchet on it . . . Some people woke up at first light, but couldn't understand what was happening—their minds didn't turn to Gabe, they thought that some madman had decided to get up early to cut wood in the early hours—and they went back to sleep. Besides, the wind was blowing and Lily couldn't hear anything in any case—were a lightning bolt to land beside her, she would have been blinded without hearing anything. As for Christoforos, he happened to be sleeping in the inn that night: the blows of the hatchet reached his ears like the distant barking of a dog when we are turning over . . . before being stifled again languidly in our sleep.

And yet, Lily, who was in the house, woke up and got out of bed on a hunch . . . Of course, she could hear nothing of what everyone else could hear, but also nothing of what everyone else couldn't hear . . . She wrapped herself in a cape, rubbed a little spittle on her eyes to open them, and quickly went downstairs. She passed through the porch, tripped on a piece of wood sticking out of the loom, went out into the yard, stumbled again on a millstone, and then, finally— between the wind pushing her back and the light of the moon that was pulling her to see—she discerned just ahead of her that stumpy monster her brother, who was struggling to get his head through a wide rent in the wooden gate, having already managed to get his right leg through and the hand holding the hatchet. *He's not going to claw his way in like that* was the thought that passed through her mind, but the hatchet scared her, made her quickly intuit what she had no time to understand. And coming up from the side so that he wouldn't see her, hugging the wall of the yard with her back, she arrived at the front gate, put her hand under his foot, and with a well-gauged, quick spiral movement, tipped him back outside—after first having taken care to relieve him of the hatchet. His squeals, when he found himself like a discarded octopus on the street, were not heard by her, of course. Then she opened the door properly, took hold of him before he could get away from her, and made him follow her to the ruins, to the wild fig tree. And there, with countless gestures and signs, with the moon's silver dust shining every so often between her mouth and her teeth, began asking him what on earth he was up to without consulting her, and she didn't stop until daybreak (and some window shutters began to be opened), didn't stop reproving him and sweet-talking him at the same time—mainly sweet-talking him.

Before midday, Christoforos had been forced to return his clothes to him, and he spent all the rest of the day cursing as he repaired the door that was smashed to *smithereens.*

Gabe calmed down for a long time, bothered no one, and they just about lost him again, just about missed him.

His relationship with his mute sister, his only sister, was filled with tenderness, reciprocal promises for something better, and, of course, reciprocal understanding, since, in addition to their common blood, they were also united by the common source of their speechlessness. When both of them were younger, children not like all the other children, and Gabe would occasionally come down from the hills, Georgiana, Christoforos's mother, would go and ask his master's mother to let him come and sleep at her house for a night, to eat with them, with his sister . . . She would let him, and Georgiana would take the little Gabe, ugly like a *trampled mushroom,* by the hand and bring him to his younger and unimaginably cute sister, Lily . . . The brother and sister smelled each other at first like animals, like two mammals that were kept apart and occasionally allowed to come into contact: they were like wolf cubs without their mother, brought up among lambs or humans, but not always tame, not completely . . . And then, passing into another mode of communication, they exchanged impressions and ins and outs as if they were describing miracles, real miracles that the ears of all the others round about were unable to grasp: if he praised her beauty, she was entranced by his ugliness—who knows, some such thing.

"Anyone would envy them seeing them together, when they *talk!*" Georgiana said to everyone.

And she put them to sleep in the same bed, putting between them, however, a long, thick, red pillow. But the following morning, she would see them making odd signs to each other: Lily showing four fingers and Gabe hitting them and showing eight of his own, then Lily pulling at his forelock and accusing him because *three of them were worthless*—and such things that no one understood what they referred to.

Till one evening, after putting them to bed, instead of going straight to bed herself Georgiana remained and hid under their bed to see what it was they got up to. And she saw nothing. But she heard! . . . "What?" the others asked her the next day. "Leave it be," she said to them. "What?" they asked again. "Leave it be," she said again. "Are you going to tell us what *or* we won't ask you again?" they said, eventually threatening her. And Georgiana, rather than have to suffer their indifference, preferred to share her secret: "*Cannon fire*, that's what! The kind that you have to be exceptionally well-equipped for . . . Like my father once upon a time when we thought he'd burst his pants . . . if we were anywhere near, we looked to the ground!"

She came out with it and the others burst into laughter, puffing up and down like seagulls from all their cackling (they truly found it exceptionally funny— especially after the seriousness they had imagined), yet the impoverished woman still couldn't believe it: two little children, two deaf-mutes, brother and sister, doing things like that! . . . Where had they learned such things? Where had they come up with it? And how did the one hear the other, as their ears were full of *cotton-wool? Boom-boom*, the place where her curiosity had led her to hide was suddenly not big enough for her, she couldn't even cross herself, while the two little farters above were coming out in spots from all their laughter and were making a rocker of the bed. "Lord above!" she thought (and had a hard time not to reveal herself). "What doesn't come out of their mouths comes out elsewhere! And do they even hear what I hear, or just sense it and amuse them-selves like that?"

And before the two of them fell asleep on the bed above so that she could escape from her stifling hiding place, she understood what they did: that they *caught* the warm smelly air in their hands so it wouldn't get away . . . and that when Gabe had exhausted his natural resources, he would begin his chicanery by squeezing his mouth in his hands or spitting on his hands and rubbing them in his armpits or in the joint behind his knees, so producing exceptionally loud sounds (albeit without any smell), which made him laugh even more and try to get his sister to laugh too, but she was not going to consent to that kind of thing. She made him move over and put the pillow back between them, something that meant in their nighttime language *ceasefire*.

This and more of the same is what the two of them would get up to when they were still small—innocent creatures, as we might say.

As they grew up, they no longer had the privilege of sleeping in the same bed whenever they met. But when he was late in coming, Lily would go and find him in the hills, and then incomprehensible *bucolic idylls* would take place: some had seen them, they said, sitting together on a ridge or on a small rock and kissing on the mouth without the slightest movement, or pretending to kiss and then turning away from each other and spitting! Spitting, in fact, over and over again, as though they were erasing all and everything, then wiping their mouths and once again joining their lips together, before spitting again and so on and so forth, while a little way off the sheep grazed and the dogs lazed.

And it wasn't so much the kissing or the spitting that left them aghast (those, that is, who were secretly watching) as the fact that a pretty albeit mute girl like Lily could, with her lips, touch the lips of a hobgoblin, even if he was her brother! This was what they would find incomprehensible, they would have to be reborn in order to understand it.

Meanwhile, however, *this* emboldened them, and they began trying to get Lily alone for their own purposes, putting their hands on her as though it were something entirely natural. But Lily was also bold enough to turn away from all the other mouths and slip like an eel from their arms. Besides, more than anyone else, and naturally more than her brother, she liked her adopted brother . . .

We already know some of what follows: when her adopted brother refused her in favor of another foster daughter, Lily found consolation in the little obedient children. And when she lost these or grew tired of them, they all learned one day that Lily had become a midwife.

But how the relationship between the deaf-and-dumb brother and sister had thenceforth developed, no one knew or was particularly concerned about. All they happened to see was that she would protect him whenever necessary, hide him or do whatever she could for him—as in the time with the hatchet—in order to placate his occasional yet always dangerous bouts of anger: she knew, they said, from herself.

And we come to that summery, sunny day when Febronia, not wanting to wait with folded arms for one more childbirth, took a broom with a long wooden handle and swept some scattered hay in the yard towards the barn—so it wouldn't get blown away by the wind and the animals could eat at least. That was the moment that a woman from one of the neighboring houses chose to come and complain about the hullabaloo being made by her children and stepchildren.

"I don't know whether you've spoiled them or you just don't care about them," she said to Febronia, waving her arms in the air, "and they come and give ideas to my own children and climb up the fig tree and jump into my house—through a window where there was once a screen so that not even a fly got in!—and they turn my cupboards inside out! Whatever I've hidden, I can't ever find again! And especially that one there, your grandson!... Do you hear me? Before, my own children were quiet, really quiet—I'd beg them to get up to some mischief, but they didn't! But since they met your kids, they've gone from bad to worse. Put a rein on them, I'm telling you, put a rein on them . . . You don't have any cupboards, and they come like mice burrowing into mine . . . All right?"

"My father-in-law was right," Febronia thought to herself, "you can get by with a bad year, but not with a bad neighbor . . ." And she swallowed her anger by sweeping away the hay with more and more care and with the hay the other woman's words, while those *fingers* contorted angrily behind her and cast dark, giant shadows in first one place then the other . . . "She'll go on, go on," she thought, "and get tired."

But the other woman got more steamed up instead of getting tired and followed her about the yard, waving her arms more and more excitedly.

"Otherwise, I'll tell my husband, and my husband doesn't talk with his mouth like me, he talks with his hand, with the holy rod, understand? And your kids are asking for it . . . Do you hear what I'm saying or don't you give a hoot?"

"I hear you," Febronia turned and said to her, "but it's summer and there's work to do. Why don't you come quarrel in the winter, when we're sitting around with nothing to pass the time?"

As she said this, she stumbled, and went to sit down on a bench nearby. She let the broom fall to the ground, and her face became distorted.

The other woman was momentarily taken aback with her arms suspended in the air.

"Did you sit down so that we can quarrel?" she asked hesitantly.

"No, so I can give birth," Febronia said *jokingly* and moved her fingers strangely, as though the knuckles had moved, as though she didn't know where so many fingers had come from . . .

Shortly afterwards, she went to lie down on her own in one of the upstairs rooms, supine on the narrow bed that had seen more labors than any other, and all the women who happened to be in the house began preparing cloths and hot water, while the woman who had come to quarrel was now mopping her brow and telling her to hold on till they could send for Lily, who knew more about these things.

■

They found Lily, but she couldn't find her bag with her instruments. We should note that since they had pulled her half-dead from the ditch near the school Lily had not been to help any woman in her time of labor. And the women themselves hesitated to call her after what had happened. At first she was completely powerless, weak-willed and terrified, didn't recall her old self at all, didn't appear to remember even the most familiar things around her. But even when Persa had come and stopped that constant nosebleed, Lily, though starting to recover, continued to keep a distance from the events around her, and in vain the others attempted to help her return to her old ways—even to some of the *bad* ones: they would send some of the little children to go and sit with her, to caress her knees, to tickle her feet or play *this little piggy went to market* on her fingers . . . But despite all this, Lily's eyes livened up very little, whereas in the past she would have tingled with pleasure.

Now Christoforos himself came (with Persa behind him) to tell her that she had to go upstairs to help Febronia, who was about to give birth—all right when it came to other women, he said, but when it was a member of the family, how could she refuse. Lily got up for his sake and went to the corner where she always put her bag, beneath a wooden couch that was fixed to the wall. But it wasn't there, and instead of looking for it elsewhere—turning the house upside-down as she would have done under other circumstances—her eyes darkened incredibly from her rage and surprise as she recalled (or who knows what) *where* her bag was, *who* had taken it from her, and *when*, and this immediately turned her into a wildcat, and she began to howl, to thrash about and gasp, as though she was the one in labor and not the woman upstairs.

Christoforos realized that Lily's spring hibernation was at an end, that the moment of revelation had arrived: the disappearance of the bag with her instruments made her *speak*—what, that is, his own pains, efforts, and pleading hadn't succeeded in doing up till then, since back in March. It was as if that bag, its disappearance, suddenly cost her more than the beating itself . . . Unless it had all been covered by a veil, as it's said happens sometimes in such cases, and now, with the loss of the bag—which, it should be noted, was for Lily what the inn was for him—the veil had been removed. And she pointed, coming out with inarticulate groans, to the mountain, and then put her finger in her mouth, deep inside till it touched the roof, and then turned it again toward the mountain, and again put it into her mouth: *The one like me, my brother, the mute, he's the one who took it! . . . He's the one who hit me and took the bag! . . .*

Christoforos swallowed his tongue: her brother was the one person he hadn't thought of.

He sent three of his sons up the mountain, and by evening they had returned with Gabe tied to a horse. They had found the bag with the instruments hidden under some fleeces and twigs in the sheepfold. So the *culprit* had been found, together with the *evidence*.

And yet nothing had become clear as to *why* he had beaten his sister like that . . . She had already told them the story half a dozen times: on the first day of the Carnival, when it was still morning, someone had come and asked her to go with him to Mavra Nera (a neighboring village) to help his wife give birth. She got her bag, made sure she had with her the amulet that Eftha had once given her when she had begun her work, got onto his horse, and went, and if—she said—no one saw her as she was leaving, it wasn't her fault: the house was empty, they were all out in the streets with the bells, and besides—we might add—it wouldn't have been the first time that Lily had gone out on a job without anyone noticing. In fact, sometimes she would take her bag and go out into the streets and the neighborhoods without anyone having called her—just like the itinerant tinkers and peddlers: she would ring a bell, one of the tools of her trade, and ask the women who came to their windows whether they needed her or whether they might need her before long . . . So she had gone that day to Mavra Nera, had spent all night there with the woman, who let out a sigh and gave birth to a plump little baby with the first light of day, and once everything was in order— after, that is, they had fed her and paid her—Lily again got onto the horse and returned, accompanied by the same man, to her own village.

When they arrived close to the school, which as we know was on the outskirts of the village in the fields, he left her in order to be home, he said, before it got dark, but in fact it was because it was the first time that he had become a father and he was impatient to set eyes again on his new offspring.

In any case, Lily too was pleased to be able to walk a bit after finishing with a delivery—she was like anyone who does creative work and, pleased with the fruit of the day's toil, goes outside to rejoice in it mentally, while walking, preferably as the sun is going down.

But while she was walking without hearing either the bells or the songs that were ringing in the air in a wide radius, she saw her brother a little way off on the side of a rise, caught up, like a badly tied bundle, in some dry, tangled roots . . . And a horde of unripe red apples that he had stolen from some apple trees farther on and stuffed in his knapsack were gleefully rolling ahead of him and waiting for him . . . When the hapless fellow finally freed himself from the roots, he went and slipped down good and proper beside the apples.

Lily laughed her heart out. She went up to him, rollicking with laughter, and began to wipe the dirt from his clothes and explain to him with her hands and her stick that now it would be much harder for him to gather them up again one by one from where they had scattered and rolled (the place was full of bushes and ditches) than it had been for him to climb the trees and steal them in the first place! . . . She simply wanted to tease him, to make him laugh too at his mishap, to laugh with him, and then she would help him pick up the apples.

But he was offended by her gestures and became angry, very angry—there's a proverb which goes *If you weren't born deaf and dumb, you've no idea from where anger can come*—and his anger came in the shape of a thick branch . . . Her laughter must have stopped very abruptly.

Every time she reached this point in her narration, Lily would put her fingers to her brow and bow her head slightly: *All this on my brow,* she meant, and at the same time it was a kind of oath concerning the truth of her words. If Eftha had been alive and had brought her Bible, she would have put them on that.

But Gabe, tied to a chair now, just as previously he had been tied to the horse, so as not to be able to get away from them, watched her relating all this and his face contorted with the most disagreeable and unappeased grimaces— *grimmifaces*, as they called them. He denied all that his sister claimed; to be exact, he denied everything, and his grimaces were an attempt to say that he had no connection whatsoever with all these fairy tales, that he had found the bag somewhere and had taken it with him into the hills to see what was inside it—he didn't know whose it was or what the things inside were used for. But he wasn't able for long to withstand Christoforos's pressure and threats (who knows what kind of threats), and he eventually admitted that yes, he was the one who had beaten his sister that day—but not because of the apples.

"Then why?" they asked him.

Gabe let out two cries of lamentation, untied the rope binding him with amazing speed and power, and hid his scrawny face in his breast, covering it with his two short, sturdy arms—a strange mass so that you couldn't see where his neck ended and his feet began.

The others shook him: "Why? Why?"—till they realized that he was crying silently and despondently. They let him cry for a while like that, not knowing themselves what to think. Then they gently tugged at his hands, gave him a handkerchief to wipe his eyes, and then heard his version of the story—much shorter and much more startling than hers: because, he said, she wouldn't let him get married to another deaf-mute!

They couldn't understand anything. It's not easy for a brother and sister to arrive at such a moment, not easy and not pleasant, but even more so when they also happen to be deaf and dumb—and if someone else deaf and dumb happens to come between them—then it's bedlam . . . Who was this other deaf-mute?

No one! Lily tried to convince them. *With a face like that, like a trampled mushroom, like a squashed snail, like an empty walnut shell, would any woman look twice at him? Don't make me laugh! I'm his own sister, and I have to take a deep breath before I can bring myself to face that midget! . . . It's his witless mind—as he gets older—that's filling with stuff and nonsense. Let him say what he wants, don't take any notice of him . . .*

And yet Gabe insisted, with the most despondent and horrid contortions, that for years he had been in love with a woman who was also a deaf-mute, but his sister wouldn't allow it, would go to the woman and slander him so that she wouldn't have him, his very own sister was stopping him, his sister who was jealous because he loved another woman . . .

And things remained there. They didn't try to find the other woman— perhaps she existed, but wasn't in fact *another*. And Lily, though finally admitting who had hit her on that Clean Monday, didn't want to divulge any more to them. Nor did she want her brother sent to live somewhere else, as Christoforos proposed. If it was in him, she said, to beat women and throw them into ditches, then there wouldn't be one ditch without a woman in it. And since she had got her bag back (it was a mystery to her too that she hadn't missed it for so long), she didn't want her hapless brother punished by others. And if she was more than generous with her comic and demeaning *figures of speech* when she was describing him to others, no one was in any doubt that she would give her own life if his life were threatened.

They recalled the profound sayings of their dear-departed Eftha: "*The abyss calling to the abyss,*" she would say (with a tinge of *finite* pomposity) when she saw these two talking together, laughing, arguing, enjoying themselves or busying themselves with something, *unheard* by everyone and forever. "Abyss . . . abyss," she would say again and again—"but that might be paradise for them."

And they had to accept it: faced with an abyss of silence such as these two experienced for more or less sixty years (more in the brother's case), they could only pass by on the outside. On the outside and at a distance.

That same day, the day of the silent revelation as we might call it, Febronia gave birth to the twins (after seven years of *truce*, they were presented with twins), and Lily—while they were bringing her brother from the mountain— helped her, albeit without her instruments . . .

And the next spring, one month after the Carnival, some of Kimon's friends—with Gabe's help—caught a wolf and hanged it on the same tree that he had hanged himself . . . The animal was in no way to blame, but this too *had to be done*. As a kind of remembrance.

And they were surprised to see one of Christoforos's daughters wandering in the area around Megali Morphina so early in the morning . . .

"It's . . . which one is it? The *shy* one?" one of them asked.

"It's the one with the red hair—is it *shy* they call her or something else?" another one said.

She, of course, went away as soon as she saw them.

But she returned when they had gone and gazed at the wolf in front of her . . .

Meanwhile, just a few months earlier, on a moonlit night in January, the inn had burned down and Cletia had been lost in the flames . . . And a few days before that, the new century had been ushered in.

Five years later, years of unforgettable rain and flooding, if we remember, Christoforos's sesame-oil mill was ready, and he tried his luck just where it had run out on him with the inn.

"I'm like a bad old dog," he said to Persa, his third wife. "Spouses, daughters, sisters, daughters-in-law, sons-in-law, and grandchildren who've all died on me—and I'm still here! Sleepless guardian . . . And now I've built a mill for sesame."

"What are you going to call it?" she confined herself to asking.

"*Sesame-oil mill*, what else? I don't want any other names," said Christoforos, "I'm afraid of them."

"And if—," Persa started to say.

"If what? If that burns down too? Then let them build a fountain with running water in my name," said Christoforos, invoking the bitter support of his irony.

Nevertheless, some of his sons had the idea of calling his new sesame-oil mill . . . the True Grit.

"Why that?" he asked them. "We're going to be grinding sesame not grit."

"Because of your endurance and courage," they said. "Everyone knows what *true grit* means and they'll bring us sesame from as far afield as Capernaum."

"Do as you think fit," he eventually said, deciding that the idea was not *unreasonable*.

And so they did, in fact, call their mill the True Grit—bringing a master craftsman to engrave it in black antique letters on a plaque that they fixed over the entrance, crowned with a triangular cover.

That same year, little Julia, the daughter of Febronia and Hesychios, from fluttering around all day like a butterfly, suddenly had to be confined to bed, and because she was around the age of twelve, just as, that is, her godmother and aunt of the same name was when she fell ill, the adults in the house became worried lest sisaibeoma were again making its appearance . . . Nevertheless, the little girl's hair didn't start to come out, she simply turned pale and developed an instability (she would unexpectedly lose her balance and fall down), and, of course, she began suffering from high temperatures at night.

"Should we call for a doctor?" Febronia (who, like a second Sarah, had after the twins given birth to that other child with the three names: Sakis-Barnabas and *Benjamin*) asked Persa one day. "Or can you with all your experience and knowledge cure her? At first I thought it would pass by itself . . ."

At first, they all thought it would pass.

Persa promised to do all she could, whatever was in her power to do.

And day and night she sat beside her step-granddaughter, crushing seeds in one hand or mixing mysterious powders with juices, and with the other, puff-puff, smoking as she pondered — it was summer and all the windows were open.

"Give that to me," Febronia said to her one evening, and took the cigarette from her mouth as though pulling off a sucker, "you can't do two jobs at once."

"If you try it before you throw it away," Persa said to her, "you'll like it. Not the first, but the second time."

Febronia barely tried it; it left her with a burning sensation, a feeling of sickness, and a cough. She threw it away. Presently, Persa took out another. And the sick little girl opened her eyes occasionally, looked at them *from elsewhere* and shut them again.

Quite often, when Persa would go into the room with herbs and smoke coming from her fingers *from the time of the Pythia* (it was Christoforos who came up with this), she would find the elder Julia there, sitting on the edge of the bed. As soon as she saw Persa, she would get up, gently stroke her niece's forehead, and go out of the room on tiptoe, clearing her throat and as though she didn't know where the door was. Or to put it another way, when Persa went out, the elder Julia would before long climb up the internal staircase and enter the little girl's room.

"It's like we're making a figure eight — the one goes this way, the other comes the other way . . . neither of us leaves her on her own," Persa said to her once, and she held her by the arm so she wouldn't leave. "Why is it really that you avoid me?" she asked her, turning her earrings a little to the side. "Is it because I took the place of your mother in this household?"

"My mother's place?" Julia responded. "No . . . I'm not . . ."

"I know that you weren't happy even *before* I married your father," Persa said, studying her eyes and mouth. "So why? And why are you avoiding me instead of telling me what's eating you?"

"No, I . . . nothing," murmured Julia, "I came to see how the little girl was doing . . . And I too . . . But then . . . O, nothing."

"*O-nothing*," came a soft echo from behind them: the little Julia was still playing, whenever she woke, with the elder one's words . . .

"Stay a while," Persa said to her in a low but warm voice, "it's only with you that she talks like that, can't you hear her?"

"I know . . . ," said Julia, and she unexpectedly leaned over towards her step-mother: she said something to her very, very softly so that it was more her breath that Persa heard than her voice. And she quickly pulled back and made for the door.

"Wait . . . what did you say?" Persa asked, going after her.

Julia wavered between bursting into tears or talking. In the end, she did what a lot of children do in group prayers, when they just open and close their mouths to the words that are said by others . . . And she waited for Persa's reaction.

"Can you say it a little bit *louder?*" said Persa very politely. "That's how Lily talks . . . and we can't always understand her."

Julia nodded her head as if in agreement and went towards the stairs. She halted . . . and turned towards her stepmother:

"When it gets dark," she said in a voice that was strangely cracked and hoarse, "I *hear.*"

"What do you hear?"

"*That wild voice,*" she whispered, and her expression was full of fear and ela-tion.

"What wild voice?" asked Persa, herself feeling something of the fear and ela-tion—something of the *way* Julia had spoken.

Again Julia made those soundless movements with her mouth, but this time she said something short and quite *readable:* a small phrase, very small—a *wu*, *w, wu* . . . in fact, the last *wu* could be heard slightly. And it was—*wul.*

"Something . . . *woolly?*" asked Persa, puzzled, because this is what it had sounded like to her—she was almost sure. "You hear . . . *the wild voice of some-thing woolly?*"

Julia smiled; no one could understand. Then she put her left hand on the rail-ing and went down the stairs like a fleeting shadow, so lightly, and twice turning her head to the side as though she had heard someone calling her.

Persa remained pensive: Woolly? She wondered—what was this woolly some-thing with the *wild voice?* . . . And a thought crept up on her—like a snake—just as had happened with Christoforos when it had seemed to him that Kimon's eyes were open beneath the cloth, black and open . . . "Wolf!" she whispered to herself, knowing one or two things about that story between Julia and the werewolf from a very few hints that Christoforos had dropped in the past: "*She hears the wild voice of the wolf! So she still hasn't forgotten him?*"

And she stood there, at the top of the stairs, confused, astounded, irresolute: should she run after the elder Julia or go back to the bedside of the younger one?

"Thank heavens for tobacco," she thought, and took the tin of cigarettes out of her pocket . . . But it was some time before she was able to light one—such was her surprise at that secretive—albeit still *open* after such a long time—affair of the elder Julia, during days and nights when they were all talking about or referring to the mysterious illness of little Julia.

That same evening, moreover, while Lily was cleaning fish in a corner of the yard and throwing the innards to the cats that had surrounded her and that were meowing softly and drooling with greed (as she was, doing the same with her mouth as she listened to them, so that anyone would have thought that there were seven cats and not six . . .), she suddenly stopped her meowing and turned her head around: Julia was standing behind her and had been waiting, for some moments, for Lily to make this movement . . . And farther behind, from a downstairs window, Persa was watching both of them.

What do you want, you-who-are-so-fond-of-tears? asked Lily, who—no matter how much work she had—was never too tired to *address* people by their chief characteristic.

I don't want to scare you, I want to tell you something, replied Julia, who was perhaps the only one in the household who spoke to the mute Lily as if she were a mute herself—all the others, no matter how many gestures and facial contortions they employed, never forgot to also make use of their vocal cords when conversing with her . . . *Something that I don't want the others to know.*

Why? Don't they love you? asked Lily.

It's not that . . .

I love you! Lily assured her, fending off the cats, which, seeing her preoccupied, became emboldened and lusted after the fish itself and not just the innards.

I want you to tell your brother . . . , Julia went on, with the same hesitation as when she spoke normally. *I mean . . .*

Come right out with it, like the others do, Lily advised her.

I . . . don't want to come right out and say it . . . I can't, Julia replied.

I thought a lot of your mother, Eftha! said Lily, who was beginning to lose track of the conversation or perhaps suddenly felt Eftha's absence . . . *But Persa's nice too . . . I'm telling you, Persa's turned out nice too, you should respect her— she's the one who saved me from that nosebleed. Heavens! All that blood, do you remember? And she stopped it with an egg! A real witch! . . . Witch, witch, no doubt about it . . .* (she always depicted Persa with a circle: sometimes elongated, which meant egg, sometimes round, which meant bracelet, but mainly with lots of circles all together in front of her eyes, which either meant cigarette smoke, or abracadabra).

"Are you talking about me, Lily?" Persa asked her, leaving the window and coming out into the yard next to them.

About you—your predecessor, said Lily, going back to her fish. But as soon as she saw that two were missing, and that half the cats were also missing, she handed the pot with the rest to Persa and ran to find the feline predators.

"Just the two of us again," said Persa, smiling.

"Yes . . ."

"Don't you want to talk to me? To tell me so I'll understand?" asked Persa, again leaning her head to the side and giving her a friendly and concerned look. "I know . . . I've taken your mother's place—"

"No, don't . . . not that!" Julia interrupted her with a wholly concerned look.

"What's gotten into you? What have I said that I shouldn't?" asked the woman with the green earrings and the yellow nails, probably pleased by the spirited reaction of this usually shy girl. She waited, however, for something more.

And this *more* was once again soundless: those movements of her arms . . . which this time stopped a rather long sentence, eight or ten words.

"*Bozi-godsputi!*" said Persa (something she said a lot and which meant something like "God above" or "Lord have mercy"). "I sometimes talk in the tongue of my Circassian grandfather; your mother, from what they tell me, spoke in a language all her own, too—and everybody, I mean, has their own way of talking . . . But you, when you open that mouth of yours like a hungry tortoise . . . Oh, my dear girl, it's easier for me to understand Lily than you! And Lily is deaf and dumb . . . But you?"

Julia's eyes misted over. And her lips moved again, voicing a sentence inside her mouth rather than outside . . . Something like—*thoul* was what Persa heard this time. She couldn't make it out. She shook the pot with the fish in her hands, but she couldn't make it out . . . *Thoul!*

"*The wolf?* . . . Is that what you're trying to say?" she asked, trying to elicit something more from her.

Julia stared at her with some surprise; then she nodded her head as though in affirmation and went off again.

So, concerning this elder Julia—who for some inexplicable reason appeared more vulnerable and defenseless than the younger one—Christoforos had searched long back and in numerous places in the hope of finding one of her exercise books, one of those with her proverbs and chronologies, which might shed a little light on his blind investigations into what had happened between her and the deceased builder. But as he had already feared would be the case, he found nothing. Later, however, quite by chance, he came across a sheet of paper with a relatively recent date which said: *As soon as night falls and a full moon rises in the sky, then it can be heard*

(Just that—there was no period or dots.)

Intrigued, he took the paper, folded it, and put it in his breast pocket, and when an appropriate moment arose he took it out and lightly touched his daughter's left earlobe with it: when she turned round to see, he moved to her right; when she turned to the right, he hid himself again on her left . . . These were the kinds of games he had played with her when she was little, and though many years had gone by since then, he continued to play the same games with his grandchildren and the other children, but with the grown-ups too, if the moment was right . . . And always, when they *caught* him, he would keep on demanding the answer to a standard crazy question: "Eleni-Eleni-her-mother's-name-what's-her-name?," a variant of a supposedly more reasonable question: "Eleni, Eleni's mother what's she called?," whereupon all you had to do was to say any woman's name for him to be content, and, what's more, for him to *re-ward* you.

Julia smiled (so as not to displease him) and waited for the question.

"What do you mean by that . . . *full moon that as soon as night falls rises in the sky?*" he asked her, waving the paper with the incomprehensible sentence, and saw her eyes mist over before the smile had even faded from her lips. "Don't get upset for no reason, I'm not going to scold you, I haven't come to scold you," he told her, "all I want to know is what you meant with this here . . . With this— look, don't turn your head away."

"Nothing . . . I didn't mean anything . . . That's how it begins . . . a story in a book and I copied it," she told him.

"And why did you copy it? Because you liked it so much? Every night we can see a full moon or a moon in one of its quarters rising in the sky. If we decided to copy it every time! . . ."

Silently, she agreed: *that wasn't reasonable.*

"And haven't you written anything about Kimon . . . he rose up there too?" he asked her presently.

"About who?" she whispered, and her eyes welled up.

"About Kimon. The builder with the blue eyes. Haven't you written anything about him? . . . It was one of our walnut trees that *helped* him to get up there! I thought you'd have written something about him, not to let all that learning you had go to waste," her father continued in a rather harsh voice . . . "So what then? Wasn't that other bane of his and Chrysanthe as well enough for him? Did he need *our walnut tree* too?"

Julia appeared to be looking at him and listening, but actually his face was quivering before her like the moon in murky water—her eyes were wet with tears, wet and blurred, they couldn't see him.

"Tell me something, my dear girl!" he said, changing tack and desperately imploring her. "What is it that can be heard then? When the full moon—"

"*The wild voice,*" she said, as though someone else were speaking in her place.

His eyes moved from side to side: had she said it to him or to someone else? He almost looked over his shoulder . . .

"What voice?" he asked her, as if not hearing well.

"The other one . . ."

He coughed and scratched the back of his neck.

"Listen here, Julia, my dear," he said to her, bending at his knees so that he would have her exactly before him at his height (she was sitting on a stool). "The years are passing, that Kimon—if it's him you're talking about—has gone. Let's not go now into the why and how of it. He's gone. He's no longer with us . . . They've already dug him up."

"I know. He's in that little building now," she said, wiping first one eye and then the other with the front and back of her hand.

"If you know, why are you still weeping?" her father asked her.

"I don't weep all the time . . . But—if Cletia were still alive . . . if we still had the inn and the hunter was still coming . . . like then when he brought the weasel . . ."

"Yes . . . so what are you getting at? Why are you suddenly talking about Cletia and the hunter?"

"Oh! . . . ," she exclaimed, and her eyes filled with tears again.

Those tears, the welling in her eyes, and her whole behavior, which had something uncertain about it, something without follow-up, something guilty—and so fixed on something—set him to thinking and perhaps instilled in him a vague, a very vague feeling of fear.

Shortly afterwards, her brother Hesychios again made a couple of attempts to bring her close to his icon-painter friend—the fact that he was called Kimon of course reminded him of the other one (especially that evening of the Carnival when the two of them had crossed paths by chance down by the gate), but he didn't give the event a second thought: his sister's confessions to his wife hadn't reached as far as him. But nor for his sister was the name alone so important as to make her forget the other one or endeavor to *resurrect* him by uniting her life with one more Kimon.

And so, one Sunday, she saw horses being decked out, loaded with textiles and embroidery, and carrying as a bride one of her young nieces, the not yet sixteen-year-old Efthalitsa, daughter of Hesychios and one of those *early affairs*—one of the infants who, when Julia was still only sixteen, some black-clad women had left outside the gate . . . She stared at her now in secret from behind a window, lifting up the corner of one of the curtains, while the girl outside in the yard, close to that same gate, was turning her adorned neck to left and right, and her waist too (thereby risking falling from the horse, which was walking friskily among the crowd of people), in order to bid farewell to all of them, not miss anyone, but also so that no one would miss the fact that she was *already* a bride . . .

Julia quietly opened the window and the young bride immediately saw her from below:

"Aunt Julia," she shouted happily, waving her hand. "Bye! . . . Won't you say good-bye to me?"

But there was no one at the window when some of the others raised their eyes to look.

"Bye! Bye! . . . I'm saying good-bye, won't you say good-bye to me?" shouted the younger Julia to the bride, almost hysterically, as a replacement, and she hopped wildly around the horse, trying as hard as she could to catch hold of her feet with their embroidered white socks.

"No, not to you—you're too little!" she said to her hurriedly, and rather meanly, without reason, and, casting a last look—of grievance? of surprise?—at the window that was still open, she left with the icon painter for his house in other parts.

And so, if Hesychios wasn't going to become his bosom friend's brother-in-law, he at least became his father-in-law. What matter if Efthalitsa was less than half the age of the groom . . . As long as the merry-go-round continued.

All the next days, little Julia complained, moaned, and remained angry.

"She called me little, called me little . . . As if I asked her!" she said to whoever she saw, as if everyone was obliged to know what had so annoyed her at her sister's wedding. "She called me little, instead of saying good-bye to me! . . ."

"Don't make a big thing out of it," her mother said to her one day, "when she comes back the next time, she'll see how much you've grown! Now run fetch me a pair of scissors so I can cut your nails—they'll grow even quicker!"

Obediently and even more indifferently, little Julia brought her the scissors.

"Sit there . . . At least you don't torment me like the other one."

"She called me little! . . . The *sakafliora!* The *gavatsa!* The *tsiotsia!*"[3]

"Shh . . . Look how I'm cutting your nails so they'll grow nicely again," her mother said.

But little Julia was not enamored of her nails as Rodanthe had been. She was much more upset by the fact that her sister had called her *little*.

Around nine months later, Petros, the last son of the deceased Petroula and Christoforos, the son who had lost his mother before even the forty days' confinement had passed, and who hadn't rushed like his brothers and sisters to get married at eighteen or twenty-five, or even thirty-five, announced to his father that he intended to do it now.

"And who's the lucky woman?" he asked him.

"The youngest daughter of So-and-So," Petros said.

Christoforos grabbed hold of his head to stop it falling off: if he wasn't very much mistaken, *the youngest daughter of So-and-So* was Kimon's sister-in-law, Chrysanthe's younger sister.

"Couldn't you find someone else?" he asked him, without beating around the bush. "Why her?"

"Why not her?" Petros asked, puzzled.

"Because her brother-in-law, have you forgotten? *built* himself into our walnut tree! I still can't look at that tree without being afraid in case I see his legs dangling! . . . And apart from that, they say that she loved him . . . Were there so few others? Why her?"

"Because she's the one I've chosen," said Petros, "and if her brother-in-law built himself into our walnut tree, what fault is it of hers? And even if she loved him as you say, he no longer exists; death erases everything."

Christoforos felt a deep sadness, something hurting him deep down, without being able to understand what. Normally, he should have been happy: bringing to mind that skinny broken girl as he'd seen her at Kimon's house on the day of his funeral, with pain tingling in her eyes and love smoldering in her words; he couldn't understand why he should feel sorrow at the fact that she was trying to break free of that pain . . . And yet, he did feel sorrow, the sorrow that someone feels who has been betrayed. And more than his sorrow, it was perhaps the muddle, that whirl of coincidences. And his secret concern about Julia: about

3. Some local *expressions*, dialect words for injudicious women.

how this news would reach her ears, even if she didn't know anything about the other woman's secret longing for Kimon—and yet how could he be sure that Julia didn't secretly know about this already?

He huffed and puffed, he didn't know where to begin to try to unravel this tangled business, how to tackle it . . .

"What's wrong with you? I thought you'd be pleased," said Petros. "She's a good woman, good-hearted, hardworking . . . she's left it a bit late, too, like me . . . I think we're a good match. And her father is not giving her without a dowry: she'll get her sister's share too, what belonged to Kimon, given that he doesn't have any other children and neither did Kimon."

"And how did you find her? When did you see her in order to fall in love with her?" Christoforos asked him. "Was it at the funeral?"

"What funeral! I saw her one evening walking in the rain all alone . . . And I said to myself: *That's her, Petros, she's the one for you.* How can I put it . . . I felt something that I haven't felt with any other woman. It was like she was fashioned from the drops of rain! I liked her! And it wasn't as if I'd never seen her before. I had seen her. I knew her. But I felt that thing for the first time that evening."

"Which evening? Before Kimon's death or afterwards?"

"Afterwards, of course," said Petros, "it's not been long, just a couple of months."

This brought some relief to Christoforos—though again without his being able to understand why. But there were still many things gnawing at him.

"And what about her? . . . How did she take it? Have you spoken to her?"

"Naturally. At first she wouldn't even hear of it. Then she said something to me that I didn't understand: that my hands resembled someone else's. *Whose?* She didn't say. I understood. To me, I told her, all hands are the same. No, she insisted, they're not the same, they differ from person to person. All right, I told her, and so does that mean that you accept or not? She hesitated . . . The next time I asked her, she hesitated again. And then the rains came and didn't stop for a whole ten days. But yesterday I went to her house—my legs led me there, otherwise I would have told you . . . I wanted to tell you what I was thinking and then go . . . I found her eating with her elderly parents. Grilled mushrooms in soup plates . . . And she basically said yes—she even mentioned you: if my father consented . . . That's what she said to me, more than once—for what reason? Why wouldn't my father consent? I said to her. For years he's been begging me to find a wife . . . Isn't it true that for years you've been telling me to get married because you haven't got enough grandchildren?"

Christoforos answered neither yes nor no.

"Of course, yes! You even wanted to pair me off with Teyim at one time, with Myra, Megaera, whatever you call her . . . Can you imagine if I'd married her? I'd have your wife as my mother-in law now—the wife of my father!" said Petros. "Be pretty confusing wouldn't it?"

"Confusing wouldn't be the word for it," Christoforos agreed, albeit unwillingly and somewhat ironically.

So they were *less* confused at least—though undoubtedly more secretly, more hypodermically—by Kimon's sister-in-law becoming Julia's sister-in-law.

It sufficed that the web grew thicker.

It was still the time of the rains, with those storms, winds, the thunder that seemed as though it would never stop—though now and again some short unexpected sunny periods made their appearance . . . amidst a dark, almost permanently nocturnal and menacing atmosphere. Sun and rain was something they had seen many times, but sun and darkness no, this was something they saw for the first time.

And it was also the period when the most children were born—all together as if the rain had brought them. "What else can we do," said the parents, "whole months inside the house, and outside that constant drizzle . . ."

So they were referred to as "the rain generation." One of these was Sakis: *Benjamin*, that is.

One day, another six or seven months later, when the rains had begun to abate and the ground to dry, or rather to bear three times as much fruit, Persa paid a visit to her daughter Myra, taking little Julia with her.

They let her play, and Julia listened to them talking in low voices, *just like mother and daughter*, and louder sometimes, sitting on straw and wide strips of leather, behind Apostolos's shop, drinking coffee with powdered chickpea in large cups in which, as well as their bread, they dipped the tips of their fingers: afterwards, the one would wipe them on her lips, the other would lick them, as though sucking marrow from a bone.

She was playing behind them with some ropes and was listening—some of what they said she missed, some not.

"My husband's grieved," said the mother to the daughter, "that you can sense earthquakes coming and pride yourself on it like a peacock, but you didn't say anything to him about that last one . . . He still talks about it."

"I did tell him, of course I told him, by God's good grace! I got the dogs and goats and everything to tell them—they cawed, howled, whinnied . . . But no one believed, have you forgotten? You were here and you know. And now he's grieved? Why? Te 'im. Evil's the last thing I wanted for him," said Myra.

"He's not saying that you wanted anything bad to happen to him, he says that you didn't tell him plainly—maybe the inn would have survived."

"Survived . . . how? The inn wasn't destroyed by the earthquake—it burnt down on its own."

"Even so. If you'd told him plainly . . ."

"Ah, plainly . . . ," said Myra, "nobody can sense those things plainly . . . Sssfff! All gone, I've finished my coffee! What about you, some more?"

"Those who smoke know how to drink slowly," said Persa, and putting her cup down on a rock turned to look at Julia. She turned suddenly to the side and began jumping in the air, with her eyes making circles like a bird . . .

Then she heard them talking about other things.

"I wasn't here then, they told me about it . . . It happened, they say, on the day you were betrothed—splats, on the stairs! . . . Bozi-godsputi! . . . And how do you feel now without that worm in your entrails?"

"Lighter . . . heavier, I don't know. I think there's another one growing inside."

"You'll be the death of Apostolakos."

"No, not at all. When I'm eating, he sits and watches me. It makes him happy."

"Spoils his appetite, more like! . . . And what about the other one? Your first?"

"He's carrying on with that other woman, how should I know—for me he's dead and buried, I've said my last good-byes."

"Have you ever seen him again since then?"

"I've just told you, for me he's dead and buried, six feet under, gone. By God's good grace."

"Where have you picked up that *By God's good grace* from? You didn't use to say it."

"From him! He missed nothing, the sly devil, just put God in front . . . Ouf! Do you mind if I dip my finger in? This coffee, by God's good grace, you can't have enough of it! The grounds are even tastier than the coffee itself!"

"Why don't you get a teaspoon? Garnok! . . . Hey, *garnok*!"[4]

"Better with the fingers."

"I don't know who you take after when it comes to food. You're like a pig, you eat everything but the stones."

"Just listen to her!"

---

4. *Jar, urn*—synecdochically *insatiable.*

At that very moment, a small dry twig dropped from the beak of some low-flying bird and fell into Persa's cup.

"What a sign!" shouted Myra.

The bird, alarmed and saddened by its loss but lighter now, flew higher, and Persa—watching its flight—again turned her gaze to see what little Julia was doing.

She jumped up a couple of times as if someone were making her do it . . . she wasn't in the mood for any more. With her hands joined behind her back and her little belly jutting out comically in front of her like a balloon (a sign, they said, that she would grow taller), she gazed at Myra, who kept moving her finger back and forth, from the cup to her mouth, taking all the thick black coffee grounds that were so sweet, bitterly sweet . . . Then—she was insatiable—she took the little twig from her mother's cup and licked that too! And then she dipped it in again and licked it again! . . . Persa hit her on the hand, Myra chortled; and the little girl started as though a cold current had passed through her . . .

"Come over here, *moumouska*,"[5] Persa called to her, "do you want some too? Do you fancy a little?"

"There's nothing left, by God's good grace," Myra answered, now running her tongue round the inside of the empty cup, "nothing, look!" and she held it upside down.

"Never mind her, I'll give you some from mine . . . Bring the ropes and come and play here next to us," Persa said again to Julia, who was still standing motionless and staring at the same spot, even though Myra had moved and was on the go all the time looking to see what else (apart from the forbidden twig) she could lick, suck, or nibble.

"Come on . . . what's got into you?" Persa called for a third time.

"I can't," the little girl replied softly from where she was, somewhat wearily, and as she was standing there, *she appeared to fall* . . .

We should point out that what we said just now might not have happened exactly like that. But neither of the other two who witnessed it could say how it happened. The little girl floated down to the ground like the most delicate tulle, in the same way that the breeze might have swept it a little higher or brought it closer to them . . . It was the movement of a bubble that played with their eyes, provoking a dozen or more different impressions and leaving them without even one when they saw her on the ground and ran over to her.

5. "Little girl," "girlie."

This was the first instance, the first strange indication that something was not right with little Julia, who until then they had marked out—or so they said—for song and dance.

When they lifted her up, and tapped her a little on the face, she was able to stand as before—except that it was clear from her face that her whole world had changed. Persa ran back to get her cup (she hid the twig from the bird's beak, kept it), and pouring whatever had remained of the cold coffee (*"sweet like love, black like hell,"* she murmured), she took a little of the grounds with two of her fingers and put them into the girl's mouth—she thought that someone might drop where he stood purely from a craving. Julia swallowed it seemingly with delight . . . She gave her some more . . .

"Enough?" she asked, when Julia had swallowed that too.

"Enough," she said, though Persa was sure that if she had asked, "Do you want some more?" Julia would have said yes.

They left the rest "for the stones to eat" and went back home a different way, through the back streets, doing triple the distance, and during this time, Persa's apricot eyes missed none of Julia's movements or steps . . . And at the same time, she spoke to her, somewhat mockingly, with a buzzing in her ears, about the greediness of Myra, who made even the birds lose their sense of direction.

And she said nothing about it to Febronia so as not to put any premature and perhaps ungrounded thoughts into her head. Of course, if the moumouska said anything herself . . . But she, at least from what transpired in the next couple of days, said nothing—she might not have even understood anything.

On the third day, she had to be dragged home by two girls from the neighborhood, Loula and Toula, who were a little older than she was.

"She just fell there where we were playing . . . She says she can't walk," they said to Febronia, who looked askance at all three of them.

"Let her go," she told them, "take your hands from under her arms."

But the moment they did so, little Julia sank between them like an invertebrate.

Her mother was ready to give her a slap—she raised her hand threateningly.

"You see this here? . . . It's summer and I'm up to the ears in work—save your antics for the winter," she told her.

Because she thought Julia was acting like that to scare them (as she had done at other times in the past: pretending to be blind or lame or dumb . . .), and Febronia's nerves were day by day becoming more frayed, so she was in no mood for the antics of either the young or the old.

On the fourth day, she was brought home by four boys from the neighborhood—they had found her, they said, on the ground beside the fountain . . . On the fifth day, it was a man who brought her, in his arms—he had found her behind his house scratching at the wall as she tried to get to her feet . . . Februnia's mouth filled with saliva: every morning, she would leave Julia with her elder stepsisters to get dressed, comb their hair, take care of their younger brothers and sisters, so that she could go off to the fields, and when she came back, she would find Julia wilting somewhere and would hear all the details of what happened from the others . . . *They'll think I'm completely callous,* she thought, *I've already got a reputation for it* . . . And she bent over her daughter, flushed as she was from the fields, even her breath smelled of sweat, and she shook her head with eyes full of confusion, without being able to utter a word, to put everything that was going through her mind into some order: *What's this now? . . . What are they telling me about you? . . .* And she held her, lifted her up, supported her legs on the ground, between her knees, and she begged her, silently, with her eyes, to stand up properly, as before, not to fall again, to make fools of all of them so the two of them could laugh together . . . "Dance! Dance like before, my precious, make them choke on their words!" she whispered in her ear. But just as her heart was trembling with fear, so Julia's legs were trembling, and just as words are often lost, so she too lost her strength.

So this, now, what was it? No one had seen it before, and they had seen so much. Little Julia, the most vivacious and nimble female in the house, was able less and less each day to stand, to walk, to control her legs: as soon as they let go of her, she would fall—while her eyes searched for the slightest shadow on their faces, the slightest whisper or nod between them, as though she were probing into them: what were they doing, thinking, imagining about her . . .

This, then, during the first few days.

And one fine morning, she showed no willingness, no compliance to get out of bed, even to try. The following day, she became scared: as soon as they went up to her, said to her, "Let us help you up, so you can walk a little," she began to cry. And they didn't ask her again the day after that so that she wouldn't call to mind the previous day and begin to cry again.

And the day eventually came when they could no longer actually remember when all this had started, when Julia had been well and when she had stopped walking. It was only Persa who couldn't forget that *first time* she had seen her fall . . . and several decades later—if by any chance she had still been alive then—she would have been able to witness the same scene more or less with a man who from being *upright* on his feet suddenly found himself *facedown* on the floor with nothing having intervened, nothing stranger or serener than the happening itself, which made him say to his friends with modest conviction: "An evil angel passed by and thought it good to touch me." Out of so many, out of a large group of friends who were drinking and chatting freely, he was *the only one* to be touched . . . In the meantime, he got up, pushed his hair back, and became again just as he was before falling.[6]

But we can't say the same about Julia: she didn't become again as she was before. As for the rest, it was a tremendous summer, a thrice-blessed year: the trees, the soil weren't able to give their fruits quickly enough, and there were many—weary from the toil, exhausted but happy—who weren't quick enough to get home at night: they fell asleep on the way, there where they halted a little to take a rest.

And at home, Persa, alone in a room that had become *hers* (in which only the ceiling was not cluttered with shelves and cupboards filled with potions and powders), was trying to talk to a twig . . . trying to get something out of it. It was the twig that had fallen from the bird's beak just before little Julia had fallen: like an evil omen it had dropped into her cup . . . Then when Myra had cried out: "What a sign!"

What might all this mean—if indeed it meant anything?

But the only thing the twig—not even a bird—could tell her was what happened . . . Just like some flowers or sentiments that prefer to die in full bloom rather than wither and decay.

It was just a little twig, and it was being asked to talk, to express itself on human matters.

Around mid-September, two doctors came to see her, since Persa held up her hands in despair, saying that the rest was not her domain. She had lotions for no end of spots and wounds, she had shavings from old skins or from deer antlers in oil for difficult wounds, she knew how to alleviate rheumatisms with the leaves of a rare parasite plant that she wrapped round the joints and it absorbed the pain (and sometimes, if the binding was too tight or if the pain had some other provenance, the leaves would eat at the flesh and open up new wounds—for which she also had the cure); in wooden jars she had spiders' webs that were used in many things; vases with roots, seeds, and liquids both precious and dangerous, like that "gouzi-krava," as it was called, which was thick and yellow from

6. An unforgettable scene from Tarkovsky's "The Sacrifice."

the stomach of a large insect and which she guarded like it was gold; she knew in which cases the fine, perfectly filtered soil from anthills could prove life-saving, as with the black powder from burnt eggshell, or the early-morning bitter saliva, before we eat or drink anything; or how beneficial were the ground—and roasted—seeds from nettles for the kidneys; or the powder from deer antlers in rose-vinegar for headaches; how much could be told from mixing a few drops of lemon with the urine of a pregnant woman, and also how effective urine from anybody was for burns.

It's true, that is, that Persa was knowledgeable concerning many practical medicines—and some of these had indisputably proved their exceptional qualities—and she could have filled a book with all her knowledge so that others might learn too.

Nevertheless, in Julia's case, after laboring for days and nights, she eventually admitted that it was not known or obvious demons she was dealing with, and she gave up the struggle—no matter how saddened she was by this and at the unfulfilled hopes they had all pinned on her.

And yet the two doctors who came said roughly the same. Though they said a little more, something hopeful that Persa, too, had somewhat vaguely mulled over: that it was perhaps to do with *her age, psychological*, and that it would pass by itself . . . They should wait a little longer and not put any pressure on Julia.

So they prayed and organized vigils round the sick girl's bed and at the same time worked (shelling corn, bundling the last leaves of tobacco, putting the summer fruits into ash or cutting it into slices so it would dry for the winter), without being able to do anything more. From all the oh-ing and ah-ing, her mother started to lose her hair, her scalp filled with bald patches, and to her horror one day she suspected that she might be pregnant again . . . It was the first time in so many years of marriage to Hesychios that she thought she would go mad, that she wanted to jump from the window, that she felt an abhorrence for her indefatigable belly, for what until then she had felt a bitter pride or thought that with this she warded off ungraspable things that threatened her . . . Now she saw it as one more punishment, as the culmination of all the catastrophes that had engulfed her since she had *wedded* him, for whom her first daughter's heart had become poisoned . . . She would recall her first daughter more and more often; she looked at Julia, and it was as though she were seeing her, but fading more slowly, at half her age we could say, a child, and without any groaning, without any curses—but for her there was no difference.

"No, Lord, no," she would say to herself in various corners of the house where no one could hear her, thinking of her age and all the rest (she had already turned fifty-five and already—*still*—had a three-year-old child). "Not this too. Sakis would be the last one, we agreed—I almost put it in writing: no more children . . . You even made me the mother—stepmother—of my grandson! . . . What else? Isn't all this enough? My daughter was sacrificed so I could wed him, who now . . . Isn't it enough? Don't take Julia from me now as well . . . *Bozi-godsputi!* Can you understand that better? Bozi-godsputi! Bozi-godsputi!"

Talking to herself like this one day, she went to find Persa.

"Bozi-godsputi!" she said to her, as though addressing her with a particularly reverent and painful name. "Give me a potion! . . . If you think anything of me, if I'm still worthy of any respect, give me a potion to get rid of the child!"

"What child?" she asked, surprised.

"The one I have inside me again! . . ."

"I don't see anything . . . you don't seem to me to have anything . . . ," Persa said to her, after examining her pelvis and pressing her belly a little with her fingers.

"Well, it seems so to me, and I'm not mistaken," said Febronia.

"And if there is no child and the dangerous potion I give you . . . goes elsewhere?"

"Where elsewhere?" Febronia said mockingly. "Where do you see that elsewhere? In any case, it will go to me . . . And I deserve it!"

"Calm yourself and get back to your daughter who needs you," the sagacious Circassian woman counseled her.

"The other one needed me too . . . ," said the much-troubled Febronia.

"I didn't know the other one, she was before my time . . . I'm talking to you about this one . . . And don't go putting ideas in your head that the other is to blame—the dead aren't like us, they don't take revenge," said Persa, "all they ask of us is that we leave them in peace, that we don't tangle them up in our affairs."

"Let's hope so," said Febronia, giving in. "But give me something for this . . ."

"I'm not giving you anything."

"Won't you be ashamed of me if I have another child?" she said, trying now in this way to soften the other woman's Circassian tenacity.

Her hanging green earrings swung back and forth: We wouldn't be ashamed—they seemed to be saying—at things far worse.

And no matter how much Febronia pleaded with her, Persa refused to give her the potion.

And at the same time, the other Julia, the one with her own concerns, would every so often push open the door of the sick little girl with the same name, the same fiery red hair, and ask her—if she was awake—whether she would like an apple . . .

No one understood what she meant with the business of the apple all the time ("Take one . . . I'll cry if you don't," she would say to her, and crying, of course, was not something difficult for her). Yet no one understood either why, if the little girl were sleeping or burning up with fever, she would turn with the apple to them: "Apple? . . . Did someone ask for an apple?" she would ask them innocently, as though they had any mind for apples amidst the decay that filled their eyes.

And it was only Persa, once again, being an outsider, who saw (before the others did, anyway, and more clearly) that though they were all fraught with anxiety for the little Julia, the other Julia would beat them to it in her own way.

This is what had been strangely worrying her that day on the stairs, when the elder Julia had said something to her that she couldn't hear—that she couldn't hear not even when she repeated it even more quietly, this time moving only her lips . . . And then suddenly—with a shortness of breath in her virginal breast, with a moonstruck gaze—she had put her on hot coals by coming out with that *wild voice* . . .

All this may have been nothing, the *peculiarities* of some recollection perhaps, but it aroused suspicion in Persa—and this same thing continued to gnaw at her, to worry her, every time Julia went into the little girl's room (now that she no longer cared whether there were others there too) and asked in her velvety voice whether anyone wanted an apple . . .

One evening she came into the room with a large lighted candle, protecting the flame with her hand so it wouldn't blow out, with a man's black hat covering half her face. They all stirred and stared: both at the candle and at the way she was holding it to protect it from the supposed breeze—as for the hat, they weren't so surprised: she had found it herself behind the house not long before, after a windy night, and evidently it had been removed from someone's head by the wind and carried as far as their plum tree—they had seen her wearing it before . . .

"Light . . . Who wants the sacred light?" she whispered, as though she were returning from the Easter service.

"We do," said Febronia automatically.

"Phhh . . . ," came from Julia's mouth as she blew on it and then handed the extinguished candle to the one who had said *we do.*

Febronia took the candle equally automatically, but stared at her sister-in-law as though staring at a complete stranger, at someone whose behavior was completely inappropriate.

"Have you lost your mind?" she asked her drily, adding with not a little bitterness: "You were the only one that I didn't suckle," leaving the others to draw their own conclusions as to the rest—including the black hat . . .

Julia covered her face and left sobbing—no one had had any time to concern themselves with her *too* or to draw any conclusions.

And if Persa followed her, if she managed, that is, to see the edges of her dress brushing against the last stairs, she wasn't able — just as before — to run and catch up with her to ask her outright what was happening. . . . The black hat, however, had dropped in the parlor and got caught up in her own long dress, and she picked it up, examined it in the dim light of the lamp, in the moonlight that, faint and cold, filtered in through the window.

The following day they had a visitor. If Persa hadn't known him well, she might have thought it was the stranger who had lost his hat and heard that some woman in that house had found it — so crabby and touchy was his expression and so suspicious the way he looked at them, as though they might steal his shoes and the clothes off his back, not to mention his precious fingers!

But it was her brother, she knew him well (it was with him that she had been living before they called her to come and save Christoforos's deaf-mute adopted sister), and she wasn't overly pleased to see him standing before her uninvited.

"What brought you here?" she asked him *in a tactful way* when the necessary introductions were over, which hadn't particularly pleased anyone, especially at times like those.

"Just passing, why all the grumbling?" he said to her abruptly.

"Who's the grumbler?" Persa murmured, irately.

Because he was a real grumbler and fractious man ("like infants who are teething," she used to say), and if she had lived with him for some years, taking care of him and putting up with him, it was simply because circumstances had dictated it. At bottom, she felt sorry for him: blood is, after all, thicker than water. He was also an old bachelor — he didn't want any woman and no woman wanted him. Despite this, he was exceptionally sensitive when it came to the female presence . . . and Persa had searched, when they lived together (and before and afterwards, from afar, without him knowing), to try to find him a woman, and because of this, she always spoke well of him, praised him to every woman she met. For this unsociable soul, this polished piece of brass, also had his good points — or one at least: he played the accordion! . . . And when he was warmed up and really played, with heart and soul, with all his being, well then he enchanted his listeners, even the bees would stop to hear him. And the fingers that God had given him for this instrument — ten slender, dark-skinned, sparkling fingers that, as they moved with marvelous speed and grace over the buttons and keys, seemed more like twenty, thirty — no . . . no one else had fingers like his.

Yet all those women who knew something of his character would say to Persa, "And what are his fingers to me? Will I be living with him or his fingers?"

"You'll be living with him, but his fingers will provide your living," Persa would reply, and tell them how her brother had made a great deal of money with those fingers of his, had filled baskets with money, as everyone called him to their weddings and festivities (without forgetting the bagpipes and drums too), and, naturally, he was well paid for it.

Now her brother had come there, so those who didn't know him might meet him and, of course, he had come with his instrument slung over his shoulder . . . He stooped from the weight of it for so many years (he only put it down when he went to bed, and he had brought it from Russia—where he had lived, so he said, *quelques années*),[7] but he was so tall and wiry, so thin that even without the accordion he would have started to stoop eventually. To be exact, he was humpbacked.

And as he was very swarthy, with glassy, jet-black eyes that reflected much of his soul's suspiciousness and vanity (but also its deep deathly bitterness), he made his sister—with her generally chestnut-colored hair and complexion—seem fair or rather *russet* next to him. In any case, they weren't very much alike in character, perhaps not at all, and only something fleeting in their expressions, in their aura as we might say, stopped you from ruling out any possibility that they might be related.

His name was Jacob, ten years or so younger than Christoforos, and when Christoforos heard Persa continually calling him Jacob instead of the more usual Iakovos, he was surprised and asked her why. "Because he was christened Jacob and that's how we always called him at home," said Persa. And she also told him, by the way, that they had a brother called Joseph, a cousin called David, a Joachim, a Moses, and other such names in their family, so Christoforos started to get the idea that he was dealing with a dynasty of Jews, who one by one were making their appearance . . . "Ts-ts-ts," he exclaimed, clicking his tongue when Persa had finished, "all the prophets have found a home with you, it seems," but the way he said it, with no lack of irony, strangely enough didn't offend the newcomer (it might very well have—Persa was afraid it would, indeed hoped it would—so that he would get up and leave) but just made him laugh, revealing the few teeth he had missing in front. But there were other reasons why Christoforos didn't really take a liking to him.

At the dinner table, whoever happened to sit to the right and left of Jacob had a hard time of it. Not only because he wouldn't dream of moving his huge accordion from under his legs (this is where he put it when he took it off his shoulder), which, at the slightest nudge, gave off a sharp, piercing sound that scared the wits out of them, but also because its owner would turn every so often

7. "For a few years."

and gaze at the person next to him with an expression as though he smelled bad or, in the worst case, as though the person next to him had dared to think that Jacob smelled bad . . . Then again, he would often blow the air through his teeth, making a hissing sound, like the whistling sound that drives dogs away, and being unused to this they turned at first to look at him (later they avoided it), something which greatly annoyed him so that he snatched at his napkin, ready to push his chair back, but . . . he would again make that *tsss-tsss* sound and remain in their midst.

And he was so difficult when it came to food and different tastes (not that — this — not this — that) that Christoforos lost his appetite, which in any case had been reduced by all the various happenings. And when, in the end, Jacob did eventually put something in his mouth, it was as though he would spit it out — such were his peculiarities and discontent . . . And this is why, of course, there wasn't an ounce of fat on him, this is why if someone accidentally touched him on his arm or thigh, it was like knocking on wood. (As to his humpback no one doubted it, but they all took great care not to touch it.)

"Tell him to put a few pounds on . . . so the women can see him!" a *gloomy* Christoforos said to Persa that evening.

"What women?" she asked, more surprised than indifferent at what she had heard.

"The ones he's going to charm with his fingers, how should I know?" he said.

"Let them try putting up with him first," murmured Persa.

At any rate, Jacob himself had a different view of all this and considered his lean build *très elegant*[8] — yes, indeed, *très elegant*, given that he knew a little French, God knows from where and when.

And yet there was a strange kind of dignity in his appearance — or perhaps it was just that strange bitterness in his eyes — that charmed you, that somehow intrigued you . . . As though he had been greatly wounded and since then had been under no illusions — but on the contrary, was full of suspicion. And although this suspicion became more noticeable (almost flickering in his eyes) when a woman's dress rustled around him, as soon as the woman looked him in the eyes — looked at him twice, that is — he became, so to speak, another person: courteous, attentive, *vulnerable*. And if this didn't pass quickly, it lasted for some time.

Besides, he possessed a sense of smell and hearing all his own if a woman were about to appear on the horizon, and with mathematical precision one could notice that whenever he fixed his eyes on a closed door or on a window

8. "Very smart."

(with the feverish intensity and awe of the recluse who is waiting to see a *vision*), always before long the door would open and a woman would walk in, or her head would pass hastily by the window, without anyone else having heard or sensed anything.

And since the house where his sister now lived was full of women—without there being any shortage of men—Jacob's eyes found very little rest that night . . . As for his heart, we can't say.

While getting his bed ready, Persa asked him when he was planning to leave.

"I've got a problem with my liver," he told her, "and I'm told the climate here is good for these things."

It was one of the few times that he answered without pulling a wry face and without getting tetchy, without, that is, taking the other person's question to be a personal insult—and his sister's question wasn't exactly *tactful*.

"I'll give you some special syrup to ease your liver," she told him, "but better that you forget about the climate here . . . We have a sick girl in the house, things are difficult, you came at a bad time."

"Why? Isn't your syrup any good for her too?" he asked her.

"It's not syrup she needs," she said. "I don't know . . . I don't know—seems to me that God's made up his mind."

"Is she old? Pretty?" Jacob wanted to know.

"No, she's a little girl who wanted to grow up. Her legs have become paralyzed—a butterfly without wings . . . Can you imagine a butterfly without wings? That's her."

"I can cure her," he said to her as though suddenly having a brainwave.

"You?" she exclaimed in complete disbelief . . .

"Yes, me—*seelance!*[9] Don't say anything to anyone."

"What shouldn't I say?"

"I'll play a couple of Russian pieces for her that no one knows . . . That Volga one and others . . . And your little butterfly will fly again, I'll make her fly again. *Compree?*"[10]

Persa sat down on the bed, resting her chin on her hands, her elbows on her knees, and for some time gazed at her toenails, which needed cutting, and at his shoes.

"If you do it," she said to him as she got up, "I'll find you a wife. This time I will—here, in this climate, perhaps even in this house. But first make the girl well, save my reputation."

9. "Silence."
10. "Understood?"

And the next morning she told Christoforos and the sick girl's parents—*though she had seen fit not to tell them this the previous evening*—that she herself had secretly told her brother to come because she hoped that his instrument and music would help Julia to walk again: she believed, she told them, in this kind of power.

They couldn't believe it at first, but they waited to see—to see and to hear in order to believe. At bottom, this is what Persa was doing too, and from this point of view, she was perhaps even more anxious than Febronia.

So when night fell, because Jacob preferred the evening hours—he considered the morning hours to be *dust*—she appeared with him in the doorway . . . They all turned to look at him, he looked like a swarthy spindleshanks in the distance like that on his ungainly pegs and his dark looks and attire, and it seems that he too wanted to look at them for a while from there, get a general feel for things and only then come inside.

"Come on . . . don't stand there in the doorway like Charon," said his sister, who had walked straight in ahead of him and now turned to go back to him. "There she is, waiting to listen to you."

Almost stumbling with vanity, Jacob got to the middle of the room and there strained his neck to look towards the bed . . . She was awake and was looking at him too.

And she had become unbelievably *littler* since the time for her had started to pass like the birds outside the window; her face was like a thimble—but she had also become unbelievably *lovelier.* Unbelievably so. It was as though loveliness had decided to become *exclusive* and invariable and had chosen the face of little Julia: a face like a beloved portrait, like personified charm, but that made you feel unhappy, unable to touch it or even approach it. This was something that her folks, who saw and caressed her every day, probably couldn't perceive, couldn't *realize*, but for someone looking at her for the first time, it was something that they couldn't forget. Nor express in words.

"It's an honor for me," he said, taking the accordion from his shoulder, and with such surprise from his twitching mouth, yet with earnestness too, with such sincerity, that is, that the little girl's mother was moved, was ashamed that she hadn't got up from her chair on seeing him in the doorway—so she got up then, looked around to find a stool for him . . . trying to hide her belly, which could no longer be hidden, as with her age.

"Have a seat, dear guest, have a seat . . . dear *in-law,* I meant to say . . . where would you like to sit?" she said to him, with one hand holding the pleated apron beneath her stomach and as though threshing or incensing the air and the floor with the other—she reminded them of the days after an earthquake or a war, when households were destroyed, houses collapsed, and they had nowhere for a stranger, a visitor to sit.

"He can have mine," said a tearful Julia, the elder one, who was sitting on a stool, cramped in the small space between the bed and the window, given that Febronia's search for a stool was confined to the main part of the room, which was taken up by others who were rather stiff and unwilling to give up their seats. And she came out of that cramped space with the stool on her head. "*Stool?* . . . *You asked for a stool?*" they were all afraid she would ask him. But she put it down silently at his feet, faltered on her way to the door, then suddenly vanished like a shadow there where a wall ends.

Of course, Jacob could only play in a high chair.

His coming was both praiseworthy and blameworthy. He appeared like a deus ex machina to stir them out of the silence and desperation of those days, yet ten evenings passed and little Julia listened to him still bedridden.

Nevertheless, the fever abated — her cheeks, which with the onset of evening would grow hot and then begin to be flushed and to burn, now remained cool and waxen day and night. And she would wait for him . . . that was something: wait with her folks for a famous virtuoso who played for her sake and only for her, instead of waiting all night for the fever to go away.

Her face would start with an uncanny longing when Persa came first into the room and announced that he was on his way, that he was coming upstairs — and with steps that sounded heavy and solid on the stairs as though he were walking on stilts: *tac* . . . and another *tac* . . . on each stair, without his lordship being in any hurry whatsoever.

"Why doesn't he walk quicker?" she asked them one evening, as though she were ready to watch him jump or something.

They smiled at her as if not hearing — better to turn a deaf ear if, in her innocence, she meant what they couldn't bear even to think.

And from nightfall to nightfall, there were always some from the houses round about who crept into theirs to hear him and see how the sick little girl was. At first they would stand discreetly on the stairs, some resting against the rail, others against the wall, leaving a passage between them for whichever member of the household had to go up or down. But gradually, as no one made them go away, they started to bring others with them and they came right up outside the little girl's door, a few even passed inside to lean against anything that was free without talking — and always with the feeling that they were doing something forbidden, that they were infringing on something . . . And it's true that there was nothing more enchanting, nothing more nostalgic or infectious as a feeling than those wonderful pieces that *the black stork* was playing for little

Julia—but also for them now, since it soon became clear that their presence, their being there, spurred his fingers, flattered him, made him surpass himself . . . As long as they didn't make any noise.

It was really strange: whereas when he played he usually had his eyes closed and seemed as if transformed, as if he were somewhere else, alone with his fingers and those rare melodies, as soon as some whispering behind him took on the dimensions of a conversation (no matter in how low a voice), he grew angry, became grumpy, and then everything stopped—the accordion and the whispering.

It's not that they did it to annoy him or to spoil the evening, but as they had begun to get to know him (and he them), they didn't think it so bad to occasionally break the devout silence to say a few words to each other: how comic his scrawny build was, for instance, with that "pumpkin" on his fleshless back or how much lovelier Julia had become (and more distant from everyday life) since the last time they had seen her running in the streets, or how the older Julia appeared a little "unbalanced" in her manners, in her ideas, and the words she mumbled now and again, and how Febronia's face had become more "harrowed and puffy" since the previous summer—they would have had to have been stones and not people (and especially not women) to have let all this go without any comment, without any *whispering*. And so, without in any way feeling disregard for his music and his talent, they didn't wait to leave the place to discuss all this at their ease.

Yet he would get angry, become grumpy (it was in his nature anyway . . .), and furiously removing his fingers from the accordion or bringing them down with force on all the keys together (creating an unprecedented cacophony), he would shout over his shoulder:

"SEELANCE!"

Seela-a-ance . . . Just this, and if he had said it to them in Chinese, they would still have understood that he meant shut up.

Shut up, then, or rather silence and reverence again so that they might enjoy his art, which was more than just music, for—whenever the time was right—there were words too, and songs, entire ballads . . . He sang them in a voice that was gruff, stiff, and quite dreary (he wasn't by any means young), the voice of an aged dog, we might say, searching for its ancestry among the rubble, with frequent pauses and deep rests (when he would frighten them: had he forgotten the words? Or had he heard them whispering again and was preparing to unleash an angry volley?) . . . a voice that always managed to find again its hazardous path, its incomparable gruffness and its bitter tones—a voice, that is, that didn't lend itself at all to lightweight festivities. And yet it allows us to suspect that if this peculiar musician had had a clear and limpid voice, the crowd around him would have disappeared as quickly as snow in mid-July.

So he was right then to come out with those murky sounds that made little Julia's face light up. And the other Julia's face too.

Some of his songs were in a strange language with a lot of *-oskaya* and *-oskoudi*, and sometimes, while he was singing, he would stop, give the accordion a break, and, randomly looking at someone, would ask him in his deep voice: "Are you conversant with all this?" (and naturally he wasn't conversant, it might as well have been a voice from above). Yet there were also songs, the words of which went straight to their hearts: "The severed, the severed bough / of pine smells sweet / and the dead live again when / some soul breathes a sigh for them . . ." Who among his listeners wouldn't sigh at such words? And what woman would remain unmoved when she heard that voice singing: "Ash I take from the fire / burning heat from my heart / and the tears from my eyes / for you to bathe in, my lady"?

They were Jacob's best moments. When you easily forgave him all his quirks and grumbling. And little Julia was now only the beginning, the spark let's say: gradually, as soon as she would start to be sleepy and turn gently on her pillow, the enchanted audience would slip into the large parlor or, weather permitting, would go down into the yard to gather there and he would again be at the center of it . . .

"Love me, don't be afraid / that it may be a sin," he sang for them one night, "and when you hear tell of hell / know that it's just . . . just a myth! Voualla!"[11] He finished the song and brought one of his fingers down heavily on a specific note—the end, they all supposed, and it was, indeed, the end. But before removing the two straps from his shoulders, before putting the accordion down at his feet and meticulously wiping the corners of his mouth and his brow a little with a handkerchief, he suddenly turned his head and, over his hump, among so many people, his eye fixed on one woman: the most hidden, the most concealed.

And just as he did every night, on closing his musical instrument with a leather latch, he said to them in his third language: "*E mante-non . . .*,"[12] adding "whatever each one feels like offering . . ."

This *offering* was something taken care of by his sister, who brought out a small plate just as in church.

And when afterwards he shut himself in the room they had given him, he

11. "There you are! I said it!"
12. "And now."

would empty out the contents of the plate on a little table, and (though he said himself that money corrupts man) he enjoyed those moments—balsam for his loneliness—as he counted out the coins and unfolded the few notes that, combined with all the rest he had, made a handsome little pile.

And in the morning, he would be late in rising—it was then that he slept, that is—and it would have to be noon, "for the sun to show its horns," as Persa shouted from outside his door, for him to make up his mind to get out of bed and go to sit at the table with them, all dressed and spruced up—till evening, which was his time, Julia's time . . . the little one and the elder one.

They had long since ceased to hope. But one evening, they didn't need him at all, and they sent him back downstairs: little Julia had asked them to take her "to the hares"—she had been asking them all afternoon . . . And her surprised father decided to take her, got the horse and cart ready, and said to Febronia, to his sister Julia, and to anyone else who wanted to come too—it looked like there would be a bright moon, an October moon, and such desires, however unexpected and inexplicable they might be, shouldn't remain unfulfilled.

The hares was not a place name; they were the hares themselves who were in abundance at that time in the meadows, and as soon as night fell and the moon came out, especially if it was full, they would come out and play with their bunnies in the moonlight. And they played so wonderfully, so wonderfully and crazily, that anyone who happened to see them—*to see hares playing in the moonlight*—said, Now *that's* happiness, *that's* paradise, and was lost for words. And if these people were hunters . . . they very soon found their words again, and that crazy playing became a dust storm and turned into writhing in the face of their shot. But if they weren't hunters, were just passing by there at that moment, then they would stand motionless, concealed behind branches and bushes, and allow their souls to be enchanted by that boundless joy— boundless—of the hares playing in the moonlight.

This is why some people would go on purpose when night fell to the edges of the meadows, either alone or with company, and wait for the hares to come out to play . . . And even those who hadn't seen them knew about their playing.

Julia had seen it—only once, but she had seen it—when she was even smaller, five or six: they were returning late from some festivity in other parts and they had her with them, together with other children, sitting two by two on some enormous fat cows . . . Strange; though there were other animals more suited to carrying live burdens on their backs, Julia clearly recalled (or we do on her account) that she was plodding along with other children on enormous fat cows

. . . Perhaps her folks had bought them then and wanted to try them out; perhaps the horses and donkeys were in short supply. And when they had reached some point and wanted to stop and rest (it was nighttime, the sky was filled with stars), in the distance, in a clearing in a wood or a depression, they saw little white animals leaping up and down like bundles of light, hugging each other and rolling about on the ground, so half of them were lost to view, then leaping up again, chasing each other, biting each other in fun, running, stopping, listening, leaping again . . . *It was the hares:* a delight to see them in that fragile hush and moonlight as they frolicked and cavorted . . . Someone next to her groaned and raised his arms in supplication: "Let my heart stop now, I can't endure any more!"—and it was the first time that she had ever seen anyone *want to die* when marveling at something, and all the others around him motioned to him with their fingers "shhh . . . ," because they too felt or wanted the same.

It was, then, this vivid (or deep) recollection, and who knows what other impulse or presentiment, that led little Julia to suddenly ask one evening to be taken again to the hares.

And they took her. They put together a rough-and-ready bed in the cart, propped her on high cushions, adorned her neck with bows and paper flowers, and wrapped her legs (all her body from the waist down) in a soft sheet, and all of them remarked on its sparkling blue color: "*Patience*—blue brings *patience*," someone had told Febronia, and she had dyed a white sheet blue and henceforth wrapped her daughter's legs in this, trying to *bind* herself too with this promise of patience . . . If the blue were to fade, she could dye it again; but if—God forbid—Julia was taken from her, who would bring her back? (Such were the thoughts she had from time to time.)

They took other blankets with them too because it would get cold later—it might have been a warm October, but it changed at night—they also took bread and quince preserve for anyone who got hungry. Next to her sat Febronia, without Sakis, her last child (because he might have suddenly started to cry and scared the hares), and all around sat a crowd of her brothers and sisters, after having sworn that they wouldn't talk, wouldn't go crazy when they saw the hares. And in front was her father in one of his shiny velvet waistcoats and the reins in his hands—"so that the hysterical women would see him again from the windows and wish that I weren't there," thought Febronia, pursing her lips . . . Febronia, who, no matter how much she felt for her daughters, unfortunately still couldn't rid herself of the other thing, the now perpetual nightmare. And as for the elder Julia, she changed her mind at the last minute and got down from the cart: she ran in front, stopped next to the ruins, and from there waved to little Julia as the cart went past—she kept waving even when the cart had disappeared from view . . .

It was still daytime, there was still light, that half-light that struggles to become dusk, and with a little luck they would arrive at a lovely meadow, Haliva, before the hares got tired of playing. With a little luck, they would even be waiting for them.

On their way, before they left the houses behind and got onto the quiet dirt roads and their real nighttime excursion began, those who encountered them and saw in the cart that now almost celestial figure of Hesychios's little daughter beside her mother crossed themselves and asked:

"Are you taking her to the doctors? To see the doctors?"

"Yes . . . to the hares," her father replied, so she wouldn't hear the same word for a third time.

And also because he really had believed that afternoon that *the hares* would save her—that there was no other miracle coming from elsewhere. So every so often he would sit up straight and whip the reins, entranced, whinnying louder than the horse, and then he would turn to see if his precious girl was watching and laughing . . . or whether she had fallen asleep.

"She's watching you, she's watching you," his wife assured him, "we're all watching you."

She wasn't lying: they were all watching him—little Julia was watching him too. Just as in the place of the horse and in front of it, she was also *watching* a line of cows that were walking languidly and steadily and taking her to the hares and lulling her . . . She was asleep by the time they arrived.

And so she didn't see Pascalis, one of her mother's godchildren, whom everyone called Pacalacou (Febronia had only been six when they had chosen her to baptize him), and who was a little touched in the head following an accident, who had arrived before them at Haliva, the outskirts of Haliva, for his own reasons, and whom they all saw down on his knees next to a walnut tree, groaning languorously almost . . . Even when he heard the wheels of the cart, even when the wheels stopped two yards in front of him, he didn't stop groaning or looking with his head completely tucked between his open knees: were his eyes fixed on a horde of treasure?

"Pacalacou! . . . What are you doing?" Hesychios asked him sternly, somewhat alarmed at his posture and at his indifference, or rather at his absorption— it being already dark and desolate there—and waving his whip in the air.

Pacalacou slowly lifted his head, saw him, saw the others who were staring at him with eyes like fireflies in the night, and equally slowly—but also in the same innocent way that he might say "Some-thing" or "No-thing"—answered quite frankly:

"Poop-ing!"

For someone to ask you what you're doing and for you to answer "pooping"! And to be actually doing it! . . . It was completely unheard of; the children in the cart, apart, that is, from Julia, who was sleeping, squealed with laughter and woke her up . . . Their father got angry: "Shut up!" he shouted, turning his whip towards them, and they cowered (yet ready to burst from their stifled laughter), while Julia stared at him ecstatically . . .

"He's attending to his bodily need, what are you getting worked up about?" Febronia said to him: she didn't like that chance encounter either, but she always managed to find a little of her own composure when Hesychios was about to lose his.

"And this is where he came to do it? Doesn't he have a lavatory at home?" he retorted, becoming even angrier.

"Come on! Who would go home just for that when he's working *kir?*"[13] Febronia reminded him. "And anyway, what home?" she remembered afterwards.

"Ki-i-ir!" said Pacalacou too, perhaps not having heard them. "Only when ki-i-ir! . . ."

"We're here tonight for another reason . . . To see the hares," Hesychios said to him, somewhat placated. "Have you seen them perhaps? Did you catch sight of them anywhere?"

Pacalacou had got up and was searching for some soft leaves . . .

Febronia tossed him a piece of bread with some dry quince preserve.

"Off with you, Pacalacou . . . ," she shouted to him with what was left of her tenderness and ostensibly for his own good. "I'm your godmother . . . Don't stay here, my boy—what are you looking for?"

"Let him tell us whether he's seen them," Hesychios said to her, resting the whip on her breast. And he again asked Pacalacou: "Have you seen them? Did they come out? Or have they already gone?"

"Ov' there," Pacalacou said, without indicating where.

"Where ov' *there?*" he asked him.

"Ov' there," he said again, pointing behind with his elbow in the direction of the meadow anyway, while he picked up from the ground the bread with his godmother's quince preserve. And heeding her advice, he sank back under cover of the walnut tree to eat it.

---

13. *Kir*—with an unusual pronunciation, somewhere between *kir* and *kiour*—was what they called staying out all night in the fields, and more generally the countryside in the light of the moon.

They left before he came out again and presently entered Haliva's magic ground.

Somewhere there, they stopped; they couldn't go with the wheels farther inside. And the children began to get down from the cart with a great many precautions and just as many antics, one moment bathed in moonlight and then in the darkness, some of them jumping over the sides and sliding down the wheels, others jumping like arrows into their father's arms, and still others straight down onto the ground, quietly and cleanly as if they didn't have any legs.

The hares were still playing a little way off . . . But in order to get a closer look at them, they had to cover quite a distance on all fours—or, rather, with their bellies to the ground—even holding their breath and begging the spirits of the night to show the same discretion.

And getting Julia out of the cart—wasn't all this being done for her?—was a little difficult, since her weak, virtually transparent legs no longer had any contact with what they were walking on, and her parents had to carry her between them, tying her like a boat, while they were forced to crawl on their knees . . . It was like the road to Calvary in a moonlit landscape.

She's paralyzed, paralyzed, what's the point? thought Febronia, terrified, ready to burst into tears, to cry out, to crack, to give up, to explode, to drive the children away from her and the hares away too. *What good will these little animals do her?* she asked herself. *What Persa did with her herbs? What Jacob did with his music? She's paralyzed! . . . And God? . . . Ah, that God—just one of him and old at that—who's he to listen to first?*

As if her thoughts had a voice, Hesychios kept mouthing "shhh . . ." through his teeth, and she would raise her eyes and look at him questioningly, sorrowfully.

And along with everything else, she made an arrangement with him, sorting out finalities: *As our hands are clasped at this moment, so let them be clasped forever, and as our fingers are joined on account of this paralyzed child, let them remain joined forever! . . . Don't join them with any other woman, don't you yourself join with any other woman—whether it's you or me who closes their eyes first (and probably it will be me), don't join with any other woman! . . . Almighty Lord, hear the sincere voice of your servant! Servant to you, servant to my jealousy—hear my sincere voice! . . .*

But as she had said herself just previously, what and who is *one* God to hear first? Hesychios was already telling her in a low voice to remove her hands; he would carry Julia on his own as it would be easier.

She took her hands away unprotestingly; peace comes to all in the end. And she was the last, following—walking upright and not crawling (not very convenient with her belly the way it was)—the procession to the hares, while he moved in front of her like a roe deer, youthful and flexible, and all that remained to her was the ultimate privilege of seeing him, seeing him in the shining light of that night and of reflecting that she was a fourteen-year-old girl when he was born, that she was already a mother when he was the same age as the little girl he was carrying . . . of reflecting on all this and of almost having forgotten *what* it was that he was carrying and *where* they were going.

Argyris, Julia's seventeen-year-old brother and the son of another of her sisters, was the first to see them . . . And as he was going on all fours, quite a way ahead of the others, he turned in the same way—though much more quickly—to tell them, Stop! You would have bet your life that something had touched him and transformed him: his eyes, movements were changed, his voice different.

"But we still can't see anything," his father whispered to him.

"They're there! . . . I saw them! . . . ," Argyris whispered in awe. "Follow me, but don't make a sound, they'll go away! . . ."

Everything that his father had been saying to him at home or on the way, he now said to his father: and it was his father's turn to heed.

So he followed Argyris with the others, all of them making every possible effort not to create the slightest noise, and they came to a spot that was ideally concealed by thick foliage, so that all you had to do was crawl inside, without brushing against anything, in order to have facing you—always at some distance but *facing you*—the enthralling spectacle: the hares at play . . .

And yet if the reflection of the moon and stars hadn't been so diffuse upon them, perhaps no one would have seen those dark animals down there . . . very dark to be hares, and also—apart from three small ones—very large . . .

At first no one said anything—whatever animals they might be, their delight in their playing was immeasurable . . . But they slowly came to realize (Hesychios and Febronia in their own way, the children in theirs) that these animals certainly weren't hares, not even ferrets or foxes. And they all broke out into a cold sweat: they were . . . wolves.

"Holy Mother!" Argyris, the eldest of the children, now whispered—with even greater awe this time.

Febronia gave him a look that those strange circumstances made rather abstruse and questioning.

"*Holy Mother!* . . . ," she said to him in a whisper and with a little spite in her voice. "Is that why you told us not to make the *slightest* noise? So that *they* wouldn't go away?"

The young lad stared at her alarmed, dumbfounded: he too hadn't realized — the first time he'd seen them — that they weren't hares . . . (Or if he had *understood* something, deep down in his conscience, he hadn't known what it was.)

It was a pair of wolves with their three cubs — and another one, bigger and in every way more imposing than the other two . . . These three held a strange posture, from which little stirred or escaped: towering in the middle was the largest, with its back turned to the frightened foliage, its tail half in the air and moving — but only to one side and languidly — and its head also turned round: towards the three cubs that were playing. (And even if it's said that wolves are incapable of turning their heads, it's not true. But in a way that renders this movement of theirs *exclusive* — and extremely impressive.) Its jaws were open: its tongue was stuck out like a poppy petal . . . Next to it, or to be precise a little behind, close up to its turned head that is, was the second one, which was ceaselessly sniffing and smelling it and occasionally licking it on the snout, indifferent to the antics of the cubs, with its ears bent back and its front legs joined in a — very elegant we have to say — V shape. Its own tail was lowered, its eyes most probably closed. And on the other side, to the left as they were looking at them, was the third, also close up and also with its front legs in that same elegant shape, the same open mouth as the first, but this one was neither licking nor being licked: it was simply gazing at the cute little cubs in front of it (most probably it was the she-wolf) and perhaps — *perhaps* — those who were hidden a little way off in the foliage wouldn't escape their attention for much longer.

They were now subject to constant streams of cold sweat: they had come looking for hares and had stumbled on a regal family of wolves. Their eyes were not even blinking, perhaps from their bewilderment and terror. As for their mouths, after the whispers between Argyris and Febronia, these had well and truly become sealed.

Since, however, they had come this far, since — by all appearances — the wolves had already exiled the hares from their meadows, and, above all, since little Julia didn't seem to be disappointed or panicked by this difference (on the contrary: she stared at them with wide-open and dazzled eyes and now and again took some deep trembling breaths as though she were about to fly) — a common and secret agreement led all the others around her to gaze in awe at the playing of the little cubs and at the simple, unadorned majesty of the other three. Besides, if they hadn't been *wolves*, if it hadn't been, that is, for the fear that their very name instills, there is no doubt that the terror of these people would have been equaled by their elation, and the bewilderment at what they were seeing would have been genuine admiration and sweetness . . . For the little cubs were no less cute and adorable than little lambs or little puppies, and as for the grown ones, these—if we might be allowed to say—are among the proudest and finest animals to be subject to such calumny and persecution . . .

When all's said and done, they are wild and wish to remain wild.

"Seems the time has come for us to be fond of wolves too," thought Hesychios, every so often casting sideways glances at his children, who were gazing—absorbed body and soul—at the scene in the clearing (the little cubs were now playing round the legs of the grown ones, provoking them to play too), and while, enclosed between his two knees, he had little Julia, whose slight and tiny movements, whose trembling and occasional spasms at the waist, and whose face filled with indescribable joy made him think that she would break free from him and set off walking! . . .

But as for the rest—and since Julia kept on proving him wrong regarding the latter—the poor man was at a complete loss, and Febronia along with him: how should they see this *lucky* encounter with the wolves? As auspicious or inauspicious? And had Pacalacou, that *warden of Haliva*, known *where* he was pointing, *where* he was sending them when he said "ov' there"? Or had he been as unsuspecting as they had been when they came full of cautious enthusiasm and unexpressed hopes to that tranquil spot?

Prompted by some unknown force or desire to *learn*, to *understand* what was happening to them, Hesychios put his mouth to his daughter's ear and asked her: "Do you want to walk, my precious . . . Now? . . ."

And he turned his ear to her so that she could say something to him.

But she didn't lean towards his ear.

"Why? . . . ," she said to him—from some distance—drawing a line across his cheek with her nail. "*Can't we see them well enough from here?*"

"Who?" he seized the opportunity to ask. "Who?"

She drew another line across his cheek with her nail and bent her neck to one side, gazing into his eyes mockingly . . . Even though it was nighttime, even though the moon is not the sun, he was certain that she was looking at him mockingly . . . teasingly, resignedly, and at the same time impatiently: as when we look at someone who asks something though he knows the answer better than we do . . .

Hesychios suddenly felt a little dizzy, a weakness in his limbs, a clouding of his mind—as though he had two heads struggling on one neck. And at the same time there came to him an *illumination* in flashes, in old images, very old—from thirty years before: a little unruly girl whom they had to chase in order to cut her nails in a yard . . . whom they caught and sat her down . . . who had looked *just like that* at her mother in her red dress when she had asked her strangely: "And why should they stay?" when he and a warden were getting ready to leave . . . *"To watch us!"* the little girl had said to her mother in an indomitable mixture of cheekiness and bashfulness, of grievance and craftiness, leaving the older woman speechless . . .

Just as he was left speechless by that same innocent craftiness, that same unpredictable mixture (of bashfulness and a thousand other things) that was in his daughter's voice and gaze at that moment: *"Can't we see them well enough from here?"* . . . The same look, the same voice, the same childlike mockery: his daughter, this very daughter, was *the daughter of the warden!* . . . Or at least she recalled her that night, greatly recalled the daughter of the warden then and of the . . . the woman in red with her big belly, with the black scissors and the brown patches on her face who had told him that unknown tale about the birds that cried *"coocoo-coo-coocooee (the little girl punished me! the little girl punished me!)"* when he was only twelve years old, when he had run from his home, when he had been found by a warden in a plum tree, when he had taken him by the hand and returned from the fields with him, when they had reached the first houses and the warden had taken him for a little time to his own house . . .

The excursion that night was taking him a long, long way: from the hares to the wolves, and from his sick little girl to his first slaughtering and the yard of the woman in red . . .

But *if that was the case*, then the woman with the umpteenth embryo inside her belly who was beside him, Febronia, the woman he had married seventeen years earlier, was the woman in red . . . Then her daughter Rodanthe was the daughter of the warden . . . So then he had fathered his son Argyris not *only* with Febronia's daughter but also with the daughter of the warden . . . But then Febronia's husband, her first husband, must have been a warden and not a cobbler! . . . Unless he was a cobbler who also worked a few days each week as a warden . . .

He felt giddy, a dizziness, ready to black out: this was no merciless merry-go-round, no spider's web, no jumble, no maze, nor even diabolical fortune. It was life itself, they themselves.

A little farther off and doubled up on her knees as he was, Febronia turned and looked at him, her eyes blinking (eyes that were now gazing at *what they hadn't seen* for so many years!), and slightly nodded her head, as though it were his thoughts that now had a voice . . . As though she wanted, tacitly and humbly, to confirm everything for him, once and for all, that the shock that he was now going through was the same shock that she had suffered from as far back as only the second day of their marriage when she had seen his younger brother, Minas, wearing Rodanthe's knitted top . . . and when for the first time her suspicion was aroused (but who was she to share it with?) that not only had she taken as her second husband the renowned and illustrious Hesychios, father of her grand-child, but also that unknown radiant boy whom her first husband had brought to their house one day, one of those days, three or four at the most, when an uncle of his who was a warden had to attend a trial in the town and had asked him to take his place.

That night, Julia and Argyris had not only brought them to the wolves, but also to the far reaches of their hearts.

On the way back—the wolves let them go, going first themselves—they picked up Pacalacou and took him with them. They saw him lying facedown under the outer branches of the walnut tree, using his two hands as a cushion for his face, which was pressed against them, so they assumed he was sleeping and decided not to disturb him. But in fact he was playing hide-and-seek with the night birds, and on hearing the wheels turned on his side and lifted one of his hands, shouting, "Godmother!" No doubt what he wanted was more bread and quince preserve . . . They took him with them.

In the cart, Febronia, after giving him a crust of bread and a little more quince preserve, being his godmother, asked him how his grandparents were (he only had the two), and he told her that his grandfather had breathed his last and they were expecting his grandmother to do the same any time.

Febronia ran her fingers through what little hair she had left.

"How, when did all this happen? I never got wind of it!" she said. "It's like I've disappeared from the world . . . I don't get wind of anything that happens. Ah Pacalacou, I'm your godmother, but better if I weren't. Cares, so many cares, my boy, they've left me a wreck . . . The answer's in my heart, I know."

This same woman who hardly said anything to anyone about her own con-cerns ("she doesn't even have a life," as others said about her), now suddenly felt an almost irresistible need to open her heart to Pacalacou, the "village idiot" (as they had christened him when he was still small), perhaps because it was only from such as him that she still hoped to find a little consolation and under-standing.

But whenever anyone said more than ten words together to Pacalacou, he appeared dejected, gazed at you hostilely (at best he was nonplussed), and unfortunately he was unable to alter this reaction even for his godmother's sake. Apart from in exceptional circumstances.

"Grandfather breathed his last," he said again, wiping the crumbs from his mouth.

And suddenly seeing how beautiful and quiet Julia was with the flowers round her neck and the blue sheet round her legs, he fell upon her and began to kiss her hair and cheeks.

"Don't, leave her! Leave her . . . it's not right for you to kiss her!" her brothers and sisters said to him, but he imagined that they were pulling his leg and only doubled his kisses, so much that Argyris picked up a stick and threatened to hit him . . . Febronia came between them, telling Argyris not to get worked up so easily and telling Pacalacou not to kiss Julia because she was tired and wanted to rest—and for her Pacalacou immediately did as he was told and backed away.

Febronia took down the lamp from the hook where it was hanging and extinguished it. And disappointed that her godchild heeded her in some things but in others didn't even listen, she sent him to sit outside, next to her husband, who was by himself. She also gave him a third piece of bread.

"And from the other . . . ," he said, waiting.

"There's no more of the other," she told him, "sweet things finish quickly, it's the bitter things that never end."

Pacalacou agreed and went outside to sit with Hesychios.

"Sit yourself down," he said to him, when he saw him coming out.

And for quite some time he didn't say anything more to him—in any case, Pacalacou rarely spoke himself. But later, he tried to get him talking about the wolves, and perhaps that's why he didn't start straightaway: in order to give Pacalacou time to forget, to lapse into his mind's numbness, because only then was there a little hope that he might say something, that you might get something out of him, even some *details* from him.

"Tell me, Pacalacou . . . I'm your godmother's husband, as you know, husband of your good ol' godmother . . . So tell me, did you know *who* comes at night to Haliva?"

"I did know," he said.

"Who?"

Pacalacou took a little time to answer. Then he said: "You."

"Yes, us. We're people—we, you . . . we're people," Hesychios said, making out that what he was saying or what he was about to say didn't interest him all that much. "But what about *animals*? Which animals come to Haliva at night to play?"

"All of them," said Pacalacou, without having to *pretend* to be uninterested.

"*All!* Don't lie to me—they don't all come! There's another meadow for all the animals."

"There is."

"But Haliva is where the *hares* often come at night to play . . . Isn't that right?"

"That's right."

Hesychios reflected that he would have been better off with a pry in his hands instead of a whip . . . Of course, the whip would do the job just as well, but he didn't want to go that far. Anyway, he went on with his questions.

"So the hares would come and play and everything was just fine . . . But perhaps wolves have been seen in Haliva of late . . . *Wolves* I said."

"Wolves have been seen," said Pacalacou, *almost* with emphasis.

"*Wolves have been seen!* What's that you say?" said Hesychios, teasing him.

"They've been seen," Pacalacou repeated. "There are wars in the hills beyond and they're driving the wolves ov' here."

"Wars?" exclaimed the driver of the cart, who was taken aback not only by what he had heard but also by Pacalacou's *eloquence*. "No one has heard anything about wars . . . Where did you hear it from? And just where are these wars?"

"Ov' there . . . in the hills beyond."

"Towards Haliva?"

"Farther, you can't see."

"And don't the hares come anymore?"

"Yes they come," said Pacalacou.

"And how does that work? Hares and wolves in the same meadow?"

"The wolves eat them so now they don't come."

"You're not making yourself clear," Hesychios complained, "first you say that they come and then that they don't come."

Pacalacou didn't reply to complaints.

"Tell me, Pacalacou, do you believe in miracles?"

"I believe in them," he said.

"Have you ever seen one? *You*, with your own eyes."

"No."

"So why do you believe in them?"

"Like you do," said Pacalacou, just as anyone might *reasonably* reply.

"And wolves? Have you ever seen wolves with your own eyes?"

"I've seen them."

"And weren't you afraid? Didn't you run and hide?"

"I was afraid . . . When they're full, they don't do any harm."

"Hmm-hmm!" retorted Hesychios, who unintentionally had started to take the conversation seriously, a conversation that recalled the chatter of monkeys—and endless chatter . . . "I was told, Pacalacou, that even when wolves are full, they still slay sheep. They don't eat them, but they still slay them. Like that, out of habit."

Pacalacou shrugged—it seems he hadn't heard anything like that or didn't believe it.

"From afar . . . ," was all he whispered.

"What do you mean from afar?" Hesychios asked.

"I saw them."

"Ah, we, too, saw them from afar," Hesychios thought to himself, "just imagine seeing them from close up! . . ." And he suddenly changed the topic.

"So then, Pacalacou . . . come a bit closer. I want to say something to you quietly . . ."

Pacalacou edged closer to him, Hesychios turned to him and, with his face almost pressing against Pacalacou's, said:

"Your godmother's first husband, do you remember him?"

"Yes, I remember him."

"What was he? A warden?"

"He was a shoemaker."

"He wasn't a warden?"

"He was a shoemaker."

"What was his name?"

Pacalacou searched his memory for a moment.

"Argyris," he said.

"Well done, so you remember that. But you don't remember if he was also a warden . . ."

" . . ."

"Do you remember how your godmother was then? . . . Do you remember what she used to wear?"

"She wore clothes."

"Thank you very much. But did she also wear a *red dress?*"

Pacalacou's eyes and mouth opened wide just as little Theagenis's had then—Hesychios caught sight of him and pulled at the reins to stop the horse so that he could see better.

"What is it?" he asked him, all excited, as when two friends are hitting the bottle and suddenly one sees he has *more* in his glass. "What is it, Pacalacou?"

Febronia stuck her head out from inside the cart—she had been jolted by the sudden halt—just like then from behind the quiet little door . . .

"Ho, ho! . . . ," laughed Pacalacou, as if he had been reminded of something very amusing.

The horse started to trot again, and Febronia went back inside the covering;

from afar, from the houses that once by one started popping up, two cocks were heard crowing together.

"It's daybreak!" said one of the children from inside, stretching.

"What else," Febronia's tired voice was heard to say.

"Tell me! . . ." her husband implored Pacalacou with some sobriety, almost wrapping the whip round his neck, round his own neck, as some people do with streamers . . . "Did your godmother use to wear a *red* dress then?"

"Yes, she wore a red dress," said Pacalacou, obliging him, and obliging him even more by adding a detail that Hesychios didn't know: "She use to go in it to the shoe shop and the kids . . . ho, ho! . . . would run after her, making fun of her. But my godmother didn't care."

That is just what the now grown-up Theagenis wanted to hear. *That.*

And he left Pacalacou near a little cottage where his grandmother lived, while Febronia once again stuck her head out to say good-bye to him and also say how sorry she was that she didn't have time to get down to see the sick old woman just for a little . . .

"But give her my warm wishes," she told him, "and tell her to expect me: I'll come another day to see her! . . . Now," she muttered to herself, putting her head back inside, "when that day will be, only God knows."

As they got nearer to their own house, she came outside and sat next to Hesychios.

"Are we going to tell the others what we saw in the meadow—or is it better not to get them alarmed?" she asked him.

Hesychios didn't give her an answer; all he did was turn his head every few moments and stare at her . . . *Stare at her.* Like then in her yard, thirty years earlier, like then at the ruins . . . *He couldn't get his fill of her.* And at the same time *he was afraid of her* . . . And he took it out with his whip on the horse's haunches.

"Why are you staring at me like that?" she asked him at one moment. "Why are you whipping the poor animal?"

"Because . . . I want you to tell me what you have to say about deep rivers!" he said to her with an expression full of greed, as though he were occupied with other things, completely different from those that were now concerning him and gnawing at him. "About the deep rivers that don't . . . what is it again that they don't do?"

"Gurgle," replied Febronia, somewhat confused, "*deep rivers don't gurgle.* Your sister Julia liked that, and she wrote it in one of her exercise books. Anyhow, are we going to tell her—and the others—what we saw in Haliva, or is it better not to rub salt in the wound?" she asked him again.

And again he didn't give her an answer. In any case, there were also the children, *the witnesses*, and most likely they wouldn't refrain from coming out with the truth: even if they were to swear them to secrecy, they'd still talk every day about the wolves . . .

As for their own secret—riding as they were like that next to each other in that noisy vehicle: a royal couple with no crown—no one would learn it.

A few days passed with lightning: that warm and gentle October with its many grapes came to an end, and little Julia was never better since the time she had fallen ill. To the point that she twice agreed to get out of bed and, holding on to the arms of one or the other, began again to walk. At least to walk stumblingly, since those shaky and unsteady steps that only just touched the ground differed in no way from the desperate efforts of a twelve-month-old infant to stand on its feet and for the first time, from this position, to look around at life and at the people who embellished it . . . Anyway, those who saw her were delighted, and some said to Febronia that they had a craving for a little *walkie pastry*: a special pie with walnuts, honey, and sesame that people made and gave to the relatives when a child of the family *walked for the first time*. (Each of the three ingredients corresponded to a wish, to an important attribute: strength, sweet days and wealth, abundance . . . Everyone's dreams, that is, that keep us on our toes.)

But Febronia took it rather as ridicule (her daughter used to dance like Salome with the *twelve* veils—so why now had they all remembered the walkie pastry?), and she didn't make any.

And one day, an ordinary autumnal day, a wind got up that grew stronger and stronger; eventually doors and windows started banging as though quarreling with each other, watering cans and brooms began racing in the yards, clothes flew away with their pegs, and all those out on the streets, passersby in the clear blue sky, clung to the walls—if they were in time—so as not to be carried away like everything else by the whirlwind.

Persa told her brother Jacob not to move, not even from one bedroom to the next, because she was in no mood to chase him through the air, but while she was speaking, a window opened behind her and the current *landed* her at his feet.

"You should be careful what you say!" he said to her with a sardonic look.

And Febronia, who was looking for something among wood and crates in a shed at the back of the house, stopped her searching and rushed to go out, but as soon as she pushed the door open, the wind blew it shut in her face. She pushed it again, and again the wind blew it shut on her.

"Ah—wind, we'll have to have words," she said to it.

She took a deep breath and pushed the door with both hands. But again the wind blew it shut in her face.

"So what do you want? Do you want us to fight?" she said to it again. And flustered and angry, she grabbed hold of a piece of wood and pushed the door with that—managing like this (though quite unprepared) to leap outside into the raging wind.

She ran into the house as though being whipped. And anxiously she rushed upstairs, to where Julia was, but before getting there, while climbing one by one those stairs that in the past she ran up so fast that no one could catch her, the breath had left her body: out of fear, the unbridled fear that if by chance the window, which was next to her daughter's bed, had blown open she would never see her daughter again, she would find the bed empty . . . It was the kind of fear that clouds your mind even if there's not a lot of substance to it: is it possible, is it feasible that the wind could carry away a little twelve-year-old girl from her bed? And yet the poor woman thought of this too as she ran up the stairs: if she's not been taken today, she'll live another thirty years!

And she reached the room and put her hand on the doorknob to push open the door (remembering the capers of the other door . . . and virtually certain that she would find herself staring at an empty bed . . .) and she halted.

"Julia? . . ." she called in a low voice, as though trying to sweet-talk her fears; and she felt herself squeezing hold of a cold hand. "*Julia!*"

No one answered, and this, for her heart, was the last breath. She stared at the door like an idiot and couldn't understand why she literally didn't scream the door down or why she didn't push it open so she could see the rest . . .

She went back as far as the stairs, without really knowing why, and then returned to the door. And this time, as though she had been locked outside, she began beating it with her fists and shouting.

She immediately heard footsteps from inside and fell silent. And when the door opened, she saw standing before her the elder Julia . . . and behind her the room, which was dim and with leaves on the floor, dry yellow leaves evidently blown in by the wind . . . She also saw little Julia in her bed looking at her anxiously from under the covers, but not with the same madness that was in her eyes: everything was quiet in there, even if the floor was covered with leaves . . .

"Why don't you answer when I call you?" she asked these two who were in a world of their own, after recovering a little from her own panic.

"It's windy . . . ," the elder one said, meaning that perhaps for this reason they hadn't heard.

"*It's windy!* That's why I lost my wits," said Febronia, looking at the bed. "And didn't you hear me either?" she asked the little girl, more softly and meaningfully.

"I heard something . . . ," she said, though looking more at her aunt, as though asking her if what she was saying was true.

"So if you heard something, why didn't you say *yes! I'm here?*" her mother asked her. "And why is it so dark in here? What happened?"

"We're listening to the wind . . . ," the younger one answered again, and the elder one added that they had closed the shutters because the wind kept blowing the window open and they were scared — she pointed to the leaves on the floor . . .

Febronia breathed a deep sigh.

"Everything frightens me these days, and even more so today," she said. "I won't be able to get any peace unless that wind dies down."

Yet before she had even finished speaking, all three of them raised their eyes to the ceiling: it was as if horses were galloping on the roof . . . that's how gusty the wind was at certain moments.

"I won't be able to get any peace," Febronia repeated aphoristically.

And for some time, she remained motionless, listening to the wind with the other two . . . Then she stooped to pick up some of the leaves from the floor, muttering: "It's one of those winds that doesn't last long, but it will rip up trees in its path. Once a wind like that," and she raised her voice, "snatched an infant from its mother's breast, can you imagine? She hadn't tried to shelter when she heard it . . . and anyway where could she shelter? She was suckling it out on the threshing floor. And the wind snatched it from her! She was fortunate it didn't snatch her breast too! . . . *And it happened.* It happened when I was little, it's not that I read it somewhere," she said, casting a fleeting glance at her sister-in-law and putting the leaves into a bowl on the table. "And a lot more has happened on account of such winds, but some things are better left unsaid."

"And what happened to the infant?" asked her sister-in-law in a stifled voice.

"It went together with her nipple . . . Just like I'll be gone one of these days," said Febronia, who now saw everything revolving around her own pain . . . But she finished the story about the infant. "They found it in some holly oak, five acres away. The holly oak saved it — it was covered in cuts and scratches, but it was saved from the wind. And by a miracle it still had a little breath left in it! . . . Otherwise they wouldn't have found it . . . not even at the other end of Serbia."

Outside, the wind was still blowing, still pounding between the walls, though something told Febronia—while she was talking—that it had already started to abate. She went over and looked through the slats of the shutter . . . A few moments passed and she went on looking . . .

"It's dying down . . . ," she said eventually, turning to the two Julias, who were also listening to the strange way that this fierce wind—*sidling* up and down— was abating. "It's going elsewhere now . . . dying down here," she said again, as if not believing it.

And when she was sure that the wind outside had, in fact, abated, that all the other things inside her had also abated, she pulled back the two latches from the closed shutter and pushed it to open it: one last gust caressed her face . . . And as she poked her head farther out—to see what was happening outside—the *remnants* of a gust brushed her cheek like a feather . . . And everything around her, and farther still, felt the same: what remains, so to speak, from what has passed.

Nevertheless, after testing its strength among the houses and the people, this wind continued its path farther afield, in the forested areas, and even today they still talk about a LINE, two yards wide and half a mile in length, without trees, bare, that it left in its wake. *The twister.*

Even today they still talk about it.

And the following day—a day of despondent calm but also of glorious sunshine—everyone was talking about this, about that *line* on the horizon that, from various vantage points, they were able to see clear and distinct from everything around, as well as if it were a straight and shorn strip on the back of a ram.

In the afternoon, in Julia's room, she and her mother were dozing: she on her pillows, Febronia lying at her side, with a broad beam of sunlight streaming slantwise over the two of them, teeming with golden particles and infusing the room with an incredible glow and warmth.

"We'll hear the cuckoo again, Julia!" her mother said to her at one moment. She said it quietly, as though it had escaped from her lips, yet with conviction, with surprising ardor.

Her daughter most likely didn't hear, or at any rate didn't answer.

Febronia gazed at the wooden floorboards that this year they still hadn't covered with the winter rugs because of the prolonged good weather; she gazed at them, at how they too looked pleased by this sunlight, and bringing before her eyes *the leaves* that she had picked up from there the day before, and bringing to her ears *the wind* that had been raging outside, she went on with this pleasant thought on her own: since that raging wind lifted us off our feet yesterday but left us safe in our beds, since the trees were enough for it, we'll hear the cuckoo again in spring! . . . She recalled one of her grandfather's sayings but of lots of other old people too: if they heard the cuckoo's song in spring, they regarded it as a good sign; that they would see out the year, that life was giving them one year more . . . They always regarded it as a good sign.

And Febronia already regarded as a good sign the fact that the previous day's gale had passed without taking little Julia with it . . . Propping herself on her elbow, she raised herself up a little to see what Julia was doing: she had her eyes closed, with her eyelids trembling occasionally as though she were dreaming. Febronia closed her eyes again.

And gradually an extremely melodic, almost feminine voice began to infiltrate its way quite effortlessly into her drowsiness: *". . . o-o-ocks . . . erwa-a-are . . . o-o-oins . . ."*

She opened her eyes again, as though by doing this she would be able to hear or understand better. And so it was: what had seemed like the distant wind-borne song of a Siren was the voice of a peddler, who was getting nearer and shouting (but without actually *shouting*, without yelling at all as others do) that he buys, in short, what they didn't want: "Broken clo-o-ocks . . . silverwa-a-are . . . o-o-old-co-o-oins . . . a-a-all your o-o-old things I buy . . ."

It had been some time since they'd heard a peddler, and a very long time since they'd heard a voice so calm and welcome that even with those extended vowels, it didn't grate on the ears. On the contrary, it flattered them, almost pandered to them, as when you caw to birds, imitating their voice . . .

And he let a few moments pass and then came out again with exactly the same words . . . And he must have been walking very slowly, or not walking at all, because his voice seemed to be coming always from the same place: from somewhere close by, perhaps from beneath their window. Too lazy to get up and go all the way around the bed to get there, Febronia climbed over Julia to get to the other side, and raised herself up with not a little difficulty, holding on to the window ledge, and looked out from behind the window—as far as she could see. She couldn't see anyone. She turned to Julia, who still had her eyes closed. The voice was heard again just at the moment that Febronia was climbing back over Julia again to avoid going all the way round the bed, but mainly to *undo* her first movement—a movement that was generally considered to be inauspicious and was in all secrecy forbidden: when you climbed over someone like that, that someone might not grow up! But if you climbed back over that someone in the opposite direction, then the danger was allayed.

". . . a-a-all your o-o-old things I buy . . ."

Julia's eyes half opened as if she were just emerging from a deep sweet sleep.

"What's he saying?" she asked her mother, "*broken clocks . . . old . . .* what did he say after *broken clocks?*"

"He's saying about coins too," said Febronia.

"And what else? He's saying about something else."

"I can't make it out . . . *o-o-old things* . . . Let's listen again."

They listened to him carefully, but once again they couldn't make out clearly what he was saying—even though he had a clear voice—after *broken clocks*.

He stopped as he had been doing every so often . . . They waited for him to start up again, but he didn't.

"Pity," said Julia, after waiting a while, sometimes with closed and sometimes with half-open eyes.

"He'll no doubt pass by tomorrow," said her mother.

And then he rewarded her: his voice came again two or three times, now putting—just imagine—an "all" before every word: an "all" that gave a more official and distinct tone to what he was asking for, but also an infinitely more solitary tone: "A-*a-all* broken clo-o-ocks . . . *a-a-all* silverwa-a-are . . . *a-a-all* old co-o-oins . . . a-a-all your o-o-old things . . ."

"All silverware," whispered Julia, contented.

"Yes, it was all silver—"

"A-a-all broken clo-o-ocks . . . a-a-all silverwa-a-are . . . a-a-all old co-o-oins . . . a-a-all your o-o-old things I buy . . . ," his melodic voice came again to interrupt her, as though correcting her for having missed half his "alls."

That *all*. One *all*, and Julia breathed her last. That's all it took.

Ninth Tale

"THE WINDS WERE BLOWING FROM ALL QUARTERS AND THE TORTOISE WENT WITH THE CANDLE ON ITS BACK"

And what things they had to remember of that golden-red butterfly who vanished with the peddler's voice . . .

A door opposite the bottom of the house's main staircase—a tall wooden door that led to a storeroom with firewood where they went only in winter—was found to be marked on the other side with a stack of horizontal pencil lines, and carefully written next to every pencil line was a different date. Some dates were very close to each other (even from one day to the next!), others were weeks or months apart, and all of them were from the past three years, more or less. The distance between some of the lines was no more than a hair's breadth, and the distance from the lowest line to the highest was not more than half a hand's span. The highest was also the most recent: around four months earlier.

They all imagined it was something thought up by the elder Julia, who, no longer content with her secret exercise books, was now also etching her chronologies on this rarely opened door . . . And yet she was the only one who knew that these pencil lines were the work of little Julia: "Here is where," she told them, "she measured her height . . . how much taller she was getting day by day . . . I was the only one she told because I caught her at it once . . . And she asked me from then on to be the one to measure her . . . I would put my hand to the point where her head reached on the door, and then we pressed hard on the pencil to mark the spot . . . And afterwards she would write the date herself: today so much, the next day so much . . . Once it was very cold in here, very cold . . . Let's be going, I said to her, the cold makes us smaller, not taller . . . She wanted to grow as tall as the door! First as tall as me, then as tall as Grandma Persa, she said, and then as tall as the door! . . . But I can't go on, I don't want to remember."

No one *could bear to remember*, yet they did nothing else.

On the evening of the day they bid farewell to her—and certainly before, when they still had her close to them and paid their respects, but especially when they returned *without her*—the house was satiated with their words and their talking and by the name *Julia*, the name *Julia*, that double name that was also the name of her living aunt, her godmother, and which by an ironic coincidence was related acoustically (essentially, that is) to *Cletia, Febronia,* and *Efthalia*. Whether present or absent, these names, people, all of them had something to say on the occasion—and to the credit—of this little girl's passing so quietly and so incomprehensibly to the other shore.

Being the one most often chosen for such blows, Febronia had the first word—and the last. Whenever anyone else interrupted her to say something, even if it were her husband or another of her children, she would come back with another ten new memories and episodes: when Julia said that, when she did the other, when she went there, when she got wet, when she was frightened, when she had stepped on a bee and the bee hadn't been happy about it, when a tortoise had crawled over her—she had been lying on her back, dozing in a field—not to harm her of course, but simply because it had encountered her on its path just as it encountered countless other minor obstacles it was able to surpass; when they had found her riding a dog and she had smacked her, and the dog had started barking, ready to tear them to pieces because they had deprived it of the little girl; when she had implored them with tears in her eyes to give *her too* a little purgative (she saw it all white and thick pouring from the bottle onto the spoon and from the spoon into someone's mouth, and she was envious, who knows what she thought about how special it must be, how tasty and desirable, and she was driven crazy by the idea that *they wouldn't give any to her*), so when one day Febronia let her have a spoonful to get some peace from all her crying, Julia had the runs for three days and couldn't even stand up, she had no intestines left . . . Or when she had fallen into a crate of tomatoes and they looked everywhere for her but couldn't find her, and when they did find her, they didn't find any tomatoes . . . Or when, still little, she hadn't been able to walk, but was already so lively that she stuck her hands in wherever you could imagine, and one day, pushing a blade this way and that, this way and that (trying to get hold of it), she had cut two of her fingers, one on each hand, and Febronia had bandaged them for her with two cloths so she wouldn't see the blood and be frightened. And yet Julia liked those *little white bonnets* on her fingers and fixed her attention on them, holding her hands out in front of her, at some distance, as though looking at an open book with images . . . She fixed her attention. For two hours, till she got hungry and thirsty, she simply gazed at her fingers just as Gabe did at the ants. And from that time on, whenever Febronia wanted to have a little peace, she would sit on the bed, pretend to cut her fingers with something, and immediately, supposedly in a panic, would bandage them for her with white cloth—and that was all it took: Julia found something to occupy her, and Febronia could get on with her work. Until, of course, Julia got fed up with this and Febronia had to think up something else. But in the meantime the little girl began to walk and to occupy herself with a pile of new and different things, which again left Febronia in peace—even amusing her or sometimes infuriating her.

Or when—to get out of the flow of all these unforgettable things—Julia did that . . . when she did the other . . .

There is nothing more natural for a grown-up than to reminisce about his childhood, and heaven forbid that this mixture of pleasure and pain should be missing from our lives—even if it leaves us with a taste of something *illusory*. But for a child to be lost and for you to reminisce about its yesterdays, to be nostalgic about what it didn't manage to be nostalgic about, this is a pain of the bitterest kind—and only those who have experienced it can be rightly said to know it.

On the contrary, everybody knows that when the mind cannot endure to dwell on some detail, it slips away and turns to a thousand other things . . . it requires time. And this is what happened that night in the big house of Christoforos after the funeral (and the complete absence) of his twelve-year-old granddaughter: their minds and their words turned to a thousand other things, to what was and wasn't anymore.

Febronia had such verve in her recollections and stories with incredible descriptive episodes about the hale and hearty young girl, had so much excitement, so many flushes and feverish shivers that every so often she would remove a cardigan from her shoulders then put it back on, looking at it strangely, would ask for water that she didn't drink, yet would reach out her hand to take it as she would to the highest branch of a tree (as though her movements had no connection with her needs or with the object she was touching), and her face seemed more rosy, restless, and entranced than in her youth—a youth that had long ceased to concern her, while Hesychios beside her was disconcerted and taken aback at seeing her like that: Was it a dead daughter they had in the house or a joyful celebration? But also (and *mainly*, for him . . .), Where for so many years had *this* been hidden, this face of the woman in red, who had once enchanted him?

She wasn't looking at him exactly, her eyes had no room to look at anyone, to take anything into account, only room to recall and bring before her little Julia, her works and days. She had them wide open, that is, and fixed on his feet, in that *abyss* of memories, and she never even noticed when it was that he went out for a while or when it was that he came back . . . And occasionally she escaped from her other recollections, those that kept her on the surface of her pain, to ask his feet: "*Was it on account of us* that she died? *Was it on account of us*, do you think, that she died?" and whoever heard her understood the harsh drama of this question, but usually none of this was heard by the others.

Or at other times, at the same moment that she was narrating something or happened to be listening to something, she would whisper to herself, "Am I asleep or alive? What a moron, am I asleep or alive?"—"I'm asleep," she would answer herself, "It's in my sleep that I'm seeing all this . . ." Yet this feeling that they were *asleep* was something that others had too—a feeling that even the most composed person has when something strange happens to him, either when it's something horribly unpleasant or an unexpected opportunity for riches.

And when the couch or the divan was no longer big enough for her, as unaware she passed from one to the other, she simply got down on the floor with her legs relaxed, her shoulders relaxed, and an indifferent *mass* in front of her, with her gaze remaining ever fixed on that abyss, wandering ceaselessly, somewhere there at Hesychios's feet, as if there were nothing else around her, as if everything had accumulated there. And nevertheless—with her hands still reaching for and refusing the same things—the vivid and joyous incidents with little Julia endlessly poured from her mouth . . . Besides, it was as though her aspect had two faces, or rather her face had two aspects: the one amazingly fixed on absence, uninvolved in any act or thought, and the other completely tangible and flexible, *here*, in all the things she was with such fervor saying about Julia, whom she now doted over for one thing, now scolded for another, pulled towards her, sent away, went out to the *parmakia*,[1] and called to come in because it was getting dark, because Julia always forgot herself at play or when in other people's houses.

And suddenly, after an upsetting silence, when all the gushing no longer allowed her to recall anything specific: "You say something too," she urged those around her (at first she didn't let them get a word in), "you all knew her too, lived beside her . . . say something!"

And it was then that Febronia laughed . . . At almost anything they said, she would laugh and flush right down to her neck since most of the episodes with the little and unforgettable Julia had—before she got ill of course—laughter either as their occasion or their consequence. Particularly when they said things that she heard for the first time, that by chance she didn't know (Julia, you see, didn't belong only to her: her pranks reached as far as the farthest houses),

---

1. "The railings," "the balconies."

well—it was then that Febronia's laughter prepared the ground for all kinds of misunderstandings, especially on the part of those women who had never forgotten what this widow had done *after* the death of her first daughter and *with whom* she had gone off and spawned all her other children.

"It's a good thing that Julia didn't manage to grow up and find a love of her own, or lose her honor . . . She would have taken him from her—she still has some elbow room to work with!" said one woman, and aware of the venom contained in her words, she took out her handkerchief and neatly wiped her thin, unsmiling lips to stop it from dripping onto her chin.

"Why look so far ahead?" said another. "She had her so many months in the house, ill and bedridden—any other mother, my poor dears, don't you agree, any other mother would have moved heaven and earth to save her—whereas she was out on the streets following her husband—as though more *susceptible* because of the worry they already had in the house—in case he happened to look at some other woman!"

"You're not serious! . . ." (There happened to be one innocent woman in the group.)

"Serious, you say—on everything that's holy!"

"And how did she have the heart? With a child in the house at death's door . . ."

"You'd better ask her, how should I know how she had the heart. *She* was the one who was following him around, not me—I couldn't care less about him!"

"As you've made your bed, so you have to lie in it," said the first woman by way of an epigram.

Far from these women, Febronia every so often became aware of her situation, and removing that incredibly apathetic gaze of hers for a while from the feet of her husband she asked him directly to his face:

"And Julia now . . . *with all that we're doing* . . . what will she say? She'll be ashamed of us, won't she be ashamed?"

Deeply preoccupied—because of the death, the emotional upset, the sick laughter, the moaning, the endless night, but also because of what had been tormenting him and getting him worked up again following that night with the wolves—he said to her: "She'll like it, she'll like it . . ."

"Do you think so?" she asked, as though seeking the greatest of help or at any rate the truth. "Do you think so or are you just saying it so I won't be ashamed?"

"She'll like it . . . how should I know? I wish she were here too to laugh louder than any of us!"

"You can say that again . . . But about who? About who?" asked Febronia.

"About Julia? About the other one? . . . About which one first?" And her gaze sank into the void again, the stories began again.

She told them about that day when she saw Julia looking at a little boy by the name of Antonakis, who was cracking walnuts in a corner and then putting them in his mouth quickly like a squirrel, as if he were afraid lest someone come and take them from him. She looked at him for some time, looked covetously. "Why are you eating walnuts?" she eventually asked him. "Because my tummy's hurting," he replied cleverly. "Ah! . . ." said Julia, going over to him. But the closer she came to him, the more the boy squeezed himself into the corner where he had chosen to eat his walnuts. Yet she didn't hold back: as he edged farther into the corner, so did she. It reached a point where he could no longer crack open the walnuts with the hammer without also hitting his own toes . . . "Go away, you stupid girl!" he said to her angrily. "Why should I go away?" she said, and her eyes opened wide, like so: "My tummy hurts too!"

Even the squirrel laughed, and he gave her a few nuts.

Really, you didn't know whether it was a funeral that had taken place or an engagement party, with the mother of the young girl praising her to the groom's family, preparing them at the same time for her vivacious character, for the surprises that lay in store for them with this bride.

So much so that it seemed to some the most unnatural thing, that little Julia was still among them just as much as the cooing of a wild dove is where grain is being sown: confused, alive and dead, shy and shameless, ready to begin dishing out slaps or nips for what they had done to her—for dressing her up as a twelve-year-old bride and putting her into the ground! . . . And it was as though her mother beside her was encouraging it all, fair or unfair.

Besides, there was also the family of a groom who had been dead for years: Febronia's first husband, Argyris F. These grave and quiet people—who from the time Febronia had married again (and married in fact the one person she shouldn't have) hadn't wanted to set eyes on her again, not even a picture of her—swallowed their hate and went all together to lend support by their presence at the death of her little daughter, though for them, it was *only* the death (and the consequences) of her first daughter that counted, of their real niece. Nevertheless, they went. But on seeing their once sister-in-law, that unfaithful and wayward woman as they had once characterized her, lamenting her dead child by narrating the most pleasant things she could remember about her and by unbosoming herself with laughter and excitement, they couldn't bear it, and one of them asked her at one point whether she didn't have anything more unpleasant to remember . . .

"Of course I have!" cried Febronia. "I've a heap of sorrows, a mountain! . . . When she told us about the hares—*take me to see the hares, I want you to take me to see the hares*—who would have thought that a quick death, one in a hurry, was already around us, and wouldn't let her slowly fade between her sheets for another forty months . . . who would have thought it? We took her to the hares. And the hares turned out to be . . . *wolves with their cubs* . . . But she laughed like they were hares, fooled us: she got to her feet, made out she was walking a few steps, her eyes shone again . . . She fooled us like she used to fool the neighborhood kids! And we thought, The girl is going to get well, we don't need to swarm round her like bees swarming round a flower. And we left her, everyone went back to their work, and a day came when she was alone in her room, in her bed, or at most with her aunt who baptized her, or at most with me . . . Because that's what she wanted: to end without us breathing all over her, without a dozen people all around her and a dozen pairs of eyes. No one dies easily when there are so many eyes around begging him to live, holding his hands to stop him from departing! The soul doesn't come out softly, it sticks in the throat, turns back, is tormented . . . That's what our Julia did. Is that enough for you? Or do you want more?"

They pursed their lips even tighter. Febronia continued:

"A whole twister passed outside and left her, didn't take her. And she ended up being taken by a peddler, one of those who go around asking for any and all old clocks, all . . . anything to be thrown away . . . it's just not possible, merciful God! It's not possible! That's how the jewel of our house went—that peddler took her soul with him! . . . Yet he had such a voice, a fine and soothing voice— must have once been a cantor—so that . . . if I'd had my wits about me at that moment, I'd have hung on to her so he'd have taken me too! It's *me* who's the useless clock after all, the silverware that's become tarnished and is beyond being polished again. *Me!* . . . Do you want more? I'll tell you: Julia paid the price for my other daughter, your niece, who was once in love with *him!*"

As if her greatest sorrow had come out of her, she pointed at her husband's feet.

They half-turned to look at him, to haughtily assess his wretched charm— and this perhaps satisfied them a little.

And Febronia continued narrating things both pleasant and unpleasant, now mixing in childhood memories from her other daughter, Rodanthe, and only those who had known her too, who remembered her, could distinguish which memory was of the one and which of the other—Febronia herself didn't appear to particularly distinguish them, or perhaps she simply didn't care about such a rudimentary difference.

"Her nails, good heavens—what I had to go through every time I tried to cut her nails! It was war! I had a pair of black scissors, as big as she was, I got hold of them and chased her, and how! Like chasing a butterfly in flight . . . By the time I caught her, my own nails had grown—I'd sit down and cut my own, while lace fans came out of hers. That's how much she loved her nails!"

Once again she burst into laughter, perhaps the sickest laughter of the whole evening, a worm gnawing at her that became a beast and devoured her, dominated her, while Hesychios got to his feet suddenly and went outside, his legs barely supporting him and supporting his head with one hand. She followed him with a fiery look, vacant from so much intensity . . . He must have been overcome by *lossness*,[2] thought the others—from so much fatigue, from so much . . . One of his sisters ran after him, Lily ran after him too . . . Febronia went on:

"I would get angry then with her vivaciousness, I'd go blue in the face with all the shouting, but now—if only she were here and let her flay me with her nails!"

"*She should have flayed you! . . . We all should have flayed you then! You she devil!*" was the spiteful comment of one of the group of women standing to one side and observing everything going on with eyes and tongues that dripped venom; one of those who were once Febronia's companions, mothers who had lost their daughters for the sake of that man, and who whirled and turned this way and that as if they'd been bitten by a tarantula with six babes in their arms . . . And whom one day Febronia had *betrayed* by going with him! And he had accepted her!

Julia was buried and an old tale was unburied, which none of these women (or any of the others generally) had ever forgotten or forgiven. Perhaps first and foremost Febronia hadn't forgiven herself for it, but her *ways* differed so much from those of the other women, so much so that whatever happened from then on, however many more daughters she lost, however much laughter tarnished her or graced her, nothing would ever make her like them.

And at one moment, Persa went up to Christoforos and quietly said to him: "There are some women out in the parlor who are lying in wait with eyes and ears open and have taken it upon themselves to speak ill of your daughter-in-law, who's laughing, they say, as though she were celebrating her daughter's marriage! . . . Go and put them in their place, today's not a day for that kind of talk."

2. *Dizziness, swooning,* feeling that you're *not all there.*

For some time Christoforos had not been able to hear well, but of late he was becoming even more hard of hearing.

"Who should I put in their place? Febronia?" he said to her. "She's like the wind . . . Her daughter's dead and she's mourning her as only she knows how. And she's right to do so."

"I'm not saying anything to the contrary," Persa replied, "but put those others outside who are speaking so ill of her in their place. Their words are cutting . . . files for sharpening knives. Find a way to get them all in here and tell them that story that you once told me, about the tortoise, that made me laugh . . . It will give your daughter-in-law a bit of respite if no one else . . . Because her laughter is costing *her* more than anyone else tonight."

Christoforos had also begun forgetting.

"What story with the tortoise?" he asked her. "When did I ever tell you stories about tortoises?"

"Then! At a funeral that we'd gone to together two or three years ago of a — distant — uncle of yours? cousin of yours? I don't recall. They were laughing there too. They were remembering some of his old ways — he was something of a prankster — and they were laughing. He was old too, of course, he'd had a good run, it didn't cost them too much to mourn him with laughter . . . But here tonight . . . they've all taken Febronia the wrong way, are making her a target. Do what you can to justify her. Tell them the story about the tortoise that went with the candle on its back! . . ."

"Ah . . . so that's the one you're talking about," said Christoforos, remembering.

And he found a way to round them all up, to ask for quiet, to ask for a little silence and attention from even the most grieving women, and to tell them an *ordinary* story with an unexpected ending.

Once, he said, in days long gone, a mother lost her son, a fine young man like cool water — there wasn't a handsomer lad or one more intelligent, kinder, or more hardworking than him. People came from all parts to pay their respects and offer comfort to his mother, but naturally nothing would comfort her — she mourned him and kept on mourning him, pulling at her hair and beating her breast beside his coffin . . . A tortoise heard all this lamentation and thought it her duty to go to the funeral too. But how could she go? Just with her shell? No, everyone else was going with candles. So she too had to go with a candle. But how was she to carry a candle? Where could she put it so that it wouldn't fall? She thought and thought and at last found the answer: She lit the candle and stuck it on her back! And she set off like that, with the lighted candle on her back, and laboriously arrived at the house where they had the dead youth. But the first people who saw her in the yard started to laugh, to laugh under their breath, to choke with laughter . . . "Where are you off to, Mrs. Tortoise?" they asked it. "To say my farewells to the young lad," she replied. "And that candle on your back, what's that for?" they asked her. "Why? Didn't you come with candles too to bid him farewell?" said the tortoise quite seriously. "Yes, we came with candles, but . . . ," *ha ha ha* and *hee hee hee*, and they choked with laughter: they had never before seen anything like that—*a tortoise coming with a candle on its back!* Never before . . . and they found it very funny—moving but funny. But the tortoise, without losing either her courage or her grief, reached the room where they had the dead youth. But once again she found her way blocked by some of the dead boy's aunts, who, seeing her in the doorway, rushed to chase her away because such a funny tortoise would make even the bereaved mother laugh . . . "Let me say my farewells, why don't you let me?" the tortoise called out complainingly. "Who is it? Who's calling out like that?" asked the mother, who was bent over her son's corpse. "A tortoise!" the other women told her. "And why don't you let it come in?" she asked, surprised. "Let it come in . . . Come inside, Mrs. Tortoise, come and grieve for him too . . ." And as soon as the grieving mother turned her head and saw the tortoise, in deep mourning though she was, *she burst out laughing too* . . .

And since that day it's always said that people at funerals should laugh, there's just no other way. This is what the wise old tortoise had come to teach them.

Late that night, when the last people had left Christoforos's house, Febronia went up to her room alone. She had neither laughter nor tears left, neither for Julia nor for the other daughter, and when she saw Hesychios stretched out on the bed, with the covers to one side, breathing deeply with eyelids closed, and a lamp burning on a stool beside him, she moved like someone lost to the world, as though it wasn't her who was moving, and simply turned down the wick in order to get undressed and lie down beside him . . . But while she was sitting on the edge of the bed with her back turned to him and had removed her garment from her shoulders without having the strength to pull it farther down, to remove it completely, she noticed that the floor around her feet, which had been dark, was slowly getting lighter . . . She thought, *Something's happening,* and mechanically raised her eyes to the wall opposite: the wall too was dimly lit, and this lighting (slowly yet constantly) grew stronger and rose towards the ceiling . . . She raised her eyes there and saw huge trembling shadows *unknown to her* . . . She was afraid of maybe seeing more—yet at the same moment, she suspected Hesychios behind her and turned round: she saw him, and from being stretched out on the bed with eyes closed he had quietly sat up (slightly turned in the other direction) and was slowly turning up the lamp wick, and from his safe place was watching her inner reactions . . .

"You scared me," she said to him breathlessly, "I thought I was about to see Julia! . . ."

"Julia is fine. Leave her for a little to herself tonight," he said to her in a soft voice, with a glint on his face, on that unfadingly attractive face, but also in his voice, his eyes, his smile, which made her think of a thousand and one things . . . A thousand and one things, but not the one thing she heard next: *"Are you the wife of the forest warden?"*

She looked at him strangely, as though she had lost her tongue. She remembered something, understood something, a loose thread found its bobbin and began to rewind itself . . . But why that night? Why *this, too,* that night? For the previous fifteen years, she had no longer thought of it, she had no longer been tormented by her daughter's little knitted top with the embroidered "R" that she had seen Minas, the youngest of her new brothers-in-law, wearing . . . During the first two years of her marriage, this suspicion had tormented her far more often, but there were so many other strange things about that marriage that she decided to forget about the knitted top, to put it out of her mind. And she really had forgotten it: her fear in case she lost Hesychios, in case she lost him before she herself was lost to the world, had helped her forget the knitted top. Besides, she had never seen Minas wearing it again: as though he had worn it once and once only—deliberately: to alarm her from only the second day of her marriage . . . From then on a life had begun, a rose-gardened *tortura*,[3] that left her with no time for thinking about what had happened in the past: her worry and her jealousy lest Hesychios went with any other women was enough for her to deal with . . .

And if it had seemed to him—then, in Haliva, with the wolves—that she had smiled at him as if to confirm everything, it was just his idea, the product of his own suspicion (so belated, but not late), which was so pricking him at that moment. . . . If she turned and looked at him, blinking her eyes and nodding her head, it was simply because she *wanted* to say to him: "Just look what this evening had in store for us . . . The sight of wolves!"

But *wolves,* when their time comes, appear on all sides, and their eyes are shiny and penetrating like nothing else . . . Wolves, not with their accustomed *attributes,* not necessarily as enemies, but as pawned memories—of that *"tender wakefulness that is mightier than the sword and is feared by those who fear to exist."*[4]

---

3. *Torment, anxious love.*
4. From lines by the poet Tassos Tanoulas.

This was how Hesychios's eyes were at that moment.

"Why don't you tell me?" he asked her again. "*Are you the wife of the forest warden?*"

Febronia pulled her dress back up, covering her shoulders.

"Listen," she started to say.

"The woman in the red dress? Who was chasing her daughter to cut her nails? The *wildling?*"

"Listen . . . ," she said again, searching for what she would say next: "If you don't think of me as your wife, then . . . *I am the wife of the forest warden.*"

"Then you're *twice mine,*" he said, ever ready and bedazzled. "Once for *then,* and once for *afterwards.*"

And he pulled her into his arms, wrestled and kissed her on the mouth the way he used to kiss her on the first nights—but above all, he "snapped her" out of that dream of hers.

She felt ashamed and tried to pull away from him, to wipe her lips, to prevent him from doing it again: she felt as though one of her own sons were kissing her—and she felt it *then* for the first time, and it was torture, it was disastrous . . .

"Who was it that you had in your belly *then?*" he asked her as they wrestled, and his "then" was much weightier.

"Konstantakis . . . I don't remember!" she replied, frightened, his now . . . just as she had always been his since then.

"Konstantakis, yes . . . now it all makes sense! . . . And how did it come about that your husband was a warden?"

"He wasn't a warden . . ."

"I know . . . But that day he was a warden—why?"

"It was an uncle of his who was the warden, not him . . . But the uncle . . . was away for a few days . . . and he took his place."

"Now it all makes sense . . . ," Hesychios repeated, unable to satiate his wish to savor that beleaguered and *distorted* body. "Now it all makes sense, now it's complete, now it all fits . . . Tell me what else you remember from that day . . ."

"Nothing . . . other than that there was a good-looking little boy . . . very good-looking."

"I remember something more . . . I was that little boy . . . But you were tall then—you seemed tall to me like Persa!"

"I was like I am now—you were still little so you thought I was tall," she told him, "I was like I am now . . . only younger."

"*Old,* not young. To me you were *old!* . . . But not *too* old . . ."

"Now I'm old," she said, and felt aggrieved, as though reminding herself of it.

Their words were a mesh around their act, an act that *lasted long,* that danced with its shadows all over the room and drowned out all the words . . .

"What are we doing? How strange it is!" she suddenly remembered, and started to weep. "We buried our daughter today! . . ."

"Our daughter's just fine, she's just fine," he whispered, "she doesn't care . . . Nor does the other one."

"I care."

"So do I . . . But let's remember all the rest . . . What was that song about the twenty-twoers?"

"I don't remember."

"It was you who told it to me . . . The little girl punished me! The little girl punished me . . ."

"I don't remember—but the little girl will punish both of us . . ."

"Where did the birds go . . . how was it? . . . to drink water from a spring and a little girl punished them . . . Tell it to me again."

"The little girls will punish both of us—they've already punished both of us, Hesychios."

"How I tried to find you! . . . I even followed a little dead foal trying to find you both! . . ."

"You remember a lot, it seems, I don't remember so much," she said between her sobs.

"I tried to *find* you both, that's why I remember . . . Where was your house? That house of yours then?"

"Where it is now . . . It's changed since then . . . Before my husband died, we knocked down the outside staircase . . . it fell down by itself . . . we knocked down other things too. But he died, and I did all the rest myself."

"And why couldn't I find it when I was looking for it?"

"Because it wasn't right, it was too soon . . . who knows?"

"I'd never seen you before apart from that day . . ."

"And I'd never seen you before . . . Such a fine boy, such a face . . ."

"Didn't you know whose son I was?"

"No . . . Our houses were a long way away, I didn't know who you were . . . And you . . . didn't you recognize Rodanthe when . . . when you met her later?"

"No, I didn't *recognize* her . . . I'd no idea who she was."

"Oh, of course . . . there weren't just one or two, there were many Rodanthes! . . ."

"Don't let all that upset you . . ."

"Didn't you even recognize me when you saw me . . . then, at the ruins?"

"I couldn't remember! . . . I didn't know who you were, when I'd seen you before! . . . Didn't you even know my mother?"

"I'd heard about her because of the snakes . . . When she became my mother-in-law, I remembered who she was . . . But I didn't know her."

"Your husband never came back to see me again . . . though he'd promised."

"I know. He forgot to bring the knitted top back too . . . the one I gave you so you wouldn't be cold, that green and gold one . . . Your little brother was wearing it when we got married . . . I saw it one day."

"Do you still have that red dress?"

"It must be somewhere . . . if I haven't thrown it away."

"I want you to show it to me one day . . . I want you to wear it again!"

"Inside out! . . . How can I still be alive? How can I still be alive and talking and . . . What more punishment am I to suffer? Remember Julia who's just died! Remember the other one too!"

"I remember them . . . Julia more so."

"How do you remember them? *Like that?* . . ."

"I remember them."

Daybreak found them sleeping like babies. They had got tired, the lamp had gone out by itself. And they had sworn not to tell anyone.

Roughly a month passed, and every day Febronia grieved for the loss of Julia, and her tears for Julia also watered again the loss of her other daughter, the forgotten one let's say, yet in the end her grief and distress were more to do with herself: the *most dangerous drink* was herself. And what was still going on between herself and Hesychios—*still* and *often* as if they were newlyweds, as if they were not the slightest bit choked by regret . . .

"The solution's in my heart," she said again and again, as if this *solution* had become an obsession, yet also independent of her. "The solution's in my heart— if only it were my mind that had something wrong with it! . . . But no. Nothing. There now. I'm worrying for nothing. Not so much as a headache! . . . The solution's in my heart, and only there, that's why it's so difficult! . . . Whereas if I were to go mad, if something was wrong with my mind . . . When I was little, my grandmother would see me restless, with something gnawing away inside me even then, and she'd say: Don't worry, when you get older, you'll see how everything will fit into place. When I got just a little older, she died, and it was my mother now who said to me: What are you like that for? When you get married, everything will be better . . . I got married, was widowed, lost my first daughter, and it was then that my father started saying to me—he was still living: Don't fret, God's good! Good? I said to him. Eh, when you die, something will change for sure! he'd say to me and smile beneath his mustache—he liked saying things like that. Till the day that he too departed, he never said anything serious . . . Anyway what's serious? That's the truth: *when I die.* So let me die! Let me be found on my back with my eyes open, with a fly on my eyebrow! . . . The solution's in my heart, I know it, and nowhere else."

Such *feverless raving* was not exhibited by anyone else in the house, not even by Lily when she was in the grip of her mute demons, nor even by the elder Julia, demure and taciturn as she was, who—nevertheless—had begun of late to murmur various things . . . But she simply murmured them, they almost couldn't hear her. Then again, they were words without substance, carried away by the wind, without the burning intensity of the words of her sister-in-law, of this weary and tormented woman, they didn't take on those hues that some swift-legged clouds suddenly take on and turn the whole sky black before you can say Jack Robinson. But until proof of the opposite, Julia's words were always (even when they were not dictated by the quintessence of logic) few and prudent.

And this is how it was that evening when she unexpectedly said to them (given that half of them were talking about other things and half of them were sitting silent round the table):

"She died in my place."

They hardly understood who had said it, even less *why* she'd said it and about *whom*. But quickly, from the way she brought the napkin to her chin and got to her feet to go out or retreat into a corner, they realized that the words had come from Julia and were referring to her little niece of the same name. Why she said them remained unknown.

Febronia stared at her, her eyes flickering with bewilderment, but ready in any case to respond.

"What do you mean?" she asked.

"I mean that . . . she died in my place," said Julia *clearly*. "She had no other reason."

"My daughter?"

"Yes . . ."

"And why in your place? Don't I exist? Why didn't she die in my place?" asked Febronia.

"All right . . . in your place too," Julia said, somewhat embarrassed and conciliatory, not wishing to worsen the situation, which was taking on a note of contention between her and her brother's wife, whom she had always respected and sympathized with, even though of late—mainly because of the ordeal of the little Julia—she had more or less ignored her and no longer talked to her as in the past, nor did she encourage her to talk.

And saying it, she left them all dumbfounded around the large table, going out with a step that was anything but steady or proud.

"Why did she say that?" Febronia, breaking the silence, asked the others, more calmly and consciously than she had asked Julia.

"Because . . . that's how she understood it to be, it seems," answered Persa, who—during those last few moments—had taken on an expression as though she had at last discovered the answer to something that had greatly puzzled her. "Yes . . . ," she went on, "she said it some time ago, before the little girl died . . . before the hares, even before Jacob . . . She said it to me, there in the doorway, on the stairs . . . and afterwards in the yard with the fish. But I hadn't heard properly then, hadn't understood, I was simply obsessed by *something*."

"What exactly did she say to you?" Febronia asked her on behalf of all those who were listening.

"She said . . . that, I think. But I couldn't hear, she didn't *say* it . . . she just kept opening and closing her mouth like a fish. But . . . now I'm sure that she said the same thing," Persa said, trying to assure herself and the others.

"*She died in my place?* But she hadn't died yet," said one of the other sisters of Hesychios and Julia.

"She said it differently then. She said she *will*—" Persa suddenly stopped, preferring not to say any more; besides, her own suspicions were simply strengthened that night, they were in no way clarified. "I don't know, I didn't hear anything," she concluded, as they all waited to see if she changed her mind.

"And how long did it take her to think about it before she came out with it just like that out of the blue?" someone asked—after having thought long about it himself.

No doubt for a long time, thought Julia's father to himself, who sometimes didn't hear much of what was being said around him, but sometimes heard everything; *for a long time* . . . And without wanting to, without thinking about it, he fixed his gaze on one of the women who had come into his house quite recently as a daughter-in-law: the woman whom Petros had married—the former sister-in-law of Kimon.

As soon as she noticed his gaze, she felt uncomfortable and did more or less the same thing as Julia, bringing the napkin to her chin and wishing more than anything else that she could retreat somewhere . . .

Christoforos moved his head slightly and looked elsewhere—after all, he didn't know, didn't understand why his eyes had fallen on her.

Yet that gaze of his (and the discomfort it caused) didn't escape Febronia's notice, and having reached a certain limit where she no longer took anything into account, like those about to die who don't really care whether others are happy or unhappy, she turned to her younger sister-in-law and said:

"Did you know, dear girl, that your former brother-in-law, Kimon, with his blue eyes, your sister's brother, was in love with the sister of your husband and of mine? . . . Her, yes, with the red hair, the one you see every day. He was in love with her! And she was in love with him, even if she didn't know it! . . . And so he hanged himself on the walnut tree and she remained just as you see her."

The woman—Nitsa was her name—flushed bright red, full of pain: those words were like a bared sword in her heart . . . But she didn't let out a sound.

Petros put his arm round her shoulders, squeezed her, whispered a couple of kind words in her ear, and then turned to Febronia and told her that from the time she'd lost "her second daughter," she'd started to speak as though she were drunk, as though she didn't know what was going on around her.

"I wish I were drunk! I wish I didn't know what was going on around me!" she said.

"What are you drinking? Has Persa been giving you something to drink that your words are so full of fire?" Petros went on, casting looks of rebuke at his younger half-brother Hesychios.

"Absinth," retorted Febronia. "It's green, isn't it? Eh, that's what I've been drinking. And it's not Persa who's been giving it to me, don't try to involve her. I find it on my own. I get it from here": and she pointed to a part of her body, perhaps her gall bladder, perhaps her heart.

"Shhh . . . ," Hesychios told her.

"Shhh . . . why? Are you telling me you didn't know that your sister, your velvety, was in love with that poor wretch the builder?" Febronia answered him.

Most likely this happened because Hesychios—from the moment his wife had said what she had to Petros's wife—seemed to have been taken aback; but he didn't want to say or to hear anything more about it. At least not then.

"Now's not the time for such things," he said to her.

"Ah! So *it's not the time for such things!*" retorted Febronia, giving him a look full of innuendo, flashing and sarcastic. "But it is for other things . . ."

"Why are you raking up all that business now?" shouted Christoforos, losing his patience and casting all the weight of his look on her, his old daughter-in-law.

"The story is *still* eating away at your daughter," she said to him, "just like other stories are still eating away at me."

Every so often there came a point of *saturation*, and yet it didn't bring satiety, it wasn't enough.

With the coming of winter, things got much worse for all the members of the household. And despite the odd *nodding and hinting* that some had picked up on and had conveyed in their turn to others, they were all unprepared and were left with their mouths open: their hills filled with wolves . . . Some dark-colored wolves, almost black, which they'd never seen before, they weren't *theirs*, they said. And Pacalacou's innocent words ("wolves have been seen"), just like those other words of his about the war in the mountains beyond, now found their justification in Hesychios's ears. And besides, Gabe, being more experienced, had been desperately nodding and hinting to Lily for some time, and she, in her turn, to the others . . . But they weren't always understood.

And we, too, a year and a half ago, while these words were being written, lost the most important source from which we were drawing these tales of old in order to transform them: the man in question (father in every sense) died quite peacefully, slowly fading over thirty-eight days, and giving us the impression that he might hang on like that for another thirty-eight months, and so . . . some aspects of this story with the black wolves that arrived when he was still a little child, and above all the cause and the consequences of certain events that followed, remained somewhat dim in our memory: as he had narrated them to us many many years before, in his prime, and we had listened with deep pleasure (he was an incomparable storyteller), yet without any concern for details, without the subsequent passion to learn everything thoroughly: we would listen to him and we were under that most natural of illusions that he would tell it all again to us whenever we so wished, and at any time we needed to hear it . . .

We managed to be with him during those final thirty-eight days, when he no longer said anything, when—in the melancholy hope that we might perhaps get him to say something more—we bent over him and *ourselves* narrated to him some of the tales he had once told us . . . And every so often he would open his eyes (once bright green . . . but now dull and whitish like those of sheep) and ask us quietly, with a distant surprise: "How can you remember all that? What memories you have!" "You're the one who told it to us once upon a time, don't you remember?" we said to him. "*Me?* . . . ," he said, somewhat astonished. "Perhaps . . . If you say so, perhaps." And he would again peacefully close his eyes for as many days as were left him.

And so we were unable to hear again from his lips this tale of the black wolves and the consequences. We asked others of his age or even younger.

And we discovered that there was some turmoil, some violent conflict in the northern Balkan provinces that was causing the wild animals to move south, forcing them from their habitat, since it's well known that no wild beast is comparable to man when he decides to give vent to his anger. So the sound of their rifles, successive sounds that began in spring and progressively intensified (and to which the wolves were not by birth accustomed), the smoke from the fires, the cries, the distant yelling that grew nearer and nearer, the uncertain present, and a future with such inauspicious allusions made these animals leave their lairs and seek refuge in more peaceful hills and forests. Sporadically at first, then en masse: every lame she-wolf, it was said, accompanied by her adopted cub arrived in those parts.

And the first victims—as winter was already setting in and these sturdy refugees began to lose their fatty tissue—were, *naturally*, the sheep and goats. And because these had left their folds high up and had come down lower, close to where there were people, the wolves too came lower and lower . . . It's said that one morning they came right down to the village square (which recently had been renamed as a *square*; before it was known as *the old main marketplace*), that some people saw black wolves in front of the bell tower, and on seeing the people the wolves had turned to go back up into the foothills, halting every so often and looking back as though displeased by this return . . . which, when all's said and done, had not been forced upon them by the people, who were struck dumb by fear.

A lot is still said even today about those wolves, by those who saw them or those who heard say about them. A lot, and we don't know how much is true and how much not true. Such as, for example, that they eventually became so satiated that they only bit the lambs on the neck and then left them—that the streets, the cobbled ways, the paths to the mountain were cluttered with dead and half-dead lambs, some of which were still bleating . . . That the wolves even went into the yards of houses (of outlying, of course, or uninhabited ones, but not all that far from where the other houses began) . . . Or that, once in a while, the wolves would steal little children—babies from their cots near the window . . . And also that—and this was the strangest, the most mysterious thing in this tale—some of the lambs from those that were left followed the wolves back to their lair *by themselves!* . . . That the wolf would simply lead the way and stop now and again to turn to look at the lamb, and it, completely obedient, as though hypnotized by those profound, shiny eyes, was there, waiting for when the wolf would continue its way up or down towards its lair, so that it would arrive there with it . . .

As to what went on there—no one talked about that. Anyway, the lips that informed us of the above-mentioned phenomenon (a phenomenon perhaps not unprecedented) did not, to our mind, seem to be uttering words that were the product of an unbridled imagination.

And it wasn't only the wolves, which, in any case, finding the pathways open and surroundings not at all unamenable, began in time to move farther south or to go farther afield to east and west. It was also the conflict itself in the north that was spreading like ink on blotting paper, was taking on a desperate aspect, and one day came very close to the sesame-oil mill, the school, and the other buildings and holdings in those parts. And coming as it did, it also left its mark wherever it passed.

Not that the inhabitants actually took up arms against the foreign intruders (as happened in other areas), no, on the contrary, some of the former were forced to hide some of the latter in their homes, with the danger, of course, of losing their heads — either from their guests, if they happened to refuse, or from their armed fellow nationals, if this *hospitality* of theirs, albeit forced, ever became known . . .

Between a rock and a hard place, then, for these people, who, for obvious reasons, happened to be the most well-off in those parts: tiny cottages could hardly be used as places of refuge; only houses with lots of corridors and rooms and as many secret ways.

Christoforos's house, which was essentially a hive of large family homes, separated by dividing walls, with fences, with double or single ceilings, was one of the first to be chosen. The same fate awaited some other houses, less renowned and more distant, but equally secure and labyrinthine. The people inside these houses doubled in the wink of an eye, and for a certain length of time — days or weeks — they lived together in a rather strange and not at all untroubled way: the foreigners were like phantoms, huddled in out-of-the-way corners, sneaky and secretive, with unusual habits and their own beliefs (you didn't know if they ate, what they ate, or if they stayed hungry, if they ever ventured out into the light or if they preferred the darkness, if they had contact with others of their own kind and how), and yet they left their mark everywhere: their boots were like adzes and damaged the floors and hitherto insignificant cracks now gaped with Balkan vigor in the ceilings of those below; or allowed the laughter to be heard, the coughing, filling the others with fear and causing them to fall silent for hours; or someone would put an eye to one of the holes and look at them, just look at them, and if that thing wasn't an eye, it was a rifle barrel that both silenced and alarmed. And much more.

At the same time, they found or had a way of reassuring them every so often: "If you don't betray us, we won't harm you." But who could sleep peacefully during those nights and under those circumstances — and with the threat following the reassurance: "If you give us away, we'll slaughter you all, every last one of you"? In their terror, they muzzled their children and kept them bound to their sides so they wouldn't go out and, being children, brag about what was *going on* in their homes — and how they wished they themselves knew what was going on and why.

There were a few, however, who knew, and who not only came to a complete understanding with the foreigners (secret or open), but had even acceded to the currents that had brought the foreigners from their revolutionary committees.

And one day the foreign intruders disappeared, cellars and attics emptied, but now the fear came from another direction—from those who were furiously hunting and searching for them, and if they didn't find them, they would, so the rumors had it, severely punish the families who had given them refuge, especially if these included Slavophones.

There were numerous Slavophones, however, or rather there were *also* Slavophones, indigenous Macedonians, that is, who knew the Slavic tongue, throughout those parts, particularly among the aged (the result, we imagine, of older invasions and fermentations), and now all these were in danger of being thought of as *Slavophiles*—something that for the others, their armed and fanatical fellow-nationals, was tantamount in those days to treachery.

So many householders were now obliged to abandon their homes, not only those who in one way or another had provided the foreign insurgents with refuge but others too: people who hadn't put even a foreign cat in their house, simply because they happened to speak (to understand, that is) Slavic. And from one day to the next, they became—like the wolves—refugees in more distant villages and towns, which, because of the distance or who knows what else, were not directly at risk from the double invasions.

They took with them whatever food and possessions they could carry and—many of them—poisoned the rest or buried it so that it wouldn't be taken by the first chance hordes, but also so that it wouldn't be appropriated by neighbors who had nothing, so they said, to fear, and who perhaps were rubbing their hands because of this mayhem, which would allow free rein to some of their designs for seizing it. The roads filled with horse-drawn carriages and oxcarts that carried in one night, or two or five, all their lives' load. The tears of children who didn't understand why they were being dragged off like that, the shouting of men who were arguing with each other, the women's heartrending pleas, old people who cried in their infirmity, and everything that recalled other times, darker ones and even more desperate, came again to the surface and filled the air. Earthquakes, disasters seemed like tranquil states—at least more natural—compared to this madness that had caught hold of them and was driving them pell-mell from their homes. It was heard that in nearby parts some families who hadn't managed to get away in time had already been punished severely (the parents had lost their heads and the children their parents), and, of course, that the whole business was provoking a chain reaction and the foreigners were responding with reprisals, or that they were the ones who had begun the massacres . . .

A whirl of events—*like a madwoman's hair*, as others would describe it.

■

"Lucky Eftha, lucky Petroula . . . And lucky you, Cletia . . . And you, little Julia, luckier than all of them! . . . So much fear that you didn't have to endure . . . So much that your fate protected you from . . . ," Christoforos murmured to himself as, almost a biblical figure now, he piled his children's children and probably their possessions on strong or pathetic carts and closed an entire sesame mill as he might close a little cardboard box. His eyes, less emotional and distracted than those of his daughter Julia, nevertheless were misted like hers. And nevertheless he struggled to hear what his elder sons were saying to him: his ears were less and less able to hear the *orders* from outside—especially when confusion prevailed.

But all they were telling him was to stand aside: "You're an old man now!" they shouted to him, not with the intention of hurting him, but those moments were not for pleasantries. "Go and sit down in a corner somewhere with your grandchildren! Don't get under our feet, you're getting in the way!"

"What's that you're saying, my fine lads?" he asked, trying to understand, while his hands were caught up in the animal hides. "Isn't all this trouble enough for me?"

"You're getting in the way!"

He heard, but he didn't want to believe what he heard.

"I'm getting in your way? Are you serious? Try putting yourselves in my place."

"Listen you old fool, you're getting in our way and that *polyglotism* of yours is a real pain!" one of them shouted in an outburst of anger and flippancy.

"In God's name, I don't understand you," Christoforos murmured bitterly— and after a short pause.

Because . . . he both understood and didn't. Because as a man whom fate had ordained to be born and to live in that melting-pot peninsula, in periods that were by no means without their turbulence or shadows, he actually did know *other languages:* that Slavic dialect, that suddenly so contentious dialect, and quite a bit of Turkish (from the Turkish kids with whom he played or argued when he was little), and, more recently, he had begun to pick up a little of Persa's Circassian . . . But of course, his mother tongue, his living language, *definitive* both for him and his descendants, was Greek and no other.

"So, then—and without God as my witness—I don't understand you," he said again to his sons.

"Leave your father alone—hasn't he had enough grief? Isn't it enough that his ears have filled with crickets?" said Persa, defending her husband.

"But we didn't say anything bad to him . . . just not to get in our way," replied, somewhat guiltily, one of her stepsons. "He took it the wrong way—that's all. As he used to say himself, *Old age brings a plague of other things as well.*"

"*All's well,* I know, *all's well* . . . anyway . . . ," this indefatigable old man went on muttering to himself.

At that same time Febronia, in the seventh month of this late and certainly the last pregnancy of hers, was closing her wardrobes without any particular haste, covering with cloth, paper, and occasionally wax whatever jars or pots were left full, pulling the sheets from the beds and putting out poison for the fleas (the fleas came in droves only in summer, now it was almost Epiphany— but she put it out anyway, as she had it), and generally was leaving all the rooms clean and tidy as though preparing for Easter. And she gazed at the results of her tidiness with the approval that visitors looking around might feel . . . Actually, she didn't want to leave it; though it no longer made such a great impression on her.

"That's how I want to find it again," she said to herself and her child, and rushed to straighten the fold in the curtain. "Otherwise . . . if someone has the desire, let them make a mess of it"—while Hesychios was calling her from the yard to come downstairs because she was the last, the only one who was still inside the house, with Sakis, her youngest child, who was clutching her hem, not letting her leave or stay.

She took one last look, closed the doors, let him cling to the side of her belly, and went down the stairs, one by one, closing the stairway *glavan*[5] behind her.

Hesychios watched her coming out of the dark porch . . . It was dusk, and there were no lamps lit any longer inside the house.

"What have you been doing all this time? Why are you so late?" he asked her.

"Julia . . . ," she said, and shuddered as she looked back at the house; "our Julia . . . we're leaving her here." And then her gaze fell on all the other children's heads that were waiting to leave with them.

"Where Julia is now, she's not in any danger," he said to her.

"People say they go into the cemeteries too . . ."

"Who says?"

"Everyone . . . How should I know?"

"Let them. What can they do?"

"They take the gold teeth, the wedding rings . . ."

5. A kind of hatch over the stairs, which, when closed, blocked the entry to the second floor and the attic rooms.

"Our Julia had neither gold teeth nor a wedding ring."

"You're right about that," said Febronia. "But then there's the injustice of it all, the injustice . . . And something tells me that I'm not going to see my home again."

"Yes you will—we may be going now but we'll be back," he told her.

"Going is in our hands—but coming back? . . ."

"Climb up now. We're going to Lake to live there for a while . . ." And offering her his arm so that she could climb up into the highest and deepest cart, he asked her quietly and quickly (his mouth brushing her ear) whether she had left the red dress behind . . .

With her leg in the air, ready to clamber up, she turned and stared at him.

"I don't know if you're playing or being serious—there are times when I've honestly no idea," she said, with apprehension in her eyes.

"Shhh . . . ," he said, as though she were the one who at such moments set the fuse alight.

A little behind them, Christoforos was handing over the keys to his adopted sister, Lily—she was in no danger, not even the angels spoke her language.

"We're going, but we're coming back, don't carry on like that," he said to her, because she was crying and clutching hold of his sleeve and wiping her eyes on the edge of his belt. "In one way or another, things will calm down again, and we'll find our homes again, we'll get back to our work again . . . Come with us if you want—I'm saying it again, come with us."

No, no, I have to stay, to take care of the house! she said, using her hands and constantly crying.

"So, bye then, Lily . . . till the next time, see you soon."

Bye . . . Safe journey, bye! My dearest! My precious! . . . Bye!

Standing farther off, at the other side of the yard, were Orhan's mother and some other women like her, in their baggy breeches and their headscarves— they, too, were not in any danger. Like dirge singers, they were shaking their heads at the sight of the *masters* leaving and in their language were quietly wishing them *Godspeed, safe return,* whenever it be Allah's will . . .

They hadn't gone far, they could still see a few houses round about, these too closed and shut, and they could hear cats meowing exactly like infants would screech if uncovered in the chill of the night, when in the light of their lamps— hanging in front of their carts—they were able to see a lonely figure, waving his arms like a castaway in the middle of the road. They stopped and let him climb up—it was Pacalacou.

Febronia called him to her and asked him where he wanted to go, where he had left his grandmother. He told her that he no longer had a grandmother, she had died that evening.

"And you've left her unburied?"

"She told me not to bury her."

Who had the time or the inclination to go against such a last wish, or even not to believe it? No one. Febronia made room for him to sit beside her, and he, bending his back, opened his hand and asked her for a little bread. She gave him some, but told him not to ask her for any more till they reached where they were going, because the bread was in short supply though there were many mouths to feed.

. . . And they had their eyes wide open, at least most of them did, though the night was almost over after so many hours on the road, and they wanted nothing but to be able to sleep. Some of the children managed to, but not the grown-ups. They were racked with concern for what they had left behind them and for the unknown that was awaiting them—one of them said: "Better that we were still in our homes even with the wolves in the yard and the jackals on the roof . . ."

"Where we're going we'll become fishermen, it's not too bad," another one replied.

"We'll become beggars, that's what I say," announced a third, despondently.

"Slow down, my sorry lad, we're not going to any palaces, we'll be among poor folk—they don't even have any salt there to savor themselves, the lake yields them fresh water."

"So much the worse—beggars from the unsavory," said the previous one, even more despondently.

"But they have peace, nothing to worry them."

"What good is peace when you're turned out of your own home . . . Anyway."

"I say we should play at *red lolly, yellow lolly!* It will pass the time," suggested another, who hadn't spoken until then, given that they were now well out of range of danger.

"Wake the children up to play? Are we going to act like children now in our old age? And with everything that's going on around us?"

"Why not? My father-in-law's last wish before he died was for me to say *red lolly, yellow lolly* to him fifteen times without getting my tongue twisted! Naturally I couldn't, but by that time his soul had departed and it went happily. And he also left me ten sovereigns!"

"Let's play it then and maybe our souls will find a bit of happiness *before* we lose them," conceded the other man, who had previously thought this game unworthy of their ill-fortune.

And they began to play *red lolly, yellow lolly*, and whoever managed to say it fifteen times without getting tongue-twisted with all the *l*'s received an apple! . . . Now they didn't have as much as a leaf—the only prize (if they managed to say it even ten times) was a few stifled yawns and a little overdue sleepiness as the horizon began to dimly glow. That was something at least.

Besides, they still had half or even a full day's journey ahead of them before they reached the lake.

In older times, the distance between their parts and the lake was measured by the knitting of a stocking up to the thigh—by the time it took, that is, to knit the stocking, starting from the toe, passing up the heel, the ankle, the calf, reaching the knee and ending high up at the selvage . . . We have no idea how this was timed: perhaps they had a woman sit on a horse or donkey, gave her plenty of yarn and five small needles, and said to her, "If you finish a long stocking by the time you arrive at the lake, you'll get to eat the freshest and tastiest freshwater fish you've ever eaten." And she must have done her level best to finish the last stitch before arriving at the lakeshore, and so eat the best-ever fish . . . We've no idea; that's what they say.

The lake itself was large and still, a gray-green polished mirror, and it was called Lake Goulgi. The village, however, built on its western shore was called Lake. And many of its inhabitants, from spring to fall, lived on floating houses, in little floating rooms with two roofs: one slanting upwards and one rocking in the water . . . And all of them fished.

And they were expecting the others, those who had been uprooted, with feelings that ranged from intense curiosity to meet *mountain folk* (particularly on the part of the younger ones) to the vague fear that these mountain folk might refresh themselves in the freshwater of their Goulgi and not want to leave again . . . Whatever the case, they were expecting them. After all, there were some family ties between the mountain folk and the lake folk, but also an old obligation that had to be taken care of: thirty years before, a terrible drought had made their lake run dry, and for a period of roughly two years—as they had no other livelihood than what came from their lake and their fishing—many of them had sought their living in neighboring mountain areas.

So friendly relations had developed between them and it was then, too, that a number acquired ties through marriage—Kimon the icon painter was, for example, from that place. The marriages between them, that is, though sporadic, didn't stop even long after the end of the drought.

So it was to Kimon's family, then, and to his relatives that Christoforos's sons with their families would go to live for a while—till affairs at home had calmed down. For the others, there were, or there would be found, other houses—or even other villages beyond Lake. As for Christoforos himself, there was no question: he could, he said, easily accommodate himself at the bottom of the Goulgi . . . After all that he'd been burdened with . . .

Once they arrived, for a long time they saw nothing but sand and marshes, marshes and reeds, and heard wild squawking that discouraged them somewhat—in their tired imaginations they wondered, What was awaiting them? For the inhabitants of Goulgi to welcome them with open arms? For them to come along with fairies? Perhaps not, but so much sand, so much marshland, and that inhospitable squawking in the gray twilight wasn't the best possible welcome. Quite simply, they had to endure this too.

Those coming behind, at any rate, saw the tracks from the cartwheels on the wet sand, tracks like silver ribbons, over which were others and still others . . . And they saw, all of them, the vast lake in the distance: a dark tranquil surface that something was causing to quiver here and there, to ripple as though invisible heavy raindrops were falling on it, and it gave them a feeling completely unknown to them.

"The water . . . ," said Christoforos, after pondering long, "the dark water . . ."

And whoever heard him could understand what he meant by this—and what that unknown feeling was that kept them all so silent: the water that they knew from taps, rain, and streams, even from the floods, wells, and waterfalls, acquired here—the water of the lake—another kind of evocativeness and *attitude*, a strange inertia which at the same time incited . . . It was the hour, it seems, and with the heavy, still weather up above. And the reasons that had brought them there . . . rather like fortune seekers.

As for the rest, they were all coming from the east and had to go round half the lake to get to the first houses, there at least where the reeds started to get a little less, where the water became a little more cheerful and the squawking took on more gentle tones.

And it was there that Kimon, the icon painter, with his young, pregnant wife, were the first in line to welcome them . . . Behind them, standing in line, were his parents, brothers and sisters, and all his relatives. They were not accompanied by fairies, not even now, but they did light their lamps for the welcoming, and a little girl, rather like Julia (but not as pretty or angelic as her), in a well-made gray dress held in her arms three loaves of bread, while beside her a boy, again in a gray outfit and with black circles beneath his unmoving eyes, which were serious and shining like a mandarin's, was carrying a tray with fried fish on a bed of fresh lettuce leaves. As soon as the first carriage halted, they went up, gave them the loaves and fish without saying a word, and withdrew to the back with short steps. The mountain folk didn't know whether they were supposed to start sharing out the food and eating it or simply to keep hold of it themselves. The only one who didn't hesitate was Pacalacou, asking his godmother for "a little bread and three flishes" . . . From his overexcitement, the poor lad was unable to say fish—he called it *flish*—and his mouth watered.

Efthalitsa ran into her father's arms, stood on tiptoe on his shoes, turned her belly outwards, to one side, and laid her delicate neck on his shoulder. She purred rather than spoke—but she soon got tired and put her cheek more comfortably against his chest.

"It's my father!" she shouted to her in-laws, but mainly so that the more distant relatives who didn't know him would hear . . .

She didn't throw herself into Febronia's arms—she wasn't her mother exactly—she simply held out her hand and gazed, with some disgust or perhaps fear, at her body, which was in the same state as hers.

"Where's the baby? Didn't you bring it?" Hesychios asked Kimon.

"The one is at home asleep," Efthalitsa hastened to say, "and the other one is here!"—and she lightly patted her swollen belly, firm with her youthfulness.

"And the other's here," Febronia added drily, showing what she had to show—because her stepdaughter's behavior had annoyed her and because, to all those strangers who were gazing at her stupidly, she had to say something instead of starting to defend herself because of her body and her age . . .

Next she called Thomas to her, who was then seven years old and his eyes were at the peak of their beauty and strangeness, and she presented him as being indicative of her children.

As soon as they realized that she hadn't chosen him at random from among her children but because his eyes were *different*, they all gathered round him, went up to him, but without daring to come into actual contact with him . . .

"Let them see your eyes!" she whispered to him, leaning over him, as the boy felt himself shriveling from their eyes, which were filled with astonishment at the sight of his. "Show them, don't be ashamed—do they think they're the only ones who . . . what? who have a lake like that? What else have they got . . . Show them your eyes!"

Thomas raised his head and surrendered like an ailing deer to the greedy pawing (by means of their eyes) of those Gouglians . . . Safi-Lisafi stood beside him to lend support.

"And this one here? . . . Who's he? Is he your son too?" another woman asked her, pointing at Pacalacou, who had set himself down at his godmother's feet and was licking the fish bones as if they were lollipops.

"Uh-ho . . . this is not going to work out well, and it's still only the first day," Febronia thought to herself. But she decided to show herself to be above all that, to ignore their barbs—besides she only had Goulgi left—and she replied to the unknown woman that this simple and innocent lad was her godson.

"Ah! . . . I'll tell you the story of how I came to baptize him! . . . But when we get to know each other better," she promised them.

Afterwards she realized that by saying "my godson" for someone who was roughly the same age as she was, it was as though she were giving them cause to regard her as being even older . . . But it was too late, or perhaps too early, to explain to them, and then again . . . did she really care? No she didn't care, she didn't care about anything anymore after Julia's death.

"And this one here is my husband," she said, pointing out Hesychios to the crowd of people who had encircled them—"my husband, yes, I'm his wife . . . ," as though she could no longer control her words or her reactions, the higher and lower levels of herself, her need for peace, but also her need for a little more *provocation*, anyway for something that would lead her to extremes, and then, finally, she could return to being serious again. That's how she felt, that's how she understood it: she would become *serious* again; she could die there, become invulnerable.

"I've fallen low, very low," she reflected.

For years, something had every day been grinding on her nerves, like the pestle going up and down and ceaselessly pounding. Even in her sleep the grinding continued—she would wake up feeling battered. And yet she held herself together. She didn't want this endurance of hers, but nor did she want him to take another woman in her place . . . And she would see other women everywhere . . .

Without being aware of what she was saying, she continued with the introductions:

"And this is my father-in-law with his third wife," she said, pointing to Christoforos and Persa, "and this . . . lake of yours, Goulgi with its fresh water, welcoming us here . . . and . . . Where's Julia?" she suddenly asked her own folk, with a lively concern.

Hesychios's eyes fixed on her despondently, full of expression; if they could, they would have talked: *Don't start again, not here among strangers, not all those stories again about Julia and the other one! . . .*

"I mean your sister," she said, as though setting his mind at ease.

"Oh . . . Where's Julia?" he asked his other brothers.

"She must be behind in one of the other carts," they told him.

"We didn't leave her, did we?"

"Well, she's hardly a little girl to need her hand held . . ."

"I think I saw her . . . she was with us this morning . . . Or was it last night? What about you?"

"I think I saw her too . . . But where was it?"

Nor could they find Persa's brother Jacob, who, after having come to cure his liver—though he cured nothing—had stayed with them, without appearing to have any such intention at first; on the contrary, he acted as if he were doing them a favor by installing himself in their house. They didn't want him, they weren't at all keen on his grouchy face, his humpback, his whims (and as for his accordion, hadn't they learned to live without it?), but they couldn't find any excuse to tell him to leave and go somewhere else. Then, the *events* had started, and they left Jacob to one side. So they wouldn't have given a second thought now to his absence from that little gathering if their redheaded sister hadn't also been missing.

They all looked at Persa, as if she were responsible for the two of them.

"I haven't seen my brother for days . . . ," she told them a little reluctantly, as though concealing half of the truth without good reason, but the other half with good reason, "and as for Julia . . . I don't know, there are other carriages coming behind, other households . . . She may have been left behind and they're bringing her—it's getting light, a new day's coming."

But the other carts, which in any case weren't many, only one, arrived at Lake the next day (the others had decided to head elsewhere), and that one only had her folk inside.

They waited three more days and then Hesychios took a horse, wrapped a black woolen scarf round his head, and went off to look for her.

The winter in that place—that particular one, at least, if not all—was not a heavy one; there was no snow or ice, but the humidity opened up holes in your bones. And when there was frost or mist, especially mist, eyes were of no use at all: you plodded on through the mist as you would through the clouds, or through a mountain of thin cotton wool, and if someone happened to be doing the same from the other direction, the one was for the other—at the moment they met—like someone emerging from the beyond. Which is why most of them carried lamps, even if it was broad daylight, or—even if someone was walking alone—he would talk loudly from time to time.

They had a strange and slightly comic dialect, in which diminutives were rife, particularly in the women's names all ending in *-itsa*. And all the Ann-itsas, Stell-itsas, and Agn-itsas or Chrysanth-itsas and Calliop-itsas were one thing.

But there were also other four-syllable names that had no need at all of that *-itsa* ending but they got it anyway. Like, for example, the grandmother of Kimon the icon painter, who was called Painemeni (this was the vaunted name they had found for her) and everyone called her *Painemen-itsa* (making her considerably less vaunted), and her two granddaughters to boot, or like another woman, who bore the seemly name Nicomache but who was called by friends and enemies alike *Nicomach-itsa* . . . It seems that this was the solution they had come up with in those parts, otherwise all the women would have been Itsa. Only their Goulgi was exempted from the rule—no one had ever thought of calling it Goulg-itsa—and, of course, all the foreign girls who got married there had to lose, together with their virginity, any *sobriety* that their name might have had. From this point of view, Efthal-itsa had come to them ready-made.

The same fate awaited most words of feminine gender, whereas, on the contrary, the men kept their names intact, as did the words of masculine gender, which were not dissipated by such *self-indulgent* currents.

But more generally, too, the way that they spoke was very different, recalling a gathering of songbirds, and—from this point of view again—as soon as Efthalitsa found herself again with her old family, and in fact as hostess this time, she started exaggerating: she wanted so much to show them how she had adapted to the customs and mores of her new land, how well she had got the hang of the speech there, perhaps also how happy she was in her new life (even if she weren't, that's what she wanted to show to those beleaguered folk) that she stressed excessively the local patois, stressed it wrongly, and her pronunciation was marked by trills and warbles that made even her in-laws knit their brows when they listened to her for some time . . .

"I can't imagine what the women here do when they want to quarrel," said Febronia one evening, confiding in two of her sisters-in-law. "They must drive each other mad with all those *-itsas* at the end of every word . . . They don't seem very serious people to me. And what do they do at funerals? . . . Can you imagine?"

They stared at her somewhat strangely. As if to say, That's something it would be better for you not to ask.

"The people here are out of their minds," commented their husbands. "They call their village a lake, Limni, and the actual lake they call something else!"

"Why do you think they called it Goulgi?"

"How should I know? Maybe because . . . whatever you throw into it, even a hazelnut, is gulped up. One gulp and gone!"

"It was once marshland—I bet it was marshland once and it's gulped up a lot . . . That's why the inhabitants today think so much of it."

"So you think, do you, that this Goulgi has one or two secrets of *that sort* too?"

"Only one or two? Ha! . . . But we won't be here long enough to find out."

"Do you think it was here maybe that Ali Pasha drowned kyra-Frosyne?"

"No, nincompoop. That Goulgi was in Yannena. As for this one here . . . like I said, we won't be here long enough to find out."

But they were there long enough, and during the month and a half approximately that they spent there they saw how the lake dwellers fished with their reed rods, how they married and died to the same accompaniment of reed pipes, how their children's baptisms didn't take place in fonts but in the lake itself, even in winter, and how—or better *that*—the work of some of them was to breed worms in special crates and sell them to the fishermen. They were unable to see the worms themselves—or how they overfed them in order to fatten them up . . .

They also had time to savor (those who weren't squeamish) some of their incredible dishes, such as the thick turtle soup, the nettle pie, the *hedgehog stew* (also a sort of soup) and the *reed pilaf*, consisting of rice, eel, raisins, plums, and young reed shoots. Digesting all these was equally incredible.

But they were really astonished and insulted when, after only their second day there, a local doctor passed by and examined their children, these refugee kids, just by looking at them, and because some of them had rashes on their cheeks, mouths, chins, boils or lichens that spring up on children's skin for no good cause, the doctor told them they would have to coat their children in quicklime—no more nor less—so they wouldn't infect the locals with an illness! . . .

"But we don't have cholera, we're not here to infect you!" they protested. "They're simple spots, boils at the most. They're from all the anxiety, the trip . . . and from the tiredness, the wind . . . the fact that the children are in a new environment. They'll have gone in a couple of days."

But the doctor—and along with him all the mistrustful inhabitants of Goulgi—insisted that there was no other way for those rashes to go . . . And so those unfortunate children discovered what it meant to be coated in quicklime in aid of health protection in the area . . .

It wasn't just the children, but their parents too who were glum and horrified; they took it badly. Especially Febronia, as almost all her little ones had to be coated with lime and stay with those white masks for hours, with their eyes looking at her with untold puzzlement and sadness. When she washed them, they gradually began to come round, wanted to eat, and the spots had totally dried up or even dropped off. But all the mothers were left with a grudge against those lake dwellers and without admitting it hoped that they too would one day become refugees—and their children would become *poppies* from all their rashes!

Following this enforced lime, and with all the other odd things that happened there, Febronia began herself to *imbibe tobacco,* in other words to smoke, because—she said—their humidity (and she emphasized *their*) affected her bones and her head, and only the smoking gave her some relief . . . It was random inspiration that provided her with this justification, but certain events that upset her deep down also played their part. As for her mother-in-law, Persa, she—needing no justification for anything she did—gladly provided her with the tobacco and all the other things she needed.

Febronia realized from the very start that Efthalitsa, whom she had raised from her cradle, must have said a few choice words about their family—words less than complimentary and who knows how exaggerated—because all her in-laws in Goulgi stared at her as though scared of her, gazing at her askance with the kind of look reserved for someone untrustworthy, someone dangerous. "If they only knew—were I to tell them—how broken I am . . . ," reflected Febronia with bitterness. And also with anger when she reflected further.

And one day (a day when Hesychios was away), when Febronia and her stepdaughter happened to be alone together outside in the yard, both equally swollen around the waist, and while Efthalitsa was pretending to tend to some ailing plants in pots (the moss on the walls and the stones looked healthier) and ignoring her presence, she said to her:

"Anyway Julia died . . . died in the fall, and she was your little sister, she was asking for you . . . She kept measuring herself to see how much taller she was so you'd find her grown up! . . . Your little *sis-itsa,* how do you say it here?"

It was as though she were asking for a little sympathy, a little attention in that wetland.

"She *was* my little sister. Half and half," said the young woman through clenched teeth, still bent over the flowerpots, and enigmatically stressing *was.*

"What do you mean?" asked Febronia, "that she's dead and isn't anymore?"

"What I mean is that—you're not my mother. And I was once scared of you, but now I'm not."

"I may not be your mother, but I'm the mother of your sister!" retorted Febronia. "And when all's said and done, who was it who raised you? Who changed your diapers? Or did you come out of an egg ready and on your own two feet?"

"Auntie Cletia who died! She was the one who raised me, she's the one who changed my diapers," replied Efthalitsa.

"Ah, so you still remember Cletia! Seems I'll have to die too for you to remember my sacrifices! I'll have to die too, to cease to exist!"

"You've got your own children to remember your sacrifices. All I remember is your shouting. And how you woke us up every morning by pinching us!"

"When was that?" asked Febronia, going over to her as though she were holding a knife in her hand—as though they were both holding knives.

"Every day, every winter . . . You had an obsession, with the cold, with pinching us to wake us up."

"When you had to get up for school and you wouldn't get up any other way, how was I supposed to wake you? With eiderdown?"

"You made us black and blue with those nails of yours! . . . All that pinching we had to put up with!" said Efthalitsa, abandoning all the trills and warbles of the other accent and with her hand going between her thigh and her neck as though she were being stung by bees. "That was your way of saying good morning—and to us, not to your own brood. To us. Sins sown elsewhere, the children of other women . . . You were jealous of us! Your jealousy even went as far as us," she added.

Febronia's eyes darkened, flashed, shot in all directions.

"Just who do you think you're talking to?" she asked her stepdaughter. "Where did you learn to sharpen your tongue like that? Goulgi?"

"Goulgi has made a human being of me. Do you know how my in-laws treat me here? Like a princess!" replied Efthalitsa.

"I can see that. You're like a chaffinch—or should I say a crow—gabbling from the treetop, and those below stand there waiting for you to fall, to pluck your fine plumage. Like a princess, she says!"

"Your jealousy will be the end of you!"

"Jealousy over what?"

"My father! That he had me with another woman! That you weren't the only one! That he did whatever he wanted with other women! That—"

"You'd do well to keep your mouth shut, because if I tell you a few things, you'll be the one who's jealous of me," Febronia warned her; "and no matter if you're thirty or forty years younger than me."

"That he did whatever he wanted with others!" Efthalitsa repeated, as if not having heard anything. "That . . . and if your first daughter, that first popped cherry, hadn't died, you'd have killed her yourself—you were a widow—so that you yourself could get your hands on him!"

That was going beyond all reason, beyond even the most diseased imagination. Not even Febronia had ever thought of that—and she had had many thoughts from the time that she had got caught up in the workings of her fate and had struggled, sometimes to break free, sometimes to get caught up even more. Beyond all reason.

She put her hand to her forehead and brought it down like a piece of wood to her belly. Perhaps she had intended to cross herself and only did half the movement, perhaps—before making the sign of the cross—she wanted to bring it down on her stepdaughter's face. To teach her not to come out with words like that again . . .

"All pointless, stuff and nonsense!" she groaned, taking a hold of herself.

And she gazed, with eyes overflowing with grief and weariness, at the damp house where they were staying, the tiny windows, the cold yard, the greenness that like slime spread everywhere, over whatever didn't move, even over shoes rarely worn . . . Yes, there were two black shoes next to the flowerpots that had started to sprout inside and out—black shoes that were covered in green from the damp, the lack of movement, the lack of use, like fig trees that spring up amid rocks and wasteland, finding—in their case—the dryness favorable . . . Someone no longer wanted those shoes, though he had removed their laces.

"Pthh!" she spat in the direction of her own shoes; the shoes her belly didn't allow her to see—was it that she didn't want to give credence to those unknown, black, and moss-filled shoes, or to her stepdaughter? This stepdaughter who until now had made her wonder how those affable women, all those incorrigible *-itsas*, quarreled in that place, and who had just shown her good and proper how vitriolic their tongues could be . . .

"Febron-itsa . . . what are you spitting for?" a voice behind her asked.

It was Efthalitsa's mother-in-law, a fat, burly woman—and elderly, she could have been Febronia's mother—whose wrinkles and folds of flesh were nothing beside her two eyebrows, which were the color of black dye, arched like bows and thick like cord: as though these two eyebrows would never succumb, as though they were mounted astride time . . . And whatever we say about the eyes or claws of the eagle, they said in Goulgi about the eyebrows of this old woman.

Beside her was one of her daughters, another Painemen-itsa, and Febronia understood, got wind somehow, that they had been there concealed somewhere and had heard everything that Efthalitsa had said to her . . . But she couldn't understand from their expression, from the way they came up to her, what they thought of her after everything they had heard, what their opinion was, and whether . . . whether, by any chance, they might have taken her side.

"I'm not spitting . . . I was saying how pointless it all is, un—"

"Was your littl' girlie complaining?" asked the one with the characteristic eyebrows.

"*Complaining? My littl' girlie?*" said Febronia with tactful curiosity . . . But she couldn't endure that dialect for long, she found it shallow—she spoke differently. And she couldn't suppress her anger for long either—it became a sea and was drowning her. "Unbearable, it's all become unbearable!" she exclaimed. "Did you hear what she said? You don't know me well enough to be able to judge, but did you hear what she said? That I . . . That she was the only one I left black and blue and the children of the other women, the other women, and mine she says, mine . . . That my first daughter . . . Where's one of mine now? Where am I? I'm not even in my own home, not even in my own home . . . to hear words like that, I don't even know where that door leads! . . . Where are the children I had with her father? . . . Leave me, it's nothing . . . Would it were my mind! . . . Would it were my mind there was something wrong with! . . . With her father, she says! . . . Perhaps she's the one who's jealous of me? Perhaps she's the one who made a gift of him to me and now she wants a share of his good looks? Just imagine! . . . *My littl' girlie!*"

While talking and waving her arms angrily, she had slipped and fallen against the plant pots, banging her head on one of them—even the plant pot felt pain. She was now holding her injured forehead and with the other hand pushing away the in-laws who were trying to console her, help her up, take her in their arms. She was in need of a tender embrace, so long as it was an embrace and not a trap, but she pushed them aside, and with some difficulty got to her feet by herself. A little blood was trickling from her lips . . . She kept touching the spot with her finger and looking at it in puzzlement.

"I hit my head and it's my lip that's bleeding," she murmured.

Then she again remembered her children and looked around her with her hair hanging over her eyes and a gaze beneath that provoked fear.

"Where's one of mine now?" she asked again, disdaining to use the word *children.*

"Febron-itsa! . . . Why would you want one?" asked the one with the eyebrows.

"Did you hear what she said?"

"Febron-itsa, yes, we heard, she's said it to us, she's always harping on about it. But . . . we understand. A stepmother, even if she's an angel, is still a stepmother. Forget it. Words are like straw, scattered by the wind."

"No, words are like pins and they prick. You were here and you heard her," said Febronia, trying to make witnesses of all of them—even though it was at her expense—and without knowing what had pricked her most in all her stepdaughter's vitriolic words: the bit about the pinching? Or the unfair insinuation about her first daughter? Certainly, this was worse, the latter, but it was easier for her to free herself from the accusations—whatever accusations, even fleeting ones—by beating all her own children black and blue . . .

"Where's one of mine now?" she asked again, taking the trouble to wipe the trickle from her lip once and for all and push her hair back.

"Why would you want one, Febron-itsa?" the other woman asked her again. "To see! I want to see one . . ."

"You'll see one this evening. The children have gone to the lake, they're playing and having a good time."

"Good time, my foot! . . . There's not even one here? They're all playing?"

"They'll be back. Let's go inside, Febron-itsa, you fell down . . . Pregnant women eat for two and talk rashly . . . And our littl' daughter-in-law is pregnant too . . . Think of the children you'll both give birth to—you'll give birth together, more or less at the same time . . . Why trouble your kind littl' hearts in this way?"

Littl' daughter-in-law, perhaps, but kind littl' hearts? Why?

"I think I'm the one who knows best when it comes to the child I'll give birth to . . . And she knows what's best for hers," said Febronia. "But if you heard what she said, if you—"

The other woman raised her arms, moistened her middle fingers, and daintily passed them over her eyebrows, twice. Febronia halted, believing she was about to see something spectacular. That's how she used to halt at first when she was with Persa, when Persa would roll and lick her cigarettes before lighting them. But then the other woman—as if having cleared her eye of something—turned to say something to Efthalitsa . . . But her daughter-in-law had dashed off, there were only four fallen plant pots in the yard. She said to her daughter, who was there doing nothing, to pick the little plant pots up from the ground. Then cajolingly she leaned over to Febronia to tell her a *secret*:

"Her littl' tongue sometimes gets the better of her . . . she's not bad really."

"Nor was I," thought Febronia, "but that's how I became."

And that touch of the other woman's breasts on her forearm drove her mad, her arched eyebrows from close up were like snakes, and all those *littl' tongues, littl' hearts, littl' trills* stirred once again her already shattered endurance—so she suddenly found herself at the front gate.

There she looked to left and right, not knowing which way to go. And the next second she was outside in the street . . . but she got caught up in her skirts, in the secret winds that were lingering around her, and Her Majesty found herself doubled-up on the ground—it was one of those days, otherwise there's no explanation for it. And as though the fall weren't enough, on her second fall, this time in the middle of the street, a dog leapt out from somewhere and began growling at her wildly, only two inches from her nose . . . She stared at it speechless, nullified, trying not to provoke anything worse, but the dog was incited by her whole stance and with every loud "grrr! grrr!" stretched its neck farther forward, forcing her to lean her head farther and farther to one side and backwards, till she buried herself in her hands on the ground, defenseless—and with the dog above her still growling . . .

She remained like that, a tangled ball of shame, panic, and humiliation, even when the dog—having accomplished its mission—left her and went away.

And then what she expected to happen happened: a crowd of people gathered around her . . . The two in-laws first, then a couple of other people from the neighboring houses, then others. They didn't ask her anything—but neither did she dare raise her eyes to look at them. She just glanced at their legs, and from that she understood roughly what they were thinking about her and what opinions they were forming . . . But when one of her children came near, to be exact the youngest one, Sakis, and—terrified by what he could see happening to his mother—nudged her and cried out in an escalating wail: "Ah, Ma-Mama, 'et up!," the most ludicrous thing happened: she grabbed hold of the child and, weeping herself, began to hit him—to hit him unaccountably, while at the same time crying and shaking.

"Now let her try and tell me that she was the only one I beat black and blue, her and the children from the other women! That I had my own wrapped in cotton wool! . . . Now it's your turn, my poor little lad, so they'll see that I'm equally capable of beating my own children black and blue! Now it's your turn! For her *littl'* sake! For all their *littl'* sakes! So they'll see just how bad a *mother* I am, never mind *stepmother!*"

Such situations had, sadly, happened before; but at home, not in a strange place, not in front of strangers who had not known her for more than four or five days . . . But what did it matter whether she was at home or elsewhere? What mattered was that Febronia was in pain—whether good or bad, she was going through the mill under her skin. And with her the children next to her, whether those she had given birth to herself or those that other women had had with her husband. Because when words reached her ears that pained her, words above all from her old circle of women friends, the grandmothers of her stepchildren, that she ill-treated them and beat them, well, it was then that her own children paid by way of atonement—her own flesh, in other words. She would take them out into the yard, it's said, and beat them mercilessly so that people would see that even if they thought her a bad stepmother, she was no better as a mother to her own children . . . "And if the others hate me," she reflected in moments of gloomy calmness, "then my own children should string me up one day, slaughter me, deny me. But they should also realize how I suffered, how I paid myself, and am still paying."

But the other children, too, the ones who were less hers, also paid a bitter price in deeper places. In other words, everyone paid—even Hesychios paid through either witnessing or hearing about scenes like this in his house . . . But she too began to sense an end to all this, a savage and quick death, particularly after the beating that her little Sakis suffered—the unfairest of all—and she swore that this would be her last humiliation, her final degradation.

She would never forget the dog, and how it hurled those growls . . . "grr! grr! . . ." at her, at her face . . . Like stones.

That evening, she gathered together all the children, hers and those only half hers, gathered them together in one of the bedrooms, squeezed them into one bed, squeezed between them herself, and while half of them were crying in her arms and the other half were staring at her anxiously and sorrowfully from the edges of the bed, she turned her head to the wall, where the lamp made the shadow of her head doubly large, and said to them:

"Pray that I die soon—be happy when I die, think to yourselves, *She's escaped.* Otherwise, we'll all go on suffering."

And that same night, when the children had gone to sleep, each sucking on a finger, even the older ones (some of them exchanged fingers: they put theirs into another mouth and put another finger into theirs), Febronia quietly slipped out of bed, carefully descended the stairs, and went into another house, the house next door but one, where her mother-in-law and father-in-law were. There she chose one of the windows with a little luck, threw a couple of small stones at it, and called up a couple of times in a hollow voice, "Persa! . . . Persa! . . . ," and when Persa opened the shutters and put her head out (with her long adorned hair let down for the nighttime: a mature Persephone from other times, other places), she asked her for a *little tobacco* . . . She couldn't say it any other way, or say anything else.

As though she had been expecting this surprise for some time, or better this *appeal* (but also having heard what Febronia had done that afternoon, what had happened to her), she withdrew inside again without asking anything, simply making a sign to Febronia that she would return, and when she did return, she threw her a handful of finely cut tobacco, some folded cigarette papers, and a heavy flint, all in a little bag, in a valuable *purse.*

It landed right at her feet. The night was a little cool, with the usual damp and a waxing moon that emitted a faint yellowish-gray light . . . She bent down, picked it up, and silently thanked Persa, who had perhaps already shut the window . . . The light of the moon fell upon her like sea spray. And she made her way to an orchard a little farther off, where she knew (she'd seen it by chance the previous day) there was a well . . . She had decided that night to jump into it . . . And she wanted—while going there—not to think more of it, to have decided it was enough . . . The fact that Hesychios was away would help her: Hesychios himself would help, her fateful husband, who was away that night . . . He would help her. And the well was full; it was a regular well, not a dried-up one. The solution really was in her heart. And in Hesychios's absence—albeit his temporary absence. Everything would be done by the time he returned, everything would be finished. Everything. And she herself before anything else. He would grieve for her, their children would grieve for her, everyone would grieve for her—she too if she could—but like this everything would be finished. She had decided. Except that she needed some absinthe, and she couldn't find anything like that. *Some absinthe!* And because she couldn't find absinthe, she thought that the cut tobacco in her little bag, when it entered her lungs as thick, strong smoke (her virgin lungs when it came to such experiences), would work like absinthe, would affect her, intoxicate her, carry her away—in other words, would help her in her decision, would push her before she changed her mind. Because she knew, imagined, that for people to kill themselves required a little boost. Something. Some boost—whatever you want to call it—*any* and *some* thing. Something that would close their eyes pleasurably, remove their will, entice them to the end! Something more than love even! . . . Otherwise life picks up the slack again and holds them back. And she didn't want to be held back anymore by life's wiles. No, she didn't want it.

She entered the orchard, and walking without haste looked around her to make sure it was empty.

"In spring you'll be in leaf and bloom," she said to it, whispering and smiling bitterly, "but I won't be here in spring to see you."

But it might just as well have been one of those barren orchards that remain fruitless both in winter or summer—what did she care? Here in this place, from what she could see, only the water of Lake Goulgi was *fertile*, the reeds on its shores and the moss on the walls. Everything else stagnated, remained soaked in that damp—what did she care about all that? And Efthalitsa's unkind words . . . and the in-law's caresses . . . and Argyris and Rodanthe . . . and Hesychios's kisses as soon as the two of them lay down together at night . . . how could she care anymore about all this? And the "grr, grr" of that stupid dog . . .

She reached the well, face to face so to speak, and it was only then that she remembered something else: the child that she still had in her womb, that she hadn't managed to give birth to, to give it a name . . . This, momentarily (and so uninvited), did seem to be something that she cared about, something that held her back . . . "Dear Lord," she prayed, "don't do this to me, I've made my mind up." She had now reached the well's surrounding wall, and groping it with her fingers, with her mind, she began to test how easy it would be for her to climb over it and jump inside. It wasn't going to be that easy. But at such an hour, nothing was impossible. She got a large stone lying nearby, a rock, stepped on it, raised herself up two hand's breadths, and leaned over the well, which was full of water: she saw the moon below.

"Why are you letting me do this?" she reflected.

It wasn't with regard to herself that she thought this, but (and once again so unexpected) with regard to that unborn creature inside her: she imagined holding it in her arms and dragging it with her, there where her fate, her destiny, was dragging her . . . And what if it didn't want to be dragged there? It's not as if she could ask it. What if it didn't want to? What if it began to . . . What if it was unable to drown like her and began struggling in her belly to survive? How could she subject it to that kind of *double* drowning?

"Why are you letting me do this, Lady Moon?" she asked weakly, raising her eyes.

"Think it over a little more," Lady Moon answered indifferently.

The woman stepped down from the rock, became two hand's breadths shorter (as she was), and remained all alone with herself: it was, in some way, as though everything had happened and passed. *A long time before.*

At the other side of the dark mass before her, the well that is, she heard a *cugh*, something like *cugh*, as though someone had coughed, as though a frog had moved. Wasn't she all alone? She walked in the direction of the noise (when you've been through a lot, there's not a lot that scares you), and then suddenly halted: "You crazy devil!" she thought. "Why did you get the cigarettes from Persa and then forget about them?"

She had forgotten about the cigarettes, the *absinthe!* . . . She almost broke into laughter. She was holding them in her hand and had forgotten about them — how ironic.

She heard that *cugh* again and she started walking again along the edge of the well. She wasn't afraid of very much that night, and it was just as well, for she saw two legs stretched out in front of her, on the dark ground . . .

"Pacalacou! . . . ," she exclaimed, as soon as she realized who it was. "You'll be the death of someone with that stillness of yours! . . . What are you doing here at this time of night? *Draculacou!*[6] . . . Waiting for ghosts?"

"Kir . . . staying outdoors," he said to her, simply moving his legs. He had his

6. "Vampire!"

back resting against the other side of the well's surrounding wall and was twice his normal size because of all the clothes he was wearing. When he noticed that she was holding something in her hand, he stretched out his hand, asking her for a crust.

"At this time of night?" she said, again ticking him off. "I don't have crusts even for the fish at nighttime . . . I've got some tobacco, do you want some?"

"What tobacco?"

"Tobacco, you'll see."

And without speaking, she motioned to him to make room for her so she could sit next to him—he wasn't sitting on the earth, exactly, but on a doubled-up piece of canvas that he unfolded and willingly shared with her.

During the few days that Pacalacou had been in Limni, he hadn't been living in a specific house. He went wherever he wanted or, more correctly, to wherever they didn't drive him away straightaway, and he would often go down to the shores of the Goulgi and wait for the fishermen to take pity on him and give him some fish. If time went by and they didn't give him any, he would go off begging and asking for some himself. And if the fish were tiny, he would put them raw straight into his mouth and, struggling to swallow them, would chortle: ho-ho . . . ho-ho-ho . . . as if they were tickling his palate. Sometimes they would fall out, jump from his mouth as though they were alive, and he would pick them up from the muddy sand. Always chortling . . . He seemed to amuse himself with the fish—no one recalled him ever being so cheerful or laughing as much as there, and perhaps, they said, there was a bride who would keep him in Goulgi.

"Pacalacou, if I tell you what I did today to my son Sakis, you'll believe me, unfortunately," Febronia began to say, while trying to separate two cigarette papers. "But if I tell you what else I was going to do tonight, you won't believe me . . . That's why it's better if I don't say anything and you can think what you like about why I'm here at this time of night . . . Look. I was struggling to separate two cigarette papers and there are four—how fine they are! Do you know how they make cigarettes, how they roll them? . . . Look who I found to ask! . . . Think what you want . . . What's got into me tonight so that I want to smoke? Lighting up now in my old age!"

"Where's Godfa'er?" he asked.

Pacalacou was in a world of his own. He might have meant Argyris, her first husband, but Febronia—looking at him out of the corner of her eye—understood that he meant the other one.

"He's gone to find his sister," she told him. "That's why you see me hanging round wells at this time of night . . . Do you know Julia, Pacalacou? Not my Julia, the little daughter we lost—the other one, the grown-up Julia. Have you seen her? Do you know where she is?"

"G-cugh!"

"What's wrong with you?" she asked him.

"The fish bones . . ."

"Have you been eating raw fish again? Have they got stuck in your throat?"

"Yes . . . If you had a bit of bread to give me . . . *Cugh!*"

"If I did, I'd give it to you," his godmother said, "but how was I to know I'd find you here going *cugh-cugh* from the fish? . . ."

Pacalacou stuck one of his fingers as far as it would go into his mouth: either he would push the bone farther down or get it out . . . Febronia tried to fix herself a cigarette, bringing to mind all the movements and tricks she'd seen Persa doing . . .

"So then," she asked him, when she was sure that he had found some relief, for the time being at least, from the bones in his throat, "have you seen Julia? Do you know where she is?"

"No. Once she was near a well."

As he said it, he tossed his head back and shoulders too . . . Febronia thought that the bone had come back into his throat, but he laughed . . . The kind of laughter that a chimpanzee, on hearing it, would reply to.

"What well? Where? Why are you laughing?" she asked him.

"One like this. Someone wanted . . . ho-ho . . . ho-ho-ho . . ."

"Someone what?"

"With a *bell.*"

"What bell?"

"Ho-ho . . . ho-ho-ho . . ."

"Pacalacou, of all the ways to laugh, why did you choose that one?"

"Ho-ho . . . ho-ho-ho . . ."

"A *well like this one, someone with a bell,*" Febronia said to herself, in a loose attempt to make something of Pacalacou's words and make sense of them, if they had any, that is. Sometimes they did—no one took him seriously, but sometimes they did. Being his godmother, she knew this, but it was only on rare occasions that she remembered it, needed it, or some such thing. And then there was that laughter . . . Where had he got that laughter from?

She managed to roll her cigarette and lit it with more than a little difficulty: the flint was being stubborn and wouldn't catch light in all that damp . . . Or the wick was dry. She was afraid, now she had got that far, making a reefer for herself after all that had gone before and all she had gone through, that she would never be able to light it . . . But eventually, after a lot of *scrits-scrats* and with her thumb hurting her, a tiny flame deigned to appear, which for an instant shot up, flummoxed her, and then went out again . . . At the fourth flame, she succeeded in lighting it and in keeping the end lit by constantly inhaling all the smoke.

"Damn thing! . . . It lit straightaway!" she said with singed tongue and burning throat.

She wanted to fool it, to fool herself, but the cigarette didn't appear to be in the mood, and at the third or fourth puff it made her feel well and truly dizzy and stupefied. She rested her head on the soft sleeves of her godson, reflecting that *now* was the time she should jump into the well, *now*, not before . . . Every so often, she swallowed a little smoke, and her lungs took it in like a fresh breeze from the woods . . . How strange: no resistance, no unpleasant feeling, on the contrary . . . Like some virgin hymens that if touched by a hot rod gladly give way . . . She looked straight ahead of her, a little higher or lower, but with all her desires magnified and blurred . . . Blue standards parading in the darkness . . . All that was hers seemed very familiar to her, excessively strange. Apart from anything else, she wasn't coughing.

"The smoke is doing something to me," she murmured. "It's that I shamed myself a lot today, a lot . . . You're the only one I have any trust in."

"And what if you give birth here?" he asked her.

"What do you mean 'here'?"

"Here. What if that harms you and you die?"

"Ah, you mean . . . No, don't be afraid, I have time yet. What do you know about all that?"

"Ho-ho . . . ," he laughed, "ho-ho-ho . . ."

"Do you know where your mother gave birth to you? No, you don't know. Well, don't worry, because no one knows. And if they do, so what?"

"Nothing, that's what."

"Nothing. That's how you should talk, like a human being, and not all that ho-ho that you come out with all the time . . . My mother-in-law was right when she said, By the second one, you'll start to like it . . . Have you ever smoked this stuff, Pacalacou? Have you ever smoked?"

"No—is that what's smelling?"

"Yes—shall I sit farther away?"

"The well is taking the smell."

"In all this open space! . . . ," said Febronia, when before it had just seemed like a *little orchard* to her. "Oh! . . . ," she sighed, filled with emotion, and looking around her. *"The light of January's moon is almost like day . . . Moon, my dear little moon, high up in the sky . . ."*

"My fingers are cold," said Pacalacou.

"And mine. That little devil only warms my innards—it leaves my hands cold . . . *Cold hands, warm heart*. What were you saying about the well before? You saw Julia at a well? When?"

"On Saint Barbara's Day."

"Dear child! How do you remember that it was on Saint Barbara's Day?"

"My *nan*[7] had her name day."

"Of course, she was called Barbara. And you left her unburied . . . Shameful that."

"She sent me to fetch wood from *Puzla-kuk* . . .[8] There's a well there, isn't there?"

"Indeed there is. And that someone you said with the bells?"

"He was there, ho-ho . . ."

"You're dreaming it up, Pacalacou, and I'm sitting here listening to you! . . . That someone with the bells is long gone. That builder, you mean, who hanged himself?"

"It wasn't him," said Pacalacou.

"There's no one else with bells as far as Julia's concerned," she said.

"He didn't have bells, he was . . . ho-ho . . . ho-ho-ho . . ."

"What was he?"

"Old."

"Has he already had time to grow old? Do people grow old there too?" asked Febronia, whose mind was fixed—a distant memory—on the idea of Kimon the builder and his bells, as Julia had once spoken to her about him . . .

But a lot of time had passed, they were all getting older. And if, by mistake, she was now saying all this to her simpleton godson, she didn't think that it would bother Julia—she too had become something of a simpleton since then . . . She brought her to mind amid a wave of tenderness and felt sorry that from the time little Julia had fallen ill, she hadn't behaved all that well to the elder Julia, had ignored her, their relationship had soured—once they had been like sisters. A lot had turned sour: she kept falling, day after day (falling literally and people gathered round her as round a dying animal), while Julia didn't speak, kept everything to herself—and what she didn't keep to herself was better not heard. Hadn't she gone so far one day as to say about little Julia that "she died in my place"? Do you say things like that? Of all those who have died up until now, has any one of them ever filled another's grave?

When she had finished her cigarette, she stubbed it out in the moist earth and rolled another—she had well and truly received her baptism. And her need to talk, to find escape, was nourished by those little movements of her hands,

7. His grandmother.

8. A place quite far from their parts, farther even than where Febronia had her first house.

hitherto unknown and suddenly so pleasant . . . Images, shadows, memories, and words came and went in her head: expanding and contracting in turn, vanishing and reappearing—"What is it about the darkness?" she thought. "What happened at that well?" Hot, glowing rods gently stroked her beneath her breast—making her almost blissful . . . Without speaking, Pacalacou gazed with secret admiration at her movements. And if she said something to him, he gazed at her mouth, at her teeth, which dimly glinted every so often like scales, and if he wanted to, he answered her, and if he wanted to, he would ask her something. They were well, both of them, communicating. It was nighttime.

"I mustn't forget myself completely!" she said to him with a sudden and slightly bashful smile. "What will anyone think if they see me with you beside a well?"

"Ho-ho . . . ho-ho-ho . . ."

"It's the first time I've set eyes on this well—is it here in daytime too?"

"Ho-ho . . . ho-ho-ho . . ."

"Of course it is, what am I saying? I saw it only yesterday afternoon—no, the day before yesterday. But it's not visible from the other house . . . What are you thinking of again that's making you do ho-ho all the time? And . . . What did you imagine? We all get old. We all get old, old, we don't ask anyone! And these people here in Goulgi . . . What was I about to say?"

"We don't ask anyone."

"I had something else in my mind! . . . But I'll tell you about these people here. They heard, then, that I was the one who christened you, and they think I'm . . . They think you're older: you look young to us, to them you look old— how old are you? And because they think you're old, imagine how old they take me for! For the godmother of my father-in-law! And then they see me with this belly . . . and a young husband to boot—what's going on? they say. What do they think is going on? I'm tired, Pacalacou . . . I wish I was like I was when I christened you, just for a little to be like then. Instead of growing completely old and having to say to my husband, *Get married again* . . . No, for Christ's sake, better the boneyard! Let the boneyard have me from now! But just for a little to be like I was then. Little, sprite, and saucy . . . How wonderful it was then! My mother was confined to bed after giving birth—she didn't give birth every year, but it just happened to be that year. And my elder sister was ill and also confined to bed. And that's why they dressed me up in white, in red: you're going to be a godmother, they said, it's fallen on you. A mere slip of a girl and they make a godmother of you! . . . You feel like climbing into the font yourself."

"Did you climb in?"

"Then? No, only you . . . But for days beforehand, our grandmother kept drumming it into me: you'll give the name Pascalis to the boy, Pascalacos, take care you don't get your tongue twisted, I'll cut it out! Sleeping and waking I kept saying it, Pascalis-Pascalacos so I wouldn't forget, so I wouldn't get my tongue twisted. Because she'd had a son called Pascalis who had died, one of my uncles, I'd never even met him. But your grandmothers — you had two then — had other sons who had died, and each of them wanted the name of her own son! That was the custom then. If you died, someone else had to be given your name, to envy you your luck — and it's still like that. It's like saying, if I give birth to a girl now, I have to name her Julia. Or like, that other Julia, who I should have named . . . Anyhow . . . Just because I didn't call her Rodanthe, it's not as though she came to a better end, is it? It's the souls that Charon is after, not their names."

"Souls are better," said Pacalacou, licking his lips as though they were talking about trout.

"I don't know if they're better, but there are more of them. Names . . . one, two, three, a thousand, eventually they run out. But souls never run out. Millions of them!"

"Why?"

Febronia stubbed out the second cigarette butt in the ground with a graceful and steady motion, as though seedlings would shoot up there in spring . . .

"Pacalacou, you're good company for me," she said to him, "but I regret talking to you. Wasting my words — it's like pouring water into a cracked pitcher. I'm telling you there are millions of souls and you ask me why."

"What should I ask you?"

"Nothing. Ask nothing, you only get me more confused. Just listen . . . Do you want me to tell you about your christening? I remember it like it was now."

"Like now?"

"Yes. The older you get, the more you recall the past. Things that happened yesterday you forget, but older things you remember . . . You were very small then — even for a godmother like me, you were very small, unbelievably, like something unreal." (At the same time she rolled a third reefer.) "And then again I'd never seen you before, I thought that all newborns were beautiful — ours at home was . . . eh, so-so, at any rate you didn't get a shock when you saw it. But when they opened your wrappings and I saw your face, I almost fell down. Pacalacou . . . I saw — how can I put it — a little brown frog inside crookedly opening its mouth . . . He recognizes you, they told me, do you see how he's smiling at you? That was a *smile*. Imagine what his crying must be like, when before long you started to cry and go green . . . I wanted to leave, but they wouldn't let me. Hold him, Febronia, caress him, he's crying because he wants you, some of your aunts said to me. They'd got used to you. And I saw them, how they pinched your cheeks—*gou, gou*—and looked sideways at me . . . And afterwards they put their fingers on your neck, on that mass of wrinkles, and brought them down, down as far as your navel, *good baby, good baby*, they kept saying . . . and again looked at me—they had understood that I was afraid. What could I do? I, too, put my finger on your neck and said *good baby* . . . And gradually I got over my fear, got used to you . . . do you want me to tell you more about that day? I remember it well. Or are you cold? Do you want us to go?"

"No, I'm not cold," Pacalacou said.

"Maybe you don't like it that I called you a little frog?"

"No, I liked it, here they make soup out of the little frogs . . . Tell me some more."

"It's the turtles they make soup out of . . . and some other things. The Painemen-itsas told me . . . The frogs they let croak."

"And they do the same with the frogs, a fisherman told me . . . Tell me some more."

She had started to get cold herself, felt the smoke from her mouth like a south wind—she wasn't cold, exactly, but she might very well become ill, find herself with a temperature before daybreak.

"Yes," she began again, "when we went into the church and the time came for me to say your name to the priest so he could announce it to the gathering of people, there was a gang of kiddies there waiting to hear it and run to your house to tell your family, to get a few pennies. Well, as soon as they heard it, I saw them jump up and—not forgetting that the godmother was only a kiddie—I jumped up too, what did I have to lose? I put you down so that I could run. They said I threw you down—I don't remember it like that, but I remember running . . . I was six years old, not even a deer could catch up with me. And we all arrived at the house, and before going in, there, there before me on the street was one of your grandmothers . . . I forgot to tell you that both your grandmas had sent secret messengers from early on, *a different one from each*, to persuade me to give you a different name! I had three names up my sleeve and I had to choose one of them . . . And I chose the one that mine wanted, because she was in our house every day, and if I'd chosen another name, I'd have gone through hellfire morning, noon, and night. But I felt sorry for the other two . . . Do you want me to tell you the story?"

"Tell it me."

"So then we arrived at the house, and there was your grandma outside on the street. *Pascalacos! Pascalacos!* the kids shouted to her and, on hearing them, it was as though she turned to stone. When she saw me among the kids, however, she was surprised and took heart and fell upon me with open arms: She's the only one who'll tell me how she christened him, she said to the other kids, She's his godmother, you others don't know! And turning to me, she said: How did you christen the baby, little girlie? *Pascalacos,* I told her. *Pascalacos?* she cried, taking a step back. Who told you to give him that name? The Holy Virgin in a dream, I told her—that's what my grandmother had told me to say. *Pascalacos?* she cried again. Did you perhaps get confused? Did the Holy Virgin perhaps tell you to say *Eleftheracos* like my son was called? No, no, *Pascalacos*... Think hard now... I am doing, I told her, *Pascalacos*. She went away saddened, just as the other one came out full of hopeful expectation. Come over here, Febronia dear, she said, what nice name did you give to our little boy today? And she jingled the pennies in her hand... *Pascalacos,* I told her, with my eyes on the pennies. *Pascalacos?* she cried out like the other one. Are you sure? Did you perhaps say *Apostolacos* and you've forgotten? No, no, *Pascalacos,* I said, knowing that I'd lose the pennies... That's how it happened with you then!... Both of them were left aggrieved, each of them with the longing to hear her own son's name... I was upset too. Why did they make me your godmother if it was like that, they should have christened you themselves... And I was left with my hands empty."

"Where was my mother?" asked Pacalacou.

"She was pushing up daisies, didn't you know? Six feet under. As soon as she gave birth to you, she was taken by God. If not, she would have kissed my hem that day and bowed and scraped before me given that I was your godmother. Do you know what it means for them to kiss your hem?"

"I know. And then what happened?"

"Then... when you'd grown up a little and could walk with your left arm dangling behind and your one foot turned inwards, your two grandmothers came one day to see my mother and began, *pss*... *pss*..., to talk to her and cast sideways glances at me... A tremor ran through me, a shudder of fear, and when they were getting ready to leave, I tried to leave first. But my mother caught hold of me by the elbow—may God show his understanding to her too—dragged me to where we kept the animals and began beating me... beat me black and blue, you've never seen such a pasting! Why, I didn't know, I didn't have time to say anything, she brought her hands down on me like someone possessed, they even fell on the animals if they got in the way, they cringed, like me... they were tied up, they had nowhere to go. And when she calmed down, do you know what she said to me? That the two old women had told her—and they'd been told by others—that on the day of the christening, I *dropped* you to run and get a few pennies, and falling like you did on the stone slabs of the church, a little drop of blood had lodged in your brain... and because of that you're soft in the head

. . . because of that. Just imagine what they came up with! . . . What about you, Pacalacou, do you believe that?"

"No."

"No, because you love me. Apart from anything else, how tall could I have been then? Even if I'd dropped you from my arms, even if it happened like they said, how tall was I for you to hurt your head as if I'd thrown you from a balcony? . . . No, they were just looking for an excuse. You were always soft in the head from birth, you walked differently, talked, looked differently, and those two — just because I didn't name you Eleftheracos or Apostolacos — put it around that *I was to blame* for the fact that you were a simpleton."

"What happened to those two?"

"They died. One of them the same year that my first daughter was born and the other one two years later. But their words remained . . . And it was a good thing that your nan Barbara, a sister of the grandfather, stepped in and brought you up . . . Your grandfather and grandmother who raised you were brother and sister, did you know?"

"No."

"You're lying, you did know, you even called her Nan and not Grandma.[9] I don't suppose you remember the other two . . ."

"No."

"Better. And you don't remember what happened when they tried to get you to slaughter a lamb . . . Do you remember?"

She expected him to say no again. But he simply gazed at the well behind him, and so Febronia continued:

"They tried to get you to slaughter a lamb to supposedly get rid of the *shadow* over your head . . . But the opposite happened, the *shadow* got bigger . . . And from that day on I shared the blame with the lamb. *Me, your godmother, and the lamb* . . . And the lamb at least was slaughtered that same day, whereas my blame since then keeps putting out shoots — for one thing or another . . . The finger has been pointed at me more than once."

She had already stubbed out her third cigarette some time ago — she didn't want a fourth, three were enough for one night. She murmured to herself, looking her godchild in the eyes:

"I've told you such a lot tonight and you don't look at all glum . . ."

"When will Godfa'er be back?" he asked her.

"When he's found his sister. If he doesn't find her, he may not come back at

9. *Nan* is what in those parts they called second or third aunts or grandmothers but also old women generally. And perhaps it's worth mentioning that their second or third uncles were called . . . Tweets! Like the sound made by birds.

all . . . The two of us will sit like this next to the well and we'll go on chatting till
we die . . . Tell me again about Julia and how you saw her at a well in Puzla-kuk
. . . What was she doing with that old man you talked about?"

"If I tell you . . . ho-ho . . . ho-ho-ho . . . Godfa'er will beat me!"

"You're laughing before he beats you . . . Anyway, you don't have a godfather,
only a godmother, and that's me. And I'm not going to beat you. So tell me."

"He was kissing her, there! Ho—"

"Stop all that laughing. Who was kissing her?"

"The old man."

"Who was he kissing?"

"Julia."

"Which old man?"

"Him that came to stay with you . . . That old man."

"You told me someone with a bell."

"And the *thing* that he had on his back, what is it?" Pacalacou asked her.

"Who are you talking about, for heaven's sake?" asked Febronia. "What about
his back?"

"On his back . . . that hump. Isn't it a *bell?*"

There were some in those parts who called humps *bells* . . . Especially if they
grew on skinny backs and it hit you in the eye, like a bell dongs in your ear . . .

"Are you talking about . . . ?"

Febronia couldn't even say the name, couldn't believe it, but at the same
time she understood—now she understood—that Pacalacou's laughter every
time that the conversation went to the *other* well had a reason, some saucy recollection . . . But then again, it was difficult for her to believe it: Julia, her red-
headed sister-in-law, always frightened, timid, distant . . . Hesychios's *velvety*,
going to Puzla-kuk with an *old crock?* It was inconceivable.

"And what was the one with the bell doing with her?" she numbly asked her
godson, as all the other stories she'd been telling him till now dissolved like
smoke around the well . . .

"He wanted to hold her, to kiss her on the mouth," said Pacalacou, who, apart
from the fact that he didn't always laugh, was also sometimes very expressive in
his choice of words and in the way he came out with them . . .

"Ah . . . he *wanted to*," said Febronia, as though mesmerized. "So he didn't
kiss her exactly?"

"He did in the end, he kissed her on the mouth . . . Kissed her, I saw them,
he covered her in saliva and she began to cry . . . But he kept kissing her and her
body was bending like an osier . . . He kept kissing her."

"Just imagine! . . . ," Febronia thought to herself as she listened to him. "She
didn't want the builder, who was a fine man, with his blue eyes, with his strong

arms that could break rope—before the wolf got him of course—and then she goes and lets herself be kissed by an old dolt! . . ."

"You know, Pacalacou," she turned and said to him, "what you're telling me all seems so incredible, so bizarre . . . Did you perhaps see them close together by the well, like you and I are now, *innocent*, and all the rest has come out of your head?"

"It's not all out of my head, I saw them," Pacalacou said with a somber expression.

"And it was on Saint Barbara's Day?"

"Yes, I'd gone to gather a little wood and I saw them."

"Was it nighttime?"

"It was getting dark. Then it was soon nighttime."

"And did they stay there . . . all night?"

"No, they separated. They went separate ways . . . and I left with the wood."

"But it was then when we still had the wolves . . . Weren't they afraid?" Febronia asked with a slight shudder.

"Yes, the wolves. Seems they weren't afraid," said Pacalacou.

"And weren't you afraid?" she asked him.

"I went to gather wood," he told her, as though the wolves only bothered strange couples who went out to kiss in secret . . . And in any case, they didn't bother these either, it seemed.

"Lord above!" she said with a shudder. "I need at least another three reefers to digest all that, smoke myself blue in the face! . . ."

"The smoke helps, but then it just vanishes into the cold sky," he said.

"How is it you're talking like that tonight! What wits all of a sudden! . . . Like some sort of seer . . . like someone risen from the dead," she said to him. "And we all thought you were in a world of your own. But I christened you, and I'm certain that you're not just in a world of your own."

"I am, I am!" he said with sudden elation, and his pile of clothes rubbed up against hers.

"All right, all right, I didn't say it for you to get worked up about it—I'm in a world of my own too," said his godmother. ". . . What is it you want? Bread?" she asked, somewhat surprised: he was snuggling up to her, groping her breast and belly like a mole.

"Can I smell you a little bit?" he said to her—and never before had he asked her for bread or anything else with such longing.

"Smell me! You call that smelling?" she said, starting to be more surprised and pulling back from him. But he continued to move closer to her . . .

Then she let him; just as so many, many things had happened to her that day, and not only that day (so many that she couldn't even bring them all to mind, or if she did she would have to disappear herself), so she let him smell her, grope her with his fingers, with his doglike breath, let him search for—who knows— his mother perhaps, while she coddled him, making circles with her hand on his back, thickly covered as it was with clothes and rags.

"My little harebrained lad . . . my poor orphan . . . are you hungry? Are you very hungry?" she whispered to him, with a distillation of motherly submission and compassion.

To put it another way, this *accumulation* of what had happened and was happening in her life, all this *fecundity,* the *burden* of it, had brought her to her knees, exhausted her: like the overly heavy branches that break in the end.

The following morning, she went to find Persa and dangling before her eyes the almost empty tobacco pouch asked her: "Did you already know what I learned last night?"

"I knew long before you learned it," Persa replied.

"I'm not talking about the tobacco," said Febronia, "I mean your . . ." She wanted to say "your brother," but something held her back from saying it just yet. Besides, Persa might have also meant the same thing.

She waited for Hesychios to return, but for the present only the time passed and brought nothing. And the images returned to her mind of what Pacalacou had told her . . . She thought of going and talking to her father-in-law, but just the thought of it scared her—she knew how much Christoforos liked the newly ar- rived Jacob . . . Meanwhile, she rolled new cigarettes and smoked (she had asked Persa to refill the pouch for her), half-unknown among all the half-unknowns in that house, and at some moment she heard Kimon scolding his wife, Efthalitsa, for the previous day's episode . . . and she was whimpering and said:

"I won't do it again, but it was her fault, she wound me up . . . why should she care if I was bent over the flowerpots and wasn't speaking to her?"

"She might not be your real mother," said the icon painter, "but your father is my best friend and she, whatever you say, is his wife!"

"Don't remind me!" shouted Efthalitsa. "Fifteen years living in that house was enough!"

"And me, what did I have to go through in that house for seventeen years?" Febronia muttered to herself, "it wasn't all *one and one makes two.*"

That evening, she again encountered Persa for a little in one of those yards belonging to others that resembled a Turkish bath given the way the dark fell together with the mist. On seeing her holding a cigarette, Persa advised her to be a little careful, not to be greedy since she was a beginner.

"Here there are no tobacco leaves or tobacconists," she said to her; "if what

I brought with me runs out, then what will we do? End up drying reeds and smoking them?"

"It'll pass, it'll pass," said Febronia, "it's that time of day . . ."

"Is anything wrong?" asked Persa.

"Nothing. I'm just waiting for Hesychios to get back—I'm suddenly without a home and without a husband, and with so many cares . . . What else could be wrong? Can you think of anything else?"

She shook her earrings and turned her red eyes to the mist.

"The wind's up and blowing from all quarters," she said, almost without moving her lips.

"I'm sure she knows," Febronia thought to herself. "She knows and she's afraid of each new day that dawns, just like me."

And when night had well and truly fallen and everyone was asleep, she went again to the well on her own. Not with the intention of . . . jumping in again, but with the hope of finding Pacalacou again in order to ask him not to say anything—not to say anything to anyone about what he knew, till Hesychios got back and they found out what had happened to Julia.

She found him in the same spot and he was overjoyed to see her again.

"Don't get beside yourself, I'm not here so you can smell me again," she said to him, and the poor wretch snuggled up in his clothes and breathed on his hands. Anyway, she sat beside him again to roll one more cigarette—there was no moon that night, and the damp was more noticeable, piercing . . . "Aren't you cold?" she asked, puzzled. "Just what are you made of?"

"Shall we go to the lake tomorrow night?" he asked her.

"To the lake? You're getting a bit bold aren't you, my lad? Isn't the well enough for you?"

"So when will Godfa'er come back?" he asked her.

"He's not come back, and I don't know when he'll come back, and that's why I'm here," she told him. "Because, till he gets back—are you listening to me, Pacalacou? Till he gets back, and afterwards too, I don't want you to say anything about what you saw at the other well . . . Do you understand?"

"I won't say anything," he promised her, and she could rely on his promise: he had so much love for her and was so obedient to her that were she to tell him to go and jump in the Goulgi he would. The question was, would anything change with that promise?

She sat beside him smoking and silent, with her stomach rumbling now and then in the stillness, while he opened his nostrils to smell her smoke . . . If he were to sidle up to her like the previous night with those nostrils, perhaps once again she would have been unable to fend him off—which is why she stubbed the cigarette out long before it began to burn her fingers, steadied herself on his knees and got to her feet. She was heavy like the weather; she who once with one step was here, there, and everywhere . . . She picked up the pouch with the rest of the tobacco and the flint and told him to be careful of the damp.

Pacalacou rubbed his back against the wall of the well and his rags got caught on one of the jagged stones . . .

"Are you going to go and sleep?" he asked her twice.

"All my joints are creaking," she replied the second time. "I'm not for places like this."

And after she had advanced a little in the empty orchard, she turned her head, saw him too on his feet: he seemed to her to be ready to run—as though he wanted to, but was hesitating to run after her . . . "Lordy," she thought, "he's a human being too, and he wants to sleep in a bed; but there's hardly a bed even for me in the house of these strangers . . ."

She put her hand to her mouth and shouted to him:

"When we leave here, when we go back to our own parts, I'll have you sleep in my house, Pacalacou!" And after a slight pause, as though someone else were listening and might misunderstand: "Now that you've lost your third grandmother and you've only got me, your godmother!" she shouted even louder.

Pacalacou waved his twisted arm, meaning that he would go to her house without a second thought, and that simple laughter that came out of his mouth left a mark in the mist.

"When we go back to our own parts . . . ," Febronia muttered to herself, speeding up her step.

From the time when the black wolves had appeared and began roaming in their parts, from then if not before, one of the strangest and most dubious of romances had begun to weave itself in Christoforos's house. And if something stops us from saying that its *target* was once again Julia, the most mysterious of all the souls in the house, it is because it might very well have been Julia herself who was the *weaver*.

And the first stirring were the eyes, those very bitter black eyes that he turned on her (after a certain time, *only* on her) like a viper—and if they didn't make her feel the way she did with Kimon's blue eyes (his had a different kind of persistence, subjection, and intensity), they did remind her of another look, a much older one: a wily, solitary one . . . It was also those long dark fingers on the accordion, so nimble, so unpredictable, it was also all those lovely songs he sang in that old, gruff voice, it was also the bed next to the window where many dead sat at the bedside of her sick niece and many living came in and out, it was those evening hours that didn't bring either a *miracle* or *liberation*, it was also his ill-tempered solitariness, which in vain sought some contact with the enigma of her own: it was all of these things, generally speaking, that led Julia to a haughty, humpbacked old man.

One evening, she saw him putting the accordion on his back, and because they no longer wanted him to play for little Julia (they had taken her to *the hares* that evening), he was going out for a walk by himself. She quickly went to one of the upstairs windows—and from that one to another one. But it was dark, she lost sight of him, and went down the stairs even quicker to catch up with him before he had gone too far. She went the same way that she had seen him go, but because the darkness was coming down between them equally quickly, she was forced to turn into various lanes at random, from one to the other, in order to find him, to see him again without his knowing . . . Just before she had given up hope, and while walking now on dirt paths in her old sandals and some old black stockings, she saw him: he was walking before her with his head down—at a distance the same as that between their front door and the ruins. She halted as though a bat had flown into her face. He was so thin and long-legged, so crooked with his hump, his pointed elbows, his cauliflower ears, so haughty, pathetic, and alone with the moon above bathing him in its light . . . A crazy idea came into her head. So crazy that he was wise to *nothing* behind him.

She let him go on walking, and the moon—in no way passive—seemed to her to be walking too, but in the opposite direction, towards her, with a *heart-breaking* smile, and only in this way did she realize that she was walking, but . . . backwards, to one side, sideways, like those who are frightened or scared, or like the children who were dancing backwards. Those children with the hoods, whoever they were.

But backwards like that, she bumped into a tree, fell against its trunk, and—turning round—embraced it. Putting her cheek to its rough bark (if not to those warm bells of Kimon), she heard coughing, spitting, and her father's voice: "*The old goat! He himself!* . . ." She was alarmed. Was her father there too? Had he seen her? Or was everything rustling in her head like the leaves in the wood when they smell a storm approaching? If it was him, if he caught her running behind an old goat (while she was seeking someone else), what would she say to him? That she regretted not having gone with the other Julia to *the hares* and was going there now? That she hadn't found them? That she was lost? What can anyone say when they're lost in any case?

She left the tree, and seeing that she was walking on dirt, removed her san-dals, slipped them over her hand, and cautiously made her way to the edge of the field where the track began. She saw some bushes on the other side . . . she had to pass over the track like lightning—and that's just what she did. But she dropped one of her sandals, right in the middle of the dirt track, and was afraid to go back for it. She left it there and hid behind the bushes and waited: the years had no meaning for her, just the minutes . . .

Returning from his lonely moonlit walk, Jacob saw the sandal, arched his back even more, and at first stared at it as if afraid he might catch fleas. But he quickly recognized it, touched it, fondled it . . . And with a resounding smack of his lips that showed great voracity (this usually dry and unenthusiastic man), he stuck out his tongue and almost licked it. Then he put it safely into one of his deep pockets . . .

"*Mon dieu!*"[10] he said in his aged voice that scratched and pitched. "Saint Demetrius wore sandals too! . . ."

It was around the time of Saint Demetrius's Feast Day and the Indian summer that usually came with it . . .

He said it in the direction of the bushes, where Julia's *feelings* were stirring if not her body.

And when he arrived back home, he showed the sandal to his sister. She recognized it too—there was no one who would doubt who the owner of that sandal was, with its suede now shiny and discolored . . .

"Where did you find it?" she asked him.

"She came to the fields with me," he told her.

"Who?"

"Who? . . . The one who was wearing it, who else?"

"Have you taken leave of your senses?" his sister exclaimed.

"No, she came to the fields with me, I'm telling you—she would hardly have escaped my notice," said Jacob, with all the pride instilled in him by this idea, this suspicion . . . and this fear—though he wasn't sure where this fear was coming from.

"She was supposed to be going with the others to the hares . . . ," murmured Persa. "Isn't that where she went?"

"The others to the hares, and she with me to the fields . . . ," said Jacob in his reverie. And he reminded her with a hint of derision: "Eh! . . . You told me that this time you'd find me a woman if I cured the little girl, isn't that what you said?"

"But you didn't cure her," Persa reminded him.

"You don't let me finish! . . . To add that you didn't have to find her; she turned up by herself."

10. "My God!"

"Shh! We'll be out of a home if her father finds out!"

"Are you scared of him, *ma ser?*"[11]

"Enough of your nonsense! He can't stomach you, even if you are my brother."

"His daughter can stomach me."

"His daughter is elsewhere. She hears *wild voices* that transport her elsewhere . . . Do you understand, Jacob? Or do you want me to spell it out for you?" Persa said to him.

"What I understand is that she was waiting for me . . . That she's starting up tendernesses with me,"[12] he said, once again in reverie.

"She started up tendernesses, as you put it, with someone else—it's not you she's waiting for," said Persa, persisting in going contrary to his fantasies. "So put your tongue back in your mouth: it's someone else that Julia's stayed single for."

"And if the other one has abandoned her?" asked Jacob.

"It wasn't him who refused her."

"I think I love her . . . ," her brother said, still in his reverie.

"Take a look at your teeth . . . they've gone rotten . . ."

"Hers will go rotten too. And so tell me . . . If she loves me too, are you saying that *you* will come between us, because your husband can't stomach me?"

Persa made a gesture with her hand to tell him that she didn't want to hear any more. She wouldn't exclude anything, but she didn't want to hear any more. She left him and tried to remember what Julia was wearing on her feet when she saw her the last time, when the others were getting ready to go to the hares just a few hours before (naturally, they still hadn't come back) and the redhead had changed her mind and not gone with them . . . What had she been wearing? Her sandals for sure—as long as it wasn't snowing, she wore her sandals. But Persa wished she had remembered *seeing* them. She hadn't seen them: we don't look to see what the other one is wearing on his feet, unless there is some reason. And there hadn't been any reason to do so. Nor had she seen Julia from the time the others had left in the cart . . . On the contrary, her brother had eaten alone, picked his teeth clean with a needle, wiped himself, scratched himself, and afterwards had told her that he was going for a walk in the fields under the moonlight . . . He had even winked at her. She had interpreted it to mean that if the others had preferred the hares on account of little Julia, he wasn't going to get upset about it: there were the empty fields . . . Yet perhaps his look had hinted that for him there was also the elder Julia?

11. "My sister."
12. Beginning a liaison . . .

She wouldn't exclude anything—except, perhaps, that Julia actually *did love* Jacob and had followed him into the fields to this end.

She went to see if she was in her room, in a room, that is, where she retired to at nights, where, that is—in a separate bed—three or four of her nieces and nephews slept. All she found was two of these sitting in front of the fire, which was barely lit, and playing their own form of backgammon: the checkers were thimbles filled with coal dust . . . And in their hands they were holding tiny catapults.

"Where's your aunt who sleeps here with you?" she asked them.

"We're not going to tell you!" said the smaller one, after first shooting with his catapult at one of the thimbles and covering the other one in coal dust.

"Why aren't you going to tell me?" she asked, somewhat annoyed.

"Because we don't know," replied the elder one. "Because they didn't take us with them where they went, that's why," he added.

They were the ones being punished: there wasn't a day or night went by without some of the children having to pay with something—their supper or exclusion—for some rash act of theirs that had annoyed someone. So these two hadn't been taken to Haliva to see the hares . . . and they were passing their time with coal dust.

Persa lifted up the bedspread—both bedspreads—and looked underneath the beds.

"Do you know where your aunt's sandals are?" she asked.

Neither of the two children deigned to answer such a question . . . Another thimble fell over.

"Did you see what she was wearing this evening, this afternoon? . . . What she had on her feet?"

They couldn't have cared less. Or they thought it only natural that she would have been wearing her blue sandals, just as it was only natural that this red-eyed woman always wore green earrings . . . And so they didn't even bother to answer her.

"They do right to punish you!" said Persa vindictively.

But when she had closed the door behind her, the elder one said to the younger one, "If our aunt has lost her blue sandals, she'll be crying all night . . . And if she hasn't lost them, she'll still be crying! . . ."

The ninth thimble was knocked over.

While Persa, her anxiety rekindled, returned to her brother . . . Going down the main staircase in order to climb up a smaller one in the west wing, she halted and asked herself what all this worry and fluster that had taken hold of her was for: Julia might have lost her sandal in the house, on one of the stairs—there were so many staircases that the women were running up and down all day, sometimes they lost much more important things; and Jacob might have found it, have taken it with him to the fields, and given how the old wretch liked to pride himself . . .

When she entered the little room where they had put him as the ineffective doctor he was, she saw Julia's sandal hanging from a hook on the wall while he was caressing the keys on his accordion with eyes closed (just before she entered, at the sound of the slight disturbance outside, he had opened them and stared at the door in awe; but he closed them again with a languorous smile on seeing who came in . . .).

She said to him:

"You might think I'm stupid, but I don't understand what you wanted to tell me with that sandal!"

"Fourteen loves I lived while I've had breath . . . ," sang Jacob.

"Why not make it forty-four," she said, mocking him.

". . . but this last one will be my death. Voualla!"

"Jacob, speak plainly," she implored him; "did anything happen out there in the fields?"

But Jacob didn't say anything more to her—he didn't know any more himself, but above all *this* didn't mean . . .

And the next morning, Julia was once again wearing both her sandals, while he had shut himself in his room. She was pale, very pale, as though she had been sucked dry. Persa couldn't remember whether she had always been so pale.

It was the time around Saint Demetrius's Day, as we said, a lovely and pleasant October which instead of the usual rains and genuine autumnal chills was still providing them with summer grapes and a wealth of black figs. And during the days when little Julia had her last glimmerings: she died on the fifth of November, along with *all the old coins, all the silverware* . . . the weather suddenly changed. And the black wolves appeared. But it took a month before there were clear signs of them and for everyone to start talking about them.

And for Julia to start with some vague and unspecified feelings (guilt mixed with desires that were constantly foiled) and for these to take a more distinct form—even if for us (and for them then) all these were totally inscrutable.

In his little room, Jacob stewed in his own juice: that same night *following the fields*, Julia went herself into that room to ask for her sandal back. She went in and stayed—standing and wearing only one sandal at the door. And she confessed that she had followed him to the fields because it was as though she had heard a voice calling her . . . Because, she said, she had been moved by those songs, because she had understood that he was singing them for her, because of that *"love me and hold nothing back"* . . .

With an air of grandeur, he got up from his bed and went over to her; and if he wasn't mistaken, she moved towards him a little too from where she was standing at the door. And she bent her head when he told her a few more songs like that "love me and hold nothing back" (without singing them necessarily), and when—breaking the silence that ensued—he asked her if she'd ever heard such songs, such words, from anyone else, she raised her head slightly (as though he had touched her chin) and smiled: a smile all her own, which nevertheless made him feel unique. And when he went a little closer to her and his fingers—in truth the most magnetic thing about him—lightly touched her clothes, she remained motionless. And when he put his hand behind on her slender waist and pulled her slightly towards him, she followed. And then she remained motionless again, more or less at his disposition, when he lowered his high neck and more or less kissed her on her hair. He said some other appropriate words to her, which she listened to . . . But when he asked for more, a real kiss, she jumped aside and left him trembling.

"Is there something wrong with you, child?" he asked her dejectedly.

Julia took her sandal from the hook and stood facing him, but at the same distance as at the beginning, and with her breast heaving.

"Only if . . . ," she said, and she seemed to need to catch her breath in order to continue.

"Only if—what?" he asked, after waiting a few moments.

"Only if you go . . . if you come . . . I'll tell you in a few days!" she promised him.

A few days later, the same things happened, again in that same room, again it was nighttime, and after she had got him excited, she again left him cold and went away saying the same things to him.

He began having problems with his liver. And not only this, but he felt dizzy whenever he saw her with others or just thought about her, yet he didn't want to talk to his sister Persa, to ask her help: not after all that mumbo-jumbo he had told her that evening, when he had returned from the fields with Julia's sandal in his pocket and his head in the clouds . . . He had his pride.

On the day of the strong wind, his sister—what irony—had fallen at his feet, while he had been fantasizing about his red-headed goddess in that position . . .

And the following day, the last drop of little Julia's life had fallen—the house had filled with lamentation. For many days and nights.

He remained shut up in his room, and the feeling that no one remembered him, no one took him into account, cost him greatly. If among all this there hadn't been the elder Julia, he would have got up and left—that inconspicuous-ness and, as well, that *subjugation* were not at all to his liking.

Yet, on the other hand, whoever passed outside his room talked about the wolves and the first lambs that were being lost . . .

"How did I get into this?" he grumbled inside the four walls they had al-lotted to him. "I'm for salons, for musical soirées, where they listen to me and all stand to attention. Here, this lot listen to the wolves singing at night . . . *Quel dommaz!*"[13]

But one evening, his door opened and in walked Julia again. She was wear-ing black because of her niece, and she had finally taken off those age-old san-dals—her legs seemed different in a pair of gray bootees that reached up to her ankles, most likely men's, from some small-footed brother, if not from one of her adolescent nephews. Yet they suited her, flattered her in a strange sort of way, given that her black dress reached down to about an inch above the bootees, and between these and her hemline, her calves appeared seemly, thin, and some-what childlike. She seemed *little* in her build, vulnerable, and cute (despite the black), as though half her years had left her with her younger niece.

Her red lips, how I'd like to kiss them . . . was the song that came into Jacob's mind—though her hair was even redder. But he had already touched her hair. What remained untouched was her lips, her heart.

"If you are what you say," she told him, "if you want . . . what it is you want . . . then . . . then tomorrow night . . . I want you to come out . . . for me . . . as far as . . . as far as . . ."

"I'm sick and tired of staying in this cell waiting for you," Jacob told her, as the gaps in her words stifled him as much as her absence.

"If that's how it is, I'll go," she said, turning towards the door but staying in the same spot, as though the room were a theater.

"Wait! You take whatever I say the wrong way!" he said. "So many days in here all alone . . ."

"Me too, I'm alone," she said, turning back to him and again leaning towards him with that sibylline face. "Don't talk too loud, I don't want anyone hearing you."

"If you ask me to hold my tongue, I'll hold my tongue," he told her, "but . . . come a little closer, or someone will hear us—even the walls have ears."

She went a little closer to him and his whole body stirred, shivered . . . and became numb at the same time, his genitals shrank, his shoulders curved even

13. "What a shame!"

more; his age suddenly *showed itself*, bothered him, just as much as that bone in his back sticking out . . . He sought to forget through his words:

"With me, great times await you," he said to her hoarsely, "don't think that . . . You find me unprepared, that's why I'm standing like this . . . But if I see to myself, if I spruce myself up as they say . . . I've traveled round half the world, yes me who you see standing here before you! Half of Europe at my feet . . . And I've had many women . . . One married woman forgot her husband on my account! . . . I know women . . . There was a Solance who wouldn't leave my side . . . She would take me home with her at night—yellow curtains on the windows, comfortable crepe armchairs, Arabic coffee—and in the mornings everyone would stare at me as I went downstairs . . . They were unable to sleep because of what they heard all night . . . And I don't only mean the accordion . . . And all that in Paris, rue Casteré . . . But you're different, made of different stuff . . . You're without guile, without experience—I don't imagine you'll get jealous because I'm speaking to you a little about the others!"

"You'll see when we get there," Julia said to him, who evidently hadn't heard anything of what he'd been saying. "Ask where M'ravita's Pit is . . . Will you remember? *M'ravita's Pit.* That's how we call it round here . . . Even if you just say M'ravita, anyone will tell you . . . I'll be waiting there . . . Ask old people, not children—children . . . might follow you . . . Though they're afraid now . . . Tomorrow night as soon as it gets dark . . . You'll have to walk a bit . . . Are you afraid?"

"Let me make sure I understand first," he mumbled, as all this—from the questionable Solance to the unknown Maravita—seemed to him *without rhyme or reason.*

"You'll understand tomorrow . . . there," she said, touching the tips of his fingers with hers, and the bootees with the black dress (black with blue glints) slipped outside the door.

As if he had seen all this in a dream, the next day he got ready, spruced himself up, drank something that smelled of aniseed, picked up his accordion, and went out of the house a long time before it got dark. Every so often he clicked his tongue. She hadn't given him much to go on—she hadn't even told him in what direction he should go to find Maravita and her pit, but he took the path that he knew towards the fields, the path he'd taken that other evening. Reaching the more distant houses, he noticed that in the yards the people were skinning the slaughtered lambs and goats—he was slightly surprised, but he was more concerned about what he was going to do himself. In one of the yards, someone saw him, recognized him, and called to him from afar, raising his bloodied hand:

"Hey there, Mister Musician, with your big harmonica! . . ."

He raised his hand and smiled humbly: sometimes humble people moved him and he became like them . . .

"Stroll?" the other shouted to him. "Stroll at dusk, in that *other* light?"

What did he mean?

Jacob didn't waste any time, he simply smiled at him again from afar and waved to him again . . .

"We're slaughtering them ourselves before the wolves get them!" said the other one, as if priding himself on it, but Jacob didn't hear him, he was already a long way off.

"Ha! Instead of the wolves eating them, let those jackals have them," the man said to himself, and his wife and some children heard him and felt sad; his wife advised him to speak more quietly, not to advertise it.

When the houses really did begin to become few and far between, Jacob stopped before a fence and asked two elderly men, who were also skinning a large sheep in their yard (they were bent over it and totally absorbed in their work), in which direction he should go to get to Maravita.

"In the direction of where the sun sets when it comes out!" answered one of them in good spirits and with perhaps some innuendo, nudging with his foot the other man, who was somewhat younger. "Show the man, Nestor, how to get to M'ravita—I'm stiff," he said with more than a little familiarity.

Wiping his hands on his sleeves, he came over to the fence and pointed Jacob in a certain direction, continually stressing how many times he had to turn right, how many left and how many he should go straight on. When he had finished his detailed instructions for a second time and was getting ready for a third, the other man behind him shouted:

"Ask him, Nestor, what business he has in M'ravita at such an hour—but see you don't make him dizzy!"

But while the man in the middle had his head turned, Jacob climbed down from the fence, and as he walked off he heard their loud conversation:

"He's a stranger, Vangelis, what can I say to him?"

"And just because he's a stranger, does that mean we can't be knowin' what he wants in M'ravita?"

"He's carrying a load, leave him in peace."

"Did you tell him that there are wolves at night?"

"Tell him about the wolves, no, I forgot."

"Ah, dear ol' Nestor . . ."

Jacob felt a chill through all his bones: for days he had been hearing people talking of wolves, though if he hadn't heard these two talking he would have made straight for Maravita just as someone might head towards his fields

. . . Without the slightest suspicion, without thinking twice about anything (this same man who was cautious even of the water he drank), simply because a mysterious girl had asked him to . . . For one of her kisses, nothing more—if she had given him more, perhaps he wouldn't have gone, perhaps he would have said *basta, c'est suffee* . . .[14] He proceeded a little farther so he wouldn't be seen by the other two or arouse the curiosity of the older one, and there he stopped, wet his lips, and put his accordion down on the ground (really, why did he need it? Was he going to a wedding?) in order to decide whether to go on in the direction of Julia's unknown wildernesses or turn back while the hour still permitted him, even though all that was waiting for him was an empty bedroom and an equally empty night.

When again he passed the double strap over his shoulder and took to his legs again, he had made up his mind that he wanted to kiss that mysterious female being—that he wanted to finish that kiss that had begun with her red hair but had never, so many days now, descended any lower: to her lips that mumbled gibberish and that made him long for them—her lips, nothing else, he longed for her lips as another might long for her body. He wasn't like the others.

He forgot, however, to pick up his *arrogance* too, his pride anyway, his inseparable companion together with his accordion, and now that he was walking out in lonely, unknown places, with the dusk gradually enveloping him and slightly mocking him, with the gray clouds slipping lower and lower and the silence of that hour *broken* every now and again by distant howling, strange lamentations, he felt rather like a servant being sent to the gallows simply so they might test the strength of the rope. That's how he felt. And—strangely enough—he accepted it, he found it quite natural . . . Except that he wished they had given him a horse too—so he could go wherever it was he was going on horseback . . . and that they had put a warm cloak over his shoulders, something that would have protected him from that bitter chill, it being the end of November.

"I'll catch my death," he thought, "I'll well and truly catch my death tonight." But he couldn't go back, whether he went on or went back, it was the same. All he did was stop now and again to cough—a sharp, dry cough that brought pain to his lungs and all the way down to his ribs. He also had the problem with his liver . . . To his left, he discerned a large hollow in the ground like a dried-up pond. Nevertheless, there were bushes here and there in the hollow and a tall tree that dominated the whole area and had shed all its leaves. If he had been a local, he would have known that this was M'ravita's Pit and that Maravita was a foreign noblewoman in times long gone who had fallen in love with a

14. "Enough, that's enough . . ."

young man of humble birth from those parts (called, according to some, Hara-
lambos and according to others Lysimachus, so let's call him Lysilambos) who
had gone to foreign lands to sell horses, and just as his horses and her lordly husband's purse had exchanged hands, so too she had exchanged her heart with his
. . . From then on, Lysilambos remained there, worked as a groom in the lord's
stables, where Maravita would come at night in secret to find him, and there in
the stables she savored the long kisses of their illicit love. All this until the lord
found them in each other's arms and immediately ordered Lysilambos's head
to be cut off, while for Maravita he reserved a slower and more dishonorable
death: he brought her and all her entourage to the land of her lover, chose the
tallest tree in a deserted spot, bound her to it, and left her there to die bound
to its trunk. One of his servants gave her a little water morn and night, which
she refused in order to die quicker; but they forced her to drink it. The lord
remained there himself and wouldn't leave while she was going through the
throes of death. And when she finally expired (after twenty-seven whole days, as
many as the years of her life), he put an end to his own life with a sword, under
the same tree, at his wife's feet. And though he had left written instructions to
his servants to take both bodies, his and his wife's, back to their own land to be
buried, they carried out only half his orders, and they left Maravita's body just
as it was, bound to the tree, in the homeland of Lysilambos: *the sun shall eat
her clothes and the wind her hair* . . . (as the locals sang in their dirges for her).
And it's said that from that time, that spot turned into a pit on its own, a form
of nest and tomb for those three (that's what was said: for those three), and that,
if you looked carefully on one side of the tree, low down close to its roots, you
could still see two marks shaped like feet: those left by Maravita who had waited
there twenty-seven days for death to come to her, thereby paying in full for her
one *mistake*.

For all married women (perhaps even up to today), that tree, that hollow,
all that place invoked fear and reticence and obliged them—whenever they
passed by, by chance or will—to bow their heads and pray for Maravita or for
their own souls, even if they hadn't themselves dared to commit adultery, not
even in their dreams. They all prayed and secretly crossed themselves to ward
off any similar fate, or perhaps—deep down and implicitly—wishing that they,
too, had savored it . . . to the extent that any god at least would permit it. And if
some of the women (very few we imagine) had savored it to that extent at least,
they, it's said, were quite capable of betraying themselves, *after the event*, simply
by passing by that place—such was the trembling that took hold of them and
such their loss of color and humor.

And so Jacob arrived there ignorant of all these tales and legends. But he didn't need to be aware of all this for his body to hunch even more from the chill of an invisible presence, or of many, as soon as he stepped onto that incline and took a few paces . . .

"Where has that half-crazy woman brought me?" he asked himself, no doubt longing for the evenings when he would count his coins in his empty room. And despite all that had happened and despite his having gone there on her account, obeying her strange demands, as soon as he saw her appearing from behind the big tree, with her back stretched and resting against the trunk and with her hands hidden, he felt even more frightened.

"And now what's going to happen? . . . ," he asked her with a very sullen expression, once using his voice and another three times with his hand, given that several moments passed and she simply stared at him.

"I heard your step and came out . . . ," she said, just as he was getting ready to speak again.

"I've been hearing other things," he told her. "I came here right as rain with my accordion and I've fallen into a wolf's lair."

"Wolves? Come closer . . . What do you know about wolves?" she asked him, moving away just a little from the tree trunk. "Come closer," she said to him again in her velvety voice, "they won't bother you . . . it's nothing, there are hundreds of strange things in life like that! . . ."

"For me it's the first, may the good Lord not deem me worthy of any more," he muttered, feeling distressed and removing the heavy instrument from his back. "You would have made me leave your parts," he said to her sternly, as though warning her, "but you've got me hooked, and all I can do is follow you."

She was wearing her gray bootees with woolen stockings—now that she had taken off her sandals, she was never without the bootees—and was wrapped up in a heavy black coat that was big enough to hold a second one like her. How had she come there on her own? As for him, okay, she had asked him herself to come. But she?

"Come . . . As you've arrived this far, come . . . *What mother devours her own children*, do you know?" she asked him, as if she wanted him to forget all the rest with entertaining riddles, and she stretched out her hand to him.

"I know nothing of all that," he replied.

"You'll learn. The earth! . . . And what is it that makes food taste better? . . . Shall I tell you? Conversation . . ."

"Conversation . . . So my sister, in one of her conversations, do you know what she said? That your little niece was touched by an angel as it was passing by on some mission, and she fell and never got up again. But you—"

"She died in my place . . . don't you feel sorry for me?" she asked him.

"Is it you I should feel sorry for or her?" he asked, puzzled.

"Oh . . ."

He had come as close to her as was necessary and looked her in the face, endeavoring by himself to forget all the rest and above all what she was saying to him . . . Her figure had become so delicate that the tip of her nose shook when she spoke, her eyelashes resembled quitch, and her gaze between them was virtually transparent—a snowy gaze with a pale green iridescence . . . "Can't her folks see what's happening to her?" he wondered, as though he could see or understand what was happening.

"And why have you brought me to this godforsaken place?" he asked her. "To accompany you?"

"Yes . . . So you can tell them . . . Oh perhaps they'll grieve for a while, till . . . till they forget . . . I want to go with them."

Her arm appeared like a stalk from inside her dark, long-sleeved coat and pointed into the distance, or rather behind her, to where the lonely and sometimes collective howling could be heard sporadically.

"If you're afraid, go," she said to him afterwards, without a trace of irrationality in her voice.

"Bah! You've not brought me here to tell me to go, have you?" he said, suddenly showing his own touchiness too, but also his burning desire for that kiss, that chimerical kiss on the lips, before and after which he wanted nothing else to exist. So he grabbed hold of her by the shoulders and set himself to capturing those lips, to achieving his aim—she jerked from left to right, fluttered around him almost, elusive—and amidst all that impatience, all that strangeness that had perplexed and irked him, he somehow found what he wanted, and his lips went back and forth, wet and insubstantial like moss, on hers . . . When he left her, he saw the night getting darker on the horizon, and Maravita's tree stood all alone beside him. He trembled from head to foot from his contact with such a girl.

A few days later, again for her sake, he went to another spot, to the well at Puzla-kuk . . . This time he didn't take his heavy instrument with him, only his hump, and he chewed on a stick of cinnamon so his breath would smell sweet . . . The same things happened there—what for him was *sublime* but for her was a momentary and sad recourse to vanity, bound as she was to other visions.

And following this, Jacob was confined to bed, and only his sister Persa went into his room to see him and bring him some of her alleviating potions, endeavoring above all not to arouse Christoforos's suspicion. But the foreigners with their rifles had already lodged themselves in their house, and no one had the time anymore to give thought to the poor accordionist.

"She gave herself to me!" he told her amid his fever, but with some traces still of his feverless vanity. "The daughter of your husband, that same man who looks the other way when I pass by, gave herself to me, gave all to me . . . I couldn't keep her in check . . . She squeezed me dry . . . I may even have left her with a little Jacoby! . . ."

Persa shook her head: Is there a blind man who doesn't dream of his eyes? she thought, knowing only too well with how much chastity her stepdaughter Julia was girded, and also how devoid of intercourse her brother's body would remain till the end.

"Never you mind, never you mind, rest now," she told him, like the elder sister she was, measuring his temperature with the palm of her hand. "Whatever happened, happened, on her part and on yours . . . rest now and don't concern yourself with anything."

And when Jacob's forehead (which, for as long as he had fever, seemed in texture like warm wood) again began to cool and his chest to recover a little from the coughing, Persa smuggled him out of one of the back doors, advising him not to return—not to return unless he were to learn that all of them in that house, including her, had been lost. But by then he, too, would have gone the way of all flesh.

"Make haste, quickly!" she shouted to him in a muffled voice, as he was dawdling and looking contemptuously at the back view of this—in many ways—renowned house that had accommodated him for some one hundred days.

"What a house!" he sneered. "It turns the artiste out by the back door so it can fill up with trash. Ha!"

"Fine, fine, make a song out of it when you're with the angels," his sister told him. "Now hurry, quickly!"

And taking hold of his hump, she pushed him away with both hands . . . He very nearly went head over heels, while his accordion (which he still hadn't put over his shoulder) fell, opened up, and let out a melodic wail that petered out before it could be heard any longer; as it fell, it hit him on the knee, his feet got tangled, went backwards instead of forwards as though he were slipping on a snow-covered incline—until he again found some sort of balance, just enough to make him think it incredible that he was upright again, master of the situation. His breathing sounded more like snoring.

"How can I hurry?" he turned and said to her.

And she felt sorry for him, sorry for many things.

Julia, meanwhile, regardless of the circumstances, would go out and walk here and there, always with a penchant for the fields, just as once she had gone to the evening school: with that same animated timidity, that same desire . . .

The cold weather had now set in, snow had fallen, and she wore the bootees that she had found in an unfrequented room (the same one in which Cletia had spent her last days with the hunter's weasel, that tiny mammal that had so surprised them all then, and where now—in this same room and after her—some gruff-looking strangers had ensconced themselves) and wrapped herself in an old black overcoat, still hard-wearing and durable, that had once belonged to her grandfather Lukas, and after him had been worn by his sons in times of need, and by his grandchildren when they became men, and now it had the honor of warming Julia's unfathomable, twilight solitude.

No one had the guts to go out after dark, and it got dark early. She, however, went out. And starting much earlier—so the darkness would find her already a good way off—and she said, if anyone were to ask her, that she was going to help in the sesame-oil mill.

And she did go first to the sesame-oil mill. As though she had to show her presence there, as though she wanted her father to see her and understand what even she herself didn't really understand and yet drew her so completely... She would go up to him with her now familiar, somewhat dreamy, gait and, her head bowed, say to him:

"Papa, I'm here... Do you have anything for me?"

"What might I have for you, my dear child?" he'd say with the same tenderness that he always showed her. "Here, even the experienced hands can't manage... Not even the inexperienced can manage anymore!"

And he would show her farther inside, the mill's complex workings and the work itself that continued—despite the adverse conditions—from hand to hand, from pail to pail, from millstone to millstone, so the sesame would become powder and the powder tahini... But he would also show her each time what he had before him, on a rectangular wooden table with thick square legs, where he sat in his old age—given that he still had his eyes left—and made *little tortoises*... Just imagine: little tortoises, since only in this way could he still channel some of his old vigor, and because of his need to do something "with his hands," but also because of that melancholy which was gradually taking root inside him and which in those times they referred to simply as *pining*. Or as a *shadow*.

And he would make these little tortoises with a coconut shell cut in two for the carapace, with a chickpea sticking out for a head and beans cut in half (or sometimes melon seeds) for feet. He added two black spots to the chickpeas for eyes; and the tiniest of sticks or a wood splinter for a tail. And he stuck all these together with resin, left it to dry, and when the table was full and preventing him from making any more, he would line them up on a shelf behind him. There were some very tiny tortoises, as big as the smallest walnut, then medium-sized ones, and the big ones, the *mothers*. Usually he placed them in order: the tiny ones first and the bigger ones behind as though they were keeping an eye on the smaller ones.

Since little Julia had died, another of his grandchildren, he more and more took refuge in this work . . . His sons shook their heads sorrowfully, called him the "poor tortoise-maker," and referred to this unusual craft as an "office without superiors," or "work outside the trade" (like saying without rivals, without competitors), though deep down they thought that this handicraft work might have some value in a manner of speaking or be sold to people like Signor Boroni . . . And at the same time they were secretly pleased that it kept him far away from more practical matters: they could at last themselves make decisions concerning both the house and the mill. Naturally, he still kept an eye on these decisions, and he was the one who had the keys, but it seemed that the little tortoises had taken over his old age. They were silent, too, didn't speak to him—even more silent than Lily. They had a patience all their own.

Some of his grandchildren saw him busying himself and learned the craft themselves (though only for as long as they thought it worthwhile); others waited for the opportunity to steal one of his tortoises (they could of course take one openly, but they preferred to steal it), and others, the tougher ones, turned them upside down, spat into the hollow of the shell and left them like that till their spittle dried and their grandfather returned them to their proper position.

". . . I'll be going then," said Julia demurely.

"Where will you go? . . . ," her father asked himself more than her. "Can you see these"—he pointed again to his little tortoises—"that all stay at my side?"

"Yes, I'll come back . . . ," she told him hesitantly. "I'll go out the other way and . . ."

Again her slender arm emerged like a stalk from her big black overcoat and pointed to the back door of the mill, not far from the spot where once there was a big fireplace and all those who came to their inn then would warm themselves . . .

Christoforos turned his head in that direction.

"What is there out the other way?" he asked himself more than her, in the same tone. "Stones, nettles, my dear girl . . . ," he told her. "Ah, yes," he remembered, "there's the tobacco house out back . . . Didn't it burn?"

And whichever children of his were anywhere nearby attributed supernatural powers to Julia since she managed, though speaking so quietly, to get him to hear her!

"Did that Circassian woman send you to find some shop-bought tobacco for her?" he asked her one time.

"No, she didn't send me . . . She has her brother sick at home . . . he doesn't go out, he's afraid to," said Julia.

"Who doesn't go out?"

"Her brother . . . the musician."

"His music was all we needed! . . . But she says to me, whenever I ask her about him, that she'll turn him out, tell him to go . . . Has she still not turned him out? We've got other *guests* in the house," said Christoforos, choosing the best chickpeas from a plate in his drawer.

"He's sick, coughing . . . She can't tell him to leave . . . He's fallen ill."

"What's he fallen ill from?"

"Seems the air's upset him," said Julia. "He wasn't used to the climate here."

"Of course he wasn't—this climate requires lungs, not huffing and puffing. And let me tell you something . . . ," her father remembered, "there are those stuck-up swaggerers like his lordship whose eyes wander all over the place. Don't think that . . . because he looks at you that it means anything."

"He doesn't look at me," Julia retorted, quite adamantly.

"And don't you go looking at him," he told her. "Do you know who he reminds me of . . . That old goat way back then in the hospital, do you remember? S'eere."

"Yes, I remember him."

"Well, they're two of a kind . . . Goats are always goats, leopards don't change their spots . . . That's what he's like too."

Only once, on that particular day, was there any direct reference to Jacob by Christoforos and Julia, and this was just by coincidence. The rest of the time, Christoforos neither had the inclination nor the occasion to talk to his daughter about him, though more than once he gave her to understand that he had no special liking for certain *crusty six-footers* like his newly arrived brother-in-law, even if he was gifted as an accordion player . . . He told her this with his eyes, whenever Jacob happened to be anywhere around them, or using some kind of code language like the time after her sisaibeoma . . . And on another occasion— again by coincidence perhaps—when hearing him singing in the yard, he had turned and said moodily to some women who were drooling (Julia happened to be standing behind them): "Ah the poor wretch . . . Even wolves sing better." The wolves still hadn't made their appearance when he said it.

And on another occasion, on one of those evening strolls of hers to the sesame-oil mill, she herself turned the conversation to the wolves while her father was bent over his little tortoises. She leaned over to his ear: "Papa . . . haven't we always had wolves here since long ago?" she asked him.

"Yes, we've always had them, of course we have," he told her, "all the hills have wolves." He raised his eyes and looked at her: "What's my daughter after? What's got into her?" he asked, apparently innocently. Tenderly, a little wearily, because for a long time he had ceased to be surprised by the often peculiar behavior of this daughter and her unexpected questions or allusions, which made everyone else feel uneasy, so that in the end they didn't even respond to them. He had long accepted her as she was (as had everyone else, more or less), and he had got used to the idea that not even he could fathom the reasons for this peculiarity. He knew, of course, that that builder, Kimon, who had committed suicide had played a decisive role in this, just as he also had the feeling that Julia had been like this from the cradle, and that she would remain unwed for the rest of her life. Yet this idea had ceased to upset him. "When all's said and done," he thought to himself, "at least I'll have one daughter in my old age who doesn't create more obligations for me." Because he was always afraid lest that *unruly fellow* take his third wife before taking him.

"Because . . . ," she told him, "when you were young . . . what was that story you used to tell us about anthills? . . . About a wolf that bit your donkey."

"It was a she-wolf. Do you want me to tell it to you again?"

She nodded affirmatively, and some of the children rushed to sit next to her so they too could hear the story.

"It was evening, then, in a field, starlight, midsummer . . . I had tied the animal to an almond tree so I could sleep. And from deep sleep, I suddenly opened my eyes and saw the animal madly going in circles round the tree, with its ears erect like horns, and another animal sitting on its haunches and watching. What, I said to myself, where did that second donkey come from? That's what I took it for, half-asleep as I was. But then I thought to myself, only dogs sit like that on their haunches, and wolfhounds. And at the word *wolfhound*, I realized that it was a wolf. I broke out in a cold sweat. In my fright I picked up a rock and threw it at it. The donkey was wild with panic, began braying, the wolf got angry too, and suddenly leapt . . . Perhaps if I hadn't thrown the rock, it wouldn't have bitten it—it didn't look hungry . . . it sank its teeth into the donkey's rump and ran off. And out of nowhere, a little wolf cub jumped after it, plonkety-plonk, like a tarantella . . . It was a she-wolf with her cub. There was no more sleeping or dreaming for me. It was a she-wolf this big," and he put his hand to his forehead, stretching out his other hand to the brazier that was beside him.

"And what about the donkey that got bitten?" asked one of Julia's nephews, before she herself even had time.

"The donkey that got bitten . . . I had a flash of inspiration and found some soil from an anthill and put it on the wound and the animal survived. It wasn't a very deep bite, it hadn't had time to sink its teeth in very deeply, yet if it wasn't for the anthill, the wound would have become infected . . . We all knew about the soil from anthills long ago, it wasn't Persa who told us. We used to know a lot more too."

"And another time . . . again with wolves . . . when you tied the animals round your body . . . ," said Julia, jogging her father's memory once more.

"Ah, that's another tale!" Christoforos exclaimed. "That's one that our father used to tell us. They used to tie the animals with rope round their waist when they were sleeping out in the open, supposedly so the wolves wouldn't eat them—there were swarms of them that year—supposedly so they'd wake up if the wolves came near, and in the morning they found only the ropes and . . . the odd leg, the odd ear belonging to their animals . . . Amazing times! And just imagine how tired the people were then, to go on sleeping while the wolves were beside them eating their animals! . . ."

"So no one likes them, then?" Julia half-asked.

"What can I say . . . If no one likes them, at least they like each other," Christoforos replied.

"And now these black ones . . . are they all black, like they say?"

"All black, like what you're wearing, no, there aren't any—all that's just hearsay," he told her. "There are tawny ones, fair-haired that is, and gray ones . . . and, of course, there are the darker ones. They're the best known—*kurt balkan* they're called in Turkey and *balkansi bilk* in Bulgaria . . . I don't know about in other languages, ask Persa if she knows. *Persa-Persa* . . . she might know in Persian."

Julia stayed a little while longer with him, silent, as though she had run out of words and questions; then she picked up one of the little tortoises from his table . . . put it down . . . picked it up again, put it in her pocket, and went deeper inside the mill.

"Where are you going, Julia?" he asked her from behind.

"Out the other side . . . I'll be back," she said.

"Yes, come back," he said simply, as a matter of course.

She went deeper inside, to the center of the mill, to where a cinnamon-colored horse was walking in circles, wearing blinkers so it wouldn't get dizzy, and helping in the grinding of the sesame seeds. She touched its wet, hot haunches, which were almost steaming, glanced at her brothers with a sense of guilt and consummate love, and proceeded to the other side. A wisp of powder enveloped her and followed her, together with the noise, or rather the monotonous creaking, of the spoked wheel going round with the horse. She suddenly reached out her hand and took a handful of roasted sesame seeds from the pan and scattered them over her red hair . . . like a bride whom they scatter with confetti. No one saw her do it, but she turned pale by herself.

"Julia! . . . Where are you off to?" shouted Hesychios; he had a powder-stained black kerchief wrapped round his head, a mark that he was in mourning for his daughter, and he was standing motionless holding a pail, making the others wait, making them stand motionless too.

"*To the wolves*," she told him.

"To the wolves?"

No one took her seriously, of course, that's how little ten-year-old girls spoke.

"Come on! . . . Let her go to the wolves!" another one shouted.

For them, Julia was *a wind that causes no harm* . . . and a wind that causes no harm, they say, should be left to blow.

Hesychios handed the pail to the next one, *left her*, and the work continued intensely; their faces gleamed like quartz.

Not long afterwards, on that evening when they all, women and children too, left their homes to go as temporary refugees to Goulgi, Julia slipped out of a door, perhaps out of one of the carts, without anyone noticing her amidst all the hubbub, and went elsewhere.

We don't know what else we can say, how else we might contribute, in what more *digestible* a way we might end such a tale: this girl, for all of them the most chaste and the most unattainable, wished to go elsewhere, to go with the voices and the shadows that were calling her . . . And it's not in our hands to hold her back.

Tenth Tale

"THE BIRD AND THE CRUMB"

The mist fell and never stopped falling over Goulgi. And when for a brief interlude it dissolved, a milky light emerged from between the dark clouds, a cold wintry light that allowed you to see just a field or so ahead—and ahead often meant to the next bank of mist that was reforming and closing in again.

Febronia lost her gruffness in that place, not simply her peace and quiet: fourteen days had passed and Hesychios hadn't returned, nor had they received word of him. A full half-month since he had gone off on his horse to find his sister Julia, and for the time being everything seemed to suggest that he had preferred to get lost himself rather than not find her.

Her spirits had grown heavy, like her body, and she spent many hours each day inside a kitchen with a black dirt floor and four or five planks thrown here and there for people to walk on but also for keeping the damp somewhat at bay. No longer afraid and most likely *unenviable* now without Hesychios's presence beside her, she sat on a stool next to the fireplace, on a white fleece that by chance she had brought from her own home and had placed over the stool, and as she imbibed the smoke from her wretched cigarettes, so also the smoke imbibed her. No one said anything to her. Occasionally, to perhaps lessen whatever bad impressions had been created at her expense, she would ask her stepdaughter Efthalitsa to give her the baby to hold—a ten-month-old little boy who gazed at her with goggling eyes—or she would ask her for needles and yarn to knit him some slip socks. These slip socks (short baby socks) were rather like the bridge of Arta: she would knit them during the day, almost finish them, but something would happen at night, and the next morning she would begin again. Nor did Efthalitsa say anything to her, she avoided any discussion with her—something that was much less *devastating* than either of them provoking a disagreement with the other, but perhaps equally sad: almost the same, in fact.

And she kept looking at the wooden door that was two steps above the kitchen floor, a door with a large *eye* in the bottom left-hand corner, through which a black cat by the name of Nina came and went at ease, as did a small yellow dog by the name of Nino, both of whom spent most of their time roaming around the kitchen, sometimes under the table, sometimes behind the curtains, and sometimes under her feet. She would stare at them: the one would pass by the other going in different directions—Nina's tail would wrap itself like morning glory round Nino's snout and Nino's round Nina's, until they tired of it or someone gave them a kick—or they would lie together on one of the planks and were so loving and playful with each other, disproving the tradition that always wanted them at each other's throats, that Febronia fully expected them before very long to bring her a puppy-cat to keep her company amidst all that tedium.

For the rest, the door rarely opened, unless it was someone coming or going who was too big to pass through that hole like the pets. They didn't open it even after the meals, when the floor would be covered with crumbs, peel, and fish bones, and Efthalitsa or one of the other women would take a broom and, swish-swish, hastily sweep everything in the direction of the fire. It wasn't that this caused a cloud of dust that got up Febronia's nostrils; rather, she was bothered by the very idea of this kitchen, which had no ventilation: the two small windows had been boarded up and their deep sills transformed into cupboards or iconostases, and as for the hole at the bottom of the door, they kept it closed with the same piece of wood that had been removed to create the opening, and only when either Nino or Nina wanted to go out would someone take the piece of wood away (it had a kind of handle) and then immediately replace it; and when the pets wanted to come back in again, they had to bang or scratch the door for quite a while from outside . . . The orifice would open for a moment and then close again.

She reflected that Hesychios would return, not see her, think that she too had got lost like his sister Julia, and leave again—such were her irrational thoughts. Nevertheless, she didn't decide to go and find some other *corner* where she might spend her free and tedious time. Perhaps because nowhere else in the house had she found a fire burning, whereas in the kitchen it was always lit, even when there was no one in it. Or perhaps because deep down she wished to avoid any encounter with her father-in-law, whom she heard went down to the lake every day with his head lowered and without talking to anyone—only coming out with a word or two to his grandchildren, when they pushed themselves into his lap and pulled his beard. He had left the little tortoises in the sesame-oil mill; he would now watch the live turtles when they came out onto the mud, and the lake dwellers, who had half-heard about his daughter's disappearance, doffed their caps to him or raised their canes when they passed by, without venturing anything more.

Febronia met with Persa, however, quite often—if for nothing else than to ask her for tobacco and to confide in her, relating some of that horde of dreams that came to her, not only in her sleep at night but also during that often momentary yet constant napping of hers while she was sitting on the stool.

"I've never had so many dreams," she told her. "The slower life unfolds in this marshland, especially now that my husband is away, the quicker and fancier these *caravans* pass before my eyes whenever I close them . . . Like loaded camels. Like someone was unloading them on me out of a cart . . . I don't know how to explain it. I forget most of them. But just as many more come in their place."

"You're enriching yourself while you're sleeping, that's all it is," Persa said to her.

"I'm enriching myself in my sleeping and losing myself in my waking, is that what you mean?" Febronia asked.

"Not everything comes to us as we might want it," Persa replied, as though trying to give an explanation for the situation in general.

"The way things come to me, I don't have time to understand what I want or don't want," said Febronia. "What a mysterious thing sleep is! . . . This morning I saw a bird, a beautiful bird colored black and blue, like an eagle it was, but not so big . . . Strange: it was alive, but it had been killed by hunters, they had cooked it. I took tiny pieces of its flesh, the lean parts, slices of it, and put them into my mouth . . . But I was ashamed because the bird was still alive, standing somewhere, with a proud air, and watching me eat . . . I swallowed the mouthfuls as though I were famished—someone was gesturing to me, I couldn't understand. But now I suspect that it might have been Julia, my sister-in-law. Whom we've given up for dead but who's still alive . . . Or the opposite: whom we *suppose* is alive . . . What do you think?"

Persa preferred to ask her what else she had seen rather than reply; she was still keeping to herself those hot-air claims of Jacob, just as Febronia had said nothing about what she had learned from Pacalacou. And quite simply each of them imagined that the other one knew something more (Persa from her brother; Febronia from Julia herself), but not enough to justify the latter's disappearance. As for Jacob's disappearance, this was no longer enveloped in a veil of mystery, since Persa had told them in the meantime that she had shown him the door herself.

"I also saw Rodanthe, my first daughter," Febronia went on, relating her dreams. "Given that we can't look at each other in any other way . . . I hadn't seen her for some time. She said to me, You waited eight years to have another child after me—she meant then, with Argyris, when I'd had her and I was still young—and now you've got old, she said . . . I was puzzled, in my sleep that is, how she remembered that it was eight years—even I'd forgotten . . . She didn't say anything else, at least I don't remember anything else . . . I also saw someone who stole babies and hung them from his fingers like peddlers do with embroidery patterns. Lots, lots of things, I don't remember . . . In another dream, I'd just given birth and honey was running from my ears. And farther off, behind the door, was a dead body. And outside there was shouting, weeping . . . Where are all these dreams coming from? Is it the damp that gives rise to them? Does it breed them? I don't even have time to collect my thoughts, I forget my living children, forget who I am."

"You left all your work and your chores behind you in the other house, that's why you have time for dreams," Persa told her.

"Are they just dreams? At lunchtime they gave me a plate with three boiled potatoes, a little rice, and a fish on top. I said thank you; I pushed the fish aside and began to mash the potatoes into the rice with my fork. But before I'd finished—it's like an illness, a complaint, it comes at any time—my eyes closed and I found myself napping . . . As for the rest, I wouldn't swear to it: I think I woke up again and went on mashing the potatoes with my fork . . . But beside me I felt something bothering me, and turning around I saw a dress and a strange woman bending over my head. I immediately recoiled. What are you doing? I said to her. Counting my gray hairs? What gray hairs, she said to me, you've got a worm on your head. A worm? A worm. They're yours, I said, you're the ones who breed worms here, I've never had a worm on my head. Well, there! she said, putting two of her fingers into my hair and taking out a gray worm. I swallowed my tongue. Can you see it? she said. And she squashed it before my very eyes, wiped her fingers on my shoulder and left. I felt ashamed. It might at least have been a bug, a louse . . . Even a horsefly . . . But a worm! . . . When I'd eaten the rice and potatoes and I handed the plate back—without having touched the fish—I asked them if they'd seen a woman searching in my hair . . . To cut a long story short, they hadn't seen any woman nor did they understand who I might be talking about. So how do you explain all that?"

"You're overly concerned with your gray hairs it seems," Persa said to her.

"Maybe so. But gray worms is another thing! . . . And how do you explain the fact that the others neither saw nor understood anything? We were all in the same kitchen—they were at the table and I was next to the fire."

"You saw that too in your sleep—how do you expect the others to see anything?" asked Persa. Now it was her turn to be puzzled.

"No, I see other things in my sleep, they're different," Febronia protested gently, as though about to be seized again by her *complaint*. And she didn't have the strength to protest or persist any further.

At lunchtime on the next day, she preferred to leave her stool and go to sit properly with the others at the table: there were Efthalitsa's in-laws, their unmarried daughter, the icon painter, and one or two more . . . and she, of course, with several of her children. The rest of them spent all their time from morning to night at the lake, while those in the kitchen were sitting all together on a long narrow bench, on the other side, and were eating, holding their plates on their knees; Sakis, who was next to her, sitting on a second stool, waited for her to feed him in order to fill his stomach. They were having vegetable soup; at least that's what they called that gray-green mush that they ate with forks, as the greens were like seaweed and slipped out of even the most dexterous spoons. She did as she saw the others doing: she wrapped it round her fork in order to put it into her mouth, and if she wanted a little soup, she lifted the clay bowl and drank it from that. She rarely managed to suck up the soup without sucking the greens with it, so that—unused to it as she was—they were left hanging over her chin and she had to suck at them again or wipe herself with her napkin. She also had to feed Sakis, and most of the time the greens slipped onto his clothes while he got a mouthful of air. In the end, she allowed him to eat with his fingers, and the others didn't say anything to her—in fact, the icon painter smiled at the boy now and again to encourage him in his great endeavor. Because in this particular case his fingers were not all that much more effective than the fork.

She was thinking about her husband, even though she pretended that she had thoughts for nothing but the soup . . . "He's forgotten me, forgotten what state I'm in, forgotten *the wife of the forest warden*, and his children, and his daughter Julia, forgotten everything on account of his sister," she thought. She would have liked to have had him in front of her, to see what his eyes would say to her . . . And if she had been fortunate enough to eat somewhere on her own, all on her own, she would have let her tears drop into the plate, she would have drunk her own tears as consolation or to feel even more crushed . . . There's no sadder thing than to be eating and choking with tears at the same time, but perhaps even worse is to have to choke back your tears in order to eat.

So she traveled with her tears inside herself . . . There she dreamed this too: that they found Julia, her sister-in-law, and put her in a bed the way they might someone who was ill, like the prodigal daughter; people went to see her, but she didn't want to see anyone: "Leave me alone," she said, "let me travel with my tears now that you've found me again" (and anyway what had she been doing before?), and she drove everyone away with her slender hand.

Let me travel with my tears. Only she could come up with things like that, and only she could dream of such things. And actually do them at the table.

Deep down, she was very saddened that Julia had been lost like that—no less so than if she had lost a real sister. She suffered whenever she brought her to mind, grief raked her innards . . . Which is why the fact that Hesychios too was missing was an *extra*.

At one moment, they saw her wiping the greens from her chin and getting up from the table. Many things happened at the same time: Nina and Nino howled with pain as, accidentally, she trod on their tails or their legs (they had both curled up under her chair), and Sakis, whom she pushed without wanting to, fell off his stool onto the animals, who howled again, more out of fright this time, and the little boy's clay bowl fell with him and smashed into a dozen pieces.

"What is it, Febron-itsa? Have you had enough?" asked those old arch-eyebrows of Goulgi in a pompous tone.

"I'm going to go and look for him, don't try to stop me," she told them, searching for her black shawl and taking care, for as many minutes as she had left, of little Sakis, who was crying because of his consternation, because of the general consternation that had come over all of them. But also because of something more specific, given that his mother's movements, these awakened movements, her old nimbleness, her quick breath, and also the dog's presence beside him (even if Nino didn't much resemble that other one, the fierce dog that had almost swallowed her up outside on the street), made him fear for the worst. His fear was transmitted to his older brothers and sisters, and all of them gazed at Febronia just as when she had doused them in quicklime . . . Thomas's eyes, his *double* gaze, made her shut her own for a moment, made her hesitate.

"No, don't try to stop me, and don't look at me like that," she said to her children, as though the other people there didn't exist—her voice was both pleading and demanding at the same time. "You're together, you're not alone, and you have your grandfather here with you . . . But as he's still not back, I have to go and look for him. Your father—that's who I have to go and look for. He went looking for his sister, and now I'll go looking for him. So that everything will work out happily, and we can all go back home. All eat roasted quince and sugar."

She covered up her mouth and half her face with her shawl, left Sakis in the arms of the icon painter, opened the door that had been closed for so many days, and the drowsiness brought languor to her eyes.

All of them followed her outside, some running, others moving rather perplexedly. Without knowing why exactly, Efthalitsa started to cry and to pick up the pieces of the broken bowl from the floor. She picked up the larger pieces, threw them into the fire, and went outside behind the others.

"Come back, where are you going?" she groaned, screwing up her eyes, through which—because of the tears and the mist—she could see almost nothing. Though she knew that even if they were to close her stepmother inside a bottle . . .

"Febronia! My dear Febr . . . wait!" shouted Kimon, who ran after her still holding Sakis in his arms. "We'll go together to look for him . . . by boat!"

Febronia halted.

"By boat?" she asked, as though it was something she had never thought of. "Why by boat?" He went off in the other direction, into the hills, that way . . . on horseback."

"Perhaps by now he's reached the other side, beyond Goulgi," said Kimon, finding no other way to make her change her mind. "He's my friend, I know him well. He's reached the other side and he can't get back across the lake."

"So you go in the boat and I'll go looking for him on my own," said Febronia, continuing on her way.

"Wait, oh! A lamp, quickly . . . bring a lamp," shouted the man, turning to the others. And when they brought him what he'd asked for, he lit it and gave it to little Sakis to take to her.

The little boy stumbled after her, holding the lamp, and every couple of steps called out, tossing his head back: "Take it! . . . Take it! . . ." When he caught up with her (she had stopped and was waiting), he lifted the lamp up above his head and went on in that same monotonous voice recalling a twenty-twoer: "Take it! . . . Take it! . . ." His eyes had that strange, almost devout stillness of the cross-eyed when they talk to you and look elsewhere.

She remembered how unfairly she had beaten him one day, how wretched she had felt afterwards, and knowing that what he was actually saying was "Take me, take me," she reached out her hand and with the other took the lamp from him. His delight at her compassion was boundless.

"She's taken the child with her!" cried the women behind her, in alarm.

"So much the better. She won't be able to get very far with the child," said Kimon.

"Come back, Febron-itsa! You'll get lost in the mist!" shouted Kimon's mother.

"So we'll get lost in the mist!" she shouted back, impatiently waving the hand that was holding the child—he was skipping along tra-la-la—as if the two of them were off to gather bluebells in the mist.

"And if he returns in the meantime?"

"If he returns in the meantime, keep him here. If I come back, I'll come back on my own . . . On our own, isn't that so? Let's not all get lost looking for each other . . . My little darling! How could I ever leave you with them . . . with only reed pilaf to eat . . ."

They could no longer hear her, she was talking to herself and to Sakis.

The only sound they heard was that of frogs from the pools of water as they passed by. All around them the mist was a white darkness that engulfed them, hiding anything else from them, yet equally hiding them from anything else. They stopped at one point, because on a rock they found an old, frayed blanket.

"The Good Lord," Febronia said, opening it and shaking it a couple of times. Perhaps she should have said something else because the blanket was damp and rotten; where it was folded the weave had turned moldy and almost tore when it was shaken. She spread it out over some low bushes, equally wet from the heavy hoarfrost, and knelt down before her son.

"You'll remember all this when you grow up," she said to him, dexterously pushing his trouser legs into his socks (fortunately he was wearing knee-length socks, woolen ones and tight-fitting) and fastening his jacket up to the top with two safety-pins. "You'll say, Where on earth did my mother take me one day! . . . ," and at the same time taking out of her bosom a large colored kerchief, she wrapped it, warm as it was, round his neck, unfastening one of the safety-pins and then fastening it again. She also tightened his shoelaces and rubbed his bottom to warm that up too. "Right . . . *all fitted out, and ready to go to God! . . .* Do you remember who used to say that? How could you. Uncle Didsios would say it when he got drunk—you were still a twinkle in your father's eye, and now he's up in the sky. Do you have any gloves? How could you . . . Never mind. Put your one hand in your pocket and give me the other. Like that. Till we find your father. Let's take this old blanket with us till we find something better. God throws them down to whoever . . . I don't know, what we're doing might be fool-hardy, but what would we gain by staying with them?"

She pulled the worthless cover from the bushes and pointed in the direction where she supposed the lake to be.

After they had walked about the same distance again, the mist began to clear, and now they could see around them the flat gray landscape with its silent and bleak appearance, and if it had been a mirror, it would still have had that gray and bleak appearance, since up above the sky was no different. But there were clusters of reeds here and there, and a little farther off there were hills and trees, and even farther the snow-covered mountain ranges of their own lands, which they couldn't see from where they were. They didn't extinguish the lamp—it was their warmth during that journey.

Evening was approaching, and their feet began to grow despondent as though they were wearing shoes made of iron . . .

"Sounds to me like rain, but I don't see any rain," Febronia said at one moment. "It's like I'm walking through a wood where the leaves have been wet first by the rain and afterwards the raindrops reach us . . ."

"It's drizzling . . . ," said Sakis after a while, perhaps to indulge her.

"Drizzling?" she asked, and stretched out her hand like a beggar. "It's not drizzling," she said, "it just seems to you like it is. Just as it seems to me like . . ."

She halted—the boy with her—and gazed at the dark sky above and the heavy unmoving clouds.

"Muted weather," she muttered, "It doesn't want to let loose."

But they saw a fire, or something that looked like fire, through the trees, a long way from them. And so they found an excuse to head in that direction, and with still a long way to go, they discerned a horse. They could also just about make out someone who was moving with amazing speed, and it was someone of very short build.

"That's not your father," Febronia announced categorically to Sakis. "Yet . . . wait a moment . . . it might very well be Gabe."

"Him that can't thpeak?"

"Yes, he's mute, he can't speak—say it clearly: *speak!* . . . Are you afraid of him?" (She said that because whenever Sakis was frightened or afraid of something, he not only lost his color, but also his s's.)

"I'm not afraid of him . . . What'th he doing here?"

"If it's him, he'll tell us himself . . . And the horse, that horse . . . I can't see it all that well, but I think I can see its eyes . . . It seems tired."

"What'th the horse doing here?"

"I don't know . . . same as us perhaps," said Febronia, and without giving it a second thought, she began waving the lamp as high as she could and with as much ease as her advanced pregnancy would allow.

There was no response: the horse remained motionless, and the man with the short build kept disappearing, and each time he reappeared he seemed to be carrying something and had his head bowed. The fire was growing weaker and weaker.

"And what if they're robbers? What if it's those madmen with the rifles?" Febronia thought suddenly, and for the first time since leaving the others round the table, she felt afraid for herself and for her little Sakis in case they were both found the next morning robbed and thrown in a ditch. "Yet what are we doing to rile them? What do we have for them to rob us of?" she kept asking herself. "Three safety-pins and a shawl; and a lamp; and this old blanket; and we're looking for my husband who's lost somewhere."

At that very same moment, Sakis turned his head back and said: "There's another one coming from over there. On a horse."

He didn't lisp at all this time, he said everything clearly.

Febronia didn't turn to look, but she too heard the hoofbeats and the splashing of water as the horse trod in puddles . . . "Oh no," she thought, "they're surrounding us—and I'm to blame for what's to befall this innocent little creature whose ignorance is making him fearless." And tightly grasping his hand, she pulled him in front of her instead of looking back. But the boy, even after he had hidden in her skirts, popped his head out and looked, full of curiosity, in the direction in which she had her back turned.

"What are you looking at like that?" she asked him. "My nerves are about to shatter."

"He's got a lamp, too," said Sakis.

"So what?"

"He's waving it."

"Stop wanting to see everything."

"Why are you afraid?" he asked, looking up at her.

"Sa-a-akis!" came the sound of a voice from behind them, and the little boy jumped in surprise and hid himself between her legs.

"Hmm!" she exclaimed.

"Sakis . . . Febra . . . Where are you off to?" came the sound of the voice again, this time gentler and familiar, tired, relieved, almost paternal.

So it wasn't a robber, it was Kimon, who had come out in search of them with a horse he had borrowed from the refugees and a lamp from the many possessed by the natives of Goulgi. They both turned towards him and watched him approaching . . . His lamp was hanging from the top of a forked rod he was holding like a standard and sometimes he raised it higher, sometimes lowered it or waved it to right and left.

"I've been looking for you," he said with a sigh of relief, when only a small distance still separated him from them.

"Why go to the trouble?" murmured Febronia, without much conviction.

And at the same moment, from the other direction, a sound like the beginning of a storm was heard, a heartrending yell, an *ou-ououou-ououou* . . .which, though also somehow familiar to her, terrified her. Sakis turned pale with fear, while Kimon put his lamp down on the ground, quickly unhooking it from the forked rod, and—not having the ability to jump down from the horse—remained crouched in his saddle. The yell from the other direction—joyful nevertheless—was heard again and again: Gabe—because it was him and none other—had seen the two lamps, had probably recognized one of them, and was turning somersaults beside the fire, or what was left of it, and a man who until then had not been visible stood up next to him and raised his hand in the air.

A tiny flame ran through Febronia's body like a salamander might have run:

the man who had stood up and was waving his hand was none other than Hesychios.

When she came close to him, instead of saying anything, she put her fingers into her mouth and then touched his with them: just as by touch they sometimes kissed the smooth surface of holy icons. That's what she tried to do, but her fingers rested upon two swollen, rough, and cracked lips.

"Lord above, what's happened to you?" she asked him, staring at him in the light of her lamp: if it had been anyone else, even her brother, she wouldn't have recognized him, not even in broad daylight. "What's happened to you? Where's your handsome face? Where were you?"

"Slow down . . . slow down," he said, taking hold of her by the shoulders and trembling a little; then he put his arms around little Sakis and shook hands with Kimon without uttering another word.

Motioning to Gabe, he asked him to build up the fire, which was going out, and he sat down—inviting the others to do the same—on soft black capes. Gabe, stumbling in his excitement and confusion, threw an armful of bare twigs onto the fire, and it was then that the few remaining flames almost went out completely; the twigs were wet because of the dampness, and the only woman among them—no less in a state of excitement herself—took some of the twigs from the pile and put them under her armpits, softening and warming them, as she sometimes did with her children's underwear before they put it on. Then, in her own way, she carefully placed them on the ailing fire and at the same time placed her hands and chin close to the cinders and began to blow and blow . . . Sakis bent down next to her—overjoyed, certain that what he was experiencing would kindle the jealousy of all his brothers and sisters—and he began puffing out his own cheeks: *pfff . . . pfff . . .* The fire, not wanting to displease such a nice boy (and even less his mother), began shooting out fiery tongues in the air, and before long it was blazing heartily instead of grumbling with itself.

Now Febronia could see her husband's face better: it seemed longer and drier, it was pitted, and the only inkling of charm she could still discern was round his eyes and in that area around his lips where a smile trembled occasionally and recalled the old Hesychios. It was perhaps the first time that she felt no rush of envy or despair troubling her heart, and this was not because he looked so haggard in his body, so alienated from himself, from what, that is, made women fall at his feet, but because of the inexpressible grief etched on his face; his expression, which made him seem as if focused on some mortal thought, brought out her maternal instincts, she felt wholly maternal and liberated from him, without feeling any reproach for this, without in any way feeling her love lessened, and without feeling the need to explain this or to begin again to be tormented or to lament her marriage. As though it had always been like this and everything had happened for no other reason.

Apart from this, however, Hesychios had things to say to them that evening which are not easily said, and so Gabe — who followed the story — supplemented with gestures and inarticulate cries whatever he left out or was unable to put into words.

For one last time, the talk was about Julia.

After searching for her all over for eight days, climbing hills, descending ravines, arriving in villages where he knew no one and no one knew him, asking the young and old about a pale red-haired woman in black clothes whom no one had seen, leaving a name behind him as someone *who had lost his wife and was looking for her from place to place,* Hesychios eventually arrived back at the family home, his own house, with his last care being whether armed men — locals or foreigners — were still lying in wait there.

There in one of the windows, he saw Lily and Gabe gesturing hammer and tongs at each other . . . he hid in order to follow, without them seeing him, this voiceless — and yet so charming — conversation: Lily was falling on the bed or against the wall and breaking into tears, lamenting, while Gabe was endeavoring to calm her by showing her that they could do nothing and that it was God's will. *And what are we going to tell the others when they return?* she asked him. *Exactly what we saw, what else?* he replied. *But how? How? How are we to tell them?* she reminded him, and most likely she wasn't referring to the fact that they were mutes, but to the event itself, which to them was unthinkable. *So then we won't tell them anything, we'll pretend we don't know,* said Gabe. *But how? How?* Lily went on wondering. *This doesn't have anything to do with you or me, it doesn't have anything to do with two deaf-mutes, it has to do with that.*

And in the way that she showed *that* as *two-eyes-from-which-tears-are-falling,* Hesychios realized, was now sure, that they were talking about his sister Julia. He rushed onto the porch, in two strides mounted the little staircase on the left, and burst into the room. The two mutes were taken aback when they saw him.

"Where's Julia? What do you know about Julia?" he started to ask them, and while they remained speechless before him (as though they were deliberately not talking, not opening their mouths to say something), he started — for the first time in his life — to lose his temper, to kick out at whatever was around him, to shake them, grabbing hold of their collars or their arms, and, finally, to threaten that he would strangle them if they didn't tell him what they knew. Black shadows passed across his eyes, and at the same time sparks flew from them, as though he had heard the most outrageous of things, as though every last suspicion were buried deep in his heart: "What do you two know? You monsters of the Apocalypse! . . . Where's my sister?"

And they told him everything they knew, at least what they had seen with their own eyes . . . what no one else had seen, not even him.

Sakis was listening to his father with his ears wide open, and seeing him Febronia pulled him to her.

"You're always popping up like a mushroom, go to sleep now," she told him, trembling with anticipation, "close your ears and your eyes and go to sleep, or I'll send you to Gabe!"

Sakis was afraid of Gabe (not because Gabe had ever hit him or chased him, but simply because he was a mute), and knowing that his mother was not joking when she talked in this way, he curled up somewhere between her and his father, covering his ears with his hands. And his hands stayed there, warming his ears a little but without preventing him from hearing. He shut his eyes.

"They had seen Julia in a well . . . next to a wolf," said Hesychios in that toneless and expressionless voice in which we sometimes announce the most dramatic or monstrous things.

"In a well? You mean . . . ," whispered Kimon, snapping the end of a twig between his fingers.

"Lying facedown, and the wolf beside her."

"In Puzla-kuk?" came the sound of Febronia's stuttering voice.

"No, farther off. A dried-up well in the hills."

"And . . . so? Where is she now?"

"Now, she's nowhere," said Hesychios.

The rest was related by Gabe, and now it was Hesychios's turn to supplement the story at times or to confirm it by his silence; or he would simply hang his arms over his bent knees and lower his head down between them to avoid seeing them again . . . Febronia turned to him and took hold of his fingers, squeezed them, cold and stiff as they were, in her own, as though urging him to get up with her and leave that place, but then she turned her eyes back again to Gabe: they had placed the two lamps at the highest point they could in order to better see his gestures, his grimaces, and when necessary his somersaults and his running around a notional well . . . Kimon the icon painter understood absolutely nothing of this language, but he found himself suddenly gripped by the desire to take wood and brush and paint something of the scenes that were being enacted in front of him, and so he tried to retain them, to keep them as alive and vivid as he could in his mind. And Sakis was able to uncover his ears.

And because of our own shortcomings but also out of respect, we will suffice ourselves with giving the bare *bones* of the story, far removed from the indescribably masterful account given by Gabe: a week or so previously, tired of guarding the empty house, Lily had gone to find her brother. First she had passed by the winter pastures, and not seeing a soul there she continued towards the sheepfold. She was carrying a basket with some provisions and a new pair of socks, and she found him with his few remaining goats and sheep and his four dogs. There were also two adopted youths with him, and because Gabe hadn't washed himself for months and his body smelled of dung, she persuaded him to leave the animals with the two young shepherds and come home with her so she might wash him and cut his nails, particularly his toenails, which were almost longer than his toes themselves. Walking with their sticks—it was still afternoon—they noticed a hedgehog beside a dry well. Gabe went up closer, and thinking her brother might kill the unfortunate creature for no other reason than that it had spikes, Lily ran after him to prevent anything happening. There they argued for a while, almost came to grips (Gabe insisted that he didn't want to kill the animal, Lily didn't believe him), and while this was going on, the hedgehog disappeared. Gabe ran around to the other side of the well, and Lily ran after him. And it was then, when Gabe leapt up onto the wall surrounding the well to escape her, that both the hedgehog and the chase were forgotten: first he and then immediately afterwards his sister saw at the bottom of the well, amid bushes and thorns, a woman lying motionless next to a large animal; she was facedown, the animal beside her, and she had her arm around the animal's neck, as though they were sleeping and didn't care in the slightest what they both were or how they had chosen to sleep. The woman had red hair, which was hanging frozen over the leaves of the bushes through which the white tip of her nose was visible: they recognized her as Julia and the animal was a wolf, a gray and tawny wolf. The brother and sister up above began yelling and clapping their hands.

But when presently they returned to the same spot with the other two shepherds and the dogs, as well as ropes and stakes that would be of use to them though they weren't sure how, they found the dry well empty, save for the bushes that had been thrown inside as happened over time: Julia and the wolf were no longer there. Their hearts stopped beating and started again: Julia and the wolf weren't there. It was the same the next day when they returned with Hesychios . . . As also the following day and the day after that when the three of them went and kept a lookout, as though their only hope was for the dead girl, the living-dead girl, to come back and fall again into the well with the wolf.

What the two deaf-mutes had seen was seen only by them and on that one afternoon. And no one else saw it.

∎

"And what makes you believe those two deaf-mutes?" Hesychios's wife asked him as they made their way back to Goulgi that same night, five people, two horses, and two lamps.

"What am I to believe? That Julia went with the wolves, as she told me herself one day and I didn't believe her, and that she'd come back to us?" asked Hesychios. "Now there's not one left in our hills . . . They came, took her, and left. What am I to believe?"

She didn't know what to say to him, and she certainly didn't want to tell him what she happened to know herself — very little from one point of view, yet enough to put the lid on all the business with the well. Deep down she too believed — though without being able to understand — what the two deaf-mutes had seen: however absurd or incomprehensible their *account* sounded, her own doubts seemed equally pointless and groundless.

It's not out of the question, she reflected, that someone had thrown a dead wolf into the well and that Julia had gone there one day and seen it . . . The well was a deep one — all wells are deep and they become even deeper when there's no water in them. And if, falling in, she didn't die on the spot, everything would have been over in a few hours or days.

And yet where did Julia and the wolf disappear to afterwards? Where did they go? How did they get out of the well that had become their grave? This was something she couldn't — neither she nor anyone else — give an answer to. And it wasn't the only thing.

"How am I going to tell my father? How am I going to find the words to tell him?" Hesychios asked.

"Do you think in his own way he's not expecting it?" she said to him. "Those little tortoises he's been making all this time —"

"How am I going to tell my father, who's expecting her?" he asked again, grief-stricken.

She reached out her hand and caressed his bowed head, still wrapped in the black kerchief, as he walked beside her, at the side of the horse, on which he had put her and Sakis.

"I'll be with you," she said. "And besides, when things go as far as they have, do you think words are necessary?"

Not long afterwards, around mid-February, they all went back with their ox-carts and carriages to their own village. The troubles had abated, temporarily at least, and they could return to their houses, return to their work, even if their hearts were filled with so much sorrow.

Returning, they took Gabe with them, but not Pacalacou: Christoforos's family had been due to leave two days earlier, but they stayed because Febronia couldn't find her godson anywhere. His absence wasn't especially important to anyone — particularly after what they had learned about Julia — but Febronia pleaded with them to delay their departure a little until they found him. He was found by two fishermen while they were guiding their boat through the shallows and it caught on something: they pulled him out from the weeds and rushes, his body in a state of dissolution, his eyes already eaten, his cheeks sponges — and an army of tiny aquatic creatures slid from his mouth like a necklace when they stretched him out on the reeds. Goulgi, though it was unknown when, had made him its own. When they told his godmother and she went to see him (not to look at him; she wasn't made of steel), she asked them to gently push him back in, and she sang her laments.

And on the way back, given the way that things had turned out, she nostalgically brought to mind, with the indolence of a pregnant woman, that sweet night in October when she had encountered her godchild with his trousers down in Haliva, on their way to the hares, their way to the wolves, with little Julia in the cart unable to move. At least they still had her then, and they had the grown-up Julia too, and they had Pacalacou to make them laugh or get angry: "In the o-o-open air, me! . . . Only in the o-o-o-pen air! . . ." And now the fish were eating him. And the earth with its deep secrets the two girls.

She bent and kissed the hem of her dress — what made her think of doing that? And with this came an appetite for quince paste on a slice of bread, and then for something else. She looked for Persa, but Persa was in another carriage, and so she put her hand into Hesychios's pocket and pulled out his tobacco pouch. He had already seen her smoking and hadn't said anything to her: he simply stared at her and remained quiet; and he did the same that day. She rolled three cigarettes: the first she gave to him, the second to one of his brothers, who was holding the reins, and, as for the third, her eyes closed again before she had even finished it. This time she saw her in-laws — a heterogeneous couple: Hesychios's mother and Argyris's father, sitting on a rafter like a couple of betrothed kids and wearing red shoes: "Well then! When is it Easter so we can have you with us for a few days, listen to some conversation, laugh, enjoy ourselves," they said, impatiently swinging their legs. Because of all the swinging, one of them lost a shoe, and Febronia immediately woke up. For years, whenever she saw shoes in her dreams, she expected them to come down on her head — she was very superstitious when it came to shoes. And above all *cautious* for a couple of days, till she forgot the dream and her fear died down, or till she satisfied herself with some minor misfortunes, of the kind that happen without dreaming about shoes.

They arrived home at nightfall, and Lily—who had been notified by others, by families who had arrived earlier—was waiting for them at the front gate and kissed them all one by one, big and small, keeping the loudest kiss for Persa (she never forgot how Persa had saved her, though she wasn't always grateful to her for that) and two warm and despondent kisses for Christoforos, who appeared to be more mute than she was.

My poor dear, gone, gone, those tearful eyes have gone—she said to him, using her hands and putting the house keys back with his—*and gone like that, it's not for us to weep.* And meanwhile she was weeping, revitalizing herself in her tears.

He nodded as though agreeing with whatever anyone said to him.

After kissing Lily too, Febronia left the unloading to the others and went upstairs to look at the rooms and the storeroom. She found them in a mess; they looked unfamiliar to her and desecrated: the cupboards were open, the curtains on the floor, the storage jars—which with such care she had sealed and hidden—were either smashed or missing, her chests were missing their lids, their contents turned upside down, the dowry she had been saving for her daughters (at least for as many as survived) was all torn, and the walls were here and there covered in black fingermarks, in filth. It hit her hard—on top of everything else—and she went back down the stairs to ask Lily who had done all this, why and when, but as she was on her way down, another thought flashed through her mind and she went back up. She gazed at everything again. And as she looked at that wreckage, as she discovered more dirty work (in the wedding garlands from her marriage to Hesychios—which she had also had in a chest, but which were now lying in a corner—there was a disgusting dried pile that, if not vomit, was something worse), she realized that all this was not the work of men—they might turn bloodthirsty when they get mad and become predators if the occasion arises, but such *imagination* when it came to causing damage was something only women had . . . And it hit her even harder: she felt certain that it was the work of her old friends, the friends who had subsequently turned into vipers and spit their venom wherever they could.

"But what have I done to them? What?" she groaned, hitting her forehead. "Did I steal their husbands? Was it their sons I led astray for them to hate me so?"

She imagined them entering the house, rushing into her rooms when Lily had gone with Gabe and Hesychios to keep a lookout at the well, she imagined them biding their time till Lily was out of the house . . .

She opened one of the windows—she didn't have the courage to go back down the stairs—and stuck her head out to call Hesychios from the yard, but a piercing pain ran through her that made her drop to her knees and almost

scream: it was her month to give birth, but not her day. And yet in the space of
a moment she was gripped by those deep pains, and she realized that what was
still waiting to happen would happen on that same night of the return home—
the signals had started some time before.

She groaned and struggled on the floor with her body, called for help, but not
loud enough for the others to hear her from down below—they were also shouting and making noise, but for other reasons. "I'm going to die," she thought,
"and no one will get wind of it, they'll find me" . . . *The solution was in her heart.*
She looked around her: among all the things strewn on the floor and trampled
on was a red sleeve that was hanging as far as the armpit from one of the chests.
She hadn't seen that garment for years or worn it for even more. She made an
effort and dragged herself over to it, pulled at the sleeve and the bust came out,
pulled at the bust and the whole dress came out—a pulsating crimson memory
. . . She crawled back to the window with this in her arms and let it fall down into
the yard: she counted one-two-three (remembering the shoe from the rafter)
and heard the terrified shriek of her youngest boy, then some laughter, cries of
surprise from ten different mouths, including Hesychios's: "What's that? . . .
Febra! . . . Who threw it down? . . . Where's your mother? Where's Febra?" and
then his running upstairs, which sounded as though it were an earthquake.

That's how he found her, and behind him came the others.

Half an hour later, someone collected together her children and shut them
in a cold room, hanging a lamp on a hook in the wall.

"Pray," he told them, "and ask God to save your mother."

From another part of the house, from somewhere high up, her screams every
so often reached down to them as they cut her open to take the child, because
the rudimentary anesthetics were not sufficient . . . She had given birth to so
many children, but this one wouldn't come like all the others, nor did it want to
wait a few days more. Lily stared unhappily at her two cauterized nails and her
instruments that sat there discarded—everything had been undertaken by two
doctors in black neckties, who, by sheer coincidence, happened to be in those
parts that night asking about a renowned inn . . . If they hadn't been there, perhaps the same work could have been undertaken by two bold twelve-year-olds.
Febronia was gushing blood.

"Dear God, I'm here, can't you see me?" she cried, fixing her eyes on the ceiling (with her eyes *twice the size* from the pain), imploring God—and all those
around her—to show pity on her at last.

"Save our mama, God! Save our mama, God!" echoed the voices of the children below in a frenzied whirl, and the prayers and the devotions followed incessantly, even when the cries from upstairs stopped. More of the night went

by with half the children still on their knees in vain, while the other half had become drowsy and were asleep.

Here, then, was one woman in that household, in these tales, who died in her bed like *a common mortal*, cut up and dripping blood. Together with her last labor—a daughter.

Hesychios demanded that they iron her old red dress, scent it, and dress her in it—not one of his sisters or his aunts could refuse him or tell him that things like this were not customary or even permitted as a garment in such circumstances. They all obeyed and dressed her in that—particularly since he was the first to lend a hand.

And because Febronia's eyes had remained open and they hadn't been quick enough (hadn't managed) to close them, and because legend has it that Death can't complete his work as long as the pupils of the eyes are still *emitting* images and reflecting the trembling and frightened *weaklings* all around, Persa covered those testifying and tormented eyes with wax, with plentiful drops of melted wax.

Neither fowl nor beast nor human ever had a look like that.

"What's wrong with her eyes? Why are they like that?" asked the children, especially the younger ones, as their father had brought them himself to see her, and to stay with her *as long as they wanted*.

"She wants to look at you some more, she's not had her fill of you," said Persa, mentally exorcising her own words, afraid lest Febronia—beneath her new eyelids—was searching for a companion from among her own children.

In the coffin, they put three eggs—a burial custom, who knows from how long ago, for women who died before succeeding in giving birth.

A few days later, Efthalitsa, her stepdaughter in Lake, gave birth to a daughter, and, as was only to be expected, they named her Febronia.

And Nitsa, Petros's wife, childless for such a long time following their marriage, also brought a baby girl into the world a few months afterwards, and they called her Julia.

And that's how things were; sometimes the flesh and sometimes the bare bones, sometimes the living souls and sometimes their shadows. Besides it was just a question of time—everything was just a question of time.

At ten years old, Sakis—who, we should note, was left-handed—was a match for two or three men when it came to the harvest. The wheat—the tips of which, their thick tufts, he could only see by craning his neck—fell into his arms from the right side, like swooning women, and one of the grown-ups had to follow behind him to take it from him and make it into sheaves.

"Stand well back," the boy would say to him, "I don't want to take your legs as well—and then who will make it into sheaves!"

One day, after finishing on his own a large section of the field (three of his brothers were still struggling to finish, all of them together, a smaller section) and having put on his jacket, he felt a strange weight, a bulge in one of the pockets, and so he put his hand inside: he touched something soft, fingered it, and for a moment was afraid that someone had stuffed a dead kitten inside. But the very next moment, a pleasant smell having reached his nostrils, he pulled out a silky pouch containing freshly cut juicy tobacco . . . This, for Sakis, was tantamount to a dream, to the smoke that came from his imagination . . . "Bah," he thought, "have I put someone else's jacket on by mistake?" He stared at himself in surprise, but the jacket he was wearing was his. Nor was it possible for his jacket to have pockets belonging to others. He sat down on a packsaddle that was lying on the ground nearby to try to solve the mystery: he stared at the lovely smooth tobacco pouch, about half-full, stared at his clothes, his small yet miraculous hands (in the meantime the smell was making him feel dizzy, it was like incense), stared at the other side of the field where his elder brothers were, at those sunburned necks that kept dipping into the wheat, till the idea suddenly came to him to look behind his back. There, between the bushes and dry twigs, he saw his father smiling and gesturing to him with his hands that what he had found in his pocket was his; he had earned it with his sickle.

"You mean I can . . . ?" Sakis asked, still unable to believe it.

"Yes, you can! It's your gift for all the work you get through," Hesychios told him, stepping away from the bushes.

And so this skilled boy harvester would before long become—with his father's blessing—a skilled smoker too. When his brothers returned, they found him on the saddle well and truly *incensing* himself, causing them to raise their eyebrows somewhat.

At twelve years old, while passionately harvesting in another field, he cut off the little finger of his right hand—not of his left, as we mistakenly wrote in another tale on the theme of some strange fingers . . . A few months previously, they had spared him his first slaughtering due to the fact that he was so dexterous with the sickle that he could, in a manner of speaking, buy off his other *cutting* duty (besides it was true that in recent years the custom had begun to wane and to be confined only to the firstborn sons), yet nevertheless, as it turned out, Sakis had to sacrifice one of his fingers in any case.

And it was this boy who, when he grew older, followed in the footsteps of his grandfather and father and acquired children from two different women, the second of whom would bring her own children from her first marriage . . . Meaning that he is the one responsible for the third successive generation—which we mentioned at the beginning—with *all manner* of brothers and sisters.

Incessant circles; yet this book will close its own circle with the characters who have supported it and accompanied it until now, with those phantom-characters, and not with the later ones.

We learned, then, that Lily died quietly one morning while drinking her coffee, after having delivered three women the night before—she had run from one house to the next. *Death on her feet* was how they called hers—something, that is, that everyone would wish for themselves—though life could have given her a bit more time, since, at sixty-five years of age, she was still in the best of health. And since, not long after Febronia's death, Lily had lain in wait behind a fountain one evening and seeing two women walking arm in arm and returning home after paying a visit to another house, had stuck out a large black umbrella, using its handle to upend the unsuspecting women. As they fell on top of each other, Lily revealed herself and began to beat them mercilessly, punching and kicking them . . . They were two of those venomous friends who had soiled Febronia's rooms when she was away in Goulgi and she, Lily (who was responsible for the house), had left it for just a few hours . . . Unfortunately, when she had returned (and during the following few days), she didn't think—in the middle of her grief—to look to see whether anything had happened to the house in her absence, and unfortunately Febronia had found her rooms just as she had found them . . .

These friends had had the gall to come to the funeral, but Lily held back—stayed her hand at any rate—till she was sure of what she suspected. And once she had confirmed her suspicions by every means possible, she simply waited for the suitable day and time . . . in order to send them home black and blue and then to go on her own and give herself up at a sort of gendarmerie that they had in the old marketplace.

They kept her for two days and nights in there and then let her go free, given that no one came forward to make a complaint; neither of those bruised and beaten women dared.

Lily was pleased that she had got her own back for Febronia—and neither Christoforos nor anyone else in the house scolded her for that.

She continued to run about with her stick and her bag of instruments, with her profuse silence and that incomparable agility wherever the need called—and about two and a half years later she bid farewell to all and everything.

Meanwhile, two peacocks had arrived in their house. Yes, two peacocks. One morning, some people had seen them roaming perplexedly in the garden behind the house, and at first had taken them for turkeys (they had never seen peacocks except in paintings), for fancy-feathered turkeys—which, in any case, were also known as *indians*.

What are those birds doing here? they wondered, and went down to get a better look at them. The birds, one of them that is, began squawking in a loud, wild voice, and at the same time opening out its paradisaical feathers, and they were amazed that such a beautiful and majestic bird, literally magnificent, could have such an unpleasant and cold squawk . . . The other one was more modest, less colorful, but as soon as it opened its mouth, it sounded just the same.

They had no idea from where they had come, and of course it was difficult for them to drive them away—and, anyway, where were they to send birds like these that couldn't fly? In addition, they confirmed that they were peacocks and not just any birds. And they discovered, among other things, that their squawking was so disturbing and sad because, it's said, in all their narcissism, they see their ugly feet below.

The peacocks arrived at the beginning of spring—just over two years after Febronia's death. A couple of months later, two bougainvilleas arrived too—they found these too, that is, one morning between the ivy and the rosebushes covering one of the walls, again at the back of the house. They were enormous, blooming, luxuriant—the one mauve, the other purple, each in its own clay pot, and each pot with embossed scenes—and the place there resembled a real paradise, filled with these stunning bougainvilleas and with the peacocks' stunning feathers resting against their flowers.

They kept the bougainvilleas too.

Towards the end of the summer, in the usual way, two large wicker beehives arrived . . . Fine, they said, and they also kept the bees that were humming inside.

But when at the end of the fall they found a beautiful mare tied to their plum tree with her foal, they started to get worried about these offerings. They were extremely original, extremely generous—but what did they conceal? Who had thought them up and carried out a plan of this sort—and why?

They thought of keeping watch at night and of keeping an eye on what was going on at the back of the house, though these weird things didn't take place every night. Not to mention the fact that it seemed silly to them to guard their house in order to prevent some unknown presence from bringing them new gifts . . .

Whatever the case, on Christmas Eve they found a basket with seasonal fruit, namely oranges, and next to it a demijohn of superb red wine. They were afraid to try it in case there was anything wrong with it, but in the end anyone who tasted it didn't want to drink anything else for the rest of his life. As for the oranges, they were so tasty that they even ate the peel.

This riddle lasted twelve months. The following spring, one of Hesychios's daughters, the only one of Febronia's left, Safi-Lisafi, found a bird so beautiful—sitting on a pumpkin leaf lying on the ground—that it took her breath away when she saw it, and naturally she was afraid that the bird would fly away as soon as it saw her. But no; it remained fixed where it was, and just made anxious circles with its eyes, while its body performed tiny movements on the spot, still sitting on the leaf. It resembled a little hen or duck when brooding, or perhaps a wild dove. The shiny red plumage, however, covering its breast, the rather long and pointed beak, its wings that formed a grid of yellow, brown, and black dots, two black marks on the sides of its pink neck, and, finally, two crimson rings around its large, round eyes, without doubt allow us to suppose that it was a rare turtledove.

Safi-Lisafi approached it, the turtledove stirred, somewhat frightened, and this movement revealed to the girl that the bird had its legs tied.

"Ah!" she exclaimed sorrowfully, and kneeling down began to caress its back, to say gentle words to it, to promise that she would free it, but first she wanted to understand. She searched with her eyes all around, looking for its mate—those gifts usually came in pairs—but another bird like that one was nowhere to be seen. And with hesitant but not at all clumsy movements, she pulled it closer to her . . . only to see, much to her surprise, that hanging from the red silk cord tying its legs together were two precious rings, one at each end.

Amazed, she reflected that things like that didn't happen even in fairy tales, and picking up the beautiful turtledove together with the rings she covered it with a rag she found hung over a wire and went first of all (managing not to let anyone see her) and showed them to her brother Thomas. He noticed that the dark-colored stones in the rings had the same shape and hue as the bird's eyes and that engraved on each stone was a letter: one was H, the other Z.

And though the twins sensed that the H had something to do with their father (and this thought caused them deep concern), they gathered up their treasure and secretly took it to their grandfather Christoforos.

"Bah!" he exclaimed, seeing as well as he had in his youth—and with the help now provided by a pair of eyeglasses. "Where's that Z sprung from?"

In other words, neither did he appear to doubt that the other letter was referring to his son Hesychios.

A few days later, the mystery was solved: an aristocratic lady, extremely wealthy, a young widow and lonely, who in recent years had been living only with her horses, her birds, and her servants in a mansion behind the hills of Dekatessara, Zina Nazareti by name and born in Egypt, had found this way, for a whole year, of proposing marriage to the widower Hesychios . . .

On account of his good looks. The kind of looks that have the same attribute as good wine, which becomes even more palatable and refined as it gets older, and also as that mythical phoenix, which, it's said, rises from its own ashes (because all the ills of recent years had ravaged Hesychios's face and rewrought it). It was impossible, then, for talk of such looks not to reach the ears of this Zina or leave her indifferent. Besides, she had seen him with her own eyes: she had come to some of the Carnival festivities, hidden behind a mask with a peacock feather, and she had seen him as a bell-wearing goat, but without his mask and calpac, dancing in the streets . . . His good looks brought a sweet pain to her body, and the image of his face had remained in her eyes throughout the seven years that had passed since then.

Nor had his wife's death left her indifferent—and no irony is intended here: she felt boundless sympathy for that woman, was saddened by her end, which made her think, think of many things. But it also filled her with the temptation to try and obtain Hesychios for herself.

She herself was no goddess of beauty, and besides, she had reached the age that makes women hold in check their great zest for life—but doesn't stop them enjoying it. After all, Zina Nazareti, from the moment that she revealed both her face and her purpose to Hesychios and his immediate family, made no attempt to conceal all the rest: she wanted this man as a companion for her loneliness and, why not, as her heir—both him and his descendants—given that she herself had no immediate family; she wasn't asking him to fall in love with her, nor, of course, to give her children.

After thinking it over for a few nights (the idea of spending a part of his life in a mansion, surrounded by horses and peacocks, by azaleas, hortensias, and bougainvilleas, but also by his children if he so wanted, as a companion to a cultivated and reclusive woman was by no means something to be looked down upon), he nevertheless sent her his polite refusal along with the two rings.

She accepted his refusal with dignity—and not a little understanding—though she sent one of the rings back to him, asking him to keep it to remember her by. It was the one with her letter, the Z, and Hesychios—who was unable to pretend to be tough without being so—kept it, though he didn't wear it. Or he wore it secretly, at certain times, and looked at his hand in the way that we look at things that don't wholly concern us, but that we like looking at . . .

And besides, a bond of friendship developed between him and Zina, a bond of companionship, and it's said that he went to visit her now and again (probably without announcing it to his family or asking their approval), which for her was a godsend.

Of course, her birds and her flowers remained at their house—the former even produced descendants and the latter cast their seeds in other pots too. The two beehives were added to their own hives, the mare had more foals with their horses, and every Christmas, someone would be entrusted by Zina to bring them a demijohn of that exceptional wine. In other words, her friendly intentions—in the end as at the beginning—embraced all of Hesychios's family.

The lovely turtledove, however, flew back to its wood.

And in any case, it wasn't only Zina who had thoughts about Hesychios. Young girls, who still hadn't been born when he was in his heyday, would have sold their souls to the devil, as the saying goes, in order to take Febronia's place in his life, in his bed, even if some god were to warn them ten times a day that this place was not without its pain. They would have risked it anyway; all they wanted was to have a child by him or simply feel his breath on their necks . . .

And it wasn't only these young girls either. One day, as he was clearing away the weeds and dry grass from around the edges of one of his fields, a woman passed who had quite recently been widowed and she greeted him. He returned the greeting, but before long the woman passed by again—in the opposite direction this time—and waving her hand said to him: "Gone . . . gone . . ."

At the same time she walked on with the small sliding steps of a sixteenth-century geisha.

Hesychios didn't understand, but he didn't attach any particular importance to what she said.

"Gone . . . gone . . . ," she shouted again, halting and making circles like a windmill with her arms.

"What are you saying over there?" he asked her, lifting up a big tuft of dry grass with his pitchfork and throwing it onto the pile behind him, which he would presently set fire to.

"Gone . . . my husband's gone too, same place as your wife went," said the woman.

"What do you mean?" he asked again, though he was starting to understand where she was going with all that "gone . . . gone . . ."

"Just that . . . where your wife went"—and she pointed with her finger to the black band round his brow—"My man's gone too . . . They've left us. And they're not coming back. And your children need a mother. Just like mine need a father . . ."

Someone, it seems, had informed this woman—rather irresponsibly—or perhaps she had deduced it for herself, that Febronia had once won Hesychios with only her boldness as a weapon and a certain *disregard* concerning their dead ones . . .

He stuck the pitchfork in the ground, rested his elbow on the handle, and stared at her for a while, just stared, narrowing his eyes. Then he got on with his work.

She saw him, saw enough, and turned to leave. But then she halted once again.

"Don't you at least appreciate what I just said to you . . ." she shouted sorrowfully. "Eh? . . . Speak, say something."

"It's not that," he said, "but you picked the wrong time . . ."

"And when is the right time?" she asked him.

She received no answer, so she asked again: "Should I have waited another three years? Till we've had our fill of mourning?"

"No, not that either," said Hesychios, as though talking more to the dry grass than to her.

"Then what?"

"Those things happen in their own good time," replied Hesychios, after remaining silent for several moments. "What else can I say . . . We're not suited to each other."

"But with Febronia you were?"

"Yes, I was."

"Well I wasn't with Panayotis . . . But I respect his memory," said the woman, suddenly deciding not to lose all her self-respect; and she left and went to her own field, with the usual steps of a peasant woman of her times.

Yet a few months later, she sent him an official proposal by two of her cousins. Hesychios again refused it. Just as he had refused so many other such proposals, just as he would refuse so many more in the future . . .

Nevertheless, five and a half years after Febronia's death, he would get married again to another widow, Penelope, who also had several children and was a few years older than him.

How strange; this man, who could have asked for the hand of any princess from North or South, from the distant East or the nearer West, or have had all the young blooms in the area falling at his feet, all the virgins, foolish ones or shrewd ones, showed an unexpected preference for women who were older and had suffered . . . At least if he were going to wed them.

Of course, Penelope may not have been fourteen years older than him, but she must have been at least four. She also happened to be a distant relative of Febronia's. And one of her eyes *bulged* as they say, wasn't in its place, so she couldn't see very well with it. As for her past, she had gone through so much poverty and hardship that for Hesychios to ask for her in marriage seemed more than incredible to her—her bulging eye, they say, almost popped out completely. But sometimes it seems that what doesn't happen in dreams happens in reality: its power for good or bad, for things both lowly and inconceivable, is without bounds. And let us not forget that without this where would imagination find room to breathe?

Concerning Hesychios's second marriage, we won't have much to say—in any case, some allusions were made to it in stories that were written later, in other books.

Anyway, no one thought that by this act he betrayed Febronia's memory— something that everyone would have thought, including her enemies, if he had taken some young hussy, which he could very easily have done.

And other children came from this marriage.

Yet day by day, Hesychios began to drink—and to drink more and more. He would get up in the middle of the night and drink on an empty stomach, till he ruined his lungs.

He died at the same age as Febronia, exactly fourteen years after her. Without, till the very last, removing from his head the black kerchief that he wrapped like a turban, or tied at the corners like a pirate.

And then, during those fourteen years, other things too had happened that justified—not to say perpetuated—that mourning. It was not only the two brothers he lost, Achilles and Zacharias, it wasn't only Aunt Polyxeni who had departed and, long before her, Aunt Lily. Nor only Stefanos, one of his first sons, born illegitimate, who was killed by a bullet in the leg in the Great War. It was many other things too.

Let's take them one by one.

A few months before he married Penelope, it was the spring when it was Thomas's turn to undertake his first slaughtering . . . Hesychios, having once gone through that ordeal himself, was not at all insistent that his own sons should also go through the ordeal on account of the custom. Nevertheless, more or less everyone in the family began saying that in recent years they had neglected the custom far too much, alluding to the fact that the particular hardships that they had faced during those years (the inexplicable and fatal illness of his daughter

Julia, the disappearance from the face of the earth of his sister Julia, his wife's painful end) were due perhaps to this negligence . . . They were evidently forgetting that all that had happened to them earlier—such as Eftha getting bitten by a snake, such as Cletia getting burned with the inn, such as Marigo expiring in the snow—was in no way less hard.

Whatever the case may be, Hesychios had not tried to persuade any of his sons at the age of twelve to slaughter a lamb or goat, and none of his sons had complained about this—but certain appearances were kept up: someone supposedly reminded the boys of their duty, the boys supposedly refused or fell ill, and they eventually entered their thirteenth year without bathing their hands in blood. This was something of an innovation.

But when Thomas's turn came to do the same, there were many who looked at him as if to say, With those different eyes of yours that God gave you, you ought to do it—for all those who didn't do it.

Thomas didn't speak—he had been from the start the least talkative of all the children in that hive. And his day arrived, *April with its love,* and he allowed them to dress him like a groom, shave him in a mock fashion, bring the musicians, give him advice, encourage him and all the rest, except that—while going down the stairs to the porch and from there to the yard—Thomas sprouted wings and vanished.

And truly, those who were waiting in the yard heard a *whoosh* and felt as if an arrow had brushed past their shoulders—and they saw nothing else.

As the twelve-year-old ran, getting farther and farther away, he heard the sound of other feet behind him and a panting that resembled his own . . . It was Safi-Lisafi, who was following him and would go wherever he was going.

And they went into the hills.

For over two days they roamed up there and ate whatever they found—not locusts and honey, of course, but unripe blackberries, dogwood berries, the *flesh* of wild mallows, even tender leaves or shoots . . . this is what they ate. While it was still light, they would sit somewhere and gaze at the landscape around them, the place where they had been born and raised . . . It was *then* that Thomas allowed Safi-Lisafi for the very first time to actually *look* at his eyes, the brown and green one, and this was a great piece of luck for her . . . But when for the second time, the sky began to be enveloped by darkness and they had no idea how long this would last, they too began to be enveloped by a wish to go home, by fear.

"If we don't return, what will happen?" Safi-Lisafi asked her brother.

"They'll find us," he told her.

"And if they don't find us?"

"If they don't find us . . ."

"Might we die?"

"No, but . . . we might."

"And won't they be upset if they find us like that?"

"Yes, they'll be upset."

"So then let's return, Thomas."

Searching for the way back, shouting whatever came into their mouths, they found themselves in the tranquil spot where an old shepherd looked after their grandfather's sheep. Having already been notified about the disappearance of the two children, he kept them with him that night and sent one of his adopted sons to tell the others below not to worry.

He was a man of roughly Christoforos's age (they were in fact second cousins) and had the same name as Thomas but was known by everyone as Thomas-the-Demon because in his youth, it's said, he used his deep blue, piercing eyes to no good end: from the time he was small he was in the employ of a lord whose only pleasure in life was not to see anyone else prospering. And because the poor and childless had no hope of prospering in any case, he set himself to destroying his own kind—and, in fact, their flocks—using the demonic eyes of his underling . . . It sounds incredible, the creation of some sick imagination, and yet all Thomas had to do, then, was fix his eyes on the eyes of a sheep for the sheep to fall down ill . . . He cast the evil eye on it, his eyes had a catastrophic effect on the innocent beast, and this effect would multiply among all the others . . .

His master would pay him for this work, for destroying others' flocks with his eyes and not for guarding his own—for his own he had other shepherds, with eyes apparently not dangerous.

But one day things changed. Thomas, who was already becoming known as Thomas-the-Demon and was feared by all, fell in love with one of his master's daughters, and because the master *laughed his heart out* on hearing this and before long gave her to someone else, Thomas—after fixing his eyes on his master's flock and destroying it—fixed them on his master himself and left him a withered buttercup.

After this, and after he had passed through many entanglements, he returned to his own parts, repentant, with sore eyes, and begged both friends and enemies alike to give him a job as a shepherd. In fact, in order to make up for the things of the past, he now cured ailing animals—he became the best vet of his times and without having a license. His uncle Lukas took pity on him and kept him with him on his pastures. And after Lukas, Christoforos.

But he remained with his name. As he did with the three fingers on his right hand: the other two—forefinger and middle finger—he had cut off himself with an ax to avoid having to go to the army(!).

These, then, were the sins of his youth (though he never regretted the second one), which he included among the many stories he told the children that night and the next day, till Hesychios arrived on horseback to take them.

Two years later, Hesychios's Thomas decided that he too wanted to be a shepherd. Since much earlier he had shown a particular liking, a great fondness, for animals (and this is why, of course, he would never agree to slaughter a lamb), but after those hours spent among so many lambs, listening to the old shepherd's tales—and after subsequently going back up into the hills, either alone or with his twin sister—he realized that he wouldn't be able to live better anywhere else. The air up there suited him . . . and no one was perplexed by his eyes.

"And what will become of me now that you've become a shepherd?" Safi-Lisafi asked him one day, after they had stopped her from going up into the hills to see him (though she did it in secret whenever she found the opportunity).

"You'll become a wife . . . you'll get married, have children," he told her.

"To whom?" she asked sorrowfully, her head bowed, making a clicking sound with her thumbnails.

"With me!" replied Thomas-the-Demon, who was listening to them and watching.

Her eyebrows moved like little snakes recoiling back into their nests.

"O you . . . but you're a granddad," she said, looking at him askance. And she again asked her brother in earnest, as though she expected him to give her there and then the name of some groom: "To whom?"

"To someone . . . Are you in a hurry?"

"No, I'm in no hurry . . . And will you get married too?"

"Perhaps I will . . . It's still too soon."

"To whom?"

"To you!" replied Thomas-the-Demon again.

Of this veritable *demon*, of his sinful past, what had remained alive and fully active was his humor and his mirth. His deep blue eyes, which had once caused so much fear, had now sunk into their sockets, his skin had become wizened, and his eight fingers resembled vine branches, but he could still come out with a couple of words—and the *couple of words* that he usually came out with were "blast it"—in order to erase many others . . . And this always constituted the *epilogue* to his own tales.

Nevertheless, hidden beneath this worn-out face with the sullen or pseudo-sullen expression it occasionally took on was a fair amount of cordiality, which he shared with the dogs and sheep (being a lonely dog himself), sometimes with his adopted sons, too, and certainly with his young namesake, who went to live with him, and his twin sister whenever she came to see them.

Life up there was not at all bad, or especially monotonous—"We're having a great time," as Thomas-the-Demon said to anyone from the *netherworld* who came up and asked them how they were getting along. "See that you do too."

Every morning they would drink a cup of fresh milk (Thomas-the-Demon would add a little salt, never sugar), but towards evening and by the time it was dark, the milk in the same cup would have turned red, and they would stretch out beside each other and the long tales would begin. The elder Thomas would talk, and the younger one would listen—though occasionally the reverse would happen. Before turning in, they would smoke two or three cigarettes, which they smoked in pipes made from the branches of cherry trees or rosebushes (these branches had a soft center that could easily be pushed out with a wire, thereby creating a channel for the smoke—and also the wood didn't burn easily if the lighted cigarette burned down to the mouth of the pipe), and when they had nothing to say, they would listen to the silence, they would listen to the night birds and to the faint bleating of the animals that were dozing not far away and most likely dreaming.

These animals—the good spirits shown by one, the low spirits shown by another—were of the same concern to them as words are to a poet or methane and nitrogen are to a chemist.

Thomas's favorite animal was that very same lamb he had refused to slaughter, now a full-grown ewe, which the other Thomas had named "Kassiani"[1] because its behavior—the way it bent its legs and sat down before its young master as soon as he called it, or the way it rubbed its head against his legs or hands and looked him in the eyes with its mouth trembling—recalled more the behavior of a faithful and intelligent dog, or, at any rate, of a repentant and devoted woman, rather than of sheep that show their feelings to human beings in ways not so *expressive*.

"She's a fine sheep, that Kassiani—the only thing she's missing is a human voice!—but she's turned out to be barren," Thomas-the-Demon would say every so often.

"Never mind, all the others give birth," said Thomas.

"And what if we get official word to send her for her meat?"

"We won't send her."

"Would you take it so much to heart?"

"We won't send her."

"Blast it. We won't send her."

1. Kassia (Greek Kassiani) was a Byzantine (ninth century) abbess, poet, composer, and hymnographer. The "Hymn of Kassiani," sung during Easter Week, is traditionally associated with the "woman fallen in many sins" (translator's note).

This Kassiani had another strange characteristic that, you might say, brought her into even closer contact and accord with her master: she too had two disparate eyes. Not, of course, with that same striking difference that surprised you with Thomas's eyes, but—and at certain moments—her one eye was much darker than the other. It became almost black, whereas the other one was always pale gray or a little yellowy-gray.

"If she were a woman, I'd wager that you'd marry her," Thomas-the-Demon said to him. "And if nothing else, your sister would click her nails, knit her eyebrows, and say to me—she'd say it to me, not you—*blast it!*" (And he imitated Safi-Lisafi's delicate and somewhat liquid voice.)

When, in the evenings, the two of them would sit and drink their wine and smoke using those cherry-wood pipes, recounting their tales (Thomas-the-Demon drank, smoked, and talked much more, but the younger one began to learn from him too), Kassiani would very often leave the other sheep and come over to be in their company.

Those moments, especially when they were silent and gazing at the sun as it was about to set, were beautiful moments, sensitive ones.

"The sun sets and we set too," said Thomas-the-Demon sometimes, shaking his head.

"Life rolls by with its delusions," said the young Thomas, going one better—one of his grandfather's *aphorisms* that found a favorable response . . .

And like this four years went by. During this time, Thomas had acquired more brothers and sisters from his father's new wife, and his brother Sakis was no longer the *Benjamin* of the family. Nevertheless, everyone still called him Benjamin—and would still do so for a long time; it was only in Goulgi that he became Sakis, and later of course, when he was grown up.

He too would come into the hills to see them, quite often, especially in spring and fall—in summer, with all the harvesting and the other chores, he had no time. And in winter, it was the two of them who would come down.

"Look . . . I'm missing a finger, too," he said to Thomas-the-Demon.

"Who cut it off?" he asked, pretending not to know.

"I did!" replied Sakis, fingering his breast with the others as though it were a harp.

"Blast it. And my two, it was me who did it," said Thomas-the-Demon.

"What with?"

"With an ax, what a fool."

"Ah, okay," said Sakis, "I did it with a sickle."

"Aha . . . And I heard that you like the odd fag too . . . that your father lets you."

"He doesn't just let me—he was the one who put it in my pocket."

"And what do you use to smoke it?"

"My mouth."

"Ah, okay. We smoke them using pipes and cherries," said Thomas-the-Demon.

"Blast it!" roared little Sakis.

That year, the same year that a big fire ravaged the seaside town close by, the sheep were afflicted by a disease that ravaged them too, wiping them out. It was *dalaki*, that's what they called the disease, and it appeared once in every forty years, but—paraphrasing the proverb "better a hawk for a day than a jackdaw for a year"—they said, "better liver fluke now and again than dalaki once in a blue moon."

Perhaps the antidote has been found now for this kind of epidemic (perhaps others have broken out), but back then not even Thomas-the-Demon could do anything to keep it at bay. He was simply able to recognize its symptoms before anyone else, when the instances were still sporadic and difficult to discern—a tottering of the sheep's legs, duller and choked bleating, a jerk of the neck as though it had momentarily lost its sight—and, without saying anything to Thomas so as not to alarm him, he hastened to isolate the ones *stricken* and began slashing them on the throat or forehead with a knife . . . Thomas saw him, of course, was horrified, and rushed at him—he imagined that the old man had lost his wits, had gone back to the ways of his demonic past. He grabbed hold of him by the shoulders and hurled him to the ground.

"Blast it!" he said. "If they have any chance at all of being saved, it's only in this way—get a knife yourself and cut them so their blood runs. Their blood, do you understand? It's diseased."

But not even the bloodletting saved them, or perhaps just temporarily, and within a few days more and more sheep started to totter where they were grazing and to lose their sight.

A few days more and over half of them had died, and not only in their sheepfold of course, but everywhere, throughout the entire region—the dalaki was taking on the proportions of a cholera epidemic. And the people—pitiful perhaps, but . . . *need knows no law*—did what they did when the wolves had appeared: they summarily slaughtered as many of the animals as were still healthy so that at least they would be left with something for themselves . . . And those dramatic cries were heard once again: "Instead of the wolf eating it, let the jackal have it" . . . And the area filled with dead sheep and the people's tables with their sacrificial victims.

Thomas took Kassiani, put her on his shoulders—this was his *need*—and left. He hadn't seen any of the symptoms in her yet (or perhaps he didn't want to see them), and he had to save her at all costs, not let the dalaki get her or any knife in only her sixth year. He was in his eighteenth.

He found a cave, a sort of cave—the same spot where he and Safi-Lisafi had spent their first night in the hills, when they had run away from home . . . It was here that he spent that night with Kassiani, far from people and animals.

But in the morning, Kassiani began to totter; she went to rub herself against his hands, but tottered and fell, and when she raised her head to look at him, her eyes were white—both the black one and the gray one were white, without any focus.

Sobbing, as though he had to cut his sister or his mother, even though she was already doomed, he took out his knife and cut her neck in two places. But . . . who knows what clouded his mind, who knows what scenes appeared before his eyes from his grandmother Eftha (whom he had never met) when she sucked the blood from arms or legs that had been bitten by a snake so as to remove the venom and spit it out, and he did the same with Kassiani's blood . . . Except that he didn't spit it out; he swallowed it. And when he realized what he'd done, he swallowed still more to hasten the end.

While watching his animal expiring, he felt the cold palm on his brow too. A few more hours passed, or was it only moments, or perhaps it was an entire night and day. He wanted to say something to Safi-Lisafi, write her something on a piece of paper, in his pocket, but he found nothing and there was no more time. He picked up a stone and—with a hand that couldn't—wrote on the damp earth: Good-bye Saf.

For the following months, all his brothers and sisters, those from other mothers too, went to the cemetery to grieve for him, but Safi-Lisafi went into the hills, to that cave where they had found him. Around that Good-bye Saf, which to her was clearly discernible in the earth, she placed some stones, and every time she went there, she would add more stones. It ended up by being a small circular wall, a small sacrificial altar or well. Then she would go outside into the light and gaze at the *most beautiful place in the world*. And then she would silently go back home.

So that this silent pining for her brother wouldn't eat away at her, they took care to betroth her to a nice young boy, a friend of Argyris and the same age as him. The wedding preparations were under way, but one day, while she was cutting a loaf of bread, the knife slipped and went through her heart, and she fell lifeless.

After this, Hesychios—who was already spending most of his time with a bottle—advanced to the ranks of the dipsomaniacs . . . He would put the bottle under his clothes, mount his horse, take a pitchfork or pickax for company, and no one knew where he was going or when he would return. Occasionally, his path brought him as far as Dekatessara, behind the hills, to Zina's house, covered as it was in flowers. He would ask her to give him another bottle—white, red, black, whatever—and . . . what woman in her place would say no to him, for anything?

Then there were the others. His son Christodoulos, his first child with Febronia, emigrated to America at the age of twenty-six, where he married Judith, though he would come back to see them every ten years, until he never came back again.

Argyris joined the merchant navy, traveled all over the world, from Antwerp to Malta and from Bristol to Buenos Aires, and got killed in a fracas in a Lisbon nightclub. He had been intending to get engaged only a few days later to Cecilia, a fado singer—he had written to tell them, "She's beautiful, like her songs. When you see her and hear her you'll understand. . . . *Minha vida é para ela.*"[2]

Persa's brother Jacob died in an asylum not long after he had come to their house with his accordion, and Lily's brother Gabe died in deep old age.

But three of the sons of Hesychios and Febronia, Zafeiris, Sterios, and Sakis, also lived long lives. Zafeiris was confined to an old people's home by the wife of one of his grandchildren, a young girl who already had two children; Sterios died in his orchard with its apple trees and cherry trees while reading books on the Great Inventors given to him by one of his nephews; and Sakis and his second wife were taken away by his children to live in the town, only three years before his end came too.

It was from Sakis that we learned the most; he was the source that still remains inexhaustible. In his hands, his grandfather's sesame-oil mill—the once renowned inn—became a large timber warehouse, then a cinema, then a timber warehouse again, and then it was leased to others, and we don't know what happened to it.

Towards the end, when he could still speak and recognize—and when he still had his old *wit*—he wasn't able to understand what house that was, what bed it was he was lying in, what ceiling it was he was staring at.

"When was this house built? Who put the doors in? How many rooms for the girls?" he would ask us.

"It's new, we didn't build it ourselves, it's not the other one," we would explain to him.

2. "My life is hers."

"Ah, now you're talking plainly so I can understand. *It's not the other one.*"

He found his tongue again after several days, after twice falling into a torpor before coming round, and twice more into his death throes before coming back again. He kept saying something intently, asking us something, but no one could understand what it was. So as not to torment him with our stupid expressions, we decided to reply "Yes, yes . . ."

He couldn't understand why we were saying this to him with such certainty, and he gazed at his precious son, in whom he had always had complete faith — and repeated the question exclusively to him . . . But he couldn't make out the words either — just three short words — and he, too, tried to reassure him by holding his hand and saying: "Yes, Dad, yes . . ."

He grew desperate and his voice became crystal clear: *"Am I dead?* I'm asking . . ."

The "no" that was heard from so many mouths together was not enough to bring him back.

Yet while he was still in his prime, in that aged prime at least, in the *spring* of his old age as he liked to call it, he was not at all averse to telling us for the tenth, for the hundredth time, whatever we wanted to hear again. And each time it was like new, as though heard for the first time.

Sometimes it was just a one-line dialogue — things about his brothers and sisters:

"What was it that you said happened to Uncle Stefanos?"

"Stefanos went with a bullet in the leg. The wars . . ."

"And Uncle Argyris?"

"Argyris, poor lad. Killed abroad in a swordfight."

"And Uncle Thomas?"

"Ah . . . Thomas, Thomas" — the name brought a light to that wrinkled face that can't be described. "Thomas, the most handsome after our father, the most modest, with one green eye and one brown . . . He died on account of a ewe."

It was one of the times he said this that became the occasion, the spark, the *tone* for us to begin our own adventurous journey . . .

Concerning Persa, we didn't need to ask a great deal because she lived long enough for us to know her; she was amazed but also skeptical when it came to the first radios that swamped the country . . .

"That thing," she said, "will stop you people talking to each other one day."

"Stop us talking?"

"Talking to each other, all you'll do is listen."

She wasn't far wrong, but she should have seen that moving necrosis in people's homes.

She lived to a grand old age, always with her apricot eyes and her hooked nose, with her herbs, her *letters of appeal*, and her green earrings, and she kept company with two of Hesychios's first daughters, two of those *sown in the wind*, who, in a manner of speaking, were her granddaughters (granddaughters of her husband), and were much younger than her, though old women themselves and, like her, made of strong stuff.

During her last couple of years, at least ten times a day she would lift up the skin, now dry and shriveled, on the back of her left hand, pinch it in a certain spot with two fingers and then let it fall back: the quicker it fell, settled back in place on her hand, the more days she had left to live; the longer it remained raised, just as her fingers left it, the less oil there was left in the lamp.

One day among all the others, that sad little *bow* on her hand stayed like that for a long time, didn't look like settling, untying itself as they say. She looked at it, looked at it, opened and closed the fingers of that hand—not to make it fall by force, but so that she could understand just how persistent it was—but the thing remained raised, resisted.

And then, as was her custom, she entwined the fingers of both hands over her belly and, after twiddling her thumbs for some time, she stopped, paused for only a short while, and began again but in the opposite direction, saying something that—in that way at least—we never heard again, never found again coming from any *voice*. Saying, "We didn't do too badly with the other obligation . . . How's it *dying* now."

Everything revolves around that; everything. And Christoforos, roughly two decades before Persa, crushed by life and yet initiated in it through and through, still used to go from the house to the sesame-oil mill, and from there he would go, taking a horse—or sometimes on foot—up into the hills. He didn't have many people of his age or station left, and one of these was Thomas-the-Demon, who was still tending a few sheep up on the slopes.

"All deaths bring sorrow till you come to terms with them, don't let me start counting them one by one," he said to him as the two of them sat gazing at the setting sun, "but Julia's death . . . that one . . . To go with the wolves like that . . ."

"Blast it, Christoforos," said Thomas-the-Demon softly. "And we who are still here with the sheep, have we gained anything?"

"I pass by her well, bend, look, search . . . *I'm an old man, dear girl, put your-self in my place*, I call to her."

"And does she hear you?"

"It's not a quirk, it's my grief."

"And does she hear you, I'm asking you?"

"Her? How should I know? But I know that I hear the echo: . . . *irl!* . . . *ace!* . . . I can hear it clearly. Just like when I was little and used to play."

"Everything's an echo, Christoforos."

"Now you're coming round to my way of thinking."

"Look over there at what's happening . . . Charon is bringing out his spawn at sunset to drink water—do you see them?"

"Yes, I see them. And our lamenting blurs it . . . The laments, the grievances, the tender accusations . . . Why?"

"Now you're the one coming round to my way of thinking."

They fell silent again as the sun sank lower and the dusk gradually began to spread—inexpressible things wrestled with them . . .

"It's the twilight hour," Thomas-the-Demon reminded him.

"It is indeed."

"A tender hour . . . blast it. You feel like slaughtering yourself."

"No one, no one will ever know."

There were days when he would stay indoors from morning to night, sitting in an armchair with a table in front of him; he would take a handkerchief from his pocket and, folded in four as it was, he would carefully place it on the edge of the table so half of it was hanging over (exactly half), hold it with his fingers so it didn't fall, and place his brow or his temple on it: he remained like that for hours, still and silent, with eyes open or closed. Those in the house spoke to him, but he didn't hear. Or if he heard something, it was rarely what they had said to him, so—if he answered—no matter how closely the others listened, they rarely understood what he was saying to them.

One day, he was stung by a wasp. It was the day when the children were going from house to house with their wooden swallows and singing seasonal songs—not Christmas carols, but songs of spring: "From the Black Sea the swallow is coming . . ." He went to lie down.

Sons, daughters, and friends came to see him—and Persa was ever at his bed-side, without her potions: there was nothing wrong with her husband, he had simply been stung by a wasp and it had given him a bit of fever. Nevertheless, they called a doctor, who was at the start of his career. He took Christoforos's pulse while looking at the second hand on his watch, listened to his heart, and pronounced his opinion.

"Nothing, Christoforos, sir, nothing. Your pulse is strong and regular, your heart is like that of a little boy. I wish we all had a constitution like yours."

The days passed and the doctor came by now as a visitor—Christoforos had some very attractive granddaughters, and they found the doctor attractive too.

During one of these visits, while he was standing over him and Christoforos was looking into his eyes with warm surprise, he said to him in a spontaneously familiar tone:

"Come on . . . don't make out that you don't recognize me."

Christoforos made no reply, he just went on looking at him.

"Don't you realize who he is?" asked an attractive red-haired girl. "We see him every day."

"It's Marcos," said Christoforos. "I've been waiting for you . . . ," he said to the doctor, making room for him to sit on the bed next to his feet, where the doctor always sat, who, of course, was not called Marcos; but he didn't want to cause him any consternation, to go contrary to the way things were. In any case, in his features—especially his profile—he resembled someone . . . someone called Marcos, a hunter.

And before he went, he again stood over him, put his hand on his shoulder, in the way that the young do to the old, and—though he knew he was not talking to someone ill—he said, voicing his words clearly:

"You'll get well, you'll get well . . . Just don't let it get you down."

Christoforos nodded his head as if in agreement. *With me, Marcos, it's not about getting well, it's about finding peace,* he said to him with his eyes.

Another day, Thomas-the-Demon came down from the hills. He placed a tiny newborn lamb at his feet, didn't stay long, but before leaving, asked him:

"What do you have to say to me, Christoforos?"

Christoforos said something to him using his hands.

The other one understood and said, "All right."

Shortly afterwards, a woman who was passing outside saw, it seems, the peacocks in all their glory, and shouted out in a voice full of affectation and excitement:

"Do they open their wings? Do they open them?"

He had his eyes closed, he opened them and closed them again. He saw in a wearisome yet fleeting dream that he became a crumb and the birds ate him . . .

But the last image that he saw was when the crumb had gone and the birds flew away.

NOTE

In the case of certain locations or places, actual place names were used, but in the main the names are imaginary or variations on names. The same is true, moreover, of all the events in the novel.

Z.Z.

ZYRANNA ZATELI, an acclaimed Greek novelist, was born in 1951 in Thessaloníki, where she attended drama school. She worked as an actor, chiefly on radio, and as a radio producer before writing several novels and works of nonfiction. In 1994 and 2002, Zateli was awarded the Greek National Prize for Literature. In 2010, Zateli received a Lifetime Achievement Award for her fiction writing from the Academy of Athens.

DAVID CONNOLLY was born in Sheffield, England. He studied Ancient Greek at the University of Lancaster, and Medieval and Modern Greek Literature at Trinity College, Oxford, and received his doctoral degree for a thesis on the theory and practice of literary translation from the University of East Anglia. A naturalized Greek, he has lived and worked in Greece since 1979 and has taught translation at the undergraduate and postgraduate levels for many years at a number of university institutions in Greece. His last position before retiring was as professor of translation studies at the Aristotle University of Thessaloníki. He has written extensively on the theory and practice of literary translation and on Greek literature in general and has published over forty books of translations featuring works by major Greek poets and novelists. His translations have received awards in Greece, the United Kingdom, and the United States.